THE DOCTOR'S WIFE

MARY ELIZABETH BRADDON was born in London in October 1835, the youngest daughter of Henry Braddon (a feckless solicitor and writer on sporting subjects) and Fanny White, his Irish wife, who left him when Mary was 4 years old and brought her daughters up alone. In 1856 Braddon began producing magazine stories in an unsuccessful attempt to augment the family income, and in 1857, using the name Mary Seyton, she began a brief career as an actress, an experience on which she was to draw in several of her novels. In 1860 she wrote her first novel, *Three Times Dead* (later published as *The Trail of the Serpent)*, met the publisher John Maxwell, and gave up the stage. From this point onwards Braddon's life and career became intertwined with Maxwell's. The first of their children was born in 1862 (they married in 1874, following the death of Maxwell's first wife), the year in which she had her first commercial success with *Lady Audley's Secret*. Partly as a result of the precariousness of Maxwell's publishing ventures, Braddon continued to produce fiction at an extraordinary rate throughout the rest of the nineteenth century as well as 'conducting' several magazines, including *Belgravia* (1866–76). One of the most notorious sensation novelists of the 1860s, Braddon later developed the satirical talents evident in some of her earlier work to produce sharply observed novels of contemporary social life. Several of Braddon's novels were adapted for the stage, and *Aurora Floyd* was made into a silent film in 1913. The last of her eighty novels was published posthumously in 1916, following her death in February 1915.

LYN PYKETT is a Professor of English at the University of Wales Aberystwyth. She is the author of numerous books and articles on nineteenth- and twentieth-century fiction, including *Emily Brontë* (1989), *The Improper Feminine: The Women's Sensation Novel and the New Woman Writing* (1992), *The Sensation Novel from 'The Woman in White' to 'The Moonstone'* (1994), and *Engendering Fictions: The English Novel in the Early Twentieth Century* (1995). She has also edited two collections of essays, *Reading Fin de Siècle Fictions* (1996) and *Wilkie Collins: A New Casebook* (1998).

D1254057

OXFORD WORLD'S CLASSICS

*For almost 100 years Oxford World's Classics have brought
readers closer to the world's great literature. Now with over 700
titles—from the 4,000-year-old myths of Mesopotamia to the
twentieth century's greatest novels—the series makes available
lesser-known as well as celebrated writing.*

*The pocket-sized hardbacks of the early years contained
introductions by Virginia Woolf, T. S. Eliot, Graham Greene,
and other literary figures which enriched the experience of reading.
Today the series is recognized for its fine scholarship and
reliability in texts that span world literature, drama and poetry,
religion, philosophy and politics. Each edition includes perceptive
commentary and essential background information to meet the
changing needs of readers.*

OXFORD WORLD'S CLASSICS

MARY ELIZABETH BRADDON

The Doctor's Wife

Edited with an Introduction and Notes by
LYN PYKETT

Oxford   New York
OXFORD UNIVERSITY PRESS
1998

Oxford University Press, Great Clarendon Street, Oxford OX2 6DP

Oxford New York

Athens Auckland Bangkok Bogotá Buenos Aires Calcutta
Cape Town Chennai Dar es Salaam Delhi Florence Hong Kong Istanbul
Karachi Kuala Lumpur Madrid Melbourne Mexico City Mumbai
Nairobi Paris São Paulo Singapore Taipei Tokyo Toronto Warsaw
and associated companies in Berlin Ibadan

Oxford is a trade mark of Oxford University Press

Editorial matter © Lyn Pykett 1998
Chronology © David Skilton 1987

First published as an Oxford World's Classics paperback 1998

British Library Cataloguing in Publication Data
Data available

Library of Congress Cataloging in Publication Data
Braddon, M. E. (Mary Elizabeth), 1837–1915.
The doctor's wife / Mary Elizabeth Braddon ; edited with an
introduction and notes by Lyn Pykett.
(Oxford world's classics)
Includes bibliographical references.
I. Pykett, Lyn.   II. Title.   III. Series: Oxford world's classics
(Oxford University Press)
PR4989.M4D63 1998   823'.8—dc21   98-6755
ISBN 0-19-283301-4

1 3 5 7 9 10 8 6 4 2

Typeset by Ace Filmsetting Ltd, Frome, Somerset
Printed in Great Britain by
The Bath Press
Bath

CONTENTS

INTRODUCTION

> If the test of genius were success, we should rank Miss Braddon
> very high in the list of our great novelists. The fertility of her
> invention is as unprecedented as the extent of her popularity.
> Month after month she produces instalments of new novels
> which attract countless readers, and are praised by not a few
> competent critics. Three years ago her name was unknown to
> the reading public. Now it is nearly as familiar to every
> novel-reader as that of Bulwer Lytton or Charles Dickens.[1]

Mary Elizabeth Braddon achieved extraordinary popular success and
excited heated (often outraged) debate among fiction reviewers with
her sensation novel *Lady Audley's Secret*. This novel, first serialized
in 1861, published in three volumes in 1862,[2] and reissued in one-
volume editions throughout the nineteenth century and down to the
present, was one of the bestsellers of its day. It was also adapted for
the stage and has remained part of the melodramatic repertoire.
Braddon immediately followed up its success with a handful of other
novels in the sensation mould: *Aurora Floyd*, *Eleanor's Victory*, and
John Marchmont's Legacy, all published in volume form in 1863. By
1864, when she produced *The Doctor's Wife*—the eighth of more
than eighty novels and collections of stories she was to publish
between 1862 and 1916 (her last novel was published posthumously)—
Braddon was already a contender for the title of queen of the circulating library. However, as her letters to her mentor the novelist
Edward Bulwer-Lytton reveal, she aspired to more than merely popular and commercial success. She wished to please discriminating
critics rather than to scandalize them, and to deflect the attacks of
those who 'have pelted me with the word "sensational"'.[3]

---

[1] W. Fraser Rae, 'Sensation Novelists: Miss Braddon', *North British Review*, 43
(1865), 180–204, 180.

[2] *Lady Audley's Secret* was published in three volumes in 1862. It was partially
serialized in *Robin Goodfellow* (July–Sept. 1861), and subsequently, following the clo-
sure of *Robin Goodfellow*, it was wholly serialized in the *Sixpenny Magazine* (Jan.–Sept.
1861). It had a further serial publication when it was re-run in the *London Journal*
(Mar.–Aug. 1863).

[3] Letter to Bulwer-Lytton written in the summer of 1864; quoted in Robert Lee
Wolff, *Sensational Victorian: The Life and Fiction of Mary Elizabeth Braddon* (New
York, 1979), 163.

On 13 April 1863 she wrote to Bulwer informing him that she had sold the two novels which she was currently writing *(Eleanor's Victory* and *John Marchmont's Legacy)* for 'the highest rate to be screwed out of a publisher for the class of book I can write', adding: 'if I live to complete these two I shall have earned enough to keep me & my mother for the rest of our lives, & I will then try and write for Fame and do something more worthy to be laid upon your altar'.[4] At the time of writing this letter Braddon seems to have been in the process of developing a strategy, which she pursued for the next couple of years, of producing pairs of novels, one of which was aimed purely at the commercial market and the other at 'Fame' and artistic recognition. *The Doctor's Wife*, Braddon's favourite among her novels, was intended as her 'literary' novel for 1864, while *Henry Dunbar*, the other novel published in that year, was produced for a market all too eager for Braddon's sensational tales of murder, deception, and intrigue. As she wrote to Bulwer-Lytton in December 1862, when she had completed her fourth novel, *Aurora Floyd*, 'it has been my good, or bad, fortune to be flung into a very rapid market, & to have everything printed & published almost before the ink with which it was written was dry' (Wolff, p. 154). Two years later she declared that she saw *The Doctor's Wife* as a change of direction, 'a kind of turning point in my life, on the issue of which it must depend whether I sink or swim' (Wolff, p. 164). Readers will decide for themselves whether or not this novel succeeded in keeping Braddon's aesthetic ambitions afloat, or indeed whether its interest and achievement lie in other directions altogether.

Certainly *The Doctor's Wife* is a self-consciously literary novel, in both its conception and execution. Braddon, an inveterate recycler of her own and other novelists' plots, borrowed this one from Gustave Flaubert's *Madame Bovary* (1857), the story of the adulterous wife of a provincial doctor which was to become one of the classics of the nineteenth-century European novel. Braddon frankly admitted her indebtedness to Flaubert's novel, which had enjoyed a *succès de scandale* in France but was, in 1864, not yet well known in England: 'The idea of the Doctor's Wife is founded on "Madame Bovary," the style of which struck me immensely in spite of its hideous immorality' (Wolff, p. 162). What struck Braddon most about

---

[4] Quoted ibid. 135. Subsequent references to this volume are given in the text.

Flaubert's style was what she described as his 'Pre-Raphaelite' power to 'make manifest a scene and an atmosphere in a few lines - almost a few words', and 'a kind of grim humour equal to Balzac'. Balzac was another of the French novelists whom Braddon admired and wished to emulate, as she indicated to the editor of *Temple Bar*, who was apparently pressing her for more of the 'right-down sensational': 'The Balzac-morbid-anatomy school is my especial delight.'[5] Although she does not rise to the heights of Flaubertian style in *The Doctor's Wife*, and she does not even attempt the studied impersonality of Flaubert's narrator, Braddon constantly strives for an effect of 'literariness', not least through her extensive use of allusions to novels, plays, poems, and paintings. It is worth noting that quite a lot of Braddon's knowledge of literature appears to have been acquired during her career as an actress, and many of the novels and poems to which she refers or from which she quotes are mediated through stage adaptations.

Another indication of the nature of Braddon's literary ambitions in this novel is her treatment of the genre in which she had achieved her own popular and financial success, through her representation of the works and views of her fictional sensation novelist Sigismund Smith. Smith, who is presented with great gusto, is the only one of her characters to appear in more than one novel (he reappears as Sigismund Smyth in *The Lady's Mile*, 1866). In many respects, Smith is Braddon's fictional *alter ego*; indeed Robert Lee Wolff went so far as to describe him as an authorial 'mouthpiece' (p. 126). Clearly Smith's pronouncements on his own writing and on sensation writing in general act as a partly insouciant, partly defiant *apologia* for Braddon's fictional practice to date, not least her penchant for using other people's plots. '[T]he next best thing you can do if you haven't got ideas of your own,' Smith confides to his bemused friend George, 'is to steal other people's ideas in an impartial manner. Don't empty one man's pocket, but take a little bit all around' (p. 45). The result is what Smith calls a 'combination story' (p. 45), a useful term for that generic hybridity which modern critics have seen as one of the distinguishing features of the sensation novel.[6]

[5] Quoted in Edmund Yates, *Fifty Years of London Life* (New York, 1885), 336-7.

[6] See Patrick Brantlinger, 'What Is "Sensational" About the Sensation Novel?', *Nineteenth Century Fiction*, 37 (1982), 1–28, and Lyn Pykett, *The Sensation Novel from 'The Woman in White' to 'The Moonstone'* (Plymouth, 1994).

This 'very mild young man' (p. 13), who has changed his name from the prosaic Sam to the more exotic Sigismund as more suited to his authorial persona, might also be seen as a device by means of which his creator simultaneously satirizes and celebrates the sensation genre, attacks its critics, and at the same time distances her own 'artistic' narrative from the low genre(s) with which she has hitherto been associated and some of whose machinery and effects she continues to employ.

In the figure of Smith a number of clichés about the artist and commercial literary production collide. Smith writes obsessively in his garret-like office in the manner of the archetypal Romantic artist. However, unlike such a figure, whose effusions are (at least in literary mythology) wrung painfully from his suffering soul, Smith's blood-curdling tales of murders and suicides are produced to order as the printer's boy waits impatiently at the door. His writing earns for him both a reasonable living and an instant fame as 'a sensation author' whose novels 'enjoyed an immense popularity amongst the classes who like their literature as they like their tobacco—very strong' (p. 11). Sigismund's is a form of alienated literary production: he 'had never in his life presented himself before the public in complete form; he appeared in weekly numbers at a penny, and was always so appearing'. Like his creator, 'He had his ambition, which was to write a great novel; and the archetype of this *magnum opus* was the dream which he . . . fondly nursed by night and day. In the mean time he wrote for his public, which was a public that bought its literature in the same manner as its pudding—in penny slices' and 'was contented' (p. 12).

Braddon draws Smith into the current sensation debates by describing his work in terms of the same metaphors of consumption - which liken the reading of sensation fiction to smoking or chewing tobacco or eating pudding—as those used by several fiction reviewers to condemn sensation novels, including her own.[7] Unsurprisingly, however, both the narrator and her character are much more tolerant than were most fiction reviewers in the 1860s of the consumption model of popular culture. (Smith declares that he actively likes writing to satisfy the appetites of the penny public.) Braddon also

---

[7] See, for example, [H. L. Mansel] 'Sensation Novels', *Quarterly Review*, 133 (1863), 482–514, 485.

aims a shaft at those who attacked sensation fiction by attributing Smith's contentment with his writing lot to the fact that 'in the fifty-second year of this present century', that 'bitter term of reproach, "sensation," had not yet been invented for the terror of romancers' (p. 11). Unburdened by the shameful label of sensation novelist, Smith pronounces gleefully on the characteristics of sensation writing. 'What the penny public want', Smith asserts, 'is plot and plenty of it; surprises and plenty of 'em; mystery, as thick as a November fog' (p. 45). The sensation-reading public also wants bodies and plenty of them—several murders and/or suicides are essential for the penny dreadful, although one murder usually suffices for a three-decker.

Braddon also uses Smith as a means of intervening in the current debate about the supposedly dangerous effects of reading sensation fiction. He gives several examples of the excesses of which he writes but repeatedly denies that there is a direct link (as many critics of sensation writing claimed) between reading about passionate deeds and crimes, and committing them. Thus, he denies that his putative rewriting of Goldsmith's *The Vicar of Wakefield* 'in the detective pre-Raphaelite style' (p. 48) would be, as 'I dare say some people would cry out . . . wicked and immoral', declaring, 'I don't suppose the clergy would take to murdering their sons by reason of my fiction, in which the rules of poetical justice would be sternly adhered to' (p. 49). Smith does concur with the prevailing fear that sensation-reading is a form of addiction, which requires ever-increasing quantities of the addictive substance to feed the craving. However, the main plot of *The Doctor's Wife* displaces the discourse of addiction from sensation fiction on to romance and from popular fiction on to high art by charting the dangerous consequences of its heroine's 'intellectual opium-eating' (p. 29) and her addiction to romantic tales and Romantic poetry.

As well as being deployed as a weapon in the current sensation wars, Smith's pronouncements on the characteristics of sensationalism together with the narrator's descriptions of his work are designed to emphasize that there is a sharp contrast between the typical sensation product and the relatively plotless and mundane story of middle-class life in 'Midlandshire' in *The Doctor's Wife*, a novel which has no imprisonments, elopements, or suicides, and only two bodies, one of which results from 'natural causes' and both of which are produced rather hurriedly at the end of the third volume. *The Doctor's Wife*, as the narrator seeks to persuade her readers on more than one occasion, is not a sensation novel: 'This is *not* a sensation novel. I write here what I know to be the truth' (p. 358). On the contrary, it is a novel of 'character', a self-conscious attempt by its author at 'going in a little for the subjective'.[8]

The Doctor's Wife is a tale of provincial life which focuses on the clash between the real and the ideal, between the mundane reality of middle-class domestic life and the world of art, the imagination, and dreams. Like Braddon's earlier sensation novels (and, indeed, the woman's sensation novel in general), *The Doctor's Wife* explores somewhat minutely the middle-class woman's dissatisfaction with the conditions of her life, her sense of entrapment in a marriage too hastily embarked upon, and of alienation from a husband who happily inhabits his own male world of work and seems incapable of understanding her (or possibly any woman's) feelings and predicament. However, both the plot and the narrative voice of this novel are more overtly moralizing than those of Braddon's more obviously sensational novels such as *Lady Audley's Secret* and *Aurora Floyd*. Indeed *The Doctor's Wife*, despite the persistence of the satirical note evident in Braddon's earlier work, has some affinities with the sentimental sensationalism of Mrs Henry Wood. It combines sin (or at least thoughts of sin) and sentiment in a manner similar to Wood's *East Lynne*, although its representation of the sufferings of its sinning heroine are more restrained than Wood's prolonged dwelling on the agonies of Isabel Carlyle. *The Doctor's Wife* is also rather less melodramatic than *East Lynne*, notwithstanding the sudden and deadly reappearance of Isabel Gilbert's father at the end of Braddon's novel. Although it has recourse to some sensational machinery, *The Doctor's Wife* is a kind of female *Bildungsroman*, which charts its heroine's sentimental education and also her moral evolution from a self-absorbed spinner of dreams into a sadder and a wiser woman who is also an altruistic, useful citizen. The novel's relative lack of sensation scenes and its rather schematic moral pattern, which has more in common with the fiction of George Eliot than it does with Braddon's earlier novels, are evident if one compares *The Doctor's Wife* with *Madame Bovary*, the text on which it is based.

[8] A letter to Bulwer of 17 Jan. 1864, quoted in Wolff, *Sensational Victorian*, 161.

Like Emma Bovary, her Flaubertian original, Isabel Gilbert, the doctor's wife, is a romanticist who lives in a world of books and dreams. However, unlike Emma Bovary, Isabel has a quality of innocence and unworldliness which she maintains, rather improbably according to some commentators, throughout her marriage and her involvement with her aristocratic 'lover', Roland Lansdell. Robert Lee Wolff describes her as 'preternaturally innocent and bland' (p. 163), a view shared by one of the novel's early reviewers, who opined that 'the limits of what is natural are clearly exceeded when we find the highly dutiful, sensitive young wife wholly insensible to anything perilous or improper in indulging the full strength of her sentimental passion, when it has at length met with a palpable embodiment in the person of Roland Lansdell'.[9] Braddon's narrator attributes Isabel's unworldliness, like so much else, to her reading: 'Isabel Gilbert was not a woman of the world. She had read novels while other people perused the Sunday papers . . . she believed in a phantasmal universe, created out of the pages of poets and romancers' (p. 253). For most of the narrative this 'phantasmal world' is more real to Isabel than the world of newspapers or the humdrum surroundings which she inhabits. Isabel desires a life of beauty, poetry, and elevated emotions. Her love of fine things is presented as a form of aestheticism rather than a merely materialist or acquisitive love of luxurious objects. For example, she does not see the prospect of a life of luxury as an inducement to elope with Roland. Emma Bovary, on the other hand, is a sensualist who craves material luxury, and after her initial seduction by the glamour of the ball at the château of Vaubyessard, she uses books and magazines as a vicarious means of experiencing fashionable life.

She bought a map of Paris and with her finger-tip traced walks about the capital. . . . She surrendered to the magic of *Corbeille*, a magazine devoted to women's interests, and of the *Sylphe des Salons*. She devoured the accounts of first-nights, race-meetings and balls, not missing a single word. She took an interest in the début of a singer or the opening of a shop. She knew the latest fashions, the names of the best dressmakers, the days on which the fashionable world drove in the Bois or went to the opera. She pored over the description of furniture in the works of Eugène Sue. She read Balzac and George Sand, seeking in their pages satisfaction by proxy for all her longings. Even at meals she sat with a book before her, turning the pages while Charles ate his food and chatted. . . . Paris, vaster than the ocean, shimmered for her in a rosy vapour. . . . the world of high diplomacy . . . the circle which revolved about the great ducal houses . . . the gay crowd, diversified by an admixture of actresses and men of letters . . . In the heat of her desire she confounded heart's happiness with the sensual pleasures of luxury, true refinement with elegance of manners.[10]

In Emma's case love is always linked to lust and luxury. Thus, in the early stages of her love for Léon the notary's clerk, 'the hunger of her senses, her greed for money, and the melancholy of passion, would all swirl together in a spasm of pain, and instead of thinking no more about him, she let her imagination dwell on him, finding stimulus in sorrow and seeking to indulge it' (p. 102). Isabel's love for Roland is altogether more ethereal than Emma's love for the succession of men with whom she becomes infatuated. It is in every sense a literary romance. When she meets him Isabel is already enraptured by Roland's volume of world-weary poems, *An Alien's Dreams* ('a sort of mixture of Tennyson and Alfred de Musset' (p. 130)), and their relationship develops around the sharing and discussion of books. Roland offers Isabel free access to his extensive library, and they regularly meet in the sequestered spot to which Isabel retreats virtually every day to read (and dream).

   Another important difference between *The Doctor's Wife* and *Madame Bovary* is their treatment of the dangers of reading, and the different reading histories which Flaubert and Braddon construct for their heroines. Isabel's reading is shown to destabilize her by making her emotionally vulnerable and dissatisfied with ordinary domestic duties and her everyday life. This was a charge which its critics frequently levelled at the sensation novel. For example, in an article which appeared in the year before the publication of *The Doctor's Wife*, the *Christian Remembrancer* attacked sensation novels for 'willingly and designedly draw[ing] a picture of life which . . . make[s] reality insipid and the routine of ordinary existence intolerable to the imagination'.[11] Emma Bovary's reading, on the other

---

[10] Gustave Flaubert, *Madame Bovary*, trans. Gerard Hopkins, ed. with an introduction by Terence Cave and notes by Mark Overstall (Oxford and New York: Oxford University Press, 1981), 53–5. Subsequent references to this edition are given in the text.

[11] 'Our Female Sensationalists', *Christian Remembrancer*, 46 (1863), 209–36, 212.

hand, does not simply make her discontented with the 'routine of ordinary existence', it directly affects her actions. On the brink of her affair with Rodolphe, Emma is lured by the siren voices of fictional adulteresses as she 'called to mind the heroines of the books that she had read; the lyrical legion of those adulterous ladies sang in her memory as sisters, enthralling her with the charm of their voices' (p. 154).

Braddon presents Isabel's addiction to a particular kind of reading as highly problematic, but in her case reading is also associated with self-improvement and education. It is the means by which Isabel transcends her sordid upbringing, and it opens her up to productive as well as dangerously seductive forms of the imagination. Moreover, the narrative which Braddon constructs for the heroine of her novel is developmental, rather than the narrative of decline which Flaubert produces. Unlike her French model, Isabel is represented as learning to read differently and to value a different kind of reading from the romances and Romantic poetry which she imbibed in her youth, as she turns to 'graver books'[12] such as biography, history, and philosophy.

The novel's treatment of Isabel's reading history, like its representation of Sigismund Smith, plays out some of its anxieties about its own status as art, as well as Braddon's anxieties about being tagged exclusively with the sensation label and consigned irrevocably to the role of producer for the marketplace rather than that of artist. It also foregrounds the class and gender inflections of contemporary debates about morality, culture, cultivation, and the effects of novel-reading. Isabel's early reading encourages her to aspire to an aristocratic mode of existence and conception of femininity inappropriate to her life as the daughter of a down-at-heel lodging housekeeper and fraudster, and the wife of a provincial doctor. However, like so many novels of this period, *The Doctor's Wife* ends with an accommodation between aristocratic and bourgeois values, as Isabel is transformed by coming to understand the importance and worth of her husband's altruistic devotion to his work and patients, by suffering, by reading serious books, and, unsurprisingly given Braddon's deep investment in Literature and Art in the very

---

[12] Braddon in a letter to Bulwer-Lytton of summer 1864, quoted in Wolff, *Sensational Victorian*, 164.

undertaking of this novel, by the refinement of mind that has been produced by the reading which had hitherto led her astray. As Kate Flint has noted, this novel does not condemn novel-reading 'as an activity in itself: what is seen to matter is the cultivation of a self-knowing and self-responsible attitude towards it'.[13] Indeed, far from condemning novel-reading, Braddon's narrative assumes a practised reader who can not only recognize the numerous literary allusions in *The Doctor's Wife* but also decode them and interpret their significance. Of course, it could be argued that the literary allusions are merely offered up for the reader's self-congratulatory consumption, or that Braddon uses them as a kind of cultural capital which she displays in order to persuade her readers and reviewers of the novel's artistic credentials. However, Kate Flint is surely right when she suggests that one of their functions is to encourage readers 'to enter into an active process of interpretation which invites recognition of their own active . . . role as readers'.[14] Among other things, the numerous literary references in *The Doctor's Wife* act to distance readers from the heroine, and engage them in an active process of judgement of her. For example, only the most resistant readers of Dickens would be likely to regard Edith Dombey (one of Isabel's frequently invoked heroines) as a happy role model for the young wife of a provincial doctor. Similarly, the attentive reader will soon work out that Isabel has miscast *Othello* if she sees Roland Lansdell in the role of Cassio.

The most glaringly obvious difference between Braddon's heroine and her Flaubertian original is that Emma Bovary, unlike Isabel, is an adulteress; indeed she is a double adulteress as she succumbs to the practised rake Rodolphe Boulanger before engaging in an affair with the object of her first infatuation, Léon Dupuis. Ironically Flaubert's novel, regarded by many as a triumph of artistry and a landmark in novelistic realism, is in many ways more sensational than the queen of the English sensation novel's reworking of it. Flaubert dwells minutely on Emma's sensations, and on the disintegration of her dreams of love and luxury as her affair with Léon declines into a sordid reality and she finds 'in adultery nothing but the platitudes of marriage' (p. 282). He uses some of the standard plot devices of the sensation novel as his heroine becomes increas-

---

[13] Kate Flint, *The Woman Reader, 1837–1914* (Oxford, 1993), 291.
[14] Ibid. 283.

ingly embroiled in debt and deceit and a prey to blackmail, and he produces a sensational death scene in which his heroine dies an agonizing death by arsenic, administered by her own hand. In Braddon's novel, on the contrary, the cupidity, sordidness, financial deceptions and entanglements, and agonizing deaths are all at one remove from the heroine. Isabel herself both redeems and is redeemed by her unworldliness, the spirituality of her love for Roland, and her faithfulness to her marriage vows.

Braddon's apparent censoring or bowdlerizing of Flaubert's novel by avoiding the adultery plot has been attributed by both nineteenth- and twentieth-century critics to the timidity of the mid-nineteenth-century English novel on sexual matters, and to the constraints imposed by contemporary popular morality on fictional form. The point is neatly made in a review of Braddon's *The Lady's Mile* in the *Christian Remembrancer* in 1866: 'In comparing themselves with French novelists, our writers must feel at a cruel disadvantage, and must often be ashamed of the clumsy expedients they are driven to by punctilio, the necessities of the publisher, or whoever else feels the pulse of popular morality.'[15] One of the 'clumsy expedients' to which sensation novelists had frequent recourse was the bigamy plot, in which a man, or, more usually, a woman remarries despite or in ignorance of the fact that his/her legal spouse is still alive, and thus wittingly or unwittingly becomes an adulterer, but (as it were) with the benefit of clergy.[16] In *The Doctor's Wife*, Isabel's preternatural innocence is the 'expedient' by means of which Braddon avoids adultery. In the case of this novel, however, the avoidance of adultery might be attributed less to a squeamishness about sex than to the author's interest in 'poetry', to her ambition to produce a 'literary' novel, and her desire to throw off the sensation label. When she published *The Doctor's Wife* Braddon was already well known as a bigamy novelist, and for many critics the term 'sensation' was synonymous with the use of an adultery or bigamy plot. Notwithstanding her creation of several heroines whom reviewers regarded as outraging morality and literary decorum with their 'equivocal talk and fleshly inclinations',[17] Braddon's notions of

---

[15] 'Youth as Depicted in Modern Fiction', *Christian Remembrancer*, 52 (1866), 185.

[16] See Jeanne Fahnestock, 'Bigamy: The Rise and Fall of a Convention', *Nineteenth Century Fiction*, 36 (1981–2), 47–71.

[17] Margaret Oliphant, 'Novels', *Blackwood's*, 102 (1867), 257–80.

the literary seem to have involved a rather conservative conception of decorum, as is evident in this admittedly defensive letter to Bulwer Lytton, in which she replies to Margaret Oliphant's anonymous attack on aspects of her work in *Blackwood's* in 1867:

[I]n 'The Doctor's Wife' I described the sentimental fancy of a young married woman for a man who seems to her the ideal of all her girlish dreams. And this study of a silly girl's romantic passion is not a story which I would care to place in the hands of 'the young person,' but I defy any critic—however nice, or however nasty—to point to one page or one paragraph in that book . . . which contains the lurking poison of sensuality.[18]

Braddon's reworking of *Madame Bovary* was noted by a few contemporary commentators, some of whom connected its indebtedness to Flaubert to the superior quality of *The Doctor's Wife* as compared to much of Braddon's other fiction. Margaret Oliphant, for example, linked the 'higher note' struck by *The Doctor's Wife* to the fact that 'it is to some extent plagiarised . . . from a French story', and observed that the plagiarism 'clearly defined wherein the amount of licence permitted by English taste differs from that which comes natural [*sic*] to the French'.[19] Several reviews, whether or not they noticed the 'plagiarism', noted that *The Doctor's Wife* represented a new direction for its author. The *Saturday Review*, for example, after thanking Braddon rather condescendingly for 'the indefatigable efforts which she makes for the amusement of the public' (efforts which are compared with those of 'an acrobat upon the high rope'), welcomed *The Doctor's Wife* as an experiment in a 'new and comparatively untried path of art'. 'This time the writer seems intent upon dazzling us by the unlooked-for versatility of her powers. The first thing we are conscious of, in taking up *The Doctor's Wife*, is the change of tone and subject-matter which it exhibits as compared with the lady's previous writings in general.[20] The most important innovation as far as the *Saturday's* reviewer was concerned is that the main interest of this novel is not, as in Braddon's previous books, 'plot and incident'. Rather, *The Doctor's Wife* 'must be described as in the strictest sense a novel of character', and one in which Braddon attempts more than hitherto 'in the way of mental

---

[18] Letter of early Sept. 1867, quoted in Wolff, *Sensation Novels*, 204.
[19] 'Novels', 263.   [20] *Saturday Review*, 18 (5 Nov. 1864), 571.

analysis and the delineation of motives'. The reviewer finds that this attempt is not entirely successful because Isabel's character is an 'exaggeration'. 'It may be questioned whether a personage so exclusively embodying a single idea could ever by possibility exist and continue acting in real life in anything like the fashion of Isabel in the fiction.'[21] However, despite what is rather revealingly described as 'this instinctive failing', the novel is pronounced to be 'wholly consistent from first to last, and artistically true to the type of human nature which the novelist has set herself to portray'.[22] The review concludes by congratulating Braddon for applying her talents 'in a new and more wholesome direction' than hitherto and 'reaching a point of moral elevation which, despite perhaps a little overstrain of fancy, shows her capable of real excellence in the highest and purest walks of art'.[23]

In its review the *Spectator* modified its earlier hostility to Braddon, commenting on the 'quite unexpected power' of this new novel. Like the reviewer in the *Saturday*, the *Spectator*'s critic classifies *The Doctor's Wife* as a novel of character, whose chief interest is 'the inner life of a girl gifted with a romantic imagination, but whose outer surroundings are of the most ordinary kind'.[24] The *Spectator*'s reviewer seems to have been persuaded that Braddon had succeeded in her attempt to move from sensation to poetry, since he detects 'a kind of poetry lurking in the over-heated silly imagination' of Isabel, and finds the scene in which she decides not to elope with Roland to be 'one of the ablest we ever read'. However, the praise is not entirely unreserved. Braddon is accused of an inartistic carelessness and haste: 'a little more pains, a little more time, a little more of the lovingness with which the author has painted single scenes', and Isabel might have joined the ranks of those fictional heroines - like Sir Walter Scott's Flora (in *Rob Roy*), Jane Austen's Emma, and Thackeray's Becky Sharp (in *Vanity Fair*)—who become 'real figures'.[25] Despite these shortcomings, it is conceded that 'Miss Braddon has at last contributed something to fiction which will be remembered' and her novels will henceforth gain entry to 'houses where [they] have not hitherto been seen'.

W. Fraser Rae, writing in the *North British Review*, was not

[21] Ibid.   [22] Ibid.   [23] Ibid. 572.
[24] *Spectator*, 22 October 1864, 1214.   [25] Ibid. 166–7.

persuaded. As far as he was concerned the doors of respectable houses ought to remain firmly closed to *The Doctor's Wife*, as they should to Braddon's earlier novels. He did allow that the novel had some virtues, and that it 'possessed fewer artistic faults' than any of Braddon's other novels to date. However, for Rae its virtues only served to amplify its defects and to demonstrate 'how very nearly Miss Braddon has missed being a novelist whom we might respect and praise without reserve', since 'it also proves how she is a slave . . . to the style which she created. "Sensation" is her Frankenstein'.[26] Rae's essay, which offers an assessment of Braddon's fiction down to *Only A Clod* (1865), affords an interesting perspective on the contemporary critical response to Braddon. His negative critique, like Margaret Oliphant's, is conducted in the language of class. As far as Rae is concerned, Braddon's achievement, and her danger, is that she has not merely seduced the 'unthinking crowd' or appealed to the tastes of 'the class . . . lowest in the social scale, as well as in mental capacity', but rather that she has 'temporarily succeeded in making the literature of the Kitchen the favourite reading of the Drawing room'. Braddon's fiction, it would seem, neither knows nor keeps to its proper station. Her 'stories of blood and lust, of atrocious crimes and hardened criminals' are not issued in penny numbers, but are written in 'easy and correct English' and published in three volumes.[27] In short, Braddon's fiction disturbs the class boundaries on which the social status quo is built.

Most contemporary attacks on Braddon's novels (and on the sensation novel more generally) were founded on a perception that they undermined or challenged the social order by misrepresenting or perverting human nature, social reality, the relations between the sexes, conventional models of conduct, and traditional conceptions of gender. Margaret Oliphant, in the course of several attacks on Braddon's fiction and its influence, finds her guilty of all of these crimes of misrepresentation, but reserves her most severe criticism for what she sees as Braddon's perverse misrepresentation of femininity:

What is held up to us as the story of the feminine soul as it really exists underneath its conventional covering is a very fleshly and unlovely record. Women driven wild with love for the man who leads them on to despera-

---

[26] 'Sensation Novelists: Mrs Braddon', 197.   [27] Ibid. 204.

tion . . . ; women who marry their grooms in fits of sensual passion [a direct reference to *Aurora Floyd*]; women who pray their lovers to carry them off from husbands and homes they hate . . . and [who] live in a voluptuous dream, either waiting for or brooding over the inevitable, lover.[28]

Like Rae's, Oliphant's critique of Braddon is couched in the language of class. She implies that the misrepresentation of the world which she detects in the novels of Braddon 'and her like' arises from ignorance of the respectable classes: she suggests that these parvenu writers 'might not be aware how young women of good blood and good training feel'.[29] Oliphant also associated Braddon's (mis)representation of middle-class women and their world with the new fiction of '"protest" against the conventionalities in which the world clothes itself'[30] which was inaugurated by *Jane Eyre* (1847). The *Christian Remembrancer* also suggests that Braddon's challenge to the way things are is both more insidious and more subversive than mere ignorance of the social niceties:

Her bad people don't only pretend to be good: they are respectable; they really work, nay slave in the performance of domestic duties . . . but the real influence of everything this lady writes is to depreciate custom, and steady work of any kind whatever . . . She disbelieves in systematic formal habitual goodness . . . She declares for what she calls a Bohemian existence.[31]

For this reviewer Braddon's fiction, and the sensation novel more generally, is 'a sign of the times—the evidence of a certain train of thought and action, of an impatience of old restraints, and a craving for some fundamental change in the working of society'.[32]

The issue of the subversiveness of her fiction, and the extent to which it challenged the social and literary norms of the nineteenth century, has dominated much of the debate about Braddon since her work was restored to critical view with the renewal of interest in the sensation novel initiated by Kathleen Tillotson in the late 1960s.[33] Elaine Showalter was one of the first feminist critics to appropriate Braddon's work as an example of subversive, radical, feminist

---

[28] Oliphant, 'Novels', 259.   [29] Ibid. 260.   [30] Ibid. 258.
[31] *Christian Remembrancer*, 46 (1863), 230.   [32] Ibid. 210.
[33] Kathleen Tillotson, 'The Lighter Reading of the Eighteen-Sixties', Introduction to Wilkie Collins, *The Woman in White* (Boston, 1969).

critique, detecting in the sound of the rapidly turning pages of the apparently endless supply of novels-with-a-secret produced by Braddon and her female contemporaries evidence of 'a broader female discontent with the institutions of family life'[34] and 'the threat of new fantasies, new expectations, and even female insurrection'.[35] In her influential reassessment of women's literary achievements in *A Literature of Their Own*, Showalter saw novels such as Braddon's as fulfilling a range of functions for their writers and female readers. They provided a vicarious experience and excitement for female readers confined to middle-class domestic life; they both drew upon and constructed a sense of shared values and experiences among those readers; they enacted women's suppressed emotions and covert anger at the limitations of their circumstances, and they provided a series of readily recognized formulae for the satirization or subversion of social and literary codes.[36] Winifred Hughes amplifies this latter point in her important monograph on the sensation novel, arguing that Braddon 'circumvents' the popular conventions, 'using them against themselves, investing them with a new ironic significance'. Ellen Miller Casey goes even further and suggests that Braddon's fiction 'sees through Victorian propriety to a counterworld of feminine rebellion'.[37]

   More recently there has been an interrogation of that supposedly radical critique of nineteenth-century bourgeois culture which critics in the 1960s and 1970s detected in popular novelists such as Braddon, Charles Reade, and Wilkie Collins. As John Kucich has observed, claims that these writers' works offered 'a challenge to mainstream bourgeois culture so fundamental that it promised a radical break from that culture' now seem 'politically and culturally naive'.[38] In fact an element of critique had been present in some of

[34] Elaine Showalter, 'Family Secrets and Domestic Subversion: Rebellion in the Novels of the Eighteen-sixties', in A. Wohl (ed.), *The Victorian Family: Structure and Stresses* (London, 1978), 105.

[35] Ibid. 114.

[36] Elaine Showalter, *A Literature of Their Own: British Women Novelists from Brontë to Lessing* (Princeton, 1977), 162.

[37] Winifred Hughes, *The Maniac in the Cellar: The Sensation Novel of the 1860s* (Princeton, 1980), 124, and Ellen Miller Casey, ' "Other People's Prudery": Mary Elizabeth Braddon', in Don Richard Cox (ed.), *Sexuality in Victorian Literature* (Tennessee, 1984), 81.

[38] John Kucich, *The Power of Lies: Transgression in Victorian Fiction* (Ithaca, NY, 1994), 75 and 76.

those earlier attempts to politicize Braddon and others. For example, Elaine Showalter's Braddon is—like her sister sensationalists—ultimately a failed or compromised radical or subversive, trapped by her own social conformity and by prevailing literary conventions and generic codes: 'By the second volume guilt has set in. In the third volume we see the heroine punished, repentant, and drained of all energy . . . the very tradition of the domestic novel opposed the heroine's development.'[39] This model seems to be more readily applicable to *Lady Audley's Secret* (whose transgressive heroine dies of boredom in the Belgian *maison à santé*, in which she has been incarcerated by her male relatives) or *Aurora Floyd* (whose dynamic and unconventional heroine is tamed by marriage and motherhood) than it is to *The Doctor's Wife*, whose heroine is transformed from a passive consumer of romanticizing literature into a rational subject who is actively engaged in practical schemes of social improvement. Subsequently (from the mid-1980s) Nancy Armstrong, D. A. Miller, Mary Poovey, and Ann Cvetkovich,[40] among others, have interrogated attempts to read particular nineteenth-century writers or genres as oppositional or subversive by exploring what they describe as the complex and contradictory ideological economies of Victorian fiction. Ann Cvetkovich has revisited the question of the subversiveness of Braddon's fiction (and that of the sensation novel more generally) by reading it in relation to what she calls 'the politics of affect'.[41] Cvetkovich's project is to 'historicize the structures of fantasy and affect',[42] and she seeks to demonstrate that in the 1860s and 1870s the representation in fiction (and elsewhere) of the 'sensationalized woman' established a 'relation between femininity and affect'[43] which was crucial in the production and reproduction of middle-class domestic ideology. Cvetkovich argues that fiction such as Braddon's, which represents women primarily as affective beings and focuses minutely on their 'psychic sufferings',[44] at once produces feminine feeling (indeed produces femininity as feeling) and

[39] Showalter, *A Literature of Their Own*, 180.

[40] See Nancy Armstrong, *Desire and Domestic Fiction: A Political History of the Novel* (Oxford and New York, 1987), D. A. Miller, *The Novel and the Police* (Berkeley and Los Angeles, 1988), Mary Poovey, *Uneven Developments: The Ideological Work of Gender in Mid-Victorian England* (Chicago, 1988), and Ann Cvetkovich, *Mixed Feelings: Feminism, Mass Culture and Victorian Sensationalism* (New Brunswick, NJ, 1992).

[41] Cvetkovich, *Mixed Feelings*, 2 and *passim*.

[42] Ibid. 42.   [43] Ibid. 2.   [44] Ibid. 40.

at the same time manages and contains it in a disciplinary or regulatory process. Cvetkovich's thesis fails to take account of the extent to which a novel such as *The Doctor's Wife* itself 'historicize[s] the structures of fantasy and affect' through its analysis of the way in which its heroine is constructed by her reading, but it offers a useful way of understanding the particular model of self-development which Braddon constructs for her female protagonist.

For the most part twentieth-century literary historians have been just as eager to contain Braddon's early fiction within the discourse of sensationalism as were those nineteenth-century reviewers whose critical terminology they have so patiently analysed and deconstructed. This critical preoccupation with the specificities of sensationalism has tended to have the effect of focusing attention on what distinguishes Braddon's novels (particularly those written in the 1860s) from the 'mainstream' realist novel, and has thus, in its own way, continued the marginalization of Braddon's fiction begun by nineteenth-century reviewers. However, there are several respects in which *The Doctor's Wife* does bear comparison with a classic of the English nineteenth-century novel such as *Middlemarch* (1871–2). To be sure, Braddon's study of provincial life lacks both the social range of Eliot's *magnum opus* and its intellectual breadth; for example, *Middlemarch* has throroughly internalized the language of modern science, whereas *The Doctor's Wife* simply refers to current scientific debates. Nevertheless, Braddon's novel, like Eliot's, succeeds in its attempt to offer (among other things) a serious analysis of the limitations of women's education, the constraints of middle-class domesticity, and the dangers for women of romantic fantasy.

Christopher Heywood noticed so many similarities between *Middlemarch* and *The Doctor's Wife* that he claimed that Braddon's novel was a direct source for Eliot's.[45] The similarities are quite striking. Both novels set their studies of provincial life in a fictional version of Warwickshire, both make use of medical debates about the causes and treatment of deadly diseases which plagued the poorer sections of the community in particular (cholera in *Middlemarch*, typhoid in *The Doctor's Wife*), both have a character based on the Coventry philanthropist Charles Bray (Mr Raymond in *The Doctor's*

---

[45] Christopher Heywood, 'A Source for *Middlemarch:* Miss Braddon's *The Doctor's Wife* and *Madame Bovary*', *Revue de littérature comparée*, 44 (1970), 184–94.

Wife, Mr Brooke *in Middlemarch*), and in Isabel Gilbert, the half-educated fantasist turned practical philanthropist, Braddon combines the characteristics which George Eliot dispersed into two characters, Rosamund Vincy and Dorothea Brooke. And *Middlemarch*, too, is indebted to *Madame Bovary.* Heywood argues that Eliot's borrowing from Flaubert is done at one remove, and that it is mediated through Braddon's reworking of Flaubert's plot in *The Doctor's Wife.* Heywood's case is not altogether convincing in this essay, nor in the series of essays in which he seeks to demonstrate (by means of rather literal-minded readings) that *The Doctor's Wife* is the intermediary between *Madame Bovary* and Hardy's *The Return of the Native* (1878) and George Moore's *A Mummer's Wife* (1885).[46] However, it is undoubtedly the case that many readers of English fiction in the nineteenth century were acquainted with Flaubert's novel through their reading of *The Doctor's Wife.* It is in this respect that Braddon's novel can be said to have played an important part in mediating Flaubert's text into English culture.

The Doctor's Wife is an interesting and important cultural document. It is also a compelling and affecting narrative told by a consummate storyteller. Even the fiercest of Braddon's contemporary critics was forced to acknowledge that she had some virtues. After attacking Braddon in a series of articles in the 1860s, Margaret Oliphant conceded that,

Miss Braddon . . . is perhaps the most complete story-teller [among the sensationalists] . . . and has not confined herself to that or any other type of character, but has ranged widely over all English scenes and subjects . . . [giving] some sense of life as a whole, and some reflection of the honest sentiments of humanity, amid the froth of flirtation and folly which has lately invaded, like a destroying flood, the realms of fiction.[47]

[46] Christopher Heywood, '*The Return of the Native* and Miss Braddon's *The Doctor's Wife*: A Probable Source', *Nineteenth Century Fiction*, 18 (1963), 91–4; 'Miss Braddon's *The Doctor's Wife*: An Intermediary between *Madame Bovary* and *The Return of the Native*', *Revue de littérature comparée*, 38 (1964), 255–61; 'Flaubert, Miss Braddon and George Moore', *Revue de littérature comparée*, 12 (1960), 151–8.

[47] Margaret Oliphant, *The Victorian Age in English Literature* (London, 1892), 494–5.

NOTE ON THE TEXT

The Doctor's Wife was first issued in serial form in monthly instalments between January and December 1864 in *Temple Bar*, a magazine which published novels, poetry, essays, and reviews. The first, three-volume edition was published by John Maxwell and Company in 1864 (Maxwell was the father of Braddon's children, and, following the death of his first wife, Braddon's husband). Starting in the mid-1860s, numerous editions of Braddon's novels were issued in various formats throughout her lifetime. Ward Lock and Tyler issued a small-format yellowback series, and more expensive series of 'stereotyped' editions were issued by John and Robert Maxwell, Spencer Blackett, and Simpkin and Marshall. The current edition is based on the three-volume first edition which reproduces the text of the serial version, except for some minor variations of paragraphing and punctuation, and one or two additions and deletions which are recorded in the notes at the end of the volume. I have compared this text with the one-volume stereotyped edition issued by Simpkin, Marshall, Hamilton, Kent and Company (undated, but Simpkin and Marshall began publishing Braddon's work with *The Fatal Three* in 1888). The stereotyped edition omits several substantial passages which are present in the serial version and the first three-volume edition, and these omissions are noted in the notes at the end.

SELECT BIBLIOGRAPHY

Bibliographies

Wolf, Robert L., *Nineteenth-Century Fiction: A Bibliographical Catalogue*, 5 vols. (London and New York, 1981–6).

Biographies, Memoirs, and Letters

Maxwell, William B., *Time Gathered* (London, 1937).

Sadleir, Michael, *Things Past* (London, 1944).

Wolff, Robert L., 'Devoted Disciple: The Letters of Mary Elizabeth Braddon to Sir Edward Bulwer-Lytton, 1862–1873', *Harvard Library Bulletin*, 22: 1 (Jan. 1974), 1–35, and 22: 2 (Apr. 1974), 129–61.

——*Sensational Victorian: The Life and Fiction of Mary Elizabeth Braddon* (New York, 1979).

Critical Studies of Braddon and General Studies of Sensation Fiction

Brantlinger, Patrick, 'What Is "Sensational" About the Sensation Novel?', *Nineteenth Century Fiction*, 37 (1982), 1–28.

Casey, Ellen Miller, ' "Other People's Prudery": Mary Elizabeth Braddon', in Don Richard Cox (ed.), *Sexuality in Victorian Literature* (Tennessee, 1984).

Cvetkovich, Ann, *Mixed Feelings: Feminism, Mass Culture and Victorian Sensationalism* (New Brunswick, NJ, 1992).

Edwards, Philip D., *Some Mid-Victorian Thrillers: The Sensation Novel, Its Friends and Foes* (St Lucia, Queensland, 1971).

Fahnestock, Jeanne, 'Bigamy: The Rise and Fall of a Convention,' *Nineteenth Century Fiction*, 36 (1981–2), 47–71.

Flint, Kate, *The Woman Reader, 1837–1914* (Oxford, 1993).

Heywood, Christopher, 'Flaubert, Miss Braddon and George Moore', *Revue de littérature comparée*, 12 (1960), 151–8.

——'*The Return of the Native* and Miss Braddon's *The Doctor's Wife*: A Probable Source', *Nineteenth Century Fiction*, 18 (1963), 91–4.

——'Miss Braddon's *The Doctor's Wife*: An Intermediary between *Madame Bovary* and *The Return of the Native*', *Revue de littérature comparée*, 38 (1964), 255–61.

——'A Source for *Middlemarch*: Miss Braddon's *The Doctor's Wife* and *Madame Bovary*', *Revue de littérature comparée*, 44 (1970), 184–94.

Hughes, Winifred, *The Maniac in the Cellar: The Sensation Novel of the 1860s* (Princeton, NJ, 1980).

Kucich, John, *The Power of Lies: Transgression in Victorian Fiction* (Ithaca, NY, 1994).

Pykett, Lyn, *The Improper Feminine: The Woman's Sensation Novel and the New Woman Writing* (London, 1992).

——*The Sensation Novel from 'The Woman in White' to 'The Moonstone'* (Plymouth, 1994).

Showalter, Elaine, 'Family Secrets and Domestic Subversion: Rebellion in the Novels of the Eighteen-sixties', in A. Wohl (ed.), *The Victorian Family: Structure and Stresses* (London, 1978).

Tillotson, Kathleen, 'The Lighter Reading of the Eighteen-sixties', Introduction to Wilkie Collins, *The Woman in White* (Boston, 1969).

Vicinus, Martha, ' "Helpless and Unfriended": Nineteenth-century Domestic Melodrama', *New Literary History*, 13 (1981), 127–43.

A CHRONOLOGY OF
MARY ELIZABETH BRADDON

1835	Born 4 October in Frith Street, Soho, third child of Henry and Fanny Braddon.
c.1840	Her parents separate owing to her father's infidelity and financial irresponsibility.
1857–60	Goes on the provincial stage as 'Mary Seyton', working mainly in Yorkshire.
1860	Publishes *Three Times Dead*, her first novel.
1861	Begins to live with publisher John Maxwell, who cannot marry her since his wife is alive, and confined in a lunatic asylum; is stepmother to his five children.
1861–2	*Lady Audley's Secret* a great success.
1862	Bears the first of her children by Maxwell.
1862–3	*Aurora Floyd*.
1864	*The Doctor's Wife*.
1866	*The Lady's Mile. Belgravia Magazine* founded by Maxwell for Braddon, and conducted by her for a decade.
1868	Publishes her twentieth novel. Death of sister and mother.
1868–9	Nervous breakdown complicated by puerperal fever.
1873	Begins to write for the stage, with only modest success.
1874	Marries Maxwell on the death of his first wife.
1876	*Joshua Haggard's Daughter*.
1880	Publishes her fortieth novel.
1884	*Ishmael*.
1888	*The Fatal Three*.
1892	*The Venetians*.
1895	Death of John Maxwell
1896	Publishes her sixtieth novel.
1907	*Dead Love Has Chains*.
1915	Dies at Richmond, 4 February.
1916	*Mary*, her last novel and eighty-fifth book, is published.

A CHRONOLOGY OF
MARY ELIZABETH BRADDON

THE
DOCTOR'S WIFE

CONTENTS

Contents

VOLUME III

VOLUME I

CHAPTER I

A YOUNG MAN FROM THE COUNTRY

There were two surgeons in the little town of Graybridge-on-the-Wayverne, in pretty pastoral Midlandshire,—Mr Pawlkatt, who lived in a big, new, brazen-faced house in the middle of the queer old High Street; and John Gilbert, the parish doctor, who lived in his own house on the outskirts of Graybridge, and worked very hard for a smaller income than that which the stylish Mr Pawlkatt derived from his aristocratic patients.

John Gilbert was an elderly man, with a young son. He had married late in life, and his wife had died very soon after the birth of this son. It was for this reason, most likely, that the surgeon loved his child as children are rarely loved by their fathers—with an earnest, over-anxious devotion, which from the very first had been something womanly in its character, and which grew with the child's growth. Mr Gilbert's mind was narrowed by the circle in which he lived. He had inherited his own patients and the parish patients from his father, who had been a surgeon before him, and who had lived in the same house, with the same red lamp over the little old-fashioned surgery-door, for eight-and-forty years, and had died, leaving the house, the practice, and the red lamp to his son.

If John Gilbert's only child had possessed the capacity of a Newton or the aspirations of a Napoleon, the surgeon would neverthe-less have shut him up in the surgery to compound aloes and conserve of roses, tincture of rhubarb and essence of peppermint. Luckily for the boy, he was only a commonplace lad, with a good-looking, rosy face; clear gray eyes, which stared at you frankly; and a thick stubble of brown hair, parted in the middle and waving from the roots. He was tall, straight, and muscular; a good runner, a first-rate cricketer, tolerably skilful with a pair of boxing-gloves or single-sticks, and a decent shot. He wrote a fair business-like hand, was an excellent arithmetician, remembered a smattering of Latin, a random line here and there from those Roman poets and philosophers whose writings had been his torment at a certain classical and commercial academy at Wareham. He spoke and wrote tolerable English, had read Shakespeare and Sir Walter Scott, and infinitely preferred the latter, though he made a point of skipping the first few chapters of the great novelist's fictions in order to get at once to the action of the story. He was a very good young man, and went to church two or three times on a Sunday; and would on no account have broken any one of the Ten Commandments on the painted tablets above the altar by so much as a thought. He was very good; and, above all, he was very good-looking. No one had ever disputed this fact: George Gilbert was eminently good-looking. No one had ever gone so far as to call him handsome; no one had ever presumed to designate him 'plain.' He had those homely, healthy good looks which the novelist or poet in search of a hero would recoil from with actual horror, and which the practical mind involuntarily associates with tenant-farming in a small way, or the sale of butcher's meat.

I will not say that poor George was ungentlemanly, because he had kind, cordial manners, and a certain instinctive Christianity, which had never yet expressed itself in any very tangible form, but which lent a genial flavour to every word upon his lips, to every thought in his heart. He was a very trusting young man, and thought well of all mankind; he was a Tory, heart and soul, as his father and grandfather had been before him; and thought especially well of all the magnates round about Wareham and Graybridge, holding the grand names that had been familiar to him from his childhood in simple reverence, that was without a thought of meanness. He was a candid, honest, country-bred young man, who did his duty well, and filled a small place in a very narrow circle with credit to himself and the father who loved him. The fiery ordeal of two years' student-life at St Bartholomew's* had left the lad almost as innocent as a girl; for John Gilbert had planted his son during those two awful years in the heart of a quiet Wesleyan family in the Seven-Sisters Road, and the boy had enjoyed very little leisure for disporting himself with the dangerous spirits of St Bartholomew's. George Gilbert was two-and-twenty, and in all the course of those two-and-twenty years which made the sum of the young man's life, his father had never had reason to reproach him by so much as a look. The young doctor was held to be a model youth in the town of

Graybridge; and it was whispered that if he should presume to lift his eyes to Miss Sophronia Burdock, the second daughter of the rich maltster, he need not aspire in vain. But George was by no means a coxcomb, and didn't particularly admire Miss Burdock, whose eyelashes were a good deal paler than her hair, and whose eyebrows were only visible in a strong light. The surgeon was young, and the world was all before him; but he was not ambitious; he felt no sense of oppression in the narrow High Street at Graybridge. He could sit in the little parlour next the surgery reading Byron's fiercest poems, sympathising in his own way with Giaours and Corsairs; but with no passionate yearning stirring up in his breast, with no thought of revolt against the dull quiet of his life. [There are prisoners and prisoners. There are some who grow flowers in the windows of their cells, who make themselves comfortable, who invent all manner of ingenious contrivances whereby to render their narrow chambers pleasant, who eat and drink and sleep, placidly indifferent to all the world outside the cruel walls that shut them in. There are other captives who sit at their barred windows staring for ever at one patch of distant sky—that lovely sky, which covers a free world and slowly consume themselves with the fire of their own souls.]*

George Gilbert took his life as he found it, and had no wish to make it better. To him Graybridge-on-the-Wayverne was all the world. He had been in London, and had felt a provincial's brief sense of surprised delight in the thronged streets, the clamour, and the bustle; but he had very soon discovered that the great metropolis was a dirty and disreputable place as compared to Graybridge-on-the-Wayverne, where you might have taken your dinner comfortably off any door-step as far as the matter of cleanliness is concerned. The young man was more than satisfied with his life; he was pleased with it. He was pleased to think that he was to be his father's partner, and was to live and marry, and have children and die at last in the familiar rooms in which he had been born. His nature was very adhesive, and he loved the things that he had long known, because they were old and familiar to him; rather than for any merit or beauty in the things themselves.

The 20th of July 1852 was a very great day for George Gilbert, and indeed for the town of Graybridge generally; for on that day an excursion-train left Wareham for London, conveying such roving spirits as cared to pay a week's visit to the great metropolis upon

very moderate terms. George had a week's holiday, which he was to
spend with an old schoolfellow who had turned author, and had
chambers in the Temple, but who boarded and lodged with a family
at Camberwell. The young surgeon left Graybridge in the maltster's
carriage at eight o'clock upon that bright summer morning, in company with Miss Burdock and her sister Sophronia, who were going
up to London on a visit to an aristocratic aunt in Baker Street, and
who had been confided to George's care during the journey.

The young ladies and their attendant squire were in very high
spirits. London, when your time is spent between St Bartholomew's
Hospital and the Seven-Sisters Road, is not the most delightful city
in the world; but London, when you are a young man from the
country, with a week's holiday, and a five-pound note and some odd
silver in your pocket, assumes quite another aspect. George was not
enthusiastic; but he looked forward to his holiday with a placid
sense of pleasure, and listened with untiring good humour to the
conversation of the maltster's daughters, who gave him a good deal
of information about their aunt in Baker Street, and the brilliant
parties given by that lady and her acquaintance. But, amiable as the
young ladies were, George was glad when the Midlandshire train
steamed into the Euston Terminus, and his charge was ended. He
handed the Misses Burdock to a portly and rather pompous lady,
who had a clarence-and-pair* waiting for her, and who thanked him
with supreme condescension for his care of her nieces. She even
went so far as to ask him to call in Baker Street during his stay in
London, at which Sophronia blushed. But, unhappily, Sophronia
did not blush prettily; a faint patchy red broke out all over her face,
even where her eyebrows ought to have been, and was a long time
dispersing. If the blush had been Beauty's bright, transient glow, as
brief as summer lightning in a sunset sky, George Gilbert could
scarcely have been blind to its flattering import; but he looked at the
young lady's emotion from a professional point of view, and mistook
it for indigestion.

'You're very kind, ma'am,' he said. 'But I'm going to stay at
Camberwell; I don't think I shall have time to call in Baker Street.'

The carriage drove away, and George took his portmanteau and
went to find a cab. He hailed a hansom, and he felt as he stepped into
it that he was doing a dreadful thing, which would tell against him in
Graybridge, if by any evil chance it should become known that he

had ridden in that disreputable vehicle. He thought the horse had a rakish, unkempt look about the head and mane, like an animal who was accustomed to night-work, and indifferent as to his personal appearance in the day. George was not used to riding in hansoms, so, instead of balancing himself upon the step for a moment while he gave his orders to the charioteer, he settled himself comfortably inside, and was a little startled when a hoarse voice at the back of his head demanded 'Where to, sir?' and suggested the momentary idea that he was breaking out into involuntary ventriloquism.

'The Temple, driver; the Temple, in Fleet Street,' Mr Gilbert said politely.

The man banged down a little trap-door, and rattled off eastwards.

I am afraid to say how much George Gilbert gave the cabman when he was set down at last at the bottom of Chancery Lane; but I think he paid for five miles at eightpence a mile, and a trifle in on account of a blockade in Holborn; and even then the driver did not thank him.

George was a long time groping about the courts and quadrangles of the Temple before he found the place he wanted, though he took a crumpled letter out of his waistcoat-pocket, and referred to it every now and then when he came to a standstill.

Wareham is only a hundred and twenty miles from London; and the excursion-train, after stopping at every station on the line, had arrived at the terminus at half-past two o'clock. It was between three and four now, and the sun was shining upon the river, and the flags in the Temple were hot under Mr Gilbert's feet.* He was very warm himself, and almost worn out, when he found at last the name he was looking for, painted very high up, in white letters, upon a black door-post,—'4th Floor: Mr Andrew Morgan and Mr Sigismund Smith.'

It was in the most obscure corner of the dingiest court in the Temple that George Gilbert found this name. He climbed a very dirty staircase, thumping the end of his portmanteau upon every stair as he went up, until he came to a landing, midway between the third and fourth stories; here he was obliged to stop for sheer want of breath, for he had been lugging the portmanteau about with him throughout his wanderings in the Temple, and a good many people had been startled by the aspect of a well-dressed young man carrying his own luggage, and staring at the names of the different rows of houses, the courts, and quadrangles in the grave sanctuary.

George Gilbert stopped to take breath; and he had scarcely done so, when he was terrified by the apparition of a very dirty boy, who slid suddenly down the baluster between the floor above and the landing, and alighted face to face with the young surgeon. The boy's face was very black, and he was evidently a child of tender years, something between eleven and twelve, perhaps; but he was in no wise discomfited by the appearance of Mr Gilbert; he ran up-stairs again, and placed himself astride upon the slippery baluster with a view to another descent, when a door above was suddenly opened, and a voice said, 'You know where Mr Manders, the artist, lives?'

'Yes, sir;—Waterloo Road, sir, Montague Terrace, No. 2.'

'Then run round to him, and tell him the subject for the next illustration in the *Smuggler's Bride*. A man with his knee upon the chest of another man, and a knife in his hand. You can remember that?'

'Yes, sir.'

'And bring me a proof of chapter fifty-seven.'

'Yes, sir.'

The door was shut, and the boy ran down-stairs, past George Gilbert, as fast as he could go. But the door above was opened again, and the same voice called aloud,

'Tell Mr Manders the man with the knife in his hand must have on top-boots.'

'All right, sir,' the boy called from the bottom of the staircase.

George Gilbert went up, and knocked at the door above. It was a black door, and the names of Mr Andrew Morgan and Mr Sigismund Smith were painted upon it in white letters as upon the door-post below.

A pale-faced young man, with a smudge of ink upon the end of his nose, and very dirty wrist-bands, opened the door.

'Sam!'

'George!' cried the two young men simultaneously, and then began to shake hands, with effusion, as the French playwrights say.

'My dear old George!'

'My dear old Sam! But you call yourself Sigismund now?'

'Yes; Sigismund Smith. It sounds well; doesn't it? If a man's evil destiny makes him a Smith, the least he can do is to take it out in his Christian name. No Smith with a grain of spirit would ever consent to be a Samuel. But come in, dear old boy, and put your portmanteau down; knock those papers off that chair—there, by the window. Don't be frightened to making 'em in a muddle; they can't be in a worse muddle than they are now. If you don't mind just amusing yourself with the *Times* for half an hour or so, while I finish this chapter of the *Smuggler's Bride,* I shall be able to strike work, and do whatever you like; but the printer's boy is coming back in half an hour for the end of the chapter.'

'I won't speak a word,' George said respectfully. The young man with the smudgy nose was an author, and George Gilbert had an awful sense of the solemnity of his friend's vocation. 'Write away, my dear Sam; I won't interrupt you.'

He drew his chair close to the open window, and looked down into the court below, where the paint was slowly blistering in the July sun.

CHAPTER II

A SENSATION AUTHOR

Mr Sigismund Smith was a sensation author.* That bitter term of reproach, 'sensation,' had not been invented for the terror of romancers in the fifty-second year of this present century; but the thing existed nevertheless in divers forms, and people wrote sensation novels as unconsciously as Monsieur Jourdain talked prose. Sigismund Smith was the author of about half a dozen highly-spiced fictions, which enjoyed an immense popularity amongst the classes who like their literature as they like their tobacco—very strong. Sigismund had never in his life presented himself before the public in a complete form; he appeared in weekly numbers at a penny, and was always so appearing; and except on one occasion when he found himself, very greasy and dog's-eared at the edges, and not exactly pleasant to the sense of smell,—on the shelf of a humble librarian and newsvendor, who dealt in tobacco and sweetstuff as well as literature,—Sigismund had never known what it was to be bound. He was well paid for his work, and he was contented. He had his ambition, which was to write a great novel; and the archetype of this *magnum opus* was the dream which he carried about with him wherever he went, and fondly nursed by night and day. In the mean time he wrote for his public, which was a public that bought its literature in the same manner as its pudding—in penny slices.

There was very little to look at in the court below the window, so George Gilbert fell to watching his friend, whose rapid pen scratched along the paper in a breathless way, which indicated a dashing and Dumas-like style of literature, rather than the polished composition of a Johnson or an Addison. Sigismund only drew breath once, and then he paused to make frantic gashes at his shirt-collar with an inky bone paper-knife that lay upon the table.

'I'm only trying whether a man would cut his throat from right to left, or left to right,' Mr Smith said, in answer to his friend's look of terror; 'it's as well to be true to nature; or as true as one can be, for a pound a page;—double-column pages, and eighty-one lines in a column. A man would cut his throat from left to right: he couldn't do it the other way, without making perfect slices of himself.'

'There's a suicide, then, in your story?' George said, with a look of awe.

'*A* suicide!' exclaimed Sigismund Smith; '*a* suicide in the *Smuggler's Bride!* why, it teems with suicides. There's the Duke of Port St Martin's, who walls himself up alive in his own cellar; and there's Leonie de Pasdebasque, the ballet-dancer, who throws herself out of Count Caesar Maraschetti's private balloon; and there's Lilia, the dumb girl,—the penny public like dumb girls,—who sets fire to herself to escape from the—in fact, there's lots of them,' said Mr Smith, dipping his pen in his ink, and hurrying wildly along the paper.

The boy came back before the last page was finished, and Mr Smith detained him for five or ten minutes, at the end of which time he rolled up the manuscript, still damp, and dismissed the printer's emissary.

'Now, George,' he said, 'I can talk to you.'

Sigismund was the son of a Wareham attorney, and the two young men had been school-fellows at the Classical and Commercial Academy in the Wareham Road. They had been school-fellows, and were very sincerely attached to each other. Sigismund was supposed to be reading for the Bar; and for the first twelve months of his sojourn in the Temple the young man had worked honestly and conscientiously; but finding that his legal studies resulted in nothing but mental perplexity and confusion, Sigismund grew weary of waiting for the briefs that never came, and beguiled his leisure by the pursuit of literature.

He found literature a great deal more profitable and a great deal easier than the law; and he abandoned himself entirely to the composition of such works as are to be seen, garnished with striking illustrations, in the windows of humble newsvendors in the smaller and dingier thoroughfares of every large town. Sigismund gave himself wholly to this fascinating pursuit, and perhaps produced more sheets of that mysterious stuff which literary people call 'copy' than any other author of his age.

It would be almost impossible for me adequately to describe the difference between Sigismund Smith as he was known to the very few friends who knew any thing at all about him, and Sigismund Smith as he appeared on paper.

In the narrow circle of his home Mr Smith was a very mild young man, with the most placid blue eyes that ever looked out of a human head, and a good deal of light curling hair. He was a very mild young man. He could not have hit any one if he had tried ever so; and if you had hit him, I don't think he would have minded—much. It was not in him to be very angry; or to fall in love, to any serious extent; or to be desperate about any thing. Perhaps it was that he exhausted all that was passionate in his nature in penny numbers, and had nothing left for the affairs of real life. People who were impressed by his fictions, and were curious to see him, generally left him with a strong sense of disappointment, if not indignation. [They had their own idea of what the author of the *Smuggler's Bride* and *Lilia the Deserted* ought to be, and Mr Smith did not at all come up to the popular standard; so the most enthusiastic admirers of his romances were apt to complain of him as an impostor when they beheld him in private life.]*

Was this meek young man the Byronic hero they had pictured? Was this the author of *Colonel Montefiasco, or the Brand upon the Shoulder-blade*? They had imagined a splendid creature, half magician, half brigand, with a pale face and fierce black eyes, a tumbled mass of raven hair, a bare white throat, a long black-velvet dressing-gown, and thin tapering hands with queer agate and onyx rings coiling up the flexible fingers.

And then the surroundings. An oak-panelled chamber, of course—black oak, with grotesque and diabolical carvings jutting out at the angles of the room; a crystal globe upon a porphyry pedestal; a mysterious picture, with a curtain drawn before it—certain death being the fate of him who dared to raise that curtain by so much as a corner. A mantelpiece of black marble, and a collection of pistols and scymitars, swords and yataghans—especially yataghans,—glimmering and flashing in the firelight. A little show of eccentricity in the way of household pets: a bear under the sofa, and a tame cobra di capella coiled upon the hearthrug. This was the sort of thing the penny public expected of Sigismund Smith; and, lo, here was a young man with perennial ink-smudges upon his face, and an untidy chamber in the Temple, with nothing more romantic than a waste-paper basket, a litter of old letters and tumbled proofs, and a cracked teapot simmering upon the hob.

This was the young man who described the reckless extravagance of a Montefiasco's sumptuous chamber, the mysterious elegance of a Diana Firmiani's dimly-lighted boudoir. This was the young man in whose works there were more masked doors, and hidden staircases, and revolving picture-frames and sliding panels, than in all the old houses in Great Britain; and a greater length of vaulted passages than would make an underground railway from the Scottish border to the Land's End. This was the young man who, in an early volume of poems—a failure, as it is the nature of all early volumes of poems to be—had cried in passionate accents to some youthful member of the aristocracy, surname unknown—

> 'Lady Mable, Lady May, no paean in your praise I'll sing;
> My shattered lyre all mutely tells
> The tortured hand that broke the string.
> Go, fair and false, while jangling bells
> Through golden waves of sunshine ring;
> Go, mistress of a thousand spells:
> But know, midst those you've left forlorn,
> *One*, lady, gives you scorn for scorn.'

'Now, George,' Mr Smith said, as he pushed away a very dirty inkstand, and wiped his pen upon the cuff of his coat,—'now, George, I can attend to the rights of hospitality. You must be hungry after your journey, poor old boy! What'll you take?'

There were no cupboards in the room, which was very bare of furniture, and the only vestiges of any kind of refreshment were a brown crockery-ware teapot upon the hob, and a roll and pat of butter upon a plate on the mantelpiece.

'Have something?' Sigismund said. 'I know there isn't much, because, you see, I never have time to attend to that sort of thing. Have some bread and marmalade?'

He drew out a drawer in the desk before which he was sitting, and triumphantly displayed a pot of marmalade with a spoon in it.

'Bread and marmalade and cold tea's capital,' he said; 'you'll try some, George, won't you? and then we'll go home to Camberwell.'

Mr Gilbert declined the bread and marmalade; so Sigismund prepared to take his departure.

'Morgan's gone into Buckinghamshire for a week's fishing,' he said, 'so I've got the place to myself. I come here of a morning, you know, work all day, and go home to tea and a chop or a steak in the evening. Come along, old fellow.'

The young men went out upon the landing. Sigismund locked the black door and put the key in his pocket. They went down-stairs, and through the courts, and across the quadrangles of the Temple, bearing towards that outlet which is nearest Blackfriars Bridge.

'You'd like to walk, I suppose, George?' Mr Smith asked.

'Oh, yes; we can talk better walking.'

They talked a great deal as they went along. They were very fond of one another, and had each of them a good deal to tell; but George wasn't much of a talker as compared to his friend Sigismund. That young man poured forth a perpetual stream of eloquence, which knew no exhaustion.

'And so you like the people at Camberwell?' George said.

'Oh, yes, they're capital people; free-and-easy, you know, and no stupid, stuck-up gentility about them. Not but what Sleaford's a gentleman; he's a barrister. I don't know exactly where his chambers are, or in what court he practises when he's in town; but he *is* a barrister. I suppose he goes on circuit sometimes, for he's very often away from home for a long time together; but I don't know what circuit he goes on. It doesn't do to ask a man those sort of questions, you see, George; so I hold my tongue. I don't think he's rich, that's to say not rich in a regular way. He's flush of money sometimes, and then you should see the Sunday dinners—salmon and cucumber, and duck and green peas, as if they were nothing.'

'Is he a nice fellow?'

'Oh, yes; a jolly, out-spoken sort of a fellow, with a loud voice and black eyes. He's a capital fellow to me, but he's not fond of company. He seldom shows if I take down a friend. Very likely you mayn't see him all the time you stay there. He'll shut himself up in his own room when he's at home, and won't so much as look at you.'

George seemed to be rather alarmed at this prospect.

'But if Mr Sleaford objects to my being in the house,' he began, 'perhaps I'd better—'

'Oh, he doesn't object, bless you!' Sigismund cried hastily; 'not a bit of it. I said to Mrs Sleaford the other morning at breakfast, "A friend of mine is coming up from Midlandshire; he's as good a fellow as ever breathed," I said, "and good-looking into the bargain,"—don't you blush, George, because it's spooney,—and I asked Mrs S. if she could give you a room and partially board you,—I'm a partial boarder, you know,—for a week or so. She looked at her husband,—she's very sharp with all of *us*, but she's afraid of *him*,—and Sleaford said yes; my friend might come and should be welcome, as long as he wasn't bothered about it. So your room's ready, George, and you come as my visitor; and I can get orders for all the theatres in London, and I'll give you a French dinner in the neighbourhood of Leicester Square every day of your life, if you like; and we'll fill the cup of dissipation to the highest top sparkle.'

It was a long walk from the Temple to Camberwell; but the two young men were good walkers, and as Sigismund Smith talked unceasingly all the way, there were no awkward pauses in the conversation. They walked the whole length of the Walworth Road, and turned to the left soon after passing the turnpike. Mr Smith conducted his friend by mazy convolutions of narrow streets and lanes, where there were pretty little villas and comfortable cottages nestling amongst trees, and where there was the perpetual sound of clattering tin pails and the slopping of milk, blending pleasantly with the cry of the milkman. Sigismund led George through these shady little retreats, and past a tall stern-looking church, and along by the brink of a canal, till they came to a place where the country was wild and sterile in the year 1852. I dare say that railways have cut the neighbourhood all to pieces by this time, and that Mr Sleaford's house has been sold by auction in the form of old bricks; but on this summer afternoon the place to which Sigismund brought his friend was quite a lonely, countryfied spot, where there was one big, ill-looking house, shut in by a high wall, and straggling rows of cottages dwindling away into pigsties upon each side of it.

Standing before a little wooden door in the wall that surrounded Mr Sleaford's garden, George Gilbert could only see that the house was a square brick building, with sickly ivy straggling here and there about it, and long narrow windows considerably obscured by dust and dirt. It was not a pleasant house to look at, however agreeable it might be as a habitation; and George compared it unfavourably with the trim white-walled villas he had seen on his way,—those neat little mansions at five-and-thirty pounds a year; those cosy little cottages, with shining windows that winked and blinked in the sunshine by reason of their cleanliness; those dazzling brass plates, which shone like brazen shields upon the vivid green of newly-painted front doors. If Mr Sleaford's house had ever been painted within Mr Sleaford's memory, the barrister must have been one of the oldest inhabitants of that sterile region on the outskirts of Camberwell; if Mr Sleaford held the house upon a repairing lease, he must have anticipated a prodigious claim for dilapidations at the expiration of his tenancy. Whatever could be broken in Mr Sleaford's house, was broken; whatever could fall out of repair, had so fallen. The bricks held together, and the house stood; and that was about all that could be said for the barrister's habitation.

The bell was broken, and the handle rattled loosely in a kind of basin of tarnished brass, so it was no use attempting to ring; but Sigismund was used to this. He stooped down, put his lips to a hole broken in the woodwork above the lock of the garden-door, and gave a shrill whistle.

'They understand that,' he said; 'the bell's been broken ever since I've lived here, but they never have any thing mended.'

'Why not?'

'Because they're thinking of leaving. I've been with them two years and a half, and they've been thinking of leaving all the time. Sleaford has got the house cheap, and the landlord won't do any thing; so between them they let it go. Sleaford talks about going to Australia some of these days.'

The garden-door was opened while Mr Smith was talking, and the two young men went in. The person who had admitted them was a boy who had just arrived at that period of life when boys are most obnoxious. He had ceased to be a boy pure and simple, and had not yet presumed to call himself a young man. Rejected on one side by his juniors, who found him arrogant and despotic, mooting strange and unorthodox theories with regard to marbles, and evincing supreme contempt for boys who were not familiar with the latest vaticinations of the sporting prophets in the *Bell's Life* and the *Sunday Times*; and flouted on the other hand by his seniors, who offered him half-pence for the purchase of hardbake, and taunted him with base insinuations when he was seized with a sudden fancy for going to look at the weather in the middle of a strong cheroot,— the hobbledehoy sought vainly for a standing-place upon the social scale, and finding none, became a misanthrope, and wrapped himself in scorn as in a mantle. For Sigismund Smith the gloomy youth cherished a peculiar hatred. The young author was master of that proud position to attain which the boy struggled in vain. He was a man! He could smoke a cigar to the very stump, and not grow ashy pale, or stagger dizzily once during the operation; but how little he made of his advantages! He could stay out late of nights, and there was no one to reprove him. *He* could go into a popular tavern, and call for gin-and-bitters, and drink the mixture without so much as a wry face; and slap his money upon the pewter counter, and call the barmaid 'Mary;' and there was no chance of *his* mother happening to be passing at that moment, and catching a glimpse of his familiar back-view through the half-open swinging door, and rushing in, red and angry, to lead him off by the collar of his jacket, amid the laughter of heartless bystanders. No; Sigismund Smith was a MAN. He might have got tipsy if he had liked, and walked about London half the night, ringing surgeons' bells, and pulling off knockers, and being taken to the station-house early in the morning, to be bailed out by a friend by and by, and to have his name in the Sunday papers, with a sensational heading, 'Another tipsy swell,' or 'A modern spring-heeled Jack.'

Yes; Horace Sleaford hated his mother's partial boarder; but his hatred was tempered by disdain. What did Mr Smith make of all his lofty privileges? Nothing; absolutely nothing. The glory of manhood was thrown away upon a mean-spirited cur, who, possessed of liberty to go where he pleased, had never seen a fight for the championship of England, or the last grand rush for the blue riband of the turf; and who, at four-and-twenty years of age, ate bread and marmalade openly in the face of contemptuous mankind. Master Sleaford shut the door with a bang, and locked it. There was one exception to the rule of no repairs in Mr Sleaford's establishment: the locks were all kept in excellent order. The disdainful boy took the key from the lock, and carried it in-doors on his little finger. He had warts upon his hands, and warts are the stigmata of boyhood; and the sleeves of his jacket were white and shiny at the elbows, and left him cruelly exposed about the wrists. The knowledge of his youth, and that shabby frouziness of raiment peculiar to middle-class hobbledehoyhood, gave him a sulky fierceness of aspect, which harmonised well with a pair of big black eyes, and a tumbled shock of blue-black hair. He suspected every body of despising him, and was perpetually trying to look down the scorn of others with still deeper scorn. He stared at George Gilbert, as the young man came into the garden, but did not deign to speak. George was six feet high, and that was in itself enough to make *him* hateful.

'Well, Horace!' Mr Smith said good-naturedly.

'Well, young 'un,' the boy answered disdainfully, 'how do *you* find yourself?'

Horace Sleaford led the way into the house. They went up a flight of steps leading to a half-glass door. It might have been pretty once upon a time, when the glass was bright, and the latticed porch sheltered by clustering roses and clematis; but the clematis had withered, and the straggling roses were choked with wild convolvulus tendrils, that wound about the branches like weedy serpents, and stifled buds and blossoms in their weedy embrace.

The boy banged open the door of the house, as he had banged-to the door of the garden. He made a point of doing every thing with a bang; it was one way of evincing his contempt for his species.

'Mother's in the kitchen,' he said; 'the boys are on the common flying a kite, and Izzie's in the garden.'

'Is your father at home?' Sigismund asked.

'No, he isn't, Clever; you might have known that without asking. When ever is he at home at this time of day?'

'Is tea ready?'

'No, nor won't be for this half-hour,' answered the boy

triumphantly; 'so, if you and your friend are hungry, you'd better have some bread and marmalade. There's a pot in your drawer, up-stairs. I haven't taken any, and I shouldn't have seen it if I hadn't gone to look for a steel pen; so, if you've made a mark upon the label, and think the marmalade's gone down lower, it isn't *me*. Tea won't be ready for half an hour; for the kitchen-fire's been smokin', and the chops can't be done till that's clear; and the kettle ain't on either; and the girl's gone to fetch a fancy loaf,—so you'll have to wait.'

'Oh, never mind that,' Sigismund said; 'come into the garden, George; I'll introduce you to Miss Sleaford.'

'Then *I* shan't go with you,' said the boy. 'I don't care for girls' talk. I say, Mr Gilbert, you're a Midlandshire man, and you ought to know something. What odds will you give me against Mr Tomlinson's brown colt, Vinegar Cruet, for the Conventford steeple-chase?'

Unfortunately Mr Gilbert was lamentably ignorant of the merits or demerits of Vinegar Cruet.

'I'll tell you what I'll do with you, then,' the boy said; 'I'll take fifteen to two against him in fourpenny-bits, and that's one less than the last Manchester quotation.'

George shook his head. 'Horse-racing is worse than Greek to me, Master Sleaford,' he said.

The 'Master' goaded the boy to retaliate.

'Your friend don't seem to have seen much life,' he said to Sigismund. 'I think we shall be able to show him a thing or two before he goes back to Midlandshire, eh, Samuel?'

Horace Sleaford had discovered that fatal name, Samuel, in an old prayer-book belonging to Mr Smith; and he kept it in reserve, as a kind of poisoned dart, always ready to be hurled at his foe.

'We'll teach him a little life, eh, Samuel?' he repeated. 'Haw, haw, haw!'

But his gaiety was cut suddenly short; for a door in the shadowy passage opened, and a woman's face, thin and vinegary of aspect, looked out, and a shrill voice cried:

'Didn't I tell you I wanted another penn'orth of milk fetched, you young torment? But, law, you're like the rest of them, that's all! *I* may slave my life out, and there isn't one of you will as much as lift a finger to help me.'

The boy disappeared upon this, grumbling sulkily; and Sigismund opened a door leading into a parlour.

The room was large, but shabbily furnished and very untidy. The traces of half a dozen different occupations were scattered about, and the apartment was evidently inhabited by people who made a point of never putting any thing away. There was a workbox upon the table, open, and running over with a confusion of tangled tapes, and bobbins, and a mass of different-coloured threads, that looked like variegated vermicelli. There was an old-fashioned desk, covered with dusty green baize, and decorated with loose brass-work which caught at people's garments or wounded their flesh when the desk was carried about; this was open, like the workbox, and was littered with papers that had been blown about by the summer breeze, and were scattered all over the table and the floor beneath it. On a rickety little table near the window there was a dilapidated box of colours, a pot of gum with a lot of brushes sticking up out of it, half a dozen sheets of Skelt's dramatic scenes and characters lying under scraps of tinsel, and fragments of coloured satin, and neatly-folded packets of little gold and silver dots, which the uninitiated might have mistaken for powders. There were some ragged-looking books on a shelf near the fire-place; two or three different kinds of ink-stands on the mantelpiece; a miniature wooden stage, with a lop-sided pasteboard proscenium and greasy tin lamps, in one corner of the floor; a fishing-rod and tackle leaning against the wall in another corner; and the room was generally pervaded by copy-books, slate pencils, and torn Latin grammars with half a brown-leather cover hanging to the leaves by a stout drab thread. Every thing in the apartment was shabby, and more or less dilapidated; nothing was particularly clean; and every where there was the evidence of boys.

I believe Mr Sleaford's was the true policy. If you have boys, 'cry havoc, and let loose the dogs of war;' shut your purse against the painter and the carpenter, the plumber and glazier, the upholsterer and gardener; 'let what is broken, so remain,'—reparations are wasted labour, and wasted money. Buy a box of carpenter's tools for your boys, if you like, and let them mend what they themselves have broken; and, if you don't mind their sawing off one or two of their fingers occasionally, you may end by making them tolerably useful.

Mr Sleaford had one daughter and four sons, and the sons were all boys. People ceased to wonder at the shabbiness of his furniture and the dilapidation of his house, when they were made aware of this fact. The limp chintz curtains that straggled from the cornice had been torn ruthlessly down to serve as draperies for Tom when he personated the ghost in a charade, or for Jack when he wanted a sail to fasten to his fishing-rod, firmly planted on the quarter-deck of the sofa. The chairs had done duty as blocks for the accommodation of many an imaginary Anne Boleyn and Marie Antoinette,* upon long winter evenings, when Horace decapitated the sofa-pillow with a smoky poker, while Tom and Jack kept guard upon the scaffold, and held the populace—of one—at bay with their halberds—the tongs and shovel. The loose carpets had done duty as raging oceans on many a night, when the easy-chair had gone to pieces against the sideboard, with a loss of two wine-glasses, and all hands had been picked up in a perishing state by the crew of the sofa, after an undramatic interlude of slaps, cuffs, and remonstrances from the higher powers, who walked into the storm-beaten ocean with cruel disregard of the unities. Mr Sleaford had a room to himself up-stairs, a Bluebeard chamber, which the boys never entered; for the barrister made a point of locking his door whenever he left his room, and his sons were therefore compelled to respect his apartment. They looked through the keyhole now and then, to see if there was any thing of a mysterious nature in the forbidden chamber; but, as they saw nothing but a dingy easy-chair and an office-table, with a quantity of papers scattered about it, their curiosity gradually subsided, and they ceased to concern themselves in any manner about the apartment, which they always spoke of as 'Pa's room.'

CHAPTER III

ISABEL

The garden at the back of Mr Sleaford's house was a large square plot of ground, with fine old pear-trees sheltering a neglected lawn. A row of hazel-bushes screened all the length of the wall upon one side of the garden; and wherever you looked, there were roses and sweet-briar, espaliered apples, and tall straggling raspberry-bushes, all equally unfamiliar with the gardener's pruning-knife; though here and there you came to a luckless bush that had been hacked at and mutilated in some amateur operations of 'the boys.'

It was an old-fashioned garden, and had doubtless once been beautifully kept; for bright garden-flowers grew up amongst the weeds summer after summer, as if even neglect or cruel usage could not disroot them from the familiar place they loved. Thus rare orchids sprouted up out of beds that were half full of chickweed, and lilies-of-the-valley flourished amongst the groundsel in a shady corner under the water-butt. There were vines, upon which no grape had ever been suffered to ripen during Mr Sleaford's tenancy, but which yet made a beautiful screen of verdant tracery all over the back of the house, twining their loving tendrils about the dilapidated Venetian shutters, that rotted slowly on their rusted hinges. There were strawberry-beds, and there was an arbour at one end of the garden in which the boys played at 'beggar my neighbour' and 'all fours' with greasy, dog's-eared cards in the long summer afternoons; and there were some rabbit-hutches—sure evidence of the neighbourhood of boys—in a sheltered corner under the hazel-bushes. It was a dear old, untidy place, where the odour of distant pigsties mingled faintly with the perfume of the roses; and it was in this neglected garden that Isabel Sleaford spent the best part of her idle, useless life.

She was sitting in a basket-chair under one of the pear-trees when Sigismund Smith and his friend went into the garden to look for her. She was lolling in a low basket-chair, with a book on her lap, and her chin resting on the palm of her hand, so absorbed by the interest of the page before her that she did not even lift her eyes when the two young men went close up to her. She wore a muslin dress, a good deal tumbled and not too clean, and a strip of black velvet was tied round her long throat. Her hair was almost as black as her brother's, and was rolled up in a great loose knot, from which a long untidy curl fell straggling on her white throat—her throat was very white, with the dead, yellowish whiteness of ivory.

'I wish that was *Colonel Montefiasco,*' said Mr Smith, pointing to the book which the young lady was reading. 'I should like to see a lady so interested in one of *my* books that she wouldn't so much as look up when a gentleman was waiting to be introduced to her.'

Miss Sleaford shut her book and rose from her low chair, abashed by this reproach; but she kept her thumb between the pages, and evidently meant to go on with the volume at the first convenient opportunity. She did not wait for any ceremonious introduction to George, but held out her hand to him, and smiled at him frankly.

'You are Mr Gilbert, I know,' she said. 'Sigismund has been talking of you incessantly for the last week. Mamma has got your room ready; and I suppose we shall have tea soon. There are to be some chops on purpose for your friend, Sigismund, mamma told me to tell you.'

She glanced downwards at the book, as much as to say that she had finished speaking, and wanted to get back to it.

'What is it, Izzie?' Sigismund asked, interpreting her look.

'Algerman Mountfort.'

'Ah, I thought so. Always *his* books.'

A faint blush trembled over Miss Sleaford's pale face.

'They are so beautiful!' she said.

'Dangerously beautiful, I'm afraid, Isabel,' the young man said gravely; 'beautiful sweet-meats, with opium inside the sugar. These books don't make you happy, do they, Izzie?'

'No, they make me unhappy; but'—she hesitated a little, and then blushed as she said—'I like that sort of unhappiness. It's better than eating and drinking and sleeping, and being happy that way.'

George could only stare at the young lady's kindling face, which lighted up all in a moment, and was suddenly beautiful, like some transparency which seems a dingy picture till you put a lamp behind it. The young surgeon could only stare wonderingly at Mr Sleaford's daughter, for he hadn't the faintest idea what she and his friend were talking about. He could only watch her pale face, over which faint blushes trembled and vanished like the roseate reflections of a sunset sky. George Gilbert saw that Isabel Sleaford had eyes that were large and black, like her brother's, but which were entirely different from his, notwithstanding; for they were soft and sleepy, with very little light in them, and what little light there was, only a dim dreamy glimmer in the depths of the large pupils. Being a very quiet young man, without much to say for himself, George Gilbert had plenty of leisure in which to examine the young lady's face as she talked to her mother's boarder, who was on cordial brotherly terms with her. George was not a very enthusiastic young man, and he looked at Miss Sleaford's face with no more emotion than if she had been a statue amongst many statues in a gallery of sculpture. He saw that she had small delicate features and a pale face, and that her great black eyes alone invested her with a kind of weird and melancholy beauty, which kindled into warmer loveliness when she smiled.

George did not see the full extent of Isabel Sleaford's beauty, for he was merely a good young man, with a tolerable commonplace intellect, and Isabel's beauty was of a poetical kind, which could only be fully comprehended by a poet; but Mr Gilbert arrived at a vague conviction that she was what he called 'pretty,' and he wondered how it was that her eyes looked a tawny yellow when the light shone full upon them, and a dense black when they were shadowed by their dark lashes.

George was not so much impressed by Miss Sleaford's beauty as by the fact that she was entirely different from any woman he had ever seen before; and I think herein lay this young lady's richest charm, by right of which she should have won the homage of an emperor. There was no one like her. Whatever beauty she had was her own, and no common property shared with a hundred other pretty girls. You saw her once, and remembered her for ever; but you never saw any mortal face that reminded you of hers.

She shut her book altogether at Sigismund's request, and went with the two young men to show George the garden; but she carried the dingy-looking volume lovingly under her arm, and she relapsed into a dreamy silence every now and then, as if she had been reading the hidden pages by some strange faculty of clairvoyance.

Horace Sleaford came running out presently, and summoned the wanderers to the house, where tea was ready.

'The boys are to have theirs in the kitchen,' he said; 'and we elders tea together in the front parlour.'

Three younger boys came trooping out as he spoke, and one by one presented a dingy paw to Mr Gilbert. They had been flying a kite, and fishing in the canal, and helping to stack some hay in the distant meadow; and they were rough and tumbled, and smelt strongly of out-door amusements. They were all three very much like their brother; and George, looking at the four boys as they clustered round him, saw eight of the blackest eyes he ever remembered having looked upon; but not one of those four pairs of eyes bore any resemblance to Isabel's. The boys were only Miss Sleaford's half-brothers. Mr Sleaford's first wife had died three years after her marriage, and Isabel's only memory of her mother was the faint shadow of a loving, melancholy face; a transient shadow, that came to the motherless girl sometimes in her sleep.

An old servant, who had come one day, long ago, to see the Sleafords, told Isabel that her mother had once had a great trouble, and that it had killed her. The child had asked what the great trouble was; but the old servant only shook her head, and said, 'Better for you not to know, my poor, sweet lamb; better for you never to know.'

There was a pencil-sketch of the first Mrs Sleaford in the best parlour; a fly-spotted pencil-sketch, which represented a young woman like Isabel, dressed in a short-waisted gown, with big balloon sleeves; and this was all Miss Sleaford knew of her mother.

The present Mrs Sleaford was a shrewish little woman, with light hair, and sharp gray eyes; a well-meaning little woman, who made every body about her miserable, and who worked from morning till night, and yet never seemed to finish any task she undertook. The Sleafords kept one servant, a maid-of-all-work, who was called the girl; but this young person very rarely emerged from the back-kitchen, where there was a perpetual pumping of water and clattering of hardware, except to disfigure the gooseberry-bushes with pudding-cloths and dusters, which she hung out to dry in the sunshine. To the ignorant mind it would have seemed that the Sleafords might have been very nearly as well off without a servant; for Mrs Sleaford appeared to do all the cooking and the greater part of the house-work, while Isabel and the boys took it in turns to go upon errands and attend to the garden-door.

The front-parlour was a palatial chamber as compared to the back; for the boys were chased away with slaps by Mrs Sleaford when they carried thither that artistic paraphernalia which she called their 'rubbish,' and the depredations of the race were, therefore, less visible in this apartment. Mrs Sleaford had made herself 'tidy' in honour of her new boarder, and her face was shining with the recent application of strong yellow-soap. George saw at once that she was a very common little woman, and that any intellectual graces inherited by the boys must have descended to them from their father. He had a profound reverence for the higher branch of the legal profession, and he wondered that a barrister should have married such a woman as Mrs Sleaford, and should be content to live in the muddle peculiar to a household where the mistress is her own cook, and the junior branches are amateur errand-boys.

After tea the two young men walked up and down the weedy pathways in the garden, while Isabel sat under her favourite pear-tree reading the volume she had been so loth to close. Sigismund and his Midlandshire friend walked up and down, smoking cigars, and talking of what they called old times; but those old times were only four or five years ago, though the young men talked like graybeards, who look back half a century or so, and wonder at the folly of their youth.

Isabel went on with her book; the light was dying away little by little, dropping down behind the pear-trees at the western side of the garden, and the pale evening star glimmered at the end of one of the pathways. She read on more eagerly, almost breathlessly, as the light grew less; for her stepmother would call her in by and by, and there would be a torn jacket to mend, perhaps, or a heap of worsted-socks to be darned for the boys; and there would be no chance of reading another line of that sweet sentimental story, that heavenly prose, which fell into a cadence like poetry, that tender, melancholy music which haunted the reader long after the book was shut and laid aside, and made the dull course of common life so dismally unendurable.

Isabel Sleaford was not quite eighteen years of age. She had been taught a smattering of every thing* at a day-school in the Albany Road; rather a stylish seminary in the opinion of the Camberwellians. She knew a little Italian, enough French to serve for the reading of novels that she might have better left unread, and just so much of modern history as enabled her to pick out all the sugarplums in the historian's pages,—the Mary Stuarts and Joan of Arcs and Anne Boleyns, the Iron Masks and La Vallières, the Marie Antoinettes and Charlotte Cordays, luckless Königsmarks and wicked Borgias; all the romantic and horrible stories scattered amid the dry records of Magna Chartas and Reform Bills, clamorous Third Estates and Beds of Justice. She played the piano a little, and sang a little, and painted wishy-washy-looking flowers on Bristol-board *from* nature, but not at all *like* nature; for the passion-flowers were apt to come out like blue muslin frills, and the fuchsias would have passed for prawns with short-sighted people.

Miss Sleaford had received that half-and-half education which is popular with the poorer middle classes. She left the Albany-Road seminary in her sixteenth year, and set to work to educate herself by means of the nearest circulating library. She did not feed upon garbage, but settled at once upon the highest blossoms in the flower-garden of fiction, and read her favourite novels over and over again, and wrote little extracts of her own choosing in penny account-books, usually employed for the entry of butcher's meat and grocery. She knew whole pages of her pet authors by heart, and used to recite long sentimental passages to Sigismund Smith in the dusky summer evenings; and I am sorry to say that the young man, going to work at Colonel Montefiasco next morning, would put neat paraphrases of Bulwer,* or Dickens,* or Thackeray* into that gentleman's mouth, and invest the heroic brigand with the genial humour of a John Brodie,* the spirituality of a Zanoni,* and the savage sarcasm of a Lord Steyne.* Perhaps there never was a wider difference between two people than that which existed between Isabel Sleaford and her mother's boarder. Sigismund wrote romantic fictions by wholesale, and yet was as unromantic as the prosiest butcher who ever entered a cattle-market. He sold his imagination, and Isabel lived upon hers. To him romance was something which must be woven into the form most likely to suit the popular demand. He slapped his heroes into marketable shape, as coolly as a butterman slaps a pat of butter into the semblance of a swan or a crown, in accordance with the requirements of his customers. But poor Isabel's heroes were impalpable tyrants, and ruled her life. She wanted her life to be like her books; she wanted to be a heroine,—unhappy perhaps, and dying early. She had an especial desire to die early, by consumption, with a hectic flush and an unnatural lustre in her eyes. She fancied every time she had a little cough that the consumption was coming, and she began to pose herself, and was gently melancholy to her half-brothers, and told them one by one, in confidence, that she did not think she should be with them long. They were slow to understand the drift of her remarks, and would ask her if she was going out as a governess; and, if she took the trouble to explain her dismal meaning, were apt to destroy the sentiment of the situation by saying, 'Oh, come now, Hookee Walker.* Who eat a plum-dumpling yesterday for dinner, and asked for more? That's the only sort of consumption *you*'ve got, Izzie; two helps of pudding at dinner, and no end of bread-and-butter for breakfast.'

It was not so that Florence Dombey's* friends addressed her. It was not thus that little Paul* would have spoken to his sister; but then, who could tolerate these great healthy boys after reading about little Paul?

Poor Izzie's life was altogether vulgar and commonplace, and she could not extract one ray of romance out of it, twist it as she would. Her father was not a Dombey,* or an Augustine Caxton,* or even a Rawdon Crawley.* He was a stout, broad-shouldered, good-tempered-looking man, who was fond of good eating, and drank three bottles of French brandy every week of his life. He was tolerably fond of his children; but he never took them out with him, and he saw very little of them at home. There was nothing romantic to be got out of him. Isabel would have been rather glad if he had ill-used her; for then she would have had a grievance, and that would have been something. If he would have worked himself up into a rage, and struck her on the stairs, she might have run out into the lane by the canal; but, alas, she had no good Captain Cuttle* with whom to take refuge, no noble-hearted Walter* to come back to her, with his shadow trembling on the wall in the dim firelight! Alas, alas! she looked north and south and east and west, and the sky was all dark, so she was obliged to go back to her intellectual opium-eating, and become a dreamer of dreams. She had plenty of grievances in a small way, such as having to mend awkward three-cornered rents in her brothers' garments, and being sent to fetch butter in the Walworth Road; but she was willing enough to do these things when once you had wrenched her away from her idolised books, and she carried her ideal world wherever she went, and was tending delirious Byron at Missolonghi,* or standing by the deathbed of Napoleon the Great, while the shop-man slapped the butter on the scale, and the vulgar people hustled her before the greasy counter.

If there had been any one to take this lonely girl in hand and organise her education, Heaven only knows what might have been made of her; but there was no friendly finger to point a pathway in the intellectual forest, and Isabel rambled as her inclination led her, now setting-up one idol, now superseding him by another; living as much alone as if she had resided in a balloon, for ever suspended in mid air, and never coming down in serious earnest to the common joys and sorrows of the vulgar life about her.

George and Sigismund talked of Miss Sleaford when they grew

tired of discoursing upon the memories of their schoolboy life in Midlandshire.

'You didn't tell me that Mr Sleaford had a daughter,' George said.

'Didn't I?'

'No. She—Miss Sleaford—is very pretty.'

'She's gorgeous,' answered Sigismund, with enthusiasm; 'she's lovely. I do her for all my dark heroines,—the good heroines, not the wicked ones. Have you noticed Isabel's eyes? People call them black; but they're bright orange colour, if you look at them in the sunshine. There's a story of Balzac's called *The Girl with the Golden Eyes*.* I never knew what golden eyes were till I saw Isabel Sleaford.'

'You seem very much at home with her?'

'Oh, yes; we're like brother and sister. She helps me with my work sometimes; at least, she throws out suggestions, and I use them. But she's dreadfully romantic. She reads too many novels.'

'Too many?'

'Yes. Don't suppose that I want to depreciate the value of the article. A novel's a splendid thing after a hard day's work, a sharp practical tussle with the real world, a healthy race on the barren moorland of life, a hearty wrestling-match in the universal ring. Sit down then and read *Ernest Maltravers*,* or *Eugene Aram*,* or the *Bride of Lammermoor*,* and the sweet romance lulls your tired soul to rest, like the cradle-song that soothes a child. No wise man or woman was ever the worse for reading novels. Novels are only dangerous for those poor foolish girls who read nothing else, and think that their lives are to be paraphrases of their favourite books. That girl yonder wouldn't look at a decent young fellow in a Government office, with three hundred a year and the chance of advancement,' said Mr Smith, pointing to Isabel Sleaford with a backward jerk of his thumb. 'She's waiting for a melancholy creature, with a murder on his mind.'

They went across the grass to the pear-tree, under which Isabel was still seated. It was growing dark, and her pale face and black eyes had a mysterious look in the dusky twilight. George Gilbert thought she was fitted to be the heroine of a romance, and felt himself miserably awkward and commonplace as he stood before her, struggling with the sensation that he had more arms and legs than he knew what to do with. I like to think of these three people gathered in this neglected suburban garden upon the 21st of July 1852, for they were on the very threshold of life, and the future lay before them like a great stage in a theatre; but the curtain was down, and all beyond it was a dense mystery. These three foolish children had their own ideas about the great mystery. Isabel thought that she would meet a duke some day in the Walworth Road: the duke would be driving his cab, and she would be wearing her best bonnet and *not* going to fetch butter; and the young patrician would be struck by her, and would drive off to her father, and there and then make a formal demand of her hand; and she would be married to him, and wear ruby velvet and a diamond coronet ever after, like Edith Dombey in Mr Hablot Browne's grand picture.* Poor George fashioned no such romantic destiny in his day-dreams. He thought that he would marry some pretty girl, and have plenty of patients, and perhaps some day be engaged in a great case which would be mentioned in the *Lancet*,* and live and die respected, as his grandfather had done before him, in the old house with the red-tiled roof and oaken gable-ends painted black. Sigismund had, of course, only one vision,—and that was the publication of that great book, which should be written about by the reviewers and praised by the public. He could afford to take life very quietly himself; for was he not, in a vicarious manner, going through more adventures than ever the mind of man imagined? He came home to Camberwell of an afternoon, and took half a pound of rump-steak and three or four cups of weak tea, and lounged about the weedy garden with the boys; and other young men, who saw what his life was, sneered at him and called him 'slow.' Slow, indeed! Is it slow to be dangling from a housetop with a frayed rope slipping through your hands and seventy feet of empty space below you? Is it slow to be on board a ship on fire in the middle of the lonely Atlantic, and to rescue the entire crew on one fragile raft, with the handsomest female passenger lashed to your waist by means of her back hair? Is it slow to go down into subterranean passages, with a dark lantern and half a dozen bloodhounds, in pursuit of a murderer? This was the sort of thing that Sigismund was doing all day, and every day—upon paper; and when the day's work was done, he was very well contented to loll in a garden-chair and smoke his cigar, while enthusiastic Isabel talked to him about Byron, and Shelley, and Napoleon the First; for the two poets and the warrior were her three idols, and tears came into her eyes when she talked of the sorrowful evening after Waterloo, or the wasted journey to Missolonghi, just as if she had known and loved these great men.

The lower windows of the house were lighted by this time, and Mrs Sleaford came to the back-parlour window to call the young people to supper. They kept primitive hours at Camberwell, and supper was the pleasantest meal in the day; for Mrs Sleaford's work was done by that time, and she softened into amiability, and discoursed plaintively of her troubles to Sigismund and her children. But to-night was to be a kind of gala, on account of the young man from the country. So there was a lobster and a heap of lettuces,—very little lobster in proportion to the green stuff,—and Sigismund was to make a salad. He was very proud of his skill in this department of culinary art, and as he was generally about five-and-twenty minutes chopping, and sprinkling, and stirring, and tasting, and compounding, before the salad was ready, there was ample time for conversation. To-night George Gilbert talked to Isabel; while Horace enjoyed the privilege of sitting up to supper chiefly because there was no one in the house strong enough to send him to bed, since he refused to retire to his chamber unless driven there by force. He sat opposite his sister, and amused himself by sucking the long feelers of the lobster, and staring reflectively at George with his elbows on the table, while Sigismund mixed the salad.

They were all very comfortable and very merry for Isabel forgot her heroes, and condescended to come down temporarily to George's level, and talk about the Great Exhibition* of the previous year, and the pantomime she had seen last Christmas. He thought her very pretty as she smiled at him across the table; but he fell to wondering about her again, and wondered why it was she was so different from Miss Sophronia Burdock and the young ladies of Graybridge-on-the-Wayverne, whom he had known all his life, and in whom he had never found cause for wonder.

The salad was pronounced ready at last, and the 'six ale,' as Horace called it, was poured out into long narrow glasses, and being a light frisky kind of beverage, was almost as good as champagne. George had been to supper-parties at Graybridge at which there had been real champagne, and jellies, and trifles, but where the talk had not been half so pleasant as at this humble supper-table, on which there were not two forks that matched one another, or a glass that was free from flaw or crack. The young surgeon enjoyed his first night at Camberwell to his heart's content; and Sigismund's spirits rose perceptibly with the six ale. It was when the little party was gayest that Horace jumped up suddenly with the empty lobster-shell in his hand, and told his companions to 'hold their noise.'

'I heard him,' he said.

A shrill whistle from the gate sounded as the boy spoke.

'That's him again!' he exclaimed, running to the door of the room. 'He's been at it ever so long, perhaps; and won't he just give it me if he has!'

Every body was silent; and George heard the boy opening the hall-door and going out to the gate. He heard a brief colloquy, and a deep voice with rather a sulky tone in it, and then heavy footsteps coming along the paved garden-walk and mounting the steps before the door.

'It's your pa, Izzie,' Mrs Sleaford said. 'He'll want a candle: you'd better take it out to him; I don't suppose he'll care about coming in here.'

George Gilbert felt a kind of curiosity about Isabel's father, and was rather disappointed when he learnt that Mr Sleaford was not coming into the parlour. But Sigismund Smith went on eating bread-and-cheese, and fishing pickled onions out of a deep stone jar, without any reference to the movements of the barrister.

Isabel took a candle, and went out into the hall to greet her father. She left the door ajar, and George could hear her talking to Mr Sleaford; but the barrister answered his daughter with a very ill grace, and the speech which George heard plainest gave him no very favourable impression of his host.

'Give me the light, girl, and don't bother!' Mr Sleaford said. 'I've been worried this day until my head's all of a muddle. Don't stand staring at me, child! Tell your mother I've got some work to do, and mayn't go to bed all night.'

'You've been worried, papa?'

'Yes; infernally. And I don't want to be bothered by stupid questions now I've got home. Give me the light, can't you?'

The heavy footsteps went slowly up the uncarpeted staircase, a door opened on the floor above, and the footsteps were heard in the room over the parlour.

Isabel came in, looking very grave, and sat down, away from the table.

George saw that all pleasure was over for that night; and even Sigismund came to a pause in his depredations on the cheese, and meditated, with a pickled onion on the end of his fork.

He was thinking that a father who ill-used his daughter would not be a bad subject for penny numbers; and he made a mental plan of the plot for a new romance.

If Mr Sleaford had business which required to be done that night, he seemed in no great hurry to begin his work; for the heavy foot-steps tramped up and down, up and down the floor overhead, as steadily as if the barrister had been some ascetic Romanist who had appointed a penance for himself, and was working it out in the solitude of his own chamber. A church-clock in the distance struck eleven presently, and a Dutch-clock in the kitchen struck three, which was tolerably near the mark for any clock in Mr Sleaford's house. Isabel and her mother made a stir, as if about to retire; so Sigismund got up, and lighted a couple of candles for himself and his friend. He undertook to show George to the room that had been prepared for him, and the two young men went up-stairs together, after bidding the ladies good-night. Horace had fallen asleep, with his elbows upon the table, and his hair flopping against the flaring tallow-candle near him. The young surgeon took very little notice of the apartment to which he was conducted. He was worn out by his journey, and all the fatigue of the long summer day; so he undressed quickly, and fell asleep while his friend was talking to him through the half-open door between the two bedrooms. George slept, but not soundly; for he was accustomed to a quiet house, in which no human creature stirred after ten o'clock at night; and the heavy tramp of Mr Sleaford's footsteps in a room near at hand disturbed the young man's slumbers, and mixed themselves with his dreams.

It seemed to George Gilbert as if Mr Sleaford walked up and down his room all night, and long after the early daylight shone through the dingy window-curtains. George was not surprised, there-fore, when he was told at breakfast next morning that his host had not yet risen, and was not likely to appear for some hours. Isabel had to go to the Walworth Road on some mysterious mission; and George overheard fragments of a whispered conversation between the young lady and her mother in the passage outside the parlour-door, in which the words 'poor's rates,' and 'summonses,' and 'silver spoons,' and 'backing,' and 'interest,' figured several times.

Mrs Sleaford was busy about the house, and the boys were scattered; so George and Sigismund took their breakfast comfortably together, and read Mr Sleaford's *Times*, which was not as yet required for that gentleman's own use. Sigismund made a plan of the day. He would take a holiday for once in a way, he said, and would escort his friend to the Royal Academy and divers other picture-galleries, and would crown the day's enjoyment by a French dinner.

The two young men left the house at eleven o'clock. They had seen nothing of Isabel that morning, nor of the master of the house. All that George Gilbert knew of that gentleman was the fact that Mr Sleaford had a heavy footstep and a deep sulky voice.

The 21st of July was a blazing summer's day, and I am ashamed to confess that George Gilbert grew very tired of staring at the pictures in the Royal Academy. To him the finest works of modern art were only 'pretty pictures,' more or less interesting according to the story they told; and Sigismund's disquisitions upon 'modelling,' and 'depth,' 'feeling,' and tone, and colour, and distance, were so much unintelligible jargon; so he was glad when the day's work was over, and Mr Smith led him away to a very dingy street a little way behind the National Gallery.

'And now I'm going to give you a regular French dinner, George, old fellow!' Sigismund said, in a triumphant tone.

Mr Gilbert looked about him with an air of mystification. He had been accustomed to associate French dinners with brilliantly lighted cafés and gorgeous saloons, where the chairs were crimson velvet and gold, and where a dozen vast sheets of looking-glass reflected you as you ate your soup. He was a little disappointed, perhaps, when Sigismund paused before a narrow doorway, on each side of which there was an old-fashioned window with queer-shaped wine and liqueur bottles neatly ranged behind the glass. A big lantern-shaped lamp hung over the door, and below one of the windows was an iron grating, through which a subtle flavour of garlic and mock-turtle soup steamed out upon the summer air.

'This is Boujeot's,' said Mr Smith. 'It's the jolliest place; no grandeur, you know, but capital wine and first-rate cooking. The

Emperor of the French used to dine here almost every day when he was in England; but he never told any one his name, and the waiters didn't know who he was till they saw his portrait as President in the *Illustrated News.*'

It is a popular fiction that the Prince Louis Napoleon was in the habit of dining, daily, at every French restaurant in London during the days of his exile;* a fiction which gives a romantic flavour to the dishes, and an aroma of poetry to the wines. George Gilbert looked about him as he seated himself at a little table chosen by his friend, and he wondered whether Napoleon the Third had ever sat at that particular table, and whether the table-cloth had been as dirty in his time. The waiters at Boujeot's were very civil and accommodating, though they were nearly harassed off their legs by the claims of desultory gentlemen in the public apartments, and old customers dining by pre-arrangement in the private rooms up-stairs. Sigismund pounced upon a great sheet of paper, which looked something like a chronological table, and on the blank margins of which the pencil records of dinners lately consumed and paid for had been hurriedly jotted down by the harassed waiters. Mr Smith was a long time absorbed in the study of this mysterious document; so George Gilbert amused himself by staring at some coffee-coloured marine views upon the walls, which were supposed to represent the Bay of Biscay and the Cape of Good Hope, with brown waves rolling tempestuously under a brown sky. George stared at these, and at a gentleman who was engaged in the soul-absorbing occupation of paying his bill; and then the surgeon's thoughts went vagabondising away from the little coffee-room at Boujeot's to Mr Sleaford's garden, and Isabel's pale face and yellow-black eyes, glimmering mysteriously in the summer twilight. He thought of Miss Sleaford because she was so unlike any other woman he had ever seen, and he wondered how his father would like her. Not much, George feared; for Mr Gilbert senior expected a young woman to be very neat about her back-hair, which Isabel was not, and handy with her needle, and clever in the management of a house and the government of a maid-of-all-work; and Isabel could scarcely be that, since her favourite employment was to loll in a wicker-work garden-chair and read novels.

The dinner came in at last, with little pewter covers over the dishes, which the waiter drew one by one out of a mysterious kind of wooden oven, from which there came a voice, and nothing more.

The two young men dined; and George thought that, except for the fried potatoes, which flew about his plate when he tried to stick his fork into them, and a flavour of garlic, that pervaded every thing savoury, and faintly hovered over the sweets, a French dinner was not so very unlike an English one. But Sigismund served out the little messes with an air of swelling pride, and George was fain to smack his lips with the manner of a connoisseur when his friend asked him what he thought of the *filets de sole à la maître d'hôtel,* or the *rognons à la* South-African sherry.

Somehow or other George was glad when the dinner was eaten and paid for, and it was time to go home to Camberwell. It was only seven o'clock as yet, and the sun was shining on the fountains as the young men went across Trafalgar Square. They took an omnibus at Charing Cross, and rode to the turnpike at Walworth, in the hope of being in time to get a cup of tea before Mrs Sleaford let the fire out; for that lady had an aggravating trick of letting out the kitchen-fire at half-past seven or eight o'clock on summer evenings, after which hour hot water was an impossibility; unless Mr Sleaford wanted grog, in which case a kettle was set upon a bundle of blazing fire-wood.

George Gilbert did not particularly care whether or not there was any tea to be procured at Camberwell, but he looked forward with a faint thrill of pleasure to the thought of a stroll with Isabel in the twilit garden. He thought so much of this, that he was quite pleased when the big, ill-looking house and the dead wall that surrounded it, became visible across the barren waste of ground that was called a common. He was quite pleased, not with any fierce or passionate emotion, but with a tranquil sense of pleasure. When they came to the wooden door in the garden-wall, Sigismund Smith stooped down and gave his usual whistle at the keyhole; but he looked up suddenly, and cried:

'Well, I'm blest!'

'What's the matter?'

'The door's open.'

Mr Smith pushed it as he spoke, and the two young men went into the front garden.

'In all the time I've lived with the Sleafords, that never happened before,' said Sigismund. 'Mr Sleaford's awfully particular about the gate being kept locked. He says that the neighbourhood's a queer one, and you never know what thieves are hanging about the place;

though, *inter nos*, I don't see that there's much to steal hereabouts,' Mr Smith added, in a confidential whisper.

The door of the house, as well as that of the garden, was open. Sigismund went into the hall, followed closely by George. The parlour-door was open too, and the room was empty—the room was empty, and it had an abnormal appearance of tidiness, as if all the litter and rubbish had been suddenly scrambled together and carried away. There was a scrap of old frayed rope upon the table, lying side by side with some tin-tacks, a hammer, and a couple of blank luggage-labels.

George did not stop to look at these; he went straight to the open window and looked out into the garden. He had so fully expected to see Isabel sitting under the pear-tree with a novel in her lap, that he started and drew back with an exclamation of surprise at finding the garden empty; the place seemed so strangely blank without the girlish figure lolling in the basket-chair. It was as if George Gilbert had been familiar with that garden for the last ten years, and had never seen it without seeing Isabel in her accustomed place.

'I suppose Miss Sleaford—I suppose they're all out,' the surgeon said rather dolefully.

'I suppose they *are* out,' Sigismund answered, looking about him with a puzzled air; 'and yet that's strange. They don't often go out; at least, not all at once. They seldom go out at all, in fact, except on errands. I'll call the girl.'

He opened the door and looked into the front-parlour before going to carry out this design, and he started back upon the threshold as if he had seen a ghost.

'What is it?' cried George.

'My luggage and your portmanteau, all packed and corded; look!'

Mr Smith pointed as he spoke to a couple of trunks, a hat-box, a carpet-bag, and a portmanteau, piled in a heap in the centre of the room. He spoke loudly in his surprise; and the maid-of-all-work came in with her cap hanging by a single hair-pin to a knob of tumbled hair.

'Oh, sir!' she said, 'they're all gone; they went at six o'clock this evenin'; and they're going to America, missus says; and she packed all your things, and she thinks you'd better have 'em took round to the greengrocer's immediant, for fear of being seized for the rent, which is three quarters doo; but you was to sleep in the house tonight, if you pleased, and your friend likewise; and I was to get you your breakfastes in the morning, before I take the key round to the Albany Road, and tell the landlord as they've gone away, which he don't know it yet.'

'GONE AWAY!' said Sigismund; 'GONE AWAY!'

'Yes, sir, every one of 'em; and the boys was so pleased that they would go shoutin' 'ooray, 'ooray, all over the garding, though Mr Sleaford swore at 'em awful, and did hurry and tear so, I thought he was a-goin' mad. But Miss Isabel, she cried about goin' so sudden, and seemed all pale and frightened like. And there's a letter on the chimbley-piece, please, which she put it there.'

Sigismund pounced upon the letter, and tore it open. George read it over his friend's shoulder. It was only two lines.

'DEAR MR SMITH,—Don't think hardly of us for going away so suddenly. Papa says it must be so.

'Yours ever faithfully,

'ISABEL.'

'I should like to keep that letter,' George said, blushing up to the roots of his hair. 'Miss Sleaford writes a pretty hand.'

CHAPTER IV

THE END OF GEORGE GILBERT'S HOLIDAY

The two young men acted very promptly upon that friendly warning conveyed in Mrs Sleaford's farewell message. The maid-of-all-work went to the greengrocer's, and returned in company with a dirty-looking boy—who was 'Mrs Judkin's son, please, sir'—and a truck. Mrs Judkin's son piled the trunks, portmanteau, and carpet-bag on the truck, and departed with his load, which was to be kept in the custody of the Judkin family until the next morning, when Sigismund was to take the luggage away in a cab. When this business had been arranged, Mr Smith and his friend went out into the garden and talked of the surprise that had fallen upon them.

'I always knew they were thinking of leaving,' Sigismund said, 'but I never thought they'd go away like this. I feel quite cut up about it, George. I'd got to like them, you know, old boy, and to feel as if I was one of the family; and I shall never be able to partial-board with any body else.'

George seemed to take the matter quite as seriously as his friend, though his acquaintance with the Sleafords was little more than four-and-twenty hours old.

'They must have known before to-day that they were going,' he said. 'People don't go to America at a few hours' notice.'

Sigismund summoned the dirty maid-of-all-work, and the two young men subjected her to a very rigorous cross-examination; but she could tell them very little more than she had told them all in one breath in the first instance.

'Mr Sleaford 'ad 'is breakfast at nigh upon one o'clock, leastways she put on the pertaturs for the boys' dinner before she biled 'is egg; and then he went out, and he come tearin' 'ome agen in one of these 'ansom cabs at three o'clock in the afternoon; and he told misuss to pack up, and he told the 'ansom cabman to send a four-wheeler from the first stand he passed at six o'clock precise; and the best part of the luggage was sent round to the greengrocer's on a truck, and the rest was took on the roof of the cab, and Master 'Orace rode alongside the cabman, and would smoke one of them nasty penny pickwicks, which they always made 'im bilious; and Mr Sleaford he didn't go in the cab, but walked off as cool as possible, swinging his stick, and 'olding his 'ead as 'igh as hever.'

Sigismund asked the girl if she had heard the address given to the cabman who took the family away.

No, the girl said; Mr Sleaford had given no address. He directed the cabman to drive over Waterloo Bridge, and that was all the girl heard.

Mr Smith's astonishment knew no bounds. He walked about the deserted house, and up and down the weedy pathways between the espaliers, until long after the summer moon was bright upon the lawn, and every trailing branch and tender leaflet threw its sharp separate shadow on the shining ground.

'I never heard of such a thing in all my life,' the young author cried; 'it's like penny numbers. With the exception of their going away in a four-wheeler cab instead of through a sliding panel and subterranean passage, it's for all the world like penny numbers.'

'But you'll be able to find out where they've gone, and why they went away so suddenly,' suggested George Gilbert; 'some of their friends will be able to tell you.'

'Friends!' exclaimed Sigismund; 'they never had any friends—at least not friends that they visited, or any thing of that kind. Mr Sleaford used to bring home some of his friends now and then, of an evening after dark generally, or on a Sunday afternoon. But we never saw much of them, for he used to take them up to his own room; and except for his wanting French brandy and cigars fetched, and chops and steaks cooked, and swearing at the girl over the balusters if the plates weren't hot enough, we shouldn't have known that there was company in the house. I suppose his chums were in the law, like himself,' Mr Smith added musingly; 'but they didn't look much like barristers, for they had straggling moustachios, and a kind of would-be military way; and if they hadn't been Sleaford's friends, I should have thought them raffish-looking.'

Neither of the young men could think of any thing or talk of any thing that night except the Sleafords and their abrupt departure. They roamed about the garden, staring at the long grass and the neglected flower-beds; at the osier arbour, dark under the shadow of a trailing vine, that was half-smothered by the vulgar luxuriance of wild hops,—the osier arbour in which the spiders made their home, and where, upon the rotten bench, romantic Izzie had sat through the hot hours of drowsy summer days, reading her favourite novels and dreaming of a life that was to be like the plot of a novel.

They went into the house, and called for candles, and wandered from room to room looking blankly at the chairs and tables, the open drawers, the disordered furniture, as if from those inanimate objects they might obtain some clue to the little domestic mystery that bewildered them. The house was pervaded by torn scraps of paper, fragments of rag and string, morsels of crumpled lace and muslin, bald hair-brushes lying in the corners of the bedrooms, wisps of hay and straw, tin-tacks, and old kid-gloves. Every where there were traces of disorder and hurry, except in Mr Sleaford's room. That sanctuary was wide open now, and Mr Smith and his friend went into it and examined it. To Sigismund a newly-excavated chamber in a long-buried city could scarcely have been more inter-esting. Here there was no evidence of reckless haste. There was not a single fragment of waste paper in any one of the half-dozen open drawers on either side of the desk. There was not so much as an old envelope upon the floor. A great heap of gray ashes upon the cold hearthstone revealed the fact that Mr Sleaford had employed himself in destroying papers before his hasty departure. The candle-stick that Isabel had given him upon the previous night stood upon his desk, with the candle burnt down to the socket. George remembered having heard his host's heavy footsteps pacing up and down the room; and the occasional opening and shutting of drawers, and slamming of the lids of boxes, which had mixed with his dreams all through that brief summer's night. It was all explained now. Mr Sleaford had of course been making his preparations for leaving Camberwell—for leaving England; if it was really true that the family were going to America.

Early the next morning there came a very irate gentleman from the Albany Road. This was the proprietor of the neglected mansion, who had just heard of the Sleaford hegira,* and who was in a towering passion because of those three quarters' rent which he was never likely to behold. He walked about the house with his hands in his pockets, kicking the doors open, and denouncing his late tenants in very unpleasant language. He stalked into the back parlour, where George and Sigismund were taking spongy French rolls and doubtful French eggs, and glared ferociously at them, and muttered something to the effect that it was like their impudence to be making themselves so 'jolly comfortable' in his house when he'd been swindled by that disreputable gang of theirs. He used other adjectives besides that word 'disreputable' when he spoke of the Sleafords; but Sigismund got up from before the dirty table-cloth, and protested, with his mouth full, that he believed in the honesty of the Sleafords; and that, although temporarily under a cloud, Mr Sleaford would no doubt make a point of looking up the three quarters' rent, and would forward post-office orders for the amount at the earliest opportunity. To this the landlord merely replied, that he hoped his—Sigismund's—head would not ache till Mr Sleaford *did* send the rent; which friendly aspiration was about the only civil thing the proprietor of the mansion said to either of the young men. He prowled about the rooms, poking the furniture with his stick, and punching his fist into the beds to see if any of the feathers had been extracted therefrom. He groaned over the rents in the carpets, the notches and scratches upon the mahogany, the entire absence of handles and knobs wherever it was possible for handles or knobs to be wanting; and every time he found out any new dilapidation in the room where the two young men were taking their breakfast, he made as if he would have come down upon them for the cost of the damage.

'Is that the best tea-pot you're a-having your teas out of? Where's the Britannia metal as I gave thirteen-and-six for seven year ago? Where did that twopenny-halfpenny blown-glass sugar-basin come from? It ain't mine; mine was di'-mond-cut. Why, they've done me two hundred pound mischief. I could afford to forgive 'em the rent. The rent's the least part of the damage they've done me.'

And then the landlord became too forcible to be recorded in these pages, and then he went groaning about the garden; whereupon George and Sigismund collected their toilet-apparatus and such trifling paraphernalia as they had retained for the night's use, and hustled them into a carpet-bag, and fled hastily and fearfully, after giving the servant-maid a couple of half-crowns, and a solemn injunction to write to Sigismund at his address in the Temple if she should hear any tidings whatever of the Sleafords.

So, in the bright summer morning, George Gilbert saw the last of the old house which for nearly seven years had sheltered Mr Sleaford and his wife and children, the weedy garden in which Isabel had idled away so many hours of her early girlhood, the straggling vines under which she had dreamed bright sentimental dreams over the open leaves of her novels. [(An inexpressible melancholy comes over me as I think of one name that I wrote in the last chapter of this story, and that I can never again write as I wrote it then; one name that must henceforth be missing out of that grand triumvirate of writers whose books were Isabel Sleaford's chief education; one bright and great name which we spoke so lightly not very long ago, and which we think of now with a sad and solemn reverence, with unalloyed regret.)]*

The young men hired a cab at the nearest cab-stand, and drove to the establishment of the friendly greengrocer who had given shelter to their goods. It was well for them, perhaps, that the trunks and portmanteau had been conveyed to that humble sanctuary; for the landlord was in no humour to hesitate at trifles, and would have very cheerfully impounded Sigismund's simple wardrobe, and the bran-new linen shirts which George Gilbert had brought to London.

They bestowed a small gratuity upon Mrs Judkin, and then drove to Sigismund's chambers, where they encamped, and contrived to make themselves tolerably comfortable, in a rough gipsy kind of way.

'You shall have Morgan's room,' Sigismund said to his friend, 'and I can make up a bed in the sitting-room; there's plenty of mattresses and blankets.'

They dined rather late in the evening at a celebrated tavern in the near neighbourhood of those sacred precincts where law and justice have their head-quarters, and after dinner Sigismund borrowed the *Law-List.**

'We may find out something about Mr Sleaford in that,' he said.

But the *Law-List* told nothing of Mr Sleaford. In vain Sigismund and George took it in turn to explore the long catalogue of legal practitioners whose names began with the letter S. There were St Johns and Simpsons, St Evremonds and Smitherses, Standishes and Sykeses. There was almost every variety of appellation, aristocratic and plebeian; but the name of Sleaford was not in that list: and the young men returned the document to the waiter, and went home wondering how it was that Mr Sleaford's name had no place among the names of his brotherhood.

I have very little to tell concerning the remaining days which the conditions of George Gilbert's excursion-ticket left him free to enjoy in London. He went to the theatres with his friend, and sat in stifling upper boxes, in which there was a considerable sprinkling of the 'order' element, during these sunshiny summer evenings. Sigismund also took him to divers *al-fresco* entertainments, where there were fire-works, and 'polking,' and bottled stout; and in the daytime George was fain to wander about the streets by himself, staring at the shop-windows, and hustled and frowned at for walking on the wrong side of the pavement; or else to loll on the window-seat in Sigismund's apartment, looking down into the court below, or watching his friend's scratching pen scud across the paper. Sacred as the rites of hospitality may be, they must yet give way before the exigencies of the penny press; and Sigismund was rather a dull companion for a young man from the country who was bent upon a week's enjoyment of London life.

For very lack of employment, George grew to take an interest in his friend's labour, and asked him questions about the story that poured so rapidly from his hurrying pen.

'What's it all about, Sigismund?' he demanded. 'Is it funny?'

'Funny!' cried Mr Smith, with a look of horror; 'I should think not, indeed. Who ever heard of penny numbers being funny? What the penny public want is plot, and plenty of it; surprises, and plenty of 'em; mystery, as thick as a November fog. Don't you know the sort of thing ? "The clock of St Paul's had just sounded eleven hours;"—it's generally a translation, you know, and St Paul's stands for Notre Dame;—"a man came to appear upon the quay which extends itself all the length between the bridges of Waterloo and London." There isn't any quay, you know; but you're obliged to have it so, on account of the plot. "This man—who had a true head of vulture, the nose pointed, sharp, terrible; all that there is of most ferocious; the eyes cavernous, and full of a sombre fire—carried a bag upon his back. Presently he stops himself. He regards with all his eyes the quay, nearly desert; the water, black and slimy, which stretches itself at his feet. He listens, but there is nothing. He bends himself upon the border of the quay. He puts aside the bag from his shoulders, and something of dull, heavy, slides slowly downwards and falls into the water. At the instant that the heavy burden sinks with a dull noise to the bottom of the river, there is a voice, loud and piercing, which seems to elevate itself out of the darkness: 'Philip Launay, what dost thou do there with the corpse of thy victim?'"—That's the sort of thing for the penny public,' said Mr Smith; 'or else a good strong combination story.'

'What do you call a combination story?' Mr Gilbert asked innocently.

'Why, you see, when you're doing four great stories a week for a public that must have a continuous flow of incident, you can't be quite as original as a strict sense of honour might prompt you to be; and the next best thing you can do if you haven't got ideas of your own, is to steal other people's ideas in an impartial manner. Don't empty one man's pocket, but take a little bit all round. The combination novel enables a young author to present his public with all the brightest flowers of fiction neatly arranged into every variety of garland. I'm doing a combination novel now—the *Heart of Midlothian** and the *Wandering Jew*.* You've no idea how admirably the two stories blend. In the first place, I throw my period back into the Middle Ages—there's nothing like the Middle Ages for getting over the difficulties of a story. Good gracious me! why, what is there that isn't possible if you go back to the time of the Plantagenets? I make Jeannie Deans* a dumb girl,—there's twice the interest in her if you make her dumb,—and I give her a goat and a tambourine, because, you see, the artist likes that sort of thing for his illustrations. I think you'd admit that I've very much improved upon Sir Walter Scott— a delightful writer, I allow, but decidedly a failure in penny numbers—if you were to run your eye over the story, George; there's only seventy-eight numbers out yet, but you'll be able to judge of the plot. Of course I don't make Aureola,—I call my Jeannie "Aureola;" rather a fine name, isn't it? and entirely my own invention,— of course I don't make Aureola walk from Edinburgh to London. What would be the good of that? why, any body *could* walk it if they only took long enough about it. I make her walk from London to Rome, to get a Papal Bull* for the release of her sister from the Tower of London. That's something like a walk, I flatter myself; over the Alps—which admits of Aureola's getting buried in the snow, and dug out again by a Mount St Bernard's dog; and then walled up alive by the monks because they suspect her of being friendly to the Lollards;* and dug out again by Caesar Borgia,* who happens to be travelling that way, and asks a night's lodging, and hears Aureola's tambourine behind the stone wall in his bedroom, and digs her out and falls in love with her; and she escapes from his persecution out of a window, and lets herself down the side of the mountain by means of her gauze scarf, and dances her way to Rome, and obtains an audience of the Pope, and gets mixed up with the Jesuits:—and that's where I work into the *Wandering Jew*,' concluded Mr Smith.

George Gilbert ventured to suggest that in the days when the Plantagenet ruled our happy isle, Ignatius Loyola* had not yet founded his wonderful brotherhood; but Mr Smith acknowledged this prosaic suggestion with a smile of supreme contempt.

'Oh, if you tie me down to facts,' he said, 'I can't write at all.'

'But you like writing?'

'For the penny public? Oh, yes; I like writing for them. There's only one objection to the style—it's apt to give an author a tendency towards bodies.'

Mr Gilbert was compelled to confess that this last remark was incomprehensible to him.

'Why, you see, the penny public require excitement,' said Mr Smith; 'and in order to get the excitement up to a strong point, you're obliged to have recourse to bodies. Say your hero murders his father, and buries him in the coal-cellar in No. 1. What's the consequence? There's an undercurrent of the body in the coal-cellar running through every chapter, like the subject in a fugue or a symphony. You drop it in the treble, you catch it up in the bass; and then it goes sliding up into the treble again, and then drops down with a melodious groan into the bass; and so on to the end of the story. And when you've once had recourse to the stimulant of bodies, you're like a man who's accustomed to strong liquors, and to whose vitiated palate simple drinks seem flat and wishy-washy. I think there ought to be a literary temperance-pledge, by which the votaries of the ghastly and melodramatic school might bind themselves to the renunciation of the bowl and dagger, the midnight rendezvous, the secret grave dug by lantern-light under a black grove of cypress, the white-robed figure gliding in the gray gloaming athwart a lonely churchyard, and all the alcoholic elements of fiction. But, you see, George, it isn't so easy to turn teetotaller,' added Mr. Smith, doubtfully; 'and I scarcely know that it is so very wise to make the experiment. Are not reformed drunkards the dullest and most miserable of mankind ? Isn't it better for a man to do his best in the style that is natural to him than to do badly in another man's line of business? *Box and Cox*** is not a great work when criticised upon sternly aesthetic principles; but I would rather be the author of *Box and Cox,* and hear my audience screaming with laughter from the rise of the curtain to the fall thereof, than write a dull five-act tragedy, in the unities of which Aristotle himself could find no flaw, but from whose performance panic-stricken spectators should slink away or ere the second act came to its dreary close. I think I should like to have been Guilbert de Pixérécourt,* the father and prince of melodrama, the man whose dramas were acted thirty thousand times in France before he died (and how many times in England?); the man who reigned supreme over the playgoers of his time, and has not yet ceased to reign. Who ever quotes any passage from the works of Guilbert de Pixérécourt, or remembers his name? But to this day his dramas are acted in every country theatre; his persecuted heroines weep and tremble; his murderous scoundrels run their two hours' career of villany, to be dragged off scowling to subterranean dungeons, or to die impenitent and groaning at the feet of triumphant virtue. Before nine o'clock to-night there will be honest country-folks trembling for the fate of Theresa, the Orphan of Geneva, and simple matrons weeping over the peril of the Wandering Boys. But Guilbert de Pixérécourt was never a great man; he was only popular. If a man can't have a niche in the Walhalla, isn't it something to have his name in big letters in the play-bills on the boulevard? and I wonder how long my friend Guilbert would have held the stage, if he had emulated Racine or Corneille.* He did what it was in him to do, honestly; and he had his reward. Who would not wish to be great? Do you think I wouldn't rather be the author of the *Vicar of Wakefield** than of *Colonel Montefiasco*? I *could* write the *Vicar of Wakefield*, too; but—'

George stared aghast at his excited friend.

'But not Oliver Goldsmith's *Vicar of Wakefield*,' Sigismund explained.

He had thrown down his pen now, and was walking up and down the room with his hands thrust deep down in his pockets, and his face scarlet with fierce excitement.

'I should do the Vicar in the detective pre-Raphaelite style.' Moses knows a secret of his father's—forged accommodation-bills, or something of that kind; sets out to go to the fair on a drowsy summer morning, not a leaf stirring in the vicarage-garden. You hear the humming of the bees as they bounce against the vicarage-windows; you see the faint light trembling about Olivia's head, as she comes to watch her brother ride along the road; you see him ride away, and the girl watching him, and feel the hot sleepy atmosphere, and hear the swoop of the sickle in the corn-fields on the other side of the road; and the low white gate swings-to with a little click, and Miss Primrose walks slowly back to the house, and says, "Papa, it's very warm;" and you know there's something going to happen.

'Then the second chapter comes, and Mr Primrose has his dinner, and goes out to visit his poor; and the two girls walk about the garden with Mr Burchell, watching for Moses, who NEVER COMES BACK. And then the serious business of the story begins, and Burchell keeps his eye upon the Vicar. Nobody else suspects good Mr Primrose; but Burchell's eye is never off him; and one night, when the curtains are drawn, and the girls are sitting at their work, and dear Mrs Primrose is cutting out comfortable flannels for the poor, the

Vicar opens his desk, and begins to write a letter. You hear the faint sound of the light ashes falling on the hearth, the slow ticking of an eight-day clock in the hall outside the drawing-room door, the sharp snap of Mrs Primrose's scissors as they close upon the flannel. Sophia asks Burchell to fetch a volume from the book-case behind the Vicar's chair. He is a long time choosing the book, and his eye looks over the Vicar's shoulder. He takes a mental inventory of the contents of the open desk, and he sees amongst the neatly-docketed papers, the receipted bills, and packets of envelopes—what? a glove, a green-kid glove sewn with white, which he distinctly remembers to have seen worn by Moses when he started on that pleasant journey from which he never returned. Can't you see the Vicar's face, as he looks round at Burchell, and knows that his secret is discovered? I can. Can't you fancy the awful silent duel between the two men, the furtive glances, the hidden allusions to that dreadful mystery, lurking in every word that Burchell utters?

'That's how *I* should do the *Vicar of Wakefield*,' said Sigismund Smith triumphantly. 'There wouldn't be much in it, you know; but the story would be pervaded by Moses's body lying murdered in a ditch half a mile from the vicarage, and Burchell's ubiquitous eye. I daresay some people would cry out upon it, and declare that it was wicked and immoral, and that the young man who could write about a murder would be ready to commit the deed at the earliest convenient opportunity. But I don't suppose the clergy would take to murdering their sons by reason of my fiction, in which the rules of poetical justice would be sternly adhered to, and Nemesis, in the shape of Burchell, perpetually before the reader.'

Poor George Gilbert listened very patiently to his friend's talk, which was not particularly interesting to him. Sigismund preached 'shop' to whomsoever would listen to him, or suffer him to talk; which was pretty much the same to this young man. I am afraid there were times when his enthusiastic devotion to his profession rendered Mr Smith a terrible nuisance to his friends and acquaintance. He would visit a pleasant country-house, and receive hospitable entertainment, and enjoy himself; and then, when all that was morbid in his imagination had been stimulated by sparkling burgundy and pale hochheimer, this wretched young traitor would steal out into some peaceful garden, where dew-laden flowers flung their odours on the still evening air, and sauntering in the shadowy groves where the nightingale's faint 'jug-jug' was beginning to sound, would plan a diabolical murder, to be carried out in seventy-five penny numbers. Sometimes he was honourable enough to ask permission of the proprietor of the country mansion; and when, on one occasion, after admiring the trim flower-gardens and ivied walls, the low turreted towers and grassy moats, of a dear old place that had once been a grange, he ventured to remark that the spot was so peaceful it reminded him of slow poisoning, and demanded whether there would be any objection to his making the quiet grange the scene of his next fiction,—the cordial cheery host cried out, in a big voice that resounded high up among the trees where the rooks were cawing, 'People it with fiends, my dear boy! You're welcome to people the place with fiends,* as far as I'm concerned.'

CHAPTER V

GEORGE AT HOME

The young surgeon went home to Midlandshire with his fellow-excursionists, when the appointed Monday came round. He met Miss Burdock and her sister on the platform in Euston Square, and received those ladies from the hands of their aunt. Sophronia did not blush now when her eyes met George Gilbert's frank stare. She had danced twice with a young barrister at the little quadrille-party which her aunt had given in honour of the maltster's daughters; a young barrister who was tall and dark and stylish, and who spoke of Graybridge-on-the-Wayverne as a benighted place, which was only endurable for a week or so in the hunting season. Miss Sophronia Burdock's ideas had expanded during that week in Baker Street, and she treated her travelling companion with an air of haughty indifference, which might have wounded George to the quick had he been aware of the change in the lady's manner. But poor George saw no alteration in the maltster's daughter; he watched no changes of expression in the face opposite to him as the rushing engine carried him back to Midlandshire. He was thinking of another face, which he had only seen for a few brief hours, and which he was perhaps never again to look upon; a pale girlish countenance, framed with dense black hair; a pale face, out of which there looked large solemn eyes, like stars that glimmer faintly through the twilight shadows.

Before leaving London, George had obtained a promise from his friend Sigismund Smith. Whatever tidings Mr Smith should at any time hear about the Sleafords, he was to communicate immediately to the young surgeon of Graybridge-on-the-Wayverne. It was, of course, very absurd of George to take such an interest in this singular family; the young man admitted as much himself; but, then, singular people are always more or less interesting; and, having been a witness of Mr Sleaford's abrupt departure, it was only natural that George should want to know the end of the story. If these people were really gone to America, why, of course, it was all over; but if they had not left London, some one or other of the family might turn up some day, and in that case Sigismund was to write and tell his friend all about it.

George Gilbert's last words upon the platform at Euston Square had relation to this subject; and all the way home he kept debating in his mind whether it was likely that Sleafords had really gone to America, or whether the American idea had been merely thrown out with a view to the mystification of the irate landlord.

Life at Graybridge-on-the-Wayverne was as slow and sleepy as the river which widened in the flat meadows outside the town; the dear old river which crept lazily past the mouldering wall of the churchyard, and licked the moss-grown tombstones that had lurched against that ancient boundary. Every thing at Graybridge was more or less old and quaint and picturesque; but the chief glory of Graybridge was the parish-church; a grand old edifice which was planted beyond the outskirts of the town, and approached by a long avenue of elms, beneath whose shadow the tombstones glimmered whitely in the sun. The capricious Wayverne, which was perpetually winding across your path wheresoever you wandered in pleasant Midlandshire, was widest here; and on still summer days the gray towers of the old church looked down at other phantasmal towers in the tranquil water.

George used to wander in this churchyard sometimes on his return from a trout-fishing expedition, and, lounging among the tombstones with his rod upon his shoulder, would abandon himself to the simple day-dreams he loved best to weave.

But the young surgeon had a good deal of work to do, now that his father had admitted him to the solemn rights of partnership, and very little time for any sentimental musings in the churchyard. The parish work in itself was very heavy, and George rode long distances on his steady-going gray pony to attend to captious patients, who gave him small thanks for his attendance. He was a very soft-hearted young man, and he often gave his slender pocket-money to those of his patients who wanted food rather than medicine. Little by little people grew to understand that George Gilbert was very different from his father, and had a tender pity for the sorrows and sufferings it was a part of his duty to behold. Love and gratitude for this young doctor may have been somewhat slow to spring up in the hearts of his parish patients; but they took a deep root, and became hardy, vigorous plants before the first year of George's service was over. Before that year came to a close the partnership between the father and son had been irrevocably dissolved, without the aid of legal practitioners, or any legal formulas whatsoever; and George Gilbert was sole master of the old house with the whitewashed plaster-walls and painted beams of massive oak.

The young man lamented the loss of his father with all that single-minded earnestness which was the dominant attribute of his character. He had been as obedient to his father at the last as he had been at the first; as submissive in his manhood as in his childhood. But in his obedience there had been nothing childish or cowardly. He was obedient because he believed his father to be wise and good, reverencing the old man with simple, unquestioning veneration. And now that the father was gone, George Gilbert began life in real earnest. The poor of Graybridge-on-the-Wayverne had good reason to rejoice at the change which had given the young doctor increase of means and power. He was elected unanimously to the post his father's death had left nominally vacant; and wherever there was sickness and pain, his kindly face seemed to bring comfort, his bright blue eyes seemed to inspire courage. He took an atmosphere of youth and hope and brave endurance with him every where, which was more invigorating than the medicines he prescribed; and, next to Mr Neate the curate, George Gilbert was the best-beloved and most popular man in Graybridge.

He had never had any higher ambition than this. He had no wish to strive or to achieve; he only wanted to be useful; and when he heard the parable of the Talents read aloud in the old church, a glow of gentle happiness thrilled through his veins as he thought of his own small gifts, which had never yet been suffered to grow rusty for lack of service.

The young man's life could scarcely have been more sheltered from the storm and tempest of the world, though the walls of some medieval monastery had encircled his little surgery. Could the tumults of passion ever have a home in the calm breast of these quiet provincials, whose regular lives knew no greater change than the slow alternation of the seasons, whose orderly existences were never disturbed by an event? Away at Conventford there were factory-strikes, and political dissensions, and fighting and rioting now and then; but here the tranquil days crept by, and left no mark by which they might be remembered.

Miss Sophronia Burdock did not long cherish the memory of the dark-haired barrister she had met in Baker Street. To do so would have been as foolish as to 'love some bright particular star, and think to wed it,'* in the young damsel's opinion. She wisely banished the barrister's splendid image, and she smiled once more upon Mr Gilbert when she met him coming out of church in the cold wintry sunlight, looking to especial advantage in his new mourning clothes. But George was blind to the sympathetic smiles that greeted him. He was not in love with Miss Sophronia Burdock. The image of Isabel's pale face had faded into a very indistinct shadow by this time; nay, it was almost entirely blotted out by the young man's grief for his father's death; but if his heart was empty enough now, there was no place in it for Miss Burdock, though it was hinted at in Graybridge that a dower of four thousand pounds would accompany that fair damsel's hand. George Gilbert had no high-flown or sentimental notions; but he would have thought it no greater shame to rifle the contents of the maltster's iron safe, than to enrich himself with the possessions of a woman he did not love.

In the mean time he lived his peaceful life in the house where he had been born, mourning with simple, natural sorrow for the old father who had so long sat at the opposite side of the hearth, reading a local paper by the light of a candle held between his eyes and the small print, and putting down the page every now and then to descant, at his ease, upon the degeneracy of the times. The weak, loving, fidgety father was gone now, and George looked blankly at the empty chair which had taken the old man's shape; but his sorrow was unembittered by vain remorse or cruel self-reproach; he had been a good son, and he could look back at his life with his dead father, and thank God for the peaceful life that they had spent together.

But he was very lonely now in the old house, which was a bare, blank place, peopled by no bright inanimate creations by which art fills the homes of wealthy hermits with fair semblances of life. The empty walls stared down upon the young man as he sat alone in the dim candlelight, till he was fain to go into the kitchen, which was the most cheerful room in the house, and where he could talk to William and Tilly, while he lounged against the quaint old angle of the high oaken chimney-piece smoking his cigar.

William and Tilly were a certain Mr and Mrs Jeffson, who had come southwards with the pretty young woman whom Mr John Gilbert had encountered in the course of a holiday-trip to a quiet Yorkshire town, where the fair towers of a minster rose above a queer old street, beyond whose gabled roofs lay spreading common-lands, fair pasture-farms, and pleasant market-gardens. It was in the homestead attached to one of these pasture-farms that John Gilbert had met the bright, rosy-faced girl whom he made his wife; and Mr and Mrs Jeffson were poor relations of the young lady's father. At Mrs Gilbert's entreaty they consented to leave the little bit of garden and meadow-land which they rented near her father's farm, and followed the surgeon's wife to her new home, where Matilda Jeffson took upon herself the duties of house-keeper, general manager, and servant-of-all-work; while her husband looked after the surgeon's stable, and worked in the long, old-fashioned garden, where the useful element very much preponderated over the ornamental.

I am compelled to admit that, in common with almost all those bright and noble qualities which can make man admirable, Mr William Jeffson possessed one failing. He was lazy. But then his laziness gave such a delicious, easy-going tone to his whole character, and was so much a part of his good-nature and benevolence, that to wish him faultless would have been to wish him something less than he was. There are some people whose faults are better than other people's virtues. Mr Jeffson was lazy. In the garden which it was his duty to cultivate, the snails crawled along their peaceful way, unhindered by cruel rake or hoe; but then, on the other hand, the toads grew fat in shadowy corners under the broad dock-leaves, and the empty shells of their slimy victims attested the uses of those ugly and venomous reptiles. The harmony of the universe asserted itself in that Midlandshire garden, unchecked by any presumptuous interference from Mr Jeffson. The weeds grew high in waste patches of ground, left here and there amongst the gooseberry-bushes and the cabbages, the raspberries and potatoes; and William Jeffson offered little hindrance to their rank luxuriance. 'There was room enough for aught he wanted,' he said philosophically; 'and ground that wouldn't grow weeds would be good for naught. Mr Gilbert had more fruit and vegetables than he could eat, or cared to give away; and surely that was enough for any body.' Officious visitors would sometimes suggest this or that alteration or improvement in the simple garden; but Mr Jeffson would only smile at them with a bland, sleepy smile, as he lolled upon his spade, and remark, 'that he'd been used to gardens all his life, and knew what could be made out of 'em, and what couldn't.'

In short, Mr Jeffson and Matilda Jeffson his wife did as they liked in the surgeon's house, and had done so ever since that day upon which they came to Midlandshire to take friendly service with their second cousin, pretty Mrs John Gilbert. They took very small wages from their kinswoman's husband, but they had their own apartments, and lived as they pleased, and ordered the lives of their master and mistress, and idolised the fair-haired baby-boy who was born by and by, and who grew day by day under their loving eyes, when the tender gaze of his mother had ceased to follow his toddling footsteps, or yearn for the sight of his frank, innocent face. Mr Jeffson may have neglected the surgeon's garden, by reason of that lymphatic temperament which was peculiar to him; but there was one business in which he never lacked energy, one pursuit in which he knew no weariness. He was never tired of any labour which contributed to the pleasure or amusement of Mr Gilbert's only son. He carried the child on his shoulders for long journeys to distant meadows in the sunshiny haymaking season, when all the air was fragrant with the scent of grass and flowers; he clambered through thorny gaps amidst the brambly underwood, and tore the flesh off his poor big hands hunting for blackberries and cob-nuts for Master 'Jarge.' He persuaded his master into the purchase of a pony when the boy was five years old, and the little fellow trotted to Wareham at Mr Jeffson's side when that gentleman went on errands for the Graybridge household. William Jeffson had no children of his own, and he loved the surgeon's boy with all the fondness of a nature peculiarly capable of love and devotion.

It was a bitter day for him when Master Jarge went to the Classical and Commercial Academy at Wareham; and but for those happy Saturday afternoons on which he went to fetch the boy for a holiday that lasted till Sunday evening, poor William Jeffson would have lost all the pleasures of his simple life. What was the good of haymaking if George wasn't in the thick of the fun, clambering on the loaded wain, or standing, flushed and triumphant, high up against the sunlit sky on the growing summit of the new-made stack? What could be drearier work than feeding the pigs, or milking the cow, unless Master Jarge was by to turn labour into pleasure by the bright magic of his presence? William Jeffson went about his work with a grave countenance during the boy's absence, and only brightened on those delicious Saturday afternoons when Master Jarge came hurrying to the little wooden gate in Dr Malder's playground, shouting a merry welcome to his friend. There was no storm of rain or hail, snow or sleet, that ever came out of the heavens, heavy enough to hinder Mr Jeffson's punctual attendance at that little gate. What did he care for drenching showers, or thunderclaps that seemed to shake the earth, so long as the little wooden gate opened, and the fair young face he loved looked out at him with a welcoming smile?

'Our boys laid any money you wouldn't come to-day, Jeff,' Master Gilbert said sometimes; 'but I knew there wasn't any weather invented that would keep you away.'

O blessed reward of fidelity and devotion! What did William Jeffson want more than this?

Matilda Jeffson loved her master's son very dearly in her own way; but her household duties were a great deal heavier than Mr Jeffson's responsibilities, and she had little time to waste upon the poetry of affection. She kept the boy's wardrobe in excellent order; baked rare batches of hot cakes on Saturday afternoons for his special gratification; sent him glorious hampers, in which there were big jars of gooseberry-jam, pork-pies, plum-loaves, and shrivelled apples. In all substantial matters Mrs Jeffson was as much the boy's friend as her husband; but that tender, sympathetic devotion which

William felt for his master's son was something beyond her comprehension.

'My master's daft about the lad,' she said, when she spoke of the two.

[I do not know what William Jeffson might have become had his destiny given him gentlemen for his kindred, and placed a pen in his hand instead of a spade; but I know that there were all the elements of poetry in his nature, and a profound depth of tenderness and sentiment underlying the slow simplicity of his talk, the gentle homeliness of his manner. He came to Midlandshire while still a young man, and he was only five-and-forty years of age at the time of John Gilbert's death; but at five-and-forty he was as simply sentimental as a schoolgirl of seventeen. He had none of the rough John Brodieism of the ordinary Yorkshireman. He was as brave and honest as Tilda Price's glorious sweetheart;* but his manner was as gentle as that of the gentlest of womankind. He was a gentleman pure and simple, fresh from the supreme hand of Nature, who creates a gentleman after her own fashion now and then, to the confusion of all theories about race and culture. If you had taken Mr Jeffson to a West-End tailor, and ordered a suit of clothes for him, you might have sent him straight into the House of Lords, and no member of that assemblage would have discovered that the intruder had been bred a market-gardener. If some wonderful hazard in the gambling game called Fortune had elevated William Jeffson to a peerage, he would have betrayed himself by no solecism; he would have omitted no duty. Fortune had done nothing for him; but he had been born a gentleman, and no power upon this earth could deprive him of his birthright. In his low, lazy accents the northern twang melted into the liquid softness of Italian. He was fond of poetry—poetry of the most sentimental order; and would entreat Master Jarge to read or recite favourite extracts from the schoolboy collection that was familiar to him. All the splendour and loveliness of the universe sank as deeply into Mr Jeffson's breast as into the soul of the greatest poet who ever charmed mankind with the magic of his verse. He lacked the sublime power of expression, but the lesser gift of appreciation had been ungrudgingly bestowed upon him. When George and his father's gardener talked about the stars and the flowers, the changing clouds, the shadows in the river, the solemn stillness of the old church, the slow plash of the willow-branches as they dipped into the water, it was the uneducated man whose thoughts were beyond the comprehension of the educated boy; the pupil's imagination soared away into bright regions, before whose shining portals the teacher shrank away bewildered, dazzled, and confounded.]*

George Gilbert taught his companion a good deal in those pleasant Saturday evenings, when the surgeon was away amongst his patients, and the boy was free to sit in the kitchen with Mr and Mrs Jeffson. He told the Yorkshireman all about those enemies of boyhood, the classic poets; but William infinitely preferred Shakespeare and Milton, Byron and Scott, to the accomplished Romans, whose verses were of the lamest as translated by George. Mr Jeffson could never have enough of Shakespeare. He was never weary of Hamlet, Lear, Othello, and Romeo, the bright young Prince who tried on his father's crown, bold Hotspur, ill-used Richard, passionate Margaret, murderous Gloster, ruined Wolsey, noble Katharine. All that grand gallery of pictures unrolled its splendours for this man, and the schoolboy wondered at the enthusiasm he was powerless to understand. He was inclined to think that practical Mrs Jeffson was right, and that her husband was a little 'daft' upon some matters.

The boy returned his humble friend's affection with a steady, honest regard, that richly compensated the gardener, whose love was not of a nature to need much recompense, since its growth was as spontaneous and unconscious as that of the wild-flowers amongst the long grass. George returned William Jeffson's affection, but he could not return it in kind. The poetry of friendship was not in his nature. He was honest, sincere, and true, but not sympathetic or assimilative; he preserved his own individuality wherever he went, and took no colour from the people amongst whom he lived.

Mr Gilbert would have been very lonely now that his father was gone, had it not been for this honest couple, who managed his house and garden, his stable and paddocks, and watched his interests as earnestly as if he had been indeed their son. Whenever he had a spare half-hour, the young man strolled into the old-fashioned kitchen, and smoked his cigar in the chimney-corner, where he had passed so much of his boyhood.

'When I sit here, Jeff,' he said sometimes, 'I seem to go back to the old school-days again, and I fancy I hear Brown Molly's hoofs upon the frosty road, and my father's voice calling to you to open the gate.'

Mr Jeffson sighed, as he looked up from the mending of a bridle or the patching of a horse-cloth.

'Them was pleasant days, Master Jarge,' he said regretfully. He was thinking that the school-boy had been more to him and nearer to him than the young surgeon could ever be. They had been children together, these two, and William had never grown weary of his childhood. He was left behind now that his companion had grown up, and the happy childish days were all over. There was a gigantic kite on a shelf in the back-kitchen; a kite that Mr Jeffson had made with his own patient hands. George Gilbert would have laughed now if that kite had been mentioned to him; but William Jeffson would have been constant to the same boyish sports until his hair was gray, and would have never known weariness of spirit.

'You'll be marrying some fine lady, maybe now, Master Jarge,' Mrs Jeffson said; 'and she'll look down upon our north-country ways, and turn us out of the old place where we've lived so long.'

But George protested eagerly that, were he to marry the daughter of the Queen of England, which was not particularly likely, that royal lady should take kindly to his old servants, or should be no wife of his.

'When I marry, my wife must love the people I love,' said the surgeon, who entertained those superb theories upon the management of a wife which are peculiar to youthful bachelors.

George further informed his humble friends that he was not likely to enter the holy estate of matrimony for many years to come, as he had so far seen no one who at all approached his idea of womanly perfection. He had very practical views upon this subject, and meant to wait patiently until some faultless young person came across his pathway; some neat-handed, church-going damsel, with tripping feet and smoothly banded hair; some fair young sage, who had never been known to do a foolish act or say an idle word. Sometimes the image of Isabel Sleaford trembled faintly upon the magic mirror of the young man's reveries, and he wondered whether, under any combination of circumstances, she would ever arrive at this standard. Oh, no; it was impossible. He looked back to the drowsy summer-time, and saw her lolling in the garden-chair, with the shadows of the branches fluttering upon her tumbled muslin dress, and her black hair pushed anyhow away from the broad low brow.

'I hope that foolish Sigismund won't meet Miss Sleaford again,'

George thought very gravely; 'he might be silly enough to marry her, and I'm sure she'd never make a good wife for any man.'

George Gilbert's father died in the autumn of '52; and early in the following spring the young man received a letter from his friend Mr Smith. Sigismund wrote very discursively about his own prospects and schemes, and gave his friend a brief synopsis of the romance he had last begun. George skimmed lightly enough over this part of the letter; but as he turned the leaf by and by, he saw a name that brought the blood to his face. He was vexed with himself for that involuntary blush, and sorely puzzled to know why he should be so startled by the unexpected sight of Isabel Sleaford's name.

'You made me promise to tell you any thing that turned up about the Sleafords,' Sigismund wrote. 'You'll be very much surprised to hear that Miss Sleaford came to me the other day here in my chambers, and asked me if I could help her in any way to get her living. She wanted me to recommend her as a nursery-governess, or companion, or something of that kind, if I knew of any family in want of such a person. She was staying at Islington with a sister of her stepmother's, she told me; but she couldn't be a burden on her any longer. Mrs Sleaford and the boys have gone to live in Jersey, it seems, on account of things being cheap there; and I have no doubt that boy Horace will become an inveterate smoker. Poor Sleaford is dead. You'll be as much astounded as I was to hear this. Isabel did not tell me this at first; but I saw that she was dressed in black, and when I asked her about her father, she burst out crying, and sobbed as if her heart would break. I should like to have ascertained what the poor fellow died of, and all about it,—for Sleaford was not an old man, and one of the most powerful-looking fellows I ever saw,— but I could not torture Izzie with questions while she was in such a state of grief and agitation. "I'm very sorry you've lost your father, my dear Miss Sleaford," I said; and she sobbed out something that I scarcely heard, and I got her some cold water to drink, and it was ever so long before she came round again and was able to talk to me. Well, I couldn't think of any body that was likely to help her that day; but I took the address of her aunt's house at Islington, and promised to call upon her there in a day or two. I wrote by that day's post to my mother, and asked her if she could help me; and she wrote back by return to tell me that my uncle, Charles Raymond, at Conventford, was in want of just such a person as Miss Sleaford (of course I had endowed Isabel with all the virtues under the sun), and if I really thought Miss S. would suit, and I could answer for the perfect respectability of her connexions and antecedents,—it isn't to be supposed that I was going to say any thing about that three quarters' rent, or that I should own that Isabel's antecedents were lolling in a garden-chair reading novels, or going on suspicious errands to the *jeweller* ("O my prophetic soul!" *et cetera*) in the Walworth Road,—why, I was to engage Miss S. at twenty pounds a year salary. I went up to Islington that very afternoon, although I was a number and a half behind with *The Demon of the Galleys* (*The D. of the G.* is a sequel to *The Brand upon the Shoulder-blade*; the proprietor of the *Penny Parthenon* insisted upon having a sequel, and I had to bring Colonel Montefiasco to life again, after hurling him over a precipice three hundred feet high),—and the poor girl began to cry when I told her I'd found a home for her. I'm afraid she's had a great deal of trouble since the Sleafords left Camberwell; for she isn't at all the girl she was. Her stepmother's sister is a vulgar woman who lets lodgings, and there's only one servant—such a miserable slavey; and Isabel went to the door three times while I was there. You know my uncle Raymond, and you know what a dear jolly fellow he is; so you may guess the change will be a very pleasant one for poor Izzie. By the by, you might call and see her the first time you're in Conventford, and write me word how the poor child gets on. I thought she seemed a little frightened at the idea of going among strangers. I saw her off at Euston Square the day before yesterday. She went by the parliamentary train; and I put her in charge of a most respectable family going all the way through, with six children, and a birdcage, and a dog, and a pack of cards to play upon a tea-tray on account of the train being slow.'

Mr Gilbert read this part of his friend's letter three times over before he was able to realise the news contained in it. Mr Sleaford dead, and Isabel settled as a nursery-governess at Conventford! If the winding Wayverne had overflowed its sedgy banks and flooded all Midlandshire, the young surgeon could have been scarcely more surprised than he was by the contents of his friend's letter. Isabel at Conventford—within eleven miles of Graybridge; within eleven miles of him at that moment, as he walked up and down the little room, with his hair tumbled all about his flushed good-looking face, and Sigismund's letter in his waistcoat!

What was it to him that Isabel Sleaford was so near? What was she to him, that he should think of her, or be fluttered by the thought that she was within his reach? What did he know of her? Only that she had eyes that were unlike any other eyes he had ever looked at; eyes that haunted his memory like strange stars seen in a feverish dream. He knew nothing of her but this; and that she had a pretty, sentimental manner, a pensive softness in her voice, and sudden flights and capricious changes of expression that had filled his mind with wonder.

George went back to the kitchen and smoked another cigar in Mr Jeffson's company. He went to that apartment fully determined to waste no more of his thoughts upon Isabel Sleaford, who was in sober truth a frivolous, sentimental creature, eminently adapted to make any man miserable; but somehow or other, before the cigar was finished, George had told his earliest friend and confidant all about Mr Sleaford's family, touching very lightly upon Isabel's attractions, and speaking of a visit to Conventford as a disagreeable duty that friendship imposed.

'Of course I shouldn't think of going all that way on purpose to see Miss Sleaford,' he said, 'though Sigismund seems to expect me to do so; but I must go to Conventford in the course of the week, to see about those drugs Johnson promised to get me. They won't make a very big parcel, and I can bring them home in my coat-pocket. You might trim Brown Molly's fetlocks, Jeff; she'll look all the better for it. I'll go on Thursday; and yet I don't know that I couldn't better spare the time to-morrow.'

'To-morrow's market-day, Master Jarge. I was thinkin' of goin' t' Conventford mysen. I might bring t' droogs for thee, and thoo couldst write a noate askin' after t' young leddy,' Mr Jeffson remarked thoughtfully.

George shook his head. 'That would never do, Jeff,' he said; 'Sigismund asks me to go and see her.'

Mr Jeffson relapsed into a thoughtful silence, out of which he emerged by and by with a slow chuckle.

'I reckon Miss Sleaford'll be a pretty girl,' he remarked thoughtfully, with rather a sly glance at his young master.

George Gilbert found it necessary to enter into an elaborate explanation upon this subject. No; Miss Sleaford was not pretty. She had no colour in her cheeks, and her nose was nothing particular,—

not a beautiful queenlike hook, like that of Miss Harleystone, the belle of Graybridge, who was considered like the youthful members of the peerage,—and her mouth wasn't very small, and her forehead was low; and, in short, some people might think Miss Sleaford plain.

'But thoo doosn't, Master Jarge!' exclaimed Mr Jeffson, slapping his hand upon his knee with an intolerable chuckle; 'thoo thinkst sommoat of her, I'll lay; and I'll trim Brown Molly's fetlocks till she looks as genteel as a thoroughbred.'

'Thoo'rt an old fondy!' cried Mrs Jeffson, looking up from her needlework. 'It isn't one of these London lasses as'll make a good wife for Master Jarge; and he'd never be that soft as to go running after nursery-governesses at Conventford when he might have Miss Burdock and all her money, and be one of the first gentlefolks in Graybridge.'

'Hold thy noise, Tilly. Thou knowst nowt aboot it. Didn't I marry thee for loove, lass, when I might have had Sarah Peglock, as was only daughter to him as kept t' Red Lion in Belminster; and didn't I come up to London, where thou wast in service, and take thee away from thy pleace; and wasn't Sarah a'most wild when she heard it? Master Jarge'll marry for loove, or he'll never marry at all. Don't you remember her as wore the pink sash and shoes wi' sandals at the dancin' school, Master Jarge; and us takin' her a ploom-loaf, and a valentine, and sugar-sticks, and oranges, when you was home for th' holidays?'

Mr Jeffson had been the confidant of all George's boyish love-affairs, the innocent Leporello* of this young provincial Juan; and he was eager to be trusted with new secrets, and to have a finger once more in the sentimental pie. But nothing could be more stern than Mr Gilbert's denial of any romantic fancy for Miss Sleaford.

'I should be very glad to befriend her in any way,' he said gravely; 'but she's the very last person in the world that I should ever dream of making my wife.'

This young man discussed his matrimonial views with the calm grandiosity of manner with which man, the autocrat, talks of his humble slaves before he has tried his hand at governing them,— before he has received the fiery baptism of suffering, and learned by bitter experience that a perfect woman is not a creature to be found at every street-corner waiting meekly for her ruler.

CHAPTER VI

TOO MUCH ALONE

Brown Molly's fetlocks were neatly trimmed by Mr Jeffson's patient hands. I fancy the old mare would have gone long without a clipping, had it not been George's special pleasure that the animal should be smartened up before he rode her to Conventford. Clipping is not a very pleasant labour; but there is no task so difficult that William Jeffson would have shrunk from it, if its achievement could give George Gilbert happiness.

Brown Molly looked a magnificent creature when George came home, after a hurried round of professional visits, and found her saddled and bridled, at eleven o'clock, on the bright March morning which he had chosen for his journey to Conventford. But though the mare was ready, and had been ready for a quarter of an hour, there was some slight delay while George ran up to his room,—the room which he had slept in from his earliest boyhood (there were some of his toys, dusty and forgotten, amongst the portmanteaus and hat-boxes at the top of the painted-deal wardrobe),—and was for some little time engaged in changing his neckcloth, brushing his hair and hat, and making other little improvements in his personal appearance.

William Jeffson declared that his young master looked as if he was going straight off to be married, as he rode away out of the stable-yard, with a bright eager smile upon his face, and the spring breezes blowing amongst his hair. He looked the very incarnation of homely, healthy comeliness, the archetype of honest youth and simple English manhood, radiant with the fresh brightness of an unsullied nature, untainted by an evil memory, pure as a new-polished mirror on which no foul breath has ever rested.

He rode away to his fate, self-deluded, and happy in the idea that his journey was a wise blending of the duties of friendship and the cares of his surgery.

I do not think there can be a more beautiful road in all England than that between Graybridge-on-the-Wayverne and Conventford, and I can scarcely believe that in all England there is an uglier town than Conventford itself. I envy George Gilbert his long ride on that bright March morning, when the pale primroses glimmered among the underwood, and the odour of early violets mingled faintly with the air. The country roads were long avenues, which might have made the glory of a ducal park; and every here and there, between a gap in the budding hedge, a white-walled country villa or grave old red-brick mansion peeped out of some nook of rustic beauty, with shining windows winking in the noontide sun.

Midway between Graybridge and Conventford there is the village of Waverly; the straggling village street over whose quaint Elizabethan roofs the ruined towers of a grand old castle cast their protecting shadows. John of Gaunt was master and founder of the grandest of those old towers, and Henry the Eighth's wonderful daughter has feasted in the great banqueting-hall, where the ivy hangs its natural garlands round the stone mullions of the Tudor window. The surgeon gave his steed a mouthful of hay and a drink of water before the Waverly Arms, and then sauntered at a foot-pace into the long unbroken arcade which stretches from the quiet village to the very outskirts of the bustling Conventford. George urged Brown Molly into a ponderous kind of canter by and by, and went at a dashing rate till he came to the little turnpike at the end of the avenue, and left fair Elizabethan Midlandshire behind him. Before him there was only the smoky, noisy, poverty-stricken town, with hideous factory-chimneys blackening the air, and three tall spires rising from amongst the crowded roofs high up into the clearer sky.

Mr Gilbert drew rein on the green, which was quiet enough to-day, though such an uproarious spot in fair-time; he drew rein, and began to wonder what he should do. Should he go to the chemist's in the market-place and get his drugs, and thence to Mr Raymond's house, which was at the other end of the town, or rather on the outskirts of the country and beyond the town; or should he go first to Mr Raymond's by quiet back lanes, which were clear of the bustle and riot of the market-people? To go to the chemist's first would be the wiser course, perhaps; but then it wouldn't be very agreeable to have drugs in his pocket, and to smell of rhubarb and camomile-flowers when he made his appearance before Miss Sleaford. After a good deal of deliberation, George decided on going by the back way to Mr Raymond's house; and then, as he rode along the lanes and back slums, he began to think that Mr Raymond would wonder why he called, and would think his interest in the nursery-governess odd, or even intrusive; and from that a natural transition of thought brought him to wonder whether it would not be better to abandon all idea of seeing Miss Sleaford, and to content himself with the purchase of the drugs. While he was thinking of this, Brown Molly brought him into the lane at the end of which Mr Raymond's house stood, on a gentle eminence, looking over a wide expanse of grassy fields, a railway-cutting, and a white high-road, dotted here and there by little knots of stunted trees. The country upon this side of Conventford was bleak and bare of aspect as compared to that fair park-like region which I venture to call Elizabethan Midlandshire.

If Mr Raymond had resembled other people, I daresay he would have been considerably surprised—or, it may be, outraged—by a young gentleman in the medical profession venturing to make a morning call upon his nursery-governess; but as Mr Charles Raymond was the very opposite of every body else in the world, and as he was a most faithful disciple of Mr George Combe,* and could discover by a glance at the surgeon's head that the young man was neither a profligate nor a scoundrel, he received George as cordially as it was his habit to receive every living creature who had need of his friendliness; and sent Brown Molly away to his stable, and set her master at his ease, before George had quite left off blushing in his first paroxysm of shyness.

'Come into my room,' cried Mr Raymond, in a voice that had more vibration in it than any other voice that ever rang out upon the air; 'come into my room. You've had a letter from Sigismund,—the idea of the absurd young dog calling himself Sigismund!—and he's told you all about Miss Sleaford. Very nice girl, but wants to be educated before she can teach; keeps the little ones amused, however, and takes them out in the meadows; a very nice, conscientious little thing; Cautiousness very large; can't get any thing out of her about her past life; turns pale and begins to cry when I ask her questions; has seen a good deal of trouble, I'm afraid. Never mind; we'll try and make her happy. What does her past life matter to us if her head's well balanced? Let me have my pick of the young people in Field Lane, and I'll find you an underdeveloped Archbishop of Canterbury; take me into places where the crimes of mankind are only known by their names in the Decalogue, and I'll find you an embryo Greenacre.* Miss Sleaford's a very good little girl; but she's got too much Wonder, and exaggerated Ideality. She opens her big eyes when she talks of her favourite books, and looks up all scared and startled if you speak to her while she's reading.'

Mr Raymond's room was a comfortable little apartment, lined with books from the ceiling to the floor. There were books every where in Mr Raymond's house; and the master of the house read at all manner of abnormal hours, and kept a candle burning by his bedside in the dead of the night, when every other citizen of Conventford was asleep. He was a bachelor, and the children whom it was Miss Sleaford's duty to educate were a couple of sickly orphans, left by a pale-faced niece of Charles Raymond's,—an unhappy young lady, who seemed only born to be unfortunate, and who had married badly, and lost her husband, and died of consumption, running through all the troubles common to womankind before her twenty-fifth birthday. Of course Mr Raymond took the children; he would have taken an accidental chimney-sweep's children, if it could have been demonstrated to him that there was no one else to take them. He buried the pale-faced niece in a quiet suburban cemetery, and took the orphans home to his pretty house at Conventford, and bought black frocks for them, and engaged Miss Sleaford for their education, and made less fuss about the transaction than many men would have done concerning the donation of a ten-pound note.

It was Charles Raymond's nature to help his fellow-creatures. He had been very rich once, the Conventford people said, in those far-off golden days when there were neither strikes nor starvation in the grim old town; and he had lost a great deal of money in the carrying out of sundry philanthropic schemes for the benefit of his fellow-creatures, and was comparatively poor in these latter days. But he was never so poor as to be unable to help other people, or to hold his hand when a mechanics' institution, or a working-men's club, or an evening-school, or a cooking-dépôt, was wanted for the benefit and improvement of Conventford.

And all this time,—while he was the moving spirit of half-a-dozen committees, while he distributed cast-off clothing, and coals, and tickets for soup, and orders for flannel, and debated the solemn question as to whether Betsy Scrubbs or Maria Tomkins was most in want of a wadded petticoat, or gave due investigation to the rival claims of Mrs Jones and Mrs Green to the largess of the soup-kitchen,—he was an author, a philosopher, a phrenologist, a meta-physician, writing grave books, and publishing them for the instruction

of mankind. He was fifty years of age; but, except that his hair was
gray, he had no single attribute of age. That gray hair framed the
brightest face that ever smiled upon mankind, and with the liberal
sunshine smiled alike on all. George Gilbert had seen Mr Raymond
several times before to-day. Every body in Conventford, or within a
certain radius of Conventford, knew Mr Charles Raymond; and Mr
Charles Raymond knew every body. He looked through the transparent screen which shrouded the young surgeon's thoughts: he
looked down into the young man's heart, through depths that were
as clear as limpid water, and saw nothing there but truth and purity.
When I say that Mr Raymond looked into George Gilbert's heart, I
use a figure of speech, for it was from the outside of the surgeon's
head he drew his deductions; but I like the old romantic fancy, that
a good man's heart is a temple of courage, love, and piety—an
earthly shrine of all the virtues.

Mr Raymond's house was a pretty Gothic building, half villa, half
cottage, with bay windows opening into a small garden, which was
very different from the garden at Camberwell, inasmuch as here all
was trimly kept by an indefatigable gardener and factotum. Beyond
the garden there were the meadows, only separated from Mr
Raymond's lawn by a low privet hedge; and beyond the meadows the
roofs and chimneys of Conventford loomed darkly in the distance.

Charles Raymond took George into the drawing-room by and by,
and from the bay window the young man saw Isabel Sleaford once
more, as he had seen her first, in a garden. But the scene had a
different aspect from that other scene, which still lingered in his
mind, like a picture seen briefly in a crowded gallery. Instead of the
pear-trees on the low disorderly grass-plat, the straggling branches
green against the yellow sunshine of July, George saw a close-cropped
lawn and trim flower-beds, stiff groups of laurel, and bare bleak
fields unsheltered from the chill March winds. Against the cold blue
sky he saw Isabel's slight figure, not lolling in a garden-chair reading
a novel, but walking primly with two pale-faced children dressed in
black. A chill sense of pain crept through the surgeon's breast as he
looked at the girlish figure, the pale joyless face, the sad dreaming
eyes. He felt that some inexplicable change had come to Isabel
Sleaford since that July day on which she had talked of her pet
authors, and glowed and trembled with childish love for the dear
books out of whose pages she took the joys and sorrows of her life.

The three pale faces, the three black dresses, had a desolate look in the cold sunlight. Mr Raymond tapped at the glass, and beckoned to the nursery-governess.

'Melancholy-looking objects, are they not?' he said to George, as the three girls came towards the window. 'I've told my housekeeper to give them plenty of roast meat, not too much done; meat's the best antidote for melancholy.'

He opened the window and admitted Isabel and her two pupils.

'Here's a friend come to see you, Miss Sleaford,' he said; 'a friend of Sigismund's; a gentleman who knew you in London.'

George held out his hand, but he saw something like terror in the girl's face as she recognised him; and he fell straightway into a profound gulf of confusion and embarrassment.

'Sigismund asked me to call,' he stammered. 'Sigismund told me to write and tell him how you were.'

Miss Sleaford's eyes filled with tears. The tears came unbidden to her eyes now with the smallest provocation.

'You are all very good to me,' she said.

'There, you children, go out into the garden and walk about,' cried Mr Raymond. 'You go with them, Gilbert, and then come in and have some stilton cheese and bottled beer, and tell us all about your Graybridge patients.'

Mr Gilbert obeyed his kindly host. He went out on to the lawn, where the brown shrubs were putting forth their feeble leaflets to be blighted by the chill air of March. He walked by Isabel's side, while the two orphans prowled mournfully here and there amongst the evergreens, and picked the lonely daisies that had escaped the gardener's scythe. George and Isabel talked a little; but the young man was fain to confine himself to a few commonplace remarks about Conventford, and Mr Raymond, and Miss Sleaford's new duties; for he saw that the least allusion to the old Camberwell life distressed and agitated her. There was not much that these two could talk about as yet. With Sigismund Smith Isabel would have had plenty to say; indeed, it would have been a struggle between the two as to which should do all the talking; but in George Gilbert's company Isabel Sleaford's fancies folded themselves like delicate buds whose fragile petals are shrivelled by a bracing northern breeze. She knew that Mr Gilbert was a good young man, kindly disposed towards her, and, after his simple fashion, eager to please her; but she felt rather than knew that he did not understand her, and that in that cloudy region where her thoughts for ever dwelt he could never be her companion. So, after a little of that deliciously original conversation which forms the staple talk of a morning call amongst people who have never acquired the supreme accomplishment called small-talk, George and Isabel returned to the drawing-room, where Mr Raymond was ready to preside over a banquet of bread-and-cheese and bottled ale; after which reflection the surgeon's steed was brought to the door.

'Come and see us again, Gilbert, whenever you've a day in Conventford,' Mr Raymond said, as he shook hands with the surgeon.

George thanked him for his cordial invitation, but he rode away from the house rather depressed in spirit, notwithstanding. How stupid he had been during that brief walk on Mr Raymond's lawn; how little he had said to Isabel, or she to him! How dismally the conversation had died away into silence every now and then, only to be revived by some lame question, some miserable remark apropos to nothing,—the idiotic emanation of despair!

Mr Gilbert rode to an inn near the market-place, where his father had been wont to take his dinner whenever he went to Conventford. George gave Brown Molly into the ostler's custody; and then walked away to the crowded pavement, where the country people were jostling each other in front of shop-windows and open stalls; the broad stony market-place, where the voices of the hawkers were loud and shrill, where the brazen boastings of quack-medicine vendors rang out upon the afternoon air. He walked through the crowd, and rambled away into a narrow back street leading to an old square, where the great church of Conventford stood amidst a stony waste of tombstones, and where the bells that played a hymn-tune when they chimed the hour were booming up in the grand old steeple. The young man went into the stony churchyard, which was lonely enough even on a market-day, and walked about among the tombs, whiling away the time—for the benefit of Brown Molly, who required considerable rest and refreshment before she set out on the return journey—and thinking of Isabel Sleaford.

He had only seen her twice, and yet already her image had fastened itself with a fatal grip upon his mind, and was planted there—an enduring picture, never again to be blotted out. That evening at

Camberwell had been the one romantic episode of this young man's eventless life; Isabel Sleaford the one stranger who had come across his pathway. There were pretty girls, and amiable girls, in Graybridge: but then he had known them all his life. Isabel came to him in her pale young beauty, and all the latent sentimentality—without which youth is hideous—kindled and thrilled into life at the magic spell of her presence. The mystic Venus rises a full-blown beauty from the sea, and man the captive bows down before his divine enslaver. Who would care for a Venus whose cradle he had rocked, whose gradual growth he had watched, the divinity of whose beauty had perished beneath the withering influence of familiarity?

It was dusk when George Gilbert went to the chemist and received his parcels of drugs. He would not stop to dine at the White Lion, but paid his eighteenpence for Brown Molly's accommodation, and took a hasty glass of ale at the bar before he sprang into the saddle. He rode homeward through the solemn avenue, the dusky cathedral-aisle, the infinite temple, fashioned by the great architect Nature. He rode through the long ghostly avenue, until the twinkling lights at Waverly glimmered on him faintly between the bare branches of the trees.

Isabel Sleaford's new life was a very pleasant one. There was no butter to be fetched, no mysterious errands to the Walworth Road. Every thing was bright and smooth and trim in Mr Raymond's household. There was a middle-aged housekeeper who reigned supreme, and an industrious maidservant under her sway. Isabel and her sickly charges had two cheerful rooms over the drawing-room, and took their meals together, and enjoyed the delight of one another's society all day long. The children were rather stupid, but they were very good. They too had known the sharp ills of poverty, the butter-fetching, the blank days in which there was no bright oasis of dinner, the scraps of cold meat and melancholy cups of tea. They told Isabel their troubles of an evening; how poor mamma had cried when the sheriff's officer came in, and said he was very sorry for her, but must take an inventory, and wouldn't leave even papa's picture or the silver spoons that had been grandmamma's. Miss Sleaford put her shoulder to the wheel very honestly, and went through Pinnock's pleasant abridgments of modern and ancient history* with her patient pupils. She let them off with a very slight dose of the Heptarchy and the Normans,* and even the early Plantagenet monarchs*; but she gave them plenty of Anne Boleyn and Mary Queen of Scots,*—fair princess Mary, Queen of France and wife of Thomas Brandon,*—Marie Antoinette and Charlotte Corday.*

The children only said 'Lor'!' when they heard of Mademoiselle Corday's heroic adventure: but they were very much interested in the fate of the young princes of the House of York, and amused themselves by a representation of the smothering business* with the pillows on the school-room sofa.

It was not to be supposed that Mr Charles Raymond, who had all the interests of Conventford to claim his attention, could give much time or trouble to the two pupils or the nursery-governess. He was quite satisfied with Miss Sleaford's head, and was content to intrust his orphan nieces to her care.

'If they were clever children, I should be afraid of her exaggerated ideality,' he said; 'but they're too stupid to be damaged by any influence of that kind. She's got a very decent moral region—not equal to that young doctor at Graybridge, certainly—and she'll do her duty to the little ones very well, I daresay.'

So no one interfered with Isabel or her pupils. The education of association, which would have been invaluable to her, was as much wanting at Conventford as it had been at Camberwell. She lived alone with her books and the dreams which were born of them, and waited for the prince, the Ernest Maltravers, the Henry Esmond,* the Steerforth*—it was Steerforth's proud image, and not simple-hearted David's gentle shadow, which lingered in the girl's mind when she shut the book. She was young and sentimental, and it was not the good people upon whom her fancy fixed itself. To be handsome and proud and miserable, was to possess an indisputable claim to Miss Sleaford's worship. She sighed to sit at the feet of a Byron, grand and gloomy and discontented, baring his white brow to the midnight blast, and raving against the baseness and ingratitude of mankind. She pined to be the chosen slave of some scornful creature, who should perhaps ill-treat and neglect her. I think she would have worshipped an aristocratic Bill Sykes,* and would have been content to die under his cruel hand, only in the ruined chamber of some Gothic castle, by moonlight, with the distant Alps shimmering whitely before her glazing eyes, instead of in poor Nancy's unromantic garret. And then the Count Guilliamme de Syques would be sorry, and put up a wooden cross on the mountain pathway, to the memory of ——, ANáΓKH;* and he would be found some morning stretched at the foot of that mysterious memorial, with a long black mantle trailing over his king-like form, and an important blood-vessel broken.

There is no dream so foolish, there is no fancy however childish, that did not find lodgment in Isabel Sleaford's mind during the long idle evenings in which she sat alone in her quiet school-room, watching the stars kindle faintly in the dusk, and the darkening shadows gathering in the meadows, while feeble lights began to twinkle in the distant streets of Conventford. Sometimes, when her pupils were fast asleep in their white-curtained beds, Izzie stole softly down, and went out into the garden to walk up and down in the fair moonlight; the beautiful moonlight in which Juliet had looked more lovely than the light of day to Romeo's enraptured eyes; in which Hamlet had trembled before his father's ghostly face. She walked up and down in the moonlight, and thought of all her dreams; and wondered when her life was going to begin. She was getting quite old; yes—she thought of it with a thrill of horror—she was nearly eighteen! Juliet was buried in the tomb of the Capulets before this age, and haughty Beatrix* had lived her life, and Florence Dombey was married and settled, and the story all over.

A dull despair crept over this foolish girl as she thought that perhaps her life was to be only a commonplace kind of existence, after all; a blank flat level, along which she was to creep to a nameless grave. She was so eager to be *something*. Oh, why was not there a revolution, that she might take a knife in her hand and go forth to seek the tyrant in his lodging, and then die; so that people might talk of her, and remember her name when she was dead?

I think Isabel Sleaford was just in that frame of mind in which a respectable, and otherwise harmless, young person aims a bullet at some virtuous sovereign, in a paroxysm of insensate yearning for distinction. Miss Sleaford wanted to be famous. She wanted the drama of her life to begin, and the hero to appear.

Vague, and grand, and shadowy, there floated before her the image of the prince; but, oh, how slow he was to come! Would he ever come? Were there any princes in the world? Were there any of those Beings whose manners and customs her books described to her, but

whose mortal semblances she had never seen? The Sleeping Beauty
in the woods slumbered a century before the appointed hero came to
awaken her. Beauty must wait, and wait patiently, for the coming of
her fate. But poor Isabel thought she had waited so long, and as yet
there was not even the distant shimmer of the prince's plumes dimly
visible on the horizon.

There were reasons why Isabel Sleaford should shut away the
memory of her past life, and solace herself with visions of a brighter
existence. A little wholesome drudgery might have been good for
her, as a homely antidote against the sentimentalism of her nature;
but in Mr Raymond's house she had ample leisure to sit dreaming
over her books, weaving wonderful romances in which she was to be
the heroine, and the hero ——?

The hero was the veriest chameleon, inasmuch as he took his
colour from the last book Miss Sleaford had been reading. Sometimes he was Ernest Maltravers, the exquisite young aristocrat, with
violet eyes and silken hair. Sometimes he was Eugene Aram, dark,
gloomy, and intellectual, with that awkward little matter of Mr Clarke's
murder preying upon his mind. At another time he was Steerforth,
selfish and haughty and elegant. Sometimes, when the orphans were
asleep, Miss Sleaford let down her long black hair before the little
looking-glass, and acted to herself in a whisper. She saw her pale
face, awful in the dusky glass, her lifted arms, her great black eyes,
and she fancied herself dominating a terror-stricken pit. Sometimes
she thought of leaving friendly Mr Raymond, and going up to London with a five-pound note in her pocket, and coming out at one of
the theatres as a tragic actress. She would go to the manager, and
tell him that she wanted to act. There might be a little difficulty at
first, perhaps, and he would be rather inclined to be doubtful of her
powers; but then she would take off her bonnet, and let down her
hair, and would draw the long tresses wildly through her thin white
fingers—so; she stopped to look at herself in the glass as she did
it,—and would cry, 'I am not mad; this hair I tear is mine!' and the
thing would be done. The manager would exclaim, 'Indeed, my
dear young lady, I was not prepared for such acting as this. Excuse
my emotion; but really, since the days of Miss O'Neill,* I don't
remember to have witnessed any thing to equal your delivery of that
speech. Come to-morrow evening and play Constance. You don't
want a rehearsal?—no, of course not; you know every syllable of the

part. I shall take the liberty of offering you fifty pounds a-night to begin with, and I shall place one of my carriages at your disposal.' Isabel had read a good many novels in which timid young heroines essay their histrionic powers, but she had never read of a dramatically-disposed heroine who had not burst forth a full-blown Mrs Siddons* without so much as the ordeal of a rehearsal.

Sometimes Miss Sleaford thought that her Destiny—she clung to the idea that she had a destiny—designed her to be a poet, an L.E.L.;* oh, above all she would have chosen to be L.E.L.; and in the evening, when she had looked over the children's copy-books, and practised a new style of capital B, in order to infuse a dash of variety into the next day's studies, she drew the candles nearer to her, and posed herself, and dipped her pen into the ink, and began to pour forth some melancholy plaint upon the lonely blankness of her life, or some vague invocation of the unknown prince. She rarely finished either the plaint or the invocation, for there was generally some rhythmical difficulty that brought her poetic musings to a dead lock; but she began a great many verses, and spoiled several quires of paper with abortive sonnets, in which 'stars' and 'streamlets,' 'dreams' and 'fountains,' recurred with a frequency which was inimical to originality or variety of style.

The poor lonely untaught child looked right and left for some anchorage on the blank sea of life, and could find nothing but floating masses of ocean verdure, that drifted her here and there at the wild will of all the winds of heaven. Behind her there was a past that she dared not look back upon or remember; before her lay the unknown future, wrapped in mysterious shadow, grand by reason of its obscurity. She was eager to push onward, to pierce the solemn veil, to tear aside the misty curtain, to penetrate the innermost chamber of the temple.

Late in the night, when the lights of Conventford had died out under the starlit sky, the girl lay awake, sometimes looking up at those mystical stars, and thinking of the future; but never once, in any dream or reverie, in any fantastic vision built out of the stories she loved, did the homely image of the Graybridge surgeon find a place.

George Gilbert thought of her, and wondered about her, as he rode Brown Molly in the winding Midlandshire lanes, where the brown hedge-rows were budding, and the whitethorn bursting into blossom. He thought of her by day and by night, and was angry with himself for so thinking; and then began straightway to consider when he could, with any show of grace, present himself once more before Mr Raymond's Gothic porch at Conventford.

CHAPTER VII
ON THE BRIDGE

While George Gilbert was thinking of Isabel Sleaford's pale face and black eyes; while, in his long rides to and fro among the cottages of his parish-patients, he solemnly debated as to whether he ought to call upon Mr Raymond when next he went to Conventford, or whether he ought to go to Conventford for the express purpose of paying his respects to Mr Raymond,—the hand of Fate turned the wavering balance; and the makeweight which she threw into the scale was no heavier than the ordinary half-ounce of original composition which Government undertakes to convey, not exactly from Indus to the Pole, but from the Land's End to the Highlands, for the small charge of a penny. While the young surgeon was hesitating on the brink of the great ocean, dipping the point of his foot into the crawling surf, only to draw back affrighted from the rush of the advancing wave; tempted by the freshness of the ocean spray, eager to plunge, yet doubtful of all that wide unknown expanse, which, in the sunshine, seemed a sea of gold, but, lashed by storms, and blackening with the darkening of the heavens, might become so terrible a grave;—while George Gilbert, in plainer words, hesitated and doubted, and argued and debated with himself, after the manner of every prudent home-bred young man who begins to think that he loves well, and sadly fears he may not love wisely,—Destiny, under the form of a friend, gave him a push, and he went souse over head and ears into the roaring ocean, and there was nothing left for him but to swim as best he might towards the undiscovered shore upon the other side.

The letter from Sigismund was dated Oakbank, Conventford, May 23d, 1853.

'Dear George,' wrote the author of *The Brand upon the Shoulder-blade*, 'I'm down here for a few days with my uncle Charles; and we've arranged a picnic in Lord Hurstonleigh's grounds, and we want you to join us. So, if your patients are not the most troublesome people in the world, you can give yourself a holiday, and meet us on Wednesday morning, at twelve, if fine, at the Waverly Road lodge-gate to Hurstonleigh Park. Mrs Pidgers—Pidgers is my uncle's housekeeper; a regular old dear, and *such* a hand at pie-crusts!—is going to pack up a basket,—and I know what Pidger's baskets are,—and we shall bring plenty of sparkling, because, when my uncle does this sort of thing, he *does* do it; and we're to drink tea at one of Lord Hurstonleigh's model cottages, in his model village, with a model old woman, who's had all manner of prizes for the tidiest dust-holes, and the whitest hearth-stones, and the neatest knife-boards, and all that kind of thing; and we're going to make a regular holiday of it; and I shall forget that there's such a creature as "the Demon of the Galleys" in the world, and that I'm a number behind with him,—which I am,—and the artist is waiting for a subject for his next cut.

'The orphans are coming, of course, and Miss Sleaford; and, oh, by the by, I want you to tell me all about poisoning by strychnine, because I think I shall do a case or two in *The D. of the G.*

'Twelve o'clock, sharp time, remember! We come in a fly. You can leave your horse at Waverly.—Yours, S.S.'

Yes; Fate, impatient perhaps of any wavering of the balance in so insignificant a matter as George Gilbert's destiny, threw this penny-post letter into the scale, and, lo! it was turned. The young man read the letter over and over again, till it was crumpled and soiled with much unfolding and refolding, and taking out of, and putting back into, his waistcoat-pocket. A picnic! a picnic in the Hurstonleigh grounds, with Isabel Sleaford! Other people were to be of the party; but George Gilbert scarcely remembered that. He saw himself, with Isabel by his side, wandering along the winding pathways, straying away into mysterious arcades of verdure, where the low branches of the trees would meet above their heads, and shut them in from all the world. He fancied himself talking to Mr Sleaford's daughter as he never had talked, nor was ever likely to talk, with any voice audible to mortal ears; he laid out and arranged that day as we are apt to arrange the days that are to come, and which—Heaven help our folly and presumption!—are so different when they do come from the dreams we have dreamed about them. Mr Gilbert lived that May holiday over and over again between the Monday afternoon on which he received Sigismund's letter, and the appointed Wednesday morning. He lay awake at night, when his day's work was done, thinking of Isabel, and what she would say to him, and how she would look at him, until those fancied words and looks thrilled him to the heart's core, and he was deluded by the thought that it was all a settled thing, and that his love was returned. His love! Did he love her, then, already—this pale-faced young person, whom he had only seen twice; who might be a Florence Nightingale, or a Madame de Laffarge,* for all that he knew either one way or the other? Yes, he loved her; the wondrous flower that never yet 'thrived by the calendar' had burst into full bloom. He loved this young woman, and believed in her, and was ready to bring her to his simple home whenever she pleased to come thither; and had already pictured her sitting opposite to him in the little parlour, making weak tea for him in a Britannia-metal teapot, sewing commonplace buttons upon his commonplace shirts, debating with Mrs Jeffson as to whether there should be roast beef or boiled mutton for the two-o'clock dinner, sitting up alone in that most uninteresting little parlour when the surgeon's patients were tiresome and insisted upon being ill in the night, waiting to preside over little suppers of cold meat and pickles, bread-and-cheese and celery. Yes; George pictured Miss Sleaford the heroine of such a domestic story as this, and had no power to divine that there was any incongruity in the fancy; no fineness of ear to discover the dissonant interval between the heroine and the story. Alas, poor Izzie! and are all your fancies, all the pretty stories woven out of your novels, all your long day-dreams about Marie Antoinette and Charlotte Corday, Edith Dombey and Ernest Maltravers,—all your foolish pictures of a modern Byron, fever-stricken at Missolonghi, and tended by you; a new Napoleon, exiled to St Helena, and followed, perhaps liberated, by you,—are they all come to this? Are none of the wonderful things that happen to women ever to happen to you? Are you never to be Charlotte Corday, and die for your country? Are you never to wear ruby velvet, and diamonds in your hair, and to lure some recreant Carker to a foreign hostelry, and there denounce and scorn him?* Are all the pages of the great book of life to be closed upon you—you, who seem to yourself predestined, by reason of so many dreams and fancies, to such a wonderful existence? Is all the mystic cloudland of your dreams to collapse and shrivel into this,—a commonplace square-built cottage at Graybridge-on-the-Wayverne, with a commonplace country surgeon for your husband?

George Gilbert was waiting at the low white gate before the ivy-covered lodge on the Waverly Road when the fly from Conventford drove up, with Sigismund Smith sitting beside the coach-man, and questioning him about a murder that had been committed in the neighbourhood ten years before; and Mr Raymond, Miss Sleaford, and the orphans inside. The surgeon had been waiting at the gate for a quarter of an hour, and he had been up ever since six o'clock that morning, riding backwards and forwards amongst his patients, doing a day's work in a few hours. He had been home to dress, of course, and wore his newest and most fashionable clothes, and was, in fact, a living realisation of one of the figures in a fly-blown fashion-plate for June 1852, still exhibited in the window of a Graybridge tailor. He wore a monthly rosebud in his buttonhole, and he carried a bunch of spring flowers,—jonquils and polyanthus, pink hawthorn, peonies, and sweetbrier,—which Mr Jeffson had gathered and tied up, with a view to their presentation to Isabel,—although there were better flowers in Mr Raymond's garden, as George reminded his faithful steward.

'Don't thee tew thyself about that, Master Jarge,' said the Yorkshireman; 'th' young wench'll like the flowers if thoo givest 'em til her.'

Of course it never for a moment entered into Mr Jeffson's mind that his young master's attentions could be otherwise than welcome and agreeable to any woman living, least of all to a forlorn young damsel who was obliged to earn her bread amongst strangers.

'I'd like to see Miss Sleaford, Master Jarge,' Mr Jeffson said, in an insinuating manner, as George gathered up the reins and patted Brown Molly's neck, preparatory to riding away from the low white gate of his domain.

George blushed like the peonies that formed the centre of his nosegay.

'I don't know why you should want to see Miss Sleaford any more than other girls, Jeff,' he said.

'Well, never you mind why, Master Jarge; I *should* like to see her; I'd give a deal to see her.'

'Then we'll try and manage it, Jeff. We're to drink tea at Hurstonleigh; and we shall be leaving there, I suppose, as soon as it's dark—between seven and eight o'clock, I daresay. You might ride the gray pony to Waverly, and bring Brown Molly on to Hurstonleigh, and stop at the alehouse—there's an alehouse, you know, though it *is* a model village—until I'm ready to come home; and you can leave the horses with the ostler, you know, and stroll about the village,—and you're sure to find us.'

'Yes, yes, Master Jarge; I'll manage it.'

So George was at his post a quarter of an hour before the fly drove up to the gate. He was there to open the door of the vehicle, and to give his hand to Isabel when she alighted. He felt the touch of her fingers resting briefly on his arm, and trembled and blushed like a girl as he met the indifferent gaze of her great black eyes. Nobody took any notice of his embarrassment. Mr Raymond and his nephew were busy with the hampers that had been stowed under the seats of the fly, and the orphans were employed in watching their elders,—for to them the very cream of the picnic was in those baskets.

There was a boy at the lodge who was ready to take the basket whithersoever Mr Raymond should direct; so all was settled very quickly. The driver received his instructions respecting the return journey, and went rumbling off to Hurstonleigh to refresh himself and his horse. The lad went on before the little party, with the baskets swinging on either side of him as he went; and in the bustle of these small arrangements George Gilbert found courage to offer Isabel his arm. She took it without hesitation, and Sigismund placed himself on the other side of her. Mr Raymond went on before with the orphans, who affected the neighbourhood of the baskets; and the three young people followed, walking slowly over the grass.

Isabel had put off her mourning. She had never had but one black dress, poor child; and that being worn out, she was fain to fall back upon her ordinary costume. If she had looked pretty in the garden at Camberwell, with tumbled hair and a dingy dress, she looked beautiful to-day, in clean muslin, fresh and crisp, fluttering in the spring breezes as she walked, and with her hair smoothly banded under a broad-leaved straw-hat. Her face brightened with the brightness of the sunshine and the charm of the landscape; her step grew light and buoyant as she walked upon the springing turf. Her eyes lit up by and by, when the little party came to a low iron gate, beyond which there was a grove, a winding woodland patch, and undulating glades, and craggy banks half hidden under foliage, and, in a deep cleft below, a brawling waterfall for ever rushing over moss-grown rockwork, and winding far away to meet the river.

'Oh, how beautiful it is!' cried Isabel; 'how beautiful!'

She was a Cockney, poor child, and had spent the best part of her life amidst the suburban districts of Camberwell and Peckham. All this Midlandshire beauty burst upon her like a sudden revelation of Paradise. Could the Garden of Eden have been more beautiful than this woodland grove?—where the ground was purple with wild hyacinths that grew under beeches and oaks centuries old; where the sunlight and shadows flickered on the mossy pathways; where the guttural warble of the blackbirds made perpetual music in the air. George looked wonderingly at the girl's rapt countenance, her parted lips, that were faintly tremulous with the force of her emotion.

'I did not think there could be any place in England so beautiful,' she said by and by, when George disturbed her with some trite remark upon the scene. 'I thought it was only in Italy and in Greece, and those sort of places—where Childe Harold* went—that it was beautiful like this. It makes one feel as if one could never go back to the world again, doesn't it?' she asked naïvely.

George was fain to confess that, although the grove was very beautiful, it inspired him with no desire to turn hermit, and take up his abode therein. But Isabel hardly heard what he said to her. She was looking away into mysterious vistas of light and shadow, and thinking that in such a spot as this the hero of a woman's life might appear in all his shining glory. If she could meet him now, this wonderful unknown being—the Childe Harold, the Lara,* of her life! What if it was to be so? what if she was to meet him now, and the story was appointed to begin to-day,—this very day,—and all her life henceforth was to be changed? The day was like the beginning of a story, somehow, inasmuch as it was unlike the other days of her life. She had thought of the holiday, and dreamt about it even more foolishly than George had done; for there had been some foundation for the young man's visions, while hers had been altogether baseless. What if Lord Hurstonleigh should happen to be strolling in his grove, and should see her and rescue her from death by drowning, or a mad bull, or something of that sort, and thereupon fall in love with her? Nothing was more life-like or likely, according to Izzie's experience of three-volume novels. Unhappily she discovered from Mr Raymond that Lord Hurstonleigh was an elderly married man, and was, moreover, resident in the south of France; so *that* bright dream was speedily shattered. But there is no point of the compass from which a hero may not come. There was hope yet; there was hope that this bright spring-day might not close as so many days had closed upon the same dull record, the same empty page.

Mr Raymond was in his highest spirits to-day. He liked to be with young people, and was younger than the youngest of them in his fresh enjoyment of all that is bright and beautiful upon earth. He devoted himself chiefly to the society of his orphan *protégées*, and contrived to impart a good deal of information to them in a pleasant easy-going manner, that took the bitterness out of those Pierian waters,* for which the orphans had very small affection. They were stupid and unimpressionable; but, then, were they not the children of that unhappy consumptive niece of his, who had acquired, by reason of her many troubles, a kind of divine right to become a burden upon happy people?

'If she had left me such an orphan as that girl Isabel, I would have thanked her kindly for dying,' Mr Raymond mused. 'That girl has mental imitation,—the highest and rarest faculty of the human brain,—ideality, and comparison. What could I not make of such a girl as that? And yet—'

Mr Raymond only finished the sentence with a sigh. He was thinking that, after all, these bright faculties might not be the best gifts for a woman. It would have been better, perhaps, for Isabel to have possessed the organ of pudding-making and stocking-darning, if those useful accomplishments are represented by an organ. The kindly phrenologist was thinking that perhaps the highest fate life held for that pale girl with the yellow tinge in her eyes was to share the home of a simple-hearted country surgeon, and rear his children to be honest men and virtuous women.

'I suppose that *is* the best,' Mr Raymond said to himself.

He had dismissed the orphans now, and had sent them on to walk with Sigismund Smith, who kindly related to them the story of *Lilian the Deserted*, with such suppressions and emendations as rendered the romance suitable to their tender years. The philosopher of

Conventford had got rid of the orphans, and was strolling by himself in those delicious glades, swinging his stick as he went, and throwing up his head every now and then to scent all the freshness of the warm spring air.

['Yes, poor little girl,' he mused; 'I suppose it *is* the best. Society wants commonplace people; and I really doubt if it might not very comfortably dispense with those gifted beings, who are perpetually running about with flaring torches men call genius, setting honest men's hayricks—in the way of old prejudices and time-honoured delusions—on fire. There are people certainly who may be trusted with one of those dangerous torches, and who straightway go to work to climb the highest mountain in the land, and set their light aloft to be a beacon for mankind; but then there are so many who are never any thing better than children playing with fire, and who are so eager to distinguish themselves, that they must needs set alight every thing they see.]*

'Poor little orphan child! will any body ever fathom her fancies or understand her dreams? Will she marry that good, sheepish country surgeon, who has fallen in love with her? He can give her a home and a shelter; and she seems such a poor friendless little creature, just the sort of girl to get into some kind of mischief if she were left to herself. Perhaps it's about the best thing that could happen to her. I should like to have fancied a brighter fate for her, a life with more colour in it. She's so pretty—*so* pretty; and when she talks, and her face lights up, a sort of picture comes into my mind of what she would be in a great saloon, with clusters of lights about her, and masses of shimmering colour, making a gorgeous background for her pale young beauty; and brilliant men and women clustering round her, to hear her talk and see her smile. I can see her like this; and then, when I remember what her life is likely to be, I begin to feel sorry for her, just as if she were some fair young nun, foredoomed to be buried alive by and by. Sometimes I have had a fancy that if *he* were to come home and see her—but that's an old busybody's dream. When did a matchmaker ever create any thing but matrimonial confusion and misery? I daresay Beatrice kept her word, and *did* make Benedick wretched.* No; Miss Sleaford must marry whom she may, and be happy or miserable, according to the doctrine of averages; and as for *him*—'

Mr Raymond stopped; and seeing the rest of the party happily engaged in gathering hyacinths under the low branches of the trees, he seated himself upon a clump of fallen timber, and took a book out of his pocket. It was a book that had been sent by post, for the paper wrapper was still about it. It was a neat little volume, bound in glistening green cloth, with uncut edges, and the gilt-letter title on the back of the volume set forth that the book contained 'An Alien's Dreams.' An alien's dreams could be nothing but poetry; and as the name of the poet was not printed under the title, it was perhaps only natural that Mr Raymond should not open the book immediately, but should sit turning and twisting the volume about in his hands, and looking at it with a contemptuous expression of countenance.

'An alien!' he exclaimed; 'why, in the name of all the affectations of the present day, should a young man with fifteen thousand a-year, and one of the finest estates in Midlandshire, call himself an alien? "An Alien's Dreams"—and such dreams! I had a look at them this morning, without cutting the leaves. It's always a mistake to cut the leaves of young people's poetry. Such dreams! Surely no alien could have been afflicted with any thing like them, unless he was perpetually eating heavy suppers of underdone pork, or drinking bad wine, or neglecting the ventilation of his bedroom. Imperfect ventilation has a good deal to do with it, I daresay. To think that Roland Lansdell should write such stuff—such a clever young man as he is, too—such a generous-hearted, high-minded young fellow, who might be—'

Mr Raymond opened the volume in a very gingerly fashion, almost as if he expected something unpleasant might crawl out of it, and looked in a sideways manner between the leaves, muttering the first line or so of a poem, and then skipping on to another, and giving utterance to every species of contemptuous ejaculation between whiles.

'Imogen!' he exclaimed; '"To Imogen!" As if any body was ever called Imogen out of Shakespeare's play and Monk Lewis's ballad!* "To Imogen:"

> "Do you ever think of me, proud and cruel Imogen
>   As I think, ah! sadly think, of thee—
> When the shadows darken on the misty lea, Imogen,
>   And the low light dies behind the sea?"

' "Broken!" "Shattered!" "Blighted!" Lively titles to tempt the general reader! Here's a nice sort of thing:

> "Like an actor in a play,
>   Like a phantom in a dream,
>   Like a lost boat left to stray
>   Rudderless adown the stream,—
> This is what my life has grown, Ida Lee,
> Since thy false heart left me lone, Ida Lee.
> And I wonder sometimes when the laugh is loud,
> And I wonder at the faces of the crowd,
> And the strange fantastic measures that they tread,
> Till I think at last I must be dead—
> Till I half believe that I am dead."

And to think that Roland Lansdell should waste his time in writing this sort of thing! And here's his letter, poor boy,—his long rambling letter,—in which he tells me how he wrote the verses, and how writing them was a kind of consolation to him,—a safety-valve for so much passionate anger against a world that doesn't exactly harmonise with the Utopian fancies of a young man with fifteen thousand a-year and nothing to do. If some rightful heir would turn up, in the person of one of Roland's gamekeepers, now, and denounce my young friend as a wrongful heir, and turn him out of doors bag and baggage, and with very little bag and baggage, after the manner of those delightful melodramas which hold the mirror up to nature so exactly, what a blessing it would be for the author of "An Alien's Dreams"! If he could only find himself without a sixpence in the world, what a noble young soldier in the great battle of life, what a triumphant hero, he might be! But as it is, he is nothing better than a colonel of militia, with a fine uniform, and a long sword that is only meant for show. My poor Roland! my poor Roland!' Mr Raymond murmured sadly, as he dropped the little volume back into his pocket; 'I am so sorry that you too should be infected with the noxious disease of our time, the fatal cynicism that transforms youth into a malady for which age is the only cure.'

But he had no time to waste upon any regretful musings about Mr Roland Lansdell, sole master of Lansdell Priory, one of the finest seats in Midlandshire, and who was just now wandering somewhere in Greece, upon a Byronic kind of tour that had lasted upwards of six months, and was likely to last much longer.

It was nearly three o'clock now, and high time for the opening of
the hampers, Mr Raymond declared, when he rejoined the rest of the
party, much to the delight of the orphans, who were always hungry,
and who ate so much, and yet remained so pale and skeleton-like of
aspect, that they presented a pair of perpetual phenomena to the
eye of the physiologist. The baskets had been carried to a little
ivy-sheltered arbour, perched high above the waterfall; and
here Mr Raymond unpacked them, bringing out his treasures one
after another; first a tongue, than a pair of fowls, a packet
of anchovy sandwiches, a great poundcake (at sight of which the
eyes of the orphans glistened), delicate caprices in the way of
pastry, semi-transparent biscuits, and a little block of stilton
cheese, to say nothing of sundry bottles of Madeira and sparkling
Burgundy.

Perhaps there never was a merrier party. To eat cold chicken and
drink sparkling Burgundy in the open air on a bright May afternoon
is always an exhilarating kind of thing, though the scene of your
picnic may be the bleakest of the Sussex Downs, or the dreariest of
the Yorkshire Wolds; but to drink the sparkling wine in that little
arbour at Hurstonleigh, with the brawling of the waterfall keeping
time to your laughter, the shadows of patriarchal oaks sheltering you
from all the outer world, is the very *ultima Thule* of bliss* in the way
of a picnic. And then Mr Raymond's companions were all so young!
It was so easy for them to leave all the Past on the threshold of that
lovely grove, and to narrow their lives into the life of that one bright
day. Isabel forgot that she had a Destiny, and consented to be happy
in a simple girlish way, without a thought of the prince who was so
long coming.

It may be that the sparkling Burgundy had something to do with
George Gilbert's enthusiasm; but, by and by, after the débris of the
dinner had been cleared away, and the little party lingered round the
rustic table, talking with that expansion of thought and eloquence of
language which is so apt to result from the consumption of effervescing wines in the open air, the young surgeon thought that all the
earth could scarcely hold a more lovely creature than the girl who
sat opposite to him, with her head resting against the rustic woodwork of the arbour, and her hat lying on her knee. She did not say
very much, in comparison with Sigismund and Mr Raymond, who
were neither of them indifferent hands at talking; but when she

spoke, there was generally something vague and dreamy in her words,—something that set George wondering about her anew, and made him admire her more than ever. He forgot all the dictates of prudence now; he was false to all the grand doctrines of young manhood; he only remembered that Isabel Sleaford was the loveliest creature upon earth; he only knew that he loved her, and that his love, like all true love, was mingled with modest doubtfulness of his own merits, and exaggerated deference for hers. He loved her as purely and truly as if he had been able to express his passion in the noblest poem ever written; but not being able to express it, his love and himself seemed alike tame and commonplace.

I must not dwell too long on this picnic, though it seemed half a lifetime to George Gilbert, for he walked with Isabel through the lanes between Hurstonleigh grove and Hurstonleigh village, and he loitered with her in the little churchyard at Hurstonleigh, and stood upon the bridge beneath which the Wayverne crept like a ribbon of silver, winding in and out among the rushes. He lingered there by her side while the orphans and Sigismund and Mr Raymond were getting tea ready at the model cottage, and putting the model old woman's wits into such a state of 'flustrification,' as she herself expressed it, that she could scarcely hold the tea-kettle, and was in imminent peril of breaking one of her best 'chaney' saucers, produced from a corner cupboard in honour of her friend and patron, Charles Raymond.

George loitered on the little stone bridge with Isabel, and somehow or other, still emboldened by the sparkling Burgundy, his passion all of a sudden found a voice, and he told her that he loved her, and that his highest hope upon earth was the hope of winning her for his wife.

I suppose that simple little story must be a pretty story, in its way; for when a woman hears it for the first time, she is apt to feel kindly disposed to the person who recites it, however poorly or tamely he may tell his tale. Isabel listened with a most delightful complacency; not because she reciprocated George's affection for her, but because this was the first little bit of romance in her life, and she felt that the story was beginning all at once, and that she was going to be a heroine. She felt this; and with this a kind of grateful liking for the young man at her side, through whose agency all these pleasant feelings came to her. [Did she love him? Alas! she had no better knowledge of that passion than the knowledge she had gathered from her books, and that was at the best so conflicting in its nature, that it was scarcely wonderful if her reading left her adrift upon a vast sea of conjecture. She thought that it was pleasant to have this young man by her side, beseeching her, and worshipping her in the most orthodox fashion. There was something contagious in George Gilbert's agitation to this inexperienced girl, who had not yet learned the highest lesson of civilisation—utter indifference to the sensations of other people. Her hand trembled a little when he took the shy fingers timidly in his own; and she stole a glance at him, and thought that he was almost as good-looking as Mr Hablot Browne's portrait of Walter Gay; and that, if she had only a father to strike her and turn her out of doors, the story of her life might be very tolerable, after all.]* And all this time George was pleading with her, and arguing, from her blushes and her silence, that his suit was not hopeless. Emboldened by the girl's tacit encouragement, he grew more and more eloquent, and went on to tell her how he had loved her from the first; yes, from that first summer's afternoon, when he had seen her sitting under the pear-trees in the old-fashioned garden, with the low yellow light behind her.

'Of course I didn't know then that I loved you, Isabel—oh, may I call you Isabel? it is such a pretty name. I have written it over and over and over on the leaves of a blotting-book at home, very often without knowing that I was writing it. I only thought at first that I admired you, because you are so beautiful, and so different from other beautiful women; and then, when I was always thinking of you, and wondering about you, I wouldn't believe that it was because I loved you. It is only to-day, this dear, happy day, that has made me understand what I have felt all along; and now I know that I have loved you from the first, Isabel, dear Isabel, from the very first.'

All this was quite as it should be. Isabel's heart fluttered like the wings of a young bird that essays its first flight.

'This is what it is to be a heroine,' she thought, as she looked down at the coloured pebbles, the floating river-weeds, under the clear rippling water; and yet knew all the time, by virtue of feminine second-sight, that George Gilbert was gazing at her and adoring her. She didn't like *him*, but she liked him to be there talking to her. The words she heard for the first time were delightful to her because of their novelty, but they took no charm from the lips that spoke them. Any other good-looking, respectably-dressed young man would have been quite as much to her as George Gilbert was. But then she did not know this. It was so very easy for her to mistake her pleasure in the 'situation;' the rustic bridge, the rippling water, the bright spring twilight, even the faint influence of that one glass of sparkling Burgundy, and, above all, the sensation of being a heroine for the first time in her life—it was so terribly easy to mistake all these for that which she did not feel,—a regard for George Gilbert.

While the young man was still pleading, while she was still listening to him, and blushing and glancing shyly at him out of those wonderful tawny-coloured eyes, which seemed black just now under the shadow of their drooping lashes, Sigismund and the orphans appeared at the distant gate of the churchyard whooping and hallooing, to announce that the tea was all ready.

'Oh, Isabel!' cried George, 'they are coming, and it may be ever so long before I see you again alone. Isabel, dear Isabel! do tell me that you will make me happy—tell me that you will be my wife!'

He did not ask her if she loved him; he was too much in love with her—too entirely impressed with her grace and beauty, and his own inferiority—to tempt his fate by such a question. If she would marry him, and let him love her, and by and by reward his devotion by loving him a little, surely that would be enough to satisfy his most presumptuous wishes.

'Dear Isabel, you will marry me, won't you? You can't mean to say no,—you would have said it before now. You would not be so cruel as to let me hope, even for a minute, if you meant to disappoint me.'

'I have known you—you have known me—such a short time,' the girl murmured.

'But long enough to love you with a love that will last all my life,' George answered eagerly. 'I shall have no thought except to make you happy, Isabel. I know that you are so beautiful that you ought to marry a very different fellow from me,—a man who could give you a grand house, and carriages and horses, and all that sort of thing; but he could never love you better than I, and he mightn't love you as well, perhaps; and I'll work for you, Isabel, as no man ever worked before. You shall never know what poverty is, darling, if you will be my wife.'

'I shouldn't mind being poor,' Isabel answered dreamily.

She was thinking that Walter Gay had been poor, and that the chief romance of Florence's life had been the quiet wedding in the little City church, and the long sea-voyage with her young husband. This sort of poverty was almost as nice as poor Edith's miserable wealth, with diamonds flung about and trampled upon, and ruby-velvet for every-day wear.

'I shouldn't so much mind being poor,' repeated the girl; for she thought, if she didn't marry a duke or a Dombey, it would be at least something to experience the sentimental phase of poverty.

George Gilbert seized upon the words.

'Ah, then, you will marry me, dearest Isabel? you will marry me, my own darling—my beautiful wife?'

He was almost startled by the intensity of his own feelings, as he bent down and kissed the little ungloved hand lying on the moss-grown stone-work of the bridge.

'Oh, Isabel, if you could only know how happy you have made me! if you could only know—'

She looked at him with a startled expression in her face. Was it all settled, then, so suddenly—with so little consideration? Yes, it was all settled; she was beloved with one of those passions that endure for a lifetime. George had said something to that effect. The story had begun, and she was a heroine.

'Good gracious me!' cried Mr Smith, as he bounded on the parapet of the little bridge, and disported himself there in the character of an amateur Blondin;* 'if the model old woman who has had so many prizes—we've been looking at her diplomas, framed and glazed, in a parlour that I couldn't have believed to exist out of *Lilian the Deserted* (who begins life as the cottager's daughter, you know, and elopes with the Squire in top-boots out of a diamond-paned window—and I've been trying the model old woman's windows, and Lilian couldn't have done it),—but I was about to remark, that if the old woman hasn't had a prize for a model temper, you two will catch it for keeping the tea waiting. Why, Izzie, what's the matter? you and George are both looking as spooney as—is it, eh?—yes, it is; isn't it? Hooray! Didn't I see it from the first?' cried Mr Smith, striking an attitude upon the balustrade, and pointing down to the two blushing faces with a triumphant finger. 'When George asked me for your letter, Izzie,—the little bit of a letter you wrote me when you left Camberwell,—didn't I see him fold it up as gingerly as if it had been a fifty-pound note, and slip it into his waistcoat-pocket, and then try to look as if he hadn't done it? Do you think I wasn't fly, then? A pretty knowledge of human nature I should have, if I couldn't see through that. The creator of Octavio Montefiasco, the Demon of the Galleys, flatters himself that he understands the obscurest diagnostic of the complaint commonly designated "spoons." Don't be downhearted, George,' exclaimed Sigismund, jumping suddenly off the parapet of the bridge, and extending his hand to his friend. 'Accept the congratulations of one who, with a heart long ber-lighted by the ber-lasting in-fer-luence of ker-rime, can-er yet-er feel a generous ther-rob in unison with virr-tue.'

After this they all left the bridge, and went straight to the little cottage, where Mr Raymond had been holding a species of Yankee levee,* for the reception of the model villagers, every one of whom knew him, and required his advice on some knotty point of law, medicine, or domestic economy. The tea was laid upon a little round table, close to the window, in the full light of the low evening sun. Isabel sat with her back to that low western light, and George sat next to her, staring at her in a silent rapture, and wondering at himself for his own temerity in having asked her to be his wife. That tiresome Sigismund called Mr Raymond aside, before sitting down to tea, on the pretence of showing him a highly-coloured representation of Joseph and his Brethren,* with a strong family likeness between the brethren; and told him in a loud whisper what had happened on the little bridge. So it was scarcely wonderful that poor George and Isabel took their tea in silence, and were rather awkward in the handling of their tea-cups. But they were spared any further congratulations from Sigismund, as that young gentleman found it was as much as he could do to hold his own against the orphans in the demolition of the poundcake, to say nothing of a lump of honeycomb which the model old woman produced for the delectation of the visitors.

The twilight deepened presently, and the stars began to glimmer faintly in an opal-tinted sky. Mr Raymond, Sigismund, and the orphans employed themselves in packing the baskets with the knives, plates, and glasses which had been used for the picnic. The fly was to pick them all up at the cottage. Isabel stood in the little doorway, looking dreamily out at the village, the dim lights twinkling in the casement windows, the lazy cattle standing in the pond upon the green, and a man holding a couple of horses before the door of the little inn.

'That man with the horses is Jeffson, my father's gardener; I scarcely like to call him a servant, for he is a kind of connexion of my poor mother's family,' George said, with a little confusion; for he thought that perhaps Miss Sleaford's pride might take alarm at the idea of any such kindred between her future husband and his servant; 'and he is *such* a good fellow! And what do you think Isabel?' the young man added, dropping his voice to a whisper; 'poor Jeffson has come all the way from Graybridge on purpose to see you, because he has heard me say that you are very beautiful; and I think he guessed ever so long ago that I had fallen in love with you. Would you have any objection to walk over yonder and see him, Isabel, or shall I call him here?'

'I'll go to him, if you like; I should like very much to see him,' the girl answered.

She took the arm George offered her. Of course it was only right that she should take his arm. It was all a settled thing now.

'Miss Sleaford has come to see you, Jeff,' the young man said, when they came to where the Yorkshireman was standing.

Poor Jeff had very little to say upon this rather trying occasion. He took off his hat, and stood bareheaded, smiling and blushing—as George spoke of him and praised him—yet all the while keeping a sharp watch upon Isabel's face. He could see that pale girlish face very well in the evening light, for Miss Sleaford had left her hat in the cottage, and stood bareheaded, with her face turned towards the west, while George rambled on about Jeff and his old school-days, when Jeff and he had been such friends and playfellows.

But the fly from Conventford came rumbling out of the inn-yard as they stood there, and this was a signal for Isabel to hurry back to the cottage. She held out her hand to Mr Jeffson as she wished him good-night, and then went back, still attended by George, who handed her into the fly presently, and wished her good-night in a very commonplace manner; for he was a young man whose feelings hid themselves from indifferent eyes, and, indeed, only appeared under the influence of extreme emotion.

CHAPTER VIII

ABOUT POOR JOE TILLET'S YOUNG WIFE

George went back to the Seven Stars, where Mr Jeffson was waiting with the horses. He went back, after watching the open vehicle drive away; he went back with his happiness, which was so new and strange, he thought a fresh life was to begin for him from this day, and would have almost expected to find the diseases of his patients miraculously cured, and a new phase of existence opening for them as well as for himself.

He was going to be married; he was going to have this beautiful young creature for his wife. He thought of her; and the image of this pale-faced girl, sitting in the little parlour at Graybridge waiting to receive him when he came home from his patients, was such an overpowering vision, that his brain reeled as he contemplated it. Was it true—could it be true—that all this inexpressible happiness was to be his?

By and by, when he was riding Brown Molly slowly along the shadowy lanes that lie between Hurstonleigh and Waverly, his silent bliss overflowed his heart and sought to utter itself in words. William Jeffson had always been George's confidant; why should he not be so now, when the young man had such need of some friendly ear to which to impart his happiness?

Somehow or other the Yorkshireman did not seem so eager as usual to take his part in his master's pleasure; he had seemed to hang back a little; for, under ordinary circumstances, George would have had no occasion to break the ice. But to-night Mr Jeffson seemed bent on keeping silence, and George was obliged to hazard a preliminary question.

'What do you think of her, Jeff?' he asked.

'What do I think to who, Master Jarge?' demanded the Yorkshireman in his simple vernacular.

'Why, Isa—Miss Sleaford, of course,' answered George rather indignantly: was there any other woman in the world whom he could possibly think of or speak of to-night?

Mr Jeffson was silent for some moments, as if the question related to so profound a subject that he had to descend into the furthest depths of his mind before he could answer it. He was silent; and the slow trampling of the horses' hoofs along the lane, and the twittering of some dissipated bird far away in the dim woodland, were the only sounds that broke the evening stillness.

'She's rare an' pretty, Master Jarge,' the philosopher said at last, in a very thoughtful tone; 'I a'most think I never see any one so pretty; though it isn't that high-coloured sort of prettiness they think so much to in Graybridge. She's still and white, somehow, like the images in York Minster; and her eyes seem far away as you look at her. Yes, she is rare an' pretty.'

'I've told her how I love her; and—and you like her, Jeff, don't you?' asked George, in a rapture of happiness that was stronger than his native shyness. 'You like her, and she likes you, Jeff, and will like you better as she comes to know you more. And she's going to be my wife, old Jeff!'

The young man's voice grew tremulous as he made this grand announcement. Whatever enthusiasm there was in his nature seemed concentrated in the emotions of this one day. He had loved for the first time, and declared his love. His true and constant heart, that wondrous aloe which was to bear a single flower, had burst into sudden blossom, and all the vigour of the root was in that one bright bloom. The aloe-flower might bloom steadily on for ever, or might fade and die; but it could never know a second blossoming.

'She's going to be my wife, Jeff,' he repeated, as if to say these words was in itself to taste an overpowering happiness.

But William Jeffson seemed very stupid to-night. His conversational powers appeared to have undergone a kind of paralysis. He spoke slowly, and made long pauses every now and then.

'You're going to marry her, Master Jarge?' he said.

'Yes, Jeff. I love her better than any living creature in this world— better than the world itself, or my own life; for I think, if she had answered me differently to-day, I should have died. Why, you're not surprised, are you Jeff? I thought you guessed at the very first— before I knew it myself, even—that I was in love with Isabel. Isabel! Isabel! what a pretty name! It sounds like a flower, doesn't it?'

'No; I'm not surprised, Master Jarge,' the Yorkshireman said thoughtfully. 'I knew you was in love with Miss Sleaford, regular fond about her, you know; but I didn't think—I didn't think—as you'd ask her to marry you so soon.'

'But why not, Jeff?' cried the young man. 'What should I wait for? I couldn't love her better than I do if I knew her for years and years, and every year were to make her brighter and lovelier than she is now. I've got a home to bring her to, and I'll work for her— I'll work for her as no man ever worked before to make a happy home for his wife.'

He struck out his arm, with his fist clenched, as if he thought that the highest round on the ladder of fortune was to be reached by any young surgeon who had the desire to climb.

'Why shouldn't I marry at once, Jeff?' he demanded, with some touch of indignation. 'I can give my wife as good a home as that from which I shall take her.'

'It isn't that as I was thinkin' of, Master Jarge,' William Jeffson answered, growing slower of speech and graver of tone with every word he spoke; 'it isn't that. But, you see, you know so little of Miss Sleaford; you know naught but that she's different, somehow, to all the other lasses you've seen, and that she seems to take your fancy like, because of that. You know naught about her, Master Jarge; and what's still worse—ever so much worse than that—you don't know that she loves you. You don't know that, Master Jarge. If you was only sure of *that*, the rest wouldn't matter so much; for there's scarcely any thing in this world as true love can't do; and a woman that loves truly can't be aught but a good woman at heart. I see Miss Sleaford when you was standin' talkin' by the Seven Stars, Master Jarge, and there wasn't any look in her face as if she knew what you was sayin', or thought about it; but her eyes looked ever so far away like: and though there was a kind of light in her face, it didn't seem as if it had any thing to do with you. And, lor bless your heart, Master Jarge, you should have seen my Tilly's face when she come up the airey-steps in the square where she was head-housemaid, and see me come up to London on purpose to surprise her. Why, it was all of a shine like with smiles and brightness, at the sight o' *me*, Master Jarge; and I'm sure *I'm* no great shakes to look at,' added Mr Jeffson, in a deprecating tone.

The reins, lying loose upon Brown Molly's neck, shook with the sudden trembling of the hand that held them. George Gilbert was seized with a kind of panic as he listened to his Mentor's discourse. He had not presumed to solicit any confession of love from Isabel Sleaford; he had thought himself more than blest, inasmuch as she

had promised to become his wife; yet he was absolutely terror-
stricken at Mr Jeffson's humiliating suggestion, and was withal very
angry at his old playmate's insolence.

'You mean that she doesn't love me?' he said sharply.

'Oh, Master Jarge, to be right down truthful with you, that's just
what I do mean. She *doan't* love you; as sure as I've seen true love
lookin' out o' my Tilly's face, I see somethin' that wasn't love lookin'
out o' hearn to-night. I see just such a look in Miss Sleaford's eyes
as I see once in a pretty young creetur that married a mate o' mine
down home; a young man as had got a little bit o' land and cottage
and every thing comfortable, and it wasn't the young creetur herself
that was in favour o' marryin' him; but it was her friends that
worried and bothered her till she said yes. She was a poor foolish
young thing, that didn't seem to have the strength to say no. And I
was at Joe Tillet's weddin',—his name was Joe Tillet,—and I see the
pretty young creetur standin', like as I saw Miss Sleaford to-night,
close alongside her husband while he was talkin', and lookin' prettier nor ever in her straw-bonnet and white ribbons; but her eyes
seemed to fix themselves on somethin' far away like; and when her
husband turned of a sudden and spoke to her, she started, like as if
she was waked out of a dream. I never forgot that look o' hearn,
Master Jarge; and I saw the same kind o' look to-night.'

'What nonsense you're talking, Jeff!' George answered, with considerable impatience. 'I dare-say your friend and his wife were very
happy?'

'No, Master Jarge, they wasn't. And that's just the very thing that
makes me remember the pretty young creetur's look that summer's
day, as she stood, dressed out in her wedding-clothes, by her loving
husband's side. He was very fond of her, and for a good two year or
so he seemed very happy, and was allus tellin' his friends he'd got
the best wife in the three Ridin's, and the quietest and most industrious; but she seemed to pine like; and by and by there was a young
soldier came home that had been to the Indies, and that was her first
cousin, and had lived neighbours with her family when she was a bit
of a girl. I won't tell you the story, Master Jarge; for it isn't the
pleasantest kind o' thing to tell, nor yet to hear; but the end of it
was, my poor mate Joe was found one summer's morning—just
such a day as that when he was married—hanging dead behind the
door of one of his barns; and as for the poor wretched young creetur

as had caused his death, nobody ever knew what came of her. And yet,' concluded Mr Jeffson, in a meditative tone, 'I've heard that poor chap Joe tell me so confident that his wife would get to love him dearly by and by, because he loved her so true and dear.'

George Gilbert made no answer to all this. He rode on slowly, with his head drooping. The Yorkshireman kept an anxious watch upon his master; he could not see the expression of the young man's face, but he could see by his attitude that the story of Joseph Tillet's misadventure had not been without a depressing influence upon him.

'Si'thee noo, Master Jarge,' said William Jeffson, laying his hand upon the surgeon's wrist, and speaking in a voice that was almost solemn, 'marryin' a pretty girl seems no more than gatherin' a wild rose out of the hedge to some men, they do it so light and careless-like,—just because the flower looks pretty where it's growin'. I'd known my Tilly six year before I asked her to be my wife, Master Jarge; and it was only because she'd been true and faithful to me all that time, and because I'd never, look at her when I might, seen any thing but love in her face, that I ventured at last to say to mysen, "William Jeffson, there's a lass that'll make thee a true wife." Doan't be in a hurry, Master Jarge; doan't! Take the advice of a poor ignor-ant chap as has one great advantage over all your learnin', for he's lived double your time in the world. Doan't be in a hurry. If Miss Sleaford loves ye true to-night, she'll love ye ten times truer this night twelvemonths, and truer still this time ten years. If she *doan't* love you, Master Jarge, keep clear of her as you would of a venom-ous serpent; for she'll bring you worse harm than ever that could do, if it stung you to the heart, and made an end of you at once. I see Joe Tillet lyin' dead after the inquest that was held upon him, Master Jarge; and the thought that the poor desperate creetur had killed hisself warn't so bad to me as the sight of the suffering on his poor dead face,—the suffering that he'd borne nigh upon two year, Master Jarge, *and had held his tongue about.*'

CHAPTER IX

MISS SLEAFORD'S ENGAGEMENT

Isabel Sleaford was 'engaged.' She remembered this when she woke on the morning after that pleasant day in Hurstonleigh grove, and that henceforward there existed a person who was bound to be miserable because of her. She thought this as she stood before the modest looking-glass, rolling the long plaits of hair into a great knot, that seemed too heavy for her head. Her life was all settled. She was not to be a great poetess or an actress. The tragic mantle of the Siddons might have descended on her young shoulders, but she was never to display its gloomy folds on any mortal stage. She was not to be any thing great. She was only to be a country surgeon's wife.

It was very commonplace, perhaps; and yet this lonely girl—this untaught and unfriended creature—felt some little pride in her new position. After all, she had read many novels in which the story was very little more than this,—three volumes of simple love-making, and a quiet wedding at the end of the chapter. She was not to be an Edith Dombey or a Jane Eyre.* Oh, to have been Jane Eyre, and to roam away on the cold moorland and starve,—wouldn't *that* have been delicious!

No, there was to be a very moderate portion of romance in her life; but still some romance. George Gilbert would be very devoted, and would worship her always, of course. She gave her head a little toss as she thought that, at the worst, she could treat him as Edith treated Dombey, and enjoy herself that way; though she was doubtful how far Edith Dombey's style of treatment might answer without the ruby velvet, and diamond coronet, and other 'properties' appertaining to the *rôle*.

In the mean while Miss Sleaford performed her duties as best she could, and instructed the orphans in a dreamy kind of way, breaking off in the middle of the preter-perfect tense of a verb to promise them that they should come to spend a day with her when she was married, and neglecting their fingering of the overture to *Masaniello**while she pondered on the colour of her wedding-dress.

And how much did she think of George Gilbert all this time? About as much as she would have thought of the pages who were to support the splendid burden of her trailing robes, if she had been about to be crowned Queen of England. He was the bridegroom, the husband; a secondary character in the play of which she was the heroine.

Poor George's first love-letter came to her on the following day,— a vague and rambling epistle, full of shadowy doubts and fears; haunted, as it were, by the phantom of poor dead-and-gone Joe Tillet, and without any punctuation whatever:

'But oh dearest ever dearest Isabel for ever dear you will be to me if you cast me from you and I should go to America for life in Graybridge would be worse than odious without you Oh Isabel if you do not love me I implore you for pity sake say so and end my misery I know I am not worthy of your love who are so beautiful and accomplished but oh the thought of giving you up is so bitter unless you yourself should wish it and oh there is no sacrifice on earth I would not make for you.'

The letter was certainly not as elegant a composition as Isabel would have desired it to be; but then a love-letter is a love-letter, and this was the first Miss Sleaford had ever received. George's tone of mingled doubt and supplication was by no means displeasing to her. It was only right that he should be miserable; it was only proper that he should be tormented by all manner of apprehensions. They would have to quarrel by and by, and to bid each other an eternal farewell, and to burn each other's letters, and be reconciled again. The quietest story could not be made out without such legitimate incidents in the course of the three volumes.

Although Isabel amused herself by planning her wedding-dress, and changed her mind very often as to the colour and material, she had no idea of a speedy marriage. Were there not three volumes of courtship to be gone through first?

Sigismund went back to town after the picnic which had been planned for his gratification, and Isabel was left quite alone with her pupils. She walked with them, and took her meals with them, and was with them all day; and it was only on a Sunday that she saw much of Mr Raymond.

That gentleman was very kind to the affianced lovers. George Gilbert rode over to Conventford every alternate Sunday, and dined with the family at Oakbank. Sometimes he went early enough to attend Isabel and the orphans to church. Mr Raymond himself was not a church-goer, but he sent his grand-nieces to perform their devotions, as he sent them to have their hair clipped by the hair-dresser, or their teeth examined by the dentist. George plunged into the wildest extravagance in the way of waistcoats, in order to do honour to these happy Sundays; and left off mourning for his father a month or so earlier than he had intended, in order to infuse variety into his costume. Every thing he wore used to look new on these Sundays; and Isabel, sitting opposite to him in the square pew, would contemplate him thoughtfully when the sermon was dull, and wonder, rather regretfully, why his garments never wore themselves into folds, but always retained a hard angular look, as if they had been originally worn by a wooden figure, and had never got over that disadvantage. He wore a watch-chain that his father had given him,—a long chain that went round his neck, but which he artfully twisted and doubled into the semblance of a short one; and on this chain he hung a lucky sixpence and an old-fashioned silver vinai-grette; which trifles, when seen from a distance, looked almost like the gold charms which the officers stationed at Conventford wore dangling on their waistcoats.

And so the engagement dawdled on through all the bright sum-mer months; and while the leaves were falling in the woods of Midlandshire, George still entreating that the marriage might speedily take place, and Isabel always deferring that ceremonial to some in-definite period.

Every alternate Sunday the young man's horse appeared at Mr Raymond's gate. He would have come every Sunday, if he had dared, and indeed had been invited to do so by Isabel's kind em-ployer; but he had sensitive scruples about eating so much beef and mutton, and drinking so many cups of tea, for which he could make no adequate return to his hospitable entertainer. Sometimes he brought a present for one of the orphans,—a workbox or a desk, fitted with scissors that wouldn't cut, and inkstands that wouldn't open (for there are no Parkins and Gotto in Graybridge or its vicinity), or a marvellous cake, made by Matilda Jeffson. Once he got up a little entertainment for his betrothed and her friends, and gave quite a dinner, with five sweets, and an elaborate dessert, and with the most plum-coloured of ports, and the brownest of sherries, procured spe-cially from the Cock at Graybridge. But as the orphans, who alone did full justice to the entertainment, were afflicted with a bilious attack on the following day, the experiment was not repeated.

But the dinner at Graybridge was not without its good effect. Isabel saw the house that was to be her home; and the future began to take a more palpable shape than it had worn hitherto. She looked at the little china ornaments on the mantelpiece, the jar of withered rose-leaves, mingled with faint odours of spices—the scent was very faint now, for the hands of George's dead mother had gathered the flowers. George took Isabel through the little rooms, and showed her an old-fashioned work-table, with a rosewood box at the top, and a well of fluted silk, that had once been rose-coloured, underneath.

'My mother used to sit at this table working, while she waited for my father; I've often heard him say so. You'll use the old workbox, won't you, Izzie?' George asked tenderly.

He had grown accustomed to call her Izzie now, and was familiar with her, and confided in her, as in a betrothed wife, whom no possible chance could alienate from him. He had ceased to regard her as a superior being, whom it was a privilege to know and worship. He loved her as truly as he had ever loved her; but not being of a poetical or sentimental nature, the brief access of romantic feeling which he had experienced on first falling in love speedily wore itself out, and the young man grew to contemplate his approaching marriage with perfect equanimity. He even took upon himself to lecture Isabel, on sundry occasions, with regard to her love of novel-reading, her neglect of plain needlework, and her appalling ignorance on the subject of puddings. He turned over her leaves, and found her places in the hymn-book at church; he made her follow the progress of the Lessons, with the aid of a church-service printed in pale ink and a minute type; and he frowned at her sternly when he caught her eyes wandering to distant bonnets during the sermon. All the young man's old notions of masculine superiority returned now that he was familiar with Miss Sleaford; but all this while he loved her as only a good man can love, and supplicated all manner of blessings for her every night when he said his prayers.

Isabel Sleaford improved very much in this matter-of-fact companionship, and in the exercise of her daily round of duty. She was no longer the sentimental young lady, whose best employment was to loll in a garden-chair reading novels, and who was wont to burst into sudden rhapsodies about George Gordon Lord Byron and Napoleon the First upon the very smallest provocation. She had tried George on both these subjects, and had found him entirely wanting in any special reverence for either of her pet heroes. Talking with him on autumn Sunday afternoons in the breezy meadows near Conventford, with the orphans loitering behind or straggling on before, Miss Sleaford had tested her lover's conversational powers to the utmost; but as she found that he neither knew nor wished to know any thing about Edith Dombey or Ernest Maltravers, and that he regarded the poems of Byron and Shelley* as immoral and blasphemous compositions, whose very titles should be unknown to a well-conducted young woman, Isabel was fain to hold her tongue about all the bright reveries of her girlhood, and to talk to Mr Gilbert about what he did understand.

He had read Cooper's* novels, and a few of Lever's;* and he had read Sir Walter Scott and Shakespeare, and was fully impressed with the idea that he could not over-estimate these latter writers: but when Isabel began to talk about Edgar Ravenswood and Lucy,* with her face all lighted up with emotion, the young surgeon could only stare wonderingly at his betrothed.

Oh, if he had only been like Edgar Ravenswood! The poor, childish, dissatisfied heart was always wishing that he could be something different from what he was. Perhaps during all that engagement the girl never once saw her lover really as he was. She dressed him up in her own fancies, and deluded herself by imaginary resemblances between him and the heroes in her books. If he was abrupt and disagreeable in his manner to her, he was Rochester; and she was Jane Eyre, tender and submissive. If he was cold, he was Dombey; and she feasted on her own pride, and scorned him, and made much of one of the orphans during an entire afternoon. If he was clumsy and stupid, he was Rawdon Crawley; and she patronised him, and laughed at him, and taunted him with little scraps of French with the Albany-Road accent, and played off all green-eyed Becky's prettiest airs upon him. But in spite of all this the young man's sober common-sense exercised a beneficial influence upon her; and by and by, when the three volumes of courtship had been prolonged to the uttermost, and the last inevitable chapter was close at hand, she had grown to think affectionately of her promised husband, and was determined to be very good and obedient to him when she became his wife.

But for the pure and perfect love which makes marriage thrice holy,—the love which counts no sacrifice too great, no suffering too bitter,—the love which knows no change but death, and seems instinct with such divinity that death can be but its apotheosis,—such love as this had no place in Isabel Sleaford's heart. Her books had given her some vague idea of this grand passion, and on comparing herself with Lucy Ashton and Zuleika,* with Amy Robsart* and Florence Dombey and Medora,* she began to think that the poets and novelists were all in the wrong, and that there were no heroes or heroines upon this commonplace earth.

She thought this, and she was content to sacrifice the foolish dreams of her girlhood, which were doubtless as impossible as they were beautiful. She was content to think that her lot in life was fixed, and that she was to be the wife of a good man, and the mistress of an old-fashioned house in one of the dullest towns in England. The time had slipped so quietly away since that spring twilight on the bridge at Hurstonleigh, her engagement had been taken so much as a matter of course by every one about her, that no thought of withdrawal therefrom had ever entered into her mind. And then, again, why should she withdraw from the engagement? George loved her; and there was no one else who loved her. There was no wandering Jamie* to come home in the still gloaming and scare her with the sight of his sad, reproachful face. If she was not George Gilbert's wife, she would be nothing—a nursery-governess for ever and ever, teaching stupid orphans, and earning five-and-twenty pounds a-year. When she thought of her desolate position, and of another subject which was most painful to her, she clung to George Gilbert, and was grateful to him, and fancied that she loved him.

The wedding-day came at last,—one bleak January morning, when Conventford wore its barest and ugliest aspect; and Mr Raymond gave his nursery-governess away, after the fashion of that simple Protestant ceremonial, which is apt to seem tame and commonplace when compared with the solemn grandeur of a Roman-Catholic marriage. He had given her the dress she wore, and the orphans had clubbed their pocket-money to buy their preceptress a bonnet as a surprise, which was a failure, after the usual manner of artfully-planned surprises.

Isabel Sleaford pronounced the words that made her George

Gilbert's wife; and if she spoke them somewhat lightly, it was because there had been no one to teach her their solemn import.
There was no taint of falsehood in her heart, no thought of revolt or
disobedience in her mind; and when she came out of the vestry,
leaning on her young husband's arm, there was a smile of quiet
contentment on her face.

'Joe Tillet's wife could never have smiled like that,' thought George,
as he looked at his bride.

The life that lay before Isabel was new; and, being little more
than a child as yet, she thought that novelty must mean happiness.
She was to have a house of her own, and servants, and an orchard
and paddock, two horses, and a gig. She was to be called Mrs
Gilbert: was not her name so engraved upon the cards which George
had ordered for her, in a morocco card-case, that smelt like new
boots and was difficult to open, as well as on those wedding-cards
which the surgeon had distributed among his friends?

George had ordered envelopes for these cards with his wife's
maiden name engraved inside; but, to his surprise, the girl had
implored him, ever so piteously, to counter-order them.

'Oh, don't have my name upon the envelopes, George,' she said;
'don't send my name to your friends; don't ever tell them what I
was called before you married me.'

'But why not, Izzie?'

'Because I hate my name,' she answered passionately. 'I hate it; I
hate it! I would have changed it if I could when—when—I first
came here; but Sigismund wouldn't let me come to his uncle's house
in a false name. I hate my name; I hate and detest it.'

And then suddenly seeing wonderment and curiosity plainly expressed in her lover's face, the girl cried out that there was no
meaning in what she had been saying, and that it was only her own
romantic folly, and that he was to forgive her, and forget all about it.

'But am I to send your name, or not, Isabel?' George asked rather
coolly. He did not relish these flights of fancy on the part of the
young lady he was training with a view to his own ideal of a wife.
'You first say a thing, and then say you don't mean it. Am I to send
the envelopes, or not?'

'No, no, George; don't send them, please; I really do dislike the
name. Sleaford *is* such an ugly name, you know.'

CHAPTER X

A BAD BEGINNING

Mr Gilbert took his young wife to an hotel at Murlington for a week's honeymoon—to a family-hotel; a splendid mansion, Isabel thought, where there was a solemn church-like stillness all day long, only broken by the occasional tinkling of silver spoons in the distance, or the musical chime of fragile glasses carried hither and thither on salvers of electro-plate. Isabel had never stayed at an hotel before; and she felt a thrill of pleasure when she saw the glittering table, the wax-candles in silver branches, the sweeping crimson curtains drawn before the lofty windows, and that delightful waiter, whose manner was such a judicious combination of protecting benevolence and obsequious humility.

Mrs George Gilbert drew a long breath as she trifled with the shining damask napkin, so wondrously folded into a bishop's mitre, and saw herself reflected in the tall glass on the opposite side of the room. She wore her wedding-dress still; a sombre brown-silk dress, which had been chosen by George himself because of its homely merit of usefulness, rather than for any special beauty or elegance. Poor Isabel had struggled a little about the choice of that dress, for she had wanted to look like Florence Dombey, on her wedding-day; but she had given way. Her life had never been her own yet, and never was to be her own, she thought; for now that her stepmother had ceased to rule over her by force of those spasmodic outbreaks of violence by which sorely-tried matrons govern their households, here was George, with his strong will and sound common-sense,— oh, how Isabel hated common-sense!—and she must needs acknowledge him as her master.

But she looked at her reflection in the glass, and saw that she was pretty. Was it only prettiness, or was it something more, even in spite of the brown dress? She saw her pale face and black hair lighted up by the wax-candles; and thought, if this could go on for ever,—the tinkling silver and glittering glass, the deferential waiter, the flavour of luxury and elegance, not to say Edith Dombeyism, that pervaded the atmosphere,—she would be pleased with her new lot. Unhappily there was only to be a brief interval of this aristocratic existence, for George had told his young wife confidentially that he didn't mean to go beyond a ten-pound note; and by and by, when the dinner-table had been cleared, he amused himself by making abstruse calculations as to how long that sum would hold out against the charges of the family-hotel.

The young couple stayed for a week at Murlington. They drove about the neighbourhood in an open fly, conscientiously admiring what the guide-books called the beauties of the vicinity; and the bleak winds of January tweaked their young noses as they faced the northern sky. George was happy—ah, how serenely happy!—in that the woman he so dearly loved was his wife. The thought of any sorrow darkling in the distance now, now that the solemn vows had been spoken, never entered into his mind. He had thought of William Jeffson's warning sometimes, it is true, but only to smile in superb contempt of the simple creature's foolish talk. Isabel loved him; she smiled at him when he spoke to her, and was gentle and obedient to his advice: he was, perhaps, a shade too fond of advising her. She had given up novel-reading, and employed her leisure in the interesting pursuit of plain needlework. Her husband watched her complacently by the light of the wax-candles while she hemmed a cambric handkerchief, threading and unthreading her needle very often, and boggling a little when she turned the corners, and stopping now and then to yawn behind her pretty little pink fingers; but then she had been out in the open air nearly all day, and it was only natural that she should be sleepy.

Perhaps it might have been better for George Gilbert if he had not solicited Mr Pawlkatt's occasional attendance upon the parish-patients, and thus secured a week's holiday in honour of his young wife. Perhaps it would have been better if he had kept his ten-pound note in his pocket, and taken Isabel straight to the house which was henceforth to be her home. That week in the hotel at Murlington revealed one dreadful fact to these young people; a fact which the Sunday-afternoon walks at Conventford had only dimly foreshadowed. They had very little to say to each other. That dread discovery, which should bring despair whenever it comes, dawned upon Isabel, at least, all at once; and a chill sense of weariness and disappointment crept into her breast, and grew there, while she was yet ignorant of its cause.

[They had very little to say to each other. Woe to the husband and wife who discover this! for though the woman is more lovely than all the houris in Mahomet's Paradise*; though the man is nobler and more splendid than Mr Tennyson's King Arthur*; they are foredoomed to be weary of one another's presence, and to loathe the lonely hour which brings them face to face, with no better resource than to stare blankly across the desolate hearth, and talk about the weather. Speech—the electric telegraph which unites the widest regions of thought and fancy—is useless for them, or can only convey polite inanities more wearisome than silence. Together day by day, they live as much apart as if an ocean rolled between them; united by a hundred bonds, they want the subtle link that would have made them one; and, at the best, are only two separate creatures chained together. Year after year they drag the chain, and are good to each other, and esteem each other, and are patient, and wonder why they are not happy. If the lady is of a sentimental turn of mind, and a reader of French novels, she settles herself comfortably, as a woman whose destiny is to be miserable and misunderstood, and, from the lonely heights amid which she dwells, looks down upon her husband with supremely contemptuous compassion; while he, looking up at her from the busy regions of this lower world, sees only a frivolous creature who neglects her household and runs long milliner's bills.

Have they ever tried to understand each other? In all the long weary years, have they ever conscientiously endeavoured to assimilate the tastes that seem so opposite? Has the woman ever said to herself, 'My husband works very hard, and comes home at night very weary from that abominable counting-house; and yet I expect that his face will light up with rapture when I talk to him about the last novel that has been sent from Mudie's,* the Beethoven quartette that I heard at the morning concert. Wouldn't it be more interesting to him if I asked whether Crashem and Smashem—that shaky firm, whose paper he has unwisely trusted in—have taken up the last bill of exchange? I don't care about Crashem and Smashem, and I have a very vague notion of the nature and properties of a bill of exchange; but then the subject is a matter of life and death to the poor hard-working creature sitting opposite to me at the long dinner-table; and it will be better for him to open his heart, and discourse at his ease upon the flatness of things in the City, the scarcity of

money, and the high rate of discount, than that he should sit patiently, sighing mournfully now and then, while I discourse about
the last volume of the novel, or the delicious *arpeggio* movement in
the quartette.'

There is no trade so vulgar or commonplace, no study so recon-
dite, no science so difficult, in which a tolerably clever woman cannot interest herself, if she seeks and wishes to be interested. She
learns very little, perhaps,—only a kind of smattering; but she learns
enough, if she learns to listen intelligently when her husband talks
to her, to hazard a judicious question that may lead him a little
farther on that pleasant road which he travels when he rides his own
hobby-horse.]*

Isabel was very young. She had not yet parted with one of her
delusions, and she ignorantly believed that she could keep those
foolish dreams, and yet be a good wife to George Gilbert. He talked
to her of his school-days; but she was not interested in those boyish
records of stand-up fights with bigger boys. (When ever was the
hero of a fight the big boy? I wonder what becomes of all those
defeated big boys in after life? Do they vanish away into empty
space, when once they pass beyond the scholastic portals? or how is
it that they are never heard of, and that every grown-up light-
weight has been victor over a craven heavy-weight?)

George Gilbert related many such experiences to his young wife,
and then branched away to his youth, his father's decline and death,
his own election to the parish duties, his lonely bachelorhood, his
hope of a better position and larger income some day. Oh, how dull
and prosaic it all sounded to that creature, whose vague fancies were
for ever wandering towards wonderful regions of poetry and romance! It was a relief to her when George left off talking, and left
her free to think her own thoughts, as she laboured on at the cambric handkerchief, and pricked the points of her fingers, and entangled her thread.

There were no books in the sitting-room at the family-hotel; and
even if there had been, this honeymoon week seemed to Isabel a
ceremonial period. She felt as if she were on a visit, and was not free
to read. She sighed as she passed the library on the fashionable par-
ade, and saw the names of the new novels exhibited on a board before
the door; but she had not the courage to say how happy three cloth-
covered volumes of light literature would have made her. George was

not a reading man. He read the local papers and skimmed the *Times* after breakfast; and then, there he was, all day long. There were two wet days during that week at Murlington; and the young married people had ample opportunity of testing each other's conversational powers, as they stood in the broad window, watching occasional passers-by in the sloppy street, and counting the rain-drops on the glass.

The week came to an end at last; and on a wet Saturday afternoon George Gilbert paid his bill at the family-hotel. The ten-pound note had held out very well; for the young bridegroom's ideas had never soared beyond a daily pint of sherry to wash down the simple repast which the discreet waiter provided for those humble guests in piti-ful regard of their youth and simplicity. Mr Gilbert paid his bill, while Isabel packed her own and her husband's things; oh, what uninteresting things!—double-soled boots, and serviceable garments of gray woollen stuff. Then, when all was ready, she stood in the window watching for the omnibus which was to carry her to her new home. Murlington was only ten miles from Graybridge, and the journey between the two places was performed in an old-fashioned stunted omnibus,—a darksome vehicle, with a low roof, a narrow door, and only one small square of glass on each side.

Isabel breathed a long sigh as she watched for the appearance of this vehicle in the empty street. The dull wet day, the lonely pave-ment, the blank empty houses to let furnished—for it was not the Murlington season now—were not so dull or empty as her own life seemed to her this afternoon. Was it to be for ever and for ever like this? Yes; she was married, and the story was all over; her destiny was irrevocably sealed, and she was tired of it already. But then she thought of her new home, and all the little plans she had made for herself before her marriage,—the alterations and improvements she had sketched out for the beautification of her husband's home. Somehow or other, even these ideas, which had beguiled her so in her maiden reveries, seemed to melt and vanish now. She had spoken to George, and he had received her suggestions doubtfully, hinting at the money which would be required for the carrying-out of her plans,—they were very simple plans too, and did not involve much expense.

Was there to be nothing in her life, then? She was only a week married; and already, as she stood at the window listening to the slop-slop of the everlasting rain, she began to think that she had made a mistake.

The omnibus came to the door presently, and she was handed into it, and her husband seated himself, in the dim obscurity, by her side. There was only one passenger—a wet farmer, wrapped in so many greatcoats that being wet outside didn't matter to him, as he only gave other people cold. He wiped his muddy boots on Isabel's dress, the brown-silk wedding-dress which she had worn all the week; and Mrs Gilbert made no effort to save the garment from his depredations. She leaned her head back in the corner of the omnibus, while the luggage was being bumped upon the roof above her, and let down her veil. The slow tears gathered in her eyes, and rolled down her pale cheeks.

It was a mistake,—a horrible and irreparable mistake,—whose dismal consequences she must bear for ever and ever. She felt no dislike of George Gilbert. She neither liked nor disliked him—only he could not give her the kind of life she wanted; and by her marriage with him she was shut out for ever from the hope of such a life. No prince would ever come now; no accidental duke would fall in love with her black eyes, and lift her all at once to the bright regions she pined to inhabit. No; it was all over. She had sold her birthright for a vulgar mess of pottage. She had bartered all the chances of the future for a little relief to the monotony of the present,—for a few wedding-clothes, a card-case with a new name on the cards contained in it, the brief distinction of being a bride.

George spoke to her two or three times during the journey to Graybridge; but she only answered him in monosyllables. She had a 'headache,' she said,—that convenient feminine complaint which is an excuse for any thing. She never once looked out of the window, though the road was new to her. She sat back in the dusky vehicle, while George and the farmer talked local politics; and their talk mingled vaguely with her own misery. The darkness grew thicker in the low-roofed carriage; the voices of George and the farmer died drowsily away; and by and by there was snoring, whether from George or the farmer Isabel did not care to think. She was thinking of Byron and of Napoleon the First. Ah, to have lived in his time, and followed him, and slaved for him, and died for him in that lonely island far out in the waste of waters! The tears fell faster as all her childish dreams came back upon her, and arrayed themselves in cruel contrast with her new life. Mr Buckstone's bright Irish hero-ine,* when she has been singing her song in the cold city street,—

the song which she has dreamt will be the means of finding her lost nursling,—sinks down at last upon a snow-covered door-step, and sobs aloud because 'it all seems so *real!*'

Life seemed 'so real' now to Isabel. She awakened suddenly to the knowledge that all her dreams were only dreams after all, and never had been likely to come true. As it was, they could never come true; she had set a barrier against the fulfilment of those bright visions, and she must abide by her own act.

It was quite dark upon that wintry afternoon when the omnibus stopped at the Cock at Graybridge; and then there was more bumping about of the luggage, before Isabel was handed out upon the pavement to walk home with her husband. Yes; they were to walk home. What was the use of a ten-pound note spent upon splendour in Murlington, when the honeymoon was to close in degradation such as this? They walked home. The streets were sloppy, and there was mud in the lane where George's house stood; but it was only five or ten minutes' walk, as he said, and nobody in Graybridge would have dreamed of hiring a fly.

So they walked home, with the luggage following on a truck; and when they came to the house, there was only a dim glimmer in the red lamp over the surgery-door. All the rest was dark; for George's letter to Mr Jeffson had been posted too late, and the bride and bridegroom were not expected. Every body knows the cruel bleakness which that simple fact involves. There were no fires in the rooms; no cheery show of preparation; and there was a faint odour of soft-soap suggestive of recent cleaning. Mrs Jeffson was up to her elbows in a flour-tub when the young master pulled his own doorbell; and she came out, with her arms white and her face dirty, to receive the newly-married pair. She set a flaring tallow-candle on the parlour-table, and knelt down to light the fire, exclaiming and wondering all the while at the unexpected arrival of Mr Gilbert and his wife.

'My master's gone over to Conventford for some groceries, and we're all of a moodle like, ma'am,' she said; 'but we moost e'en do th' best we can, and make all coomfortable. Master Jarge said Moonday as plain as words could speak when he went away, and th' letter's not coom yet; so you must joost excuse things not bein' straight.'

Mrs Jeffson might have gone on apologising for some time longer; but she jumped up suddenly to attend upon Isabel, who had burst into a passion of hysterical sobbing. She was romantic, sensitive, impressionable—selfish, if you will; and her poor untutored heart revolted against the utter ruin of her dreams.

'It is *so* miserable!' she sobbed; 'it all seems so miserable!'

George came in from the stables, where he had been to see Brown Molly, and brought his wife some sal-volatile, in a wine-glass of water; and Mrs Jeffson comforted the poor young creature, and took her up to the half-prepared bedroom, where the carpets were still up, and where the white-washed walls—it was an old-fashioned house, and the upper rooms had never been papered—and the bare boards looked cheerless and desolate in the light of a tallow-candle. Mrs Jeffson brought her young mistress a cup of tea, and sat down by the bedside while she drank it, and talked to her and comforted her, though she did not entertain a very high opinion of a young lady who went into hysterics because there was no fire in her sitting-room.

'I daresay it *did* seem cold and lonesome and comfortless like,' Mrs Jeffson said indulgently; 'but we'll get things nice in no time.'

Isabel shook her head.

'You are very kind,' she said; 'but it wasn't that made me cry.'

She closed her eyes, not because she was sleepy, but because she wanted Mrs Jeffson to go away and leave her alone. Then, when the good woman had retired with cautious footsteps, and closed the door, Mrs George Gilbert slowly opened her eyes, and looked at the things on which they were to open every morning for all her life to come.

There was nothing beautiful in the room, certainly. There was a narrow mantelpiece, with a few blocks of Derbyshire spar and other mineral productions; and above them there hung an old-fashioned engraving of some scriptural subject, in a wooden frame painted black. There was a lumbering old wardrobe—or press, as it was called—of painted wood, with a good deal of the paint chipped off; there was a painted dressing-table, a square looking-glass, with brass ornamentation about the stand and frame,—a glass in which George Gilbert's grandfather had looked at himself seventy years before. Isabel stared at the blank white walls, the gaunt shadows of the awkward furniture, with a horrible fascination. It was all so ugly, she thought; and her mind revolted against her husband, as she remembered that he could have changed all this, and yet had left it in its bald hideousness.

And all this time George was busy in his surgery, grinding his pestle in so cheerful a spirit that it seemed to fall into a kind of tune, and thinking how happy he was now that Isabel Sleaford was his wife.

CHAPTER XI

'SHE ONLY SAID, "MY LIFE IS WEARY!"'*

When the chill discomfort of that first evening at Graybridge was past and done with, Isabel felt a kind of remorseful regret for the mute passion of discontent and disappointment that had gone along with it. The keen sense of misery passed with the bad influence of the day and hour. In the sunlight her new home looked a little better, her new life seemed a little brighter. Yes, she would do her duty, she would be a good wife to dear George, who was so kind to her, and loved her with such a generous devotion.

She went to church with him at Graybridge for the first time on the morning after that dreary wet Saturday evening; and all through the sermon she thought of her new home, and what she should do to make it bright and pretty. The Rector of Graybridge had chosen one of the obscurest texts in St Paul's Epistle to the Hebrews for his sermon that morning, and Isabel did not even try to understand him. She let her thoughts ramble away to carpets and curtains, and china flower-pots and Venetian blinds, and little bits of ornamentation, which should transform George's house from its square nakedness into a bowery cottage. Oh, if the trees had only grown differently! if there had been trailing parasites climbing up to the chimneys, and a sloping lawn, and a belt of laurels, and little winding pathways, and a rustic seat half-hidden under a weeping willow, instead of that bleak flat of cabbages and gooseberry-bushes, and raw clods of earth piled in black ridges across the dreary waste!

After church there was an early dinner of some baked meat, prepared by Mrs Jeffson. Isabel did not take much notice of what she ate. She was at that early period of life when a young person of sentimental temperament scarcely knows roast beef from boiled veal; but she observed that there were steel forks on the surgeon's table, —steel forks with knobby horn-handles suggestive of the wildest species of deer,—and a metal mustard-pot lined with blue glass, and willow-pattern plates, and a brown earthenware jug of home-brewed beer; and that every thing was altogether commonplace and vulgar.

After dinner Mrs Gilbert amused herself by going over the house with her husband. It was a very tolerable house, after all; but it wasn't pretty; it had been inhabited by people who were fully satisfied so long as they had chairs to sit upon, and beds to sleep on, and tables and cups and plates for the common purposes of breakfast, dinner, and supper; and who would have regarded the purchase of a chair that was not intended to be sat upon, or a cup that was never designed to be drunk out of, as something useless and absurd, or even, in an indirect manner, sinful, because involving the waste of money that might be devoted to a better use.

'George,' said Isabel, gently, when she had seen all the rooms, 'did you never think of re-furnishing the house?"

'Re-furnishing it! How do you mean, Izzie?'

'Buying new furniture, I mean, dear. This is all so old-fashioned.'

George the conservative shook his head.

'I like it all the better for that, Izzie,' he said; 'it was my father's, you know, and his father's before him. I wouldn't change a stick of it for the world. Besides, it's such capital substantial furniture; they don't make such chairs and tables nowadays.'

'No,' Izzie murmured with a sigh; 'I'm very glad they don't.'

Then she clasped her hands suddenly upon his arm, and looked up at him with her eyes opened to their widest extent and shining with a look of rapture.

'O George,' she cried, 'there was an ottoman in one of the shops at Conventford with seats for three people, and little stands for people to put their cups and saucers upon, and a place in the middle for FLOWERS! And I asked the price of it,—I often ask the price of things, for it's almost like buying them, you know,—and it was only eleven pounds ten, and I daresay they'd take less; and oh, George, if you'd make the best parlour into a drawing-room, and have that ottoman in the centre, and chintz-curtains lined with rose-colour, and a white watered paper on the walls, and Venetian shutters outside—'

George put his hand upon the pretty mouth from which the eager words came so rapidly.

'Why, Izzie,' he said, 'you'd ruin me before the year was out. All that finery would make a hole in a hundred pounds. No, no, dear; the best parlour was good enough for my father and mother, and it ought to be good enough for you and me. By and by, when my practice extends, Izzie, as I've every reason to hope it will, we'll talk about a new Kidderminster carpet,—a nice serviceable brown ground with a drab spot, or something of that kind,—but until then—'

Isabel turned away from him with a gesture of disgust.

'What do I care about new carpets?' she said; 'I wanted it all to look pretty.'

Yes; she wanted it to look pretty; she wanted to infuse some beauty into her life, something which, in however remote a degree, should be akin to the things she read of in her books. Every thing that was beautiful gave her a thrill of happiness; every thing that was ugly gave her a shudder of pain; and she had not yet learned that life was never meant to be all happiness, and that the soul must struggle towards the upper light out of a region of pain and darkness and confusion, as the blossoming plant pushes its way to the sunshine from amongst dull clods of earth. She wanted to be happy, and enjoy herself in her own way. She was not content to wait till her allotted portion of joy came to her; and she mistook the power to appreciate and enjoy beautiful things for a kind of divine right to happiness and splendour.

To say that George Gilbert did not understand his wife is to say very little. Nobody, except perhaps Sigismund Smith, had ever yet understood Isabel. She did not express herself better than other girls of her age; sometimes she expressed herself worse; for she wanted to say so much, and a hopeless confusion would arise every now and then out of that entanglement of eager thought and romantic rapture which filled her brain. In Miss Sleaford's own home people had been a great deal too much occupied with the ordinary bustle of life to trouble themselves about a young lady's romantic reveries. Mrs Sleaford thought that she had said all that was to be said about Isabel when she had denounced her as a lazy selfish thing, who would loll on the grass and read novels if the house was blazing and all her family perishing in the flames. The boys looked upon their half-sister with all that supercilious mixture of pity and contempt with which all boys are apt to regard any fellow-creature who is so weak-minded as to be a girl.

Mr Sleaford was very fond of his only daughter; but he loved her chiefly because she was pretty, and had eyes whose like he had never seen except in the face of that young broken-hearted wife so early lost to him.

Nobody had ever quite understood Isabel; and least of all could George Gilbert understand the woman whom he had chosen for his wife. He loved her and admired her, and he was honestly anxious that she should be happy; but then he wanted her to be happy according to his ideas of happiness, and not her own. He wanted her to be delighted with stiff little tea-parties, at which the Misses Pawlkatt, and the Misses Burdock, and young Mrs Henry Palmer, wife of Mr Henry Palmer junior, solicitor, discoursed pleasantly of the newest patterns in crochet, and the last popular memoir of some departed Evangelical curate. Isabel did not take any interest in these things, and could not make herself happy with these people. Unluckily she allowed this to be seen; and, after a few tea-parties, the Graybridge aristocracy dropped away from her, only calling now and then, out of respect to George, who was heartily compassionated on account of his most mistaken selection of a wife.

So Isabel was left to herself, and little by little fell back into very much the same kind of life as that which she had led at Camberwell.

She had given up all thought of beautifying the house which was now her home. After that struggle about the ottoman, there had been many other struggles, in which Isabel had pleaded for smaller and less expensive improvements, only to be blighted by that hard common-sense with which Mr George Gilbert was wont—on principle—to crush his wife's enthusiasm. He had married this girl because she was unlike other women; and now that she was his own property, he set himself conscientiously to work to smooth her into the most ordinary semblance of everyday womanhood, by means of that moral flat-iron called common-sense.

Of course he succeeded to admiration. Isabel abandoned all hope of making her new home pretty, or transforming George Gilbert into a Walter Gay. She had made a mistake, and she accepted the consequences of her mistake; and fell back upon the useless dreamy life she had led so long in her father's house.

The surgeon's duties occupied him all day long, and Isabel was left to herself. She had none of the common distractions of a young matron. She had no servants to scold, no china to dust, no puddings or pies or soups or hashes to compound for her husband's dinner.

Mrs Jeffson did all that kind of work, and would have bitterly resented any interference from the 'slip of a girl' whom Mr Gilbert had chosen for his wife. Isabel did as she liked; and this meant reading novels all day long, or as long as she had a novel to read, and writing unfinished verses of a lachrymose nature on half-sheets of paper.

When the spring came, she went out—alone; for her husband was away among his patients, and had no time to accompany her. She went for long rambles in that lovely Elizabethan Midlandshire, and thought of the life that never was to be hers. She wandered alone in the country lanes where the hedgerows were budding; and sat alone, with her book on her lap, among the buttercups and daisies in the shady angle of a meadow, where the untrimmed hawthorns made a natural bower above her head. Stray pedestrians crossing the meadows near Graybridge often found the doctor's young wife sitting under a big green parasol, with a little heap of gathered wild-flowers fading on the grass beside her, and with an open book upon her knees. Sometimes she went as far as Thurston's Crag, the Midlandshire seat of Lord Thurston; a dear old place, an island of medieval splendour amidst a sea of green pasture-land, where, under the very shadow of a noble mansion, there was a waterfall and a mill, and a miller's cottage that was difficult to believe in out of a picture. There was a wooden bridge across that noisiest of waterfalls, and a monster oak, whose spreading branches shadowed all the width of the water; and it was on a rough wooden bench under this dear old tree that Isabel loved best to sit.

The Graybridge people were not slow to remark upon Mrs Gilbert's habits, and hinted that a young person who spent so much of her time in the perusal of works of fiction could scarcely be a model wife. Before George had been married three months, the ladies who had been familiar with him in his bachelorhood had begun to pity him, and had already mapped out for him such a career of domestic wretchedness as rarely falls to the lot of afflicted man.

Mrs Gilbert was *not* pretty. The Graybridge ladies settled that question at the very first tea-party from which George and his wife were absent. She was not pretty—when you looked into her. That was the point upon which the feminine critics laid great stress. At a distance, certainly, Mrs Gilbert might look showy. The lady who hit upon the adjective 'showy' was very much applauded by her friends.

At a distance Isabel might be called showy; always provided you like eyes that are so large as only by a miracle to escape from being goggles, and lips that are so red as to be unpleasantly suggestive of scarlet-fever. But *look into* Mrs Gilbert, and even this show of beauty vanished, and you only saw a sickly young person, with insignificant features and coarse black hair—so coarse and common in texture, that its abnormal length and thickness—of which Isabel was no doubt inordinately proud—were very little to boast of.

But while the Graybridge ladies criticised his wife and prophesied for him all manner of dismal sufferings, George Gilbert, strange to say, was very happy. He had married the woman he loved, and no thought that he had loved unwisely or married hastily ever entered his mind. When he came home from a long day's work, he found a beautiful creature waiting to receive him—a lovely and lovable creature, who put her arms around his neck and kissed him, and smiled at him. It was not in his nature to see that the graceful little embrace, and the welcoming kiss, and the smile, were rather mechanical matters that came of themselves. He took his dinner, or his weak tea, or his supper, as the case might be, and stretched his long legs across the familiar hearthrug, and talked to his wife, and was happy. If she had an open book beside her plate, and if her eyes wandered to the page every now and then while he was talking to her, she had often told him that she could listen and read at the same time; and no doubt she could do so. What more than sweet smiles and gentle looks could the most exacting husband demand? And George Gilbert had plenty of these; for Isabel was very grateful to him, because he never grumbled at her idleness and novel-reading, or worried and scolded as her stepmother had done. She was fond of him, as she would have been fond of a big elder brother, who let her have a good deal of her own way; and so long as he left her unassailed by his common-sense, she was happy, and tolerably satisfied with her life. Yes; she was satisfied with her life, which was the same every day, and with the dull old town, where no change ever came. She was satisfied as an opium-eater is satisfied with the common everyday world; which is only the frame that holds together all manner of splendid and ever-changing pictures. She was content with a life in which she had ample leisure to dream of a different existence.

Oh, how she thought of that other and brighter life! that life in which there was passion, and poetry, and beauty, and rapture, and despair! Here, among these meadows, and winding waters, and hedge-rows, life was a long sleep: and one might as well be a brown-eyed cow, browsing from week's end to week's end in the same pastures, as a beautiful woman with an eager yearning soul.

Mrs Gilbert thought of London—that wonderful West-End, May-Fair London, which has no attribute in common with all the great metropolitan wilderness around and about it. She thought of that holy of holies, that inner sanctuary of life, in which all the women are beautiful and all the men are wicked, in which existence is a perpetual whirlpool of balls and dinner-parties and hothouse flowers and despair. She thought of that untasted life, and pictured it, and thrilled with the sense of its splendour and brightness, as she sat by the brawling waterfall, and heard the creaking wheel of the mill, and the splashing of the trailing weeds. She saw herself amongst the light and music of that other world; queen of a lamplit boudoir, where loose patches of ermine gleamed whitely upon carpets of velvet-pile; where, amid a confusion of glitter and colour, she might sit, nestling among the cushions of a low gilded chair—a kind of indoor Cleopatra's galley*—and listen contemptuously (she always imagined herself contemptuous) to the eloquent compliments of a wicked prince. And then the Row!* She saw herself in the Row sometimes, upon an Arab—a black Arab—that would run away with her at the most fashionable time in the afternoon, and all-but kill her: and then she would rein him up as no mortal woman ever reined-in an Arab steed before, and would ride slowly back between two ranks of half-scared, half-admiring faces, with her hair hanging over her shoulders and her eyelashes drooping on her flushed cheeks. And then the wicked prince, goaded by an unvarying course of contemptuous treatment, would fall ill, and be at the point of death: and one night, when she was at a ball, with floating robes of cloud-like lace and diamonds glimmering in her hair, he would send for her—that wicked, handsome, adorable creature would send his valet to summon her to his deathbed, and she would see him there in the dim lamplight, pale and repentant, and romantic and delightful; and as she fell on her knees in all the splendour of her lace and dia-monds, he would break a blood-vessel and die! And then she would go back to the ball, and would be the gayest and most beautiful creature in all that whirlpool of elegance and beauty. Only, the next morning, when her attendants came to awaken her, they would find her—*dead!*

Amongst the books which Mrs Gilbert most often carried to the bench by the waterfall was the identical volume which Charles Raymond had looked at in such a contemptuous spirit in Hurstonleigh Grove—the little thin volume of poems entitled *An Alien's Dreams*. Mr Raymond had given his nursery-governess a parcel of light literature soon after her marriage, and this poor little book of verses was one of the volumes in the parcel; and as Isabel knew her Byron and her Shelley by heart, and could recite long melancholy rhapsodies from the works of either poet by the hour together, she fastened quite eagerly upon this little green-covered volume by a nameless writer.

The Alien's dreams seemed like her own fancies, somehow; for they belonged to that bright *other* world which she was never to see. How familiar the Alien was with that delicious region; and how lightly *he* spoke of the hothouse flowers and diamonds, the ermine carpets and Arab steeds! She read the poems over and over again in the drowsy June weather, sitting in the shabby little common parlour when the afternoons were too hot for outdoor rambles, and getting up now and then to look at her profile in the glass over the mantelpiece, and to wonder whether she was like any of those gorgeous but hollow-hearted creatures upon whom the Alien showered such torrents of melodious abuse.

Who was the Alien? Isabel had asked Mr Raymond that question, and had been a little crushed by the reply. The Alien was a Midlandshire squire, Mr Raymond had told her; and the word 'squire' suggested nothing but a broad-shouldered, rosy-faced man, in a scarlet coat and top-boots. Surely no squire could have written those half-heartbroken, half-cynical verses, those deliciously scornful elegies upon the hollowness of lovely woman and things in general! Isabel had her own image of the writer—her own ideal poet, who rose in all his melancholy glory, and pushed the red-coated country squire out of her mind when she sat with the *Alien's Dreams* in her lap, or scribbled weak imitations of that gentleman's poetry upon the backs of old envelopes and other scraps of waste paper.

Sometimes, when George had eaten his supper, Isabel would do him the favour of reading aloud one of the most spasmodic of the Alien's dreams. But when the Alien was most melodiously cynical, and the girl's voice tremulous with sudden exaltation of feeling, her eyes, wandering by chance to where her husband sat, would catch him yawning behind his glass of ale, or reckoning a patient's account on the square tips of his fingers. On one occasion poor George was terribly perplexed to behold his wife suddenly drop her book upon her lap and burst into tears. He could imagine no reason for her weeping, and he sat aghast, staring at her for some moments before he could utter any word of consolation.

'You don't care for the poetry, George,' she cried, with the sudden passion of a spoiled child. 'Oh, why do you let me read to you, if you don't care for the poetry?'

'But I do care for it, Izzie dear,' Mr Gilbert murmured soothingly,—'at least I like to hear you read, if it amuses *you*.'

Isabel flung the 'Alien' into the remotest corner of the little parlour, and turned from her husband as if he had stung her.

'You don't understand me,' she said; 'you don't understand me.'

'No, my dear Isabel,' returned Mr Gilbert with dignity (for his common-sense reasserted itself after the first shock of surprise); 'I certainly do *not* understand you when you give way to such temper as this without any visible cause.'

He walked over to the corner of the room, picked up the little volume, and smoothed the crumpled leaves; for his habits were orderly, and the sight of a book lying open upon the carpet was unpleasant to him.

Of course poor George was right, and Isabel was a very capricious, ill-tempered young woman when she flew into a passion of rage and grief because her husband counted his fingers while she was reading to him. But then such little things as these make the troubles of people who are spared from the storm and tempest of life. Such sorrows as these are the Scotch mists, the drizzling rains of existence. The weather doesn't appear so very bad to those who behold it from a window; but that sort of scarcely perceptible drizzle chills the hapless pedestrian to the very bone. I have heard of a lady who was an exquisite musician, and who, in the dusky twilight of a honeymoon evening, played to her husband,—played as some women play, pouring out all her soul upon the keys of the piano, breathing her fined and purest thoughts in some master-melodies of Beethoven or Mozart.

'That's a very *pretty tune*,' said the husband complacently.

She was a proud reserved woman, and she closed the piano with-out a word of complaint or disdain; but she lived to be old, and she never touched the keys again.

CHAPTER XII

SOMETHING LIKE A BIRTHDAY

It happened that the very day after Isabel's little outbreak of passion was a peculiar occasion in George Gilbert's life. It was the 2nd of July, and it was his wife's birthday,—the first birthday after her marriage; and the young surgeon had planned a grand treat and surprise, quite an elaborate festival, in honour of the day. He had been, therefore, especially wounded by Isabel's ill-temper. Had he not been thinking of her and of her pleasure at the very moment when she had upbraided him for his lack of interest in the Alien? He did *not* care about the Alien. He did not appreciate

> 'Clotilde, Clotilde, my dark Clotilde!
>   With the sleepy light in your midnight glance,
>   We let the dancers go by to dance;
>   But we stayed out on the lamplit stair,
>   And the odorous breath of your trailing hair
>   Swept over my face as your whispers stole
>   Like a gush of melody through my soul;
>   Clotilde, Clotilde, my own Clotilde!'

But he loved his wife, and was anxious to please her; and he had schemed and plotted to do her pleasure. He had hired a fly—an open fly—for the whole day, and Mrs Jeffson had prepared a basket with port and sherry from the Cock, and all manner of north-country delicacies; and George had written to Mr Raymond, asking that gentleman, with the orphans of course, to meet himself and his wife at Warncliffe Castle, the show-place of the county. This Mr Raymond had promised to do; and all the arrangements had been carefully planned, and had been kept profoundly secret from Isabel.

She was very much pleased when her husband told her of the festival early on that bright summer morning, while she was plaiting her long black hair at the little glass before the open lattice. She ran to the wardrobe to see if she had a clean muslin dress. Yes, there it was; the very lavender-muslin which she had worn at the Hurstonleigh picnic. George was delighted to see her pleasure; and he sat on the window-sill watching her as she arranged her collar and fastened a little bow of ribbon at her throat, and admired herself in the glass.

'I want it to be like that day last year, Izzie; the day I asked you to marry me. Mr Raymond will bring the key of Hurstonleigh Grove, and we're to drive there after we've seen the castle, and picnic there as we did before; and then we're to go to the very identical model old woman's to tea; and every thing will be exactly the same.'

Ah, Mr George Gilbert, do you know the world so little as to be ignorant that no day in life ever has its counterpart, and that to endeavour to bring about an exact repetition of any given occasion is to attempt the impossible?

It was a six-mile drive from Graybridge to Warncliffe, the grave old county town,—the dear old town, with shady pavements, and abutting upper stories, pointed gables, and diamond-paned casements; the queer old town, with wonderful churches, and gloomy archways, and steep stony streets, and above all, the grand old castle, the black towers, and keep, and turrets, and gloomy basement dungeons, lashed for ever and for ever by the blue rippling water. I have never seen Warncliffe Castle except in the summer sunshine, and my hand seems paralysed when I try to write of it. It is easy to invent a castle, and go into raptures about the ivied walls and mouldering turrets; but I shrink away before the grand reality, and can describe nothing; I see it all too plainly, and feel the tameness of my words too much. But in summer-time this Elizabethan Midlandshire is an English paradise, endowed with all the wealth of natural loveliness, enriched by the brightest associations of poetry and romance.

Mr Raymond was waiting at the little doorway when the fly stopped, and he gave Isabel his arm and led her into a narrow winding alley of verdure and rockwork, and then across a smooth lawn, and under an arch of solid masonry to another lawn, a velvety grass-plat, surrounded by shrubberies, and altogether a triumph of landscape gardening.

They went into the castle with a little group of visitors who had just collected on the broad steps before the door; and they were taken at once under the convoy of a dignified housekeeper in a rustling silk-gown, who started off into a *vivâ-voce* catalogue of the contents of the castle-hall, a noble chamber with armour-clad effigies of dead-and-gone warriors ranged along the walls, with notched battle-axes, and cloven helmets, and monster antlers, and Indian wampum, and Canadian wolf-skins, and Australian boomerangs hanging against the wainscot, with carved oak and ebony muniment-chests upon the floor, and with three deep-embayed windows overhanging the brightest landscape, the fairest streamlet in England.

While the housekeeper was running herself down like a musical box that had been newly wound up, and with as much animation and expression in her tones as there is in a popular melody interpreted by a musical box, Mr Raymond led Isabel to the window, and showed her the blue waters of the Wayverne tumbling head foremost over craggy masses of rockwork, green boulders, and pebbles that shimmered in the sunlight, and then, playing hide-and-seek under dripping willows, and brawling away over emerald moss and golden sand, to fall with a sudden impetus into the quiet depths beneath the bridge.

'Look at that, my dear,' said Mr Raymond; 'that isn't in the catalogue. I'll tell you all about the castle: and we'll treat the lady in the silk-dress as they treat the organ-boys in London. We'll give her half-a-crown to move on, and leave us to look at the pictures, and the boomerangs, and the armour, and the tapestry, and the identical toilet-table and pincushion in which her gracious Majesty stuck the pin she took out of her bonnet-string when she took luncheon with Lord Warncliffe a year or two ago. That's the gem of the catalogue in the housekeeper's opinion, I know. We'll look at the pictures by ourselves, Mrs Gilbert, and I'll tell you all about them.'

To my mind Warncliffe Castle is one of the pleasantest show-places in the kingdom. There are not many rooms to see, nor are they large rooms. There are not many pictures; but the few in every room are of the choicest, and are hung on a level with the eye, and do not necessitate that straining of the spinal column which makes the misery of most picture-galleries. Warncliffe Castle is like an elegant little dinner; there are not many dishes, and every thing is so good that you wish there were more. [I have been at Hampton Court with people who give you forty minutes to *do* all the rooms, and I have done a Sunday-afternoon scamper over Versailles with a cicerone who, whenever my eyes rested on a picture, reminded me sharply that I had eighty more rooms to see before dinner. But at Warncliffe you lounge through a suite of sunny chambers that have the extra charm of looking as if people lived in them.]* You see not only Murillos and Titians, Lelys and Vandykes upon the walls; you see tables scattered with books, and women's handiwork here and there; and whichever way you turn, there is always the noisy Wayverne brawling and rippling under the windows, and the green expanse of meadow and the glory of purple woodland beyond.

Isabel moved through the rooms in a silent rapture; but yet there was a pang of anguish lurking somewhere or other amid all that rapture.

Her dreams were all true, then; there were such places as this, and people lived in them. Happy people, for whom life was all loveliness and poetry, looked out of those windows, and lolled in those antique chairs, and had caskets of Florentine mosaic, and portraits by Vandyke,* and marble busts of Roman emperors, and Gobelin tapestries,* and a hundred objects of art and beauty, whose very names were a strange language to Isabel, surrounding them on every side *always*.

For some people life was like this; and for her—! She shuddered as she remembered the parlours at Graybridge,—the shabby carpet, the faded moreen curtains edged with rusty velvet, the cracked jars and vases on the mantelpiece; and even if George had given her all that she had asked—the ottoman, and the Venetian blind, and the rose-coloured curtains—what would have been the use? her room would never have looked like *this*. She gazed about her in a sort of walking dream, intoxicated by the beauty of the place. She was looking like this when Mr Raymond led her into one of the larger rooms, and showed her a little picture in a corner, a Tintoretto,* which he said was a gem.

She looked at the Tintoretto in a drowsy kind of way. It was a very brown gem, and its beauties were quite beyond Mrs Gilbert's appreciation. She was not thinking of the picture. She was thinking if, by some romantic legerdemain, she could 'turn out' to be the rightful heiress of such a castle as this, with a river like the Wayverne brawling under her windows, and trailing willow-branches dipping into the water. There were some such childish thoughts as these in her mind while Mr Raymond was enlarging upon the wonderful finish and modelling of the Venetian's masterpiece; and she was aroused from her reverie not by her companion's remarks, but by a woman's voice on the other side of the room.

'You so rarely see that contrast of fair hair and black eyes,' said the voice; 'and there is something peculiar in those eyes.'

There was nothing particular in the words: it was the tone in which they were spoken that caught Isabel Gilbert's ear—the tone in which Edith Dombey or Lady Clara Vere de Vere* might have spoken; a tone in which there was a lazy hauteur softened by womanly gentleness,—a drawling accent which had yet no affectation, only a kind of liquid carrying on of the voice, like a _legato_ passage in music.

'Yes,' returned another voice, which had all the laziness and none of the hauteur, 'it is a pretty face. Joanna of Naples, isn't it? she was an improper person, wasn't she? threw some one out of a window, and made herself altogether objectionable.'

Mr Raymond wheeled round as suddenly as if he had received an electric shock, and ran across the room to a gentleman who was lounging in a half-reclining attitude upon one of the broad window-seats.

'Why, Roland, I thought you were at Corfu!'

The gentleman got up, with a kind of effort and the faintest suspicion of a yawn; but his face brightened nevertheless, as he held out his hand to Isabel's late employer.

'My dear Raymond, how glad I am to see you! I meant to ride over to-morrow morning, for a long day's talk. I only came home last night, to please my uncle and cousin, who met me at Baden, and insisted on bringing me home with them. You know Gwendoline? ah, yes, of course you do.'

A lady with fair banded hair and an aquiline nose—a lady in a bonnet which was simplicity itself, and could only have been produced by a milliner who had perfected herself in the supreme art of concealing her art—dropped the double eye-glass through which she had been looking at Joanna of Naples,* and held out a hand so exquisitely gloved that it looked as if it had been sculptured out of gray marble.

'I'm afraid Mr Raymond has forgotten me,' she said; 'papa and I have been so long away from Midlandshire.'

'And Lowlands was beginning to look quite a deserted habitation. I used to think of Hood's haunted house* whenever I rode by your gates, Lady Gwendoline. But you have come home for good now? as if *you* could come for any thing *but* good,' interjected Mr Raymond gallantly. 'You have come with the intention of stopping, I hope?'

'Yes,' Lady Gwendoline answered, with something like a sigh; 'papa and I mean to settle in Midlandshire; he has let the Clarges-Street house for a time; sold his lease, at least, I think; or something of that sort. And we know every nook and corner of the Continent. So I suppose that really the best thing we can do is to settle at Lowlands. But I suppose we sha'n't keep Roland long in the neighbourhood. He'll get tired of us in a fortnight, and run away to the Pyrenees, or Cairo, or Central Africa; "any where, any where, out of the world!"'

'It isn't of *you* that I shall get tired, Gwendoline,' said the gentleman called Roland, who had dropped back into his old lounging attitude on the window-seat. 'It's myself that bores me; the only bore a man can't cut. But I'm not going to run away from Midlandshire. I shall go in for steam-farming,* and agricultural implements, and drainage. I should think drainage now would have a very elevating influence upon a man's mind; and I shall send my short-horns to Smithfield next Christmas. And you shall teach me political economy, Raymond; and we'll improve the condition of the farm-labourer; and we'll offer a prize for the best essay on, say, classical agriculture as revealed to us in the writings of Virgil—that's the sort of thing for the farm-labourer, I should think—and Gwendoline shall give the prizes: a blue ribbon and a gold medal, and a frieze coat, or a pair of top-boots.'

Isabel still lingered by the Tintoretto. She was aghast at the fact that Mr Raymond knew, and was even familiar with, these beings. Yes; Beings—creatures of that remote sphere which she only knew in her dreams. Standing near the Tintoretto, she ventured to look very timidly towards these radiant creatures.

What did she see? A young man half reclining in the deep embrasure of a window, with the summer sunshine behind him, and the summer breezes fluttering his loose brown hair—that dark rich brown which is only a warmer kind of black. She saw a man upon whom beneficent or capricious nature, in some fantastic moment, had lavished all the gifts that men most covet and that women most admire. She saw one of the handsomest faces ever seen since Napoleon, the young conqueror of Italy, first dazzled regenerated France; a kind of face that is only familiar to us in a few old Italian portraits; a beautiful, dreamy, perfect face, exquisite alike in form and colour. I do not think that any words of mine can realise Roland Lansdell's appearance; I can only briefly catalogue the features, which were perfect in their way, and yet formed so small an item in the homogeneous charm of this young man's appearance. The nose was midway betwixt an aquiline and a Grecian, but it was in the chiselling of the nostril, the firmness and yet delicacy of the outline, that it differed from other noses; the forehead was neither high nor low, but broad, and full at the temples; the head was strong in the perceptive faculties, very strong in benevolence, altogether wanting in destructiveness; but Mr Raymond could have told you that veneration and conscientiousness were deficient in Roland Lansdell's cranium,—a deficiency sorely to be lamented by those who knew and loved the young man. His eyes and mouth formed the chief beauty of his face; and yet I can describe neither, for their chief charm lay in the fact that they were indescribable. The eyes were of a nondescript colour; the mouth was ever varying in expression. Sometimes you looked at the eyes, and they seemed to you a dark bluish-gray; sometimes they were hazel; sometimes you were half beguiled into fancying them black. And the mouth was somehow in harmony with the eyes; inasmuch as looking at it one minute you saw an expression of profound melancholy in the thin flexible lips; and then in the next a cynical smile. Very few people ever quite understood Mr Lansdell, and perhaps this was his highest charm. When Lord Dundreary declares that he likes to wonder, he only gives utterance to a universal attribute of the mind.* To be puzzled is the next thing to being interested; to be interested is to be charmed. Yes, capricious Nature had showered her gifts upon Roland Lansdell. She had made him handsome, and had attuned his voice to a low melodious music, and had made him sufficiently clever; and, beyond all this, had bestowed upon him that subtle attribute of grace, which she and she alone can bestow. He was always graceful. Involuntarily and unconsciously he fell into harmonious attitudes. He could not throw himself into a chair, or rest his elbow upon a table, or lean against the angle of a doorway, or stretch himself full-length upon the grass to fall asleep with his head upon his folded arms, without making himself into a kind of picture. He looked like a picture just now as he lounged in the castle-window, with his face turned towards Mr Raymond.

The lady, who was called Lady Gwendoline, put up her eyeglass to look at another picture; and in that attitude Isabel had time to contemplate her, and saw that she too was graceful, and that in every fold of her simple dress—it was only muslin, but quite a different fabric to Isabel's muslin—there was an indescribable harmony which stamped her as the creature of that splendid sphere which the girl only knew in her books. She looked longer and more earnestly at Lady Gwendoline than at Roland Lansdell, for in this elegant being she saw the image of herself, as she had fancied herself so often—the image of a heartless aristocratic divinity, for whose sake people cut their throats, and broke blood-vessels, and drowned themselves.

George came in while his wife was looking at Lady Gwendoline, and Mr Raymond suddenly remembered the young couple whom he had taken upon himself to chaperone.

'I must introduce you to some new friends of mine, Roland,' he said; 'and when you are ill you must send for Mr Gilbert of Graybridge, who, I am given to understand, is a very clever surgeon, and whom I *know* to have the best moral region I ever had under my hand. Gilbert, my dear boy, this is Roland Lansdell of Mordred Priory; Lady Gwendoline, Mrs Gilbert—Mr Lansdell. But you know something about my friend Roland, I think, don't you, Isabel?'

Mrs Gilbert bowed and smiled and blushed in a pleasant bewilderment. To be introduced to two Beings in this off-hand manner was almost too much for Mr Sleaford's daughter. A faint perfume of jasmine and orange-blossom floated towards her from Lady Gwendoline's handkerchief, and she seemed to see the fair-haired lady who smiled at her, and the dark-haired gentleman who had risen at her approach, through an odorous mist that confused her senses.

'I think you know something of my friend Roland,' Mr Raymond repeated; 'eh, my dear?'

'Oh, n—no indeed,' Isabel stammered; 'I never saw—'

'You never saw *him* before to-day,' answered Mr Raymond, laying his hand on the young man's shoulder with a kind of protecting tenderness in the gesture. 'But you've read his verses; those pretty drawing-room Byronics, that refined and anglicised Alfred-de-Musset-ism,* that you told me you are so fond of:—don't you remember asking me who wrote the verses, Mrs Gilbert? I told you the Alien was a country squire; and here he is—a Midlandshire squire of high degree, as the old ballad has it.'

Isabel's heart gave a great throb, and her pale face flushed all over with a faint carnation. To be introduced to a Being was something, but to be introduced to a Being who was also a poet, and the very poet whose rhapsodies were her last and favourite idolatry! She could not speak. She tried to say something—something very commonplace, to the effect that the verses were very pretty, and she liked them very much, thank you—but the words refused to come, and her lips only trembled. Before she could recover her confusion, Mr Raymond had hooked his arm through that of Roland Lansdell, and the two men had walked off together, talking with considerable animation; for Charles Raymond was a kind of adopted father to the owner of Mordred Priory, and was about the only man that Roland had ever loved or trusted.

Isabel was left by the open window with Lady Gwendoline and George, whose common-sense preserved him serene and fearless in the presence of these superior creatures.

'You like my cousin's poetry, then, Mrs Gilbert?' said Lady Gwendoline.

Her cousin! The dark-haired being was cousin to this fair-haired being in the Parisian bonnet,—a white-chip bonnet, with just one feathery sprig of mountain heather, and broad thick white-silk strings tied under an aristocratic chin—a determined chin, Mr Raymond would have told Isabel.

Mrs Gilbert took heart of grace now that Roland Lansdell was out of hearing, and said, 'Oh, yes; she was very, very fond of the *Alien's Dreams*; they were so sweetly pretty.'

'Yes, they are pretty,' Lady Gwendoline said, seating herself by the window, and playing with her bonnet-strings as she spoke; 'they are very graceful. Do sit down, Mrs Gilbert; these show-places are so fatiguing. I am waiting for papa, who is talking politics with some Midlandshire people in the hall. I am very glad you like Roland's verses. They're not very original; all the young men write the same kind of poetry nowadays—a sort of mixture of Tennyson and Alfred de Musset.* It reminds me of Balfe's music,* somehow; it pleases, and one catches the melody without knowing how or why. The book made quite a little sensation. The *Westminster* was very complimentary, but the *Quarterly* was dreadful. I remember Roland reading the article and laughing at it; but he looked like a man who tries to be funny in tight boots; and he called it by some horrible slang term—"a slate," I think he said.'

Isabel had nothing to say to this. She had never heard that the *Quarterly* was a popular review; and, indeed, the adjective 'quarterly' had only one association for her, and that was rent, which had been almost as painful a subject as taxes in the Camberwell household. Lady Gwendoline's papa came in presently to look for his daughter. He was Angus Pierrepoint Aubrey Amyott Pomphrey, Earl of Ruysdale; but he wore a black coat and gray trousers and waistcoat, just like other people, and had thick boots, and didn't look a bit like an earl, Isabel thought.

He said, 'Haw, hum—yes, to be sure, my dear,' when Lady Gwendoline told him that she was ready to go home; 'been talking to Witherston—very good fellow, Witherston—wants to get his son returned for Conventford, gen'ral 'lection next year, lib'ral int'rest— very gentlemanly young f'ler, the son;' and then he went to look for Roland, whom he found in the next room with Charles Raymond; and then Lady Gwendoline wished Isabel good-morning, and said something very kind, to the effect that they should most likely meet again before long, Lowlands being so near Graybridge; and then the Earl offered his arm to his daughter.

She took it, but she looked back at her cousin, who was talking to Mr Raymond, and glancing every now and then in a half-amused, half-admiring way at Isabel.

'I am so glad to think you like my wretched scribble, Mrs Gilbert,' he said, going up to her presently.

Isabel blushed again, and said, 'Oh, thank you; yes, they are very pretty;' and it was as much as she could do to avoid calling Mr Lansdell 'Sir' or 'Your lordship.'

'You are coming with us, I suppose, Roland?' Lady Gwendoline said.

'Oh, yes,—that is to say, I'll see you to the carriage.'

'I thought you were coming to luncheon.'

'No; I meant to come, but I must see that fellow Percival, the lawyer, you know, Gwendoline, and I want to have a little more talk with Raymond. You'll go on and show Mrs Gilbert the Murillo* in the next room, Raymond? and I'll run and look for my cousin's carriage, and then come back.'

'We can find the carriage very well without you, Roland,' Lady Gwendoline answered quickly. 'Come, papa.'

The young man stopped, and a little shadow darkened over his face.

'Did you really ask me to luncheon?' he said.

'You really volunteered to come, after breakfast this morning, when you proposed bringing us here.'

'Did I? Oh, very well; in that case I shall let the Percival business stand over; and I shall ride to Oakbank to-morrow morning, Raymond, and lie on the grass and talk to you all day long, if you'll let me waste your time for once in a way. Good-by; good-morning, Mrs Gilbert. By the by, how do you mean to finish the day, Raymond?'

'I'm going to take Mr and Mrs Gilbert to Hurstonleigh Grove; or rather they take me, for they've brought a basket that reminds one of the Derby-day. We're going to picnic in the grove, and drink tea at a cottage in honour of Isabel's—Mrs Gilbert's birthday.'

'You must come and picnic at Mordred some day. It's not as pretty as Hurstonleigh, but we'll manage to find a rustic spot. If you care for partridges, Mr Gilbert, you'll find plenty in the woods round Mordred next September.'

The young man put on his hat, and went after his cousin and her father. Isabel saw him walk along the bright vista of rooms, and disappear in a burst of sunshine that flooded the great hall when the door was opened. The beings were gone. For a brief interval she had been breathing the poetry of life; but she fell back now into the sober prose, and thought that half the grandeur of the castle was gone with those aristocratic visitors.

'And how do you like my young kinsman?' Mr Raymond asked presently.

Isabel looked at him with surprise.

'He is your relation—Mr Lansdell?'

'Yes. My mother was a Lansdell. There's a sort of cousinship between Roland and me. He's a good fellow—a very noble-hearted, high-minded young fellow; but—'

But what? Mr Raymond broke off with so deep a sigh, that Isabel imagined an entire romance upon the strength of the inspiration. Had he done any thing wicked? that dark beautiful creature, who only wanted the soul-harrowing memory of a crime to render him perfect. Had he fled his country, like Byron? or buried a fellow-creature in a cave, like Mr Aram? Isabel's eyes opened to their widest extent; and Charles Raymond answered that inquiring glance.

'I sigh when I speak of Roland,' he said, 'because I know the young man is not happy. He stands quite alone in the world, and has more money than he knows how to spend; two very bad things for a young man. He's handsome and fascinating,—another disadvantage; and he's brilliant without being a genius. In short, he's just the sort of man to dawdle away the brightest years of his life in the drawing-rooms of a lot of women, and take to writing cynical trash about better men in his old age. I can see only one hope of redemption for him, and that is a happy marriage; a marriage with a sensible woman, who would get the whip-hand of him before he knew where he was. All the luckiest and happiest men have been henpecked. Look at the fate of the men who *won't* be henpecked. Look at Swift: he was a lord of the creation, and made the women mind him; look at him drivelling and doting under the care of a servant-maid. Look at Sterne; and Steele, who would fain have been good and loyal, but who was tempted away from his allegiance; and Byron, who outraged his wife in fact, and satirised her in fiction.* Was his life so much the better because he scorned the gentle guidance of the apron-string? Depend upon it, Mrs Gilbert, the men who lead great lives, and do noble deeds, and die happy deaths, are married men who mind their wives. I'm a bachelor; so of course I speak without prejudice. I do most heartily wish that Roland Lansdell may marry a good and sensible woman.'

'A good and sensible woman!'

Isabel gave an involuntary shudder. Surely, of all the creatures upon this over-populated earth, a sensible woman was the very last whom Roland Lansdell ought to marry. He should marry some lovely being in perpetual white muslin, with long shimmering golden hair,—the dark men always married fair women in Isabel's novels,— a creature who would sit at his feet, and watch with him, as Astarte watched with Manfred,* till dismal hours in the silent night; and who should be consumptive, and die some evening—promiscuously, as Mrs Gamp* would say—with flowers upon her breast, and a smile upon her face.

Isabel knew very little more of the pictures, or the men in armour, or the cannon in the chambers that yet remained to be seen at

Warncliffe Castle. She was content to let Mr Raymond and her husband talk. George admired the cannon, and the old-fashioned locks and keys, and the model of a cathedral made by a poor man out of old champagne-corks, and a few other curiosities of the same order; and he enjoyed himself, and was happy to see that his wife was pleased. He could tell that, by the smile upon her lips, though she said so little.

The drive from Warncliffe to Hurstonleigh Grove was as beautiful as the drive from Graybridge to Warncliffe; for this part of Midlandshire is a perpetual park. Isabel sat back in the carriage, and thought of Lady Gwendoline's artistocratic face and white-chip bonnet, and wondered whether she was the sensible woman whom Roland Lansdell would marry. They would be a very handsome couple. Mrs Gilbert could fancy them riding Arabs—nobody worth speaking of ever rode any thing but Arab horses, in Isabel's fancy—in Rotten Row. She could see Lady Gwendoline with a cavalier hat and a long sweeping feather, and Roland Lansdell bending over her horse's neck to talk to her, as they rode along. She fancied them in that glittering saloon, which was one of the stock scenes always ready to be pushed on the stage of her imagination. She fancied them in the midst of that brilliant supernumerary throng who wait upon the footsteps of heroes and heroines. She pictured them to herself going down to the grave through an existence of dinner-parties, and Rotten Row, and balls, and Ascot cups.* Ah, what a happy life! what a glorious destiny!

The picnic seemed quite a tame thing after these reveries in the carriage. The orphans met their uncle at the lodge-gate; and they all went across the grass, just as they had gone before, to the little low iron-gate which Mr Raymond was privileged to open with a special key; and into the grove, where the wonderful beeches and oaks made a faint summer darkness.

Was it the same grove? To Isabel it looked as if it had been made smaller since that other picnic; and the waterfall, and the woodland vistas, and the winding paths, and the arbour where they were to dine,—it was all very well for the orphans to clap their hands, and disport themselves upon the grass, and dart off at a tangent every now and then to gather inconvenient wild-flowers; but, after all, there was nothing so very beautiful in Hurstonleigh Grove.

Isabel wandered a little way by herself, while Mr Raymond and

George and the orphans unpacked the basket. She liked to be alone, that she might think of Lady Gwendoline and her cousin. Lady Gwendoline Pomphrey—oh, how grand it sounded! Why, to have such a name as that would alone be bliss; but to be called Gwendoline Pomphrey, and to wear a white-chip bonnet with that heavenly sprig of heather just trembling on the brim, and those broad, carelessly-tied, unapproachable strings! And then, like the sudden fall of a curtain in a brilliant theatre, the scene darkened, and Isabel thought of her own life—the life to which she must go back when it was dark that night: the common parlour, or the best parlour,—what was the distinction, in their dismal wretchedness, that one should be called better than the other?—the bread-and-cheese, the radishes,—and, oh, how George could eat radishes, crunch, crunch, crunch!—till madness would have been relief. This unhappy girl felt a blank despair as she thought of her commonplace home,—her home for ever and ever,—unbrightened by a hope, unsanctified by a memory; her home, in which she had a comfortable shelter, and enough to eat and to drink, and decent garments with which to cover herself; and where, had she been a good or a sensible young woman, she ought of course to have been happy.

But she was not happy. The slow fever that had been burning so long in her veins was now a rapid and consuming fire. She wanted a bright life, a happy life, a beautiful life; she wanted to be like Lady Gwendoline, and to live in a house like Warncliffe Castle. It was not that she envied Lord Ruysdale's daughter, remember; envy had no part in her nature. She admired Gwendoline Pomphrey too much to envy her. She would like to have been that elegant creature's younger sister, and to have worshipped her and imitated her in a spirit of reverence. She had none of the radical's desire to tear the trappings from the bloated aristocrat; she only wanted to be an aristocrat too, and to wear the same trappings, and to march through life to the same music.

George came, very much out of breath, to fetch her back to the arbour presently, where there was a lobster-salad, and that fine high-coloured Graybridge sherry, and some pale German wine, which Mr Raymond contributed to the feast.

The orphans and the two gentlemen enjoyed themselves very much. Mr Raymond could talk about medicine as well as political economy; and he and George entered into a conversation in which there were a great many hard words. The orphans ate—to do that was to be happy; and Isabel sat in a corner of the arbour, looking dreamily out at the shadows on the grass, and wondering why Fate had denied her the privilege of being an earl's daughter.

The drowsy atmosphere of the hot summer's afternoon, the Rhine wine, and the sound of his companion's voice, had such a pleasant influence upon Mr Raymond, that he fell asleep presently while George was talking; and the young man, perceiving this, produced a Midlandshire newspaper, which he softly unfolded, and began to read.

'Will you come and gather some flowers, Izzie?' whispered one of the orphans. 'There are wild-roses and honeysuckle in the lane outside. Do come!'

Mrs Gilbert was very willing to leave the arbour. She wandered away with the two children along those lovely paths, which now sloped downwards into a kind of ravine, and then wound upwards to the grove. The orphans had a good deal to say to their late governess. They had a new instructress, and 'she isn't a bit like you, dear Mrs Gilbert,' they said; 'and we love you best, though she's very kind, you know, and all that; but she's old, you know, very old,—more than thirty; and she makes us hem cambric frills, and does *go on so* if we don't put away our things; and makes us do such horrid sums; and instead of telling us stories when we're out with her, as you used,—oh, don't you remember telling us Pelham? how I love Pelham and Dombey!—about the little boy that died, and Florence, she tells us botany and jology' (the orphans called it 'jology'), 'and tertiary sandstone, and old red formations, and things like that; and oh, dear Izzie, I wish you never had been married.'

Isabel smiled at the orphans when they entwined themselves about her, and kissed them. But she was thinking of the Alien's dreams, and whether Lady Gwendoline was the 'Duchess, with the glittering hair and cruel azure eyes,' regarding whom the Alien was cynical, not to say abusive. Mrs Gilbert felt as if she had never read the Alien half enough. She had seen him, and spoken to him,—a real poet, a real, living, breathing poet, who only wanted to lame himself, and turn his collars down, to become a Byron.

She was walking slowly along the woodland pathway, with the orphans round about her, like a modern Laocoon family without the serpents,* when she was startled by a rustling of the branches a few paces farther on, and looking up, with a sudden half-frightened glance, she saw the tall figure of a man between her and the sun-light.

The man was Mr Roland Lansdell, the author of *An Alien's Dreams*.

'I'm afraid I startled you, Mrs Gilbert,' he said, taking off his hat and standing bareheaded, with the shadows of the leaves flickering and trembling about him like living things. 'I thought I should find Mr Raymond here, as he said you were going to picnic, and I want so much to talk to the dear old boy. So, as they know me at the lodge, I got them to let me in.'

Isabel tried to say something; but the orphans who were in no way abashed by the stranger's presence, informed Mr Lansdell that their Uncle Charles was asleep in the arbour where they had dined,—'up there.' The elder orphan pointed vaguely towards the horizon as she spoke.

'Thank you; but I don't think I shall find him very easily. I don't know half the windings and twistings of this place.'

The younger orphan informed Mr Lansdell that the way to the arbour was quite straight,—he couldn't miss it.

'But you don't know how stupid I am,' the gentleman answered, laughing. 'Ask your uncle if I'm not awfully deficient in the organ of locality. Would you mind—but you were going the other way, and it seems so selfish to ask you to turn back; yet if you would take compassion upon my stupidity, and show me the way—?'

He appealed to the orphans, but he looked at Isabel. He looked at her with those uncertain eyes,—blue with a dash of hazel, hazel with a tinge of blue,—eyes that were always half-hidden under the thick fringe of their lashes, like a glimpse of water glimmering among a forest of rushes.

'Oh, yes, if you like,' the orphans cried simultaneously; 'we don't mind going back a bit.'

They turned as they spoke, and Isabel turned with them. Mr Lansdell put on his hat, and walked amongst the long grass beside the narrow pathway.

The orphans were very lively, and fraternised immediately with Mr Lansdell. 'They were Mr Raymond's nieces? then they were his poor cousin Rosa Harlow's children, of whom he had heard so much from that dear good Raymond? If so, they were almost cousins of his,' Mr Lansdell went on to say, 'and they must come and see him at Mordred. And they must ask Mrs Gilbert to come with them, as they seemed so fond of her.' One of the orphans was doing the Laocoon business at that moment.

The girls had plenty to say for themselves. Yes; they would like very much to come to Mordred Priory; it was very pretty; their Uncle Charles had shown them the house one day when he took them out for a drive. It would be capital fun to come, and have a picnic in the grounds, as Mr Lansdell proposed. The orphans were ready for any thing in the way of holiday-making. And for Isabel, she only blushed, and said, 'Thank you,' when Roland Lansdell talked of her visiting Mordred with her late charges. She could not talk to this grand and beautiful creature, who possessed in his own person all the attributes of her favourite heroes.

How often this young dreamer of dreams had fancied herself in such companionship as this; discoursing with an incessant flow of brilliant persiflage, half-scornful, half-playful; holding her own against a love-stricken marquis; making as light of a duke as Mary Queen of Scots ever made of a presumptuous Chastelar!* And now that the dream was realised; now that this splendid Byronic creature was by her side, talking to her, trying to make her answer him, looking at her athwart those wondrous eyelashes,—she was stricken and dumb-founded; a miserable, stammering school-girl; a Pamela,* amazed and bewildered by the first complimentary address of her aristo-cratic persecutor.

She had a painful sense of her own deficiency; she knew all at once that she had no power to play the part she had so often fancied herself performing to the admiration of supernumerary beholders. But with all this pain and mortification there mingled a vague deli-cious happiness. The dream had come true at last. *This* was romance —*this* was life. She knew now what a pallid and ghastly broker's copy of a picture that last year's business had been; the standing on the bridge to be worshipped by a country surgeon; the long tedious courtship; the dowdy, vulgar, commonplace wedding,—she knew now how poor and miserable a mockery all that had been. She looked with furtive glances at the tall figure bending now and then under the branches of the trees; the tall figure in loose garments, which, in the careless perfection of their fashion, were so unlike any thing she had ever seen before; the wonderful face, in which there was the mellow light and colour of a Guido.* She stole a few timid glances at Mr Lansdell, and made a picture of him in her mind, which, like or unlike, must be henceforth the only image by which she would recognise or think of him. Did she think of him as what he was,—a young English gentleman, idle, rich, accomplished, and with no better light to guide his erratic wanderings than an uncertain glimmer which he called honour? Had she thought of him thus, she would have been surely wiser than to give him so large a place in her mind, or any place at all. But she never thought of him in this way. He was the incarnation of all the dreams of her life; he was Byron alive again, and come home from Missolonghi. He was Napoleon the First, restored to the faithful soldiers who had never believed that fiction of perfidious England, the asserted death of the immortal hero. He was all this; he was a shadowy and divine creature, amenable to no earthly laws. He was here now, in this brief hour, under the flickering sunlight and trembling shadows, and to-morrow he would melt away for ever and ever into the regions of light, which were his everyday habitation.

What did it matter, then, if she was fluttered and dazed and intoxicated by his presence? What did it signify if the solid earth became empyrean air under this foolish girl's footsteps? Mrs Gilbert did not even ask herself these questions. No consciousness of wrong or danger had any place in her mind. She knew nothing, she thought nothing; except that a modern Lord Byron was walking by her side, and that it was a very little way to the arbour.

END OF VOLUME I

VOLUME II

CHAPTER I

'OH, MY COUSIN, SHALLOW-HEARTED!'*

Roland Lansdell dined with his uncle and cousin at Lowlands upon the day after the picnic; but he said very little about his afternoon ramble in Hurstonleigh Grove. He lounged upon the lawn with his cousin Gwendoline, and played with the dogs, and stared at the old pictures in the long dreary billiard-room, where the rattle of the rolling balls had been unheard for ages; and he entered into a languid little political discussion with Lord Ruysdale, and broke off—or rather dropped out of it—in the middle with a yawn, declaring that he knew very little about the matter, and was no doubt making a confounded idiot of himself, and would his uncle kindly excuse him, and reserve his admirable arguments for some one better qualified to appreciate them.

The young man had no political enthusiasm. He had been in the great arena, and had done his little bit of wrestling, and had found himself baffled, not by the force of his adversaries, but by the *vis inertiae** of things in general. Eight or nine years ago Roland Lansdell had been very much in earnest,—too much in earnest, perhaps, — for he had been like a race-horse that goes off with a rush and makes running for all the other horses, and then breaks down ignominiously midway betwixt the starting-post and the judge's chair. There was no 'stay' in this bright young creature. If the prizes of life could have been won by that fiery rush, he would have won them; but as it was, he was fain to fall back among the ranks of the nameless, and let the plodders rush on towards the golden goal.

Thus it was that Roland Lansdell had been a kind of failure and disappointment. He had begun so brilliantly, he had promised so much. 'If this young man is so brilliant at one-and-twenty,' people had said to one another, 'what will he be by the time he is forty-five?' But at thirty Roland was nothing. He had dropped out of public life altogether, and was only a drawing-room favourite; a lounger in gay Continental cities; a drowsy idler in fair Grecian islands; a scribbler of hazy little verses about pretty women, and veils, and fans, and daggers, and jealous husbands, and moonlit balconies, and withered orange-flowers, and poisoned chalices, and midnight revels, and despair; a beautiful useless, purposeless creature; a mark for manoeuvering mothers; a hero for sentimental young ladies,—altogether a mockery, a delusion, and a snare.

This was the man whom Lady Gwendoline and her father had found at Baden Baden, losing his money *pour se distraire*.* Gwendoline and her father were on their way back to England. They had gone abroad for the benefit of the Earl's income; but Continental residence is expensive nowadays, and they were going back to Lowlands, Lord Ruysdale's family seat, where at least they would live free of house-rent, and where they could have garden-stuff and dairy produce, and hares and partridges, and silvery trout from the fish-ponds in the shrubberies, for nothing; and where they could have long credit from the country tradesfolk, and wax or composition candles for something less than tenpence apiece.

Lord Ruysdale persuaded Roland to return with them, and the young man assented readily enough. He was tired of the Continent; he was tired of England too, for the matter of that; but those German gaming-places, those Grecian islands, those papist cities where the bells were always calling the faithful to their drowsy devotions in darksome old cathedrals, were his last weariness, and he said, Yes; he should be glad to see Mordred again; he should enjoy a month's shooting; and he could spend the winter in Paris. Paris was as good as any other place in the winter.

He had so much money and so much leisure, and so little knew what to do with himself. He knew that his life was idle and useless; but he looked about him, and saw that very little came of other men's work; he cried with the Preacher, the son of David, king in Jerusalem, 'Behold, all is vanity and vexation of spirit, and there is no profit under the sun: that which is crooked cannot be made straight, and that which is wanting cannot be numbered: the thing that has been it is that which shall be.'

Do you remember that saying of Mirabeau's* which Mr Lewes has put upon the title-page of his wonderful Life of Robespierre:* 'This man will do great things,' said the statesman,—I quote loosely from memory,—'for he believes in himself'? Roland Lansdell did not believe in himself; and lacking that grand faculty of self-confidence, he had grown to doubt and question all other things, as he doubted and questioned himself. Nature, which had bestowed her gifts upon him with such a wantonly lavish hand, had refused him the greatest gift of all,—the sublime power of faith. He was no arrogant sceptic, who sets his own intellect above the divine mysteries of the universe. He had tried to believe, he had wrestled with himself, and had prayed earnestly but ignorantly for help; but the help had never come; and when, in the aching void of his heart, there grew a dreary conviction that no help ever could come to him, he bowed his head, and resigned himself to live in the darkness, since for him the light was never to shine. Heaven knows how he had striven to pierce the veil—how patiently he had watched for the star; but there was no lessening of the dreadful darkness, there was no glimmer of the mystic glory. He who scoffed at most things had never scoffed at this one supreme mystery, whose splendour had never been revealed to him. He envied the simple worshippers before taper-lit shrines in the dusky aisles of foreign cathedrals; he envied them his childlike and unquestioning faith, which could recognise the glory of God amongst all that faded splendour of artificial flowers and gilded candle-sticks and waxen images. He asked no better gift than this great power of belief, and would fain have given all his worldly wisdom could he have made himself like unto one of those little children whom he saw on festival-days with white wreaths upon their heads and sanctified candles in their hands.

Roland Lansdell could not believe. Sometimes on great festival-days he entered those solemn cathedrals, and stood amongst the pious crowd, as hushed and reverent in his manner as any worshipper present; for he was a gentleman, and respected the creeds of other people. He liked the grand music of the organ, the pure tones of the swelling voices; he was penetrated with the devotional spirit of the place and the hour; but he could not believe. He believed in the existence of a great and good Man, who taught the purest system of morality that was ever conceived by genius, and who gave His life in testimony of His truth: but he could understand no more than this; and being without the power of faith, he could only believe that which he could understand. The Redeemer of mankind was for him only a great teacher: the sacrifice on Calvary was only another form of the death of Socrates; another immolation of genius and truth to the besotted ignorance of mankind.

'I will do my best to lead a good life, and be useful to my fellow-creatures,' Mr Lansdell said, when he left Magdalen College, Oxford, with a brilliant reputation, and the good wishes of all the magnates of the place.

He began life with this intention firmly implanted in his mind. He knew that he was a rich man, and that there was a great deal expected of him. The parable of the Talents was not without its import to him, though he had no belief in the divinity of the Teacher. There was no great enthusiasm in his nature, but he was very sincere; and he went into Parliament as a progressive young Liberal, and set to work honestly to help his fellow-creatures.

Alas for poor humanity! he found the task more wearisome than the labour of Sisyphus,* or the toil of the daughters of Danäus.* The stone was always rolling back upon the labourer; the water was perpetually pouring out of the perforated buckets. He cultivated the working man, and founded a club for him, where he might have lectures upon geology and astronomy, and where, after twelve hours' bricklaying or road-making, he might improve his mind with the works of Stuart Mill* or Maculloch,* and where he could have almost any thing; except those two simple things which he especially wanted,—a pint of decent beer and a quiet puff at his pipe. Roland Lansdell was the last man to plan any institution upon puritanical principles; but he *did not believe in himself*, so he took other people's ideas as the basis of his work; and by the time he opened his eyes to the necessity of beer and tobacco, the workman had grown tired and had abandoned him.

This was only one of many schemes which Mr Lansdell attempted while he was still very young, and had a faint belief in his fellow-creatures: but this is a sample of the rest. Roland's schemes were not successful; they were not successful because he had no patience to survive preliminary failure, and wade on to ultimate success through a slough of despond and discouragement. He picked his fruit before it was ripe, and was angry when he found it sour, and would hew down the tree that bore so badly, and plant another. His fairest projects fell to the ground, and he left them there to rot: while he went away somewhere else to build new schemes and make fresh failures.

Moreover, Mr Lansdell was a hot-headed, impulsive young man, and there were some things which he could not endure. He could bear ingratitude better than most people, because he was generous-minded, and set a very small price upon the favours he bestowed; but he could not bear to find that the people whom he sought to benefit were bored by his endeavours to help them. He had no ulterior object to gain, remember. He had no solemn conviction of a sacred duty to be performed at any cost to himself, in spite of every hindrance, in the face of every opposition. He *only* wanted to be useful to his fellow-creatures; and when he found that they repudiated his efforts, he fell away from them, and resigned himself to be useless, and to let his fellow-creatures go their own wilful way. So, almost immediately after making a brilliant speech about the poor-laws, at the very moment when people were talking of him as one of the most promising young Liberals of his day, Mr Lansdell abruptly turned his back upon St Stephen's,* accepted the Chiltern Hundreds,* and went abroad.

He had experienced another disappointment besides the failure of his philanthropic schemes,—a disappointment that had struck home to his heart, and had given him an excuse for the cynical indifference, the hypochondriacal infidelity, which grew upon him from this time.

Mr Lansdell had been his own master from his earliest manhood, for his father and mother had died young. The Lansdells were not a long-lived race; indeed, there seemed to be a kind of fatality attached to the masters of Mordred Priory: and in the long galleries where the portraits of dead-and-gone Lansdells looked gravely down upon the frivolous creatures of to-day, the stranger was apt to be impressed by the youth of all the faces,—the absence of those gray beards and bald foreheads which give dignity to most collections of family-portraits. The Lansdells of Mordred were not a long-lived race, and Roland's father had died suddenly when the boy was away at Eton; but his mother, Lady Anna Lansdell, only sister of the present Earl of Ruysdale, lived to be her son's companion and friend in the best and brightest years of his life. His life seemed to lose its brightness when he lost her; and I think this one great grief, acting upon a naturally pensive temperament, must have done much to confirm that morbid melancholy which over-shadowed Mr Lansdell's mind.

His mother died; and the grand inducement to do something good and great, which might have made her proud and happy, died with her. Roland said that he left the purest half of his heart behind him in the Protestant cemetery at Nice. Alas! the great misery of his life afflicted him most terribly here. He did not believe! For him there was no sweet whisper of hope amid the tempest of despair. In vain, in vain he strove to look beyond that grave in the South of France. He prayed: but it may be that he prayed amiss, for the light never came to him. He went back to England, and made those brilliant speeches of which I have spoken; and was not too proud to seek for sympathy and consolation from the person whom he loved next best to her whom he had lost,—that person was Lady Gwendoline Pomphrey, his betrothed wife, the beloved niece of his dead mother.

There had been so complete a sympathy between Lady Anna Lansdell and her son, that the young man had suffered himself, half unconsciously, to be influenced by his mother's predilections. She was very fond of Gwendoline; and when the two families were in Midlandshire, Gwendoline spent the greater part of her life with her aunt. She was two years older than Roland, and she was a very beautiful young woman. A fragile-looking, aristocratic beauty, with a lofty kind of gracefulness in all her movements, and with cold blue eyes that would have frozen the very soul of an aspiring young Lawrence. She was handsome, self-possessed, and accomplished; and Lady Anna Lansdell was never tired of sounding her praises. So young Roland, newly returned from Oxford, fell—or imagined himself to have fallen—desperately in love with her; and while his brief access of desperation lasted, the whole thing was arranged, and Mr Lansdell found himself engaged.

He was engaged, and he was very much in love with his cousin. That two years' interval between their ages gave Gwendoline an immense advantage over her lover; she practised a thousand feminine coquetries upon this simple generous lad, and was proud of her power over him, and very fond of him after her own fashion, which was not a very warm one. She was by no means a woman to consider the world well lost for love. Her father had told her all about Roland's circumstances, and that the settlements would be very handsome. She was only sorry that poor Roland was a mere nobody, after all; a country gentleman, who prided himself upon the length of his pedigree and the grandeur of his untitled race; but whose name looked very insignificant when you saw it at the tail of a string of dukes and marquises in the columns of the *Morning Post*.

But then he might distinguish himself in Parliament. There was something in that; and Lady Gwendoline brought all her power to bear upon the young man's career. She fanned the faint flames of his languid ambition with her own fiery breath. This girl, with her proud Saxon beauty, her cold blue eyes, her pale auburn hair, was as ardent and energetic as Joan of Arc or Elizabeth of England. She was a grand ambitious creature, and she wanted to marry a ruler, and to rule him; and she was discontented with her cousin because a crown did not drop on to his brows the moment he entered the arena. His speeches had been talked about; but, oh, what languid talk it had been! Gwendoline wanted all Europe to vibrate with the clamour of the name that was so soon to be her own.

At the end of his second session Roland went abroad with his dying mother. He came back alone, six weeks after his mother's death, and went straight to Gwendoline for consolation. He found her in deep mourning; all a-glitter with bracelets and necklaces of shining jet; looking very fair and stately in her trailing black robes; but he found her drawing-room filled with callers, and he left her wounded and angry. He thought her so much a part of himself, that he had expected to find her grief equal to his own. He went to her again, in a passionate outbreak of grief and anger; told her that she was cold-hearted and ungrateful, and that she had never loved the aunt who had been almost a mother to her. Lady Gwendoline was the last woman in the world to submit to any such reproof. She was astounded by her lover's temerity.

'I loved my aunt very dearly, Mr Lansdell,' she said; 'so dearly that I could endure a great deal for her sake; but I can *not* endure the insolence of her son.'

And then the Earl of Ruysdale's daughter swept out of the room, leaving her cousin standing alone in a sunlit window, with the spring breezes blowing in upon him, and the shrill voice of a woman crying primroses sounding in the street below.

He went home, dispirited, disheartened, doubtful of himself, doubtful of Lady Gwendoline, doubtful of all the world; and early the next morning he received a letter from his cousin coolly releasing him from his engagement. The experience of yesterday had proved that they were unsuited to each other, she said; it was better that they should part now, while it was possible for them to part friends. Nothing could be more dignified or more decided than the dismissal.

Mr Lansdell put the letter in his breast; the pretty perfumed letter, with the Ruysdale arms emblazoned on the envelope, the elegant lady-like letter, which recorded his sentence without a blot or a blister, without one uncertain line to mark where the hand had trembled. The hand may have trembled, nevertheless; for Lady Gwendoline was just the woman to write a dozen copies of her letter rather than send one that bore the faintest evidence of her weakness. Roland put the letter in his breast, and resigned himself to his fate. He was a great deal too proud to appeal against his cousin's decree; but he had loved her very sincerely, and if she had recalled him, he would have gone back to her and would have forgiven her. He lingered in England for a week or more after all the arrangements for his departure had been made; he lingered in the expectation that his cousin would recall him: but one morning, while he was sitting in the smoking-room at his favourite club, with his face hidden behind the pages of the *Post*, he burst into a harsh strident laugh.

'What the deuce is the matter with you, Lansdell?' asked a young man who had been startled by that sudden outbreak of unharmonious hilarity.

'Oh, nothing particular; I was looking at the announcement of my cousin Gwendoline's approaching marriage with the Marquis of Heatherland. I'm rejoiced to see that our family is getting up in the world.'

'Oh, yes, that's been in the wind a long time,' the lounger answered coolly. 'Every body saw that Heatherland was very far gone six months ago. He's been mooning about your cousin ever since they met at The Bushes, Sir Francis Luxmoor's Leicestershire place. They used to say you were rather sweet in that quarter; but I suppose it was only a cousinly flirtation.'

'Yes,' said Mr Lansdell, throwing down the paper, and taking out his cigar-case; 'I suppose it was only what Gwendoline would call a flirtation. You see, I have been abroad six months attending the deathbed of my mother. I could scarcely expect to be remembered all that time. Will you give me a light for my cigar?'

The faces of the two young men were very close together as Roland lighted his cigar. Mr Lansdell's pale-olive complexion had blanched a little, but his hand was quite steady, and he smoked half his Trabuco before he left the clubroom. The blow was sharp and unexpected, but Lady Gwendoline's lover bore it like a philosopher.

'I am unhappy because I have lost her,' he thought: 'but should I have been happy with her, if I had married her? Have I ever been happy in my life, or is there such a thing as happiness upon this unequally divided earth? I have played all my cards, and lost the game. Philanthropy, ambition, love, friendship—I have lost upon every one of them. It is time that I should begin to enjoy myself.'

Thus it was that Mr Lansdell accepted the Chiltern Hundreds, and turned his back upon a country in which he had never been especially happy. He had plenty of friends upon the Continent; and being rich, handsome, and accomplished, was fêted and caressed wherever he went. He was very much admired, and he might have been beloved; but that first disappointment had done its fatal work, and he did not believe that there was in all the world any such thing as pure and disinterested affection for a young man with a landed estate and fifteen thousand a-year.

So he lounged and dawdled away his time in drawing-rooms and boudoirs, on moonlit balconies, in shadowy orange-groves, beside the rippling Arno, in the colonnades of Venice, on the Parisian boulevards, under the lime-trees of Berlin, in any region where there was life and colour and gaiety, and the brightness of beautiful faces, and where a man of a naturally gloomy temperament might forget himself and be amused. He started with the intention of doing no harm; but with no better guiding principle than the intention to be harmless, a man can contrive to do a good deal of mischief.

Mr Lansdell's life abroad was neither a good nor a useful one. It was an artificial kind of existence, with spurious pleasures, spurious brilliance,—a life whose brightest moments but poorly compensated for the dismal reaction that followed them. And in the mean while Lady Gwendoline did not become Marchioness of Heatherland; for only a month before the day appointed for the wedding, young Lord Heatherland broke his neck in an Irish steeple-chase.

It was a terrible and bitter disappointment; but Lady Gwendoline showed her high breeding and her philosophy at the same time. She retired from the world in which her career had been hitherto so brilliantly successful, and bore her sorrow in silence. She, too, had played her best card, and had lost; and now that the Marquis was dead, and Roland Lansdell far away, people began to say that the lady had jilted her cousin, and that the loss of her titled lover was Heaven's special judgment upon her iniquity,—though why poor Lord Heatherland should be sacrificed to Lady Gwendoline Pomphrey's sin is rather a puzzling question.

It may be that Lord Ruysdale's daughter hoped her cousin would return when he heard of the Marquis's death. She knew that Roland had loved her: and what was more likely than that he should come back to her, now that he knew she was once more free to be his wife? Lady Gwendoline kept the secrets of her own heart, and no one knew which of her two lovers had been dearest to her. She kept her own secrets; and by and by, when she reappeared in the world, people saw that her beauty had suffered very little from her sorrow for her disappointment.

She was still very handsome, but her prestige was gone. Impertinent young débutantes of eighteen called this splendid creature of four-and-twenty 'quite old.' Wasn't she engaged to a Mr Lansdell ever so long ago, and then to the Marquis of Heatherland? Poor thing, how very sad! They wondered she did not go over to Rome, or join Miss Sellon's sisterhood, or something of that kind. Lady Gwendoline's portrait still held its place in books of beauty, and she could see herself smiling in West-end print-shops, with a preternaturally high forehead, and ringlets down to her knees; but she felt that she was old—very old. Gossipping dowagers talked aristocratic scandal openly before her, and said, 'We don't mind *your* hearing it, you know, Gwendoline dear;' and a woman has seen the last of her youth when people say that sort of thing to her.

She felt that she was very old. She had led a high-pressure kind of existence, in which a year stands for a decade; and now in her lonely old age she discovered that her father was very poor, and that his estates were mortgaged, and that henceforth her existence must be a wretched hand-to-mouth business, unless some distant relation, from whom Lord Ruysdale had expectations, would be good enough to die.

The distant relation had died within the last twelvemonth, and the fortune inherited from him, though by no means a large one, had set the Earl's affairs tolerably straight; so he had returned to Lowlands, after selling the lease and furniture of his town-house. It

was absurd to keep the town-house any longer for the sake of
Gwendoline, who was two-and-thirty years of age, and never likely
to marry, Lord Ruysdale argued. So he had paid his debts, and had
released his estate from some of its many incumbrances, and had
come back to the home of his boyhood, to set up as a model farmer
and country gentleman.

So, in the bright July sunshine, Gwendoline and her cousin lounged
upon the lawn, and talked of old pleasures and old acquaintances,
and the things that happened to them when they were young. If the
lady ever cherished any hope that Roland would return to his allegiance, that hope has now utterly vanished. He has forgiven her for
all the past, and they are friends and first-cousins again; but there is
no room for hope that they can ever be again what they have been.
A man who can forgive so generously must have long ceased to love:
that strange madness, so nearly allied to hatred, and jealousy, and
rage, and despair, has no kindred with forgiveness. Lady Gwendoline
knew that her chance was gone. She knew this; and there was a
secret bitterness in her heart when she thought of it, and she was
jealous of her cousin's regard, and exacting in her manner to him.
He bore it all with imperturbable good temper. He had been hot-
headed and fiery-tempered long ago, when he was young and chivalrous, and eager to be useful to his fellow-creatures: but now he
was only a languid loiterer upon the earth, and his creed was the
creed of the renowned American who has declared that 'there is
nothing new, and nothing true; and it don't signify.'

What did it matter? The crooked sticks would never be straight:
that which was wanting would never be numbered. Roland Lansdell
suffered from a milder form of that disease in a wild paroxysm of
which Swift wrote *Gulliver*, and Byron horrified society with *Don
Juan*. He suffered from that moody desperation of mind which came
upon Hamlet after his mother's wedding, and neither man nor woman
delighted him.

But do not suppose that this young man gave himself melancholy
or Byronic airs upon the strength of the aching void at his own
weary heart. He was a sensible young man; and he did not pose
himself *à la* Lara, or turn down his collars, or let his beard grow. He
only took life very easily, and was specially indulgent to the follies
and vices of people from whom he expected so very little.

He had gone back to Midlandshire because he was tired of his

Continental wanderings; and now he was tired of Mordred already, before he had been back a week. Lady Gwendoline catechised him rather closely as to what he had done with himself upon the previous afternoon; and he told her very frankly that he had strolled into Hurstonleigh Grove to see Mr Raymond, and had spent an hour or two talking with his old friend, while Mr and Mrs Gilbert and the children enjoyed themselves, and prepared a rustic tea, which would have been something like Watteau,* if Watteau had been a Dutchman.

'It was very pretty, Gwendoline, I assure you,' he said. 'Mrs Gilbert made tea, and we drank it in a scalding state; and the two children were all of a greasy radiance with bread-and-butter. The doctor seems to be an excellent fellow; his moral region is something tremendous, Raymond tells me, and he entertained us at tea with a most interesting case of fester.'

'Oh, the doctor? that's Mr Gilbert, is it not?' said Lady Gwendoline; 'and what do you think of his wife, Roland? You must have formed some opinion upon that subject, I should think, by the manner in which you stared at her.'

'Did I stare at her?' cried Mr Lansdell, with supreme carelessness. 'I daresay I did; I always stare at pretty women. Why should a man go into all manner of stereotyped raptures about a Raffaelle* or a Guido, and yet feel no honest thrill of disinterested admiration when he looks at a picture fresh from the hands of the supreme painter, Nature? who, by the way, makes as many failures, and is as often out of drawing, as any other artist. Yes, I admire Mrs Gilbert, and I like to look at her. I don't suppose she's any better than other people, but she's a great deal prettier. A beautiful piece of animated wax-work, with a little machinery inside, just enough to make her say, "Yes, if you please," and "No, thank you." A lovely nonentity with yellow-black eyes. Did you observe her eyes?'

'No!' Lady Gwendoline answered sharply; 'I observed nothing except that she was a very dowdy-looking person. What, in heaven's name, is Mr Raymond's motive for taking her up? He's always taking up some extraordinary person.'

'But Mrs Gilbert is not an extraordinary person; she's very stupid and commonplace. She was nursery-maid, or nursery-governess, or something of that kind, to that dear good Raymond's penniless nieces.'

There was no more said about Mr and Mrs Gilbert. Lady

Gwendoline did not care to talk about these common people, who came across her dull pathway, and robbed her of some few accidental rays of that light which was now the only radiance upon earth for her,—the light of her cousin's presence.

Ah, me! with what a stealthy step, invisible in the early sunshine, pitiless Nemesis* creeps after us, and glides past us, and goes on before to wait for us upon the other side of the hill, amidst the storm-clouds and the darkness! From the very first Gwendoline had loved her cousin Roland better than any other living creature upon this earth; but the chance of bringing down the bird at whose glorious plumage so many a fair fowler had levelled her rifle had dazzled and tempted her. The true wine of life was not that mawkish, sickly-sweet compound of rose-leaves and honey called Love, but an effervescing, intoxicating beverage known as Success, Lady Gwendoline thought: and in the triumph of her splendid conquest it seemed such an easy thing to resign the man she loved. But now it was all different. She looked back, and remembered what her life might have been: she looked forward, and saw what it was to be: and the face of Nemesis was very terrible to look upon.

Thus it was that Lady Gwendoline was exacting of her cousin's attention, impatient of his neglect. Oh, if she could have brought him back! if she could have kindled a new flame in the cold embers! Alas! she knew that to do that would be to achieve the impossible. She looked in the glass, and saw that her aristocratic beauty was pale and faded; she felt that the story of her life was ended. The sea might break against the crags for ever and for ever; but the tender grace of a day that was dead could never return to her.

'He loved me once,' she thought, as she sat in the summer twilight, watching her cousin strolling on the lawn, smoking his after-dinner cigar, and looking so tired—so tired of himself and every thing in the world. 'He loved me once; it is something to remember that.'

The day was very dull at Lowlands, Mr Lansdell thought. There was a handsome house, a little old and faded, but very handsome notwithstanding; and there was a well-cooked dinner, and good wines; and there was an elegant and accomplished woman always ready to talk to him and amuse him;—and yet, somehow, it was all flat, stale, and unprofitable to this young man, who had lived the same kind of life for ten years, and had drained its pleasures to the very dregs. [It was all weary, flat, stale, unprofitable: because the soul of man cannot be satisfied in a state of sin: and a purposeless idle existence *is* a state of sin. Mr Lansdell did not believe this. He recognised no higher standard for his actions than the common standard of man's morality; and judging himself by that standard, he fancied that he had done well enough. He had done his best, and had failed ignominiously, and had won the right to be idle ever after that failure.]*

'We should laugh at a man who went on writing epic poems all his life, though people refused to read a line of his poetry; and no man can be expected to go on trying to improve the position of people who don't want to be improved. I've tried my hand at the working-man, and he has rejected me as an intrusive nuisance. I've no doubt he was "in his right." How should I like a reformer who wanted to set *me* straight, and lay out my leisure-hours by line and rule, and spend my money for me, and show me how to get mild Turkish, and German wines, in the best and cheapest market?'

Mr Lansdell often thought about his life. It is not natural that a man, originally well disposed, should lead a bad and useless life without thinking of it. Mr Lansdell was subject to gloomy fits of melancholy, in which the Present seemed a burden, and the Future a blank,—a great blank desert, or a long dreary bridge, like that which the genius showed to Mirza in his morning vision, with dreadful pitfalls every here and there, down which unwary foot-passengers sank, engulfed in the dreadful blackness of a bottomless ocean.

[Alas for Roland Lansdell! he could see no further shore, no sunny slopes or gleaming cliffs, beyond that dreadful ocean. There was the terrible agony of the plunge, and then there was no more. He thought this, and his life seemed dreary to him because of this. To what end were the brief pleasures of an existence which at any moment might come to a sudden end, like the shutting of a black door upon a sunlit chamber? Who could deem love a blessing, when at any moment the fond eyes might grow dim, the tender voice might fail, the gentle hand might loose its loving grasp for ever and for ever? For ever! There was no hope for this young man, who saw miracles performed every day upon this earth, who beheld death and resurrection for ever exemplified in a thousand common shapes, and yet could not believe that a Creator, who had implanted in every soul a universal yearning for a life beyond the grave, might, in His bountiful mercy, appoint a spring-time of resurrection for man as well as for the lilies of the field.]*

CHAPTER II

UNDER LORD THURSTON'S OAK

While Mr Lansdell remembered Isabel Gilbert as a pretty automaton, who had simpered and blushed when he spoke to her, and stammered shyly when she was called upon to answer him, the Doctor's Wife walked up and down the flat commonplace garden at Graybridge-on-the-Wayverne, and thought of her birthday afternoon, whose simple pleasures had been embellished by the presence of a demigod. Yes, she walked up and down between two rows of straggling gooseberry-bushes, in a rapturous day-dream; a dangerous day-dream, in which Roland Lansdell's dark face shone dazzling and beautiful. Was it wrong to think of him? She never asked herself that question. She had read sentimental books all her life, and had been passionately in love with heroes in three volumes, ever since she could remember. What did it matter whether she was in love with Sir Reginald Glanville* or Mr Roland Lansdell? One passion was as hopeless as the other, and as harmless therefore. She was never likely to see the lord of Mordred Priory again. Had she not heard him tell Mr Raymond that he should spend the winter in Paris? Mrs Gilbert counted the months upon her fingers. Was November the winter? If so, Mr Lansdell would be gone in four months' time. And in all those four months what likelihood was there that she should see him,—she, who was such a low degraded wretch as compared with this splendid being and those with whom it was his right to associate? Never, no, never until now had she understood the utter hideousness and horror of her life. The square miserable parlour, with little stunted cupboards on each side of the fireplace, and shells and peacock's feathers, and penny bottles of ink, and dingy unpaid bills, upon the mantelpiece. She sat there with the July sun glaring in upon her through the yellow-white blind; she sat there and thought of her life and its squalid ugliness, and then thought of Lady Gwendoline at Lowlands, and rebelled against the hardness of a Providence that had not made her an earl's daughter. And then she clasped her hands upon her face, and shut out the vulgar misery of that odious parlour—a *parlour*!—the very word was unknown in those bright regions of which she was always dreaming—and thought of Roland Lansdell.

She thought of him, and she thought what her life might have been—if—

If what? If any one out of a hundred different visions, all equally childish and impossible, could have been realised. If she had been an earl's daughter, like Lady Gwendoline. If she had been a great actress, and Roland Lansdell had seen her and fallen in love with her from a stage-box. If he had met her in the Walworth Road two or three years ago; she fancied the meeting,—he in a cab, with the reins lightly held between the tips of his gloved fingers, and a tiny tiger swinging behind; and she standing on the curbstone waiting to cross the road, and not out to fetch any thing vulgar, only going to pay a water-rate, or to negotiate some mysterious 'backing' of the spoons, or some such young-ladylike errand. And then she got up and went to the looking-glass to see if she really was pretty; or if her face, as she saw it in her day-dreams, was only an invention of her own, like the scenery and the dresses of those foolish dreams. She rested her elbows on the mantelpiece, and looked at herself, and pushed her hair about, and experimented with her mouth and eyes, and tried to look like Edith Dombey in the grand Carker scene,* and acted the scene in a whisper.

No, she wasn't a bit like Edith Dombey; she was more like Juliet, or Desdemona. She lowered her eyelids, and then lifted them slowly, revealing a tender penetrating glance in the golden black eyes.

'I'm *very* sorry that you are not well!'*

she whispered. Yes, she would do for Desdemona. Of, if instead of marrying George Gilbert, she had only run away to London, and gone straight to that enterprising manager, who would have been so sure to engage her! If she had done this, she might have played Desdemona, and Mr Lansdell might have happened to go to the theatre, and might have fallen desperately in love with her on the spot.

She took a dingy volume of the immortal William's from a dusty row of books on one of the cupboards, and went up to her room and locked the door, and pleaded for Cassio,* and wept and protested opposite the looking-glass, before which three matter-of-fact generations of Gilberts had shaved themselves.

She was only nineteen, and she was a child, with all a child's eagerness for something bright and happy. It seemed only a very short time since she had longed for a gaily-dressed doll that adorned one of the Walworth-Road shop-windows. Her married life had not as yet invested her with any matronly dignity. She had no domestic cares or duties; for the simple household was kept in order by Mrs Jeffson, who would have resented any interference from the young mistress. Isabel went into the kitchen sometimes, when she was very much at a loss as to what she should do with herself, and sat in an old rocking-chair swinging languidly backwards and forwards, and watching kind-hearted Tilly making a pie.

There are some young women who take kindly to a simple do-mestic life, and have a natural genius for pies and puddings, and cutting and contriving, in a cheery, pleasant way, that invests pov-erty with a grace of its own; and when a gentleman wishes to marry on three hundred a year, he should look out for one of those bright household fairies. Isabel had no liking for these things; to her the making of pastry was a wearisome business. It was all very well for Ruth Pinch to do it for once in a way, and to be admired by John Westlock,* and marry a rich and handsome young husband in next to no time. No doubt Miss Pinch knew instinctively that Mr Westlock would come that morning while the beef-steak pudding was in progress. But to go on making puddings for Tom Pinch for ever and ever, with no John Westlock! Isabel left the house affairs to Mrs Jeffson, and acted Shakespearian heroines and Edith Dombey be-fore her looking-glass, and read her novels, and dreamed her dreams, and wrote little scraps of poetry, and drew pen-and-ink profile por-traits of Mr Lansdell—always looking from right to left. She gave him very black eyes with white blanks in the centre, and streaky hair; she drew Lady Gwendoline and the chip bonnet also very often, if not quite as often as the gentleman; so there was no harm in it. Mrs Gilbert was strictly punctilious with herself, even in the matter of her thoughts. She only thought of what *might* have hap-pened if Mr Lansdell had met her long ago before her marriage.

It is not to be supposed that she forgot Roland's talk of some picnic or entertainment at Mordred. She thought of it a great deal, some-times fancying that it was too bright a thing to come to pass; at other times thinking that Mr Lansdell was likely to call at any moment with a formal invitation for herself and her husband. The weather was very warm just now, and the roads very dusty; so Mrs Gilbert stayed at home a good deal. He might come,—he might come at any unexpected moment. She trembled and turned hot at the sound of a double knock, and ran to the glass to smoothe her disordered hair: but only the most commonplace visitors came to Mr Gilbert's mansion; and Isabel began to think that she would never see Roland Lansdell again.

And then she plunged one more into the hot-pressed pages of the *Alien*, and read Mr Lansdell's plaints, on toned paper, with long *s*'s that looked like *f*'s. And she copied his verses, and translated them into bad French. They were very difficult: how was she to render even such a simple sentence as 'My own Clotilde?' She tried such locutions as '*Ma propre Clotilde*,' '*Ma Clotilde particulière*;' but she doubted if they were quite academically correct. And she set the *Alien* to tunes that he didn't match, and sang him in a low voice to the cracked notes of an old harpsichord which George's mother had imported from Yorkshire.

One day when she was walking with George,—one dreary afternoon, when George had less to do than usual, and was able to take his wife for a nice dusty walk on the high-road,—Mrs Gilbert saw the man of whom she had thought so much. She saw a brown horse and a well-dressed rider sweep past her in a cloud of dust: and she knew, when he had gone by, that he was Roland Lansdell. He had not seen her any more than if there was no such creature upon this earth. He had not seen her. For the last five weeks she had been thinking of him perpetually, and he rode by and never saw that she was there. No doubt Lord Byron would have passed her by in much the same manner if he had lived: and would have ridden on to make a morning call upon that thrice-blessed Italian woman, whose splendid shame it was to be associated with him. Was it not always so? The moon is a cold divinity, and the brooks look up for ever and win no special radiance in recompense for their faithful worship: the sunflower is always turning to the sun, and the planet takes very little notice of the flower. Did not Napoleon snub Madame de Staël?* And if Isabel could have lived thirty years earlier, and worked her passage out to St Helena* as ship's needle-woman, or something of that kind, and expressed her intention of sitting at the exile's feet for the rest of her natural life, the hero would have doubtless sent her back by the first homeward-bound vessel with an imperially proportioned flea in her ear.

No, she must be content to worship after the manner of the

brooks. No subtle power of sympathy was engendered out of her worship. She drew rather fewer profile views of Mr Lansdell after that wretched dusty afternoon, and she left off hoping that he would call and invite her to Mordred.

She resumed her old habits, and went out again with Shelley and the Alien, and the big green parasol.

One day—one never-to-be-forgotten day, which made a kind of chasm in her life, dividing all the past from the present and the future—she sat on her old seat under the great oak-tree, beside the creaking mill-wheel and the plashing water; she sat in her favourite spot, with Shelley on her lap and the green parasol over her head. She had been sitting there for a long time in the drowsy midday atmosphere, when a great dog came up to her, and stared at her, and snuffed at her hands, and made friendly advances to her; and then another dog, bigger, if any thing, than the first, came bouncing over a stile and bounding towards her; and then a voice, whose sudden sound made her drop her book all confused and frightened, cried, 'Hi, Frollo! this way, Frollo.' And in the next minute a gentleman, followed by a third dog, came along the narrow bridge that led straight to the bench on which she was sitting.

Her parasol had fallen back as she stooped to pick up her book, and Roland Lansdell could not avoid seeing her face. He thought her very pretty, as we know, but he thought her also very stupid; and he had clean forgotten his talk about her coming to Mordred.

'Let me pick up the book, Mrs Gilbert,' he said. 'What a pretty place you have chosen for your morning's rest! This is a favourite spot of mine.' He looked at the open pages of the book as he handed it to her, and saw the title; and glancing at another book on the seat near her, he recognised the familiar green cover and beveled edges of the Alien. A man always knows the cover of his own book, especially when the work has hung rather heavily on the publisher's hands.

'You are fond of Shelley,' he said. (He was considerably surprised to find that this pretty nonentity beguiled her morning walks with the perusal of the *Revolt of Islam*.)*

'Oh, yes, I am very, very fond of him. Wasn't it a pity that he was drowned!'

She spoke of that calamity as if it had been an event of the last week or two. These things *were* nearer to her than all that common business of breakfast and dinner and supper which made up her daily life. Mr Lansdell shot a searching glance at her from under cover of his long lashes. 'Was this feminine affectation, provincial Rosa-Matilda-ism, or what?'

'Yes, it was a pity,' he said; 'but I fancy we're beginning to get over the misfortune. And so you like all that dreamy, misty stuff?' he added, pointing to the open book which Isabel held in her hands. She was turning the leaves about, with her eyes cast down upon the pages. So would she have sat, shy and trembling, if Sir Reginald Glanville, or Eugene Aram, or the Giaour,* or Napoleon the Great, or any other grand melancholy creature, could have been conjured into life and planted by her side. But she could not tolerate the substantive 'stuff' as applied to the works of the lamented Percy Bysshe Shelley.

'I think it is the most beautiful *poetry* that was ever written,' she said.

'Better than Byron's?' asked Mr Lansdell. 'I thought most young ladies made Byron their favourite.'

'Oh, yes, I love Byron. But then he makes one so unhappy, because one feels that *he* was so unhappy when he wrote. Fancy his writing the *Giaour* late at night, after being out at parties, where every body adored him; and if he hadn't written it, he would have gone mad,' said Mrs Gilbert, opening her eyes very wide. 'Reading Shelley's poetry seems like being amongst birds and flowers and blue rippling water and summer. It always seems summer in his poetry. Oh, I don't know which I like best!'

Was all this affectation, or was it only simple childish reality? Mr Lansdell was so much given to that dreadful disease, disbelief, that he was slow to accept even the evidence of those eloquent blushes, the earnest shining light in those wonderful eyes, which could scarcely be assumed at will, however skilled in the light comedy of everyday life Mrs Gilbert might be. The dogs, who had no misanthropical tendencies, had made friends with Izzie already, and had grouped themselves about her, and laid their big paws and cold wet noses on her knee.

'Shall I take them away?' asked Mr Lansdell. 'I am afraid they will annoy you.'

'Oh, no, indeed; I am so fond of dogs.'

She bent over them and caressed them with her ungloved hands, and dropped Shelley again, and was ashamed of her awkwardness.

Would Edith Dombey have been perpetually dropping things? She bent over a big black retriever till her lips touched his forehead, and he was emboldened to flap his great slimy tongue over her face in token of his affection. *His* dog! Yes, it had come to that already. Mr Lansdell was that awful being, the mysterious 'Lui' of a thousand romances. Roland had been standing upon the bridge all this time; but the bridge was very narrow, and as a labouring man came across at this moment with a reaping-hook across his shoulders, Mr Lansdell had no choice except to go away or else sit down on the bench under the tree. So he sat down at a respectful distance from Mrs Gilbert, and picked up Shelley again; and I think, if it had not been for the dogs, Isabel would have been likely to drop over into the brawling mill-stream in the intensity of her confusion.

He was there by her side, a real living hero and poet, and her weak sentimental little heart swelled with a romantic rapture; and yet she felt that she ought to go away and leave him. Another woman might have looked at her watch, and exclaimed at the lateness of the hour, and gathered up her books and parasol, and departed with a sweeping curtsey and a dignified adieu to Mr Lansdell. But Isabel was planted to the spot, held by some fearful but delicious charm,—a magic and a mystic spell,—with which the plashing of the water and the slow creaking of the mill-wheel, and a faint fluttering of leaves and flowers, the drowsy buzz of multitudinous insects, the thrilling song of Shelley's own skylark* in the blue heaven high above her head, blended in one sweet confusion.

I acknowledge that all this was very hard upon the honest-hearted parish-doctor, who was at this moment sitting in the faint atmosphere of a cottage chamber, applying fresh layers of cotton wool to the poor tortured arm of a Sunday-school pupil, who had been all but burnt to death in the previous week. But then, if a man chooses to marry a girl because her eyes are black and large and beautiful, he must be contented with the supreme advantage he derives from the special attribute for which he has chosen her: and so long as she does not become a victim to cataract, or aggravated inflammation of the eyelids, or chronic sty, he has no right to complain of his bargain. If he selects his wife from amongst other women because she is true-hearted and high-minded and trustworthy, he has ample right to be angry with her whenever she ceases to be any one of these things.

Mr Lansdell and his dogs lingered for some considerable time under the shadow of the big oak. The dogs were rather impatient, and gave expression to their feelings by sundry yawns that were like half-stifled howls, and by eager pantings, and sudden and purpose-less leaps, and short broken-off yelps or snaps; but Roland Lansdell was in no hurry to leave the region of Thurston's Crag. Mrs Gilbert was not stupid, after all; she was something better than a pretty waxen image, animated by limited machinery. That pretty head was filled with a quaint confusion of ideas, half-formed childish fancies, which charmed and amused this elegant loiterer, who had lived in a world where all the women were clever and accomplished, and able to express all they thought, and a good deal more than they thought, with the clear precision and self-possession of creatures who were thoroughly convinced of the infallibility of their own judgment. Yes, Mr Lansdell was amused by Isabel's talk; and he led her on very gently, till her shyness vanished, and she dared to look up at his face as she spoke to him; and he attuned his own talk to the key of hers, and wandered with her in the Valhalla of her heroes, from Eugene Aram to Napoleon Buonaparte. But in the midst of all this, she looked all in a hurry at the little silver watch that George had given her, and found that it was past three.

'Oh, I must go, if you please,' she said; 'I have been out ever since eleven o'clock, and we dine at half-past four.'

'Let me carry your books a little way for you, then,' said Mr Lansdell.

'But are you going that way?'

'Yes, that is the very way I am going.'

The dogs were all excitement at the prospect of a move; they barked and careered about Isabel, and rushed off as if they were going to run ten miles at a stretch, and then wheeled round with alarming suddenness and flew back to Mrs Gilbert and their master.

The nearest way to Graybridge lay across all that swelling sea of lovely meadow-land, and there were a good many stiles to be crossed and gates to be opened and shut, so the walk occupied some time; and Mr Lansdell must have had business to transact in the immedi-ate neighbourhood of Graybridge, for he walked all the way through those delicious meadows, and only parted with Isabel at a gate that opened into the high-road near the entrance of the town.

'I suppose you often stroll as far as Thurston's Crag?' Mr Lansdell said.

'Oh, yes, very often. It isn't too long a walk, and it is *so* pretty.'

'It is pretty. Mordred is quite as near to you, though, and I think that you would like the gardens at Mordred; there are ruins, you know, and it's altogether very romantic. I will give you and Mr Gilbert a key, if you would like to come there sometimes. Oh, by the by, I hope you haven't forgotten your promise to come to luncheon and see the pictures, and all that sort of thing.'

No, Isabel had not forgotten; her face flushed suddenly at the thought of this rapturous vista opening before her. She was to see *him* again, once more, in his own house, and then—and then it would be November, and he would go away, and she would never see him again. No, Isabel had not forgotten; but until this moment all recollection of that invitation to the Priory had been blotted out of Mr Lansdell's mind. It flashed back upon him quite suddenly now, and he felt that he had been unduly neglectful of these nice simple-hearted Gilberts, in whom his dear good Raymond was so much interested.

'I daresay you are fond of pictures?' he said interrogatively.

'Oh, yes, I am very, very fond of them.'

This was quite true. She was fond of every thing that was beautiful,—ready to admire every thing with ignorant childish enthusiasm,—pictures, and flowers, and fountains, and moonlit landscapes, and wonderful foreign cities, and every thing upon this earth that was romantic, and different from her own life.

'Then will you ask Mr Gilbert to accept an unceremonious invitation, and to bring you to the Priory to luncheon,—say next Tuesday, as that will give me time to invite my cousin Gwendoline, and your old friend Mr Raymond, and the two little girls who are so fond of you?'

Isabel murmured something to the effect that she would be very happy, and she was sure her husband would be very happy. She thought that no creature in the world could be otherwise than enraptured by such an invitation: and then she began to think of what she would wear, and to remember that there were greasy streaks and patches upon her brown-silk wedding-dress, which was the best and richest garment her wardrobe contained. Oh, if George would only give her a pale pearly-coloured silk that she had seen in a shop-window at Murlington, and a black-lace shawl, and white bonnet, and pearly gloves and boots and parasol to match the dress! There were people in the world rich enough to have all these things, she thought,—thrice-blessed creatures, who always walked in silk attire.

Mr Lansdell begged her to write him a line to say if Tuesday would suit Mr Gilbert. They were at the last gate by this time, and he lifted his hat with one hand while he held out the other to Isabel. She touched it very lightly, with fingers that trembled a little at the thrilling contact. Her gloves were rolled up in a little ball in her pocket. She was at an age when gloves are rather a nuisance than otherwise; it is only when women come to years of discretion that they are learned as to the conflicting merits of Houbigant and Piver.

'Good-by. I shall see Gwendoline this afternoon; and I shall rely upon you for Tuesday. Hi, Frollo, Quasimodo, Caspar!'

He was gone, with his dogs and a cloud of dust about his heels. Even the dust imparted a kind of grandeur to him. He seemed a being who appeared and disappeared in a cloud, after the manner of some African genii.

Graybridge-church clock chimed the half-hour after four, and Mrs Gilbert hurried home, and went into the common parlour, where dinner was laid, with her face a little flushed, and her dress dusty. George was there already, whistling very loudly, and whittling a stick with a big knobby-handled clasp-knife.

'Why, Izzie,' he said, 'what *have* you been doing with yourself?'

'*Oh*, George!' exclaimed Mrs Gilbert, in a tone of mingled triumph and rapture, 'I have met Mr Lansdell, and he was *so* polite, and he stopped and talked to me *ever* so long; and we're to go there on Tuesday, and Lady Gwendoline Pomphrey is to be there to meet us,—only think of that!'

'Where?' cried George.

'Why, at Mordred Priory, of course. We're to go to luncheon; and, oh, George, remember you must never call it "lunch." And I'm to write and say if you'll go; but *of course* you will go, George.'

'Humph!' muttered Mr Gilbert reflectively; 'Tuesday's an awkward day, rather. But still, as you say, Izzie, it's a splendid connexion, and a man oughtn't to throw away such a chance of extending his practice. Yes, I think I'll manage it, my dear. You may write to say we'll go.'

And this was all; no rapture, no spark of enthusiasm. To tell the truth, the surgeon was hungry, and wanted his dinner. It came in presently, smelling very savoury,—but, oh, so vulgar! It was Irish stew,—a low horrid dinner, such as Hibernian labourers might devour after a day's bricklaying. Isabel ate very little, and picked out all the bits of onion and put them aside on her plate. Come what might, she would never, never eat onions again. *That* degradation, at least, it was in her own power to avoid.

After dinner, while George was busy in the surgery, Mrs Gilbert set to work to compose her letter to Mr Lansdell. She was to write to him—to him! It was to be only a ceremonious letter, very brief and commonplace: 'Mr and Mrs Gilbert present their compliments to Mr Lansdell, and will be happy to' &c. &c. But even such a letter as this was a critical composition. In that sublime region in which Mr Lansdell lived, there might be certain words and phrases that were indispensable,—there might be some arbitrary mode of expression, not to know which would argue yourself unknown. Isabel looked into *Dombey*, but there was no help for her there. She would have been very glad if she could have found 'Mrs Grainger presents her compliments to Mr Dombey,' or 'Miss F. Dombey has the pleasure to inform Mr Gay—' or something of that kind, any where amongst those familiar pages. However, she was obliged to write her letter as best she might, on a sheet of paper that was very thick and slippery, and strongly impregnated with patchouli; and she sealed the envelope with a profile of Lord Byron imprinted upon white wax,—the only stick that was to be had in Graybridge, and to find which good-natured Mr Jeffson scoured the town, while Isabel was writing her letter.

Roland Lansdell, Esqre
Mordred Priory.

To write such an address was in itself a pleasure. It was dark by the time Mrs Gilbert had finished her letter, and then she began to think of her dress,—her dress for Tuesday,—the Tuesday which was henceforth to stand out from amongst all the other days in her life.

Would George give her a new silk dress? No; that was impossible. He would give her a sovereign, and she might 'do up' the old one. She was fain to be content, and thankful for so much; and she went upstairs with a candle, and came down presently with two or three dresses on her arm. Among them there was a white muslin, a good deal the worse for wear, but prettier than the silk; a soft transparent fabric, and with lace about it. Mrs Gilbert determined upon wearing this dress; and early the next morning she went out and consulted with a little dressmaker, and brought the young woman home with her, and sat down with her in the sunny parlour to unpick and refashion and improve this white-muslin robe. She told the dress-maker that she was going on a visit to Mordred Priory, and by nightfall almost every body in Graybridge knew that Mr and Mrs Gilbert had received an invitation from Mr Lansdell.

CHAPTER III

ROLAND SAYS, 'AMEN'

Isabel had met Mr Lansdell on Thursday; and by Saturday night all her preparations were made, and the white dress, and a white-muslin mantle to match it, were in the hands of Mrs Jeffson, who was to get them up in the highest style of clear-starching. The sovereign had done a great deal. Isabel had bought a new ribbon for her straw-hat, and a pair of pale straw-coloured gloves, and all manner of small matters necessary to the female toilette upon gala occasions. And now that every thing was done, the time between Saturday night and Tuesday lay all before them,—a dreary blank, that must be endured somehow or other. I should be ashamed to say how very little of the Rector's sermon Isabel heard on Sunday morn-ing. She was thinking of Mordred Priory all the time she was in church, and the beautiful things that Mr Lansdell would say to her, and the replies that she would make. She imagined it all, as it was her habit to do.

And on this summer Sunday, this blessed day of quiet and re-pose, when there was no sound of the sickle in the corn-fields, and only the slow drip, drip, drip of the water-drops from the motion-less mill-wheel at Thurston's Crag, Roland Lansdell lounged all day in the library at Mordred Priory, reading a little, writing a little, smoking and pondering a great deal. What should he do with him-self? That was the grand question which this young man found himself very often called upon to decide. He would stop at Mordred till he was tired of Mordred, and then he would go to Paris; and when he was weary of that brilliant city, whose best delights familiarity had rendered indifferent to him, he would go Rhine-ward, over all the old ground again, amongst all the old people. Ten years is a very long time when you have fifteen thousand a-year and nothing particular to do with yourself or your money. Roland Lansdell had used up all the delights of civilised Europe; and the pleasures that seemed so freshly effervescent to other men were to him as champagne that has grown flat and vapid in the unemptied glasses on a deserted banquet-table.

He sat to-day in the great window of the library—a deeply-embayed Tudor window, jutting out upon a broad stone terrace, along whose balustrade a peacock stalked slowly in the sunshine. There were books on either side of the window; solid ranges of soberly-bound volumes, that reached from floor to ceiling on every side of the room; for the Lansdells had been a studious and book-learned race time out of mind, and the library at Mordred was worthy of its name.

There was only one picture—a portrait by Rembrandt, framed in a massive border of carved oak—above the high chimney-piece; a grave grand face, with solemn eyes that followed you wherever you went; a splendid earnest face, with the forehead mysteriously shad-owed by the broad brim of a steeple-crowned hat.

In the dark melancholy of that sombre countenance there was some vague resemblance to the face of the young man lounging in the sunny window this afternoon, smoking and pondering, and looking up now and then to call to the peacock on the balustrade.

Beyond that balustrade there was a fair domain, bounded far away by a battlemented wall; a lofty ivy-mantled wall, propped every here and there with mighty buttresses; a wall that had been built in the days when William of Normandy enriched his faithful followers with the fairest lands of his newly-conquered realm. Beyond that grand old boundary arose the square turret of the village church, coeval with the oldest part of Mordred Priory. The bells were swinging in the turret now, and the sound of them floated towards Roland Lansdell as he lounged in the open window.

'Only thirty years of age,' he thought; 'and how long it seems since I sat on my mother's knee in the shadowy, sleepy old pew yonder, and heard the vicar's voice humming under the sounding-board above our heads! Thirty years—thirty profitless, tiresome years; and there is not a reaper in the fields, or a shock-headed country lad that earns sixpence a day by whooping to the birds amongst the corn, that is not of more use to his fellow-creatures than I am. I suppose though, at the worst, I'm good for trade. And I try my best not to do any harm—Heaven knows I don't want to do any harm.'

It must have been a strange transition of ideas that at this moment led Mr Lansdell to think of that chance meeting with the doctor's dark-eyed wife under the dense foliage of Lord Thurston's oak.

'She's a pretty creature,' he thought; 'a pretty, inexperienced, shy little creature. Just the sort of woman that a hardened profligate or a *roué* would try to pervert and entangle. There's something really bewitching in all that enthusiastic talk about Byron and Shelley. "What a pity he was drowned!" and, "Oh! if he had only fought for Greece, and been victorious, like Leonidas,* you know,"—poor little thing! I wonder how much she knows about Leonidas?—"how splendid that would have been! but, oh, to think that he should have a fever—a fever just such as kills common people—and die, just when he had proved himself so great and noble!" It's the newest thing to find all these silly school-girl fancies confusing the brain of a woman who ought to be the most practical person in Graybridge,— a parish-surgeon's wife, who should not, according to the fitness of things, have an idea above coarse charity flannels and camomile-tea and gruel. How she will open her eyes when she sees this room, and all the books in it! Poor little thing! I shall never forget what a pretty picture she made sitting under the oak, with the greenish gray of the great knotted trunk behind her, and the blue water in the foreground.'

And then Mr Lansdell's ideas, which seemed especially irrelevant this afternoon, broke off abruptly. 'I hope I may never do any harm,' he thought. 'I am not a good man, or a useful man; but I don't think I have ever done much harm.'

He lit another cigar, and strolled out upon the terrace, and from the terrace to the great quadrangular stable-yard. Upon one side of the quadrangle there was a cool arched way that had once been a cloister; and I regret to say that the stone cells in which the monks of Mordred had once spent their slow quiet days and meditative nights now did duty as loose-boxes for Mr Lansdell's hunters. Openings had been knocked through the dividing walls; for horses are more socially-disposed creatures than monks, and are apt to pine and sicken if entirely deprived of companionship with their kind. Roland went into three or four of the boxes, and looked at the horses, and sighed for the time when the hunting-season should commence and Midlandshire might be tolerable.

'I want occupation,' he thought, 'physical wear and tear, and all that sort of thing. I let my mind run upon all manner of absurd things for want of occupation.'

He yawned and threw away his cigar, and strode across the yard towards the open window of a harness-room, at which a man was sitting in his shirt-sleeves, and with a Sunday paper before him.

'You may bring the Diver round in half an hour, Christie,' said Mr Lansdell; 'I shall ride over to Conventford this afternoon.'

'Yes, sir.'

Roland Lansdell did ride to Conventford; galloping his hardest into Waverly, to the scandal of the sober townspeople, who looked up from their tea-tables half scared at the sound of the clattering hoofs upon the uneven pavement; and then dawdling at a foot-pace all along the avenue which extends in unbroken beauty from Waverly to Conventford. The streets of this latter town were crowded with gaily-dressed factory-girls, and the bells from three separate spires were clanging loudly in the summer air. Mr Lansdell rode very slowly, thinking of 'all manner of absurd things' as he went along; and he entered Mr Raymond's pretty drawing-room at Oakbank just in time to catch that gentleman drinking tea with the orphans.

Of course Roland had forgotten that his friend dined at an early hour on Sundays, and he had come to dine; but it wasn't of the least consequence, he would have some tea; yes, and cold beef, by all means, if there was cold beef.

A side-table was laid for him, and a great sirloin was brought in. But Mr Lansdell did not make much havoc with the joint. He and Mr Raymond had a good deal to say to each other: and Mr Lansdell took very kindly to the orphans, and asked them a good many questions about their studies, and their present governess, who was a native of Conventford, and had gone out that evening to drink tea with her friends: and then, somehow or other, the conversation rambled on to their late governess, Isabel Sleaford, and the orphans had a great deal to say about her. She was so nice, and she told them such pretty things: *Eugene Aram* and the *Giaour*—how wicked Black Hassan was to tie his poor 'sister' up in a sack and drown her, because he didn't wish her to marry the Giaour! Miss Sleaford had modified the romantic story in deference to the tender ages of her pupils. Yes, the young ladies said, they loved Miss Sleaford *dearly*. She was *so nice*; and sometimes, at night, when they begged her very, very hard, she would ACT (the orphans uttered this last word in an awfully distinct whisper); and, oh, that was beautiful! She would do Hamlet and the Ghost: when she stood one way, with a black-velvet cloak over her shoulder, she was Hamlet; when she stood the other way, with a mahogany ruler in her hand, she was the Ghost. And she acted the Ghost so beautifully, that sometimes they were frightened, and wouldn't go outside the schoolroom-door without a candle, and somebody's hand to hold—tight.

And then Mr Raymond laughed, and told Roland what he thought of Isabel, phrenologically and otherwise.

'Poor little thing! I think there must be something sad about the story of her early life,' he said; 'for she so evidently shrinks from all allusion to it. It's the old story, I suppose,—an unkind stepmother and an uncomfortable home. Under these circumstances, I was very glad to see her married to a well-disposed, honest-hearted young man.'

'She was very fond of Mr Gilbert, I suppose,—very much in love with him?' said Roland, after a little pause.

'In love with him! not a bit of it. She was very fond of him, I daresay—not in the sentimental manner in which she discourses about her poets and her heroes; but she has every reason to be fond of him as a faithful protector and a good friend.'

Mr Raymond looked up suddenly, and fixed his eyes upon the face of his young kinsman. But it was dusk by this time; and in the dim light of the room Charles Raymond could not see the expression of Roland's face; he could only see the attitude of his head, which drooped a little forward, supported by his hand.

'I lent my voice to the bringing about of Isabel Gilbert's marriage,' Mr Raymond said slowly; 'and God grant that no man may ever be base enough or cruel enough to interpose himself between those two!'

'Amen!' answered Roland Lansdell, in a deep solemn voice.

And then he walked to the window and looked out into the twilit garden, above which the faint summer moon had newly arisen.

'If I could have believed in that splendid fable of a future life, that grand compensating balance for all the sorrows and mistakes of this lower world, what a good man I might have been!' he thought, as he stood there looking out, with his arm resting upon the broad wooden sash, and his head upon his arm.

CHAPTER IV

MR LANSDELL RELATES AN ADVENTURE

The Tuesday was a fine day. The August sunshine—the beautiful harvest-time sunshine which was rejoicing the hearts of all the farmers in Midlandshire—awoke Mrs Gilbert very early. She was going to Mordred Priory. For once she forgot to notice the ugliness of the shabby furniture, the bare whitewashed walls upon which her eyes opened. She was going to Mordred Priory. There are moments in our lives in which all the great expanse of the past and future seems as nothing compared with the consummate felicity of the present. It was very early; but not too early for her to get up, Mrs Gilbert thought. She seated herself before the little glass at the open window, and brushed her long black hair; while the birds twittered and shook themselves in the sunshine, and the faint lowing of cattle came like a long drowsy murmur from the distant fields.

The surgeon and his wife had held solemn conference with each other as to the hour at which they ought to arrive at Mordred Priory. Luncheon might be eaten at any time from one until three, Mr Gilbert said; and it was decided, therefore, that they should present themselves at the gates of the Priory a short time before one o'clock.

How pretty the village of Mordred looked in the sleepy August atmosphere, the hazy, Cuyp-like* sunshine! How beautiful every thing looked just at the entrance to the village, where there was a long straggling inn with a top-heavy roof, all dotted over with impossible little windows, a dear old red-tiled roof, with pouters and fantails brooding and cooing to themselves in the sunshine, and yellow stone-crop creeping here and there in patches of gold! To the right of the inn a shady road led away below the walls of the Priory to the square-turreted church; and, grander than the church itself, the lofty gates of Mordred dominated over all.

Isabel almost trembled as Mr Gilbert got out of the gig and pulled the iron ring that hung at the end of a long chain on one side of those formidable oaken gates. It seemed like ringing at the door of the past, somehow; and the Doctor's Wife half expected to see quaintly-costumed servants, with long points to their shoes and strange parti-coloured garments, and a jester with a cap and bells, when those great gates were opened. But the person who opened the gates was only a very harmless old woman, who inhabited some stony chambers on one side of the ponderous archway. George drove slowly under that splendid Norman gateway, and Isabel looked with a shiver at the portcullis and the great rusty chains high above her head. If it should fall some day upon Mr Lansdell, as he was riding out of his grand domain! Her mind was like a voluminous picture-book, full of romantic incidents and dreadful catastrophes; and she was always imagining such events as these. Brown Molly jogged slowly along the winding drive,—oh, the beautiful shrubberies, and banks of verdure, and dark shining foliage, and spreading cedars making solemn shadows yonder on the lawn, and peeps of glistening water in the distance; how beautiful! how beautiful!—and stopped before a Norman porch, a gray old ivy-covered porch, beneath which there was an open doorway that revealed a hall with armour on the walls, and helmed classic heads of white marble on black marble pedestals, and skins of savage beasts upon dark oak floors. Isabel had only caught a brief glimpse of the dusky splendour of this interior, when a groom appeared from behind a distant angle of the house and ran forward to take George Gilbert's horse; and in the next moment Mr Lansdell came out of the porch, and bade his visitors welcome to Mordred.

'I am so glad to see you! What a lovely morning, is it not? I'm afraid you must have found the roads rather dusty, though. Take care of Mr Gilbert's horse, Christie; you'd better put him into one of the loose-boxes. You see my dogs know you, Mrs Gilbert.' A liver-coloured pointer and a great black retriever were taking friendly notice of Isabel. 'Will you come and see my pictures at once? I expect Gwendoline and her father, and your friend Mr Raymond, and the children, presently.'

There was no special brilliancy or eloquence in all this, but it sounded different to other people's talk, somehow. The languid, lingering tones were very cordial in spite of their languor; and then how splendid the speaker looked in his loose black-velvet morning coat, which harmonised so exquisitely with the Rembrandt hues* of his complexion! There was a waxen-looking hothouse flower in his button-hole, and across that inspiration of a West-end tailor, his waistcoat, there glimmered a slender chain of very yellow gold, with onyx cameos and antique golden coins hanging to it,—altogether different from the big clumsy yellow lockets and fusee-boxes* which dangled on the padded chests of the officers at Coventford, whom Isabel had until lately so implicitly believed in.

Mr Lansdell led the way into a room, beyond which there were other rooms opening one into the other in a long vista of splendour and sunshine. Isabel had only a very faint idea of what she saw in those beautiful rooms. It was all a confusion of brightness and colour, which was almost too much for her poor sentimental brain. It was all a splendid chaos, in which antique oak cabinets, and buhl* and marqueterie,* and carved ebony chairs, and filigree-work* and ivory, old Chelsea, Battersea, Copenhagen, Vienna, Dresden, Sèvres, Derby, and Salopian china, Majolica and Palissy ware,* pictures and painted windows, revolved like the figures in a kaleidoscope before her dazzled eyes. Mr Lansdell was very kind, and explained the nature of some of these beautiful things as he loitered here and there with his guests. George walked softly, with his hat in his hand, as if he had been in church, and stared with equal reverence at every thing. He was pleased with a Vandevelde* because the sea was so nice and green, and the rigging so neatly made out; and he stopped a minute before a Fyt* to admire the whiskers of a hare; and he thought that a plump-shouldered divinity by Greuze,* with melting blue eyes and a gray-satin gown, was rather a fine young woman; but he did not particularly admire the Murillos or the Spagnolettis,* and thought that the models who sat to those two masters would have done better had they washed their faces and combed their hair before doing so.

Mr Gilbert was not enthusiastic about the pictures; but Isabel's eyes wandered here and there in a rapture of admiration, and by and by those great dark eyes filled with tears before the gem of Mr Lansdell's collection, a Raffaelle, a picture of the Man of Sorrows half-fainting under the cruel burden of His cross, sublime in resignation, unspeakably sorrowful and tender; an exquisite half-length figure, sharply defined against a vivid blue sky. 'My father believed in that picture,' said Mr Lansdell; 'but connoisseurs shrug their shoulders and tell me that it never stood upon the easel of Raffaelle Sanzio d'Urbino.'

'But it is so beautiful,' Isabel answered, in a low, awe-stricken voice. She had been very inattentive to the Rector's sermon on the previous Sunday, but her heart filled with tender devotion as she looked at this picture. 'Does it matter much who painted it, if it is only beautiful?'

And then Mr Lansdell began to explain in what manner the picture differed from the best-authenticated productions of the prince of painters; but in the middle of his little lecture Mr Raymond and the orphans came trooping through the rooms, and the conversation became general. Soon after this Lady Gwendoline and her father made their appearance, and then a very neatly-dressed maid conducted the ladies to a dressing-room that had once belonged to Roland's mother, where the window-curtains were sea-green silk, and the looking-glass was framed in white Sèvres, and where there were ivory-backed brushes, and glittering bottles of rich yellow-looking perfume in a casket of gold and enamel.

Isabel took off her bonnet, and smoothed her hair with one of the brushes, and remembered her dressing-table at home, and a broken black brush of George's with all the unprotected wires sticking out at the back. She thought of the drawer in the looking-glass, with a few bent hair-pins, and her husband's razors with coloured bone handles, and a flat empty bottle that had once held lavender-water, all jostling one another when the drawer was pulled open. Mrs Gilbert thought of these things while Lady Gwendoline removed her bonnet—another marvellous bonnet—and drew off the tightest coffee-with-plenty-of-milk-in-it-coloured gloves, and revealed long white hands, luminous with opals and diamonds. The Doctor's Wife had time to contemplate Lady Gwendoline's silk dress—that exquisitely-fitting dress, whose soft golden tint was only a little darker than the lady's hair; and the tiny embroidered collar, fitting closely to the long slender throat, and clasped by one big turquoise in a wide rim of lustreless gold, and the turquoise earrings just peeping out under rich bands of auburn hair. Mrs Gilbert admired all these things, and she saw that Lady Gwendoline's face, which was so handsome in profile, was just a little faded and wan when you had a full view of it.

The orphans took the gold tops off the bottles one by one, and sniffed energetically at the different perfumes, and disputed in whispers as to which was the nicest. Lady Gwendoline talked very kindly to Mrs Gilbert. She did not at all relish being asked to meet the Doctor's Wife, and she was angry with her cousin for noticing these people; but she was too well bred to be otherwise than kind to Roland's visitor.

They all went down-stairs presently, and were ushered into an oak-panelled room, where there was an oval table laid for luncheon, and where Isabel found herself seated presently on Mr Lansdell's right hand, and opposite to Lady Gwendoline Pomphrey.

This was life. There was a Lance-like* group of hothouse grapes and peaches, crowned with a pine-apple, in a high Dresden basket in the centre of the table. Isabel had never seen a pine-apple out of the celebrated Edith-Dombey picture until to-day. There were flowers upon the table, and a faint odour of orange-blossoms and apricots pervaded the atmosphere. There were starry white glasses, so fragile-looking that it seemed as if a breath would have blown them away; cup-shaped glasses, broad shallow glasses like water-lily leaves, glasses of the palest green, and here and there a glimpse of ruby glass flashing in the sunshine. Mrs Gilbert had a very vague idea of the nature of the viands which were served to her at that wonderful feast. Somebody dropped a lump of ice into the shallow glass, and filled it afterwards with a yellow bubbling wine, which had a faint flavour of ripe pears, and which some one said was Moselle. Mr Lansdell put some white creamy compound on her plate, which might or might not have been chicken; and one of the servants brought her an edifice of airy pastry, filled with some mysterious concoction in which there were little black lumps. She took a spoonful of the concoction, seeing that other people had done so; but she was very doubtful of the little black lumps, which she conjectured to be a mistake of the cook's. And then some one brought her an ice, a real ice,—just as if Mordred Priory had been a perpetual pastrycook's shop,—a pink ice in the shape of a pear, which she ate with a pointed gold spoon; and then the pine-apple was cut, and she had a slice of it, and was rather disappointed in it, as hardly realising the promise of its appearance.

But all the dishes in that banquet were of 'such stuff as dreams are made of.'* So may have tasted the dew-berries which Titania's

attendants gave to Bottom.* To Isabel there was a dream-like flavour in every thing. Was not *he* by her side, talking to her every now
and then? The subjects of which he spoke were commonplace enough,
certainly, and he talked to other people as well as to her. He talked
about the plans of the Cabinet and the hunting-season to Lord
Ruysdale, and he talked of books and pictures with Mr Raymond
and Lady Gwendoline, and of parish matters with George Gilbert.
He seemed to know all about every thing in the world, Isabel thought.
She could not say much; *how* to admire was all the art she knew. As
to the orphans, those young ladies sat side by side, and nudged each
other when the sacrificial knife was plunged into any fresh viand,
and discoursed together every now and then in rapturous whispers;
nothing came amiss to them, from rout-cakes* and preserved ginger
to lobster-salad or the wall of a fricandeau.*

It was four o'clock by the time the pine-apple had been cut, and
the banquet concluded. The oak-painted room was lighted by one
window—a great square window—which almost filled one side of
the room; a splendid window, out of which you could walk into a
square garden—an old-fashioned garden—divided from the rest of
the grounds by cropped hedges of dense box; wonderful boundaries,
that had taken a century or two to grow. The bees were humming in
this garden all luncheon-time, and yellow butterflies shot backwards
and forwards in the sunshine: tall hollyhocks flowered gorgeously in
the prim beds, and threw straight shadows on the smooth grass.

'Shall we go into the garden?' said Lady Gwendoline, as they rose
from the table, and every body assented: so presently Isabel found
herself amidst a little group upon the miniature lawn, in the centre
of which there was a broad marble basin, filled with gold fish, and a
feeble little fountain, that made a faint tinkling sound in the still
August atmosphere.

Mr Raymond and Roland Lansdell both having plenty to say for
themselves, and Lord Ruysdale and Lady Gwendoline being able to
discourse pleasantly upon any possible subject, there had been no
lack of animated conversation, though neither the doctor nor his
wife had done much to keep the ball rolling.

Mr Lansdell and his guests had been talking of all manner of
things; flying off at tangents to all kinds of unlikely subjects; till
they had come, somehow or other, to discuss the question of length
of days.

'I can't say that I consider long life an inestimable blessing,' said Roland, who was amusing himself with throwing minute morsels of a macaroon to the gold fish. 'They're not so interesting as Sterne's donkey,* are they, Mrs Gilbert? No, I do *not* consider long life an advantage, unless one can be "warm and young" for ever, like our dear Raymond. Perhaps I am only depreciating the fruit because it hangs out of my reach, though; for every body knows that the Lansdells never live to be old.'

Isabel's heart gave a bump as Roland said this, and involuntarily she looked at him with just one sudden startled glance. Of course he would die young; Beings always have so died, and always must. A thrill of pain shot through her breast as she thought of this; yet I doubt if she would have had it otherwise. It would be almost better that he should break a blood-vessel, or catch a fever, or commit suicide, than that he should ever live to have gray hair, and wear spectacles and double-soled boots.

Brief as that sudden look of alarm had been, Roland had seen it, and paused for a moment before he went on talking.

'No, we are not a long-lived race. We have been consumptive; and we have had our heads cut off in the good old days, when to make a confidential remark to a friend was very often leze majesty, or high-treason; and we have been killed in battle,—at Flodden,* to wit, and at Fontenoy,* and in the Peninsular*; and one of us was shot through the lungs, in an Irish duel, on the open sward of the "Phaynix".* In short, I almost fancy some fearful ban must have been set upon us in the Dark Ages, when one of our progenitors, a wicked prior of Mordred, who had been a soldier and a renegade before he crept into the bosom of the Church, appropriated some of the sanctified plate to make a dowry for his handsome daughter, who married Sir Anthony Lansdell, Knight, and thus became the mother of our race; and we are evidently a doomed race, for very few of us have ever lived to see a fortieth birthday.'

'And how is your doom to be brought about, Roland?' asked Lady Gwendoline.

'Oh, *that's* all settled,' Mr Lansdell answered; 'I know my destiny.'

'It has been predicted to you?'

'Yes.'

'How very interesting!' exclaimed the lady, with a pretty silvery laugh. Isabel's eyes opened wider and wider, and fixed themselves on Roland Lansdell's face.

'Pray tell us all about it,' continued Lady Gwendoline. 'We won't promise to be very much frightened, because the accessories are not quite the thing for a ghost-story. If it were midnight now, and we were sitting in the oak room, with the lights burning low, and the shadows trembling on the wall, you might do what you liked with our nerves. And yet I really don't know that a ghost might not be more awful in the broad sunshine—a ghost that would stalk across the grass, and then fade slowly, till it melted into the water-drops of the fountain. Come, Roland, you must tell us all about the prediction; was it made by a pretty girl with a dove on her wrist, like the phantom that appeared to Lord Lyttleton? Shall we have to put back the clock for an hour, in order to foil the designs of your impalpable foe? Or was it a black cat, or a gentleman-usher, or a skeleton; or all three?'

'I daresay it was an abnormal state of the organs of form and colour,' said Mr Raymond. 'That's the foundation of all ghost-stories.'

'But it isn't by any means a ghost-story,' answered Roland Lansdell. 'The gentleman who predicted my early death was the very reverse of a phantom; and the region of the prediction was a place which has never yet been invested with any supernatural horrors. Amongst all the legends of the Old Bailey I never heard of any ghostly record.'

'The Old Bailey!' exclaimed Lady Gwendoline.

'Yes. The affair was quite an adventure, and the only adventure I ever had in my life.'

'Pray tell us the story.'

'But it's rather a long one, and not particularly interesting.'

'I insist upon hearing it,' said Mr Raymond; 'you've stimulated our organs of wonder, and you're bound to restore our brains to their normal state by satisfying our curiosity.'

'Most decidedly,' exclaimed Lady Gwendoline, seating herself upon a rustic bench, with the shining folds of her silk dress spread round her like the plumage of some beautiful bird, and a tiny fringed parasol sloping a little backward from her head, and throwing all manner of tremulous pinky shadows upon her animated face.

She was very handsome when she was animated; it was only when her face was in repose that you saw how much her beauty had faded since the picture with the high forehead and the long curls was first exhibited to an admiring public. It may be that Lady Gwendoline knew this, and was on that account rather inclined to be animated about trifles.

'Well, I'll tell you the story, if you like,' said Roland; 'but I warn you that there's not much in it. I don't suppose you—any of you—take much interest in criminal cases; but this one made rather a sensation at the time.'

'A criminal case?'

'Yes. I was in town on business a year or two ago. I'd come over from Switzerland to renew some leases, and look into a whole batch of tiresome business matters, which my lawyer insisted upon my attending to in my own proper person, very much to my annoyance. While I was in London I dropped into the United Joint-Stock Bank, Temple-Bar Branch, to get circular notes and letters of credit upon their correspondent at Constantinople, and so on. I was not in the office more than five minutes. But while I was talking to one of the clerks at the counter, a man came in, and stood close at my elbow while he handed in a cheque for eighty-seven pounds ten, or some such amount—I know it came very close upon the hundred—received the money, and went out. He looked like a groom out of livery. I left the bank almost immediately after him, and as he turned into a little alley leading down to the Temple, I followed a few paces behind him, for I had business in Paper Buildings. At the bottom of the alley my friend the groom was met by a big black-whiskered man, who seemed to have been waiting for him, for he caught him suddenly by the arm, and said, "Well, did they do it?" "Yes," the other man answered, and began fumbling in his waist-coat-pocket, making a chinking sound as he did so. I had seen him put his money, which he took in notes and gold, into this waistcoat-pocket. "You needn't have pounced upon me so precious sharp," he said rather sulkily; "I wasn't going to bolt with it, was I?" The black-whiskered man had seen me by this time, and he muttered something to his companion, which evidently meant that he was to hold his tongue, and then dragged him off without further ceremony in the opposite direction to that in which I was going. This was all I saw of the groom or the black-whiskered gentleman on that occasion. I thought their method of cashing a cheque was rather a queer one; but I thought no more about it, until three weeks afterwards, when I went into the Temple-Bar Office of the United Joint-Stock again to complete my Continental arrangements, and was told that the cheque for eighty-seven pounds ten, more or less, which had been cashed in my presence, was a forgery; one of a series of most audacious frauds, perpetrated by a gang whose plans had only just come to light, and none of whom had yet been arrested. "They've managed to keep themselves dark in the most extra-ordinary manner," the clerk told me; "the cheques are supposed to have been all fabricated by one man, but three or four men have been employed to get hold of the original signatures of our customers, which they have obtained by a complicated system. No two cheques have been presented by the same person,—that's the point that has beaten the detectives; they don't know what sort of men to look for." "Don't they?" said I; "then I think I can assist them in the matter." Whereupon I told my little story of the black-whiskered gentleman.'

Mr Lansdell paused to take breath, and stole a glance at Isabel. She was pale always,—but she was very pale now, and was watching him with an eager breathless expression.

'Silly romantic little thing,' he thought, 'to be so intensely absorbed in my story.'

'You're getting interesting, Roland,' said Lady Gwendoline. 'Pray, go on.'

'The upshot of the matter was, that at eight o'clock that evening a grave little gentleman in a pepper-and-salt waistcoat came to me at Mivart's, and cross-questioned me closely as to what I knew of the man who had cashed the cheque. "You think you could recognise this man with the black whiskers?" he said. "Yes; most decidedly I could.' 'And you'll swear to him, if necessary?" "With pleasure." On this the detective departed, and came to me the next day, to tell me that he fancied he was on the track of the man he wanted, but he was at a loss for means of identification. He knew, or thought that he knew, who the man was; but he didn't know the man himself from Adam. The gang had taken fright, and it was believed that they had all started for Liverpool, with the intention of getting off to America by a vessel that was expected to sail at eight o'clock the following morning. The detective had only just got his information, and he came to me for help. The result of the business was, that I put on my greatcoat, sent for a cab, and started for Euston Square with my friend the detective, with a view to identifying the black-whiskered gentleman. It was the first adventure I had ever had in my life, and I assure you I most heartily enjoyed it.

'Well, we travelled by the mail, got into Liverpool in the dead of the night, and in the bleak early dawn of the next morning I had the supreme pleasure of pointing out my black-whiskered acquaintance, just as he was going to step on board the steamer that was to convey him to the *Atalanta* screw-steamship, bound for New York. He looked very black at first; but when he found that my companion was altogether *en règle*, he went away with him, meekly enough, declaring that it was all a mistake, and that it would be easily set right in town. I let the two go back together, and returned by a later train, very well pleased with my adventure.

'I was not so well pleased, however, when I found that I was wanted as a witness at preliminary examinations, and adjourned examinations, and on and off through a trial that lasted four days and a half; to say nothing of being badgered and browbeaten by Old-Bailey practitioners,—who were counsel for the prisoner,—and who asked me if it was my friend's whiskers I recognised, or if I had never seen any other whiskers exactly like his? if I should know him without his whiskers? whether I could swear to the colour of his waistcoat? whether any member of my family had ever been in a lunatic asylum? whether I usually devoted my leisure-time to travelling about with detective officers? whether I had been plucked at Oxford? whether I should be able to recognise an acquaintance whom I had only seen once in twenty years? whether I was short-sighted? could I swear I was not short-sighted? would I be kind enough to read a verse or so from a diamond edition of the works of Thomas Moore?* and so on. But question me as they would, the prisoner at the bar,—commonly known as Jack the Scribe, *alias* Jack the Gentleman, *alias* ever so many other names, which I have completely forgotten,—was the identical person whom I had seen meet the groom at the entrance to the Temple. My evidence was only a single link in a long chain; but I suppose it was eminently damaging to my black-whiskered friend; for, when he and two of his associates had received their sentence—ten years' penal servitude—he turned towards where I was standing, and said:

' "I don't bear any grudge against the gentlemen of the jury, and I don't bear any malice against the judge, though his sentence isn't a light one; but when a languid swell mixes himself up in business that doesn't concern him, he deserves to get it hot and strong. If ever I come out of prison alive, I'll *kill you!*"

'He shook his fist at me as he said it. There wasn't much in the words, but there was a good deal in the way in which they were spoken. He tried to say more; but the warders got hold of him and held him down, panting and gasping, and with his face all of a dull livid white. I saw no more of him; but if he *does* live to come out of prison, I most firmly believe he'll keep his word.'

'Izzie,' cried George Gilbert suddenly, 'what's the matter?'

All the point of Mr Lansdell's story was lost; for at this moment Isabel tottered and fell slowly backward upon the sward, and all the gold fish leaped away in a panic of terror as the doctor dipped his hat into the marble basin. He splashed the water into his wife's face, and she opened her eyes at last, very slowly, and looked round her.

'Did he say that—' she said,—'did he say that he'd kill ——?'

CHAPTER V

THE FIRST WARNING

Mrs Gilbert recovered very quickly from her fainting-fit. She had been frightened by Mr Lansdell's story, she said, and the heat had made her dizzy. She sat very quietly upon a sofa in the drawing-room, with one of the orphans on each side of her, while Brown Molly was being harnessed.

Lady Gwendoline went away with her father, after bidding Mrs Gilbert rather a cool good-morning. The Earl of Ruysdale's daughter did not approve of the fainting-fit, which she was pleased to call Mrs Gilbert's extraordinary demonstration.

'If she were a single woman, I should fancy she was trying to fascinate Roland,' Lady Gwendoline said to her father as they drove homewards. 'What can possibly have induced him to invite those people to Mordred? The man is a clod, and the woman a nonentity; except when she chooses to make an exhibition of herself by fainting away. That sort of person is always fainting away, and being knocked down by feathers, and going unexpectedly into impossible hysterics; and so on.'

But if Lady Gwendoline was unkind to the Doctor's Wife, Roland was kind; dangerously, bewilderingly kind. He was *so* anxious about Isabel's health. It was his fault, entirely his fault that she had fainted. He had kept her standing under the blazing sun while he told his stupid story. He should never forgive himself, he said. And he would scarcely accept George Gilbert's assurance that his wife was all right. He rang the bell, and ordered strong tea for his visitors. With his own hands he closed the Venetian shutters, and reduced the light to a cool dusky glimmer. He begged Mr Gilbert to allow him to order a close carriage for his wife's return to Graybridge.

'The gig shall be sent home to you to-night,' he said; 'I am sure the air and dust will be too much for Mrs Gilbert.'

But Mr Raymond hereupon interfered, and said the fresh air was just the very thing that Isabel wanted, to which opinion the lady herself subscribed. She did not want to cause trouble, she said: she would not for all the world have caused *him* trouble, she thought: so the gig was brought round presently, and George drove his wife away, under the Norman archway by which they had entered in the fresh noonday sun. The young man was in excellent spirits, and declared that he had enjoyed himself beyond measure—these undemonstrative people always declare that they enjoy themselves—but Isabel was very silent and subdued; and when questioned upon the subject, said that she was tired.

Oh, how blank the world seemed after that visit to Mordred Priory! It was all over. This one supreme draught of bliss had been drained to the very dregs. It would be November soon, and Roland Lansdell would go away. He would go before November, perhaps: he would go suddenly, whenever the fancy seized him. Who can calculate the arrangements of the Giaour or Sir Reginald Glanville? At any moment, in the dead darkness of the moonless night, the hero may call for his fiery steed, and only the thunder of hurrying hoofs upon the hard high-road may bear witness of his departure.

Mr Lansdell might leave Mordred at any hour in the long summer day, Isabel thought, as she stood at the parlour-window looking out at the dusty lane, where Mrs Jeffson's fowls were pecking up stray grains of wheat that had been scattered by some passing wain. He might be gone now—yes, now, while she stood there thinking of him. Her heart seemed to stop beating as she remembered this. Why had he ever invited her to Mordred? Was it not almost cruel to open the door of that paradise just a little way, only to shut it again when she was half blinded by the glorious light from within? Would he ever think of her, this grand creature with the dark pensive eyes, the tender dreamy eyes that were never the same colour for two consecutive minutes? Was she any thing to him, or was that musical lowering of his voice common to him when he spoke to women? Again and again, and again and again, she went over all the shining ground of that day at Mordred; and the flowers, and glass, and pictures, and painted windows, and hot-house fruit, only made a kind of variegated background, against which *he* stood forth paramount and unapproachable.

She sat and thought of Roland Lansdell, with some scrap of never-to-be-finished work lying in her lap. It was better than reading. A crabbed little old woman who kept the only circulating-library in Graybridge noted a falling-off in her best customer about this time. It was better than reading, to sit through all the length of a hot August afternoon thinking of Roland Lansdell. What romance had ever been written that was equal to this story; this perpetual fiction, with a real hero dominant in every chapter? There was a good deal of repetition in the book, perhaps; but Isabel was never aware of its monotony.

It was all very wicked of course, and a deep and cruel wrong to the simple country surgeon, who ate his dinner, and complained of the under-done condition of the mutton, upon one side of the table, while Isabel read the inexhaustible volume on the other. It was very wicked; but Mrs Gilbert had not yet come to consider the wickedness of her ways. She was a very good wife, very gentle and obedient; and she fancied she had a right to furnish the secret chambers of her mind according to her own pleasure. What did it matter if a strange god reigned in the temple, so long as the doors were for ever closed upon his awful beauty; so long as she rendered all due service to her liege lord and master? He *was* her lord and master, though his fingers were square at the tips, and he had an abnormal capacity for the consumption of spring-onions. Spring-onions! all-the-year-round onions, Isabel thought; for those obnoxious bulbs seemed always in season at Graybridge. She was very wicked; and she thought perpetually of Roland Lansdell, as she had thought of Eugene Aram, and Lara, and Ernest Maltravers—blue-eyed Ernest Maltravers. The blue-eyed heroes were out of fashion now, for was not *he* dark of aspect?

She was very wicked, she was very foolish, very childish. All her life long she had played with her heroines and heroes as other children play with their dolls. Now Edith Dombey was the favourite, and now dark-eyed Zuleika, kneeling for ever at Selim's feet* with an unheeded flower in her hand. Left quite to herself through all her idle girlhood, this foolish child had fed upon three-volume novels and sentimental poetry: and now that she was married and invested with the solemn duties of a wife, she could not throw off the sweet romantic bondage all at once , and take to pies and puddings.

So she made no endeavour to banish Mr Lansdell's image from her mind. If she had recognised the need of such an effort, she would have made it perhaps. But she thought that *he* would go away, and her life would drop back to its dead level, and would be 'all the same as if he had not been.'

But Mr Lansdell did not leave Mordred just yet. Only a week after the never-to-be-forgotten day at the Priory, he came again to Thurston's Crag, and found Isabel sitting under the oak with her books in her lap. She started up as he approached her, looking rather frightened, and with her face flushed and her eyelids drooping. She had not expected him. Demi-gods do not often drop out of the clouds. It is only once in a way that Castor and Pollux* are seen fighting in a mortal fray. Mrs Gilbert sat down again, blushing and trembling; but, oh, so happy, so foolishly, unutterably happy; and Roland Lansdell seated himself by her side and began to talk to her.

He did not make the slightest allusion to that unfortunate swoon which had spoiled the climax of his story. That one subject, which of all others would have been most embarrassing to the Doctor's Wife, was scrupulously avoided by Mr Lansdell. He talked of all manner of things. He had been a *flâneur** pure and simple for the last ten years, and was a consummate master of the art of conversation; so he talked to this ignorant girl of books, and pictures, and foreign cities, and wonderful people, living and dead, of whom she had never heard before. He seemed to know every thing, Mrs Gilbert thought. She felt as if she was before the wonderful gates of a new fairy-land, and Mr Lansdell had the keys, and could open them for her at his will, and could lead her through the dim mysterious pathways into the beautiful region beyond.

Mr Lansdell asked his companion a good many questions about her life at Graybridge, and the books she read. He found that her life was a very idle one, and that she was perpetually reading the same books,—the dear dilapidated volumes of popular novels that were to be had at every circulating-library. Poor little childish creature, who could wonder at her foolish sentimentality? Out of pure philanthropy Roland offered to lend her any of the books in his library.

'If you can manage to stroll this way tomorrow morning, I'll bring you the Life of Robespierre, and Carlyle's *French Revolution.** I don't suppose you'll like Carlyle at first; but he's wonderful when you get accustomed to his style—like a monster brass-band, you know, that stuns you at first with its crashing thunder, until, little by little, you discover the wonderful harmony, and appreciate the beauty of the instrumentation. Shall I bring you Lamartine's *Girondists** as well? That will make a great pile of books, but you need not read them laboriously; you can pick out the pages you like here and there, and we can talk about them afterwards.'

The French Revolution was one of Isabel's pet oases in the history of the universe. A wonderful period, in which a quiet country-bred young woman had only to make her way up to Paris and assassinate a tyrant, and, lo, she became 'a feature' throughout all time. Mr Lansdell had discovered this special fancy in his talk with the Doctor's Wife, and he was pleased to let in the light of positive knowledge on her vague ideas of the chiefs of the Mountain and the martyrs of the Gironde.* Was it not an act of pure philanthropy to clear some of the sentimental mistiness out of that pretty little head? Was it not a good work rather than a harmful one to come now and then to this shadowy resting-place under the oak, and while away an hour or so with this poor little half-educated damsel, who had so much need of some sounder instruction than she had been able to glean, unaided, out of novels and volumes of poetry?

There was no harm in these morning rambles, these meetings, which arose out of the purest chance. There was no harm whatever: especially as Mr Lansdell meant to turn his back upon Midlandshire directly the partridge-shooting was over.

He told Isabel, indirectly, of this intended departure, presently.

'Yes,' he said, 'you must ask me for whatever books you would like to read: and by and by, when I have left Mordred—'

He paused for a moment involuntarily, for he saw that Isabel gave a little shiver.

'When I leave Mordred, at the end of October, you must go to the Priory, and choose the books for yourself. My housekeeper is a very good woman, and she will be pleased to wait upon you.'

So Mrs Gilbert began quite a new course of reading, and eagerly devoured the books which Mr Lansdell brought her; and wrote long extracts from them, and made profile sketches of the heroes, all looking from right to left, and all bearing a strong family resemblance to the master of Mordred Priory. The education of the Doctor's Wife took a grand stride by this means. She sat for hours together reading in the little parlour at Graybridge; and George, whose life was a very busy one, grew to consider her only in her normal state with a book in her hand, and was in no wise offended when she ate her supper with an open volume by the side of her plate, or responded vaguely to his simple talk. Mr Gilbert was quite satisfied. He had never sought for more than this: a pretty little wife to smile upon him when he came home, to brush his hat for him now and then in the passage after breakfast, before he went out for his day's work, and to walk to church twice every Sunday hanging upon his arm. If any one had ever said that such a marriage as this in any way fell short of perfect and entire union, Mr Gilbert would have smiled upon that person as on a harmless madman.

Mr Lansdell met the Doctor's Wife very often: sometimes on the bridge beside the water-mill; sometimes in the meadow-land which surged in emerald billows all about Graybridge and Mordred and Warncliffe. He met her very often. It was no new thing for Isabel to ramble here and there in that lovely rustic paradise: but it was quite a new thing for Mr Lansdell to take such a fancy for pedestrian exercise. The freak could not last long, though: the feast of St Partridge the martyr* was close at hand, and then Mr Lansdell would have something better to do than to dawdle away his time in country lanes and meadows, talking to the Doctor's Wife.

Upon the very eve of that welcome morning which was to set all the breech-loading rifles in Midlandshire popping at those innocent red-breasted victims, George Gilbert received a letter from his old friend and comrade Mr Sigismund Smith, who wrote in very high spirits, and with a great many blots.

'I'm coming down to stop a few days with you, dear old boy,' he wrote, 'to get the London smoke blown out of my hyacinthines, and to go abroad in the meadows to see the young lambs;—are there any young lambs in September, by the by? I want to see what sort of a matron you have made of Miss Isabel Sleaford. Do you remember that day in the garden when you first saw her? A palpable case of spoons there and then! K-k-c-k-k! as Mr Buckstone remarks when he digs his knuckles into the walking-gentleman's ribs. Does she make puddings, and sew on buttons, and fill up the holes in your stockings with wonderful trelliswork? She never would do that sort of thing at Camberwell. I shall give you a week, and I shall spend another week in the bosom of my family; and I shall bring a gun, because it looks well in the railway carriage, you know, especially if it doesn't go off, which I suppose it won't, if it isn't loaded; though, to my mind, there's always something suspicious about the look of firearms, and I should never be surprised to see them explode by spontaneous combustion, or something of that kind. I suppose you've heard of my new three-volume novel—a legitimate three-volume romance, with all the interest concentrated upon one body,—*The Mystery of Mowbray Manor*,—pleasant alliteration of M's, eh?— which is taking the town by storm; that's to say, Camden Town, where I partial-board, and have some opportunity of pushing the book myself by going into all the circulating-libraries I pass, and putting my name down for an early perusal of the first copy. Of course I never go for the book; but if I am the means of making any one simple-minded librarian take a copy of *The M. of M. M.* more than he wants, I feel I have not laboured in vain.'

Mr Smith arrived at Warncliffe by an early train next morning, and came on to Graybridge in an omnibus, which was all spiky with guns. He was in very high spirits, and talked incessantly to Isabel, who had stayed at home to receive him; who had stayed at home when there was just a faint chance that Mr Lansdell might take his morning walk in the direction of Lord Thurston's Crag,—only a faint chance, for was it not the 1st of September; and might not he prefer the slaughter of partridges to those lazy loiterings under the big oak?

Mrs Gilbert gave her old friend a very cordial welcome. She was fond of him, as she might have been of some big brother less ob-jectionable than the ordinary run of big brothers. He had never seen Mr Sleaford's daughter looking so bright and beautiful. A new ele-ment had been introduced into her life. She was happy, unutterably happy, on the mystical threshold of a new existence. She didn't want to be Edith Dombey any longer. Not for all the ruby-velvet gowns and diamond-coronets in the world would she have sacrificed one accidental half-hour on the bridge under Lord Thurston's oak.

She sat at the little table smiling and talking gaily, while the author of *The Mystery of Mowbray Manor* ate about half a quartern of dough made up into puffy Yorkshire cakes, and new-laid eggs and frizzled bacon in proportion. Mr Smith deprecated the rampant state of his appetite by and by, and made a kind of apology for his ravages.

'You see, the worst of going into society is *that*,' he remarked vaguely, 'they see one eat; and it's apt to tell against one in three volumes. It's a great pity that fiction is not compatible with a healthy appetite; but it isn't; and society is so apt to object to one, if one doesn't come up to its expectations. You've no idea what a lot of people have invited me out to tea—ladies, you know—since the publication of *The Mystery of Mowbray Manor*. I used to go at first. But they generally said to me, 'Lor, Mr Smith, you're not a bit like what I fancied you were! I thought you'd be TALL, and DARK, and HAUGHTY-LOOKING, like Montague Manderville in *The Mystery of* —' &c. &c.; and that sort of thing is apt to make a man feel himself an impostor. And if a writer of fiction can't drink hot tea without colouring up, as if he had just pocketed a silver spoon, and it was his guilty conscience, why, my idea is, he'd better stay at home. I don't think any man was ever as good or as bad as his books,' continued Sigismund, reflectively, scraping up a spoonful of that liquid-grease which Mrs Jeffson tersely entitled 'dip.' 'There's a kind of righteous indignation, and a frantic desire to do something splendid for his fellow-creatures, like vaccinating them all over again, or founding a hospital for every body, which a man feels when he's writing—especially late at night, when he's been keeping himself awake with bitter-ale—that seems to ooze away somehow when his copy has gone to the printers. And it's pretty much the same with one's scorn and hate and cynicism. Nobody ever quite comes up to his books. Even Byron, but for turning-down his collars, and walking lame, and dining on biscuits and soda-water, might have been a social failure. I think there's a good deal of Horace Walpole's Inspired Idiocy* in this world. The morning sun shines, and the statue is musical; but all the day there is silence; and at night—in society, I suppose—the sounds are lugubrious. How I do talk, Izzie, and *you* don't say any thing! But I needn't ask if you're happy. I never saw you looking so pretty.'

Isabel blushed. Was she pretty? Oh, she wanted so much to be pretty!

'And I think George may congratulate himself upon having secured the dearest little wife in all Midlandshire.'

Mrs Gilbert blushed a deeper red; but the happy smile died away on her lips. Something, a very vague something as yet, was lurking in what Mr Raymond would have called her 'inner consciousness;' and she thought perhaps George had not such very great reason for self-gratulation.

'I always do as he tells me,' she said naïvely; 'and he's kinder than mamma used to be, and doesn't mind my reading at meals. You know how ma used to go on about it. And I mend his socks— sometimes.' She drew open a drawer, where there were some little bundles of gray woollen stuff, and balls of worsted with big needles stuck across them. 'And, oh, Sigismund,' she exclaimed rather inconsecutively, 'we've been to Mordred—to Mordred Priory—to a luncheon; quite a grand luncheon—pine-apple and ices, and nearly half-a-dozen different kinds of glasses for each person.'

She could talk to Sigismund about Mordred and the master of Mordred. He was not like George, and he would sympathise with her enthusiasm about that earthly paradise.

'Do you know Mordred?' she asked. She felt a kind of pleasure in calling the mansion 'Mordred,' all short, as *he* called it.

'I know the village of Mordred well enough,' Mr Smith answered, 'and I *ought* to know the Priory precious well. The last Mr Lansdell gave my father a good deal of business; and when Roland Lansdell was being coached-up in the Classics by a private tutor, I used to go up to the Priory and read with him. The governor was very glad to get such a chance for me; but I can't say I intensely appreciated the advantage myself, on hot summer afternoons, when there was cricketing on Warncliffe meads.'

'You knew him—you knew Mr Roland Lansdell when he was a boy?' said Isabel, with a little gasp.

'I certainly did, my dear Izzie; but I don't think there's any thing wonderful in that. You couldn't open your eyes much wider if I said I'd known Eugene Aram when he was a boy. I remember Roland Lansdell,' continued Mr Smith, slapping his breakfast-napkin across his dusty boots, and a very jolly young fellow he was; a regular young swell, with a chimney-pot hat and dandy boots, and a gold hunter in his waistcoat-pocket, and no end of pencil-cases, and cricket-bats, and drawing-portfolios, and single-sticks, and fishing-tackle. He taught me fencing,' added Sigismund, throwing himself suddenly into a position that covered one entire side of the little parlour, and making a postman's knock upon the carpet with the sole of his foot.

'Come, Mrs Gilbert,' he said, presently, 'put on your bonnet and come out for a walk. I suppose there's no chance of our seeing George till dinner-time.'

Isabel was pleased to go out. All the world seemed astir upon this bright September morning; and out of doors there was always just a chance of meeting *him*. She fetched her hat, the broad-leaved straw that cast such soft shadows upon her face, and she took up the big green parasol, and was ready to accompany her old friend in a minute.

'I don't want the greetings in the market-place,' Mr Smith said, as they went out into the lane, where it was always very dusty in dry weather, and very muddy when there was rain. 'I know almost every body in Graybridge; and there'll be a round of stereotyped questions and answers to go through as to how I'm getting on "oop in London." I can't tell those people that I earn my bread by writing *The Demon of the Galleys*, or *The Mystery of Mowbray Manor*. Take me for a country walk, Izzie; a regular rustic ramble.'

Mrs Gilbert blushed. That habit of blushing when she spoke or was spoken to had grown upon her lately. Then, after a little pause, she said shyly:

'Thurston's Crag is a pretty place; shall we go there?'

'Suppose we do. That's quite a brilliant thought of yours, Izzie. Thurston's Crag *is* a pretty place, a nice drowsy, lazy old place, where one always goes to sleep, and wishes one had bottled beer. It reminds one of bottled beer, you know, the waterfall,—bottled beer in a rampant state of effervescence.'

Isabel's face was all lighted up with smiles.

'I am so glad you have come to see us, Sigismund,' she said.

She was very glad. She might go to Thurston's Crag now as often as she could beguile Sigismund thitherward, and that haunting sense of something wrong would no longer perplex her in the midst of her unutterable joy. It was unutterable! She had tried to write poetry about it, and had failed dismally, though her heart was making poetry all day long, as wildly, vaguely beautiful as Solomon's Song. She had tried to set her joy to music; but there were no notes on the harpsichord that could express such wondrous melody; though there was indeed one little simple theme, an old-fashioned air, arranged as a waltz, ''Twere vain to tell thee all I feel,' which Isabel would play slowly, again and again, for an hour together, dragging the melody out in lingering legato notes, and listening to its talk about Roland Lansdell.

But all this was very wicked, of course. To-day she could go to Thurston's Crag with a serene front, an unburdened conscience. What could be more intensely proper than this country walk with her mother's late partial-boarder?

They turned into the meadows presently, and as they drew nearer and nearer to the grassy hollow under the cliff, where the miller's cottage and the waterfall were nestled together like jewels in a casket of emerald velvet, the ground seemed to grow unsubstantial under her feet, as if Thurston's Crag had been a phantasmal region suspended in mid air. Would he be there? Her heart was perpetually beating out the four syllables of that simple sentence: Would he be there? It was the 1st of September, and he would be away shooting partridges, perhaps. Oh, was there even the remotest chance that he would be there?

Sigismund handed her across the stile in the last meadow, and then there was only a little bit of smooth verdure between them and the waterfall; but the overhanging branches of the trees intervened, and Isabel could not see yet whether there was any one on the bridge.

But presently the narrow winding path brought them to a break in the foliage. Isabel's heart gave a tremendous bound, and then the colour, which had come and gone so often on her face, faded away altogether. He was there: leaning with his back against the big knotted trunk of the oak, and making a picture of himself, with one arm above his head, plucking the oak-leaves and dropping them into the water. He looked down at the glancing water and the hurrying leaves with a moody dissatisfied scowl. Had he been any thing less than a hero, one might have thought that he looked sulky.

But when the light footsteps came rustling through the long grass, accompanied by the faint fluttering of a woman's garments, his face brightened as suddenly, as if the dense foliage above his head had been swept away by a Titan's axe, and all the sunshine let in upon him. That very expressive face darkened a little when Mr Lansdell saw Sigismund behind the Doctor's Wife; but the cloud was transient. The jealous delusions of a monomaniac could scarcely have transformed Mr Smith into a Cassio. Desdemona might have pleaded for him all day long,* and might have supplied him with any number of pocket-handkerchiefs hemmed and marked by her own fair hands, without causing the Moor a single apprehensive pang.

Mr Lansdell did not recognise the youthful acquaintance, who had stumbled a little way in the thorny path of knowledge by his side; but he saw that Sigismund was a harmless creature; and after he had bared his handsome head before Isabel, he gave Mr Smith a friendly little nod of general application.

'I have let the keepers shoot the first of the partridges,' he said, dropping his voice almost to a whisper as he bent over Mrs Gilbert, 'and I have been here ever since ten o'clock.'

It was past one now. He had been there three hours, Isabel thought, waiting for her.

Yes, it had gone so far as this already. But he was to go away at the end of October. He was to go away, it would all be over, and the world come to an end by the 1st of November.

There was a little pile of books upon the seat under the tree. Mr Lansdell pushed them off the bench, and tumbled them ignominiously among the long grass and weeds beneath it. Isabel saw them fall, and uttered a little exclamation of surprise.

'You have brought me——' she began; but to her astonishment Roland checked her with a frown, and began to talk about the waterfall, and the trout that were to be caught in the season lower down in the stream. Mr Lansdell was more worldly wise than the Doctor's Wife, and he knew that the books brought there for her might seem slightly suggestive of an appointment. There had been no appointment, of course; but there was always a chance of finding Isabel under Lord Thurston's oak. Had she not gone there constantly, long ago, when Mr Lansdell was lounging in Grecian Islands, and eating ices under the colonnades of Venice? and was it strange that she should go there now?

I should become very wearisome, were I to transcribe all that was said that morning. It was a very happy morning,—a long, idle sun-shiny pause in the business of life. Roland recognised an old ac-quaintance in Sigismund Smith presently, and the two young men talked gaily of those juvenile days at Mordred. They talked pleas-antly of all manner of things. Mr Lansdell must have been quite ardently attached to Sigismund in those early days, if one might judge of the past by the present; for he greeted his old acquaintance with absolute effusion, and sketched out quite a little royal progress of rustic enjoyment for the week Sigismund was to stay at Graybridge.

'We'll have a picnic,' he said: 'you remember we talked about a picnic, Mrs Gilbert. We'll have a picnic at Waverly Castle; there isn't a more delightfully inconvenient place for a picnic in all Midlandshire. One can dine on the top of the western tower, in actual danger of one's life. You can write to your uncle Raymond, Smith, and ask him to join us, with the two nieces, who are really most amiable children; so estimably unintellectual, and no more in the way than a little extra furniture: you mayn't want it; but if you've space enough for it in your rooms, it doesn't in the least inconvenience you. This is Thursday; shall we say Saturday for my picnic? I mean it to be my picnic, you know; a bachelor's picnic, with all the most obviously necessary items forgotten, I daresay. I think the salad-dressing and the champagne-nippers are the legiti-mate things to forget, are they not? Do you think Saturday will suit you and the Doctor, Mrs Gilbert? I should like it to be Saturday, because you must all dine with me at Mordred on Sunday, in order that we may drink success and a dozen editions to the—what's the name of your novel, Smith? Shall it be Saturday, Mrs Gilbert?'

Isabel only answered by deepening blushes and a confused mur-mur of undistinguishable syllables. But her face lighted up with a look of rapture that was wont to illumine it now and then, and which Mr Lansdell thought was the most beautiful expression of the human countenance that he had ever seen, out of a picture or in one. Sigismund answered for the Doctor's Wife. Yes, he was sure Saturday would do capitally. He would settle it all with George, and he would answer for his uncle Raymond and the orphans; and he would answer for the weather even, for the matter of that. He further accepted the invitation to dine at Mordred on Sunday, for himself and his host and hostess.

'You know you can, Izzie,' he said, in answer to Mrs Gilbert's deprecating murmur; 'it's mere nonsense talking about prior engagements in a place like Graybridge, where nobody ever does go out to dinner, and a tea-party on a Sunday is looked upon as wickedness. Lansdell always was a jolly good fellow, and I'm not a bit surprised to find that he's a jolly good fellow still; because if you train up a twig in the way it's inclined, the tree will not depart from it, as the philosopher has observed. I want to see Mordred again, most particularly; for, to tell you the truth, Lansdell,' said Mr Smith, with a gush of candour, 'I was thinking of taking the Priory for the scene of my next novel. There's a mossy kind of gloom about the eastern side of the house and the old square garden, that I think would take with the general public; and with regard to the cellarage,' cried Sigismund, kindling with sudden enthusiasm, 'I've been through it with a lantern, and I'm sure there's accommodation for a perfect regiment of bodies; which would be a consideration if I was going to do the story in penny numbers; for in penny numbers one body always leads on to another, and you never know, when you begin, how far you may be obliged to go. However, my present idea is three volumes. What do you think now, Lansdell, of the eastern side of the Priory; deepening the gloom, you know, and letting the gardens all run to seed, with rank grass and a blasted cedar or so, and introducing rats behind the panelling, and a general rottenness, and perhaps a ghostly footstep in the corridor, or a periodical rustling behind the tapestry? What do you say, now, to Mordred, taken in connexion with twin brothers hating each other from infancy, and both in love with the same woman, and one of them—the darkest twin, with a scar on his forehead—walling up the young female in a deserted room, while the more amiable twin without a scar devotes his life to searching for her in foreign climes, accompanied by a detective officer and a bloodhound? It's only a rough idea at present,' concluded Mr Smith modestly; 'but I shall work it out in railway trains and pedestrian exercise. There's nothing like railway travelling or pedestrian exercise for working out an idea of that kind.'

Mr Lansdell declared that his house and grounds were entirely at the service of his young friend; and it was settled that the picnic should take place on Saturday, and the dinner-party on Sunday; and George Gilbert's acquiescence in the two arrangements was guaranteed by his friend Sigismund. And then the conversation wandered away into more fanciful regions; and Roland and Mr Smith talked of men and books, while Isabel listened, only chiming in now and then with little sentimental remarks, to which the master of Mordred Priory listened as intently as if the speaker had been a Madame de Staël. She may not have said any thing very wonderful; but those were wonderful blushes that came and went upon her pale face as she spoke, fluttering and fitful as the shadow of a butterfly's wing hovering above a white rose; and the golden light in her eyes was more wonderful than any thing out of a fairy tale.

But he always listened to her, and he always looked at her from a certain position which he had elected for himself in relation to her. She was a beautiful child; and he, a man of the world, very much tired and worn out by the ordinary men and women of the world, was half-amused, half-interested, by her simplicity and sentimentality. He did no wrong, therefore, by cultivating her acquaintance when accident threw her, as had happened so often lately, in his way. There was no harm, so long as he held firmly to the position he had chosen for himself; so long as he contemplated this young gushing creature from across all the width of his own wasted youth and useless days; so long as he looked at her as a bright unapproachable being, as much divided from him by the differences in their natures, as by the fact that she was the lawful wife of Mr George Gilbert of Graybridge-on-the-Wayverne.

Mr Lansdell tried his uttermost to hold firmly to this self-elected position with regard to Isabel. He was always alluding to his own age; an age not to be computed, as he explained to Mrs Gilbert, by the actual number of years in which he had inhabited this lower world, but to be calculated rather by the waste of those wearisome years, and the general decadence that had fallen upon him thereby.

'I suppose, according to the calendar, I am only your senior by a decade,' he said to Izzie one day; 'but when I hear you talk about your books and your heroes, I feel as if I had lived a century.'

He took the trouble to make little speeches of this kind very often, for Mrs Gilbert's edification; and there were times when the Doctor's Wife was puzzled, and even wounded, by his talk and his manner, which were both subject to abrupt transitions, that were perplexing to a simple person. Mr Lansdell was capricious and fitful in his moods, and would break off in the middle of some delicious little bit of sentiment, worthy of Ernest Maltravers or Eugene Aram himself, with a sneering remark about the absurdity of the style of conversation into which he had been betrayed; and would sit moodily pulling his favourite retriever's long ears for ten minutes or so, and then get up and wish Isabel an abrupt good-morning. Mrs Gilbert took these changes of manner very deeply to heart. It was her fault, no doubt; she had said something silly; or affected, perhaps. Had not her brother Horace been apt to jeer at her as a mass of affectation, because she preferred Byron to *Bell's Life*,* and was more interested in Edith Dombey than in the favourite for the Oaks?* She had said something that had sounded affected, though uttered in all simplicity of heart; and Mr Lansdell had been disgusted by her talk. Contempt from *him*—she always thought of him in italics—was very bitter! She would never, never go to Thurston's Crag again. But then, after one of these abruptly-unpleasant 'good-mornings,' Mr Lansdell was very apt to call at Graybridge. He wanted Mr Gilbert to go and see one of the men on the home-farm, who seemed in a very bad way, poor fellow, and ought not to be allowed to go on any longer without medical advice. Mr Lansdell was very fond of looking-up cases for the Graybridge surgeon. How good he was! Isabel thought; he in whom goodness was in a manner a superogatory attribute; since heroes who were dark, and pensive, and handsome were not called upon to be otherwise virtuous. How good he was! he who was as scornfully depreciative of his own merits as if the bones of another Mr Clarke had been bleaching in some distant cave in imperishable evidence of his guilt. How good he was! and he had not been offended or disgusted with her when he left her so suddenly; for to-day he was kinder to her than ever, and lingered for nearly an hour in the unshaded parlour, in the hope that the surgeon would come in.

But when Mr Lansdell walked slowly homeward after such a visit as this, there was generally a dissatisfied look upon his face, which was altogether inconsistent with the pleasure he had appeared to take in his wasted hour at Graybridge. He was inconsistent. It was in his nature, as a hero, to be so, no doubt. There were times when he forgot all about that yawning chasm of years which was supposed to divide him from any possibility of sympathy with Isabel Gilbert; there were times when he forgot himself so far as to be very young and happy in his loitering visits at Graybridge, playing idle scraps of extempore melody on the wizen old harpsichord, sketching little bunches of foliage and frail Italian temples, and pretty girlish faces

with big black eyes, not altogether unlike Isabel's, or strolling out
into the flat old-fashioned garden, where Mr Jeffson lolled on his
spade, and made a rustic figure of himself, between a middle distance of brown earth and a foreground of cabbage-plants. I am
bound to say that Mr Jeffson, who was generally courtesy itself to
every living creature, from the pigs to whom he carried savoury
messes of skim-milk and specky potatoes, to the rector of Graybridge, who gave him 'good-evening' sometimes as he reposed
himself in the cool twilight upon the wooden gate leading into
George Gilbert's stable-yard,—I am bound to say that Mr Jeffson
was altogether wanting in politeness to Roland Lansdell, and
was apt to follow the young man with black and evil looks as he
strolled by Izzie's side along the narrow walks, or stooped now and
then to extricate her muslin dress from the thorny branches of a
gooseberry-bush.

Once, and once only, did Isabel Gilbert venture to remonstrate
with her husband's retainer on the subject of his surly manner to
the master of Mordred Priory. Her remonstrance was a very faint
one, and she was stooping over a rose-bush while she talked, and
was very busy plucking off the withered leaves, and now and then
leaves that were not withered.

'I'm afraid you don't like Mr Lansdell, Jeff,' she said. She had
been very much attached to the gardener, and very confidential to
him, before Roland's advent, and had done a little amateur gardening under his instructions, and had told him all about Eugene Aram
and the murder of Mr Clarke. 'You seemed quite cross to him this
morning when he called to see George, and to inquire about the
man that had the rheumatic fever; I'm afraid you don't like him.'

She bent her face very low over the rose-bush; so low that her
hair, which, though much tidier than of old, was never quite as
neatly or compactly adjusted as it might have been, fell forward like
a veil, and entangled itself amongst the spiky branches.

'Oh, yes, Mrs George; I like him well enough. There's not a
young gentleman that I ever set eyes on as I think nobler to look at,
or pleasanter to talk to, than Mr Lansdell, or more free and open-
like in his manner to poor folk. But, like a many other good things,
Mrs George, Mr Lansdell's only good, to my mind, when he's in his
place; and I tell you, frank and candid, as I think he's never more
out of his place than when he's hanging about yon house, or idling

away his time in this garden. It isn't for me, Mrs George, to say who should come here, and who shouldn't; but there was a kind of relationship between me and my master's dead mother. I can see her now, poor young thing, with her bright fair face, and her fair hair blowing across it, as she used to come towards me along the very pathway on which you're standing now, Mrs George; and all that time comes back to me as if it was yesterday. I never knew any one lead a better or a purer life. I stood beside her deathbed, and I never saw a happier death, nor one that seemed to bring it closer home to a man's mind that there was something happier and better still to come afterwards. But there was never no Mr Roland Lansdell in those days, Mrs George, scribbling heads with no bodies to 'em, and trees without any stumps, on scraps of paper, or playing tunes, or otherwise dawdling like, while my master was out o' doors. And I remember, as almost the last words that sweet young creature says, was something about having done her duty to her dear husband, and never having known one thought as she could wish to keep hid from him or Heaven.'

Mrs Gilbert dropped down on her knees before the rose-bush, with her face still shrouded by her hair, and her hands still busy among the leaves. When she looked up, which was not until after a lapse of some minutes, Mr Jeffson was ever so far off, digging potatoes, with his back turned towards her. There had been nothing unkind in his manner of speaking to her; indeed there had even been a special kindness and tenderness in his tones, a sorrowful gentleness, that went home to her heart.

She thought of her husband's dead mother a good deal that night, in a reverential spirit, but with a touch of envy also. Was not the first Mrs Gilbert specially happy to have died young? was it not an enormous privilege so to die, and to be renowned ever afterwards as having done something meritorious, when, for the matter of that, other people would be very happy to die young if they could? Isabel thought of this with some sense of injury. Long ago, when her brothers had been rude to her, and her stepmother had upbraided her on the subject of a constitutional unwillingness to fetch butter, and 'back' teaspoons, she had wished to die young, leaving a legacy of perpetual remorse to those unfeeling relatives. But the gods had never cared any thing about her. She had kept on wet boots sometimes after 'backing' spoons in bad weather, in the fond hope that she might thereby fall into a decline. She had pictured herself in the little bedroom at Camberwell, fading by inches, with becoming hectic spots on her cheeks, and imploring her step-mother to call her early; which desire would have been the converse of the popular idea of the ruling passion, inasmuch as in her normal state of health Miss Sleaford was wont to lie late of a morning, and remonstrate drowsily, with the voice of the sluggard, when roughly roused from some foolish dream, in which she wore a ruby-velvet gown that *wouldn't* keep hooked, and was beloved by a duke who was always inconsistently changing into the young man at the butter-shop.

All that evening Isabel pondered upon the simple history of her husband's mother, and wished that she could be very, very good like her and die early with holy words upon her lips. But in the midst of such thoughts as these she found herself wondering whether the hands of Mr Gilbert the elder were red and knobby like those of his son, whether he employed the same bootmaker, and entertained an equal predilection for spring-onions and Cheshire cheese. And from the picture of her deathbed Isabel tried in vain to blot away a figure that had no right to be there,—the figure of some one who would be fetched post-haste, at the last moment, to hear her dying words, and to see her die.

CHAPTER VI

THE SECOND WARNING

Mr Roland Lansdell did not invite Lady Gwendoline or her father to that bachelor picnic which he was to give at Waverly Castle. He had a kind of instinctive knowledge that Lord Ruysdale's daughter would not relish that sylvan entertainment.

'She'd object to poor Smith, I daresay,' Roland said to himself, 'with his sporting-cut clothes and his slang-phrases, and his perpetual talk about three-volume novels and penny numbers. No, I don't think it would do to invite Gwendoline; she'd be sure to object to Smith.'

Mr Lansdell said this, or thought this, a good many times upon the day before the picnic; but it may be that there was a lurking idea in his mind that Lady Gwendoline might object to the presence of some one other than Mr Smith in the little assembly that had been planned under Lord Thurston's oak. Perhaps Roland Lansdell,—who hated hypocrisy as men who are by no means sinless are yet apt to hate the base and crawling vices of mankind,—had become a hypocrite all at once, and wanted to deceive himself; or it may be that the weak slope of his handsome chin, and the want of breadth in a certain region of his skull, were the outward and visible signs of such a weak and vacillating nature, that what was true with regard to him one minute was false the next; so that out of this perpetual changefulness of thought and purpose there grew a confusion in the young man's mind, like the murmur of many streamlets rushing into one broad river, along whose tide the feeble swimmer was drifted to the very sea he wanted so much to avoid.

'The picnic will be a pleasant thing for young Smith,' Mr Lansdell thought; 'and it'll please the children to make themselves bilious amongst ruins; and that dear good Raymond always enjoys himself with young and happy people. I cannot see that the picnic can be any thing but pleasant; and, for the matter of that, I've a good mind to send the baskets early by Stephens, who could make himself useful all day, and not go at all myself. I could run up to town under pretence of particular business, and amuse myself somehow for a day or two. Or, for that matter, I might go over to Baden or Hombourg, and finish the autumn there. Heaven knows I don't want to do any harm.'

But, in spite of all this uncertainty and vacillation of mind, Mr Lansdell took a great deal of interest in the preparations for the picnic. He did not trouble himself about the magnificent game-pie which was made for the occasion, the crust of which was as highly glazed as a piece of modern Wedgwood. He did not concern himself about the tender young fowls, nestling in groves of parsley; nor the tongue, floridly decorated with vegetable productions chiselled into the shapes of impossible flowers; nor the York ham, also in a high state of polish, like fine Spanish mahogany, and encircled about the knuckle by pure white fringes of cut paper.

The comestibles to which Mr Lansdell directed his attention were of a more delicate and fairy-like description, such as women and children are apt to take delight in. There must be jellies and creams, Mr Lansdell said, whatever difficulty there might be in the convey-ance of such compositions. There must be fruit; he attended himself to the cutting of hothouse grapes and peaches, the noblest pine-apple in the long range of forcing-houses, and picturesque pears with leaves still clinging to the stalk. He ordered bouquets to be cut, one a very pyramid of choice flowers, chiefly white and innocent-looking; and he took care to select richly-scented blossoms, and he touched the big nosegay caressingly with his slim white fingers, and looked at it with a tender smile on his dark face, as if the flowers had a language for him,—and so they had; but it was by no means that stereotyped dictionary of substantives and adjectives popularly called the language of flowers.

It was nothing new for him to choose a bouquet. Had he not dispensed a small fortune in the Rue de la Paix and in the Faubourg St Honoré, in exchange for big bunches of roses and myosotis, and Cape-jasmine and waxy camellias; which he saw afterwards lying on the velvet cushion of an opera-box, or withering in the warm atmosphere of a boudoir? He was not a good man,—he had not led a good life. Pretty women had called him 'Enfant!' in the dim mysterious shades of lamplit conservatories, upon the curtain-shrouded thresholds of moonlit balconies. Arch soubrettes in little Parisian theatres, bewitching Marthons and Margots and Jeannettons, with brooms in their hands and diamonds in their ears, had smiled at him, and acted at him, and sung at him, as he lounged in the dusky recesses of a cavernous box. He had not led a good life. He was not a good man. But he was a man who had never sinned with impunity. With him remorse always went hand-in-hand with wrong-doing. [Heaven knows that I write of him in sober earnest and sincerity. I have seen and known him, or such as him. He is no lay-figure upon which I would hang cheap commonplace moralities; but a creature of real flesh and blood, and mind and soul, whose picture I would paint— if I can. If he does not seem real after all, it is because my pen is feeble, and not because this man has not really lived and suffered, and sinned and repented.]*

In all his life, I doubt if there was any period in which Mr Lansdell had ever so honestly and truly wished to do aright as he did just now. His mind seemed to have undergone a kind of purification in the still atmosphere of those fair Midlandshire glades and meads. There was even a purifying influence in the society of such a woman as Isabel Gilbert; so different from all the other women he had known, so deficient in the merest rudiments of worldly wisdom.

*

Mr Lansdell did not go to London. When the ponderous old fly from Graybridge drove up a narrow winding lane and emerged upon the green rising ground below the gates of Waverly Castle, Roland was standing under the shadow of the walls with a big bunch of hothouse flowers in his hand. He was in very high spirits; for to-day he had cast care to the winds. Why should he not enjoy this innocent pleasure of a rustic ramble with simple country-bred people and children? He laid some little stress upon the presence of the orphans. Yes, he would enjoy himself for to-day; and then to-morrow—ah! by the by, to-morrow Mr and Mrs Gilbert and Sigismund Smith were to dine with him. After to-morrow it would be all over, and he would be off to the Continent again, to begin the old wearisome rounds once more; to eat the same dinners at the same restaurants; the same little suppers after the opera, in stuffy entresol chambers,* all crimson-velvet, and gaslight, and glass, and gilding; to go to the same balls in the same gorgeous saloons, and to see the same beautiful faces shining upon him in their monotonous splendour.

'I might have turned country gentleman, and have been good for something in this world,' thought Roland Lansdell, 'if—'

Mr Lansdell was not alone. Charles Raymond and the orphans had arrived; and they all came forward together to welcome Isabel and her companions. Mr Raymond had always been very kind to his nieces' governess, but he seemed especially kind to her to-day. He interposed himself between Roland and the door of the fly, and assisted Isabel to alight. He slipped her hand under his arm with a pleasant friendliness of manner, and looked with a triumphant smile at the rest of the gentlemen.

'I mean to appropriate Mrs Gilbert for the whole of this day,' he said cheerily; 'and I shall give her a full account of Waverly, looked upon from an archaeological, historical, and legendary point of view. Never mind your flowers now, Roland; it's a very charming bouquet, but you don't suppose Mrs Gilbert is going to carry it about all day? Take it into the lodge yonder, and ask them to put it in water; and in the evening, if you're very good, Mrs Gilbert shall take it home to ornament her parlour at Graybridge.'

The gates were opened, and they went in; Isabel arm-in-arm with Mr Raymond.

Roland placed himself presently on one side of Isabel; but Mr

Raymond was so very instructive about John of Gaunt* and the Tudors,* that all Mrs Gilbert's attention was taken up in the effort to understand his discourse, which was very pleasant and lively, in spite of its instructive nature. George Gilbert looked at the ruins with the same awful respect with which he had regarded the pictures at Mordred. He was tolerably familiar with those empty halls, those roofless chambers, and open doorways, and ivy-festooned windows; but he always looked at them with the same reverence, mingled with a vague wonder as to what it was that people admired in ruins, seeing that they generally made such short work of inspecting them, and seemed so pleased to get away and take refreshment. Ruins and copious refreshment were associated in Mr Gilbert's mind; and, indeed, there does seem to be a natural union between ivied walls and lobster-salad, crumbling turrets and cold chicken; just as the domes of Greenwich Hospital, the hilly park beyond, and the rippling water in the foreground must be for ever and ever associated with flounder souchy and devilled whitebait. Mr Sigismund Smith was delighted with Waverly. He had rambled amongst the ruins often enough in his boyhood; but to-day he saw every thing from a new point of view, and he groped about in all manner of obscure corners, with a pencil and pocket-book in his hand, laying the plan of a thrilling serial, and making himself irrecognisable with dust. His friends found him on one occasion stretched at full length amongst crisp fallen leaves in a recess that had once been a fireplace, with a view to ascertain whether it was long enough to accommodate a body. He climbed fearful heights, and planned perilous leaps and 'hairbreadth 'scapes,' deadly dangers in the way of walks along narrow cornices high up above empty space; such feats as hold the reader with suspended breath, and make the continued expenditure of his weekly penny almost a certainty.

The orphans accompanied Mr Smith, and were delighted with the little chambers that they found in nooks and corners of the mouldering castle. How delightful to have chairs and tables and kitchen utensils, and to live there for ever and ever, and keep house for themselves! They envied the vulgar children who lived in the square tower by the gate, and saw ruins every day of their lives.

It was a very pleasant morning altogether. There was a strangely mingled feeling of satisfaction and annoyance in Roland Lansdell's mind, as he strolled beside Isabel, and listened, or appeared to

listen, to Mr Raymond's talk. He would like to have had Isabel's
little hand lying lightly on *his* arm; he would like to have seen those
wondering black eyes lifted to his face; he would like her to have
heard the romantic legends belonging to the ruined walls and roofless
banquet-chambers from him. And yet, perhaps, it was better as it
was. He was going away very soon—immediately indeed; he was
going where that simple pleasure would be impossible to him, and it
was better not to lull himself in soft delights that were so soon to be
taken away from his barren life. Yes, his barren life. He had come to
think of his fate with bitter repining, and to look upon himself as,
somehow or other, cruelly ill-used by Providence.

But, in spite of Mr Raymond, he contrived to sit next Isabel at
dinner, which was served by and by in a lovely sheltered nook under
the walls, where there was no chance of the salt being blown into the
green-gage tart, or the custards spilt over the lobster-salad. Mr
Lansdell had sent a couple of servants to arrange matters; and the
picnic was not a bit like an ordinary picnic, where things are lost
and forgotten, and where there is generally confusion by reason of
every body's desire to assist in the preparations. This was altogether
a *recherché* banquet; but scarcely so pleasant as those more rural
feasts, in which there is a paucity of tumblers, and no forks to speak
of. The champagne was iced, the jellies quivered in the sunlight,
every thing was in perfect order; and if Mr Raymond had not insisted upon sending away the two men, who wanted to wait at table,
with the gloomy solemnity of everyday life, it would scarcely have
been worthy the name of picnic. But with the two solemn servants
out of the way, and with Sigismund, very red and dusty and noisy,
to act as butler, matters were considerably improved.

The sun was low when they left the ruins of the feast for the two
solemn men to clear away. The sun was low, and the moon had
risen, so pale as to be scarcely distinguishable from a faint summer-
cloud high up in the clear opal heaven. Mr Raymond took Isabel up
by a winding staircase to the top of a high turret, beneath which
spread green meads and slopes of verdure, where once had been a
lake and pleasaunce. The moon grew silvery before they reached the
top of the turret, where there was room enough for a dozen people.
Roland went with them, of course, and sat on one of the broad stone
battlements looking out at the still night, with his profile defined as
sharply as a cameo against the deepening blue of the sky. He was

very silent, and his silence had a distracting influence on Isabel, who made vain efforts to understand what Mr Raymond was saying to her, and gave vague answers every now and then; so vague that Charles Raymond left off talking presently, and seemed to fall into as profound a reverie as that which kept Mr Lansdell silent.

To Isabel's mind there was a pensive sweetness in that silence, which was in some way in harmony with the scene and the atmosphere. She was free to watch Roland's face now that Mr Raymond had left off talking to her, and she did watch it; that still profile whose perfect outline grew more and more distinct against the moonlit sky. If any body could have painted his portrait as he sat there, with one idle hand hanging listless among the ivy-leaves, blanched in the moonlight, what a picture it would have made! What was he thinking of? Were his thoughts far away in some foreign city with dark-eyed Clotilde? or the Duchess with the glittering hair, who had loved him and been false to him long ago, when he was an alien, and recorded the history of his woes in heart-breaking verse, in fitful numbers, larded with scraps of French and Latin, alternately despairing and sarcastic? Isabel solemnly believed in Clotilde and the glittering Duchess, and was steeped in self-abasement and humiliation when she compared herself with those vague and splendid creatures.

Roland spoke at last: if there had been any thing commonplace or worldly wise in what he said, there must have been a little revulsion in Isabel's mind; but his talk was happily attuned to the place and the hour; incomprehensible and mysterious,—like the deepening night in the heavens.

'I think there is a point at which a man's life comes to an end,' he said. 'I think there is a fitting and legitimate close to every man's existence, that is as palpable as the falling of a curtain when a play is done. He goes on living; that is to say, eating and drinking, and inhaling so many cubic feet of fresh air every day, for half a century afterwards, perhaps; but that is nothing. Do not the actors live after the play is done, and the curtain has fallen? Hamlet goes home, and eats his supper, and scolds his wife and snubs his children; but the exaltation and the passion that created him Prince of Denmark have died out like the coke-ashes of the green-room fire. Surely that after-life is the penalty, the counter-balance, of brief golden hours of hope and pleasure. I am glad the Lansdells are not a long-lived race,

Raymond; for I think the play is finished, and the dark curtain has
dropped, for me!'

'Humph!' muttered Mr Raymond; 'wasn't there something to
that effect in the *Alien*? It's very pretty, Roland,—that sort of dismal
prettiness which is so much in fashion nowadays; but don't you
think if you were to get up a little earlier in the morning, and spend
a couple of hours amongst the stubble with your dogs and gun, so as
to get an appetite for your breakfast, you might get over that sort of
thing?'

Isabel turned a mutely reproachful gaze upon Mr Raymond, but
Roland burst out laughing.

'I daresay I talk like a fool,' he said; 'I feel like one sometimes.'

'When are you going abroad again?'

'In a month's time. But why should I go abroad?' asked Mr
Lansdell, with a dash of fierceness in the sudden change of his tone;
'why should I go? what is there for me to do there better than here?
what good am I there more than I am here?' He asked these questions of the sky as much as of Mr Raymond; and the philosopher of
Conventford did not feel himself called upon to answer them. Mr
Lansdell relapsed into the silence that so puzzled Isabel; and nothing more was said until the voice of George Gilbert sounded from
below, deeply sonorous amongst the walls and towers, calling to
Isabel.

'I must go,' she said; 'I daresay the fly is ready to take us back.
Good-night, Mr Raymond; good-night, Mr Lansdell.'

She held out her hand, as if doubtful to whom she should first
offer it; Roland had never changed his position until this moment,
but he started up suddenly now, like a man awakened from a dream.
'You are going?' he said; 'so soon!'

'So soon! it is very late, I think,' Mrs Gilbert answered; 'at least,
I mean we have enjoyed ourselves very much; and the time has
passed so quickly.'

She thought it was her duty to say something of this kind to him,
as the giver of the feast; and then she blushed and grew confused,
thinking she had said too much.

'Good-night, Mr Lansdell.'

'But I am coming down with you to the gate,' said Roland; 'do
you think we could let you go down those slippery stairs by yourself, to fall and break your neck and haunt the tower by moonlight

for ever afterwards, a pale ghost in shadowy muslin drapery? Here's Mr Gilbert,' he added, as the top of George's hat made itself visible upon the winding staircase; 'but I'm sure I know the turret better than he does, and I shall take you under my care.'

He took her hand as he spoke, and led her down the dangerous winding-way as carefully and tenderly as if she had been a little child. Her hand did not tremble as it rested in his; but something like a mysterious winged creature that had long been imprisoned in her breast, seemed to break its bonds all at once, and float away from her towards him. She thought it was her long-imprisoned soul, perhaps, that so left her to become a part of his. If that slow down-ward journey could have lasted for ever—if she could have gone down, down, down with Roland Lansdell into some fathomless pit, until at last they came to a luminous cavern and still moonlit water, where there was a heavenly calm—and death! But the descent did not last very long, careful as Roland was of every step; and there was the top of George's hat bobbing about in the moonlight all the time; for the surgeon had lost his way in the turret, and only came down at last very warm and breathless when Isabel called to him from the bottom of the stairs.

Sigismund and the orphans appeared at the same moment. Mr Raymond had followed Roland and Isabel very closely, and they all went together to the fly.

'Remember to-morrow,' Mr Lansdell said generally to the Graybridge party as they took their seats. 'I shall expect you as soon as the afternoon service is over. I know you are regular church-goers at Graybridge. Couldn't you come to Mordred for the afternoon service, by the by?—the church is well worth seeing.' There was a little discussion; and it was finally agreed that Mr and Mrs George Gilbert and Sigismund should go to Mordred church on the follow-ing afternoon; and then there was a good deal of hand-shaking be-fore the carriage drove away, and disappeared behind the sheltering hedges that screened the winding road.

'I'll see you and the children off, Raymond,' Mr Lansdell said, 'before I go myself.'

'I'm not going away just this minute,' Mr Raymond answered gravely; 'I want to have a little talk with you first. There's some-thing I particularly want to say to you. Mrs Primshaw,' he cried to the landlady of the little inn just opposite the castle-gates, a good-natured rosy-faced young woman, who was standing on the thresh-old of her door watching the movements of the gentlefolks, 'will you take care of my little girls, and see whether their wraps are warm enough for the drive home, while I take a moonlight stroll with Mr Lansdell?'

Mrs Primshaw declared that nothing would give her greater pleasure than to see to the comfort of the young ladies. So the orphans skipped across the moonlit road, nowise sorry to take shelter in the pleasant bar-parlour, all rosy and luminous with a cosy handful of bright fire in the tiniest grate ever seen out of a doll's-house.

Mr Lansdell and Mr Raymond walked along the lonely road under the shadow of the castle-wall, and for some minutes neither of them spoke. Roland evinced no curiosity about, or interest in, that unknown something which Mr Raymond had to say to him; but there was a kind of dogged sullenness in the carriage of his head, the fixed expression of his face, that seemed to promise badly for the pleasantness of the interview.

Perhaps Mr Raymond saw this, and was rather puzzled how to commence the conversation; at any rate, when he did begin, he began very abruptly, taking what one might venture to call a conversational header.

'Roland,' he said, 'this won't do!'

'What won't do?' asked Mr Lansdell, coolly.

'Of course, I don't set up for being your Mentor,' returned Mr Raymond, 'or for having any right to lecture you, or dictate to you. The tie of kinsmanship between us is a very slight one; though, as far as that goes, God knows that I could scarcely love you better than I do, if I were your father. But if I *were* your father, I don't suppose you'd listen to me, or heed me. Men never do, in such matters as these. I've lived my life, Roland, and I know too well how little good advice can do in such a case as this. But I can't see you going wrong without trying to stop you: and for that poor, honest-hearted fellow yonder, for his sake, I must speak, Roland. Have you any consciousness of the mischief you're doing? have you any knowledge of the bottomless pit of sin, and misery, and shame, and horror that you are digging before that foolish woman's feet?'

'Why, Raymond,' cried Mr Lansdell, with a laugh,—not a very hearty laugh, but something like that hollow mockery of merriment with which a man greets the narration of some old Joe-Millerism that has been familiar to him from his childhood,—'why, Raymond, you're as obscure as a modern poet? What do you mean? Who's the honest-hearted fellow? and who's the foolish woman? and what's the nature of the business altogether?'

'Roland, let us be frank with each other, at least. Do you remember how you told me once that, when every bright illusion had dropped away from you one by one, honour still remained,—a poor pallid star, compared to those other lights that had perished in the darkness, but still bright enough to keep you in the straight road? Has that last light gone out with the rest, Roland, my poor melancholy boy,—my boy whom I have loved as my own child?— will the day ever come when I shall have to be ashamed of Anna Lansdell's only son?'

His mother's name had always something of a spell for Roland. His head, so proudly held before, drooped suddenly, and he walked on in silence for some little time. Mr Raymond was also silent. He had drawn some good augury from the altered carriage of the young man's head, and was loth to disturb the current of his thoughts. When Roland did at last raise his head, he turned and looked his friend and kinsman full in the face.

'Raymond,' he said, 'I am not a good man;' he was very fond of making this declaration, and I think he fancied that in so doing he made some vague atonement for his shortcomings: 'I am not a good man, but I am no hypocrite; I will not lie to you, or prevaricate with you. Perhaps there may be some justification for what you said just now, or there might be if I were a different sort of man. But, as it is, I give you my honour you are mistaken. I have been digging no pit for a woman's innocent footsteps to stray into. I have been plotting no treachery against that honest fellow yonder. Remember, I do not by any means hold myself blameless. I have admired Mrs Gilbert just as one admires a pretty child, and I have allowed myself to be amused by her sentimental talk, and have lent her books, and may perhaps have paid her a little more attention that I ought to have done. But I have done nothing deliberately. I have never for one moment had any purpose in my mind, or mixed her image with so much as a dream of—of—any tangible form. I have drifted into a dangerous position, or a position that might be dangerous to an-other man; but I can drift out of it as easily as I drifted in. I shall leave Midlandshire next month.'

'And to-morrow the Gilberts dine with you at Mordred; and all through this month there will be the chance of your seeing Mrs Gilbert, and lending her more books, and paying her more attention; and so on. It is not so much that I doubt you, Roland; I cannot think so meanly of you as to doubt your honour in this business. But you are doing mischief; you are turning this silly girl's head. It is no kindness to lend her books; it is no kindness to invite her to Mordred, and to show her brief glimpses of a life that never can be hers. If you want to do a good deed, and to elevate her life out of its present dead level, make her your almoner, and give her a hundred a year to distribute amongst her husband's poor patients. The weak unhappy child is perishing for want of some duty to perform upon this earth; some necessary task to keep her busy from day to day, and to make a link between her husband and herself. Roland, I do believe that you are as good and generous-minded a fellow as ever an old bachelor was proud of. My dear boy, let me feel prouder of you than I have ever felt yet. Leave Midlandshire to-morrow morning. It will be easy to invent some excuse for going. Go to-morrow, Roland.'

'I will,' answered Mr Lansdell, after a brief pause; 'I will go, Raymond,' he repeated, holding out his hand, and clasping that of his friend. 'I suppose I *have* been going a little astray lately; but I only wanted the voice of a true-hearted fellow like you to call me back to the straight road. I shall leave Midlandshire to-morrow, Raymond; and it may be a very long time before you see me back again.'

'Heaven knows I'm sorry enough to lose you, my boy,' Mr Raymond said with some emotion; 'but I feel that it's the only thing for you to do. I used sometimes to think, before George Gilbert offered to marry Isabel, that you and she would have been suited to each other somehow; and I have wished that—'

And here Mr Raymond stopped abruptly, feeling that this speech was scarcely the wisest he could have made.

But Roland Lansdell took no notice of that unlucky observation. 'I shall go to-morrow,' he repeated. 'I'm very glad you've spoken to me, Raymond; I thank you most heartily for the advice you have given me this night; and I shall go to-morrow.'

And then his mind wandered away to his boyish studies in mythical Roman history; and he wondered how Marcus Curtius* felt just after making up his mind to take the leap that made him famous.

And then, with a sudden slip from ancient to modern history, he thought of poor tender-hearted Louise la Vallière* running away and hiding herself in a convent, only to have her pure thoughts and aspirations scattered like a cluster of frail wood-anemones in a storm of wind—only to have her holy resolutions trampled upon by the ruthless foot of an impetuous young king.

CHAPTER VII

WHAT MIGHT HAVE BEEN!

Mrs Gilbert spoke very little during the homeward drive through the moonlight. In her visions of that drive—or what that drive might be—she had fancied Roland Lansdell riding by the carriage-window, and going a few miles out of his way in order to escort his friends back to Graybridge.

'If he cared to be with us, he would have come,' Isabel thought, with a pensive reproachful feeling about Mr Lansdell.

It is just possible that Roland might have ridden after the fly from Graybridge, and ridden beside it along the quiet country roads, talking as he only in all the world could talk, according to Mrs Gilbert's opinion. It is possible that, being so sorely at a loss as to what he should do with himself, Mr Lansdell might have wasted an hour thus, had he not been detained by his old friend Charles Raymond.

As it was, he rode straight home to Mordred Priory, very slowly, thinking deeply as he went along; thinking bitter thoughts about himself and his destiny.

'If my cousin Gwendoline had been true to me, I should have been an utterly different man,' he thought; 'I should have been a middle-aged steady-going fellow by this time, with a boy at Eton, and a pretty fair-haired daughter to ride her pony by my side. I think I might have been good for something if I had married long ago, when my mother died, and my heart was ready to shelter the woman she had chosen for me. Children! A man who has children has some reason to be good, and to do his duty. But to stand quite alone in a world that one has grown tired of; with every pleasure exhausted, and every faith worn threadbare; with a dreary waste of memory behind, a barren desert of empty years before;—to be quite

alone in the world, the last of a race that once was brave and generous; the feeble worn-out remnant of a lineage that once did great
deeds, and made a name for itself in this world;—that indeed is
bitter!'

Mr Lansdell's thoughts dwelt upon his loneliness to-night, as
they had never dwelt before, since the day when his mother's death
and cousin's inconstancy first left him lonely.

'Yes, I shall go abroad again,' he thought presently, 'and go over
the old dreary beat once more—like Marryat's phantom captain turned
landsman,* like the Wandering Jew in a Poole-built travelling-dress.
I shall eat fish at Philippe's again, and buy more bouquets in the
Rue Castiglione, and lose more money at Hombourg, and shoot
more crocodiles on the banks of the Nile, and be laid up with
another fever in the Holy Land. It will be all the same over again,
except that it will be a great deal more tiresome this time.'

And then Mr Lansdell began to think what his life might have
been, if the woman he loved, or rather the woman for whom he had
a foolish sentimental fancy,—he did not admit to himself that his
predilection for Isabel Gilbert was more than this,—had been free
to become his wife. He imagined himself returning from those tiresome Continental wanderings a twelve-month earlier than he had
actually returned. Had he not been on the point of so doing half-a-
dozen times? and had changed that ever-changing mind of his again
and again—now turning his face homeward for a time, now wandering farther a-field; always uncertain and dissatisfied and restless;
tired of himself and the wonderful universe, from off which all the
gloss of novelty had been worn long ago. He imagined himself coming back to Midlandshire a twelvemonth sooner. 'Ah, me!' he thought,
'only one little year earlier, and all things would have been different!' He would have gone to Conventford to see his dear old friend
George Raymond, and there, in the sunny drawing-room, he would
have found a pale-faced, dark-eyed girl bending over a child's les-
son-book, or listening while a child strummed on the piano. He
could fancy that scene,—he could see it all, like a beautiful cabinet-
picture;* ah, how different, how different every thing would have
been then! It would have been no sin then to be inexplicably happy
in that girlish presence; there would have been no vague remorseful
pang, no sting of self-reproach, mingling with every pleasant emotion, contending with every thrill of mystic joy. And then—and

then, some night in the twilit garden, when the stars were hovering dim about the city-roofs still and hushed in the distance, he would have told her that he loved her; that, after a decade of indifference to all the brightest things of earth, he had found a pure unutterable happiness in the hope and belief that she would be his wife. He fancied her shy blushes, her drooping eyes suddenly tearful in the depth of her joy; and he fancied what his life might have been for ever afterwards, transformed and sublimated by its new purpose, its new delights; transfigured by a pure and exalted affection. He fancied all this as it all might have been; and turned and bowed his face before an image that bore his own likeness, and yet was not himself—the image of a good man, happy husband and father, true friend and gentle master, dwelling for ever and ever amidst that peaceful English landscape; beloved, respected, the centre of a happy circle, the key-stone of a fair domestic arch,—a necessary link in the grand chain of human love and life.

'And instead of all this, I am a wandering nomad, who never has been, and never can be, of any use in this world; who fills no place in life, and will leave no blank when he dies. When Louis the Well-beloved* was disinclined for the chase, the royal huntsmen were wont to announce that to-day his majesty would do nothing. I have been doing nothing all my life, and cannot even rejoice in a stag-hunt.'

Mr Lansdell beguiled his homeward way with many bitter reflections of this kind. But, inconsistent and vacillating in his thoughts, as he had been ever inconsistent and vacillating in his actions, he thought of himself at one time as being deeply and devotedly in love with Isabel Gilbert, and at another time as being only the victim of a foolish romantic fancy, which would perish by a death as speedy as its birth.

'What an idiot I am for my pains!' he said to himself presently. 'In six weeks' time this poor child's pale face will have no more place in my mind than the snows of last winter have on this earth, or only in far-away nooks and corners of memory, like the Alpine peaks, where the snows linger undisturbed by the hand of change. Poor little girl! how she blushes and falters sometimes when she speaks to me, and how pretty she looks then! If they could get such an Ingénue at the Français,* all Paris would be mad about her. We are very much in love with each other, I daresay; but I don't think it's a passion to outlast six weeks' absence on either side, not on her side certainly, dear romantic child! I have only been the hero of a story-book; and all this folly has been nothing more than a page out of a novel set in action. Raymond is very right. I must go away; and she will go back to her three-volume novels, and fall in love with a fair-haired hero, and forget me.'

He sighed as he thought this. It was infinitely better that he should be forgotten, and speedily; and yet it is hard to have *no* place in the universe—not even one hidden shrine in a foolish woman's heart. Mr Lansdell was before the Priory gates by this time. The old woman stifled a yawn as she admitted the master of the domain. He went in past the little blinking light in the narrow Gothic window, and along the winding roadway, between cool shrubberies that shed an aromatic perfume on the still night-air. Scared fawns flitted ghost-like away into deep recesses amid the Mordred oaks; and in the distance the water-drops of a cascade, changed by the moonbeams into showers of silver, fell with a little tinkling sound amongst great blocks of moss-grown granite and wet fern.

Mordred Priory, seen in the moonlight, was not a place upon which a man would willingly turn his back. Long ago Roland Lansdell had grown tired of its familiar beauties; but to-night the scene seemed transformed. He looked at it with a new interest; he thought of it with a sad tender regret, that stung him like a physical pain.

As he had thought of what his life might have been under other circumstances, he thought now of what the place might have been. He fancied the grand old rooms resonant with the echoes of children's voices; he pictured one slender white-robed figure on the moonlit terrace; he fancied a tender earnest face turned steadily towards the path along which he rode; he felt the thrilling contact of a caressing arm twining itself shyly in his; he heard the low murmur of a loving voice—his wife's voice!—bidding him welcome home.

But it was never to be! The watch-dog's honest bark—or rather the bark of several watchdogs—made the night clamorous presently, when Mr Lansdell drew rein before the porch; but there was no eye to mark his coming, and be brighter when he came; unless, indeed, it was the eye of his valet, which had waxed dim over the columns of the *Morning Post*, and may have glimmered faintly in evidence of that functionary's satisfaction at the prospect of being speedily released from duty.

If it was so, the valet was doomed to disappointment; for Mr

Lansdell—usually the least troublesome of masters—wanted a great deal done for him to-night.

'You may set to work at once with my portmanteau, Jadis,' he said, when he met his servant in the hall. 'I must leave Mordred to-morrow morning in time for the seven-o'clock express from Warncliffe. I want you to pack my things, and arrange for Wilson to be ready to drive me over. I must leave here at six. Perhaps, by the by, you may as well pack one portmanteau for me to take with me, and you can follow with the rest of the luggage on Monday.'

'You are going abroad, sir?'

'Yes, I am tired of Mordred. I shall not stop for the hunting-season. You can go upstairs now and pack the portmanteau. Don't forget to make all the arrangements about the carriage; for six precisely. You can go to bed when you've finished packing. I've some letters to write, and shall be late.'

The man bowed and departed, to grumble, in an undertone, over Mr Lansdell's shirts and waistcoats, while Roland went into the library to write his letters.

How blank the room seemed! how empty and lonely! It was no new thing for him to find that handsome chamber tenantless, and to sit down alone in the stillness and the lamplight, to brood over his books, when the household was at rest. It was no new thing for him to sit alone; and yet to-night he felt his desolation as keenly as a young widower newly mourning the loss of an idolised wife. Had he not suffered himself to dream of a life that was different from this life? He had peopled that empty chamber with a vision that had made it luminous; and now, remembering that the dream was only a dream, and never, never could be more, he felt almost as sharp a pang as if he had been mourning for the dead.

The letters which he had to write turned out to be only one letter, or rather a dozen variations upon the same theme, which he tore up, one after another, almost as soon as they were written. He was not wont to be so fastidious in the wording of his epistles, but to-night he could not be satisfied with what he wrote. He wrote to Mrs Gilbert; yes, to her! Why should he not write to her when he was going away to-morrow morning; when he was going to offer up that vague bright dream which had lately beguiled him, a willing sacrifice, on the altar of duty and honour?

'I am not much good,' he said: for ever excusing his shortcomings by his self-depreciation. 'I never set up for being a good man; but I have some feeling of honour left in me at the worst.' He wrote to Isabel, therefore, rather than to her husband, and he destroyed many letters before he wrote what he fancied suitable to the occasion. Did not the smothered tenderness, the regret, the passion, reveal itself in some of those letters, in spite of his own determination to be strictly conventional and correct? But the letter which he wrote last was stiff and commonplace enough to have satisfied the sternest moralist.

'DEAR Mrs GILBERT,—I much regret that circumstances, which only came to my knowledge after your party left last night, will oblige me to leave Mordred early to-morrow morning. I am therefore compelled to forego the pleasure which I had anticipated from our friendly little dinner to-morrow evening; but pray assure Smith that the Priory is entirely at his disposal whenever he likes to come here, and that he is welcome to make it the scene of half-a-dozen fictions, if he pleases. I fear the old place will soon look gloomy and desolate enough to satisfy his ideas of the romantic, for it may be some years before I again see the Midlandshire woods and meadows.'

('The dear old bridge across the waterfall, the grand old oak under which I have spent such pleasant hours,' Mr Lansdell had written here in one of the letters which he destroyed.)

'I hope you will convey to Mr Gilbert my warmest thanks, with the accompanying cheque, for the kindness and skill which have endeared him to my cottagers. I shall be very glad if he will continue to look after them, and I will arrange for the carrying out of any sanitary improvements he may suggest to Hodgeson, my steward.

'The library will be always prepared for you whenever you feel inclined to read and study there, and the contents of the shelves will be entirely at the service of yourself and Mr Gilbert.

'With regards to your husband, and all friendly wishes for Smith's prosperity and success,

'I remain, dear Mrs Gilbert,

'Very truly yours,

'ROLAND LANSDELL.

'*Mordred Priory, Saturday night.*'

'It may be some years before I again see the Midlandshire woods and meadows!' This sentence was the gist of the letter, the stiff unmeaning letter, which was as dull and laboured as a schoolboy's holiday missive to his honoured parents.

'My poor, innocent, tender-hearted darling! will she be sorry when she reads it?' thought Mr Lansdell, as he addressed his letter. 'Will this parting be a new grief to her, a shadowy romantic sorrow, like her regret for drowned Shelley, or fever-stricken Byron? My darling, my darling! if fate had sent me here a twelve-month earlier, you and I might have been standing side by side in the moonlight, talking of the happy future before us. Only a year! and there were so many accidents that might have caused my return. Only one year! and in that little space I lost my one grand chance of happiness.'

Mr Lansdell had done his duty. He had given Charles Raymond a promise which he meant to keep; and having done so, he gave his thoughts and fancies a license which he had never allowed them before. He no longer struggled to retain the attitude from which he had hitherto endeavoured to regard Mrs Gilbert. He no longer considered it his duty to think of her as a pretty, grown-up child, whose childish follies amused him for the moment. No; he was going away now, and had no longer need to set any restraint upon his thoughts. He was going away, and was free to acknowledge to himself that this love which had grown up so suddenly in his breast was the one grand passion of his life, and, under different circumstances, might have been his happiness and redemption.

CHAPTER VIII

'OCEANS SHOULD DIVIDE US'*

Mr and Mrs Gilbert went to church arm-in-arm as usual on the morning after the picnic; but Sigismund stayed at home to sketch the rough outline of that feudal romance which he had planned among the ruins of Waverly. The day was very fine,—a real summer-day, with a blazing sun and a cloudless blue sky. The sunshine seemed like a good omen, Mrs Gilbert thought, as she dressed herself in the white-muslin robe that she was to wear at Mordred. An omen of what? She did not ask herself that question; but she was pleased to think that the heavens should smile upon her visit to Mordred. She was thinking of the dinner at the Priory while she sat

by her husband's side in the church, looking demurely down at the
Prayer-Book in her lap. It was a common thing for her now to be
thinking of *him* when she ought to have been attending to the sermon. To-day she did not even try to listen to the rector's discourse.
She was fancying herself in the dusky drawing-room at Mordred,
after dinner, hearing *him* talk. She saw his face turned towards her in
the twilight—the pale dark face—the dreamy, uncertain eyes. When
the congregation rose suddenly, at the end of the sermon, she sat
bewildered for a moment, like a creature awakened from a dream; and
when the people knelt, and became absorbed in silent meditation on
the injunctions of their pastor, Mrs Gilbert remained so long in a
devotional attitude, that her husband was fain to arouse her by a
gentle tap upon the shoulder. She had been thinking of *him* even on
her knees. She could not shut his image from her thoughts; she
walked about in a perpetual dream, and rarely awakened to the consciousness that there was wickedness in so dreaming; and even when
she did reflect upon her sin, it was very easy to excuse it and make
light of it. *He* would never know. In November he would be gone,
and the dream would be nothing but a dream.

It was only one o'clock, by the old-fashioned clock in the passage,
when they went home after church. The gig was to be ready at a
quarter before three, and at that hour they were to start for Mordred.
George meant to put-up his horse at the little inn near the Priory
gates, and then they could walk quietly from the church to Mr
Lansdell's after the service. Mr Gilbert felt that Brown Molly appeared rather at a disadvantage in Roland's grand stables.

Sigismund was still sitting in the little parlour, looking very warm,
and considerably the worse for ink. He had tried all the penny
bottles in the course of his labours, and had a little collection of
them clustered at his elbow.

'I don't think any one ever imagined so many ink-bottles compatible with so little ink,' he said, plaintively. 'I've had my best ideas
balked by perpetual hairs in my pen, to say nothing of flies' wings,
and even bodies. There's nothing like unlimited ink for imparting
fluency to a man's language; you cut short his eloquence the moment you limit his ink. However, I'm down here for pleasure, old
fellow,' Mr Smith added, cheerfully; 'and all the printing-machines
in the city of London may be waiting for copy for aught I care.'

An hour and three-quarters must elapse before it would be time even to start for Mordred. Mrs Gilbert went upstairs and re-arranged her hair, and looked at herself in the glass, and wondered if she was pretty. *He* had never told her so. He had never paid her any compliment. But she fancied, somehow, that he thought her pretty, though she had no idea whence that fancy was derived. She went downstairs again, and out into the garden, whence Mr Smith was calling to her—the little garden in front of the house, where there were a few common flowers blooming dustily in oval beds like dishes; and where, in a corner, there was an erection of shells and broken bits of coloured glass, which Mr Jeffson fondly imagined to be the exact representation of a grotto.

Mr Smith had a good deal to say for himself, as indeed he had on all occasions; but as his discourse was entirely of a personal charac-ter, it may have been rather wanting in general interest. Isabel strolled up and down the narrow pathway by his side, and turned her face politely towards him, and said, 'Yes,' and 'Did you really!' and 'Well, how very strange!' now and then. But she was thinking as she had thought in church; she was thinking of the wonderful happiness that lay before her,—an evening in *his* companionship, amongst pic-tures and hothouse flowers and marble busts and trailing silken curtains, and with glimpses of a moonlit expanse of lawn and shrub-bery gleaming through every open window.

She was thinking of this when a bell rang loud and shrill in her ear; and looking round suddenly she saw a man in livery—a man who looked like a groom—standing outside the garden-gate.

She was so near the gate that it would have been a mere affecta-tion to keep the man waiting there while Mrs Jeffson made her way from the remote premises at the back of the house. The Doctor's Wife turned the key in the lock and opened the gate; but the man only wanted to deliver a letter, which he handed her with one hand while he touched the brim of his hat with the other.

'From Mr Lansdell, ma'am,' he said.

In the next moment he was gone, and the open gate and the white dusty lane seemed to reel before Isabel Gilbert's eyes.

There had been no need for the man to tell her that the letter was from his master. She knew the bold dashing hand, in which she had read pencil annotations upon the margins of those books which Mr Lansdell had lent her. And even if she had not known the hand, she would have easily guessed whence the letter came. Who else should write so grand-looking a missive, with that thick cream-coloured envelope (a big official-looking envelope), and the broad coat-of-arms with tall winged supporters on the seal? But why should he have written to her? It was to put off the dinner, no doubt. Her lips trembled a little, like the lips of a child who is going to cry, as she opened the letter.

She read it very hurriedly twice, and then all at once comprehended that Roland was going away for some years,—for ever,—it was all the same thing; and that she would never, never, never, never,—the word seemed to repeat itself in her brain like the dreadful clanging of a bell—never see him again!

She knew that Sigismund was looking at her, and asking her some question about the contents of the letter. 'What did Lansdell say? was it a put-off, or what?' Mr Smith demanded; but Isabel did not answer him. She handed him the open letter, and then, suddenly turning from him, ran into the house, upstairs, and into her room. She locked the door, flung herself face downwards upon the bed, and wept as a woman weeps in the first great agony of her life. The sound of those passionate sobs was stifled by the pillows amidst which her face was buried, but the anguish of them shook her from head to foot. It was very wicked to have thought of him so much, to have loved him so dearly. The punishment of her sin came to her all at once, and was very bitter.

Mr Smith stood for some moments staring at the doorway through which Isabel had disappeared, with the open letter in his hand, and his face a perfect blank in the intensity of his amazement.

'I suppose it *is* a put-off,' he said to himself; 'and she's disappointed because we're not going. Why, what a child she is still! I remember her behaving just like that once at Camberwell, when I'd promised her tickets for the play, and couldn't get 'em. The manager of the T. R. D. L.* said he didn't consider the author of *The Brand upon the Shoulder-blade* entitled to the usual privilege. Poor little Izzie! I remember her running away, and not coming back for ever so long; and when she did make her appearance her eyelids were all red and swollen.'

Mr Smith stooped to pick up a narrow slip of lavender-tinted paper from the garden-walk. It was the cheque which Roland Lansdell had written in payment of the Doctor's services. Sigismund read the letter, and reflected over it.

'I'm almost as much disappointed as Izzie, for the matter of that,' he thought to himself; 'we should have had a jolly good dinner at the Priory, and any amount of sparkling; and Chateau what's-its-name and Clos de thingamy to follow, I daresay. I'll take George the letter and the cheque—it's just like Izzie to leave the cheque on the ground—and resign myself to a dullish Sunday.'

It was a dull Sunday. The unacademical 'ish' with which Mr Smith had qualified the adjective was quite unnecessary. It was a very dull Sunday. Ah, reader, if Providence has some desperate sorrow in store for you, pray that it may not befall you on a Sunday, in the blazing sunshine, when the church-bells are ringing on the still drowsy air. Mr Gilbert went upstairs by and by, when the bells were at their loudest, and, finding the door of his chamber locked, knocked on the panel, and asked Isabel if she did not mean to go to church. But she told him she had a dreadful headache, and wanted to stay at home. He asked her ever so many questions, as to why her head ached, and how long it had ached, and wanted to see her, from a professional point of view.

'Oh, no, no!' she cried, from the bed upon which she was lying; 'I don't want any medicine; I only want to rest my head; I was asleep when you knocked.'

Ah, what a miserable falsehood that was! as if she could ever hope to sleep again!

'But, Izzie,' remonstrated Mr Gilbert, 'you've had no dinner. There's cold lamb, you know; and we're going to have that and a salad after church. You'll come down to dinner, eh?'

'No, no; I don't want any dinner. Please, leave me alone. I *only* want to rest,' she answered piteously.

Poor honest George Gilbert little knew how horrible an effort it had cost his wife to utter even these brief sentences without breaking down in a passion of sobbing and weeping. She buried her face in the pillows again as her husband's footsteps went slowly down the narrow stairs. She was very wretched, very foolish. It was only a dream—nothing more than a dream—that was lost to her. Again, had she not known all along that Roland Lansdell would go away, and that all her bright dreams and fancies must go with him? Had she not counted upon his departure? Yes; but in November, not in September; not on the day that was to have been such a happy day.

'Oh, how cruel, how cruel!' she thought. 'How cruel of him to go

away like that! without even saying good-by,—without even saying
he was sorry to go. And I fancied that he liked to talk to me; I
fancied that he was pleased to see me sometimes, and would be
sorry when the time came for him to go away. But to think that he
should go away two months before the time he spoke of,—to think
that he should not even be sorry to go!'

Mrs Gilbert got up by and by, when the western sky was all one
lurid glow of light and colour. She got up because there was little
peace for a weary spirit in that chamber; to the door of which some
considerate creature came every half-hour or so to ask Isabel if her
head was any better by this time, if she would have a cup of tea, if
she would come downstairs and lie on the sofa, and to torment her
with many other thoughtful inquiries of the like nature. She was not
to be alone with her great sorrow. Sooner or later she must go out
and begin life again, and face the blank world in which *he* was not.
Better, since it must be so, that she should begin her dreary task at
once. She bathed her face and head, she plaited her long black hair
before the little glass, behind which the lurid sky glared redly at her.
Ah, how often in the sunny morning she had stood before that
shabby old-fashioned glass thinking of him, and the chance of meeting him beside the mill-stream, under the flickering shadows of the
oak-leaves at Thurston's Crag! And now it was all over, and she
would never, never, never, never see him again! Her life was finished. Ah, how truly he had spoken on the battlements of the ruined
tower! and how bitterly the meaning of his words came home to her
to-day! Her life was finished. The curtain had fallen, and the lights
were out; and she had nothing more to do but to grope blindly
about upon a darkened stage until she sank in the great vampire-
trap—the grave. A pale ghost, with sombre shadowy hair, looked
back at her from the glass. Oh, if she could die, if she could die! She
thought of the mill-stream. The wheel would be idle; and the water
low down in the hollow beyond the miller's cottage would be still
to-night, still and placid and glassy, shining rosy red in the sunset
like the pavement of a cathedral stained with the glory of a painted
window. Why should she not end her sorrows for ever in that glassy
pool, so deep, so tranquil? She thought of Ophelia, and the miller's
daughter on the banks of Allan Water.* Would she be found floating
on the stream, with weeds of water-lilies tangled in her long dark
hair? Would she look pretty when she was dead? Would *he* be sorry

when he heard of her death? Would he read a paragraph in the newspapers some morning at breakfast, and break a blood-vessel into his coffee-cup? Or would he read and not care? Why should he care? If he had cared for her, he could never have gone away, he could never have written that cruel formal letter, with not a word of regret—no, not one. Vague thoughts like these followed one another in her mind. If she could have the courage to go down to the water's brink, and to drop quietly into the stream where Roland Lansdell had once told her it was deepest? It was not any consciousness of the suicide's sin that held this ignorant girl back from the desperate deed, which took a soft and sentimental shape in her mind. It was only a shuddering horror of the plunge, a vague and shapeless terror of the 'something after,' familiar to every creature who ponders (even in the most frivolous spirit) upon Hamlet's solemn question;* it was only dim fear and apprehension that saved this girl from the rash impulse of her sorrow-stricken heart. I know that she was alike wicked and silly; I know that it must be difficult to win sympathy for a grief so foolish, an anguish so self-engendered; but her sorrow was none the less real to her because it seems foolish in the eyes of wisdom. It was not so long since she had lain awake for many weary nights weeping for the death of a pet spaniel; it was not so long since she had gone to bed sorrowful because the second volume of one of her favourite romances was unobtainable at the little Camberwell library. All the sterner business of life lay before her as yet, all the harder lessons yet remained to be learned.

She went downstairs by and by, in the dusk, with her face as white as the tumbled muslin that hung about her in limp and flabby folds. She went down into the little parlour, where George and Sigismund were waiting for their tea, and where two yellow mould-candles were flaring in the faint evening breeze.

She told them that her head was better; and then began to make the tea, scooping up vague quantities of congou and gunpowder with the little silver scollop-shell, which had belonged to Mr Gilbert's grandmother, and was stamped with a puffy profile of George the Third.

'But you've been crying, Izzie!' George exclaimed presently, for Mrs Gilbert's eyelids looked red and swollen in the light of the candles.

'Yes, my head was so bad it made me cry; but please don't ask me any more about it,' Isabel pleaded piteously. 'I suppose it was the p-picnic'—she nearly broke down upon the word, remembering how good *he* had been to her all through the happy day—'yesterday that made me ill.'

'I daresay it was that lobster-salad,' Mr Gilbert answered briskly; 'I ought to have told you not to eat it. I don't think there's any thing more bilious than lobster-salad dressed with cream.'

Sigismund Smith watched his hostess with a grave countenance, while she poured out the tea and handed the cups right and left. Poor Isabel managed it all with tolerable steadiness; and then, when the miserable task was over, she sat by the window alone, staring blankly out at the dusty shrubs distinct in the moonlight, while her husband and his friend smoked their cigars in the lane outside.

How was she to bear her life in that dull dusty lane—her odious life, which would go on and on for ever, like a slow barge crawling across dreary flats upon the black tideless waters of a canal? How was she to endure it? All its monotony, all its misery, its shabby dreariness, its dreary shabbiness, rose up before her with redoubled force; and the terror of that hideous existence smote her like a stroke from a giant's hand.

It all came back. Yes, it came back. For the last two months it had ceased to be; it had been blotted out, hidden, forgotten; there had been no such thing. An enchanter's wand had been waved above that dreary square-built house in the dusty lane, and a fairy palace had arisen for her habitation; a fairyland of beauty and splendour had spread itself around her, a paradise in which she wandered hand in hand with a demigod. The image of Roland Lansdell had filled her life, to the exclusion of every other shape, animate or inanimate. But the fairyland melted away all at once, like a mirage in the desert; like the last scene of a pantomime, the rosy and cerulean lights* went out in foul sulphurous vapours. The mystic domes and mina-rets melted into thin air; but the barren sands remained real and dreary, stretching away for ever and for ever before the wanderer's weary feet.

In all Mrs Gilbert's thoughts there was no special horror or aver-sion of her husband. He was only a part of the dullness of her life; he was only one dreary element of that dreary world in which Roland Lansdell was not. He was very good to her, and she was vaguely sensible of his goodness, and thankful to him. But his image had no abiding place in her thoughts. At stated times he came home and ate his dinner, or drank his tea, with substantial accompaniment of bread and butter and crisp garden-stuff; but, during the last two months, there had been many times when his wife was scarcely conscious of his presence. She was happy in fairyland, with the prince of her perpetual fairy tale, while poor George Gilbert munched bread and butter, and crunched overgrown radishes. But the fairy tale was finished now, with an abrupt and cruel climax; the prince had vanished; the dream was over. Sitting by that open window, with her folded arms resting on the dusty sill, Mrs Gilbert wondered how she was to endure her life.

And then her thoughts went back to the still pool below the mill-stream. She remembered the happy, drowsy summer afternoon on which Roland Lansdell had stood by her side and told her the depth of the stream. She closed her eyes, and her head sank forward upon her folded arms, and all the picture came back to her. She heard the shivering of the rushes, the bubbling splash of a gudgeon leaping out of the water: she saw the yellow sunlight on the leaves, the beautiful sunlight creeping in through every break in the dense foliage; and she saw his face turned towards her with that luminous look, that bright and tender smile, which had only seemed another kind of sunshine.

Would *he* be sorry if he opened the newspaper and read a little paragraph in a corner to the effect that she had been found floating amongst the long rushes in that very spot? Would he remember the sunny afternoon, and the things he had said to her? His talk had been very dreamy and indefinite; but there had been, or had seemed to be, an undercurrent of mournful tenderness in all he said, as vague and fitful, as faint and mysterious, as the murmuring of the summer-wind among the rushes.

[I think the youthful mind hankers naturally after suicide. Does not the youthful mind pine wildly for distinction, distinction at any price, even the temporary notoriety appertaining to a coroner's inquest and a paragraph in the Sunday papers? It was not so much the blank quiet of the grave for which Isabel languished; she wanted to die in order that Roland Lansdell might be sorry. To inspire one pang of remorse in that hard heart, she would have freely given her life. But when a sentimental young lady of nineteen is half inclined to make herself briefly famous by the crime of self-murder, she is apt to be deterred not so much by any pious horror of the crime, as by a difficulty in getting to the water.

'I cannot be allowed even to die!' thought the Doctor's Wife, as she heard the steady tramp of her husband's footsteps in the lane, and knew that he would come in presently, and the doors would be locked, and all chance of death by drowning would be over for that night at least. There was laudanum in the surgery; Mrs Gilbert knew the bottle in which it was kept: but she had taken laudanum for the toothache once or twice, and had found that opiate very nauseous. And death by poison was only a matter-of-fact business as compared to the still water and the rushes, and would have a very inferior effect in the newspapers.]*

The two young men came in presently, smelling of dust and tobacco-smoke. They found Isabel lying on the sofa, with her face turned to the wall. Did her head still ache? Yes, as badly as ever.

George sat down to read his Sunday paper. He was very fond of a Sunday paper; and he read all the accidents and police-reports, and the indignant letters from liberal-minded citizens, who signed themselves Aristides,* and Diogenes,* and Junius Brutus,* and made fiery protests against the iniquities of a bloated aristocracy. While the surgeon folded the crackling newspaper and cut the leaves, he told Isabel about Roland Lansdell's cheque.

'He has sent me five-and-twenty pounds,' he said. 'It's very liberal; but of course I can't think of taking such a sum. I've been a good deal about amongst his farm-people,—for there's been so much low fever this last month,—but I've been looking over the account I'd made out against him, and it doesn't come to a five-pound note. I suppose he's been used to deal with physicians, who charge a guinea for every visit. I shall send him back his cheque.'

Isabel shuddered as she listened to her husband's talk. How low and mean all this discussion about money seemed! Had not the enclosure of the cheque in that cruel letter been almost an insult? What was her husband better than a tradesman, when there could be this question of accounts and payment between him and Roland Lansdell?

And then she thought of Clotilde and the Duchess,—the Duchess with the glittering hair and the cruel azure eyes. She thought of 'marble pillars gleaming white against the purple of the night;' of 'crimson curtains starred with gold, and high-bred beauty brightly cold.' She thought of all that confusion of colour and glitter and perfume and music which was that staple commodity in Mr Lansdell's poetic wares; and she wondered, in self-abasement and humiliation, how she could have ever for a moment deluded herself with the idea that he could feel one transient sentiment of regard or admiration for such a degraded being as herself. She thought of her scanty dresses, that never had the proper number of breadths in the skirt; she thought of her skimpy sleeves made in last year's fashion, her sunburnt straw-hat, her green parasol faded like sickly grass at the close of a hot summer. She thought of the gulf between herself and Edith Dombey, and wondered at her madness and presumption.

[Ah, what a sweet dream it had been, and how sad was the waking! During that happy dream she had forgotten all about Edith Dombey; she had ceased to languish for ruby-velvet gowns, and diamond tiaras, and splendid apartments; she had been transformed for the time from a silly sentimental girl into a woman; simple and confiding; blindly forgetful of all things in the world except her love. But now all the old feverish longing for splendour and beauty came back upon her. If she had been like Edith Dombey, he could never have treated her thus. But she was only a poor pale-faced little Florence, created to look pretty and to be snubbed.]*

Poor George Gilbert was quite puzzled by his wife's headache, which was of a peculiarly obstinate nature, lasting for some days. He gave her cooling draughts, and lotions for her forehead, which was very hot under his calm professional hand. Her pulse was rapid, her tongue was white, and the surgeon pronounced her to be bilious. He had not the faintest suspicion of any mental ailment lurking at the root of these physical derangements. He was very simple-minded, and, being incapable of wrong himself, measured all his decent fellow-creatures by a fixed standard. He thought that the good and the wicked formed two separate classes as widely apart as the angels of heaven and the demons of the fiery depths. He knew that there were, somewhere or other in the universe, wives who wronged their husbands and went into outer darkness, just as he knew that in dismal dens of crime there lurked robbers and murderers, forgers and pickpockets, the newspaper record of whose evil deeds made no unpleasant reading for quiet Sunday afternoons. But of vague sentimental errors, of shadowy dangers and temptations, he had no conception. He had seen his wife pleased and happy in Roland Lansdell's society; and the thought that any wrong to himself, how small soever, could arise out of that companionship had never entered his mind. Mr Raymond had remarked of the young surgeon that a man with such a moral region was born to be imposed upon.

The rest of the week passed in a strange dreary way for Isabel. The weather was very fine, cruelly fine; and to Mrs Gilbert the universe seemed all dust and sunshine and blankness. Sigismund was very kind to her, and did his best to amuse her, reciting the plots of numerous embryo novels, which were to take Camden Town by storm in the future. But she sat looking at him without seeing him, and his talk sounded a harsh confusion on her ear. Oh, for the sound of that other voice,—that other voice, which had attuned itself to such a tender melody! Oh, for the beautiful cynical talk about the hollowness of life, and the wretchedness of things in general! Poor simple-hearted Mr Smith made himself positively hateful to Isabel during that dismal week by reason of his efforts to amuse her.

'If he would only let me alone!' she thought. 'If people would only have mercy upon me and let me alone!'

But that was just what every one seemed determined not to do. Sigismund devoted himself exclusively to the society of his young hostess. William Jeffson let the weeds grow high amongst the potatoes while he planted standard rose-bushes, and nailed up graceful creepers, and dug, and improved, and transplanted in that portion of the garden which made a faint pretence to prettiness. Was it that he wished to occupy Mrs Gilbert's mind, and to force her to some slight exertion? He did not prune a shrub, or trim a scrap of box, without consulting the Doctor's Wife upon the subject; and Isabel was called out into the garden half-a-dozen times in an hour.

And then during his visit Sigismund insisted upon taking Mrs Gilbert to Warncliffe to dine with his mother and sisters. Mr Smith's family made quite a festival for the occasion: there was a goose for dinner,—a vulgar and savoury bird; and a big damson-pie, and apples and pears in green leaf-shaped dishes for dessert; and of course Isabel's thoughts wandered away from that homely mahogany, with its crimson worsted d'oyleys* and dark-blue finger-glasses, to the oval table at Mordred and all its artistic splendour of glass and fruit and flowers.

The Smith family thought Mrs Gilbert very quiet and insipid; but luckily Sigismund had a great deal to say about his own achievements, past, present, and future; so Isabel was free to sit in the twilight listening dreamily to the slow footsteps in the old-fashioned street outside—the postman's knock, growing fainter and fainter in the distance—and the cawing of the rooks in a grove of elms on the outskirts of the town.

Mr Smith senior spent the evening in the bosom of his family, and was put through rather a sharp examination upon abstruse questions in chancery and criminal practice by his aspiring son, who was always getting into morasses of legal difficulty, from which he required to be extricated by professional assistance.

The evening seemed a very long one to poor Isabel; but it was over at last, and Sigismund conducted her back to Graybridge in a jolting omnibus; and during that slow homeward drive she was free to sit in a corner and think of *him*.

Mr Smith left his friends on the following day; and before going, he walked with Isabel in the garden, and talked to her a little of her life.

'I daresay it *is* a little dull at Graybridge,' he said, as if in answer to some remark of Isabel's, and yet she had said nothing. 'I daresay you do find it a little dull, though George is one of the best fellows that ever lived, and devoted to you; yes, Izzie, devoted to you, in his quiet way. He isn't one of your demonstrative fellows, you know; can't go into grand romantic raptures, or any thing of that kind. But we were boys together, Izzie, and I know him thoroughly; and I know that he loves you dearly, and would break his honest heart if any thing happened to you; or he was—anyhow to take it into his head that you didn't love him. But still I daresay you do find life rather slow work down here; and I can't help thinking that if you were to occupy yourself a little more than you do, you'd be happier. Suppose now,' cried Mr Smith, palpably swelling with the importance of his idea,—'suppose you were to WRITE A NOVEL! THERE! You don't know how happy it would make you. Look at me. I always used to be sighing and lamenting, and wishing for this, that, or the other; wishing I had ten thousand a year, or a Grecian nose, or some wordly advantage of that sort; but since I've taken to writing novels, I don't think I've a desire unsatisfied. There's nothing I haven't done—on paper. The beautiful women I've loved and married; the fortunes I've come into, always unexpectedly, and when I was at the lowest ebb, with a tendency to throw myself into the Serpentine in the moonlight; the awful vengeance I've wreaked upon my enemies; the murders I've committed would make the life of a Napoleon Buonaparte seem tame and trivial by comparison. I suppose it isn't I that steal up the creaking stair, with a long knife tightly grasped and gleaming blue in the moonbeams that creep through a chink in the shutter; but I'm sure I enjoy myself as much as if it was. And if I were a young lady,' continued Mr Smith, speaking with some slight hesitation, and glancing furtively at Isabel's face,— 'if I were a young lady, and—and had a kind of romantic fancy for a person I ought not to care about, I'll tell you what I'd do with him,—I'd put him into a novel, Izzie, and work him out in three volumes; and if I wasn't heartily sick of him by the time I got to the last chapter, nothing on earth would cure me.'

This was the advice which Sigismund gave to Isabel at parting. She understood his meaning, and resented his interference. She was beginning to feel that people guessed at her wickedness, and tried to cure her of her madness. Yes; she was very wicked—very mad. She acknowledged her sin, but she could not put it away from her. And now that he was gone, now that he was far away, never to come back, never to look upon her face again, surely there could be no harm in thinking of him. She did think of him, daily and hourly; no longer with any reservation, no longer with any attempt at self-deception. Eugene Aram and Ernest Maltravers, the Giaour and the Corsair,* were alike forgotten. The real hero of her life had come, and she bowed down before his image, and paid him perpetual worship. What did it matter? He was gone! He was as far away from her life now as those fascinating figments of the poetic brain, Messrs Aram and Maltravers. He was a dream, like all the other dreams of her life; only he could never melt away or change as they had done.

CHAPTER IX

'ONCE MORE THE GATE BEHIND ME FALLS'*

All through the autumnal months, all through the dreary winter, George Gilbert's wife endured her existence, and hated it. The days were all alike, all 'dark and cold and dreary;'* and her life was 'dark and cold and dreary' like the days. She did not write a novel. She did not accomplish any task, or carry out any intention; but she began a great many undertakings, and grew tired of them, and gave them up in despair. She wrote a few chapters of a novel; a wild weird work of fiction, in which Mr Roland Lansdell reigned paramount over all the rules of Lindley Murray,* and was always nominative when he ought to have been objective, and *vice versâ*, and did altogether small credit to the university at which he was described to have gained an impossible conglomeration of honours. Mrs Gilbert very soon grew tired of the novel, though it was pleasant to imagine it in a complete form taking the town by storm. *He* would read it, and would know that she had written it. Was there not a minute description of Lord Thurston's oak in the very first chapter? It was pleasant to think of the romance, neatly bound in three volumes. But Mrs Gilbert never got beyond a few random chapters, in which the grand crises of the work—the first meeting of the hero and heroine, the death of the latter by drowning and of the former by rupture of a blood-vessel, and so on—were described. She could not do the everyday work; she could erect a fairy-palace, and scatter lavish splendour in its spacious halls; but she could not lay down the stair-carpets, or fit the window-blinds, or arrange the planned furniture. She tore up her manuscript; and then for a little time she thought that she would be very good; kind to the poor, affectionate to her husband, and attentive to the morning and afternoon sermons at Graybridge church. She made a little book out of letter-paper, and took notes of the vicar's and the curate's discourses; but both those gentlemen had a fancy for discussing abstruse points of doctrine far beyond Mrs Gilbert's comprehension, and the Doctor's Wife found the business of a reporter very difficult work. She made her poor little unaided effort to repent of her sins, and to do good. She cut up her shabbiest dresses and made them into frocks for some poor children, and she procured a packet of limp tracts from a Conventford bookseller, and distributed them with the frocks; having a vague idea that no charitable benefaction was complete unless accompanied by a tract.

Alas for this poor sentimental child! the effort to be good, and pious, and practical did not sit well upon her. She got on very well with some of the cottagers' daughters, who had been educated at the national school,* and were as fond of reading novels as herself; she fraternised with these damsels, and lent them odd volumes out of her little library, and even read aloud to them on occasion; and the vicar of Graybridge, entering one day a cottage where she was sitting, was pleased to hear a humming noise, as of the human voice, and praised Mrs Gilbert for her devotion to the good cause. He might not have been quite so well pleased had he heard the subject of her lecture, which had relation to a gentleman of loose principles and buccaneering propensities, a gentleman who

> 'left a Corsair's name to other times,
> Link'd with one virtue and a thousand crimes.'*

But even these feeble attempts to be good—ah! how short a time it seemed since Isabel Gilbert had been a child, subject to have her ears boxed by the second Mrs Sleaford! how short a time since to 'be good' meant to be willing to wash the tea-cups and saucers, or to darn a three-cornered rent in a hobbledehoy's jacket!—even these feeble efforts ceased by and by, and Mrs Gilbert abandoned herself to the dull monotony of her life, and solaced herself with the thought of Roland Lansdell as an opium-eater beguiles his listless days with the splendid visions that glorify his besotted stupor. She resigned herself to her life, and was very obedient to her husband, and read novels as long as she could get one to read, and was for ever thinking of what might have been—if she had been free, and if Roland Lansdell had loved her. Alas, he had only too plainly proved that he did not love her, and had never loved her. He had made this manifest by cruelly indisputable evidence at the very time when she was beginning to be unutterably happy in the thought that she was somehow or other nearer and dearer to him than she ought to have been.

The dull autumn days and the dark winter days dragged themselves out and Mr Gilbert came in and went out, and attended to his duties, and ate his dinner, and rode Brown Molly between the leafless hedgerows, beside the frozen streams, as contentedly as he had done in the bright summer time, when his rides had lain through a perpetual garden. His was one of those happy natures which are undisturbed by any wild yearnings after the unattainable. He had an idea of exchanging his Graybridge practice for a better one by and by, and he used to talk to Isabel of this ambitious design; but she took little interest in the subject. She had evinced very little interest in it from the first, and she displayed less now. What would be the use of such a change? It could only bring her a new kind of dreariness; and it was something to stand shivering on the little bridge under Lord Thurston's oak, so bare and leafless now; it was something to see even the chimney-pots of Mordred, the wonderful clusters of dark red-brick chimneys, warm against the chill December sky.

Mrs Gilbert did not forget that passage in Roland Lansdell's letter, in which he had placed the Mordred library at her disposal. But she was very slow to avail herself of the privilege thus offered to her. She shrank away shyly from the thought of entering *his* house, even though there was no chance of meeting him in the beautiful rooms; even though he was at the other end of Europe, gay and happy, and forgetful of her. It was only by and by, when Mr Lansdell had been gone some months, and when the dulness of her life had grown day by day more oppressive, that Isabel Gilbert took courage to enter the noble gates of Mordred. Of course she told her husband whither she was going—was it not her duty so to do?—and George good-naturedly approving—'though I'm sure you've got books enough already,' he said; 'for you seem to be reading all day'—she set out upon a wintry afternoon, and walked alone to the Priory. The old housekeeper received her very cordially.

'I've been expecting to see you every day, ma'am, since Mr Lansdell left us,' the worthy woman exclaimed: 'for he said as you were rare and fond of books, and was to take away any that you fancied; and John's to carry them for you, ma'am; and I was to pay you every attention. But I was beginning to think you didn't mean to come at all, ma'am.'

There were fires in many of the rooms, for Mr Lansdell's servants had a wholesome terror of that fatal blue mould which damp engenders upon the surface of a picture. The firelight glimmered upon golden frames, and glowed here and there in the ruby depths of rich Bohemian glass, and flashed in fitful gleams upon rare porcelain vases and groups of stainless marble; but the rooms had a desolate look, somehow, in spite of the warmth and light and splendour.

Mrs Warman, the housekeeper, told Isabel of Mr Lansdell's whereabouts. He was at Milan, Lady Gwendoline Pomphrey had been good enough to tell Mrs Warman; somewheres in Italy that was, the housekeeper believed; and he was to spend the rest of the winter in Rome, and then he was going on to Constantinople, and goodness

knows where! For there never was such a traveller, or any one so
restless-like.

'Isn't it a pity he don't marry his cousin Lady Gwendoline, and
settle down like his pa?' said Mrs Warman. 'It do seem a shame for
such a place as this to be shut up from year's end to year's end, till
the very pictures get quite a ghastly way with them, and seem to
state at one reproachful-like, as if they was asking, over and over
again, "Where is he? Why don't he come home?"'

Isabel was standing with her back to the chill winter sky outside
the window, and the housekeeper did not perceive the effect of her
discourse. That simple talk was very painful to Mrs Gilbert. It
seemed to her as if Roland Lansdell's image receded farther and
farther from her in this grand place, where all the attributes of his
wealth and station were a standing evidence of the great gulf between them.

'What am I to him?' she thought. 'What can such a despicable
wretch as I am ever be to him? If he comes home, it will be to marry
Lady Gwendoline. Perhaps he will tell her how he used to meet me
by the mill-stream, and they will laugh together about me.'

The hot blood surged up to her face as she thought of that brief
summer-time, that one glorious glimpse of happiness, that one bright
peep into paradise, which had only served to render the dull earth
uglier and duller than it had been before.

Had her conduct been shameless and unwomanly, and would he
remember her only to despise her? She hoped that if Roland Lansdell
ever returned to Midlandshire, it would be to find her dead. He
could not despise her if she was dead. The only pleasant thought
she had that afternoon was the fancy that Mr Lansdell might come
back to Mordred, and engage himself to his cousin, and the marriage would take place at Graybridge church; and as he was leading
his bride along the quiet avenue, he would start back, anguish-
stricken, at the sight of a newly-erected headstone—'To the memory
of Isabel Gilbert, aged 20.' 20! that seemed quite old, Mrs Gilbert
thought. She had always fancied that the next best thing to marrying a duke would be to fade into an early grave before the age of
eighteen.

The first visit to Mordred made the Doctor's Wife very unhappy.
Was it not a reopening of all the old wounds? Did it not bring too
vividly back to her the happy summer-day when *he* had sat beside

her at luncheon, and bent his handsome head and subdued his deep voice as he talked to her?

Having broken the ice, however, she went very often to the Priory; and on one or two occasions even condescended to take an early cup of tea with Mrs Warman the housekeeper, though she felt that by so doing she in some small measure widened the gulf between Mr Lansdell and herself. Little by little she grew to feel quite at home in the splendid rooms. It was very pleasant to sit in a low easy-chair in the library,—*his* easy-chair,—with a pile of books on the little reading-table by her side, and the glow of the great fire subdued by a noble screen of ground-glass and brazen scroll-work. Mrs Gilbert was honestly fond of reading, and in the library at Mordred her life seemed less bitter than elsewhere. She read a great deal of the lighter literature upon Mr Lansdell's bookshelves,—poems and popular histories, biographies and autobiographies, letters, and travels in bright romantic lands. To read of the countries through which Mr Lansdell wandered seemed almost like following him.

As Mrs Gilbert grew more and more familiar with the grand old mansion, and more and more friendly with Mrs Warman the housekeeper, she took to wandering in and out of all the rooms at pleasure, sometimes pausing before one picture, sometimes sitting before another for half-an-hour at a time lost in reverie. She knew all the pictures, and had learned their histories from Mrs Warman, and ascertained which of them were most valued by Mr Lansdell. She took some of the noble folios from the lower shelves of the library, and read the lives of her favourite painters, and stiff translations of Italian disquisitions on art. Her mind expanded amongst all the beautiful things around her, and the graver thoughts engendered out of grave books pushed away many of her most childish fancies, her simple sentimental yearnings. Until now she had lived too entirely amongst poets and romancers; but now grave volumes of biography opened to her a new picture of life. She read the stories of real men and women, who had lived and suffered real sorrows, prosaic anguish, hard commonplace trial and misery. Do you remember how, when young Caxton's heart has been wrung by youth's bitterest sorrows, the father sends his son to the *Life of Robert Hall** for comfort? Isabel, very foolish and blind as compared with the son of Austin Caxton, was yet able to take some comfort from the stories of good men's sorrows. The consciousness of her ignorance increased

as she became less ignorant; and there were times when this romantic girl was almost sensible, and became resigned to the fact that
Roland Lansdell could have no part in the story of her life. [It is
impossible to live in the constant companionship of great writers
without growing wiser and better in their grave and genial company.
Slow and subtle is the influence that is exercised, unconscious the
improvement that is wrought; but not the less certain. Isabel Gilbert
went home from Mordred by and by with a cheerful countenance,
and greeted her husband pleasantly, and was tolerably reconciled to
a life whose dull monotony was in some manner counterbalanced by
the leisure that left her free to read delightful books.]* If the drowsy
life, the quiet afternoons in the deserted chambers of the Priory,
could have gone smoothly on for ever, I firmly believe that Isabel
Gilbert would have, little by little, developed into a clever and sensible woman; but the current of her existence was not to glide with
one dull motion to the end. There were to be storms and peril of
shipwreck, and fear and anguish, before the waters flowed into a
quiet haven, and the story of her life was ended.

One day in March, one bleak day, when the big fires in the rooms
at Mordred seemed especially comfortable, Mrs Gilbert carried her
books into an inner apartment, half boudoir, half drawing-room, at
the end of a long suite of splendid chambers. She took off her
bonnet and shawl, and smoothed her dark hair before the glass. She
had altered a little since the autumn, and the face that looked out at
her to-day was thinner and older than that passionate tear-blotted
face which she had seen in the glass on the night of Roland Lansdell's
departure. Her sorrow had not been the less real because it was
weak and childish, and had told considerably upon her appearance.
But she was getting over it. She was almost sorry to think that it was
so. She was almost grieved to find that her grief was less keen than
it had been six months ago, and that the splendour of Roland
Lansdell's image was perhaps a trifle faded.

But to-day Mrs Warman was destined to undo the good work so
newly effected by grave books, and to awaken all Isabel's regrets for
the missing squire of Mordred. The worthy housekeeper had received a letter from her master, which she brought in triumph to
Mrs Gilbert. It was a very brief epistle, enclosing cheques for divers
payments, and giving a few directions about the gardens and stables.
'See that pines and grapes are sent to Lord Ruysdale's, whenever he

likes to have them; and I shall be glad if you send hothouse fruit and
flowers occasionally to Mr Gilbert, the surgeon of Graybridge. He
was very kind to some of my people. Be sure that every attention is
shown to Mrs Gilbert whenever she comes to Mordred.'

Isabel's eyes grew dim as she read this part of the letter. He
thought of her far away—at the other end of the world almost, as it
seemed to her, for his letter was dated from Corfu; he remembered
her existence, and was anxious for her happiness! The books were
no use to her that day. She sat, with a volume open in her lap,
staring at the fire, and thinking of *him*. She went back into the old
italics again. His image shone out upon her in all its ancient splendour. Oh, dreary, dreary life where he was not! How was she to
endure her existence? She clasped her hands in a wild rapture. 'Oh,
my darling, if you could know how I love you!' she whispered, and
then started, confused and blushing. Never until that moment had
she dared to put her passion into words. The Priory clocks struck
three succeeding hours, but Mrs Gilbert sat in the same attitude,
thinking of Roland Lansdell. The thought of going home and facing
her daily life again was unutterably painful to her. That fatal letter—so commonplace to a common reader—had revived all the old
exaltation of feeling. Once more Isabel Gilbert floated away upon
the wings of sentiment and fancy, into that unreal region where the
young squire of Mordred reigned supreme, beautiful as a prince in
a fairy tale, grand as a demigod in some classic legend.

The French clock on the mantelpiece chimed the half hour after
four, and Mrs Gilbert looked up, aroused for a moment from her
reverie.

'Half-past four,' she thought; 'it will be dark at six, and I have a
long walk home.'

Home! she shuddered at the simple monosyllable which it is the
special glory of our language to possess. The word is very beautiful,
no doubt; especially so to a wealthy country magnate,—happy owner
of a grand old English mansion, with fair lands and covers, home-
farm and model-farm buildings, shadowy park and sunlit pleasaunce,
and wonderful dairies lined with majolica ware, and musical with
the plashing of a fountain.

But for Mrs Gilbert 'home' meant a square-built house in a dusty
lane, and was never to mean any thing better or brighter. She got up
from her low seat, and breathed a long-drawn sigh as she took her

bonnet and shawl from a table near her, and began to put them on before the glass.

'The parlour at home always looks ugliest and barest and shabbiest when I have been here,' she thought, as she turned away from the glass and moved towards the door.

She paused suddenly. The door of the boudoir was ajar: all the other doors in the long range of rooms were open, and she heard a footstep coming rapidly towards her: a man's footstep! Was it one of the servant's? No; no servant's foot ever touched the ground with that firm and stately tread. It was a stranger's footstep, of course. Who should come there that day except a stranger? *He* was far away—at the other end of the world almost. It was not within the limits of possibility that *his* footfall should sound on the floors of Mordred Priory.

And yet! and yet! Isabel stopped, with her heart beating violently, her hands clasped, her lips apart and tremulous. And in the next moment the step was close to the threshold, the door was pushed open, and she was face to face with Roland Lansdell; Roland Lansdell, whom she never thought to see again upon this earth! Roland Lansdell, whose face had looked at her in her dreams by day and night any time within these last six months!

'Isabel—Mrs Gilbert!' he said, holding out both his hands, and taking hers, which were as cold as death.

She tried to speak, but no sound came from her tremulous lips. She could utter no word of welcome to this restless wanderer, but stood before him breathless and trembling. Mr Lansdell drew a chair towards her, and made her sit down.

'I startled you,' he said; 'you did not expect to see me. I had no right to come to you so suddenly; but they told me you were here, and I wanted so much to see you,—I wanted so much to speak to you.'

The words were insignificant enough, but there was a warmth and earnestness in the tones that was new to Isabel. Faint blushes flickered into her cheeks, so deathly pale a few moments before; her eyelids fell over the dark unfathomable eyes; a look of sudden happiness spread itself upon her face and made it luminous.

'I thought you were at Corfu,' she said. 'I thought you would never, never, never come back again.'

'I have been at Corfu, and in Italy, and in innumerable places. I meant to stay away; but—but I changed my mind, and I came back. I hope you are glad to see me again?'

What could she say to him? Her terror of saying too much kept her silent; the beating of her heart sounded in her ears, and she was afraid that he too must hear that tell-tale sound. She dared not raise her eyes, and yet she knew that he was looking at her earnestly, scrutinisingly even.

'Tell me that you are glad to see me,' he said. 'Ah, if you knew why I went away—why I tried so hard to stay away—why I have come back after all—after all—so many resolutions made and bro-ken—so many deliberations—so much doubt and hesitation! Isabel! tell me you are glad to see me once more!'

She tried to speak, and faltered out a word or two, and broke down, and turned away from him. And then she looked round at him again with a sudden impulse, as innocently and childishly as Zuleika may have looked at Selim; forgetful for a moment of the square-built house in the dusty lane, of George Gilbert, and all the duties of her life.

'I have been so unhappy,' she exclaimed; 'I have been so miser-able; and you will go away again by and by, and I shall never, never see you any more!'

Her voice broke, and she burst into tears; and then, remembering the surgeon all in a moment, she brushed them hastily away with her handkerchief.

'You frightened me so, Mr Lansdell,' she said; 'and I'm very late, and I was just going home, and my husband will be waiting for me. He comes to meet me sometimes when he can spare time. Good-by.'

She held out her hand, looking at Roland nervously as she did so. Did he despise her very much? she wondered. No doubt he had come home to marry Lady Gwendoline Pomphrey, and there would be a fine wedding in the bright May weather. There was just time to go into a consumption between March and May, Mrs Gilbert thought; and her tombstone might be ready for the occasion, if the gods who bestow upon their special favourites the boon of early death would only be kind to her.

'Good-by, Mr Lansdell,' she repeated.

'Let me walk with you a little way. Ah, if you knew how I have travelled night and day; if you knew how I have languished for this hour, and for the sight of—'

For the sight of what? Roland Lansdell was looking down at the pale face of the Doctor's Wife as he uttered that unfinished sentence. But amongst all the wonders that ever made the story of a woman's life wonderful, it could never surely come to pass that a demigod would descend from the ethereal regions which were his common habitation, on *her* account, Mrs Gilbert thought. She went home in the chill March twilight; but not through the bleak and common atmosphere which other people breathed that afternoon; for Mr Lansdell walked by her side, and, not encountering the surgeon, went all the way to Graybridge, and only left Mrs Gilbert at the end of the dusty lane in which the doctor's red lamp already glimmered faintly in the dusk. Would the master of Mordred Priory have been stricken with any sense of shame if he had met George Gilbert? There was an air of decision in Roland Lansdell's manner which seemed like that of a man who acts upon a settled purpose, and has no thought of shame.

CHAPTER X

'MY LOVE'S A NOBLE MADNESS'*

Mr Lansdell did not seem in a hurry to make any demonstration of his return to Mordred. He did not affect any secrecy, it is true; but he shut himself a good deal in his own rooms, and seldom went out except to walk in the direction of Lord Thurston's oak, whither Mrs Gilbert also rambled in the chilly spring afternoons, and where Mr Lansdell and the Doctor's Wife met each other very frequently: not quite by accident now; for, at parting, Roland would say, with supreme carelessness, 'I suppose you will be walking this way tomorrow,—it is the only walk worth taking hereabouts,—and I'll bring you the other volume.'

Lord Ruysdale and his daughter were still at Lowlands; but Mr Lansdell did not betake himself thither to pay his respects to his uncle and cousin, as he should most certainly have done in common courtesy. He did not go near the gray old mansion where the Earl and his daughter vegetated in gloomy and economical state; but Lady Gwendoline heard from her maid that Mr Lansdell had come home; and bitterly resented his neglect. She resented it still more bitterly by and by, when the maid, who was a little faded like her mistress, and perhaps a little spiteful into the bargain, let drop a scrap of news she had gleaned in the servants'-hall. Mr Lansdell had been seen walking on the Graybridge road with Mrs Gilbert, the doctor's wife; 'and it wasn't the first time either; and people do say it looks odd when a gentleman like Mr Lansdell is seen walking and talking oftentimes with such as her.'

The maid saw her mistress's face turn pale in the glass. No matter what the rank or station or sex of poor Othello; he or she is never suffered to be at peace, or to be happy—knowing nothing. There is always 'mine ancient,' male or female, as the case may be, to bring home the freshest information about the delinquent.*

'I have no wish to hear the servants' gossip about my cousin's movements,' Lady Gwendoline said, with supreme hauteur. 'He is the master of his own actions, and free to go where he pleases and with whom he pleases.'

'I'm sure I beg pardon, my lady, and meant no offence,' the maid answered meekly.—'But she don't like it, for all that,' the damsel thought, with an inward chuckle.

Roland Lansdell kept himself aloof from his kindred; but he was not suffered to go his own way unmolested. The road to perdition is not quite so smooth and flower-bestrewn a path as we are sometimes taught to believe. A merciful hand often flings stumbling-blocks and hindering brambles in our way. It is our own fault if we insist upon clambering over the rocky barriers, and scrambling through the briery hedges, in a mad eagerness to reach the goal. Roland had started upon the fatal descent, and was of course going at that rapid rate at which we always travel downhill; but the road was not all clear for him. Charles Raymond of Conventford was amongst the people who heard accidentally of the young man's return; and about a week after Roland's arrival, the kindly philosopher presented himself at the gates of the Priory, and was fortunate enough to find his kinsman at home. In spite of Mr Lansdell's desire to be at his ease, there was some restraint in his manner as he greeted his old friend.

'I am very glad to see you, Raymond,' he said. 'I should have ridden over to Conventford in a day or two. I've come home, you see.'

'Yes, and I am very sorry to see it. This is a breach of good faith, Roland.'

'Of what faith? with whom?'

'With me,' answered Mr Raymond gravely. 'You promised me that you would go away.'

'I did; and I went away.'

'And now you have come back again.'

'Yes,' replied Mr Lansdell, folding his arms and looking full at his kinsman, with an ominous smile upon his face,—'yes; the fact is a little too evident for the basis of an argument. I have come back.'

Mr Raymond was silent for a minute or so. The younger man stood with his back against the angle of the embayed window, and he never took his eyes from his friend's face. There was something like defiance in the expression of his face, and even in his attitude, as he stood with folded arms leaning against the wainscot.

'I hope, Roland, that since you have come home, it is because the reason which took you away from this place has ceased to exist. You come back because you are cured. I cannot imagine it to be otherwise, Roland; I cannot believe that you have broken faith with me.'

'What if I have come home because I find my disease is past all cure! What if I have kept faith with you, and have tried to forget, and come back at last because I cannot!'

'Roland!'

'Ah! it is a foolish fever, is it not? very foolish, very contemptible to the solemn-faced doctor who looks on and watches the wretched patient tossing and writhing, and listens to his delirious ravings. Have you ever seen a man in the agonies of *delirium tremens*, catching imaginary flies, and shrieking about imps and demons capering on his counterpane? What a pitiful disease it is!—only the effect of a few extra bottles of brandy: but you can't cure it. You may despise the sufferer; but you shrink back terror-stricken before the might of the disease. You've done your duty, doctor: you tried honestly to cure my fever, and I submitted honestly to your remedies: but you're only a quack, after all: and you pretended—what all charlatans pretend—to be able to cure the incurable.'

'You have come back with the intention of remaining, then, Roland?'

'*C'est selon!* * I have no present idea of remaining here very long.'

'And in the mean time you allow people to see you walking on the Graybridge road and loitering about Thurston's Crag with Mrs Gilbert. Do you know that already that unhappy girl's name is compromised? The Graybridge people are beginning to couple her name with yours.'

Mr Lansdell laughed aloud, but not with the pleasant laugh which was common to him.

'Did you ever look in a British atlas for Graybridge-on-the-Wayverne?' he asked. 'There are some atlases which do not give the name of the place at all: in others you'll find a little black dot, with the word "Graybridge" printed in very small letters. The *British Gazetteer** will tell you that Graybridge is interesting on account of its church, which &c. &c.; that an omnibus plies to and fro between the village and Warncliffe station; and that the nearest market-town is Wareham. In all the literature of the world, that's about all the student can learn of Graybridge. What an affliction it must be to a traveller in the Upper Pyrenees, or on the banks of the Amazon, to know that people at Graybridge mix his name sometimes with their tea-table gossip! What an enduring torture for a loiterer in fair Grecian isles—an idle dreamer beside the blue depths of a Southern sea—to know that Graybridge disapproves of him!'

'I had better go away, Roland,' Mr Raymond said, looking at his kinsman with a sad reproachful gaze, and stretching out his hand to take up the hat and gloves he had thrown upon a chair near him; 'I can do no good here.'

'You cannot separate me from the woman I love,' answered Roland boldly. 'I am a scoundrel, I suppose; but I am not a hypocrite. I might tell you a lie, and send you away hoodwinked and happy. No, Raymond, I will not do that. If I am foolish and wicked, I have not sinned deliberately. I have striven against my folly and my wickedness. When you talked to me that night at Waverly, you only echoed the reproaches of my own conscience. I accepted your counsel, and ran away. My love for Isabel Gilbert was only a brief infatuation, I thought, which would wear itself out like other infatuations, with time and absence. I went away, fully resolved never to look upon her face again; and then, and then only, I knew how truly and how dearly I loved her. I went from place to place; but I could no more fly from her image than from my own soul. In vain I argued with myself—as better men have done before my time—that this woman was in no way superior to other women. Day by day I took my lesson deeper to heart. I cannot talk of these things to you. There is a kind of profanation in such a discussion. I can only tell you that I came back to England with a rooted purpose in my mind. Do not thrust yourself upon me; you have done your duty, and may wash

your hands of me with Christian-like self-satisfaction; you have nothing further to do in this *galère*.'*

'Oh, Roland, that you should ever come to talk to me like this!
Have you no sense of truth or honour? not even the common instinct of a gentleman? Have you no feeling for that poor honest-
hearted fellow who has judged you by his own simple standard, and
has trusted you implicitly? have you no feeling for him, Roland?'

'Yes, I am very sorry for him; I am sorry for the grand mistake of
his life. But do you think he could ever be happy with that woman?
I have seen them together, and know the meaning of that grand
word "union" as applied to them. All the width of the universe
cannot divide them more entirely than they are divided now. They
have not one single sentiment in common. Charles Raymond, I tell
you I am not entirely a villain; I do still possess some lingering
remnant of that common instinct of which you spoke just now. If I
had seen Isabel Gilbert happy with a husband who loved her, and
understood her, and was loved by her, I would have held myself
aloof from her pure presence; I would have stifled every thought
that was a wrong to that holy union. I am not base enough to steal
the lamp which lights a good man's home. But if I find a man who
has taken possession of a peerless jewel, as ignorant of its value, and
as powerless to appreciate its beauty, as the soldier who drags a
Raffaelle from the innermost shrine of some ransacked cathedral and
makes a knapsack for himself out of the painted canvas; if I find a
pig trampling pearls under his ruthless feet,—am I to leave the
gems for ever in his sty, in my punctilious dread that I may hurt the
feelings of the animal by taking his unvalued treasure away from
him?'

'Other men have argued as you argue to-day, Roland,' answered
Mr Raymond. [He was not at all angry. He had made human nature,
and human folly and frailty, his special study for the last thirty
years, and was as tender and pitiful of the diseases of the mind as a
great physician is of the ailments of the body. Had he not dissected
the mind, and discovered it to be subject to quite as many and as
complicated disorders as those which beset the wonderful structure
of flesh and blood and bone in which it has its mysterious lodgment?]* 'Other men have reasoned as you reason, Roland; but they
have not the less brought trouble and shame and anguish and remorse upon themselves and upon the victims of their sin. Did not

Rousseau* declare that the first man who enclosed a plot of ground and called it "mine" was the enemy of the human race? You young philosophers of our modern day twist the argument another way, and are ready to avow that the man who marries a pretty woman is the foe to all unmarried mankind. He should have held himself aloof, and waited till *the* man arrived upon the scene,—the man with poetic sympathies and sublime appreciation of womanly grace and beauty, and all manner of hazy attributes which are supposed to be acceptable to sentimental womanhood. Bah, Roland! all this is very well on toned paper, in a pretty little hotpressed volume published by Messrs Moxon;* but the universe was never organised for the special happiness of poets. There must be jog-trot existences, and commonplace contentment, and simple everyday households, in which husbands and wives love each other, and do their duty to each other in a plain prosaic manner. Life can't be all rapture and poetry. Ah, Roland, it has pleased you of late years to play the cynic. Let your cynicism save you now. Is it worth while to do a great wrong, to commit a terrible sin, for the sake of a pretty face and a pair of black eyes, for the gratification of a passing folly?'

'It is not a passing folly,' returned Mr Lansdell, fiercely. 'I was willing to think that it was so last autumn, when I took your advice and went away from this place. I know better now. If there is depth and truth any where in the universe, there is depth and truth in my love for Isabel Gilbert. Do not talk to me, Raymond. The arguments which would have weight with other men, have no power with me. It is my fault or my misfortune that I cannot believe in the things in which other men believe. Above all, I cannot believe in formulas. I cannot believe that a few words shuffled over by a parson at Conventford last January twelvemonth can be strong enough to separate me for ever from the woman I love, and who loves me. Yes, she loves me, Raymond!' cried the young man, his face lighting up suddenly with a smile, which imparted a warmth to his dark complexion like the rich glow of a Murillo. 'She loves me, my beautiful unvalued blossom, that I found blooming all alone and unnoticed in a desert—she loves me. If I had discovered coldness or indifference, coquetry or pretence of any kind in her manner the other day when I came home, I would have gone back even then; I would have acknowledged my mistake, and would have gone away to suffer alone. My dear old Raymond, it is your duty, I know, to lecture me and argue with me; but I tell you again it is only wasted labour; I am past all that. Try to pity me, and sympathise with me, if you can. Solitude is not such a pleasant thing, and people do not go through the world alone without some sufficient reason for their loneliness. There must have been some sorrow in your life, dear old friend, some mistake, some disappointment. Remember that, and have pity upon me.'

Mr Raymond was silent for some minutes; he sat with his face shaded with his hand, and the hand was slightly tremulous.

'There was a sorrow in my life, Roland,' he said by and by, 'a deep and lasting one; and it is the memory of that sorrow which makes you so dear to me; but it was a sorrow in which shame had no part. I am proud to think that I suffered, and suffered silently. I think you can guess, Roland, why you have always been, and always must be, as dear to me as my own son.'

'I can,' answered the young man, holding out his hand; 'you loved my mother.'

'I did, Roland, and stood aloof and saw her married to the man she loved. I held her in my arms and blessed her on her wedding-day in the church yonder; but never from that hour to this have I ceased to love and honour her. I have worshipped a shadow all my life; but her image was nearer and dearer to me than the living beauty of other women. I can sympathise with a wasted love, Roland; but I cannot sympathise with a love that seeks to degrade its object.'

'Degrade her!' cried Roland; 'degrade Isabel! There can be no degradation in such a love as mine. But, you see, we think differ-ently, we see things from a different point of view. You look through the spectacles of Graybridge, and see an elopement, a scandal, a paragraph in the county papers. I recognise only the immortal right of two free souls, who know that they have been created for each other.'

'Do you ever think of your mother, Roland? I remember how dearly she loved you, and how proud she was of the qualities that made you worthy to be her son. Do you ever think of her as a living presence, conscious of your sorrows, compassionate of your sins? I think, if you considered her thus, Roland, as I do,—she has never been dead to me; she is the ideal in my life, and lifts my life above its common level,—if you thought of her as I do, I don't think you could hold to the bad purpose that has brought you back to this place.'

'If I believed what you believe,' cried Mr Lansdell, with sudden animation, 'I should be a different man from what I am—a better man than you are, perhaps. I sometimes wonder at such as you, who believe in all the glories of unseen worlds, and yet are so eager and so worldly in all your doings upon this shabby commonplace earth. If *I* believed, I think I should be blinded and intoxicated by the splendour of my heritage; I would turn Trappist, and live in a dumb rapture from year's end to year's end. I would go and hide myself amid the mountain-tops, high up amongst the eagles and the stars, and ponder upon my glory. But you see it is my misfortune not to believe in that beautiful fable. I must take my life as it is; and if, after ten foolish unprofitable years, Fate brings one little chance of supreme happiness in my way, who shall tell me to withhold my hand? who shall forbid me to grasp my treasure?'

Mr Raymond was not a man to be easily put off. He stayed at Mordred for the remainder of the day and dined with his young cousin, and sat talking with him until late at night; but he went away at last with a sad countenance and a heavy heart. Roland's disease was past the cure of philosophy. What chance have Friar Lawrence* and philosophy ever had against Miss Capulet's Grecian nose and dark Italian eyes, the balmy air of a warm Southern night, the low harmonious murmur of a girlish voice, the gleaming of a white arm on a moonlit balcony?

CHAPTER XI

A LITTLE CLOUD

Isabel was happy. He had returned; he had returned to her; never again to leave her! Had he not said something to that effect? He had returned, because he had found existence unendurable away from her presence. Mr Lansdell had told the Doctor's Wife all this, not once, but twenty times; and she had listened, knowing that it was wicked to listen, and yet powerless to shut her ears against the sweet insidious words. She was beloved; for the first time in her life really, truly, sentimentally beloved, like the heroine of a novel. She was beloved; despite of her shabby dresses, her dowdy bonnets, her clumsy country-made boots. All at once, in a moment, she was elevated into a queen, crowned with woman's noblest diadem, the love of a poet. She was Beatrice, and Roland Lansdell was Dante;* or she was Leonora, and he was Tasso*; she did not particularly care which. Her ideas of the two poets and their loves were almost as vague as the showman's notion of the rival warriors of Waterloo.* She was the shadowy love of the poet, the pensive impossible love, who never could be more to him than a perpetual dream.

This was how Isabel Gilbert thought of the master of Mordred, who met her so often now in the chill spring sunshine. There was a kind of wickedness in these stolen meetings no doubt, she thought; but her wickedness was no greater than that of the beautiful princess who smiled upon the Italian poet. In that serene region of romance, that mystic fairyland in which Isabel's fancies dwelt, sin, as the world comprehends it, had no place. There was no such loathsome image in that fair kingdom of fountains and flowers. It was very wrong to meet Mr Lansdell; but I doubt if the happiness of those meetings would have had quite such an exquisite flavour to Isabel had that faint *soupçon* of wickedness been wanting. [Is there not a legend of an elegant Frenchwoman who cried out, 'Oh, if it were only a sin to eat ices!' This one charm was needed to make even a strawberry-ice entirely delicious.]*

Did Mrs Gilbert ever think that the road which seemed so pleasant, the blossoming pathway along which she wandered hand in hand with Roland Lansdell, was all downhill, and that there was a black and hideous goal hidden below in the farthermost valley? No; she was enraptured and intoxicated by her present happiness, blinded by the glory of her lover's face. [She could not have been so guilty had she been less innocent, or let me rather say, less ignorant. It would all go on for ever and ever, she thought, this delicious sentimental happiness. The *blasé* man of the world would never tire of playing this charming part of lover-poet. Lord Thurston's oak would put forth its tender leaflets, and fade, and bloom again; and Roland would never grow weary of loitering beneath the dense umbrageous branches.]* It had been very difficult for her to realise the splendid fact of his love and devotion; but once believing, she was ready to believe for ever. She remembered a sweet sentimental legend of the Rhineland: the story of a knight who, going away to the wars, was reported as dead: whereon his lady-love, despairing, entered a convent, and consecrated the sad remainder of her days to heaven. But by and by the knight, who had not been killed, returned, and finding that his promised bride was lost to him, devoted the remainder of *his* days to constancy and solitude; building for himself a hermitage upon a rock high above the convent where his fair and faithful Hildegonde* spent her pure and pious days. And every morning with the earliest flush of light in the low Eastern sky, and all day long, and when the evening-star rose pale and silvery beneath the purpling heavens, the hermit of love sat at the door of his cell gazing upon the humble casement behind which it pleased him to fancy his pure mistress kneeling before her crucifix, sometimes mingling his name with her prayers. And was not the name of the knight Roland—*his* name? It was such a love as this which Isabel imagined she had won for herself. It is such a love as this which is the dearest desire of womankind,—a beautiful, useless, romantic devotion,—a wasted life of fond regretful worship. Poor weak sentimental Mary of Scotland accepts Chastelar's poetic homage, and is pleased to think that the poet's heart is breaking because of her grace and loveliness, and would like it to go on breaking for ever. But the love-sick poet grows weary of that distant worship, and would scale the royal heavens to look nearer at the brightness of his star; whence come confusions and troubles, and the amputation of that foolish half-demented head.

So there was no thought of peril to herself or to others in Mrs Gilbert's mind when she stood on the bridge above the mill-stream talking with Roland Lansdell. She had a vague idea that she was not exactly doing her duty to her husband; but poor George's image only receded farther and farther from her. Did she not still obey his behests, and sit opposite to him at the little dinner-table, and pour out his tea at breakfast, and assist him to put on his overcoat in the passage before he went out? Could she do more for him than that? No; he had himself rejected all further attention. She had tried to brush his hat once in a sudden gush of dutiful feeling; but she had brushed the nap the wrong way, and had incurred her husband's displeasure. She had tried to read poetry to him, and he had yawned during her lecture. She had put flowers on his dressing-table— white fragile-looking flowers—in a tall slender vase, with a tendril of convolvulus twined artfully round the stem, like a garland about a classic column; and Mr Gilbert had objected to the perfumed blossoms as liable to generate carbonic-acid gas. What could any one do for such a husband as this? The tender sentimental raptures, the poetic emotions, the dim aspirations, which Isabel revealed to Roland, would have been as unintelligible as the Semitic languages to George. Why should she not bestow this other half of her nature upon whom she chose? If she gave her duty and obedience to Othello, surely Cassio might have all the poetry of her soul, which the matter-of-fact Moor despised and rejected.

It was something after this wise that Isabel reasoned, when she did reason at all about her platonic attachment for Roland Lansdell. She was very happy, lulled to rest by her own ignorance of all danger, rather than by any deeply-studied design on the part of her lover. His manner to her was more tender than a father's manner to his favourite child,—more reverential than Raleigh's* to Elizabeth of England,—but in all this he had no thought of deception. The settled purpose in his mind took a firmer root every day; and he fancied that Isabel understood him, and knew that the great crisis of her life was fast approaching, and had prepared herself to meet it.

One afternoon, late in the month, when the March winds were bleaker and more pitiless than usual, Isabel went across the meadows where the hedgerows were putting forth timid little buds to be nipped by the chill breezes, and where here and there a violet made a tiny speck of purple on the grassy bank. Mr Lansdell was standing on the bridge when Isabel approached the familiar trysting-place, and turned with a smile to greet her. But although he smiled as he pressed the slender little hand that almost always trembled in his own, the master of Mordred was not very cheerful this afternoon. It was the day succeeding that on which Charles Raymond had dined with him, and the influence of his kinsman's talk still hung about him and oppressed him. He could not deny that there had been truth and wisdom in his friend's earnest pleading; but he could not abandon his purpose now. Long vacillating and irresolute, long doubtful of himself and all the world, he was resolved at last, and obstinately bent upon carrying out his resolution.

'I am going to London, Isabel,' he said, after standing by Mrs Gilbert for some minutes, staring silently at the water: 'I am going to London to-morrow morning, Isabel.' He always called her Isabel now, and lingered with a kind of tenderness upon the name. Edith Dombey would have brought confusion upon him for this presumption, no doubt, by one bright glance of haughty reproof; but poor

Isabel had found out long ago that she in no way resembled Edith Dombey.

'Going to London!' cried the Doctor's Wife, piteously; 'ah, I knew, I knew that you would go away again, and I shall never see you any more.' She clasped her hands in her sudden terror, and looked at him with a world of sorrow and reproach in her pale face. 'I knew that it would be so!' she repeated; 'I dreamt the other night that you had gone away, and I came here; and, oh, it seemed such a dreadful way to come, and I kept taking the wrong turnings, and going through the wrong meadows; and when I came, there was only some one—some stranger, who told me that you were gone, and would never come back.'

'But, Isabel—my love—my darling—' the tender epithets did not startle her; she was so absorbed by the fear of losing the god of her idolatry; 'I am only going to town for a day or two to see my lawyer—to make arrangements—arrangements of vital importance;— I should be a scoundrel if I neglected them, or incurred the smallest hazard by delaying them an hour. You don't understand these sort of things, Isabel; but trust me, and believe that your welfare is dearer to me than my own. I must go to town; but I shall only be gone a day or two—two days at the most—perhaps only one. And when I come back, Izzie, I shall have something to say to you— something very serious—something that had better be said at once— something that involves all the happiness of my future life. Will you meet me here two days hence,—on Wednesday, at three o'clock? You will, won't you, Isabel? I know I do wrong in exposing you to the degradation of these stolen meetings. If I feel the shame so keenly, how much worse it must be for you—my own dear girl—my sweet innocent darling! But this shall be the last time, Isabel,—the last time I will ask you to incur any humiliation for me. Henceforward we will hold our heads high, my love; for at least there shall be no trickery or falsehood in our lives.'

Mrs Gilbert stared at Roland Lansdell in utter bewilderment. He had spoken of shame and degradation, and had spoken in the tone of a man who had suffered, and still suffered, very bitterly. This was all Isabel could gather from her lover's speech, and she opened her eyes in blank amazement as she listened to him. Why should he be ashamed, or humiliated, or degraded? Was Dante degraded by his love for Beatrice? was Waller degraded by his devotion to

Sacharissa*—for ever evidenced by so many charming versicles, and never dropping down from the rosy cloud-land of poetry into the matter-of-fact regions of prose? Degraded! ashamed!—her face grew crimson all in a moment as these cruel words stung her poor sentimental heart. She wanted to run away all at once, and never see Mr Lansdell again. Her heart would break, as a matter of course; but how infinitely preferable to shame would be a broken heart and early death with an appropriate tombstone! The tears rolled down her flushed cheek, as she turned away her face from Roland. She was almost stifled by mingled grief and indignation.

'I did not think you were ashamed to meet me here sometimes,' she sobbed out; 'you asked me to come. I did not think that you were humiliated by talking to me—I—'

'Why, Izzie—Isabel darling!' cried Roland, 'can you misunderstand me so utterly? Ashamed to meet you—ashamed of your society! Can you doubt what would have happened had I come home a year earlier than it was my ill-fortune to come? Can you doubt for a moment that I would have chosen you for my wife out of all the women in the universe, and that my highest pride would have been the right to call you by that dear name? I was too late, Izzie, too late; too late to win that pure and perfect happiness which would have made a new man of me, which would have transformed me into a good and useful man, as I think. I suppose it is always so; I suppose there is always one drop wanting in the cup of joy, that one mystic drop which would change the commonplace potion into an elixir. I came too late! Why should I have every thing in this world? Why should I have fifteen thousand a-year, and Mordred Priory, and the right to acknowledge the woman I love in the face of all creation, while there are crippled wretches sweeping crossings for the sake of a daily crust, and men and women wasting away in great prison-houses called Unions, whose first law is the severance of every earthly tie? I came too late, and I suppose it was natural that I should so come. Millions of destinies have been blighted by as small a chance as that which has blighted mine, I daresay. We must take our fate as we find it, Isabel; and if we are true to each other, I hope and believe that it may be a bright one even yet—even yet.'

A woman of the world would have very quickly perceived that Mr Lansdell's discourse must have relation to more serious projects than future meetings under Lord Thurston's oak, with interchange of divers volumes of light literature. But Isabel Gilbert was not a woman of the world. She had read novels while other people perused the Sunday papers; and of the world out of a three-volume romance she had no more idea than a baby. She believed in a phantasmal universe, created out of the pages of poets and romancers; she knew that there were good people and bad people—Ernest Maltravers's and Lumley Ferrers's,* Walter Gays and Carkers; but beyond this she had very little notion of mankind; and having once placed Mr Lansdell amongst the heroes, could not imagine him to possess one attribute in common with the villains. If he seemed intensely in earnest about these meetings under the oak, she was in earnest too; and so had been the German knight, who devoted the greater part of his life to watching the casement of his lady-love.

'I shall see you sometimes,' she said with timid hesitation,—'I shall see you sometimes, sha'n't I, when you come home from town? Not often, of course: I daresay it isn't right to come here often, away from George; and the last time I kept him waiting for his dinner; but I told him where I had been, and that I'd seen you, and he didn't mind a bit.'

Roland Lansdell sighed.

'Ah, don't you understand, Isabel,' he said, 'that doubles our degradation? It is for the very reason that he "doesn't mind," it is precisely because he is so simple-hearted and trusting, that we ought not to deceive the poor fellow any longer. *That's* the degradation, Izzie; the deception, not the deed itself. A man meets his enemy in fair fight and kills him, and nobody complains. The best man must always win, I suppose; and if he wins by fair means, no one need grudge him his victory. I mystify you, don't I, my darling, by all this rambling talk? I shall speak plainer on Wednesday. And now let me take you homewards,' added Mr Lansdell, looking at his watch, 'if you are to be at home at five.'

He knew the habits of the doctor's little household, and knew that five o'clock was Mr Gilbert's dinner-hour. There was no conversation of any serious nature during the homeward walk—only dreamy talk about books and poets and foreign lands. Mr Lansdell told Isabel of bright spots in Italy and Greece, wonderful villages upon the borders of blue lakes deeply hidden among Alpine slopes, and snow-clad peaks like stationary clouds—beautiful and picturesque regions which she must see by and by, Roland added gaily.

But Mrs Gilbert opened her eyes very wide and laughed aloud. How should she ever see such places? she asked, smiling. George would never go there: he would never be rich enough to go; nor would he care to go, were he ever so rich.

And while she was speaking, Isabel thought that, after all, she cared very little for those lovely lands; much as she had dreamed about them and pined to see them, long ago in the Camberwell garden, on still moonlight nights, when she used to stand on the little stone step leading from the kitchen, with her arms resting on the water-butt, like Juliet's on the balcony, and fancy it was Italy. Now she was quite resigned to the idea of never leaving Graybridge-on-the-Wayverne. She was content to live there all her life, so long as she could see Mr Lansdell now and then: so long as she could know that he was near her, thinking of her and loving her, and that at any moment his dark face might shine out of the dulness of her life. A perfect happiness had come to her—the happiness of being beloved by the bright object of her idolatry: nothing could add to that perfection: the cup was full to the very brim, filled with an inexhaustible draught of joy and delight.

Mr Lansdell stopped to shake hands with Isabel when they came to the gate leading into the Graybridge road.

'Good-by,' he said softly; 'good-by, until Wednesday, Isabel. Isabel—what a pretty name it is! You have no other Christian name?'

'Oh, no.'

'Only Isabel—Isabel Gilbert. Good-by.'

He opened the gate, and stood watching the Doctor's Wife as she passed out of the meadow, and walked at a rapid pace towards the town. A man passed along the road as Mr Lansdell stood there, and looked at him as he went by, and then turned and looked after Isabel.

'Raymond is right, then,' thought Roland; 'they have begun to stare and chatter already. My poor darling, henceforward it is my duty to protect you from such as these. Graybridge, Graybridge!— the place looks like a gaol. How I long for the free atmosphere of Switzerland; the blue sky, the purple waters, the rainbow-tinted clouds, and shadowy mountain-tops! It is like climbing half-way to heaven to live there. And I am to stop at home in this narrow patch of English landscape, and chain myself down to suit the requirements of Graybridge. I am to be a prisoner for life, with Graybridge for my gaoler; and I am to see my darling's lovely face looking sadly at me from behind the prison-bars, growing paler every day, until it fades away for ever,—rather than outrage the feelings of Graybridge? Let them talk about me at their tea-tables, and paragraph me in their newspapers, to their heart's content! My soul is as much above them as the eagle soaring sunward is above the sheep that stare up at him from the valleys. I have set my foot upon the fiery ploughshare, but my darling shall be carried across it scatheless in the strong arms of her lover.'

Mrs Gilbert went home to her husband, and sat opposite to him at dinner as usual; but Roland's words, dimly as she had comprehended their meaning, had in some manner influenced her, for she blushed when George asked her where she had been that cold afternoon. Mr Gilbert did not see the blush; for he was carving the joint as he asked the question, and indeed had asked it rather as a matter of form than otherwise. This time Mrs Gilbert did not tell her husband that she had met Roland Lansdell. The words 'shame and degradation' were ringing in her ears all dinner-time. She had tasted, if ever so little, of the fruit of the famous tree, and she found the flavour thereof very bitter. It must be wrong to meet Roland under Lord Thurston's oak, since he said it was so; and the meeting on Wednesday was to be the last; and yet their fate was to be a happy one: had he not said so, in eloquently mysterious words, whose full meaning poor Isabel was quite unable to fathom? She brooded over what Mr Lansdell said all that evening, and a dim sense of impending trouble crept into her mind. He was going away for ever, perhaps; and had only told her otherwise in order to lull her to rest with vain hopes, and thus spare himself the trouble of her lamentations. Or he was going to London to arrange for a speedy marriage with Lady Gwendoline. Poor Isabel could not shake off her jealous fears of that brilliant high-bred rival, whom Mr Lansdell had once loved. Yes; he had once loved Lady Gwendoline. Mr Raymond had taken an opportunity of telling Isabel all about the young man's early engagement to his cousin; and he had added a hope that, after all, a marriage between the two might yet be brought about; and had not the housekeeper at Mordred said very much the same thing?

'He will marry Lady Gwendoline,' Isabel thought, in a sudden access of despair; 'and that is what he is going to tell me on Wednesday. He was different to-day from what he has been since he came back to Mordred. And yet—and yet—' And yet what? Isabel tried in vain to fathom the meaning of all Roland Lansdell's wild talk—now earnestly grave—now suddenly reckless—one moment full of hope, and in the next tinctured with despair. What was this simple young novel-reader to make of a man of the world, who was eager to defy the world, and knew exactly what a terrible world it was that he was about to outrage and defy?

Mrs Gilbert lay awake all that night, thinking of the meeting by the waterfall. Roland's talk had mystified and alarmed her. The ignorant happiness, the unreflecting delight in her lover's presence, the daily joy that in its fulness had no room for a thought of the morrow, had vanished all at once like a burst of sunlight eclipsed by the darkening clouds that presage a storm. Eve had listened to the first whispers of the serpent, and Paradise was no longer entirely beautiful.

CHAPTER XII

LADY GWENDOLINE DOES HER DUTY

Mrs Gilbert stayed at home all through the day which succeeded her parting from Roland Lansdell. She stayed in the dingy parlour, and read a little, and played upon the piano a little, and sketched a few profile portraits of Mr Lansdell, desperately inky and sentimental, with impossibly enormous eyes. She worked a little, wounding her fingers, and hopelessly entangling her thread; and she let the fire out two or three times, as she was accustomed to do very often, to the aggravation of Mrs Jeffson. That hard-working and faithful retainer came into the parlour at two-o'clock, carrying a little plate of seed-cake and a glass of water for her mistress's frugal luncheon; and finding the grate black and dismal for the second time that day, fetched a bundle of wood and a box of matches, and knelt down to rekindle the cavernous cinders in no very pleasant humour.

'I'm sorry I've let the fire out again, Mrs Jeffson,' Isabel said meekly. 'I think there must be something wrong in the grate somehow, for the fire always *will* go out.'

'It usen't to go out in Master George's mother's time,' Mrs Jeffson answered, rather sharply; 'and it was the same grate then. But my dear young mistress used to sit in yon chair, stitch, stitch, stitch at the Doctor's cambric shirt-fronts, and the fire was always burning bright and pleasant when he came home. She was a regular stay-at-home, she was,' added the housekeeper, in a musing tone; 'and it was very rare as she went out beyond the garden, except on a summer's evening, when the Doctor took her for a walk. She didn't like going out alone, poor dear; for there was plenty of young squires about Graybridge as would have been glad enough to follow her and talk to her, and set people's malicious tongues chattering about her, if she'd have let 'em. But she never did; she was as happy as the day was long, sitting at home, working for her husband, and always ready to jump up and run to the door when she heard his step outside—God bless her innocent heart!'

Mrs Gilbert's face grew crimson as she bent over a sheet of paper on which the words 'despair' and 'prayer,' 'breath' and 'death,' were twisted into a heartrending rhyme. Ah, this was a part of the shame and degradation of which Roland had spoken. Every body had a right to lecture her, and at every turn the perfections of the dead were cast reproachfully in her face. As if *she* did not wish to be dead and at rest, regretted and not lectured, deplored rather than slandered and upbraided. These vulgar people laid their rude hands upon her cup of joy, and changed its contents into the bitter waters of shame. These commonplace creatures set themselves up as the judges of her life, and turned all its purest and brightest poetry into a prosaic record of disgrace. The glory of the Koh-i-noor* would have been tarnished by the print of such base hands as these. How could these people read her heart, or understand her love for Roland Lansdell? Very likely the serene lady of the Rhineland, praying in her convent-cell, was slandered and misrepresented by vulgar boors, who, passing along the roadway beneath, saw the hermit-knight sitting at the door of his cell and gazing fondly at his lost love's casement.

Such thoughts as this arose in Isabel's mind, and she was angry and indignant at the good woman who presumed to lecture her. She pushed away the plate of stale cake, and went to the window flushed and resentful. But the flush faded all in a moment from her face when she saw a lady in a carriage driving slowly towards the gate,— a lady who wore a great deal of soft brown fur, and a violet-velvet bonnet with drooping feathers, and who looked up at the house as if uncertain as to its identity. The lady was Lord Ruysdale's daughter; and the carriage was only a low basket-phaeton, drawn by a stout bay cob, and attended by a groom in a neat livery of dark blue. But if the simple equipage had been the fairy-chariot of Queen Mab* herself, Mrs Gilbert could scarcely have seemed more abashed and astounded by its apparition before her door. The groom descended from his seat at an order from his mistress, and rang the bell at the surgeon's gate; and then Lady Gwendoline, having recognised Isabel at the window, and saluted her with a very haughty inclination of the head, abandoned the reins to her attendant, and alighted.

Mrs Jeffson had opened the gate by this time, and the visitor swept by her into the little passage, and thence into the parlour, where she found the Doctor's Wife standing by the table, trifling nervously with that scrap of fancy-work whose only progress was to get grimier and grimier day by day under Isabel's idle fingers.

Oh, what a dingy shabby place that Graybridge parlour was always! how doubly and trebly dingy it seemed to-day by contrast with that gorgeous Millais-like figure* of Gwendoline Pomphrey, rich and glorious in violet velvet and Russian sable, with the yellow tints of her hair contrasted by the deep purple shadows under her bonnet. Mrs Gilbert almost sank under the weight of all that aristocratic splendour. She brought a chair for her visitor, and asked in a tremulous voice if Lady Gwendoline would be pleased to sit. There was a taint of snobbishness in her reverential awe of the Earl's handsome daughter. Was not Lady Gwendoline the very incarnation of all her own foolish dreams of the beautiful? Long ago, in the Camberwell garden, she had imagined such a creature; and now she bowed herself before the splendour, and was stricken with fear and trembling in the dazzling presence. And then there were other reasons that she should tremble and turn pale. Might not Lady Gwendoline have come to announce her intended marriage with Mr Lansdell, and to smite the poor wretch before her with sudden madness and despair? Isabel felt that some calamity was coming down upon her: and she stood pale and silent, meekly waiting to receive her sentence.

'Pray sit down, Mrs Gilbert,' said Lady Gwendoline; 'I wish to have a little conversation with you. I am very glad to have found you at home, and alone.'

The lady spoke very kindly, but her kindness had a stately coldness that crept like melted ice through Isabel's veins, and chilled her to the bone.

'I am older than you, Mrs Gilbert,' said Lady Gwendoline, after a little pause, and she slightly winced as she made the confession; 'I am older than you; and if I speak to you in a manner that you may have some right to resent as an impertinent interference with your affairs, I trust that you will believe I am influenced only by a sincere desire for your welfare.'

Isabel's heart sank to a profounder depth of terror than before when she heard this. She had never in her life known any thing but unpleasantness to come from people's desire for her welfare: from the early days in which her stepmother had administered salutary boxes on the ear, and salts-and-senna, with an equal regard to her moral and physical improvement. She looked up fearfully at Lady Gwendoline, and saw that the fair Saxon face of her visitor was almost as pale as her own.

'I am older than you, Mrs Gilbert,' repeated Gwendoline, 'and I know my cousin Roland Lansdell much better than you can possibly know him.'

The sound of the dear name, the sacred name, which to Isabel's mind should only have been spoken in a hushed whisper, like a tender pianissimo* passage in music, shot home to the foolish girl's heart. Her face flushed crimson, and she clasped her hands together, while the tears welled slowly up to her eyes.

'I know my cousin better than you can know him; I know the world better than you can know it. There are some women, Mrs Gilbert, who would condemn you unheard, and who would consider their lips sullied by any mention of your name. There are many women in my position who would hold themselves aloof from you, content to let you go your own way. But I take leave to think for myself in all matters. I have heard Mr Raymond speak very kindly of you; I cannot judge you as harshly as other people judge you; I cannot believe you to be what your neighbours think you.'

'Oh, what, what can they think me?' cried Isabel, trembling with a vague fear, an ignorant fear of some deadly peril utterly unknown to her, and yet close upon her; 'what harm have I done, that they should think ill of me? what can they say of me? what *can* they say?'

Her eyes were blinded by tears, that blotted Lady Gwendoline's stern face from her sight. She was still so much a child, that she made no effort to conceal her terror and confusion. She bared all the foolish secrets of her heart before those cruel eyes.

'People say that you are a false wife to a simple-hearted and trusting husband,' Lord Ruysdale's daughter answered, with pitiless calmness; 'a false wife in thought and intention, if not in deed; since you have lured my cousin back to this place; and are ready to leave it with him as his mistress whenever he chooses to say "Come." That is what people think of you; and you have given them only too much cause for their suspicion. Do you imagine that you could keep any secret from Graybridge? do you think your actions or even your thoughts could escape the dull eyes of these country people, who have nothing better to do than watch the doings of their neighbours?' demanded Lady Gwendoline bitterly. Alas! she knew that her name had been bandied about from gossip to gossip; and that her grand disappointment in the matter of Lord Heatherland, her increasing years, and declining chances of a prize in the matrimonial lottery, had been freely discussed at all the tea-tables in the little country-town.

'Country people find out every thing, Mrs Gilbert,' she said presently. 'You have been watched in your sentimental meetings and rambles with Mr Lansdell; and you may consider yourself very fortunate if no officious person has taken the trouble to convey the information to your husband.'

Isabel had been crying all this time, crying bitterly, with her head bent upon her clasped hands; but to Lady Gwendoline's surprise she lifted it now, and looked at her accuser with some show of indignation, if not defiance.

'I told George every—almost every time I met Mr Lansdell,' she exclaimed; 'and George knows that he lends me books; and he likes me to have books—nice, in-st-structive books,' said Mrs Gilbert, stifling her sobs as best she might; 'and I n-never thought that any body could be so wicked as to fancy there was any harm in my meeting him. I don't suppose any one ever said any thing to Beatrice Portinari, though she was married, and Dante loved her very dearly; and I only want to see him now and then, and to hear him talk; and he has been very, very kind to me.'

'Kind to you!' cried Lady Gwendoline, scornfully. 'Do you know the value of such kindness as his? Did you ever hear of any good coming of it? Did such kindness ever bear any fruit but anguish and misery and mortification? You talk like a baby, Mrs Gilbert, or else like a hypocrite. Do you know what my cousin's life has been? Do you know that he is an infidel, and outrages his friends by opinions which he does not even care to conceal? Do you know that his name has been involved with the names of married women before to-day? Are you besotted enough to think that his new fancy for you is any thing more than the caprice of an idle and dissipated man of the world, who is ready to bring ruin upon the happiest home in England for the sake of a new sensation, a little extra aliment for the vanity which a host of foolish women have pampered into his ruling vice?'

'Vanity!' exclaimed Mrs Gilbert; 'oh, Lady Gwendoline, how can you say that *he* is vain? It is you who do not know him. Ah, if you could only know how good he is, how noble, how generous! I know that he would never try to injure me by so much as a word or a thought. Why should I not love him: as we love the stars, that are so beautiful and so distant from us? Why should I not worship him as Helena worshipped Bertram,* as Viola loved Zanoni?* The wicked Graybridge people may say what they like; and if they tell George any thing about me, I will tell him the truth; and then—and then— if I was only a Catholic, I would go into a convent like Hildegonde! Ah, Lady Gwendoline, you do not understand such love as mine!' added Isabel, looking at the Earl's daughter with an air of superiority that was superb in its simplicity.

She was proud of her love, which was so high above the comprehension of ordinary people. It is just possible that she was even a little proud of the slander which attached to her. She had all her life been pining for the glory of martyrdom, and lo, it had come upon her. The fiery circlet had descended upon her brow; and she assumed a dignified *pose* in order to support it properly, and wondered if the insignia was becoming.

'I only understand that you are a very foolish person,' Lady Gwendoline answered coldly; 'and I have been extremely foolish to trouble myself about you. I considered it my duty to do what I have done, and I wash my hands henceforward of you and your affairs. Pray go your own way, and do not fear any further interference from me. It is quite impossible that I can have the smallest association with my cousin's mistress.'

She hurled the cruel word at the Doctor's Wife, and departed with a sound of silken rustling in the narrow passage. Isabel heard the carriage drive away, and then flung herself down upon her knees, to sob and lament her cruel destiny. That last word had stung her to the very heart. It took all the poetry out of her life: it brought before her, in its fullest significance, the sense of her position. If she met Roland under Lord Thurston's oak,—if she walked with him in the meadows, that his footsteps beautified into the smooth lawns of Paradise,—people, vulgar ignorant people, utterly unable to comprehend her or her love, would say that she was his mistress. His mistress! To what people she had heard that word applied! And Beatrice Portinari, and Viola, and Leila, and Gulnare, and Zelica,* what of them? The visions of all those lovely and shining creatures arose before her; and beside them, in letters of fire, blazed the odious word that transformed her fond platonic worship, her sentimental girlish idolatry, into a shame and disgrace.

'I will see him to-morrow and say farewell to him,' she thought. 'I will bid him good-by for ever and ever, though my heart should break,—ah, how I hope it may, as I say the bitter word!—and never, never will see him again. I know now what he meant by shame and humiliation; I can understand all he said now.'

Mrs Gilbert had another of her headaches that evening, and poor George was obliged to dine alone. He went upstairs once or twice in the course of the evening to see his wife, and found her lying very quietly in the dimly-lighted room with her face turned to the wall. She held out her hand to him as he bent over her, and pressed his broad palm with her feverish fingers.

'I'm afraid I've been neglectful of you sometimes, George,' she said; 'but I won't be so again. I won't go out for those long walks, and keep you waiting for dinner; and if you would like a set of new shirts made—you said the other day that yours were nearly worn out—I should like to make them for you myself. I used to help to make the shirts for my brothers, and I don't think I should pucker so much now; and, oh, George, Mrs Jeffson was talking of your poor mother to-day, and I want you to tell me what it was she died of.'

Mr Gilbert patted his wife's hand approvingly, and laid it gently down on the coverlet.

'That's a melancholy subject, my love,' he said, 'and I don't think it would do either of us any good to talk about it. As for the shirts, my dear, it's very good of you to offer to make them; but I doubt if you'd manage them as well as the workwoman at Wareham, who made the last. She's very reasonable; and she's lame, poor soul; so it's a kind of charity to employ her. Good-by for the present, Izzie; try to get a nap, and don't worry your poor head about any thing.'

He went away, and Isabel listened to his substantial boots creaking down the stairs, and away towards the surgery. He had come thence to his wife's room, and he left a faint odour of drugs behind him. Ah, how that odious flavour of senna and camomile-flowers brought back a magical exotic perfume that had floated towards her one day from *his* hair as he bent his head to listen to her foolish talk! And now the senna and camomile were to flavour all her life. She was no longer to enjoy that mystical double existence, those delicious glimpses of dreamland, which made up for all the dulness of the common world that surrounded her.

If she could have died, and made an end of it all! There are moments in life when death seems the *only* issue from a dreadful labyrinth of grief and horror. I suppose it is only very weak-minded people—doubtful vacillating creatures like Prince Hamlet of Denmark—who wish to die, and make an easy end of their difficulties; but Isabel was not by any means strong-minded, and she thought with a bitter pang of envy of the commonplace young women whom she had known to languish and fade in the most interesting pulmonary diseases, while she so vainly yearned for the healing touch which makes a sure end of all mortal fevers. But there was something—one thing in the world yet worth the weariness of existence—that meeting with *him*—that meeting which was to be also an eternal parting. She would see him once more; he would look down at her with his mysterious eyes—the eyes of Zanoni himself could scarcely have been more mystically dark and deep. She would see him, and perhaps that strangely intermingled joy and anguish would be more fatal than earthly disease, and she would drop dead at his feet, looking to the last at the dark splendour of his face—dying under the spell of his low tender voice. And then, with a shudder, she remembered what Lady Gwendoline had said of her demi-god. Dissipated and an infidel; vain, selfish! Oh, cruel, cruel slander,— the slander of a jealous woman, perhaps, who had loved him and been slighted by him. The Doctor's Wife would not believe any treasonous whisper against her idol. Only from his own lips could come the words that would be strong enough to destroy her illusions. She lay awake all that night, thinking of her interview with Lady Gwendoline, acting the scene over and over again; hearing the cruel words repeated in her ears with dismal iteration throughout the dark slow hours. The pale cheerless spring daylight came at last, and Mrs Gilbert feel asleep just when it was nearly time for her to think of getting up.

The doctor breakfasted alone that morning, as he had dined the day before. He begged that Isabel might not be disturbed. A good long spell of rest was the best thing for his wife's head, he told Mrs Jeffson; to which remark that lady only replied by a suspicious kind of sniff, accompanied by a jerk of the head, and followed by a plaintive sigh, all of which were entirely lost upon the parish-surgeon.

'Females whose headaches keep 'em a-bed when they ought to be seeing after their husband's meals hadn't ought to marry,' Mrs Jeffson remarked, with better sense than grammar, when she took George's breakfast-paraphernalia back to the kitchen. 'I heard down the street just now, as *he* come back to the Priory late last night, and I'll lay she'll be goin' out to meet him this afternoon, William.'

Mr Jeffson, who was smoking his matutinal pipe by the kitchen-fire, shook his head with a slow melancholy gesture as his wife made this remark.

'It's a bad business, Tilly,' he said, 'a bad business first and last. If *he* was any thing of a man, he'd keep away from these parts, and 'ud be above leadin' a poor simple little thing like that astray. Them poetry-books and suchlike, as she's allus a-readin' has half-turned her head long ago, and it only needs a fine chap like him to turn it altogether. I mind what I say to Muster Jarge the night as I fust see her; and I can see her face now, Tilly, as I see it then, with the eyes fixed, and lookin' far away like; and I knew then what I know better still now, my lass,—them two'll never get on together. They warn't made for one another. I wonder sometimes to see the trouble a man 'll take before he gets a pair o' boots, to find out as they're a good fit and won't gall his foot when he comes to wear 'em; but t' same man 'll go and get married as careless and off-hand like, as if there weren't the smallest chance of his wife's not suiting him. I was took by thy good looks, lass, I won't deny, when I first saw thee,' Mr Jeffson added, with diplomatic gallantry; 'but it wasn't because of thy looks as I asked thee to be my true wife, and friend, and companion, throughout this mortal life and all its various troubles.'

CHAPTER XIII

'FOR LOVE HIMSELF TOOK PART AGAINST HIMSELF'*

It was eleven o'clock when Isabel woke; and it was twelve when she sat down to make some pretence of eating the egg and toast which Mrs Jeffson set before her. The good woman regarded her young mistress with a grave countenance, and Mrs Gilbert shrank nervously from that honest gaze. Shame and disgrace—she had denied the application of those hideous words to herself: but the cup which she had repudiated met her lips at every turn, and the flavour of its bitter waters was intermingled with every thing she tasted. She turned away from Mrs Jeffson, and felt angry with her. Presently, when the faithful housekeeper was busy in the kitchen, Mrs Gilbert went softly up stairs to her room, and put on her bonnet and shawl.

She was not to meet *him* till three o'clock in the afternoon, and it was now only a little after twelve; but she could not stay in the house. A terrible fever and restlessness had taken possession of her lately. Had not her life been altogether one long fever since Roland Lansdell's advent in Midlandshire? She looked back, and remembered that she had lived once, and had been decently contented, in utter ignorance of this splendid being's existence. She had lived, and had believed in the shadowy heroes of books, and in great clumsy gray-coated officers stationed at Conventford, and in a sickly curate at Camberwell; and long, long ago—oh, unutterable horror!—in a sentimental-looking young chemist's-apprentice in the Walworth Road, who had big watery-looking blue eyes, and was not so *very* unlike Ernest Maltravers, and who gave more liberal threepenny-worths of lavender-water or hair-oil than any other chemist on the Surrey side of the water—to Isabel! not to other people! Miss Sleaford sent one of the boys for the usual threepenny-worth on one occasion, and the chemist's measure was very different, and the young lady was not a little touched by this proof of her admirer's devotion.

And looking back now she remembered these things, and wondered at them, and hated herself because of them. There was no low image of a chemist's-assistant lurking dimly in the background of Viola's life when she met her fate in the person of Zanoni. All

Isabel's favourite heroines seemed to look out at her reproachfully from their cloudland habitations, as she remembered this portion of her existence. She had lived, and there had been no prophetic vision of *his* face among all her dreams. And now there was nothing for her but to try to go back to the same dull life again, since to-day she was to part from him for ever.

The day was a thorough March day—changeable in mood—now brightened by a sudden glimpse of the sun, now gray and threatening, dull and colourless as the life which lay before Isabel Gilbert when *he* should be gone, and the sweet romance of her existence closed abruptly, like a story that is never to be finished. The Doctor's Wife shuddered as she went out into the lane, where the dust was blown into eddying circles every now and then by a frolicsome north-easter. She closed the gate safely behind her and went away, and to-day for the first time she felt that her errand was a guilty one. She went into the familiar meadow-pathway: she tried to walk slowly, but her feet seemed to carry her towards Thurston's Crag in spite of herself; and when she was far from Graybridge, and looked at her watch, it was only one o'clock, and there were two long hours that must elapse before Roland Lansdell's coming. It was only a quarter past one when she came in sight of the miller's cottage—the pretty little white-walled habitation nestling low down under big trees, which made a shelter even in winter-time. A girl was standing at a door feeding chickens and calling to them in a loud cheerful voice. There was no sorrowful love-story in *her* life, Mrs Gilbert thought, as she looked at the bouncing red-elbowed young woman. She would marry some floury-visaged miller's-man, most likely, and be happy ever after. But it was only a momentary thrill of envy that shot through Isabel's breast. Better to die for Roland Lansdell than to live for a miller's-man in thick clumpy boots and elaborately stitched smock-frock. Better to have lived for the briefest summer time of joy and triumph, and then to stand aloof upon a rock for ever afterwards, staring at the wide expanse of waters, and thinking of the past, like Napoleon at St Helena.

'He has loved me!' thought Isabel; 'I ought never to be unhappy, when I remember that.'

She had brought Shelley with her, and she seated herself upon the bench under the oak; but she only turned the leaves over and over, and listened to the brawling waters at her feet, and thought of

Roland Lansdell. Sometimes she tried to think of what her life would be after she had parted from him; but all the future after four o'clock that afternoon seemed to recede far away from her, beyond the limits of her understanding. She had a vague idea that after this farewell meeting she would be like Louise de la Vallière in the days of her seclusion and penitence. If Father Newman,* or any other enthusiastic Romanist, could have found her sitting by the brawling water that afternoon, he would have secured a willing convert to his tender sentimental creed. The poor bewildered spirit pined for the shadowy aisles of some conventual sanctuary, the low and solemn music, the glimmering shrines, the dreamy exaltation and rapture, the separation from a hard commonplace world. But no sympathetic stranger happened to pass that way while Isabel sat there, watching the path by which Roland Lansdell must come. She took out her watch every now and then, always to be disappointed at the slow progress of the time; but at last—at last—just as a sudden gleam of sunshine lighted the waterfall, and flickered upon the winding path-way, a distant church-clock struck three, and the master of Mordred Priory pushed open a little gate, and came in and out among the moss-grown trunks of the bare elms. In the next minute he was on the bridge; in the next moment, as it seemed, he was seated by Isabel's side, and had taken her passive hand in his. For the last time—for the last time! she thought. Involuntarily her fingers closed on his. How closely they seemed linked together now; they who so soon were to be for ever parted; they between whom all the expanse of the Atlantic would have been only too narrow a barrier!

Mrs Gilbert looked up sadly and shrinkingly at Roland's face, and saw that it was all flushed and radiant. These was just the faintest expression of nervous hesitation about his mouth; but his dark eyes shone with a resolute glance, and seemed more definite in colour than Isabel had ever seen them yet.

'My darling,' he said, 'I am very punctual, am I not? I did not think you would be here before me. You can never guess how much I have thought of our meeting to-day, Isabel:—seriously; solemnly even. Do you remember the garden-scene in *Romeo and Juliet*, Izzie? What pretty sportive boy-and-girl gallantry the love-making seems; and yet what a tragedy comes of it directly after! When I look at you to-day, Isabel, and think of my sleepless nights, my restless weary days, my useless wanderings, my broken vows and wasted resolutions, I look back and remember our first meeting at Warncliffe Castle—our chance meeting. If I had gone away ten minutes sooner, I might not have seen you—I might never have seen you. I look back and see it all. I looked up so indifferently when poor Raymond introduced you to us; it was almost a bore to get up and bow to you. I thought you were very pretty, a beautiful pale-faced automaton, with wonderful eyes that belonged of right to some Italian picture, and not to a commonplace little person like you. And then—having so little to do, being altogether such an idle purposeless wretch, and being glad of any excuse for getting away from my stately cousin and my dear prosy old uncle—I must needs stroll to Hurstonleigh Grove, and meet you again under the changing shadows of the grand old trees. Oh, what was it, Isabel? why was it? Was it only idle curiosity, as I believed, that took me there? Or had the cruel arrow shot home already; was my destiny sealed even then? I don't know— I don't know. I am not a good man, Izzie; but I am not utterly bad either. I went away from you, my dear; I *did* try to avoid the great peril of my life; but—you remember the monk in Hugo's *Notre Dame*.* It seems a grand story in that book, Izzie, but it's the commonest story in all the world. Some day—some careless day—we look out of the window and see the creature dancing in the sunshine, and from that moment every other purpose of our life is done with and forgotten; we can do nothing but go out and follow her wherever she beckons us. If she is a wicked siren, she may lure us into the dark recesses of her cave and pick our bones at her leisure. If she is Undine,* and plunges deep down into the blue water, we can only take a header and go to the bottom after her. But if she is a dear little innocent creature, worthy of our best love and worship, why should we not be happy with her ever afterwards, like the good people in the story-books? why should we not plan a bright life of happiness and fidelity? Isabel, my darling, I want to talk very seriously to you to-day. The crisis has come in our lives, and I am to find out to-day whether you are the true woman I believe you to be, or only a pretty little village coquette, who has fooled me to the top of my bent, and who can whistle me off and let down the wind to prey at fortune directly I become a nuisance. Izzie, I want you to answer a serious question to-day, and all the happiness of my future life depends upon your answer.'

'Mr Lansdell!'

She looked up at him—very much frightened by his manner, but with her hand still clasping his. The link must so soon be broken for ever. Only for a little while longer might she retain that dear hand in hers. Half an hour more, and they would be parted for ever and ever. The pain of that thought was strangely mingled with the delicious joy of being with him, of hearing from his lips that she was beloved. What did she care for Lady Gwendoline now?—cruel jealous Lady Gwendoline, who had outraged and insulted the purity of her love.

'Isabel,' Roland said, very gravely, bending his head to a level with hers, as he spoke, but looking at the ground rather than at her, 'it is time that we ended this farce of duty and submission to the world; we have tried to submit, and to rule our lives by the laws which other people have made for us. But we cannot—we cannot, my dear. We are only hypocrites who try to mask our revolt under the pretence of submission. You come here and meet me, and we are happy together—unutterably and innocently happy. But you leave me and go home to your husband, and smile at him, and tell him that, while you were out walking, you met Mr Lansdell, and so on; and you hoodwink and fool him, and act a perpetual lie for his delusion. All that must cease, Isabel. That Preacher, whom *I* think the noblest reformer, the purest philosopher whose voice was ever heard upon this earth, said that we cannot serve two masters. You cannot go on living the life you have lived for the last three weeks, Isabel. *That* is impossible. You have made a mistake. The world will tell you that, having made it, you must abide by it, and atone for your folly by a life of dissimulation. There are women brave enough—good enough, if you like—to do this, and to bear their burden patiently; but you are not one of them. You cannot dissimulate. Your soul has flown to me like a bird out of a cage; it is mine henceforth and for ever; as surely as that I love you,—fatally, unaccountably, mysteriously, but eternally. I know the strength of my chain, for I have tried to break it. I have held aloof, and tested the endurance of my love. If I ask you now to accept that love, it is because I know that it is true and pure,—the true metal, Izzie, the real virgin gold! I suppose a narrow vein of it runs through every man's nature; but it is only one woman's hand that has power to strike upon the precious ore. I love you, Isabel; and I want you to make an end of your present life, and leave this place for ever. I

have written to an agent to get me a little villa on the outskirts of
Naples. I went there alone, Izzie, two months ago, and set up your
image in the empty rooms, and fancied you hovering here and there
in your white dress, upon the broad marble terrace, with the blue sea
below you, and the mountains above. I have made a hundred plans for
our life, Izzie. There is not a whim or fancy of yours that I have not
remembered. Ah, what happiness! to show you wonderful things and
beautiful scenes! What delicious joy to see your eyes open their widest
before all the fairest pictures of earth! I fancy you with me, Isabel,
and, behold, my life is transformed. I have been so tired of every
thing in the world; and yet, with you by my side, all the world will be
as fresh as Eden was to Adam on the first day of his life. Isabel, you
need have no doubt of me. I have doubted myself, and tested myself.
Mine is no light love, that time or custom can change or lessen: if it
were, I would have done my duty, and stayed away from you for ever.
I have thought of your happiness as well as my own, darling; and I ask
you now to trust me, and leave this place for ever.'

Something like a cry of despair broke from Isabel's lips. 'You ask
me to go away with you!' she exclaimed, looking at Roland as if she
could scarcely believe the testimony of her own ears. 'You ask me to
leave George, and be your—mistress! Oh, Lady Gwendoline only
spoke the truth, then. You don't understand—no one understands
how I love you!'

She had risen as she spoke, and flung herself passionately against
the balustrade of the bridge, sobbing bitterly, with her face hidden
by her clasped hands.

'Isabel, for heaven's sake, listen to me. Can you doubt the purity
of my love—the truth, the honesty of my intentions? I ask you to
sign no unequal compact. Give me your life, and I'll give you mine
in exchange—every day—every hour. Whatever the most exacting
wife can claim of her husband, you shall receive from me. Whatever
the truest husband can be to his wife, I swear to be to you. It is only
a question of whether you love me, Isabel. You have only to choose
between me and that man yonder.'

'Oh, Roland! Roland! I have loved you so—and you could think
that I—. Oh, you must despise me—you must despise me very
much, and think me very wicked, or you would never—'

She couldn't say any more; but she still leant against the bridge,
sobbing for her lost delusion.

Lady Gwendoline had been right, after all,—this is what Isabel thought,—and there had been no Platonism, no poet-worship on Roland Lansdell's side; only the vulgar everyday wish to run away with another man's wife. From first to last she had been misunderstood; she had been the dupe of her own fancies, her own dreams. Lady Gwendoline's cruel words were only cruel truths. It was no Dante, no Tasso,* who had wandered by her side: only a dissipated young country squire, in the habit of running away with other people's wives, and glorying in his iniquity. There was no middle standing-place which Roland Lansdell could occupy in this foolish girl's mind. If he was not a demi-god, he must be a villain. If he was not an exalted creature, full of poetic aspirations and noble fancies, he must be a profligate young idler, ready to whisper any falsehood into the ears of foolish rustic womanhood. All the stories of aristocratic villany that she had ever read flashed suddenly back upon Mrs Gilbert's mind, and made a crowd of evidence against Lady Anna Lansdell's son. If he was not the one grand thing which she had believed him to be—a poetic and honourable adorer—he was in nothing the hero of her dreams. She loved him still, and must continue to love him, in spite of all his delinquencies: but she must love him henceforward with fear and trembling, as a splendid iniquitous creature, who had not even one virtue to set against a thousand crimes. Such thoughts as these crowded upon her, as she leaned sobbing on the narrow wooden rail of the bridge; while Roland Lansdell stood by, watching her with a grave and angry countenance.

'Is this acting, Mrs Gilbert? Is this show of surprise and indignation a little comedy, which you play when you want to get rid of your lovers? Am I to accept my dismissal, and bid you good afternoon, and put up patiently with having been made the veriest fool that ever crossed this bridge?'

'Oh, Roland!' cried Isabel, lifting her head and looking piteously round at him, 'I loved you so—I l-loved so!'

'You love me so, and prove your love by fooling me with tender looks and blushes, till I believe that I have met the one woman in all the world who is to make my life happy. Oh, Isabel, I have loved you because I thought you unlike other women. Am I to find that it is only the old story after all—falsehood, and trick, and delusion? It was a feather in your cap, to have Mr Lansdell of the Priory madly in love with you; and now that he grows troublesome, you send him about his business. I am to think this, I suppose. It has all been coquetry and falsehood from first to last.'

'Falsehood! Oh, Roland, when I love you so dearly—so dearly and truly; not as you love me,—with a cruel love that would bring shame and disgrace upon me. You never can be more to me than you are now. We may part; but there is no power on earth that can part my soul from yours, or lessen my love. I came to you this afternoon to say good-by for ever, because I have heard that cruel things have been said of me by people who do not understand my love. Ah, how should those common people understand, when even you do not, Roland? I came to say good-by; and then, after to-day, my life will be finished. You know what you said that night: "The curtain goes down, and all is over!" I shall think of you for ever and ever, till I die. Ah, is there any kind of death that can ever make me forget you? but I will never come here again to see you. I will always try to do my duty to my husband.'

'Your husband!' cried Mr Lansdell with a strident laugh; 'had we not better leave *his* name out of the question? Oh, Isabel!' he exclaimed, suddenly changing his tone, 'so help me Heaven, I cannot understand you. Are you only an innocent child, after all, or the wiliest coquette that ever lived? You must be one or the other. You speak of your husband. My poor dear, it is too late in the day now to talk of him. You should have thought of him when we first met; when your eyelids first drooped beneath my gaze; when your voice first grew tremulous as you spoke my name. From the very first you have lured me on. I am no trickster or thief, to steal another man's property. If your heart had been your husband's when first I met you, the beauty of an angel in a cathedral fresco would not have been farther away from me than yours. Depend upon it, Eve was growing tired of Eden when the serpent began to talk to her. If you had loved your husband, Isabel, I should have bowed my head before the threshold of your home, as I would at the entrance to a chapel. But I saw that you did not love him; I very soon saw that you did love, or seemed to love, me. Heaven knows I struggled against the temptation, and only yielded at last when my heart told me that my love was true and honest, and worthy of the sacrifice I ask from you. I do ask that sacrifice; boldly, as a man who is prepared to give measure for measure. The little world to which you

will say good-by, Isabel, is a world whose gates will close on me in
the same hour. Henceforth your life will be mine, with all its forfeitures.
I am not an ambitious man; and have long ceased to care about
making any figure in a world which has always seemed to me more
or less like a show at a fair, with clanging cymbals and brazen trumpets, and promise and protestation and boasting outside, and only
delay and disappointment and vexation within. I do not give up very
much, therefore; but what I have I freely resign. Come with me,
Isabel, and I will take you away to the beautiful places you have been
pleased to hear me talk about. All the world is ours, my darling,
except this little corner of Midlandshire. Great ships are waiting to
waft us away to far Southern shores, and tropical paradises, and deep
unfathomable forests. All the earth is organised for our happiness.
The money that has been so useless to me until now shall have a new
use henceforward, for it shall be dedicated to your pleasure. Do you
remember opening your eyes very wide the other day, Isabel, and
crying out that you would like to see Rome, and poor Keats's grave,
and the Colosseum,—Byron's Colosseum,—where the poetic gladia-
tor thought of his wife and children, eh, Izzie? I made such a dream
out of that little childish exclamation. I know the balcony in which
we will sit, darling, after dark nights in Carnival time, to watch the
crowd in the streets below, and, on one grandest night of all, the big
dome of St Peter's shining like a canopy of light, and all the old
classic pediments and pillars blazing out of the darkness, as in a city
of living fire. Isabel, you cannot have been ignorant of the end to
which our fate was drifting us; you must have known that I should
sooner or later say what I have said to-day.'

'Oh, no, no, no!' cried Mrs Gilbert despairingly, 'I never thought
that you would ask me to be more to you than I am now: I never
thought that it was wicked to come here and meet you. I have read
of people, who by some fatality could never marry, loving each
other, and being true to others for years and years—till death, sometimes; and I fancied that you loved me like that: and the thought of
your love made me so happy; and it was such happiness to see you
sometimes, and to think of you afterwards, remembering every word
you had said, and seeing your face as plainly as I see it now. I
thought, till yesterday, that this might go on for ever, and never,
never believed that you would think me like those wicked women
who run away from their husbands.'

'And yet you love me?'

'With all my heart.'

She looked at him with eyes still drowned in tears, but radiant with the truth of her sentimental soul, which had never before revealed itself so artlessly as now. Fondly as she worshipped her idol, his words had little power to move her, now that he was false to his attributes, and came down upon common ground and wooed her as an everyday creature. If Mr Lansdell had declared his intention of erecting a marble mausoleum in the grounds of Mordred, and had requested Isabel to commit suicide in order to render herself competent to occupy it with him immediately, she would have thought his request both appropriate and delightful, and would have assented on the spot. But his wild talk of foreign travel had no temptation for her. True, she saw as in a bright and changing vision a picture of what her life might be far away amidst wild romantic regions in that dear companionship. But between herself and those far-away visions there was a darkly-brooding cloud of shame and disgrace. The Graybridge people might say what they chose of her: she could afford to hold her head high and despise their slanderous whispers: but she could *not* afford to tarnish her love—her love which had no existence out of bright ideal regions wherein shame could never enter.

Roland Lansdell watched her face in silence for some moments, and faintly comprehended the exaltation of spirit which lifted this foolish girl above him to-day. But he was a weak vacillating young man, who was unfortunate enough not to believe in any thing: and he was, in his own fashion, truly and honestly in love,—too much in love to be just or reasonable,—and he was very angry with Isabel. The tide of his feeling had gathered strength day by day, and had relentlessly swept away every impediment, only to be breasted at last by a rocky wall; here, where he thought to meet only the free boundless ocean, ready to receive and welcome him.

'Isabel,' he said at last, 'have you ever thought what your life is to be, always, after this parting of to-day? You are likely to live forty years, and even when you have got through them, you will not be an old woman. Have you ever contemplated those forty years, with three hundred and sixty-five days in every one of them; every day to be spent with a man you don't love—a man with whom you have not one common thought? Think of that, Isabel; and then, if you do love me, think of the life I offer you, and choose between them.'

'I can only make one choice,' Mrs Gilbert answered, in a low sad voice. 'I shall be very unhappy, I daresay; but I will do my duty to my husband and—think of you.'

'So be it!' exclaimed Mr Lansdell, with a long-drawn sigh. 'In that case, good-by.' He held out his hand, and Isabel was startled by the coldness of its touch.

'You are not angry with me?' she asked piteously.

'I have no right to be angry with any one but myself. I do not suppose you meant any harm; but you have done me the deepest wrong a woman can do to a man. I have nothing to say to you except good-by. For mercy's sake go away, and leave me to myself.'

She had no pretence for remaining with him after this; so she went away, very slowly, frightened and sorrowful. But when she had gone a few yards along the pathway under the trees, she felt all at once that she could not leave him thus. She must see his face once more: she must know for certain whether he was angry with her or not.

She crept slowly back to the spot where she had left him, and found him lying at full length upon the grass, with his face hidden on his folded arms. With a sudden instinct of grief and terror she knew that he was crying, and falling down on her knees by his side, murmured, amidst her sobs—

'Oh, pray forgive me! Pray do not be angry with me! I love you so dearly and so truly! Only say that you forgive me.'

Roland Lansdell lifted his face and looked at her. Ah, what a reproachful look it was, and how long it lived in her memory and disturbed her peace!

'I will forgive you,' he answered sternly, 'when I have learnt to endure my life without you.'

He dropped his head again upon his folded arms, and Isabel knelt by his side for some minutes watching him silently; but he never stirred; and she was too much frightened and surprised by his anger, and remorsefully impressed with a vague sense of her own wrong-doing, to dare address him further. So at last she got up and went away. She began to feel that she had been, somehow or other, very wicked, and that her sin had brought misery upon this man whom she loved.

END OF VOLUME II

VOLUME III

CHAPTER I

A POPULAR PREACHER

What could Isabel Gilbert do? The fabric of all her dreams was shivered like a cobweb in a sudden wind, and floated away from her for ever. Every body had misunderstood her. Even *he*, who should have been a demigod in power of penetration as in every other attribute,—even he had wronged and outraged her, and never again could she look trustfully upward to the dark beauty of his face; never again could her hand rest, oh, so lightly, for one brief instant on his arm; never again could she tell him in childish confidence all the vague yearnings, the innocently-sentimental aspirations, of her childish soul.

Never any more. The bright ideal of her life had melted away from her like a spectral cloud of silvery spray hovering above an Alpine waterfall, and had left behind only a cynical man of the world, who boldly asked her to run away from her husband, and was angry with her because she refused to comply with his cruel demand.

Not for one moment did the Doctor's Wife contemplate the possibility of taking the step which Roland Lansdell had proposed to her. Far off—as far away from her as some dim half-forgotten picture of fairyland—there floated a vision of what her life might have been with him, if she had been Clotilde, or the glittering Duchess, or Lady Gwendoline, or some one or other utterly different from herself. But the possibility of deliberately leaving her husband to follow the footsteps of this other man, was as far beyond her power of comprehension as the possibility that she might steal a handful of arsenic out of one of the earthenware jars in the surgery, and mix it with the sugar that sweetened George Gilbert's matutinal coffee.

She wandered away from Thurston's Crag, not following the meadow pathway that would have taken her homeward; but going any where, half-unconscious, wholly indifferent where she went; and thinking, with unutterable sadness, of her broken dreams.

She had been so childish, so entirely childish, and had given herself up so completely to that one dear day-dream. I think her childhood floated away from her for ever in company with that broken dream; and that the gray dawn of her womanhood broke upon her, cold and chill, as she walked slowly away from the spot where Roland Lansdell lay face downwards on the grass, weeping over the ruin of *his* dream. It seemed as if in that hour she crossed Mr Longfellow's typical rivulet* and passed on to the bleak and sterile country beyond. Well may the maiden linger ere she steps across that narrow boundary; for the land upon this hither side is very bare and desolate as compared with the fertile gardens and pleasant meads she abandons for ever. The sweet age of enchantment is over; the fairy companions of girlhood, who were loveliest even when most they deluded, spread their bright wings and flutter away; and the grave genius of common-sense—a dismal-looking person, who dresses in gray woollen stuff, warranted not to shrink under the ordeal of the wash-tub, and steadfastly abjures crinoline—stretches out her hand, and offers, with a friendly but uncompromising abruptness, to be the woman's future guide and monitress.

Isabel Gilbert was a woman all at once; ten years older by that bleak afternoon's most bitter discovery. Since there was no one in the world who understood her, since even *he* so utterly failed to comprehend her, it must be that her dreams were foolish and impossible of comprehension to any one but herself. But those foolish dreams had for ever vanished. She could never think of Roland Lansdell again as she had thought of him. All her fancies about him had been so many fond and foolish delusions. He was not the true and faithful knight who could sit for ever at the entrance of his hermitage gazing fondly at the distant convent-casement, which might or might not belong to his lost love's chamber. No: he was quite another sort of person. He was the fierce dissolute cavalier, with a cross-handled sword a yard and a half long, and pointed shoes with long cruel spurs and steel chain-work jingling and clanking as he strode across his castle-hall. He was the false and wicked lover who would have scaled the wall of Hildegonde's calm retreat some fatal night, and would have carried the shrieking nun away, to go mad and throw herself into the Rhine on the earliest opportunity. He was a heartless Faust, ready to take counsel of Mephistopheles and betray poor trusting Gretchen.* He was Robert the Devil,* about whose accursed footsteps a whole graveyard of accusing spirits might arise at any moment. He was Steerforth, handsome, heartless, irresistible Steerforth, with no pity for simple Em'ly or noble Pegotty's broken heart.*

It may be that Isabel did not admire Mr Lansdell less when she thought of him thus; but there was an awful shuddering horror mingled with her admiration. She was totally unable to understand him as he really was—a benevolently-disposed young man, desirous of doing as little mischief in the world as might be compatible with his being tolerably happy himself; and fully believing that no great or irreparable harm need result from his appropriation of another man's wife.

The tears rolled slowly down Mrs Gilbert's pale cheeks as she walked along the Midlandshire lanes that afternoon. She did not weep violently, or abandon herself to any wild passion of grief. As yet she was quite powerless to realise the blankness of her future life, now that her dream was broken for ever. Her grief was not so bitter as it had been on the day of Roland's sudden departure from Mordred. He had loved her—she knew that now; and the supreme triumph of that thought supported her in the midst of her sorrow. He had loved her. His love was not the sort of thing she had so often read of, and so fondly believed in; it was only the destroying passion of the false knight, the cruel fancy of the wicked squire in top-boots, whom she had frequently seen—per favour of a newspaper-order—from the back-boxes of the Surrey Theatre.* But he *did* love her! He loved her so well as to cast himself on the ground and weep because she had rejected him; and the wicked squire in top-boots had never gone so far as that, generally contenting himself with more practical evidences of his vexation, such as the levying of an execution on the goods and chattels of the heroine's father, or the waylaying and carrying off of the heroine herself by hired ruffians. How oddly it happens that the worthy farmer in the chintz-waistcoat is *always* in arrear with his rent, and always stands in the relation of tenant to the dissolute squire!

Would Mr Lansdell do any thing of that kind? Isabel gave a little shiver as she glanced at the lonely landscape, and thought how a brace of hireling scoundrels might spring suddenly across the hedge, and bear her off to a convenient postchaise. Were there any postchaises in the world now, Isabel wondered. A strange confusion of thoughts filled her mind. She could not become *quite* a woman all in a moment; the crossing of the mystic brook is not so rapid an operation as that. Some remnants of the old delusions hung about her, and merely took a new form. Only the hand of wisdom could pluck the bandage from her eyes, and enable her to see things as they really were.

She sat down on the lower step of a stile to rest herself by and by, and smoothed back her hair, which had been blown about her face by the March wind, and retied the strings of her bonnet, before she went out on the high-road, that lay on the other side of the stile. When she did emerge upon the road, she found herself ever so far from home, and close to the model village where Mr Raymond had given his simple entertainment of tea and pound-cake, and in which George Gilbert had stood by her side pleading to her with such profound humility. Poor George! The quiet aspect of the village-green, the tiny cottages, trim and bright in the fading March sunshine; the low wooden gate opening into the churchyard,—all these, so strange and yet so familiar, brought back the memory of a time that seemed unspeakably far away now. She remembered the faint thrill of pleasure which had stirred her breast when the young surgeon asked her to be his wife. She did not for a moment think of what might have happened to her had she refused to hear his prayer. She could not imagine herself free, and Roland Lansdell her honourable suitor. She had thought of him as a remotely-grand and star-like creature to be worshipped for ever by kneeling devotees offering perpetual incense, and entirely happy in the radiance of his countenance. She thought of him now as a dark and destroying angel, in whose presence there was woe and ruin. She could not regard him without exaggeration; her imagination was a kind of magnifying glass, through which she had always seen him,—a dimly-gorgeous figure, vaguely grand and wonderful, in the misty atmosphere of her girlish fancies.

It was Passion-week,—for Easter fell very late in March this year,—and the model village being a worthy model in the matter of piety as well as in all other virtues, there was a great deal of church-going among the simple inhabitants. The bells were ringing for evening-service now, as Mrs Gilbert lingered in the road between the village and the churchyard; and little groups of twos and threes, and solitary old women in black bonnets, passed her by, as she loitered quite at a loss whither to go, or what to do. They looked at her with solemn curiosity expressed in their faces. She was a stranger there, though Graybridge was only a few miles away; she was a stranger, and that alone, in any place so circumscribed as the model village, was enough to excite curiosity; and it may be that, over and above this, there was something in the look of her pale face and heavy eyelids, and a certain absent expression in her downcast eyes, calculated to arouse suspicion. Even in the midst of her trouble she could see that people looked at her suspiciously; and all in a moment there flashed back upon her mind the cruel things that Lady Gwendoline Pomphrey had said to her. Yes; all at once she remembered those bitter sentences. She had made herself a subject for slanderous tongues, and the story of her wicked love for Roland Lansdell was on every lip. If *he*, who should have known her—if he before whom she had bared all the secrets of her sentimental soul—if even he thought so badly of her as to believe that she could abandon her husband and become the thing that Mr Dombey believed his wife to be when he struck his daughter on the stairs—the sort of creature whom grave Judge Brandon* met one night under a lamp-post in a London street—how could she wonder that other people slandered and despised her? Very suddenly had the gates of Paradise closed upon her: very swiftly had she been dropped down from the fairy regions of her fancy to this cold, hard, cruel workaday world; and being always prone to exaggeration, she fancied it even colder, harder, and more cruel than it was. She fancied the people pointing at her in the little street at Graybridge; the stern rector preaching at her in his Sunday sermon. She pictured to herself every thing that is most bitterly demonstrative in the way of scorn and contumely. The days were past in which solemn elders of Graybridge could send her out to wander here and there with bare bleeding feet and a waxen taper in her hand. There was no scarlet letter* with which these people could brand her as the guilty creature they believed her to be; but short of this, what could they *not* do to her? She imagined it all: her husband would come to know what was thought of her, and to think of her as others thought, and she would be turned out of doors. [The day had been when she thought it must be rather a nice thing to be turned out of doors, to wander Florence-Dombey-like through the streets of a great city; but Miss Dombey had Captain Cuttle's cosy little home for her haven of shelter, and the belief in 'drownded

Wal'r's' excellence to support her in the hour of trial. Poor Isabel had no friend on earth, except indeed that weak querulous stepmother far away in cheap untaxed Jersey, and already all but devoured out of house and home by boys. Isabel had no friend: for was not *he* in whom she had trusted her cruel enemy now, inasmuch as he had done her the deepest wrong of all by his inability to understand her? Who would believe in her or help her, if all Graybridge was against her? She fancied the door of that square house in the dusty lane shut upon her for ever, and only a blank and harsh-judging universe before her.]*

The groups of quiet people—almost all of them were women, and very few of them were young—melted slowly into the shadowy church-porch, like the dusky unsubstantial figures in a dioramic picture.* The bells were still ringing in the chill twilight; but the churchyard was very lonely now; and the big solemn yew-trees looked weird and ghost-like against the darkening gray sky. Only one long low line of pale yellow light remained of the day that was gone! the day in which Isabel had said farewell to Roland Lansdell! It was a real farewell; no lovers' quarrel, wherefrom should spring that renewal of love so dismally associated with the Eton Latin-Grammar. It was an eternal parting; for had he not told her to go away from him—to leave him for ever? Not being the wicked thing for which he had mistaken her, she was nothing in the world for him. He did not require perpetual worship; he did not want her to retire to a convent, in order that he might enjoy himself for the rest of his existence by looking up at her window; he did not want her to sit beside a brasier of charcoal with her hand linked in his—and die. He was not like that delightful Henry von Kleist,* who took his Henriette to a pleasant inn about a mile from Potsdam, supped gaily with her, and then shot her and himself beside a lake in the neighbourhood. Mr Lansdell wanted nothing that was poetical or romantic, and had not even mentioned suicide in the course of his passionate talk.

She went into the churchyard, and walked towards the little bridge upon which she had stood with George Gilbert by her side. The Wayverne flowed silently under the solid moss-grown arch; the wind had gone down by this time, and there was only now and then a faint shiver of the long dark rushes, as if the footsteps of the invisible dead, wandering in the twilight, had stirred them. She stood on the bridge, looking down at the quiet water. The opportunity had come now, if she really wanted to drown herself. Happily for weak mankind, self-destruction is a matter in which opportunity and in-clination very seldom go together. The Doctor's Wife was very miserable; but she did not feel quite prepared to take that decisive plunge which might have put an end to her earthly troubles. Would they hear the splash yonder in the church, if she dropped quietly in among the rushes from the sloping bank under the shadow of the bridge? Would they hear the water surging round her as she sank, and wonder what the sound meant, and then go on with their prayers, indifferent to the drowning creature, and absorbed by their devo-tions? She wondered what these people were like, who kept their houses so tidily, and went to church twice a day in Passion-week, and never fell in love with Roland Lansdell. Long ago, in her child-hood, when she went to see a play, she had wondered about the people she met in the street; the people who were not going to the theatre. Were they very unhappy? did they know that she had a free admission to the upper-boxes of the Adelphi, and envy her? How would *they* spend the evening,—they who were not going to weep with Mr Benjamin Webster, or Miss Sarah Woolgar?* Now she wondered about people who were not miserable like herself—simple commonplace people, who had no yearnings after a life of poetry and splendour. She thought of them as a racer, who had just run second for the Derby, might think of a quiet pack-horse plodding along a dusty road and not wanting to win any race whatsoever.

'Even if they knew him, they wouldn't care about him,' she thought. They did know him, perhaps,—saw him ride by their open win-dows, on a summer's afternoon, gorgeous on a two-hundred-guinea hack, and did not feel the world to be a blank desert when he was gone.

Did she wish to be like these people? No! Amid all her sorrow she could acknowledge, in the words of the poet,* that it was better to have loved and lost him, than never to have loved him at all. Had she not lived her life, and was she not entitled to be a heroine for ever and ever by reason of her love and despair?

For a long time she loitered on the bridge, thinking of all these things, and thinking very little of how she was to go back to Graybridge, where her absence must have created some alarm by this time. She had often kept the surgeon waiting for his dinner before to-day; but she had never been absent when he ate it. There was a station at the model village; but there was no rail to Graybridge; there was only a lumbering old omnibus, that conveyed railway-passengers thither. Isabel left the churchyard, and went to the little inn before which George had introduced her to his gardener and factotum. A woman standing at the door of this hostelry gave her all needful information about the omnibus, which did not leave the station till half-past eight o'clock; until that time she must remain where she was. So she went slowly back to the churchyard, and being tired of the cold and darkness without, crept softly into the church.

The church was very old and very irregular. There were only patches of yellow light here and there, about the pulpit and reading-desk, up in the organ-loft, and near the vestry-door. A woman came out of the dense obscurity as Isabel emerged from the porch, and hustled her into a pew; scandalised by her advent at so late a stage of the service, and eager to put her away somewhere as speedily as possible. It was a very big pew, square and high, and screened by faded curtains, hanging from old-fashioned brass-rods. There were a great many hassocks, and a whole pile of prayer and hymn books in the darkest corner; and Isabel, sitting amongst these, felt as completely hidden as if she had been in a tomb. The prayers were just finished,—the familiar prayers, which had so often fallen like a drowsy cadence of meaningless words upon her unheeding ears, while her erring and foolish thoughts were busy with the master of Mordred Priory.

She heard the footsteps of the clergyman coming slowly along the matted aisle—the rustling of his gown as he drew it on his shoulders; she heard the door of the pulpit closed softly; and then a voice, a low earnest voice, that sounded tender and solemn in the stillness, recited the preliminary prayer. There are voices which make people cry,—voices which touch too acutely on some hidden spring within us, and open the flood-gates of our tears; and the voice of the curate of Hurstonleigh was one of these. He was only a curate; but he was very popular in the model village, and the rumour of his popularity had already spread to neighbouring towns and villages. People deserted their parish-churches on a Sunday afternoon and came to hear Mr Austin Colborne preach one of his awakening sermons. He was celebrated for awakening sermons. The stolid country-people wept aloud sometimes in the midst of one of his discourses. He was always in earnest; tenderly earnest, sorrowfully earnest, terribly earnest sometimes. His life, too, outside the church was in perfect harmony with the precepts he set forth under the shadow of the dark oaken sounding-board. There are some men who *can* believe, who can look forward to a prize so great and wonderful as to hold the pain and trouble of the race of very small account when weighed against the hope of victory. Austin Colborne was one of these men. The priestly robes he wore had not been loosely shuffled on by him because there was no other lot in life within his reach. He had assumed his sacred office with all the enthusiasm of a Loyola or an Irving,* and he knew no looking back. It was such a man as this whom people came to hear at the little church beside the wandering Wayverne. It was such a man as this whose deep-toned voice fell with a strange power upon Isabel Gilbert's ears to-night. Ah, now she could fancy Louise de la Vallière low on her knees in the black shadow of a gothic pillar, hearkening to the cry of the priest who called upon her to repent and be saved. For some little time she only heard the voice of the preacher—the actual words of his discourse fell blankly on her ear. At first it was only a beautiful voice, a grand and solemn voice, rising and sinking on its course like the distant murmur of mighty waves for ever surging towards the shore. Then, little by little, the murmurs took a palpable form, and Isabel Gilbert found that the preacher was telling a story. Ah, that story, that exquisite idyll, that solemn tragedy, that poem so perfect in its beauty, that a sentimental Frenchman has only to garnish it with a few flowery periods, and lo, all the world is set reading it on a sudden, fondly believing they have found something new. Mr Austin Colborne was very fond of dwelling on the loveliness of that sublime history, and more frequently founded his discourse upon some divine incident in the records of the four Evangelists than on an obscure saying in St Paul's Epistles to the Corinthians or the Hebrews. This is no place in which to dwell upon Mr Austin Colborne, or the simple Christian creed it was his delight to illustrate. He was a Christian, according to the purest and simplest signification of the word. His sermons were within the comprehension of a rustic or a child, yet full and deep enough in meaning to satisfy the strictest of logicians, the sternest of critics. Heaven knows I write of him and of his teaching in all sincerity, and yet the subject seems to have so little harmony with the history of a foolish girl's errors and shortcomings, that I approach it with a kind of terror. I only know that Isabel Gilbert, weeping silently in the dark corner of the curtained pew, felt as she had never felt in all her Graybridge church-going; felt at once distressed and comforted. A new hero dawned upon her life; and, amid a very flood of blinding light, she saw the image of One who was worthy of all worship; a God whom women, from the hour of His advent upon earth until this sceptical, critical to-day, have ever followed with a special love and reverence; a God who held it no shame to count Mary Magdalene* among His worshippers; and who, for ever vested with an unmistakable divinity, was never more entirely divine than in His pitying tenderness for woman. Amidst all the arguments to be used against strong-minded claimants for the equality of the sexes, I wonder no one has ever urged the evidence of the Redeemer's treatment of those women whose names are eternally intermingled with His history.

Was it strange that, all at once, Isabel Gilbert should open her ears to the sublime story, which, in one shape or other, she had heard so often? Surely the history of all popular preachers goes far to demonstrate that Heaven gives a special power to some voices. When Whitefield preached the Gospel to the miners at Kingswood,*— to rugged creatures who were little better than so many savages, but who, no doubt, in some shape or other, had heard that Gospel preached to them before,—the scalding tears ploughed white chan- nels upon the black cheeks as the men listened. At last the voice of all others that had power to move them arose, and melted the stub- born ignorant hearts. Is it inspiration or animal-magnetism which gives this power to some special persons? or is it not rather the force of faith, out of which is engendered a will strong enough to take hold of the wills of other people, and bend them howsoever it pleases? When Danton,* rugged and gigantic, thundered his hideous de- mands for new hecatombs of victims, there must have been some- thing in the revolutionary monster strong enough to trample out the common humanity in those who heard him, and mould a mighty populace to his own will and purposes as easily as a giant might fashion a mass of clay. Surely Mirabeau was right. There can be nothing impossible to the man who believes in himself. The masses of this world, being altogether incapable of lasting belief in any thing, are always ready to be beaten into any shape by the chosen individual who *believes*, and is thus of another nature—something so much stronger than all the rest as to seem either a god or a demon. Cromwell* appears, and all at once a voice is found for the wrongs of a nation. See how the king and his counsellors go down like corn before the blast of the tempest, while the man with a dogged will, and a sublime confidence in his own powers, plants himself at the helm of a disordered state, and wins for himself the name of Tiger of the Seas. Given Mr John Law,* with ample confidence in his own commercial schemes, and all France is rabid with a sudden madness, beating and trampling one another to death in the Rue Quincampoix. Given a Luther,* and all the old papistical abuses are swept away like so much chaff before the wind. Given a Wesley,* the believer, the man who is able to preach forty thousand sermons and travel a hundred thousand miles, and, behold, a million disciples exist in this degenerate day to bear testimony to his power.

[Mr Austin Colborne's influence no doubt proceeded in some wise from the same source. He believed in himself; for, looking down into the pure depths of his own soul, he saw no vague and shifting monsters, called reservations, doubts, cross-purposes, unstable desires, hurrying away to hide themselves, in darksome caves and crannies, from his scrutinising eye. He believed in his creed, because, study it as he might, he found no crack or flaw in it. The history, which to Roland Lansdell seemed only an exquisite legend, a sublime theme for Italian painters or dreamy-minded poets, was to Austin Colborne a grand indisputable fact, written upon the very face of the universe. He was thoroughly happy in his faith and in his life; and a benign influence seemed to radiate from him, in which hard ignorant men and women grew better and wiser.]*

Was it strange, then, that Isabel Gilbert, so dangerously susceptible of every influence, should feel this influence, as she had felt others?* She had not been religiously brought up. In the Camberwell household Sunday had been a day on which people got up later than usual, and there were pies or puddings to be made. It had been a day associated with savoury baked meats, and a beer-stained *Weekly Dispatch* newspaper borrowed from the nearest tavern. It had been a day on which Mr Sleaford slept a good deal on the sofa, excused himself from the trouble of shaving, and very rarely put on his boots. Raffish-looking men had come down to Camberwell in the Sunday twilight, to sit late into the night smoking and drinking, and discoursing in a mysterious jargon known to the household as 'business talk.' Sometimes of a summer evening, Mrs Sleaford, awakened to a sense of her religious duties, would suddenly run a raid amongst the junior branches of the family, and hustle off Isabel and one or two of the boys to evening-service at the big bare church by the canal. But the spasmodic attendance at divine service had very little effect upon Miss Sleaford, who used to sit staring at the holes in her gloves; or calculating how many yards of ribbon, at how much per yard, would be required for the trimming of any special bonnet to which her fancy leaned; or thinking how a decent-looking young man up in the gallery might be a stray nobleman, with a cab and tiger* waiting somewhere outside the church, who would perhaps fall in love with her before the sermon was finished. She had not been religiously brought up; and the church-going at Graybridge had been something of a bore to her; or at best a quiet lull in her life, which left her free to indulge the foolish vagaries of her vagabond fancy. But now, for the first time, she was touched and melted: the weak sentimental heart was caught at the rebound. She was ready to be any thing in the world except a commonplace matron, leading a dull purposeless life at Graybridge. She wanted to find some shrine, some divinity, who would accept her worship; some temple lifted high above the sordid workaday earth, in which she might kneel for ever and ever. If not Roland Lansdell, why then Christianity. She would have commenced her novitiate that night had she been in a Roman-Catholic land, where convent-doors were open to receive such as her. As it was, she could only sit quietly in the pew and listen. She would have liked to go to the vestry when the service came to an end, and cast herself at the feet of the curate, and make a full confession of her sins; but she had not sufficient courage for that. The curate might misunderstand her, as Roland Lansdell had done. He might see in her only an ordinarily wicked woman, who wanted to run away from her husband. Vague yearnings towards Christian holiness filled her foolish breast; but as yet she knew not how to put them into any shape. When the congregation rose to leave the church, she lingered to the last, and then crept slowly away, resolved to come again to hear this wonderful preacher. She went to the little station whence the Graybridge omnibus was to start at half-past eight; and after waiting a quarter of an hour took her place in a corner of the vehicle. It was nearly ten when she rang the bell at her husband's gate, and Mrs Jeffson came out with a grave face to admit her.

'Mr George had his dinner and tea alone, ma'am,' she said in tones of awful reproof, while Isabel stood before the little glass in the sitting-room taking off her bonnet; 'and he's gone out again to see some sick folks in the lanes on the other side of the church. He was right down uneasy about you.'

'I've been to Hurstonleigh, to hear Mr Colborne preach,' Isabel answered, with a very feeble effort to appear quite at her ease. 'I had heard so much about his preaching, and I wanted so to hear him.'

It was true that she had heard Austin Colborne talked of amongst her church-going acquaintance at Graybridge; but it was quite untrue that she had ever felt the faintest desire to hear him preach. Had not her whole life been bounded by a magic circle, of which Roland Lansdell was the resplendent centre?

CHAPTER II

'AND NOW I LIVE, AND NOW MY LIFE IS DONE!'*

George Gilbert accepted his wife's explanation of her prolonged absence upon that March afternoon. She had carried her books to Thurston's Crag, and had sat there reading, while the time slipped by unawares, and it was too late to come back to dinner; and so she had bethought herself that there was evening-service at Hurstonleigh during Passion-week, and she might hear Mr Colborne preach. George Gilbert received this explanation as he would have received any other statement from the lips in whose truth he believed. But Mrs Jeffson treated her young mistress with a stately politeness that wounded Isabel to the quick. She endured it very meekly, however; for she felt that she had been wicked, and that all her sufferings were the fruit of her own sin. She stayed at home for the rest of the week, except when she attended the Good-Friday's services at Graybridge church with her husband; and on Sunday afternoon she persuaded George to accompany her to Hurstonleigh. She was making her feeble effort to be good, and if the enthusiasm awakened in her breast by Mr Colborne's preaching died out a little after she left the church, there was at the worst something left which made her a better woman than she had been before. But did she forget Roland Lansdell all this time? No; with bitter anguish and regret she thought of the man who had been as powerless to comprehend her as he was intellectually her superior.

'He knows so much, and yet did not know that I was not a wicked woman,' she thought in simple wonder. She did not understand Roland's sceptical manner of looking at every thing, which could perceive no palpable distinction between wrong and right. She could not comprehend that this man had believed himself justified in what he had done.

But she thought of him incessantly. The image of his pale reproachful face—so pale, so bitterly reproachful—never left her mental vision. The sound of his voice bidding her leave him was perpetually in her ears. He had loved her: yes; however deep his guilt, he had loved her, and had wept because of her. There were times when the memory of his tears, flashing back upon her suddenly, nearly swept away all her natural purity, her earnest desire to be good; there were times when she wanted to go to him and fall at his feet, crying out, 'Oh, what am I, that my life should be counted against your sorrow? How can it matter what becomes of me, if you are happy?'

There were times when the thought of Roland Lansdell's sorrow overcame every other thought in Isabel Gilbert's mind. Until the day when he had thrown himself upon the ground in a sudden passion of grief, she had never realised the possibility of his being unhappy because of her. For him to love her in a patronising far-off kind of manner was very much. Was it not the condescension of a demigod, who smiles upon some earthly creature? Was it not a reversal of the story of Diana and Endymion?* It was not the goddess, but the god, who came down to earth. But that he should love her desperately and passionately, and be grief-stricken because he could not win her for his own,—this was a stupendous fact, almost beyond Isabel Gilbert's comprehension. Sometimes she thought he was only the wicked squire who pretends to be very much in earnest in the first act, and flings aside his victim with scorn and contumely in the second. Sometimes the whole truth burst upon her, sudden as a thunder-clap, and she felt that she had indeed done Roland Lansdell a great and cruel wrong.

*

And where was he all this time? The man who had judged Isabel
Gilbert by a common standard, and had believed her quite ready to
answer to his summons whenever he chose to call her to his side.
Who shall tell the bitter sinful story of his grief and passion? Never
once in all his anger against Lady Gwendoline Pomphrey, when she
jilted him for the sake of young Lord Heatherland, had he felt so
desperate a rage, so deep an indignation, as that which now possessed
him when he thought of Isabel Gilbert. Wounded in his pride, his
vanity; shaken in the self-confidence peculiar to a man of the world;
he could not all at once forgive this woman who had so entirely
duped and deceived him. He was mad with mingled anger and disappointment when he thought of the story of the last twelvemonth. The
bitterness of all his struggles with himself; his heroic resolutions—
young and fresh in the early morning, old and gray and wasted before
the brief day was done—came back to him: and he laughed aloud to
think how useless all those perplexities and hesitations had been,
when the obstacle, the real resistance, to his sinful yearnings was
here—here, in the shape of a simple woman's will.

There may be some men who would not have thought the story
finished with that farewell under Lord Thurston's oak; but Roland
Lansdell was not one of those men. He had little force of mind or
strength of purpose with which to fight against temptation: but he
had, on the other hand, few of the qualifications which make a
tempter. So long as he had been uncertain of himself and the strength
of his love for Isabel, he had indeed dissembled so far as to make a
poor show of indifference. So long as he meant to go away from
Midlandshire without 'doing any harm,' he had thought it a venial
sin to affect some little friendship for the husband of the woman he
loved. But from the moment in which all vacillation gave way before
a settled purpose—from the hour of his return to Midlandshire—he
had made no secret of his feelings or intentions. He had urged this
girl to do a dishonourable act; but he had used no dishonourable
means. No words can tell how bitterly he felt his disappointment.
For the first time in his life this favourite of bountiful nature, this
spoiled child of fortune, found there was something in the world he
could not have, something that was denied to his desire. It was such
a very little time since he had bewailed the extinction of all youthful
hope and ardour in pretty cynical little verses, all sparkling with
scraps of French and Latin, and Spanish and Italian, cunningly

woven into the native pattern of the rhyme. It was only a few
months since he had amused himself by scribbling melodious lamentations upon the emptiness of life in general, and that 'mortal
coldness of the soul' to which a young man of seven-and-twenty,
with a great deal of money and nothing particular to do, is especially
subject. Ah, how pitilessly he had laughed at other men's tenderest
sentiments! What cruel aphorisms from Scarron and Rochefoucauld,
and Swift and Voltaire, and Wilkes and Mirabeau,* he had quoted
upon the subject of love and woman! How resolutely he had refused
to believe in the endurance of passion! how coldly he had sneered at
the holy power of affection! He had given himself cynical airs upon
the strength of his cousin's falsehood: and had declared there was no
truth in woman, because Lady Gwendoline Pomphrey had been
true to the teaching of her life, and had tried to make the best
market of her Saxon face and her long ringlets. And now he was
utterly false to his own creed. He was in love, passionately, earnestly
in love, with a foolish sentimental little woman, whose best charm
was—What? That was the question which he tried in vain to answer. He gnashed his teeth in an access of rage when he sought to
discover why he loved this woman. Other women more beautiful,
and how much more accomplished, had spread enchanted webs of
delicious flattery and tenderness about him; and he had broken through
the impalpable meshes, and had gone away unscathed from the
flashing glances of bright eyes, unmoved by the smiles for which
other men were ready to peril so much. Why was it that his heart
yearned for this woman's presence? She was in no way his intellectual equal: she was not a companion for him, even at her best, when
she murmured pretty little feminine truisms about Shelley and Byron. In all his loiterings by Lord Thurston's waterfall, he could
recall no wise or witty saying that had ever fallen from those childish lips. And yet, and yet—she was something to him that no other
woman had ever been, or, as he firmly believed, ever could become.
Oh, for one upward glance of those dark eyes, so shyly tender, so
pensively serene! Oh, for the deep delight of standing by her side
upon the border of a still Italian lake; for the pure happiness of
opening all the wild realms of wisdom and poetry before those youthful
feet! And then in after years, when she had risen little by little to the
standard which the world would deem befitting his wife,—then,
fate, or chance, the remote abstraction most men call Providence,

having favoured the truest and purest love upon this earth,—then he might proclaim his ownership of the prize he had won for himself; then he might exhibit before shallow, sceptical mankind one bright and grand example of a perfect union.

Mr Lansdell's thoughts wandered very much after this fashion as he wore out the long dreary days in his solitary home. He went no where; he received no one. He gave the servants standing orders to say that he was out, or engaged, to whomsoever came to Mordred. His portmanteaus were packed, and had been packed ever since the night of his last meeting with Isabel Gilbert. Every day he gave fresh orders respecting his departure. He would have the carriage at such an hour, to catch a certain train: but when the hour came, the groom was sent back to the stables, and Mr Lansdell lingered yet another day at Mordred Priory.

He could not go away. In vain, in vain he wrestled with himself: most bitterly did he despise and hate himself for his unmanly weakness; but he could not go away. She would repent: she would write to summon him to another meeting beneath the bare old oak. With an imagination as ardent as her own, he could picture that meeting; he could almost hear her voice as he fancied the things she would say. 'My love, my love!' she would cry, clasping those slender hands about his arm; 'I cannot live without you: I cannot, I cannot!'

[All manner of vague fashionable fancies which he had taken up one by one, in common with the frivolous circles in which he had been a favourite, only to drop them with a sneer and a shrug of his shoulders when the whim was over; all manner of foolish spiritualist frivolities came back upon him now, and were frail straws to which his mind clung with a something that was almost faith. Must there not be something more than common in the attraction that bound him to Isabel Gilbert? Was it odic force?* was it animal-magnetism?* was it to be explained by this, that, or the other newfangled theory that had served to make conversation for a Parisian winter and a London spring? What was it? He could find a hundred answers to that question; but not one which satisfied him. He only knew that he was false to all the philosophy of his age, and that he was eating his heart out because of a country surgeon's half-educated wife.]*

The weeks went slowly by, and Mr Lansdell's body-servant had what that individual was pleased to designate 'a precious time of it.'

Never was gentleman's gentleman so tormented by the whims and vagaries of his master. One day 'we' were off to Swisserland—Mr Lansdell's valet always called it Swisserland—and we were to go as fast as the railway service could carry us, and not get a wink of sleep any wheres, except in railway-carriages, until we got to Paw or Bas-el—the valet called it Bas-el. Another day we were going to St Petersburg, with our friend Hawkwood, the Queen's messenger; and a pretty rate we were going at, knocking the very lives out of us. Sometimes we were for tearing across the Balkan range, on those blessed Turkish horses, that jolt a man's life half out of him; or we were going on a yachting-cruise in the Mediterranean; or fishing in the wildest regions of Norway. And all about a trumpery minx at Graybridge! Mr Lansdell's body-servant would wind up, with un-mitigated contempt: all about a young person who was not fit to hold a candle to Sarah Jane the housemaid, or Eliza in the laundry! Alas for Roland Lansdell, the servants who waited upon him knew quite as well as he knew himself the nature of the fever which had made him so restless! They knew that he was in love with a woman who could never be his wife; and they despised him for his folly, and discussed all the phases of his madness over their ponderous meat-suppers in the servants' hall.

The weeks went slowly by. To Roland the days were weary and the nights intolerable. He went up to London several times, always leaving Mordred alone and at abnormal hours, and every time in-tending to remain away. But he could not: a sudden fever seized him as the distance grew wider between him and Midlandshire. She would repent to her stern determination: she would write to him, avowing that she could not live without him. Ah, how long he had expected that letter! She would grow suddenly unable to endure her life perhaps, and would be rash and desperate enough to go to Mordred in the hope of seeing him. This would happen while he was away: the chance of happiness would be offered to him, and he would not be there to seize it. She, his love, the sole joy and treasure of his life, would be there, trembling on his threshold, and he would not be near to welcome and receive her. The people at the Clarendon thought that Mr Lansdell had gone mad, so sudden were his flights from their comfortable quarters.

And all this time he could hear nothing of the woman he loved. He could not talk to his servants, and he had closed his doors against all visitors. What was she doing? Was she at Graybridge still? Was she leading the old quiet life, sitting in that shabby parlour, where he had sat by her side? He remembered the pattern of the Kidderminster carpet, the limp folds of the muslin-curtains, the faded crimson silk that decorated the front of the piano upon which she had sometimes played to him, oh, so indifferently. Day after day he haunted the bridge under Lord Thurston's oak; day after day he threw tribute of cigar-ends into the waterfall, while he waited in the faint hope that the Doctor's Wife might wander thither. Oh, how cruel she was; how cruel! If she had ever loved him, she too would have haunted that spot. She would have come to the place associated with his memory: she would have come, as he came, in the hope of another meeting.

Sometimes Mr Lansdell ventured to ride along the little street at Graybridge and through the dusty lane in which the doctor's house stood. On horseback the master of Mordred Priory was almost on a level with the bedroom windows of George Gilbert's habitation, and could look down into the little parlour where Isabel was wont to sit. Once and once only he saw her there, sitting before the table with some needlework in her hands, so deeply absorbed, as it seemed, in her commonplace labour that she did not see the cavalier who rode so slowly past her window. How should he know how often she had run eagerly to that very window—her face pale, her heart beating tempestuously—only to find that it was not *his* horse whose hoofs she had heard in the lane?

Perhaps the sight of George Gilbert's wife sitting at her needlework gave Roland Lansdell a sharper pang than he would have felt had he seen two mutes from Wareham keeping guard at the gate, and Mrs Gilbert's coffin being carried out at the door. She was not dead, then: she could live and be happy, while he—! Well, he was not dead himself, certainly; but he was the very next thing to being dead; and he felt indignant at the sight of Isabel's apparent composure.

He walked to Lowlands in the course of a week or so after this, and strolled into the drawing-room with some undefined intention of flirting desperately with his cousin Gwendoline; of making her an of marriage, perhaps. Why should he not marry? He could scarcely be more miserable than he was; and a marriage with Gwendoline would be some kind of revenge upon Isabel. He was inclined to do any thing desperate and foolish, if by so doing he could sting that cruel obdurate heart. Was this generous? Ah, no. But then, in spite of all that is said and sung in its honour, love is *not* such a very generous passion. Roland found his cousin alone, in the long low morning-room looking out into her flower-garden. She was making wax-flowers, and looked almost as tired of her employment as if she had been some poor little artizan toiling for scanty wages.

'I'm very glad you have interrupted me, Roland,' she said, pushing away all the paraphernalia of her work; 'they are very tiresome; and, after all, the roses are as stiff as camellias, and at the very best a vase of wax-flowers only reminds one of an hotel at a watering-place. They always have wax-flowers and Bohemian-glass candelabra at sea-side hotels. And now tell me what you have been doing, Roland; and why you have never come to us. We are so terribly dull.'

'And do you think my presence would enliven you?' demanded Mr Lansdell, with a sardonic laugh. 'No, Gwendoline; I have lived my life, and I am only a dreary bore, whom people tolerate in their drawing-rooms out of deference to the West-end tailor who gets me up. I am only so much old clothes, and I have to thank Mr Poole for any position that I hold in the world. What is the use of me, Gwendoline? what am I good for? Do I ever say any thing new, or think any thing new, or do any thing for which any human creature has cause to say, Thank you? I have lived my life. Does this kind of thing usually grow old, I wonder?' he asked, striking himself lightly on the breast. 'Does it wear well? Shall I live to write gossiping old letters and collect china? Will Christie and Manson* sell my pictures when I am dead? and shall I win a posthumous reputation by reason of the prices given for my wines, especially Tokay*?—all connoisseurs go in for Tokay. What is to become of me, Gwendoline? Will any woman have pity upon me and marry me, and transform me into a family-man, with a mania for short-horned cattle and subsoil-drainage? Is there any woman in all the world capable of caring a little for such a worn-out wretch as I?'

It almost depended upon Gwendoline Pomphrey whether this speech should constitute an offer of marriage. A pretty lackadaisical droop of the head; a softly-murmured, 'Oh, Roland, I cannot bear to hear you talk like this; I cannot bear to think such qualities as yours can be so utterly wasted;' any sentimental, womanly little speech, however stereotyped; and the thing would have been done. But Lady Gwendoline was a great deal too proud to practise any of those feminine arts affected by manoeuvring mothers. She might jilt a commoner for the chance of winning a marquis; but even that she would only do in a grand off-hand way befitting a daughter of the house of Ruysdale. She looked at her cousin now with something like contempt in the curve of her thin upper-lip. She loved this man perhaps as well as the Doctor's Wife loved him, or it may be even with a deeper and more enduring love: but she was of his world, and could see his faults and shortcomings as plainly as he saw them himself.

'I am very sorry you have sunk so low as this, Roland,' she said gravely. 'I fancy it would be much better for you if you employed your life half as well as other men, your inferiors in talent, employ their lives. You were never meant to become a cynical dawdler in a country-house. If *I* were a man, a fortnight in the hunting-season would exhaust the pleasures of Midlandshire for me; I would be up and doing among my compeers.'

She looked, not at Roland, but across the flower-beds in the garden as she spoke, with an eager yearning gaze in her blue eyes. Her beauty, a little sharp of outline for a woman, would have well become a young reformer, enthusiastic and untiring in a noble cause. There are these mistakes sometimes—these mesalliances of clay and spirit. A bright ambitious young creature, with the soul of a Pitt,* sits at home and works sham roses in Berlin wool; while her booby brother is thrust out into the world to fight the mighty battle.

The cousins sat together for some time, talking of all manner of things. It was a kind of relief to Roland to talk to some one—to some one who was not likely to lecture him, or to pry into the secrets of his heart. He did not know how very plainly those secrets were read by Gwendoline Pomphrey. He did not know that he had aroused a scornful kind of anger in that proud heart by his love for Isabel Gilbert.

'Have you seen any thing of your friends lately—that Graybridge surgeon and his wife, whom we met one day last summer at Mordred?' Lady Gwendoline asked by and by with supreme carelessness. She had no intention of letting Roland go away with his wound unprobed.

'No; I have seen very little of them,' Mr Lansdell answered. He was not startled by Lady Gwendoline's question: he was perpetually thinking of Isabel, and felt no surprise at any allusion made to her by other people. 'I have not seen Mr Gilbert since I returned to England.'

'Indeed! I thought he had inspired you with an actual friendship for him; though I must confess, for my own part, I never met a more commonplace person. My maid, who is an intolerable gossip, tells me that Mrs Gilbert has been suddenly seized with a religious mania, and attends all the services at Hurstonleigh. The Midlandshire people seem to have gone mad about that Mr Colborne. I went to hear him last Sunday myself, and was very much pleased. I saw Mr Gilbert's wife sitting in a pew near the pulpit, with her great unmeaning eyes fixed upon the curate's face all through the sermon. She is just the sort of person to fall in love with a popular preacher.'

Mr Lansdell's face flushed a vivid scarlet, and then grew pale. 'With her great unmeaning eyes fixed upon the curate's face.' Those wondrous eyes that had so often looked up at him, mutely eloquent, tenderly pensive. Oh, had he been fooled by his own vanity? was this woman a sentimental coquette, ready to fall in love with any man who came across her path, learned in stereotyped schoolgirl phrases about platonic affection? Lady Gwendoline's shaft went straight home to his heart. He tried to talk about a few common-place subjects with a miserable assumption of carelessness; and then, looking suddenly up at the clock on the chimney-piece, made a profuse apology for the length of his visit, and hurried away. It was four o'clock when he left the gates of Lowlands, and the next day was Sunday.

'I will see for myself,' he muttered, as he walked along a narrow lane, slashing the low hedge-rows with his stick as he went; 'I will see for myself to-morrow.'

CHAPTER III

TRYING TO BE GOOD

The Sunday after Roland Lansdell's visit to his cousin was a warm May day, and the woodland lanes and meadows through which the master of Mordred Priory walked to Hurstonleigh were bright with wild-flowers. Nearly two months had gone by since he and the

Doctor's Wife had parted on the dull March afternoon which made a crisis in Isabel's life. The warm breath of the early summer fanned the young man's face as he strolled through the long grass under the spreading branches of elm and beech. He had breakfasted early, and had set out immediately after that poor pretence of eating and drinking. He had set out from Mordred in feverish haste; and now that he had walked two or three miles, he looked wan and pale in the vivid light of the bright May morning. To-day he looked as if his cynical talk about himself was not altogether such sentimental nonsense as genial, practical Mr Raymond thought it. He looked tired, worn, mentally and physically, like a man who has indeed lived his life. Looking at him this morning, young, handsome, clever, and prosperous though he was, there were very few people who would have ventured to prophesy for him a bright and happy existence, a long and useful career. He had a wan, faded, unnatural look in the summer daylight, like a lamp that has been left burning all night. He had only spoken the truth that day in the garden at Mordred. The Lansdells had never been a long-lived race; and a look that lurked somewhere or other in the faces of all the portraits at the Priory might have been seen in the face of Roland Lansdell to-day. He was tired, very tired. He had lived too fast, and had run through his heritage of animal spirits and youthful enthusiasm like the veriest spendthrift who squanders a fortune in a few nights spent at a gaming-house. The nights are very brilliant while they last, riotous with a wild excitement that can only be purchased at this monstrous cost. But, oh, the blank gray mornings, the freezing chill of that cheerless dawn, from which the spendthrift's eyes shrink appalled when the night is done!

Roland Lansdell was most miserably tired of himself, and all the world except Isabel Gilbert. Life, which is so short when measured by art, science, ambition, glory: life, which always closes too soon upon the statesman or the warrior, whether he dies in the prime of life like Peel,* or flourishes a sturdy evergreen like Palmerston;* whether he perishes like Wolfe* on the heights of Quebec, or sinks to his rest like Wellington* in his simple dwelling by the sea: life, so brief when estimated by a noble standard, is cruelly long when measured by the empty pleasures of an idle worldling with fifteen thousand a-year. Emile Augier* has very pleasantly demonstrated that the world is much smaller for a rich man than it is for a poor one. My lord the millionaire rushes across wide tracks of varied landscape asleep in the padded corner of a first-class carriage, and only stops for a week or so here and there in great cities, to be bored almost to death by cathedrals and valhallas, picture-galleries and ruined Roman baths, 'done' in the stereotyped fashion. While the poorer traveller, jogging along out-of-the-way country roads, with his staff in his hand and his knapsack on his shoulder, drops upon a hundred pleasant nooks in this wide universe, and can spend a lifetime agreeably in seeing the same earth that the millionaire, always booked and registered all the way through, like his luggage, grows tired of in a couple of years. We have only to read Sterne's *Sentimental Journey** and Dickens's *Uncommercial Traveller*,* in order to find out how much there is in the world for the wanderer who has eyes to see. Read the story of Mr Dickens's pedestrian rambles, and then read William Beckford's delicious discontented *blasé* letters, and see the difference between the great writer, for whom art is long and life is only too short, and the man of pleasure, who squandered all the wealth of his imagination upon the morbid phantasma of *Vathek*,* and whose talent could find no higher exercise than the planning of objectionable towers.

The lesson which Mr Lansdell was called upon to learn just now was a very difficult one. For the first time in his life he found that there was something in the world that he could not have; for the first time he discovered what it was to wish wildly, madly for one precious treasure out of all the universe; and to wish in vain.

This morning he was not such a purposeless wanderer as he usually was; he was going to Hurstonleigh church, in the hope of seeing Isabel Gilbert, and ascertaining for himself whether there was any foundation for Lady Gwendoline's insinuation. He wanted to ascertain this; but above all, he wanted to *see* her—only to see her; to look at the pale face and the dark eyes once more. Yes; though she were the basest and shallowest-hearted coquette in all creation.

Mr Lansdell was doomed to be disappointed that morning, for the Doctor's Wife was not at Hurstonleigh church. Graybridge would have been scandalised if Mr and Mrs Gilbert had not attended morning-service in their own parish; so it was only in the afternoon or evening that Isabel was free to worship at the feet of the popular preacher.

The church was very full in the morning, and Roland sat in a pew near the door, waiting patiently until the service concluded. Isabel might be lurking somewhere in the rambling old edifice, though he had not been able to see her. He listened very attentively to the sermon, and bent his head approvingly once or twice during Mr Colborne's discourse. He had heard so many bad sermons, delivered in divers languages, during his wandering existence, that he had no wish to depreciate a good one. When all was over, he stood at the door of his pew, watching the congregation file slowly and quietly out of the church, and looking for Isabel. But she was not there. When the church was quite empty, he breathed a long regretful sigh, and then followed the rest of the congregation.

'She will come in the afternoon, perhaps,' he thought. 'Oh, how I love her! what a weak pitiful wretch I must be to feel like this; to feel this sinking at my heart because she is not here; to consider all the universe so much emptiness because her face is missing!'

He went away into a secluded corner of the churchyard, a shadowy corner, where there was an angle in the old wall, below which the river crept in and out among the sedges. Here the salutations of the congregation loitering about the church-door seemed only a low distant hum; here Mr Lansdell could sit at his ease upon the bank, staring absently at the blue Wayverne, and thinking of his troubles.

The distant murmur of voices, the sound of footsteps, and the rustling of women's light garments in the summer-breeze died away presently, and a death-like stillness fell upon the churchyard. All Hurstonleigh was at dinner, being a pious village that took its sabbath meal early, and dined chiefly on cold meats and crisp salads. The place was very still; and Roland Lansdell, lolling idly with his back against the moss-grown wall, had ample leisure for contemplation.

What did he think of during those two long hours in which he sat in the churchyard waiting for the afternoon service? What did he think of? His wasted life; the good things he might have done upon this earth? No! His thoughts dwelt with a fatal persistency upon one theme. He thought of what his life might have been, if Isabel Gilbert had not baulked all his plans of happiness. He thought of how he might have been sitting, that very day, at that very hour, on one of the fairest islands in the Mediterranean, with the woman he loved by his side: if she had chosen, if she had only chosen that it should be so. And he had been so mistaken in her, so deluded by his own fatuity, as to believe that any obstacle on her part was utterly out of the question. He had believed that it was only for him to weigh the matter in the balance and decide the turning of the scale.

He sat by the water listening to the church-bells as they rang slowly out upon the tranquil atmosphere. It was one of those bright summer-days which come sometimes at the close of May, and the sky above Hurstonleigh church was cloudless. When the bells had been ringing for a long time, slow footsteps sounded on the gravel-walks upon the other side of the churchyard, with now and then the creaking of a gate or the murmur of voices. The people were coming to church. Roland's heart throbbed heavily in his breast. Was *she* amongst them? Ah, surely he would have recognised her lightest footfall even at that distance. Should he go and stand by the gate, to make sure of seeing her as she came in? No, he could not make a show of himself before all those inquisitive country-people; he would wait till the service began, and then go into the church. That half-hour, during which the bells swung to and fro in the old steeple with a weary monotonous clang, seemed intolerably long to Roland Lansdell: but at last, at last, all was quiet, and the only bell to be heard in the summer stillness was the distant tinkle of a sheep-bell far away in the sunlit meadows. Mr Lansdell got up as the clock struck three, and walked at a leisurely pace to the church.

Mr Colborne was reading that solemn invitation to the wicked man to repent of his wickedness as the squire of Mordred went into the low porch. The penetrating voice reached the remotest corners of the old building; and yet its tone was low and solemn as an exhortation by a dying man's bed. The church was not by any means so full as it had been in the morning; and there was none of that fluttering noise of bonnet-strings and pocket-handkerchiefs which is apt to disturb the quiet of a crowded edifice. The pew-opener— always on the look-out to hustle stray intruders into pews—pounced immediately upon Mr Lansdell.

'I should like to sit up-stairs,' he whispered, dropping a half-crown into her hand; 'can you put me somewhere up-stairs?'

He had reflected that from the gallery he should be better able to see Isabel, if she was in the church. The woman curtsied and nodded, and then led the way up the broad wooden stairs: where would she not have put Mr Lansdell for such a donation as that which he had bestowed upon her!

The gallery at Hurstonleigh church was a very special and

aristocratic quarter. It consisted only of half-a-dozen roomy old pews at one end of the church, immediately opposite the altar, and commanding an excellent view of the pulpit. The chief families of the neigbourhood occupied these six big open pews; and the common herd in the aisles below contemplated these aristocratic persons admiringly in the pauses of the service. As the grand families in the outskirts of Hurstonleigh were not quite such unbating churchgoers as the model villagers themselves, these gallery-pews were not generally filled of an afternoon; and it was into one of these that the grateful pew-opener ushered Mr Lansdell.

She was there; yes, she was there. She was alone, in a pew near the pulpit, on her knees, with her hands clasped and her eyes looking upwards. The high old-fashioned pew shut her in from the congregation about her, but Mr Lansdell could look down upon her from his post of observation in the gallery. Her face was pale and worn, and her eyes looked larger and brighter than when he had last seen her. Was she in a consumption? Ah, no; it was only the eager yearning soul which was always consuming itself; it was no physical illness, but the sharp pain of a purely mental struggle that had left those traces on her face. Her lover watched her amidst the kneeling congregation; and a kind of holy exaltation in her face reminded him of pictures of saints and angels that he had seen abroad. Was it real, that exalted expression of the pale still face? was it real, or had she begun a new flirtation, a little platonic sentimentalism in favour of the popular preacher?

'The fellow has something in him, and is not by any means badlooking,' thought Mr Lansdell; 'I wonder whether she is laying traps for him with her great yellow-black eyes?' And then in the next moment he thought how, if that look in her pale face were real, and she was really striving to be good,—how then? Had he any right to come into that holy place? for the place was holy, if only by virtue of the simple prayers so simply spoken by happy and pious creatures who were able to believe. Had he any right to come there and trouble this girl in the midst of her struggle to forget him?

'I think she loved me,' he mused; 'surely I could not be mistaken in that; surely I have known too many coquettes in my life to be duped by one at the last! Yes, I believe she loved me.'

The earlier prayers and the psalms were over by this time; and Mrs Gilbert was seated in her pew facing the gallery, but with the

pulpit and reading-desk between. Mr Colborne began to read the
first lesson; and there was a solemn hush in the church. Roland was
seized with a sudden desire that Isabel should see him. He wanted
to see the recognition of him in her face. Might he not learn the
depth of her love, the strength of her regret, by that one look of
recognition? A green serge curtain hung before him. He pushed the
folds aside; and the brazen rings made a little clanging noise as they
slipped along the rod. The sound was loud enough to startle the
woman whom Mr Lansdell was watching so intently. She looked up
and recognised him. He saw a white change flit across her face; he
saw her light muslin garments fluttered by a faint shiver; and then
in the next moment she was looking demurely downwards at the
book on her lap, something as she had looked on that morning when
he first met her under Lord Thurston's oak.

All through the service Roland Lansdell sat watching her. He
made no pretence of joining in the devotions of the congregation;
but he disturbed no one. He only sat, grim and sombre-looking,
staring down at that one pale face in the pew near the pulpit. A
thousand warring thoughts and passionate emotions waged in his
breast. He loved her so much that he could not be chivalrous; he
could not even be just or reasonable. [It is all very well for cold
impassable King Arthur to address the fallen Queen with all the
pitiful tenderness, the dignified grandeur of the finest gentleman in
Christendom. Has he not the supreme consciousness of his own
rectitude; the knowledge that all heaven and earth are with him, to
support him in his hour of trial? It is easy for the good man to be
magnanimous; but not so easy for the sinner. Launcelot,* sinful,
passionate, unhappy Launcelot, can find no such noble phrases.
Only rugged lamentations and vain upbraidings arise from the heart
of the man who knows he is in the wrong.]* All through the service
Roland Lansdell sat watching the face of the woman he loved. If
Austin Colborne could have known how strangely his earnest, pleading
words fell upon the ears of two of his listeners that afternoon! Isabel
Gilbert sat very quietly under all the angry fire of that dark gaze.
Only now and then were her eyelids lifted; only now and then did
her eyes steal one brief imploring glance at the face in the gallery. In
all the church she could see nothing but that face. It absorbed and
blotted out all else; and shone down upon her, grand and dazzling,
as of old.

She was trying to be good. For the last two months she had been earnestly trying to be good. There was nothing else for her in the world but goodness, seeing that *he* was lost to her—seeing that a romantic Beatrice-Portinari kind of existence was an impossibility. If she had been a dweller in a Catholic country, she would have gone into a convent; as it was, she could only come to Hurstonleigh to hear Mr Colborne, whose enthusiasm answered to the vague aspirations of her own ignorant heart. She was trying to be good. She and worthy plain-spoken Mrs Jeffson were on the best possible terms now, for the Doctor's Wife had taken to staying at home a great deal, and had requested honest Tilly to instruct her in the art of darning worsted socks.

Would the sight of the wicked squire's dark reproachful face undo all the work of these two months? Surely not. To meet him once more—to hear his voice—to feel the strong grasp of his hand—ah, what deep joy! But what good could come of such a meeting? She could never confide in him again. It would be only new pain—wasted anguish. Besides, was there not some glory, some delight, in trying to be good? She felt herself a Louise de la Vallière standing behind a grating in the convent-parlour, while a kingly Louis pleaded and stormed on the other side of the iron bars.

Some such thoughts as these sustained her all through that afternoon service. The sermon was over; the blessing had been spoken; the congregation began to disperse slowly and quietly. Would *he* go now? Would he linger to meet her and speak to her? would he go away at once? He did linger, looking at her with an appealing expression in his haggard face. He stood up, as if waiting until she should leave her pew, in order to leave his at the same moment. But she never stirred. Ah, if Louise de la Vallière suffered as much as that! What wonder that she became renowned for ever in sentimental story!

Little by little the congregation melted out of the aisle. The charity-boys from the neighbourhood of the organ-loft came clumping down the stairs. Still Mr Lansdell stood waiting and watching the Doctor's Wife in the pew below. Still Isabel Gilbert kept her place, rigid and inflexible, until the church was quite empty.

Then Mr Lansdell looked at her—only one look—but with a world of passion concentrated in its dark fury. He looked at her, slowly folding his arms, and drawing himself to his fullest height.

He shrugged his shoulders, with one brief contemptuous movement, as if he flung some burden off him by the gesture, and then
turned and left the pew. Mrs Gilbert heard his firm tread upon the
stairs, and she rose from her seat in time to see him pass out of the
porch. It is very nice to have a place in romantic story: but there are
some bitter pangs to be endured in the life of a Mademoiselle de la
Vallière.

CHAPTER IV

THE FIRST WHISPER OF THE STORM

There was no omnibus to take Mrs Gilbert back to Graybridge after
the service at Hurstonleigh; but there had been some Graybridge
people at church, and she found them lingering in the churchyard
talking to some of the model villagers, enthusiastic in their praises
of Mr Colborne's eloquence.

Amongst these Graybridge people was Miss Sophronia Burdock,
the maltster's daughter, very radiant in a bright-pink bonnet, so
vivid as almost to extinguish her freckles, and escorted by young Mr
Pawlkatt, the surgeon's son, and his sister, a sharp-nosed, high-
cheek-boned damsel, who looked polite daggers at the Doctor's Wife.
Was not Mr George Gilbert a rising man in Graybridge? and was it
likely that the family of his rival should have any indulgence for the
shortcomings of his pale-faced wife?

But Miss Sophronia was in the humour to heap coals of fire on
the head of the nursery-governess whom George Gilbert had chosen
to marry. Sophronia was engaged, with her father's full consent, to
the younger Pawlkatt, who was to insure his life for the full amount
of the fair damsel's dower, which was to be rigidly tied up for her
separate use and maintenance, &c., and who looked of so sickly and
feeble a constitution that the maltster may have reasonably regarded
the matrimonial arrangement as a very fair speculation. Sophronia
was engaged, and displayed the little airs and graces that Graybridge
considered appropriate to the position of an engaged young lady.
'The only way to make love *now*,' said Mr Nash to Goldsmith, 'is to
take no manner of notice of the lady.'* And Graybridge regarded
the art of polite courtship very much in this fashion, considering

that a well-bred damsel could not possibly be too contemptuously frigid in her treatment of the man whom she had chosen from all other men to be her partner for life. Acting on this principle, Miss Burdock, although intensely affectionate in her manner to Julia Pawlkatt, and warmly gushing in her greeting of the Doctor's Wife, regarded her future husband with a stony glare, only disturbed by a scornful smile when the unfortunate young man ventured to make any remark. To reduce a lover to a state of coma, and exhibit him in that state to admiring beholders for an entire evening, was reckoned high art in Graybridge.

Every body in the little Midlandshire town knew that Miss Burdock and Mr Pawlkatt were engaged; and people considered that Augustus Pawlkatt had done a very nice thing for himself by becoming affianced to a young lady who was to have four thousand pounds tightly tied up for her separate use and maintenance.

The consciousness of being engaged and having a fortune combined to render Sophronia especially amiable to every body but the comatose 'future.' Was Isabel alone, and going to walk back? 'Oh, then, in that case you *must* go with us!' cried Miss Burdock, with a view to the exhibition of the unfortunate Augustus in peripatetic coma.

What could Mrs Gilbert say, except that she would be delighted to go home with them? She was thinking of *him*; she was looking to see his head towering above the crowd. Of course it would tower above that crowd, or any crowd; but he was like the famous Spanish fleet in the *Critic*,* inasmuch as she could not see him because he was not to be seen. She went with Miss Burdock and her companions out of the churchyard, towards the meadow-path that led across country towards Graybridge. They walked in a straggling, uncomfortable manner, for Sophronia resolutely refused all offers of her future husband's arm; and he was fain to content himself with the cold comfort of her parasol, and a church-service of ruby-velvet with a great many ribbons between the pages.

The conversation during that sabbath afternoon walk was not very remarkable for liveliness or wisdom. Isabel only spoke when she was spoken to, and even then like a bewildered creature newly awakened from a dream. Miss Julia Pawlkatt, who was an intellectual young person, and prided herself upon not being frivolous, discoursed upon the botanical names and attributes of the hedge-blossoms beside the path, and made a few remarks on the science of medicine as adapted to female study, which would have served for the ground-work of a letter in a Sunday paper.

Miss Burdock, who eschewed intellectual acquirements, and affected to be a gushing thing of the Dora Spenlow* stamp, entreated her future sister-in-law not to be 'dreadful,' and asked Isabel's opinion upon several 'dears' of bonnets exhibited that afternoon in Hurstonleigh church; and the comatose future, who so rarely spoke that it seemed hard he should always commit himself when he did speak, ventured a few remarks, which were received with black and frowning looks by the idol of his heart.

'I say, Sophronia, weren't you surprised to see Mr Lansdell in the gallery?' the young man remarked, interrupting his betrothed in a discussion of a bunch of artificial may on the top of a white-tulle bonnet so sweet and innocent-looking. 'You know, dear, he isn't much of a church-goer, and people *do* say that he's an atheist; yet there he was as large as life this afternoon, and I thought him looking very ill. I've heard my father say that all those Lansdells are consumptive.'

Miss Burdock made frowning and forbidding motions at the unhappy youth with her pale-buff eyebrows, as if he had mentioned an improper French novel, or started some other immoral subject. Poor Isabel's colour went and came. Consumptive! Ah, what more likely, what more proper, if it came to that? These sort of people were intended to die early. Fancy the Giaour pottering about in his eightieth year, and boasting that he could read small-print without spectacles! Imagine the Corsair on the parish; or Byron, or Keats, or Shelley grown old, and dim, and gray! Ah, how much better to be erratic and hapless Shelley, drowned in an Italian lake, than worthy respectable Samuel Rogers,* living to demand, in feeble bewilderment, 'And who are you, ma'am?' of an amiable and distinguished visitor! Of course Roland Lansdell would die of consumption; he would fade little by little, like that delightful Lionel in *Rosalind and Helen*.*

Isabel improved the occasion by asking Mr Augustus Pawlkatt, if many people died of consumption. She wanted to know what her own chances were. She wanted so much to die, now that she was good. The unhappy Augustus was quite relieved by this sudden opening for a professional discourse, and he and his sister became scientific, and neglected Sophronia, while they gave Isabel a good deal of useful information respecting tubercular disease, phthisis, &c. &c.; whereon Miss Burdock, taking offence, lapsed into a state of sullen gloom highly approved by Graybridge as peculiarly befitting an engaged young lady who wished to sustain the dignity of her position.

At last they came out of a great corn-field into the very lane in which George Gilbert's house was situated; and Isabel's friends left her at the gate. She had done something to redeem her character in Graybridge by her frequent attendance at Hurstonleigh church, which was as patent to the gossips as ever her visits to Lord Thurston's oak had been. She had been cured of running after Mr Lansdell, people said. No doubt George Gilbert had discovered her goings-on, and had found a means of clipping her wings. It was not likely that Graybridge would credit her with any such virtue as repentance, or a wish to be a better woman than she had been. Graybridge regarded her as an artful and presuming creature, whose shameful goings-on had been stopped by marital authority.

She went into the parlour, and found the tea-things laid on the little table, and Mr Gilbert lying on the sofa, which was too short for him by a couple of feet, and was eked-out by a chair, on which his clumsy boots rested. Isabel had never seen him give way to any such self-indulgence before; but as she bent over him, gently enough, if not tenderly, he told her that his head ached and he was tired, very tired; he had been in the lanes all the afternoon,—the people about there were very bad,—and he had been at work in the surgery since coming in. He put his hand in Isabel's, and pressed hers affectionately. A very little attention from his pretty young wife gratified him and made him happy.

'Why, George,' cried Mrs Gilbert, 'your hand is as hot as a burning coal!'

Yes, he was very warm, he told her; the weather was hot and oppressive; at least, he had found it so that afternoon. Perhaps he had been hurrying too much, walking too fast; he had upset himself somehow or other.

'If you'll pour out the tea, Izzie, I'll take a cup, and then go to bed,' he said; 'I'm regularly knocked up.'

He took not one cup only, but four cups of tea, pouring the mild beverage down his throat at a draught; and then he went up to the room overhead, walking heavily, as if he were very tired.

'I'm sure you're ill, George,' Isabel said, as he left the parlour; 'do take something—some of that horrid medicine you give me sometimes.'

'No, my dear; there's nothing the matter with me. What should there be amiss with me, who never had a day's illness in my life? I must have an assistant, Izzie; my work's too hard—that's what is the matter.'

Mrs Gilbert sat in the dusk for a little while after her husband had left her, thinking of that last look which Roland Lansdell had given her in the church.

Heaven knows how long she might have sat thinking of him, if Mrs Jeffson had not come in with those two miserable mould-candles, which were wont to make feeble patches of yellow haze, not light, in the doctor's parlour. After the candles had been brought, Isabel took a book from the top of the little chiffonier by the fire-place. It was a religious book. Was she not trying to be good now, and was not goodness incompatible with the perusal of Shelley's poetry on a Sunday? It was a very dry religious book, being in fact a volume of Tillotson's sermons,* with more hard logic, and firstly, secondly, and thirdly, than ordinary human nature could support. Isabel sat with the volume open before her, staring hopelessly at the pale old-fashioned type, and going back a little way every now and then when she caught her thoughts far away from the Reverend Tillotson. She sat thus till after the clock had struck ten. She was all alone in the lower part of the house at that hour, for the Jeffsons had gone clumping upstairs to bed at half-past eight. She sat alone, a poor childish, untaught, unguided creature, staring at Tillotson, and thinking of Roland Lansdell; yet trying to be good all the time in her own feeble way. She sat thus, until she was startled by a cautious single knock at the door. She started from her seat at the sound; but she went boldly enough, with the candle in her hand, to answer the summons.

There was nothing uncommon in a late knocking at the doctor's door,—some one from the lanes wanted medicine, no doubt; the people in the lanes were always wanting medicine. Mrs Gilbert opened the door, and looked out into the darkness. A man was standing there, a well-clad rather handsome-looking man, with broad shoulders, bold black eyes, and a black beard that covered all the lower part of his face. He did not wait to be invited to enter, but walked across the threshold like a man who had a right to come into that house, and almost pushed Isabel on one side as he did so. At first she only stared at him with a blank look of wonder, but all at once her face grew as white as the plaster on the wall behind her.

'You!' she gasped, in a whisper; 'you here!'

'Yes, me! You needn't stare as if you saw a ghost. There's nothing so very queer about me, is there? You're a nice young lady, I don't think, to stand there shivering and staring. Where's your husband?'

'Up-stairs. Oh, why, why did you come here?' cried the Doctor's Wife, piteously, clasping her hands like a creature in some extremity of fear and trouble: 'how could you be so cruel as to come here; how could you be so cruel as to come?'

'How could I be so—fiddlesticks!' muttered the stranger with supreme contempt. 'I came here because I had nowhere else to go, my lassie. You needn't whimper: for I shan't trouble you very long— this is not exactly the sort of place I should care to hang-out in: if you can give me a bed in this house for to-night, well and good; if not, you can give me a sovereign, and I'll find one elsewhere. While I *am* here, remember my name's Captain Morgan, and I'm in the merchant service,—just home from the Mauritius.'

CHAPTER V

THE BEGINNING OF A GREAT CHANGE

George Gilbert was something more than 'knocked up.' There had been a great deal of typhoid fever amongst the poorer inhabitants of Graybridge and the neighbouring villages lately—a bad infectious fever, which hung over the narrow lanes and little clusters of cottages like a black cloud; and the parish surgeon, working early and late, subject to sudden chills when his work was hottest, exposed to every variety of temperature at all times, fasting for long hours, and altogether setting at naught those very first principles of health, wherein it was his duty to instruct other people, had paid the common penalty to which all of his profession are, more or less, subject. Ah, how much we think of the soldier, who rides out amidst the blasts of trumpets and clashing of swords, and all the intoxicating magic of war; and how small an account we set upon the quiet courage of the village doctor, who meets death face to face every day, and never shirks the dangerous encounter! George Gilbert had caught a touch of the fever. Mr Pawlkatt senior called early on Monday morning,—summoned by poor terrified Isabel, who was a strange to sickness, and was frightened at the first appearance of the malady,—and spoke of his rival's illness very lightly, as a 'touch of the fever.'

'I always said it was infectious,' he remarked; 'but your husband would have it that it wasn't. It was all the effect of dirty habits and low living, he said, and not any special and periodical influence in the air. Well, poor fellow, he knows now who is right. You must keep him very quiet. Give him a little toast-and-water, and the lime-draughts I shall send you;' and Mr Pawlkatt went on to give all necessary directions about the invalid.

Unhappily for the patient, it was not the easiest matter in the world to keep him quiet. There was not much in George Gilbert, according to any poetic or sentimental standard; but there was a great deal in him, when you came to measure him by the far nobler standard of duty. He was essentially 'thorough;' and in his own quiet way he was very fond of his profession. He was attached to those rough Midlandshire peasants, whom it had been his duty to attend from his earliest manhood until now. Never before had he known what it was to have a day's illness; and he could not lie tranquilly watching Isabel sitting at work near the window, with the sunlight creeping in at the edges of the dark curtain that had been hastily nailed up to shut out the glaring day;—he could not lie quietly there, while there were mothers of sick children, and wives of sick husbands, waiting for hope and comfort from his lips. True, Mr Pawlkatt had promised to attend to George's patients; but then, unhappily, George did not believe in Mr Pawlkatt,—the two sur-geons' views were in every way opposed; and the idea of Mr Pawlkatt attending the sick people in the lanes, and seizing with delight on the opportunity of reversing his rival's treatment, was almost harder to bear than the thought of the same sufferers being altogether unattended. And, beyond this, Mr Gilbert, so clever while other people were concerned, was not the best possible judge of his own case; and he would not consent to believe that he had the fever.

'I daresay Pawlkatt likes to see me laid by the heels here, Izzie,' he said to his wife, 'while he goes interfering with my patients, and bringing his old-fashioned theories to bear. He'll shut up the poor wretched little windows of all those cottages in the lanes, I daresay; and make the rooms even more stifling than they have been made by the builder. He'll frighten the poor women into shutting out every breath of fresh air, and then take every atom of strength away from those poor wasted creatures by his drastic treatment. Dr Robert James Graves* said he only wanted three words for his epitaph, and those words were, 'HE FED FEVERS.' Pawlkatt will be for starving these poor feeble creatures in the lanes. It's no use talking, my dear; I'm a little knocked up; but I've no more fever about me than you have, and I shall go out this evening. I shall go round and see those people. There's a woman in the lane behind the church, a widow, with three children lying ill; and she seems to believe in me, poor creature, as if I was Providence itself. I can't forget the look she gave me yesterday, when she stood on the threshold of her wretched hovel, asking me to save her children, as if she thought it rested with me to save them. I can't forget her look, Izzie. It haunted me all last night, when I lay tossing about; for I was too tired to sleep, somehow or other. And when I think of Pawlkatt pouring his drugs down those children's throats, I—I tell you it's no use, my dear; I'll take a cup of tea, and then get up and dress.'

It was in vain that Isabel pleaded; in vain that she brought to her aid Mrs Jeffson, the vigorous and outspoken, who declared that it would be nothing short of self-murder if Mr Gilbert insisted on going out that evening; equally in vain the threat of summoning Mr Pawlkatt. George was resolute: these quiet people always are resolute, not to say obstinate. It is your animated, impetuous, impulsive creatures who can be turned by a breath from the pursuit or purpose they have most vehemently sworn to accomplish. Mr Gilbert put aside all arguments in the quietest possible manner. He was a medical man, and he was surely the best judge of his own health. He was wanted yonder among his patients, and he must go. Isabel and Mrs Jeffson retired in melancholy resignation to prepare the tea, which was to fortify the surgeon for his evening's work. George came down stairs half an hour afterwards, looking, not ill, or even weak; but at once flushed and haggard.

'There's nothing whatever the matter with me, my dear Izzie,' he said, as his wife followed him to the door; 'I'm only done up by very hard work. I feel tired and cramped in my limbs, as if I'd caught cold somehow or other. I was out all day in the wet last week, you know; but there's nothing in that. I shall just look in at those people at Briargate, and come back by the lanes; and then an hour or so in the surgery will finish my work, and I shall be able to get a good night's rest. I must have an assistant, my dear. The agricultural population gets very thick about Graybridge; and unless some one takes pity on the poor people, and brings about some improvement in the places they live in, we may look for plenty of fever.'

He went out at the little gate, and Isabel watched him going along the lane. He walked a little slower than usual, and that was all. She watched him with a quiet affection on her face. There was no possible phase of circumstance by which she could ever have been brought to love him: but she knew that he was good, she knew that there was something praiseworthy in what he was doing to-night,— this resolute visiting of wretched sick people. It was not the knightly sort of goodness she had adored in the heroes of her choice: but it was good: and she admired her husband a little, in a calm unenthusiastic manner,—as she might have admired a very estimable grandfather, had she happened to possess such a relative. She was trying to be good, remember; and all the sentimental tenderness of her nature had been aroused by George's illness. He was a much more agreeable person lying faint and languid in a shaded room, and requiring his head constantly bathed with vinegar-and-water, than when in the full vigour of health and clumsiness.

Mr Pawlkatt came in for his second visit half an hour after George had left the house. He was very angry when he was told what had happened, and inveighed solemnly upon his patient's imprudence.

'I sent my son round amongst your husband's patients,' he said; 'and I must say, I am a little hurt by the want of confidence in me which Mr Gilbert's conduct exhibits.'

Isabel was too much occupied by all manner of contending thoughts to be able to do much towards the soothing of Mr Pawlkatt's indignation. That gentleman went away with his heart full of bitterness against the younger practitioner.

'If your husband's well enough to go about amongst his patients, he can't want *me*, Mrs Gilbert,' he said, as Isabel opened the gate for him; 'but if you find him much worse, as you are very likely to do after his most imprudent conduct, you know where to send for me. I shall not come again till I'm sent for. Good-night.'

Isabel sighed as she shut the gate upon the offended surgeon. The world seemed to her quite full of trouble just now. Roland Lansdell was angry with her. Ah! what bitter anger and contempt had been exhibited in his face in the church yesterday! George was ill, and bent on making himself worse, as it seemed; a Person—the person whom of all others the Doctor's Wife most feared—had dropped as it were from the clouds into Midlandshire; and here, added to all this trouble, was Mr Pawlkatt indignant and offended. She did not go in-doors at once; the house seemed gloomy and hot in the summer dusk. She lingered by the gate, looking over the top of the rails at the dusty lane,—the monotonous uninteresting lane, of whose changeless aspect she was so very tired. She was sorry for her husband now that he was ill. It was her nature to love and pity every weak thing in creation. The same kind of tenderness that she had felt long ago for a sick kitten, or a wounded bird, or a forlorn street-wanderer of the canine species looking pleadingly at her with great hungry eyes, filled her heart now, as she thought of George Gilbert. Out of the blank emptiness into which he had melted long ago at Roland Lansdell's advent, he emerged now, distinct and palpable, as a creature who wanted pity and affection.

'Is he very ill?' she wondered. 'He says himself that he is not; and he is much cleverer than Mr Pawlkatt.'

She looked out into the lane, watching for her husband's coming. Two or three people went slowly by at considerable intervals; and at last, when it was growing quite dark, the figure of a boy, a slouching country-built lad, loomed out of the obscurity.

'Be this Muster Gilbert's the doctor's?' he asked of Isabel.

'Yes; do you want him?'

'I doan't want him; but I've got a letter for his wife, from a man that's staying up at our place. Be you she?'

'Yes; give me the letter,' answered Isabel, putting her hand over the gate.

She took the missive from the hand of the boy, who resigned it in a slow unwilling manner, and then slouched away. Mrs Gilbert put the letter in her pocket, and went into the house. The candles had just been taken into the parlour. The Doctor's Wife seated herself at the little table, and took the letter from her pocket and tore it open. It was a very brief and unceremonious kind of epistle, containing only these words:

'I've found comfortable quarters, for the nonce, in a little crib called the Leicester Arms, down in Nessborough Hollow, to the left of the Briargate Road. I suppose you know the place; and I shall expect to see you in the course of to-morrow. Don't forget the sinews of war; and be sure you ask for Captain Morgan.

'Yours truly.'

There was no signature. The letter was written in a big dashing hand, which had sprawled recklessly over a sheet of old-fashioned letter-paper; it seemed a riotous improvident kind of writing, that gloried in the wasted space and squandered ink.

'How cruel of him to come here!' muttered Isabel, as she tore the letter into a little heap of fragments; 'how cruel of him to come! As if I had not suffered enough already; as if the misery and disgrace had not been bitter enough and hard enough to bear.'

She rested her elbows on the table, and sat quite still for some time with her face hidden in her hands. Her thoughts were very painful; but, for once in a way, they were not entirely devoted to Roland Lansdell; and yet the master of Mordred Priory did figure in that long reverie. George came in by and by, and found her sitting in the attitude into which she had fallen after destroying the letter. She had been very anxious about her husband some time ago; but for the last half-hour her thoughts had been entirely removed from him; and she looked up at him confusedly, almost startled by his coming, as if he had been the last person in the world whom she expected to see. Mr Gilbert did not notice that look of confusion, but dropped heavily into the nearest chair, like a man who feels himself powerless to go one step further.

'I'm very ill, Izzie,' he said; 'it's no use mincing the matter; I *am* ill. I suppose Pawlkatt is right after all, and I've got a touch of the fever.'

'Shall I send for him?' asked Isabel, starting up; 'he said I was to send for him if you were worse.'

'Not on any account. I know what to do as well as he does. If I should happen to get delirious by and by, you can send for him, because I daresay you'd be frightened, poor girl, and would feel more comfortable with a doctor pottering about me. And now listen to me, my dear, while I give you a few directions; for my head feels like a ton-weight, and I don't think I shall be able to sit upright much longer.'

The doctor proceeded to give his wife all necessary instructions for the prevention of infection. She was to have a separate room prepared for herself immediately; and she was to fumigate the room in which he was to lie, in such and such a manner. As for any attendance upon himself, that would be Mrs Jeffson's task.

'I don't believe the fever is infectious,' Mr Gilbert said; 'I've caught it from the same causes that give it to the poor people: hard work, exposure to bad weather, and the foul air of the places I have to visit. Still we can't be too careful. You'd better keep away from my room as much as possible, Izzie; and let Mrs Jeffson look after me. She's a strong-minded sort of a woman, who wouldn't be likely to catch a fever, because she'd be the last in the world to trouble her head about the risk of catching it.'

But Isabel declared that she herself would wait upon her sick husband. Was she not trying to be good; and did not all Mr Colborne's sermons inculcate self-sacrifice and compassion, tenderness and pity? The popular curate of Hurstonleigh was perhaps the kind of teacher that some people would have designated a sentimentalist; but his tender, loving exhortations had a fascination which could surely never belong to the terrible threats and awful warnings of a sterner preacher. In spite of Austin Colborne's deep faith in an infinitely grand and beautiful region beyond this lower earth, he did not look upon the world as a howling wilderness, in which Providence intended people to be miserable. He might certainly behold in it a place of probation, a kind of preparatory school, in which very small virtues were expected of ignorant and helpless scholars, wandering dimly towards a starry future: but he did not consider it a universal Dotheboys Hall, presided over by a Providence after the model of Mr Squeers.* He looked into the simple narratives of four historians who flourished some eighteen centuries ago; and in those solemn pages he saw no possible justification for the gloomy view of life entertained by many of his clerical compeers. He found in those sacred histories a story that opened like an idyl; he found bright glimpses of a life in which there were marriage festivals and pleasant gatherings, social feasts and happy Sabbath wanderings through rustic paths betwixt the standing corn; he found pure earthly friendship counted no sin against the claims of Heaven, and passionate parental love not reproved as an unholy idolatry of the creature, but hallowed for ever by two separate miracles, that stand eternal records of a love so entirely divine as to be omnipotent, so tenderly human as to change the sternest laws of the universe in pity for weak human sorrow.

Mr Pawlkatt was summoned to his rival's bedside early on the following morning. George's case was quite out of his own hands by this time; for he had grown much worse in the night, and was fain to submit to whatever people pleased to do to him. He was very ill. Isabel sat in the half-darkened room, sometimes reading, sometimes working in the dim light that crept through the curtain, sometimes sitting very quietly wrapt in thought—painful and perplexing thought. Mr Gilbert was wakeful all through the day, as he had been all through the night, tossing uneasily from side to side, and now and then uttering half-suppressed groans that wrung his wife's heart. She was very foolish—she had been very wicked—but there was a deep fount of tenderness in that sentimental and essentially feminine breast; and I doubt if George Gilbert was not more lovingly watched by his weak erring young wife than ever he could have been by a strong-minded helpmate, who would have frozen any lurking sentiment in Mr Lansdell's breast by one glance from her pitiless eyes. The Doctor's Wife felt a remorseful compassion for the man who, after his own matter-of-fact fashion, had been very good to her.

'He has never, never been cross to me, as my stepmother used to be,' she thought; 'he married me without even knowing who I was, and never asked any cruel questions; and even now, if he knew, I think he would have pity upon me and forgive me.'

She sat looking at her husband with an earnest yearning expression in her eyes. It seemed as if she wanted to say something to him, but lacked the courage to approach the subject. He was very ill; it was no time to make any unpleasant communication to him. He had been delirious in the night, and had fancied that Mr Pawlkatt was present, at an hour when that gentleman was snoring comfortably in his own bed. Isabel had been specially enjoined to keep her husband as quiet as it was possible for an active industrious man, newly stricken down by some unlooked-for malady, to be kept. No; whatever she might have to say to him must be left unspoken for the present. Whatever help he might, under ordinary circumstances, have given her, he was utterly powerless to give her now.

The day in that sick chamber seemed terribly long. Not because

Isabel felt any selfish weariness of her task; she was only too anxious to be of use to the man she had so deeply wronged; she was only too eager to do something,—something that Mr Colborne himself might approve,—as an atonement for her sin. But she was quite unused to sickness; and, being of a hypersensitive nature, suffered keenly at the sight of any suffering whatever. If the invalid was restless, she fancied directly that he was worse—much worse—in imminent danger perhaps: if he rambled a little in his talk betwixt sleeping and waking, she sat with his burning hands clasped in hers, trembling from head to foot: if he fell into a profound slumber, she was seized with a sudden terror, fancying him unnaturally quiet, and was fain to disturb him, in her fear lest he should be sinking into some ominous lethargy.

The Doctor's Wife was not one of those excellent nurses who can settle themselves with cheerful briskness in a sick-room, and improve the occasion by the darning of a whole basketful of invalided stockings, reserved for some such opportunity. She was not a nurse who could accept the duties of her position in a businesslike way, and polish off each separate task as coolly as a clerk in a banking-house transacts the work assigned to him. Yet she was very quiet withal,—soft of foot, gentle-handed, tender; and George was pleased to see her sitting in the shadowy room, when he lifted his heavy eyelids a little now and then; he was pleased in a dim kind of way to take his medicine from her hand,—the slender little white hand with tapering fingers,—the hand he had admired as it lay lightly on the moss-grown brick-work of the bridge in Hurstonleigh churchyard on the afternoon when he asked her to be his wife.

Mrs Gilbert sat all day in her husband's room; but about five in the afternoon George fell into a deep slumber, in which Mr Pawlkatt found him a little after six o'clock. Nothing could be better than that tranquil sleep, the surgeon said; and when he was gone, Mrs Jeffson, who had been sitting in the room for some time, anxious to be of use to her master, suggested that Isabel should go down stairs and out into the garden to get a breath of fresh air.

'You must be a'most stifled, I should think, sitting all day in this room,' Tilly said compassionately. Mrs Gilbert's face crimsoned all over, as she answered in a timid hesitating way:

'Yes; I should like to go down stairs a little, if you think that George is sure to sleep soundly for a long time; and I know you'll take good care of him. I want to go out somewhere—not very far; but I must go to-night.'

The Doctor's Wife sat with her back to the light; and Mrs Jeffson did not see that sudden tide of crimson that rushed into her face, and faded, as she said this; but George Gilbert's housekeeper gave a sniff of disapproval notwithstanding.

'I should have thought if you was the greatest gadderabout that ever was, you'd have stayed quietly at home while your husband was lying ill, Mrs Gilbert,' she said sharply; 'but of course you know your own business best.'

'I'm not going far: only—only a little way on the Briargate Road,' Isabel answered, piteously; and then her head sank back against the wall behind her, and she sighed a plaintive, almost heart-broken sigh. Her life was very hard just now,—hard and difficult,—begirt with terror and peril, as she thought.

She put on her bonnet and shawl—the darkest and shabbiest she possessed. Mrs Jeffson watched her, as she stood before the old-fashioned looking-glass, and perceived that she did not even take the trouble to brush the rumpled hair which she pushed under her dingy bonnet. 'She can't be going to meet *him* in that plight, any-how,' thought honest Matilda, considerably pacified by the contem-plation of her mistress's toilette. She lifted the curtain and looked out of the window as the garden-gate closed on Isabel, and she saw the Doctor's Wife hurrying away with her veil pulled over her face. There was some kind of mystery about this evening walk: something that filled the Yorkshire woman's mind with vague disquietude.

The 'touch of the fever,' alluded to so lightly by Mr Pawlkatt, turned out to be a great deal more serious in its nature than either he or George Gilbert had anticipated. The week came to an end, and the parish surgeon was still a prisoner in the room in which his father and mother had died. It seemed quite a long time now since he had been active and vigorous, going about his work all day, mixing medicines in the surgery, and coming into the parlour at stated times to eat hearty meals of commonplace substantial food. Now that he was so weak, and that it was a matter for rejoicing when he took a couple of spoonfuls of beef-tea, Isabel's conscience smote her cruelly as she remembered how she had despised him because of his healthy appetite; with what bitter scorn she had regarded him when he ate ponderous slices of underdone meat, and mopped up the last drop of the goriest-looking gravy with great pieces of bread. He had been ill for only a week, and yet already it seemed quite a normal state of things for him to be lying in that darkened chamber, helpless and uneasy, all through the long summer day. The state of the doctor's health was common talk in Graybridge; as common a subject for idle people's converse as the heat of the weather, or the progress of the green corn in the fields beyond the little town. All manner of discreditable-looking parish patients came every day to the surgery-door to inquire after the surgeon's health; and went away downcast and lamenting, when they were told that he grew daily worse. Mrs Gilbert, going down to answer these people's questions, discovered for the first time how much he was beloved; he who had not one of the attributes of a hero. She wondered sometimes whether it might not be better to wear thick boots, and go about doing good, than to be a used-up aristocratic wanderer, with white hands, and, oh, such delightful varnished boots wrinkled over an arched instep. She was trying to be good herself now—pleased and fascinated by Mr Colborne's teaching as by some newly-discovered romance—she wanted to be good, and scarcely knew how to set about the task; and, behold, here was the man whom she had so completely ignored and despised, infinitely above her in the region she had entered. But was her romantic attachment to Roland Lansdell laid down at the new altar she had found for herself? Ah, no; she tried very hard to do her duty; but the old sentimental worship still held its place in her heart. She was like some classic pagan newly converted to Christianity, and yet entertaining a lurking love and reverence for the old heathen deities, too grand and beautiful to be cast off all at once.

The first week came to an end, and still Mr Pawlkatt came twice a day to visit his patient; and still he gave very much the same directions to the untiring nurses who waited on George Gilbert. He was to be kept very quiet; he was to continue the medicine; all the old stereotyped rules were to be observed.

Throughout her husband's illness, Isabel had taken very little rest; though Mr and Mrs Jeffson would gladly have kept watch alternately with her in the sick-room, and were a little wounded when banished therefrom. But Mrs Gilbert wanted to be good; the harder the task was, the more gladly did she undertake it. Very often, quite alone in that quiet room, she sat watching through the stillest hours of the night.

During all those solemn watches did any bad thoughts enter her mind? did she ever think that she might be free to marry Roland Lansdell if the surgeon's illness should terminate fatally? Never— never once did such a dark and foul fancy enter the regions of her imagination. Do not believe that because she had been a foolish woman she must necessarily be a vicious woman. Again and again, on her knees by her husband's bed, she supplicated that his life might be spared. She had never encountered death, and her imagination shrank appalled from the thought of that awful presence. A whole after life of happiness could not have atoned to her for the one pang of seeing a dreadful change come upon the familiar face. Sometimes, in spite of herself, though she put away the thought from her with shuddering horror, the idea that George Gilbert might not recover *would* come into her mind. He might not recover: the horror which so many others had passed through might overtake her. Oh, the hideous tramp of the undertaker's men upon the stairs; the knocking, unlike all other knocking; the dreadful aspect of the shrouded house! [She thought of all the deaths in her favourite books: of Paul Dombey, fading slowly, day by day, with the golden water rippling on the wall; of David Copperfield, sitting weeping in the dusk; and Agnes, with her holy face and quiet uplifted hand.]* If—if any such sorrow came upon her, Mrs Gilbert thought that she would join some community of holy women, and go about doing good until she died. Was it so very strange, this sudden conversion? Surely not! In these enthusiastic natures sentiment may take any unexpected form. It is a question whether a Madame de Chantal shall write hazy devotional letters to a St Francis de Sales,* or peril her soul for the sake of an earthly lover.

CHAPTER VI

FIFTY POUNDS

After that scene in the church at Hurstonleigh, Roland Lansdell went back to Mordred; to think, with even greater bitterness, of the woman he loved. That silent encounter—the sight of the pale face, profoundly melancholy, almost statuesque in its air of half-despairing resignation—had exercised no softening influence on the mind of this young man, who could not understand why the one treasure for which he languished should be denied to him. He could not be generous or just towards the woman who had fooled him with false hopes, and then left him to despair; he could not have pity upon the childish creature who had wandered unawares upon the flowery margin of a hideous gulf, and had fled, aghast and horrified, at the first glimpse of the yawning depths below. No; his anger against Isabel could not have been more intense had she been a hardened and practised coquette who had deliberately lured him to his ruin.

'I suppose this is what the world calls a virtuous woman,' he cried, bitterly. 'I daresay Lucretia was this sort of person; and dropped her eyelids to show-off the dark lashes, and made the most of her tapering arms over the spinning-wheel, and summoned conscious blushes into her cheeks when Tarquin looked at her.* These virtuous women delight in clamour and scandal. I've no doubt Mrs Gilbert profoundly enjoyed herself during our rencontre in the church, and went away proud of the havoc she had made in me—the haggard lines about my mouth, and the caverns under my eyes.'

[You see, Mr Lansdell could be very brutal sometimes, when he thought of the woman whose weak hand had so completely shattered the airy palace he had built for himself. There is perhaps a good deal of the savage past lurking under the civilised present. Scratch the fine gentleman's waistcoat, and you may come upon the brindled hide of the tiger. He could not forgive her. Had he not fought against the temptation which her love—so naïvely confessed in every look and tone—had offered to him? had he not fought the good fight of honour, bravely and manfully, as he himself believed, only to succumb at last; and when vanquished, to find that there had been no need for any battle at all? He thought of the life which he had planned for himself and the woman he loved; the bright erratic existence, spent wherever the earth was loveliest. A thousand schemes that he had built in that romantic future faded away, like Mireille's phantom city,* beneath the withering influence of this woman's pitiful cowardice.]*

'It is *not* because she is a good woman, it is not because she loves her husband, that she refuses to listen to me,' he thought; 'it is only a paltry provincial terror of an esclandre that ties her to this wretched place. And when she has broken my heart, and when she has ruined my life, she goes to church at Hurstonleigh, and sits in a devotional pose, with her big eyes lifted up to the parson's face, like a Madonna by Giorgione,* in order that she may rehabilitate herself in the consideration of Graybridge.'

He could neither be just nor patient. Sometimes he laughed aloud at his own folly. Was he, who had prided himself on his cynical disbelief in the depth of endurance of any emotion—was he the man to go mad for love of a pale face and darkly pensive eyes? Ah, yes! it is just these scoffers who take the fever most deeply, when the infection seizes them. Venus, the implacable goddess, mocked so long by the lip of the scorner, attaches herself at last to her prey; and the victim succumbs all at once, aghast and confounded, and acknowledges her awful power. The beautiful smiling creature, so fair to look upon, newly arisen out of the sunlit waters, with dripping hair and rosy limbs, is transformed all at once into a Nemesis, from whose dread sentence there is no escape.

'I—I, who have lived my life out, as I thought, wherever life is most worth living,—I suffer like this at last for the sake of a village surgeon's half-educated wife? I—who have given myself the airs of a Lauzun or a Brummel*—am perishing for the love of a woman who doesn't even know how to put on her gloves!'

Every day Mr Lansdell resolved to leave Midlandshire to-morrow; but to-morrow found him still lingering at the Priory in a hopeless, purposeless way,—lingering for he knew not what,—lingering, perhaps, for want of the mere physical energy required for the brief effort of departure. He would go to Constantinople over-land; there would be more fatigue in the journey that way. Might not a walk across Mount Cenis cure him of his foolish love for Isabel Gilbert? Did not D'Alembert retire from the world and all its troubles into the peaceful pleasures of geometry?* Did not Goethe seek relief from some great sorrow in the study of a new language? Roland Lansdell made a faint effort to acquire the Arabic alphabet during those wretched idle days and nights at Mordred. He would study the Semitic languages: all of them. He would go in for the Book of Job. Many people had got plenty of hard work out of the Book of Job. But the curly little characters in the Arabic alphabet slipped out of Mr Lansdell's brain as if they had been so many lively young serpents; and he only made so much headway in the attainment of the Semitic languages as enabled him to scrawl an Arabic rendering of Isabel Gilbert's name over the leaves of a blotting-book. He was in love. No schoolboy, bewitched by a pretty blue-eyed, blue-ribboned, white-robed partner at a dancing-school, was ever more foolishly in love than the young squire of Mordred, who had filled a whole volume with various metrical versions of his profound contempt for his species in general, and the feminine portion of them in particular. He had set up that gladsome halloo before he was safely out of the wood; and now he found to his cost that he had been premature; for lo, the dense forest hemmed him in on every side, and there seemed no way of escape out of the sombre labyrinth.

George Gilbert had been ill nearly a fortnight, and the master of Mordred Priory still lingered in Midlandshire. He had heard nothing of the surgeon's illness, for he had never been much given to gossiping with his body-servant; and that gentleman was especially disinclined to offer his master any unasked-for information just now; for, as he expressed himself in the servants' hall, 'Mr Lansdell's been in a devil of a temper almost ever since we come back to the Priory; and you might as lief talk to a tiger as speak to him, except when you're spoken to, and goodness knows *that* ain't very often; for any thing so gloomy as his ways has become of late, I never remember to have met with; and if it wasn't that the remuneration is high, and the perquisites never greasy about the elbows, or frayed at the edges,—which I've been with a member of the peerage that wore his clothes till they was shamefully shabby,—it wouldn't be very long as I should trouble this dismal old dungeon with my presence.'

Only from Lady Gwendoline was Roland likely to hear of George Gilbert's illness; and he had not been to Lowlands lately. He had a vague idea that he would go there some morning, and ask his cousin to marry him, and so make an end of it; but he deferred the carrying out of that idea indefinitely, as a man who contemplates suicide may postpone the ghastly realisation of his purpose, keeping his loaded pistol or his prussic acid handy against the time when it shall be wanted. He had never ridden past the surgeon's house since that day on which he had seen Isabel seated in the parlour. He had indeed shunned Graybridge and the Graybridge road altogether.

'She shall not triumph in the idea that I pursue her,' he thought;

'her vain shallow heart shall not be gratified by the knowledge of my pitiful weakness. I bared my foolish breast before her once, and she sat in her pew playing at devotion, and let me go away with my despair. She might have thrown herself in my way that afternoon, if only for a few moments. She might have spoken to me, if only half-a-dozen commonplace words of comfort; but it pleased her better to exhibit her piety. I daresay she knows as well as I do how that devotional air harmonises with her beauty; and she went home happy, no doubt, in the knowledge that she had made one man miserable. And that's the sort of woman whom the world calls virtuous,—a creature in whom vanity is strong enough to usurp the place of every other passion. For a really good woman, for a true-hearted wife who loves her husband, and before whose quiet presence the veriest libertine bows his head abashed and reverent,—for such a woman as that I have no feeling but respect and admiration; but I hate and despise these sentimental coquettes, who preach secondhand platonism, borrowed from the pages of a poet who at his best was ten times more immoral than the author of Don Juan at his worst.'*

But it was not always that Roland Lansdell was thus bitter against the woman he loved. Sometimes in the midst of his rage and anger a sudden current of tenderness swept across the dark waters of his soul, and for a little while the image of Isabel Gilbert appeared to him in its true colours. He saw her as she really was; foolish, but not base; weak, but not hypocritical; sentimental, and with some blemish of womanly vanity perhaps, but not designing. Sometimes amidst all contending emotions, in which passion, and selfishness, and wounded pride, and mortified vanity made a very whirlpool of bitter feeling,— sometimes amidst such baser emotions as these, true love— the sublime, the clear-sighted—arose for a brief interval triumphant, and Roland Lansdell thought tenderly of the woman who had shattered his future.

'My poor little girl,—my poor innocent childish love,' he thought, in these moments of purer feeling; 'if I could only be noble, and go away, and forgive you, and leave you to grow into a good woman, with that well-meaning commonplace husband, whom it is your duty to honour and obey. [Good heavens! I have heard and read of men whose lives were one long sacrifice, who never knew what it was to win the peculiar object of their desires, who were perpetual Abrahams for ever offering new Isaacs on the altar of an insatiable deity, and who derived a kind of happiness after all,—a sublimated ethereal joy,—from the pangs of their martyrdom. Surely there are Trappists in May Fair as well as amid the sombre mountain-tops of Valombrosa; men who are dumb for ever as regards the only words they *want* to speak; galley-slaves, who go about smiling, galled by invisible chains, and bound eternally to a companion they loathe; men who never know what it is to speak their own words, or take their own pleasure, who live perpetually under the eye of a *garde-chiourme*,* and are awakened out of every peaceful slumber by the striking of the cruel hammer with which he tests the strength of their irons. There are creatures who begin the experience of suffering with the first letters of their alphabet, who are drudges at a cheap school, servitors at college, bear-leaders to a snob who insults and humiliates them; tied hand and foot by the wants of a half-starved mother and ravenous younger brothers, and helpless, penniless sisters; in love, and with not so much as daily bread to offer to the woman they love; obliged to stand aloof and stifle the noblest feelings of their hearts, while a meaner man wins and misuses the prize that for them would have made all the earth glorious; compelled at last, for the sake of other people, to marry a woman they despise, and who are brave enough to keep the secret of their contempt for ever, and do their duty to the last; going down to the grave under the pressure of perpetual drudgery; never, never, never knowing what it is to have a single wish gratified while the bloom is on it; doomed to disgrace a new coat by a shabby hat, a decent hat by doubtful boots; never in any one object of life realising the complete or the beautiful. There are such men as these; and here am I, who have outbid the Marquis of Lambethia for a Murillo at Christie's; I, who never knew what sorrow was till my mother died, and who fret myself to death like a sick tiger, because the woman I love is refused to me!']*

Nothing could be more irregular than Mr Lansdell's habits during this period. The cook at Mordred declared that such a thing as a *soufflé* was a simple impossibility with an employer who might require his dinner served at any time between the hours of seven and nine. The fish was flabby, the joints were leathery; and all the hot-water reservoirs in the Mordred dinner-service could not preserve the cook's most special *plats* from stagnation. That worthy artist shrugged his shoulders over the ruins of his work, and turned

his attention to the composition of a *menu* in which the best things
were to be eaten cold. He might have spared himself the trouble.
The young man, who, naturally careless as to what he ate, had, out
of pure affectation, been wont to out-rival the insolence of the oldest *bon-vivants*, now scarcely knew the nature of the dishes that were
set before him. He ate and drank mechanically; and it may be drank
a little deeper than he had been accustomed to drink of the famous
clarets his father and grandfather had collected. But eating delighted
him not, nor drinking neither. The wine had no exhilarating effect
upon him; he sat dull and gloomy after a magnum of the famous
claret—sat with the Arabic grammar open before him, wondering
what was to become of him, now that his life was done.

He was sitting thus in the library, with the sombre Rembrandt
face that was something like his own looking gravely down upon
him; he was sitting thus by the lamplit table one sultry June evening,
when George Gilbert had been ill nearly a fortnight. The light of
the lamp—a soft subdued light, shining dimly through a great moon-
like orb of thick ground-glass—fell chiefly on the open book, and
left the student's face in shadow. But even in that shadow the face
looked wan and haggard, and the something that lurked somewhere
in all the Lansdell portraits—the something that you may see in
every picture of Charles the First of England and Marie Antoinette
of France, whensoever and by whomsoever painted—was very visible in Roland's face to-night. He had been sitting brooding over his
books, but scarcely reading half-a-dozen pages, ever since nine o'clock,
and it was now half-past eleven. He was stretching his hand towards
the bell in order to summon his valet, and release that personage
from the task of sitting up any longer, yawning alone in the housekeeper's room,—for the habits of Mordred Priory had never lost the
sobriety of Lady Anna Lansdell's regime, and all the servants except
Roland's valet went to bed at eleven,—when that gentleman entered
the library.

'Would you please to see any one, sir?' he asked.

'Would I please to see any one?' cried Roland, turning in his low
easy-chair, and staring at the solemn face of his valet; 'who should
want to see me at such a time of night? Is there any thing wrong? Is
it any one from—from Lowlands?'

'No, sir, it's a strange lady; leastways, when I say a strange lady,
I *think*, sir—though, her veil being down, and a very thick veil, I

should not like to speak positive,—I think it's Mrs Gilbert, the doctor's lady, from Graybridge.'

Mr Lansdell's valet coughed doubtfully behind his hand, and looked discreetly at the carved oaken bosses in the ceiling. Roland started to his feet.

'Mrs Gilbert,' he muttered, 'at such an hour as this! It can't be; she would never—Show the lady here, whoever she is,' he added aloud to his servant. 'There must be something wrong; it must be some very important business that brings any one to this place to-night.'

The valet departed, closing the door behind him, and Roland stood alone upon the hearth, waiting for his late visitor. All the warmer tints—he never had what people call 'a colour'—faded out of his face, and left him very pale. Why had she come to him at such a time? What purpose could she have in coming to that house save one? She had come to revoke her decision. For a moment a flood of rapture swept into his soul, warm and revivifying as the glory of a sudden sunburst on a dull gray autumn day; but in the next moment,—so strange and subtle an emotion is that which we call love,—a chill sense of regret crept into his mind, and he was almost sorry that Isabel should come to him thus, even though she were to bring him the promise of future happiness.

'My poor ignorant, innocent girl—how hard it seems that my love must for ever place her at a disadvantage!' he thought.

The door was opened by the valet, with as bold a sweep as if a duchess had been entering in all the glory of her court-robes, and Isabel came into the room. One glance showed Mr Lansdell that she was very nervous, that she was suffering cruelly from the terror of his presence; and it may be that even before she had spoken he understood that she had not come to announce any change in her decision, any modification of the sentiments that had led to their parting at Thurston's Crag. There was nothing desperate in her manner—nothing of the dramatic *aplomb* that belongs to the grand crises of life. She stood before him pale and irresolute, with pleading eyes lifted meekly to his face.

Mr Lansdell wheeled forward a chair, but he was obliged to ask her to sit down; and even then she seated herself with the kind of timid irresolution he had so often seen in a burly farmer come to supplicate abnormal advantages in the renewal of a lease.

'I hope you are not angry for me with coming here at such a

time,' she said, in a low tremulous voice; 'I could not come any earlier, or I—'

'It can never be any thing but a pleasure to me to see you,' Roland answered gravely, 'even though the pleasure is strangely mingled with pain. You have come to me, perhaps, because you are in some kind of trouble, and have need of my services in some way or other. I am very much pleased to think that you can so far confide in me; I am very glad to think you can rely on my friendship.'

Mr Lansdell said this because he saw that the doctor's wife had come to demand some favour at his hands, and he wished to smooth the way for that demand. Isabel looked up at him with something like surprise in her gaze. She had not expected that he would be like this—calm, self-possessed, reasonable. A mournful feeling took possession of her heart. She thought that his love must have perished altogether, or he could not surely have been so kind to her, so gentle and dispassionate. She looked at him furtively as he lounged against the further angle of the massive mantelpiece. His transient passion had worn itself out, no doubt, and he was deep in the tumultuous ocean of a new love-affair,—a glittering duchess, a dark-eyed Clotilde,—some brilliant creature after one of the numerous models in the pages of the 'Alien.'

'You are very, very good not to be angry with me,' she said; 'I have come to ask you a favour—a very great favour—and I—'

She stopped, and sat silently twisting the handle of her parasol— the old green parasol under whose shadow Roland had so often seen her. It was quite evident that her courage had failed her altogether at this crisis.

'It is not for myself I am going to ask you this favour,' she said, still hesitating, and looking down at the parasol; 'it is for another person, who—it is a secret, in fact, and—'

'Whatever it is, it shall be granted,' Roland answered, 'without question, without comment.'

'I have come to ask you to lend me,—or at least I had better ask you to give it me, for indeed I don't know when I should ever be able to repay it,—some money, a great deal of money,—fifty pounds.'

She looked at him as if she thought the magnitude of the sum must inevitably astonish him, and she saw a tender half-melancholy smile upon his face.

'My dear Isabel—my dear Mrs Gilbert—if all the money I

possess in the world could secure your happiness, I would willingly leave Midlandshire to-morrow a penniless man. I would not for the world that you should be embarrassed for an hour, while I have more money than I know what to do with. I will write you a cheque immediately,—or, better still, half-a-dozen blank cheques, which you can fill up as you require them.'

But Isabel shook her head at this proposal. 'You are very kind,' she said; 'but a cheque would not do. It must be money, if you please; the person for whom I want it would not take a cheque.'

Roland Lansdell looked at her with a sudden expression of doubt,— of something that was almost terror in his face.

'The person for whom you want it,' he repeated. 'It is not for yourself, then, that you want this money?'

'Oh, no, indeed. What should I want with so much money?'

'I thought you might be in debt. I thought that— Ah, I see; it is for your husband that you want the money.'

'Oh, no: my husband knows nothing about it. But, oh, pray, pray don't question me. Ah, if you knew how much I suffered before I came here to-night! If there had been any other person in the world who could have helped me, I would never have come here; but there is no one, and I *must* get the money.'

Roland's face grew darker as Mrs Gilbert spoke. Her agitation, her earnestness, mystified and alarmed him.

'Isabel,' he cried, 'God knows I have little right to question you; but there is something in the manner of your request that alarms me. Can you doubt that I am your friend,—next to your husband your best and truest friend, perhaps?—forget every word that I have ever said to you, and believe only what I say to-night—to-night, when all my better feelings are aroused by the sight of you. Believe that I am your friend, Isabel, and for pity's sake trust me. Who is this person who wants money of you? Is it your stepmother? if so, my cheque-book is at her disposal.'

'No,' faltered the Doctor's Wife, 'it is not for my stepmother, but—'

'But it is for some member of your family?'

'Yes,' she answered, drawing a long breath; 'but, oh, pray do not ask me any more questions. You said just now that you would grant me the favour I asked without question or comment. Ah, if you knew how painful it was to me to come here!'

'Indeed! I am sorry that it was so painful to you to trust me.'

'Ah, if you knew—' Isabel murmured in a low voice, speaking to herself rather than to Roland.

Mr Lansdell took a little bunch of keys from his pocket, and went across the room to an iron safe, cunningly fashioned after the presentment of an antique ebony cabinet. He opened the ponderous door, and took a little cashbox from one of the shelves.

'My steward brought me a bundle of notes yesterday. Will you take what you want?' he asked, handing the open box to Isabel.

'I would rather you gave me the money; I do not want more than fifty pounds.'

Roland counted five ten-pound notes and handed them to Isabel. She rose and stood for a few moments, hesitating as if she had something more to say,—something almost as embarrassing in its nature as the money-question had been.

'I—I hope you will not think me troublesome,' she said; 'but there is one more favour that I want to ask of you.'

'Do not hesitate to ask any thing of me; all I want is your confidence.'

'It is only a question that I wish to ask. You talked some time since of going away from Midlandshire—from England; do you still think of doing so?'

'Yes, my plans are all made for an early departure.'

'A very early departure? You are going almost immediately?'

'Immediately,—to-morrow perhaps. I am going to the East. It may be a long time before I return to England.'

There was a little pause, during which Roland saw that a faint flush kindled in Isabel Gilbert's face, and that her breath came and went rather quicker than before.

'Then I must say good-by to-night,' she said.

'Yes, it is not likely we shall meet again. Good-night—good-by. Perhaps some day, when I am a pottering old man, telling people the same anecdotes every time I dine with them, I shall come back to Midlandshire, and find Mr Gilbert a crack physician in Kylmington, petted by rich old ladies, and riding in a yellow barouche;—till then, good-by.'

He held Isabel's hand for a few moments,—not pressing it ever so gently,—only holding it, as if in that frail tenure he held the last link that bound him to love and life. Isabel looked at him wonderingly.

How different was this adieu from that passionate farewell under Lord Thurston's oak, when he had flung himself upon the ground and wept aloud in the anguish of parting from her! The melodramas she had witnessed at the Surrey Theatre were evidently true to nature. Nothing could be more transient than the wicked squire's love.

'Only one word more, Mrs Gilbert,' Roland said, after that brief pause. 'Your husband—does he know about this person who asks for money from you?'

'No—I—I should have told him—I think—and asked him to give me the money, only he is so very ill; he must not be troubled about any thing.'

'He is very ill—your husband is ill?'

'Yes,—I thought every one knew. He is very, very ill. It is on that account I came here so late. I have been sitting in his room all day. Good-night.'

'But you cannot go back alone; it is such a long way. It will be two o'clock in the morning before you can get back to Graybridge. I will drive you home; or it will be better to let my coachman—my mother's old coachman—drive you home.'

It was in vain that Mrs Gilbert protested against this arrangement. Roland Lansdell reflected that as the doctor's wife had been admitted by his valet, her visit would of course be patent to all the other servants at their next morning's breakfast. Under these circumstances Mrs Gilbert could not leave Mordred with too much publicity; and a steady old man, who had driven Lady Anna Lansdell's fat white horses for slow jogtrot drives along the shady highways and byways of Midlandshire, was aroused from his peaceful slumbers and told to dress himself, while a half-somnolent stable-boy brought out a big bay horse and an old-fashioned brougham. In this vehicle Isabel returned very comfortably to Graybridge; but she begged the coachman to stop at the top of the lane, where she alighted and bade him good-night.

She found all dark in the little surgery, which she entered by means of her husband's latch-key; and she crept softly up the stairs to the room opposite that in which George Gilbert lay, watched over by Mrs Jeffson.

CHAPTER VII

'I'LL NOT BELIEVE BUT DESDEMONA'S HONEST'*

'See that some hothouse grapes and a pine are sent to Mr Gilbert at Graybridge,' Roland said to his valet on the morning after Isabel's visit. 'I was very sorry to hear of his serious illness from his wife last night.'

Mr Lansdell's valet, very busily occupied with a hatbrush, smiled softly to himself as his employer made this speech. The master of Mordred Priory need scarcely have stained his erring soul by any hypocritical phrases respecting the Graybridge surgeon.

'I shouldn't mind laying a twelvemonth's wages that if her husband dies, he marries her within six months,' Roland's man-servant remarked, as he sipped his second cup of coffee; 'I never did see such an infatuated young man in all my life.'

A change came over the spirit of Mr Lansdell's dreams. The thought, the base and cruel thought, which had never entered Isabel's mind, was not to be shut out of Roland's breast after that midnight interview in the library. Do what he would, struggle against the foul temptation as he might,—and he was not naturally wicked, he was not utterly heartless,—he could not help thinking of what might happen—if—if Death, who carries in his fleshless hand so many orders for release, should cut the knot that bound Isabel Gilbert.

'God knows I am not base enough to wish any harm to that poor fellow at Graybridge,' thought Mr Lansdell; 'but if—'

And then the Tempter's hand swept aside a dark curtain, and revealed a lovely picture of the life that might be, if George Gilbert would only be so obliging as to sink under that tiresome low fever which had done so much mischief in the lanes about Graybridge. Roland Lansdell was not a hero; he was only a very imperfect, vacillating young man, with noble impulses for ever warring against the baser attributes of his mind; a spoiled child of fortune, who had almost always had his own way until just now.

'I ought to go away,' he thought; 'I ought to go away all the more because of this man's illness. There seems something horrible in my stopping here watching and waiting for the result, when I should gain such an unutterable treasure by George Gilbert's death.'

But he lingered, nevertheless. A man may fully appreciate the enormity of his sin, and yet go on sinning. Mr Lansdell did not go away from Mordred; he contented himself with sending the Graybridge surgeon a basket of the finest grapes and a couple of the biggest pines to be found in the Priory hothouses; and it may be that his conscience derived some small solace from the performance of this courtesy.

Lord Ruysdale called upon his nephew in the course of the bright summer morning that succeeded Isabel's visit to the Priory; and as the young man happened to be smoking his cigar in front of the porch at the moment when the Earl's quiet cob came jogging along the broad carriage-drive, there was no possibility of avoiding the elderly gentleman's visit. Roland threw aside his cigar, and resigned himself to the prospect of an hour's prosy discussion of things in which he felt no kind of interest, no ray of pleasure. What was it to him that there was every prospect of a speedy dissolution, unless—? There almost always was every prospect of a dissolution unless something or other took place; but nothing special ever seemed to come of all the fuss and clamour. The poor people were always poor, and grumbled at being starved to death; the rich people were always rich, and indignant against the oppression of an exorbitant income-tax. Poor Roland behaved admirably during the infliction of his uncle's visit; and if he gave vague answers and asked irrelevant questions now and then, Lord Ruysdale was too much engrossed by his own eloquence to find out his nephew's delinquencies. Roland only got rid of him at last by promising to dine at Lowlands that evening.

'If there's a dissolution, our party must inevitably come in,' the Earl said at parting; 'and in that case you must stand for Wareham. The Wareham people look to you as their legitimate representative. I look forward to great things, my boy, if the present ministry go out. I've been nursing my little exchequer very comfortably for the last twelve months; and I shall take a furnished house in town, and begin life again next year, if things go well; and I expect to see you make a figure in the world yet, Roland.'

And in all that interview Lord Ruysdale did not once remark the tired look in his nephew's face; that nameless look which gave a sombre cast to all the Lansdell portraits, and which made the *blasé* idler of thirty seem older of aspect than the hopeful country gentleman of sixty.

Roland went to Lowlands in the evening. Why should he not do this to please his uncle? inasmuch as it mattered so very little what he did, or where he went, in a universe where every thing was weariness. He found Lady Gwendoline in the drawing-room, look-ing something like Marie Antoinette in a *demi-toilette* of gray silk, with a black-lace scarf crossed upon her stately shoulders, and tied in a careless bow at the back of her waist. Mr Raymond was estab-lished in a big chintz-covered easy-chair, turning over a box of books newly arrived from London, and muttering scornful com-ments on their titles and contents.

'At last!' he exclaimed, as Mr Lansdell's name was announced. 'I've called at Mordred about half-a-dozen times within the last two months; but as your people always said you were out, and as I could always see by their faces that you were at home, I have given up the business in despair.'

Lord Ruysdale came in presently with the *Times* newspaper open in his hand, and insisted on reading a leader, which he delivered with amazing energy, and all the emphasis on the beginnings of the sentences. Dinner was announced before the leader was finished, and Mr Raymond led Lady Gwendoline to the dining-room, while Roland stayed to hear the Thunderer's* climax murdered by his uncle's defective elocution. The dinner went off very quietly. The Earl talked politics, and Mr Raymond discoursed very pleasantly on the principles of natural philosophy as applied to the rulers of the nation. There was a strange contrast between the animal spirits of the two men who had passed the meridian of life, and were jogging quietly on the shady slope of the hill, and the dreamy languor ex-hibited by the two young people who sat listening to them. George Sand* has declared that nowadays all the oldest books are written by the youngest authors; might she not go even further, and say that nowadays the young people are older than their seniors? We have got rid of our Springheeled Jacks and John Mittons, and Tom and Jerry* are no more popular either on or off the stage; our young aristocrats no longer think it a fine thing to drive a hearse to Epsom races, or to set barrels of wine running in the Haymarket; but in place of all this foolish riot and confusion a mortal coldness of the soul seems to have come down upon the youth of our nation, a deadly languor and stagnation of spirit, from which nothing less than a Crimean war* or an Indian rebellion* can arouse the worn-out idlers in a weary world.

The dinner was drawing to a close, when Lord Ruysdale mentioned a name that awakened all Mr Lansdell's attention.

'I rode into Graybridge after leaving you, Roland,' he said, 'and made a call or two. I was sorry to hear that Mr Gilmore—Gilson—Gilbert,—ah, yes, Gilbert,—that very worthy young doctor, whom we met at your house the other day—last year, by the by—Egad, how the time spins round!—I was sorry to hear that he is ill. Low fever—really in a very dangerous state, Saunders the solicitor told me. *You'll* be sorry to hear it, Gwendoline.'

Lady Gwendoline's face darkened, and she glanced at Roland before she spoke.

'I am sorry to hear it,' she said. 'I am sorry for Mr Gilbert, for more than one reason. I am sorry he has so very bad a wife.'

Roland's face flushed crimson, and he turned to his cousin as if about to speak; but Mr Raymond was too quick for him.

'I think the less we say upon that subject the better,' he exclaimed eagerly; 'I think, Lady Gwendoline, that is a subject that had much better not be discussed here.'

'Why should it not be discussed?' cried Roland, looking—if people can look daggers—a perfect arsenal of rage and scorn at his cousin. 'Of course, we understand that slander of her own sex is a woman's privilege. Why should not Lady Gwendoline avail herself of her special right? Here is only a very paltry subject, certainly—a poor little provincial nobody; but she will serve for want of a better: lay her on the table, by all means, and bring out your dissecting-tools, Lady Gwendoline. What have you to say against Mrs Gilbert?' He waited, breathless and angry, for his cousin's answer, looking at her with sullen defiance in his face.

'Perhaps Mr Raymond is right, after all,' Gwendoline said quietly. She was very quiet, but very pale, and looked her cousin as steadily in the eyes as if she had been fighting a small-sword duel with him. 'The subject is one that will scarcely bear discussion here or elsewhere; but since you accuse me of feminine malice, I am bound to defend myself. I say that Mrs Gilbert is a very bad wife and a very wicked woman. A person who is seen to attend a secret rendezvous with a stranger, not once, but several times, with all appearance of stealth and mystery, while her husband lies between life and death, must surely be one of the worst and vilest of women.'

Mr Lansdell burst into a discordant laugh.

'What a place this Midlandshire is!' he cried; 'and what a miraculous power of invention lies uncultivated amongst the inhabitants of our country towns! I withdraw any impertinent insinuations about your talent for scandal, my dear Gwendoline; for I see you are the merest novice in that subtle art. The smallest rudimentary knowledge would teach you to distinguish between the stories that are *ben trovato** and those that are not; their being true or false is not of the least consequence. Unfortunately, this Graybridge slander is one of the very lamest of canards.* A newspaper correspondent sending it in to fill the bottom of a column would be dismissed for incompetency, on the strength of his blunder. Tell your maid to be a little more circumspect in future, Gwendoline.'

Lady Gwendoline did not condescend to discuss the truth or probability of her story. She saw that her cousin was ashy pale to the lips, and she knew that her shot had gone home to the very centre of the bull's-eye. After this there was very little conversation. Lord Ruysdale started one or two of his favourite topics; but he understood dimly that there was something not quite pleasant at work amongst his companions. Roland sat frowning at his plate; and Charles Raymond watched him with an uneasy expression in his face; as a man who is afraid of lightning might watch the gathering of a storm-cloud. The dinner drew to a close amidst dense gloom and awful silence, dismally broken by the faint chinking of spoons and jingling of glass. Ah, what funeral-bell can fall more solemnly upon the ear than those common everyday sounds amidst the awful stillness that succeeds or precedes a domestic tempest! There is nothing very terrible in the twittering of birds; yet how ominous sound the voices of those innocent feathered warblers in the dread pauses of a storm!

Lady Gwendoline rose from the table when her father filled his second glass of Burgundy, and Mr Raymond hurried to open the door for her. But Roland's eyes were never lifted from his empty plate; he was waiting for something: now and then a little convulsive movement of his lower lip betrayed that he was agitated; but that was all.

Lord Ruysdale seemed relieved by his daughter's departure. He had a vague idea that there had been some little passage-at-arms between Roland and Gwendoline, and fancied that serenity would be restored by the lady's absence. He went twaddling on with his vapid discourse upon the state of the political atmosphere, placid as some babbling stream, until the dusky shadows began to gather in the corners of the low old-fashioned chamber. Then the Earl pulled out a fat ponderous old hunter, and exclaimed at the lateness of the hour.

'I've some letters to write that must go by to-night's post,' he said. 'Raymond, I know you'll excuse me if I leave you for an hour or so. Roland, I expect you and Raymond to do justice to that Chambertin.'

Charles Raymond murmured some polite little conventionality as the Earl left the room; but he never removed his eyes from Roland's face. He had watched the brewing of the storm, and was prepared for a speedy thunder-clap. Nor was he mistaken in his calculations.

'Raymond, is this true?' Mr Lansdell asked, as the door closed upon his uncle. He spoke as if there had been no break or change in the conversation since Mrs Gilbert's name had been mentioned.

'Is what true, Roland?'

'This dastardly slander against Isabel Gilbert. Is it true? Pshaw! I know that it is not. But I want to know if there is any shadow of an excuse for such a scandal. Don't trifle with me, Raymond; I have kept no secrets from you; and I have a right to expect that you will be candid with me.'

'I do not think you have any right to question me upon this subject,' Mr Raymond answered, very gravely: 'when last it was mentioned between us, you rejected my advice, and protested against my further interference in your affairs. I thought we finished with the subject then, Roland, at your request; and I certainly do not care to renew it now.'

'But things have changed since then,' Mr Lansdell said, eagerly. 'It is only common justice to Mrs Gilbert that I should tell you as much as that, Raymond. I was very confident, very presumptuous, I suppose, when I last discussed this business with you. It is only fair that you should know that the schemes I had formed, when I came back to England, have been entirely frustrated by Mrs Gilbert herself.'

'I am very glad to hear it.'

There was very little real gladness in Mr Raymond's tone as he said this; and the uneasy expression with which he had watched Roland for the last hour was, if any thing, intensified now.

'Yes; I miscalculated when I built all those grand schemes for a happy future. It is not so easy to persuade a good woman to run away from her husband, however intolerable may be the chain that binds her to him. These provincial wives accept the marriage-service in its sternest sense. Mrs Gilbert is a good woman. You can imagine, therefore, how bitterly I felt Gwendoline's imputations against her. I suppose these women really derive some kind of pleasure from one another's destruction. And now set my mind quite at rest: there is not one particle of truth—not so much as can serve as the foundation for a lie—in this accusation, is there, Raymond?'

If the answer to this question had involved a sentence of death, or a reprieve from the gallows, Roland Lansdell could not have asked it more eagerly. He ought to have believed in Isabel so firmly as to be quite unmoved by any village slander; but he loved her too much to be reasonable: Jealousy the demon—closely united as a Siamese twin to Love the god—was already gnawing at his entrails. It could not be, it could not be, that she had deceived and deluded him: but *if* she had—ah, what baseness, what treachery!

'*Is* there any truth in it, Raymond?' he repeated, rising from his chair, and glowering across the table at his kinsman.

'I decline to answer that question. I have nothing to do with Mrs Gilbert, or with any reports that may be circulated against her.'

'But I insist upon you telling me all you know; or, if you refuse to do so, I will go to Lady Gwendoline, and obtain the truth from her.'

Mr Raymond shrugged his shoulders, as if he would have said, 'All further argument is useless; this demented creature must go to perdition his own way.'

'You are a very obstinate young man, Roland,' he said aloud; 'and I am very sorry you ever made the acquaintance of this Doctor's Wife, than whom there are scores of prettier women to be met with in any summer-day's walk; but I daresay there were prettier women than Helen,* if it comes to that. However, as you insist upon hearing the whole of this village scandal— which may or may not be true—you must have your own way; and I hope, when you have heard it, you will be contented to turn your back for some time to come upon Midlandshire and Mrs George Gilbert. I *have* heard something of the story Lady Gwendoline told you at dinner; and from a tolerably reliable source. I have heard—'

'What? That she—that Isabel has been seen with some stranger?'

'Yes.'

'With whom? when? where?'

'There is a strange man staying at a little rustic tavern in Nessborough Hollow. You know what gossips these country people are: Heaven knows I have never put myself out of the way to learn other people's business; but these things get bruited about in all manner of places.'

Roland chafed impatiently during this brief digression.

'Tell your story plainly, Raymond,' he said. 'There is a strange man staying in Nessborough Hollow—well; what then?'

'He is rather a handsome-looking fellow; flashily dressed—a Londoner, evidently—and—'

'But what has all this to do with Mrs Gilbert?'

'Only this much,—she has been seen walking alone with this man, after dark, in Nessborough Hollow.'

'It must be a lie; a villanous invention! or if—if she has been seen to meet this man, he is some relation. Yes, I have reason to think she has some relation staying in this neighbourhood.'

'But why, in that case, should she meet the man secretly, at such an hour, while her husband is lying ill?'

'There might be a hundred reasons.'

Mr Raymond shrugged his shoulders. 'Can you suggest one?' he asked.

Roland Lansdell's head sank forward on his breast. No; he could think of no reason why Isabel Gilbert should meet this stranger secretly—unless there were some kind of guilt involved in their association. Secrecy and guilt go so perpetually together, that it is almost difficult for the mind to dissever them.

'But *has* she been seen to meet him?' cried Roland, suddenly. 'No; I will not believe it. Some woman has been seen walking with some man; and the Graybridge vultures, eager to swoop down upon my poor innocent dove, must have it that the woman is Isabel Gilbert. No: I will not believe this story.'

'So be it, then,' answered Mr Raymond. 'In that case we can drop the subject.'

But Roland was not so easily to be satisfied. The poisoned arrow had entered far into his soul, and he must needs drag the cruel barb backwards and forwards in the wound.

'Not till you have given me the name of your authority,' he said.

'Pshaw! my dear Roland, have I not already told you that my authority is the common Graybridge gossip?'

'I'll not believe that. You are the last man in the world to be influenced by paltry village scandal. You have better grounds for what you told me. Some one has seen Isabel and this man. Who was that person?'

'I protest against this cross-examination. I have been weak enough to sympathise with a dishonourable attachment, so far as to wish to spare you pain. You refuse to be spared, and must take the consequences of your own obstinacy. *I* was the person who saw Isabel Gilbert walking with a stranger—a showily-dressed, disreputable-looking fellow—in Nessborough Hollow. I had been dining with Hardwick the lawyer at Graybridge, and rode home across country by the Briargate and Hurstonleigh Road, instead of going through Waverly. I heard the scandal about Mrs Gilbert at Graybridge,— heard her name linked with that of some stranger staying at the Leicester Arms, Nessborough Hollow, who had been known to send letters to her and to meet her after dark. Heaven only knows how country people find out these things; but these things always are discovered somehow or other. I defended Isabel,—I know her head is a good one, though by no means so well-balanced as it might be,—I defended Isabel throughout a long discussion with the lawyer's wife; but riding home by the Briargate road, I met Mrs Gilbert walking arm-in-arm with a man who answered to the description I had heard at Graybridge.'

'When was this?'

'The night before last. It must have been some time between ten and eleven when I met them; for it was broad moonlight, and I saw Isabel's face as plainly as I see yours.'

'And did she recognise you?'

'Yes; and turned abruptly away from the road into the waste grass between the highway and the tall hedgerow beyond.'

For some moments after this there was a dead silence, and Raymond saw the young man standing opposite him in the dusk, motionless as a stone figure—white as death. Then after that pause, which seemed so long, Roland stretched out his hand and groped among the decanters and glasses on the table for a water-jug; he filled a goblet with water; and Charles Raymond knew, by the clashing of the glass, that his kinsman's hand was shaken by a convulsive trembling. After taking a long draught of water, Roland stretched his hand across the table.

'Shake hands, Raymond,' he said, in a dull, thick kind of voice; 'I thank you heartily for having told me the truth; it was much better to be candid; it was better to let me know the truth. But, oh, if you could know how I loved her—if you could know! You think it was only the dishonourable passion of a profligate, who falls in love with a married woman, and pursues his fancy, heedless of the ruin he may entail on others. But it was not, Raymond; it was nothing like that. So help me Heaven, amidst all selfish sorrow for my own most bitter disappointment, I have sometimes felt a thrill of happiness in the thought that my poor girl's name was still untarnished. I have felt this, in spite of my ruined life, the cruel destruction of every hope that had grown up out of my love for her; and to think that she,—that she who saw my truth and my despair, saw my weak heart laid bare in all its abject folly,—to think that she could dismiss me with schoolgirl speeches about duty and honour; and then,—then, while my grief was new,—while I still lingered here, too infatuated to leave the place in which I had so cruelly suffered,—to think that she should fall into some low intrigue, some base and secret association with——It is too bitter, Raymond; it is too bitter!'

The friendly dusk sheltered him as he dropped into a chair and buried his face upon the broad-cushioned elbow. The tears that gathered slowly in his eyes now were even more bitter than those that he had shed two months ago under Lord Thurston's oak. If this sort of thing is involved in a man's being in earnest, he had not need be in earnest about any thing more than once in his life. Happily for us, the power to suffer, like every other power, becomes enfeebled and wears out at last by extravagant usage. If Othello had survived to marry a second time, he would not have dropped down in a fit when a new Iago began to whisper poisonous hints about the lady.

'I never loved any one but her,' murmured Roland Lansdell; 'I have been a hard judge of other women; but I believed in her.'

'My poor boy, my poor impetuous Roland,' Mr Raymond said softly, 'men have to suffer like this once in a lifetime. Fight it out, and have done with it. Look the foul phantasm straight in the eyes, and it will melt into so much empty air; and then "being gone," you are "a man again." My dear boy, before this year is out, you will be sipping absinth—most abominable stuff!—after a supper at the Maison Dorée, and entertaining your companions with a satirical history of your little caprice for the Doctor's Wife.'

'And Heaven forgive me for talking like Major Pendennis,* or any other wicked old worldling!' Mr Raymond added mentally.

Roland Lansdell got up by and by, and walked to the open French window. There was a silvery shimmer of moonlight upon the lawn, and the great clock in the stables was striking ten.

'Good-night, Raymond,' said Mr Lansdell, turning on the threshold of the window. 'You can make some kind of apology for me to my uncle and Gwendoline. I won't stop to say good-night to them.'

'But where are you going?'

'To Nessborough Hollow.'

'Are you mad, Roland?'

'That's a great deal too subtle a question to be answered just now. I am going to Nessborough Hollow, to see Isabel Gilbert and her lover.'

CHAPTER VIII

KEEPING A PROMISE

The moon was slowly rising behind a black belt of dense foliage,— a noble screen of elm and beech that sheltered Lord Ruysdale's domain from the common world without,—as Roland Lansdell crossed the lawn, and went in amongst the thickest depths of the park. At Lowlands there were no smooth glades and romantic waterfalls, no wonderful effects of landscape-gardening, such as adorned Mordred Priory. The Earls of Ruysdale had been more or less behind the world for the last century and a half; and the land about the old red-brick mansion was only a tangled depth of forest, in which the deer browsed peacefully, undisturbed by the ruthless handiwork of trim modern improvement.

The lonely wildness of the place suited Roland Lansdell's mood to-night. At first he had walked very rapidly, even breaking into a run now and then; so feverishly and desperately did he desire to reach the spot where he might perhaps find that which would con-firm his despair. But all at once, when he had gone some distance from the house, and the lights in Lady Gwendoline's drawing-room were shut from him by half the width of the park, he stopped suddenly, leaning against a tree, faint and almost breathless. He

stopped for the first time to think of what he had heard. The hot
passion of anger, the fierce sense of outraged pride, had filled his
breast so entirely as to sweep away every softer feeling, as flowers
growing near a volcanic mountain may be scattered by the rolling
lava-flood that passes over them. Now, for the first time, he lingered
a little to reflect upon what he had heard. Could it be true? Could it
be that this woman had deceived him,—this woman for whom he
had been false to all the teaching of his life,—this woman, at whose
feet he had offered up that comfortable philosophy which found an
infallible armour against sorrow in supreme indifference to all things
under heaven,—this woman, for whose sake he had consented to
resume the painful heritage of humanity, the faculty of suffering?

'And she is like the rest, after all,' he thought; 'or only a little
worse than the rest. And I had forgotten so much for her sake. I had
blotted out the experience of a decade in order that I might believe
in the witchery of her dark eyes. I, the man of half-a-dozen seasons
in London and Paris, Vienna and St Petersburg, had sponged away
every base record in the book of my memory, so that I might scrawl
her name upon the blank pages; and now I am angry with her—with
her, poor pitiful creature, who I suppose is only true to her nature
when she is base and false. I am angry with her, when I have only
my own folly to blame for the whole miserable business. I am angry
with *her*, just as if she were a responsible being; as if she *could* be
any thing but what she is. And yet there have been good women in
the world,' he thought, sadly. 'My mother was a good woman. I
used to fancy sometimes what might have happened if I had known
her in my mother's life-time. I have even made a picture in my mind
of the two women, happy together, and loving each other. Heaven
forgive me! And after all her pretty talk about platonism and poetry,
she betrays me for a low intrigue, and a rendezvous kept at an alehouse.'

In all his anger against the Doctor's Wife, no thought of her
husband's far deeper wrong ever entered into Mr Lansdell's mind.
It was *he*—Roland—who had been betrayed: it was he whose love
was outraged, whose pride was humiliated to the very dust. That
there was a man, now lying ill and helpless at Graybridge, who had
a better right to resent Isabel Gilbert's treachery, and wreak vengeance upon the unknown wretch for whose sake she was thus base
and guilty, never occurred to this angry young man. It had been, for

a long time past, his habit to forget George Gilbert's existence; he had resolutely shut from his mind the image of the Graybridge surgeon ever since his return to Midlandshire; ever since the wrong he was doing against George Gilbert had fallen into a deliberate and persistent course, leading steadily to a foregone conclusion. He had done this, and little by little it had become very easy for him to forget so insignificant and unobtrusive a person as the simple-hearted parish surgeon, whose only sin against mankind was that he had chosen a pretty woman for his wife.

So now it was of his own wrongs, and of those wrongs alone, that Mr Lansdell thought. All the circumstances of Isabel's visit to the Priory came back to him. Came back? When had they left his mind, except for that brief interval of passion during which his mind had been a chaos?

'The money she wanted was for this man, of course!' he thought. 'For whom else should it be? for whom else should she come to ask for money—of her rejected lover—in the dead of the night, with all the mean miserable circumstances of a secret and guilty action? If she had wanted money from me for any legitimate purpose—in any foolish feminine confusion of debt and difficulty—why should she not have written to me boldly for the sum she required? She must have known that my purse was hers to command whenever she required it. But that she should come secretly, trembling like a guilty creature,—compromising herself and me by a midnight visit,—afraid to confess why she wanted the money,—answering my straight questions by hesitation and prevarication! What construction can I put upon her conduct of last night except one—except one? And yet, even after last night, I believed in her. I thought that she might have wanted the money for some relation. Some relation! What relation should she meet alone, secretly, late at night, in such a place as Nessborough Hollow? She who never, in all the course of our acquaintance, mentioned a living creature beyond her stepmother who had any claim upon her; and all at once some one comes—some one for whom she must have fifty pounds; not in the form of a cheque, which might be traced home to the person who received it. I cannot forget that; I cannot forget that she refused to take my cheque for the money she wanted. That alone makes a mystery of the business; and the meeting that Raymond witnessed tells all the rest. This strange man is some old lover; some jilted admirer of a bygone era, who comes now and is clamorous and dangerous, and will only be bought-off by a bribe. Oh, shame, shame, shame upon her, and upon my own folly! And I thought her an innocent child, who had ignorantly broken a strong man's heart!'

He walked on slowly now, and with his head bent, no longer trying to make a short cut for himself among the trees, but absently following a narrow winding path worn by slow peasants' feet upon the grass.

'Why should I be so eager to see this man?' he thought. 'What can I discover that I do not already know? If there is any one upon earth whose word I can trust in, it is Raymond. He would be the very last to slander this wretched woman, or to be self-deluded by a prejudice; and he saw her—he saw her. And even beyond this, the base intrigue has become common talk. Gwendoline would not have dared to say what she said to-day without good grounds for her statement. It is only I,—I who have lived apart from all the world to think and dream about her,—it is only I who am the last to be told of her shame. But I will try to see this fellow notwithstanding. I should like to see the man who has been preferred to me.'

Nessborough Hollow was some distance from Lowlands; and Mr Lansdell, who was familiar with almost every inch of his native county, made his way thither by shadowy lanes and rarely trodden byways, where the summer wild-flowers smelt sweetly in the dewy night. Never surely had brighter heavens shone upon a fairer earth. The leaves and blossoms, the long lush-grasses faintly stirred by lazy summer winds, made a perpetual whisper that scarcely broke the general stillness: and now and then the gurgling notes of a nightingale sounded amongst the clustering foliage that loomed darkly above tangled hedgerows, and broad wastes of moonlit grass.

'I wonder why people are not happy,' mused Mr Lansdell, impressed in spite of himself by the quiet beauty of the summer landscape. Intensely subjective though our natures may be, external things will not be quite put away, strive as we may to shut them out. Did not Fagin* think about the broken rail while he stood in the dock, and wonder who would mend it? Was not Manfred,* the supremely egotistical and subjective, perpetually dragging the mountain-tops and Alpine streamlets into his talk of his own troubles? So to-night, deeply absorbed though he was by the consciousness of his own wrongs, there was a kind of double action in Roland Lansdell's mind, by means of which he was conscious of every flickering shadow of the honeysuckle blossoms dark upon the silver smoothness of the moonlit grass.

'I wonder how it is that people cannot be happy,' he thought; 'why can't they take a sensuous pleasure out of this beautiful universe, and enjoy the moonlight, and the shadows, and the perfume of new-mown hay upon the summer air; and then, when they are tired of one set of sensations, move on to another: from rural England to tropical India; from the southern prairies to the snow-mantled Alps; playing a game at hide-and-seek with the disagreeable seasons, and contriving to go down to the grave through the rosy sunsets of a perpetual summer, indifferent as to who dies or suffers, so long as the beauty of the world endures? Why can't people be reasonable, and take life wisely? I begin to think that Mr Harold Skimpole* was the only true philosopher. If he had been rich enough to indulge his sensuous simplicity out of his own pocket, he would have been perfect. It is only when the Skimpole philosopher wants other people's pounds that he becomes objectionable. Ah, how pleasantly life might glide by, taken à la Skimpole;—a beautiful waveless river, drifting imperceptibly on to darkness! But we make our own election. When we are wise enough to abjure all the glittering battle-grounds of man's ambition, we must needs fall in love, and go mad because a shallow-hearted woman has black eyes and a straight nose. With red hair and freckles Mrs Gilbert might go to perdition, unwept and unhindered; but because the false creature has a pretty face we want to tear her all to pieces for her treachery.'

In that moonlight walk from Lowlands to Nessborough Hollow there was time enough for Mr Lansdell to fall into many moods. At one time he was ready to laugh aloud, in bitter contempt for his own weakness; at another time, moved almost to tears by the contemplation of his ruined dreams. It was so difficult for him to separate the ideal Isabel of yesterday from the degraded creature of to-night. He believed what Charles Raymond had told him, but he could not realise it: the hard and cruel facts slipped away from him every now and then, and he found himself thinking of the Doctor's Wife with all the old tenderness. Then suddenly, like a glare of phosphoric light, the memory of her treachery would flash back upon him. Why should he lament the innocent idol of his dreams? There was not, there never had been, any such creature. But he could not hold this in his mind. He could not blot out of his brain the Isabel of the past. It was easier for him to think of her as he might have thought of the dead, dwelling fondly on vain dreams of happiness which once might have been, but now could never be, because *she* was no more.

There was not a scheme that he had ever made for that impossible future which did not come back to his mind to-night. The places in which he had fancied himself lingering in tranquil happiness with the woman he loved arose before him in all their brightest colouring; fair lonely Alpine villages, whose very names he had forgotten, emerged from the dim mists of memory, bright as an eastern city rising out of night's swiftly-melting vapours into the clear light of morning; and he saw Isabel Gilbert leaning from a rustic balcony jutting out upon broad purple waters, screened and sheltered by the tall grandeur of innumerable snow-peaks. Ah, how often he had painted these things; the moonlit journeys on nights as calm as this, under still bluer skies lit by a larger moon; the varied ways and waters by which they might have gone, always leading them further and further away from the common world and the base thoughts of common people; the perfect isolation in which there should have been no loneliness! And all this might have been, thought Mr Lansdell, if she had not been so base and degraded a creature as to cling blindly to a vulgar lover, whose power over her most likely lay in some guilty secret of the past.

Twenty times in the course of that long summer-night's walk Roland Lansdell stopped for a minute or so, doubtful whether he should go further or not. What motive had he in seeking out this stranger staying at a rustic public-house? What right had he to interfere in a wicked woman's low intrigue? If Isabel Gilbert was the creature she was represented to be,—and he could not doubt his authority,—what could it matter to him how low she sank? Had she not coolly and deliberately rejected his love—his devotion, so earnestly and solemnly offered to her? Had she not left him to his despair and desolation, with no better comfort than the stereotyped promise that she would 'think of him'? What was she to him, that he should trouble himself about her, and bring universal scorn upon his name, perhaps, by some low tavern brawl? No; he would go no further; he would blot this creature out of his mind, and turn his back upon the land which held her. Was not all the world before him, and all creation designed for his pleasure? Was there any thing upon earth denied him, except the ignis-fatuus light* of this woman's black eyes?

'Perhaps this is a turning-point in my life,' he thought, during one of these pauses; 'and there may be some chance for me after all. Why should I not have a career like other men, and try like them to be of some use to my species? Better, perhaps, to be always trying and always failing, than to stand aloof for ever, wasting my intellect upon vain calculations as to the relative merits of the game and the candle. An outsider cannot judge the merits of the strife. To a man of my temperament it may have seemed a small matter whether Spartans or Persians were victors in the pass of Thermopylae;* but what a glorious thing the heat and din of the struggle must have been for those who were in it! I begin to think it is a mistake to lounge luxuriously on the grand-stand, looking down at the riders. Better, perhaps, wear a jockey's jacket; even to be thrown and trampled to death in the race. I will wash my hands of Mrs George Gilbert, and go back to the Priory and sleep peacefully; and to-morrow morning I will ask Lady Gwendoline to be my wife; and then I can stand for Wareham, and go in for liberal-conservatism and steam-farming.'

But the picture of Isabel Gilbert and the stranger meeting in Nessborough Hollow was not to be so easily erased from Mr Lansdell's brain. The habit of vacillation, which had grown out of the idleness of his life, was stronger in him to-night than usual; but the desire to see for himself how deeply he was wronged triumphed over every other feeling, and he never turned his face from the direction in which Nessborough Hollow lay,—a little rustic nook in fertile Midlandshire, almost as beautiful, after its own simple English fashion, as those sublime Alpine villages which shone upon Roland Lansdell in his dreams. He came near the place at last; a little tired by the long walk from Lowlands; a good deal wearied by all the contending emotions of the last few hours. He came upon the spot at last, not by the ordinary roadway, but across a strip of thickly-wooded waste land lying high above the hollow—a dense and verdant shelter, in which the fern grew tall beneath the tangled branches of the trees. Here he stopped, upon the topmost edge of a bank that sloped down into the rustic roadway. The place beneath him was a kind of glen, sheltered from all the outer world, solemnly tranquil in that silent hour. He saw the road winding and narrowing under the trees until it reached a little rustic bridge. He heard the low ripple of the distant brook; and close beside the bridge he saw the white wall of the little inn, chequered with broad black beams, and crowned by high peaked gables jutting out above quaint latticed casements. In one low window he saw a feeble candle gleaming behind a poor patch of crimson curtain, and through the half-open door a narrow stream of light shone in a slanting line upon the ground.

He saw all this; and then from the other end of the still glade he saw two figures coming slowly towards the inn. Two figures, one of which was so familiar and had been so dear that despair, complete and absolute, came upon him for the first time, in that one brief start of recognition. Ah, surely he had never believed in her falsehood until this moment; surely, if he had believed Charles Raymond, the agony of seeing her here could not have been so great as this!

He stood upon the crown of the steep slope, with his hands grasping the branches on each side of him, looking down at those two quiet figures advancing slowly in the moonlight. There was nothing between him and them except the grassy bank, broken here and there by patches of gorse and fern, and briers and saplings; there was nothing to intercept his view, and the moonlight shone full upon them. He did not look at the man. What did it matter to him what *he* was like? He looked at *her*—at her whom he had loved so tenderly—at her for whose sake he had consented to believe in woman's truth and purity. He looked at her, and saw her face, very pale in the moonlight,—blanched, no doubt, by the guilty pallor of fear. Even the pattern of her dress was familiar to him. Had she not worn it in one of their meetings at Thurston's Crag?

'Fool!' he thought, 'to think that she, who found it so easy a matter to deceive her husband, must needs be true to *me. I* was ill at ease and remorseful when I went to meet her; but *she* came to me smiling, and went away, placid and beautiful as a good angel, to tell her husband that she had been to Thurston's Crag, and had happened to meet Mr Lansdell.'

He stood as still as death; not betraying his presence by so much as the rustling of a leaf, while the two figures approached the spot above which he stood. But a little way off they paused, and were parting, very coolly, as it seemed, when Mrs Gilbert lifted up her face, and said something to the man. He stood with his back turned towards Roland, to whom the very expression of Isabel's face was visible in the moonlight.

It seemed to him as if she was pleading for something, for he had never seen her face more earnest,—no, not even when she had decided the question of his life's happiness in that farewell meeting beneath Thurston's oak. She seemed to be pleading for something, since the man nodded his head once or twice while she was speaking, with a churlish gesture of assent; and when they were about to part he bent his head and kissed her. There was an insolent indifference about his manner of doing this that stung Roland more keenly than any display of emotion could have done.

After this the Doctor's Wife went away. Roland watched her as she turned once, and stood for a moment looking back at the man from whom she had just parted, and then disappeared amongst the shadows in the glade. Ah; if she had been nothing more than a shadow—if he could have awakened to find all this the brief agony of a dream! The man stood where Isabel had left him, while he took a box of fusees from his waistcoat-pocket and lighted a cigar; but his back was still turned to Mr Lansdell.

He drew two or three puffs of smoke from the cigar, assured himself that it was fully lighted, and then strolled slowly towards the spot above which Roland stood.

All that was left of the original savage in the fine gentleman arose at that moment in Roland Lansdell's breast. He had come there, only to ascertain for himself that he had been betrayed and deluded; he had come with no vengeful purpose in his mind; or, at any rate, with no consciousness of any such purpose. He had come to be cool, indifferent, ironical; to slay with cruel and cutting words, perhaps, but to use no common weapons. But in a moment all his modern philosophy of indifference melted away, and left him with the original man's murderous instincts and burning sense of wrong raging fiercely in his breast.

He leapt down the sloping bank with scarcely any consciousness of touching the slippery grass; but he dragged the ferns and brambles from the loose earth in his descent, and a shower of torn verdure flew up into the summer air. He had no weapon, nothing but his right arm, wherewith to strike the broad-chested black-bearded stranger. But he never paused to consider that, or to count the chances of a struggle. He only knew that he wanted to kill the man for whose sake Isabel Gilbert had rejected and betrayed him. In the next moment his hands were on the stranger's throat.

'You scoundrel!' he gasped hoarsely, 'you consummate coward and scoundrel, to bring that woman to this place!'

There was a brief struggle, and then the stranger freed himself from Mr Lansdell's grasp. There was no comparison between the physical strength and weight of the two men; and the inequality was sensibly increased by a stout walking-stick of the bludgeon order carried by the black-bearded stranger.

'Hoity, toity!' cried that gentleman, who seemed scarcely disposed to take Mr Lansdell's attack seriously; 'have you newly escaped from some local lunatic asylum, my friend, that you go about the country flying at people's throats in this fashion? What's the row? Can't a gentleman in the merchant navy take a moonlight stroll with his daughter for once in a way, to wish her good-by before he fits out for a fresh voyage, without all this hullabaloo?'

'Your daughter!' cried Roland Lansdell. 'Your daughter?'

'Yes, my daughter Isabel, wife of Mr Gilbert, surgeon.'

'Thank God!' murmured Roland slowly, 'thank God!'

And then a pang of remorse shot through his heart, as he thought how little his boasted love had been worth, after all; how ready he had been to disbelieve in her purity; how easily he had accepted the idea of her degradation.

'I ought to have known,' he thought,—'I ought to have known that she was innocent. If all the world had been banded together against her, I should have been her champion and defender. But my love was only a paltry passion after all. The gold changed to brass in the fire of the first ordeal.'

He thought this, or something like this, and then in the next moment he said courteously:

'Upon my word, I have to apologise for my—' he hesitated a little here, for he really was ashamed of himself; all the murderous instincts were gone, as if they had never been, and the Englishman's painfully-acute perception of the ridiculous being fully aroused, he felt that he had made a consummate fool of himself. 'I have to apologise for my very absurd behaviour just now; but having heard a very cruel and slanderous report, connecting you as a stranger, and not as a near relation, with Mrs Gilbert, and entertaining a most sincere respect for that lady and her husband, to say nothing of the fact that I had been lately dining,'—Mr Lansdell had not drunk so much as one glassful of wine during the last four-and-twenty hours;

but he would have been quite willing to admit himself a drunkard, if that could have lessened the ridiculous element of his position,—'in point of fact I completely lost my head. I am very happy to think you are so nearly related to the lady I so much esteem; and if I can be of service to you in any manner, I—'

'Stop a bit,' cried Mr Sleaford the barrister,—'stop a bit! I thought I knew your voice. *You're* the languid swell, who were so jolly knowing at the Old Bailey,—the languid swell who had nothing better to do than join the hunt against a poor devil that never cheated you out of sixpence. I said, if ever I came out of prison alive, *I'd kill you*; and I'll keep my promise.'

He hissed out these last words between his set teeth. His big muscular hands were fastened on Roland Lansdell's throat; and his face was pushed forward until it almost touched that other handsome face which defied him in the proud insolence of a moral courage that rose above all physical superiority. The broad bright moonlight streaming through a wide gap in the foliage fell full upon the two men; and in the dark face glowering at his, Mr Lansdell recognised the man who he had followed down to Liverpool for the mere amusement of the chase,—the man described in the police records by a dozen aliases, and best known by his familiar soubriquet of 'Jack the Scribe.'

'You dog!' cried Mr Sleaford, 'I've dreamt about such a meeting as this when I was working the pious dodge at Portland. I've dreamt about it; and it did me good to feel my fingers at your throat, even in my dreams. You dog! I'll do for you, if I swing for this night's work.'

There was a struggle,—a brief and desperate struggle, in which the two men wrestled with each other, and the chances of victory seemed uncertain. Then Mr Sleaford's bludgeon went whirling up into the air, and descended with a dull thud, once, twice, three times upon Roland Lansdell's bare head. After the third blow, Jack the Scribe loosed his grasp from the young man's throat, and the master of Mordred Priory fell crashing down among the fern and wild-flowers, with a shower of opal-tinted rose-petals fluttering about him as he fell.

He lay very quietly where he had fallen. Mr Sleaford looked about him right and left along the pleasant moonlighted glade. There was not a living creature to be seen either way. The light behind the red curtain in the little rustic tavern still glimmered feebly in the distance; but the stillness of the place could scarcely have seemed more profound had Nessborough Hollow been a hidden glade in some primeval forest.

Jack the Scribe knelt down beside the figure lying so quietly amongst the tangled verdure, and laid his strong bare hand very gently above Mr Lansdell's waistcoat.

'He'll do,' muttered the Scribe; 'I've spoiled him for some time to come, any how. Perhaps it's all for the best if I haven't gone too far.'

He rose from his knees, looked about him again, and assured himself of the perfect loneliness of the place. Then he walked slowly towards the little inn.

'A low blackguard would have taken the fellow's watch,' he mused, 'and got himself into trouble that way. What did he mean by flying at me about Isabel, I wonder; and how does he come to know her? He belongs to this part of the country, I suppose. And to think that I should have been so near him all this time without knowing it. I knew his name, and that's about all I did know; but I thought he was a London swell.'

He pushed open the door of the little tavern presently—the door through which the slanting line of light had streamed out upon the pathway. All within was very quiet, for the rustic owners of the habitation had long since retired to their peaceful slumbers, leaving Mr Sleaford what he called 'the run of the house.' They had grown very familiar with their lodger, and placed implicit confidence in him as a jolly outspoken fellow of the seafaring order; for these Midlandshire rustics were not very keen to detect any small short-comings in Mr Sleaford's assumptions of the mercantile mariner.

He went into the room where the light was burning. It was the room which he had occupied during his residence at the Leicester Arms. He seated himself at the table, on which there were some writing materials, and scrawled a few lines to the effect that he found himself obliged to go away suddenly that night, on his way to Liverpool, and that he left a couple of sovereigns, at a rough guess, to pay his score. He wrapped the money up in the letter, sealed it with a great sprawling red seal, directed it to the landlord, and placed it on a conspicuous corner of the mantelpiece. Then he took off his boots, and crept softly up the creaking corkscrew staircase leading to his bedroom, with the candle in his hand. He came down stairs again about ten minutes afterwards carrying a little valise, which he slung across his shoulder by a strap; then he took up his bludgeon and prepared to depart.

But before leaving the room he bent over the table, and examined the heaviest end of his stick by the light of the candle. There was blood upon it, and a little tuft of dark hair, which he burned in the flame of the candle; and when he looked at his waistcoat he saw that there were splashes of blood on that and on his shirt.

He held the end of the stick over the candle till it was all smoked and charred; he buttoned his cut-away coat over his chest, and then took a railway-rug from a chair in a corner and threw it across his shoulder.

'It's an ugly sight to look at, that is,' he muttered; 'but I don't think I went too far.'

He went out at the little door, and into the glade, where a nightingale was singing high up amongst the clustering foliage, and where the air was filled with the faint perfume of honeysuckle and starry wild roses. Once he looked with something like terror in his face, towards the spot where he had left his prostrate enemy; and then he turned and walked away at a rapid pace, in the other direction, crossing the rustic wooden bridge, and ascending the rising ground that led towards the Briargate Road.

CHAPTER IX

RETROSPECTIVE

The parish surgeon lay in his darkened bedchamber at Graybridge day after day and night after night, and Mr Pawlkatt, coming twice a day to look at him, could give very small comfort to the watchers. George Gilbert had been ill nearly a fortnight—not quite a fortnight—but it seemed now a common thing for the house to be hushed and darkened, and the once active master lying dull, heavy, and lethargic, under the shadow of the dimity bed-curtains. Those who watched him lost all count of time. It seemed almost as if the surgeon had always been ill. It was difficult, somehow, to remember that not quite two weeks ago he had been one of the most active inhabitants of Graybridge; it was still more difficult to imagine that he could ever again be what he had been.

No patient, in the dull anguish of an obstinate fever, could have desired better or more devoted nurses than those who waited on George Gilbert. To Isabel this experience of a sick-room was altogether a new thing. She had known her father to be laid up for the space of a day with a vague sort of ailment which he called 'bile,' but which generally arose after a dinner in London with certain choice spirits of his acquaintance, and a stealthy return to the sanctuary of his Camberwell home in the chill gray glimmer of early morning. She had known her step-mother to complain perpetually of divers aches, and pains, and 'stitches,' and stiffnesses of her ribs and shoulder-blades and loins, and other complicated portions of her bony structure, and to throw out dismal prophecies to the effect that she would be worried into a premature grave by the breakage and waste of boys, and the general aggravation of a large family. But illness, a real and dangerous malady, with all its solemn accompaniments of hushed voices and darkness, and grave faces and stealthy footsteps, was quite new to the Doctor's Wife.

If she had loved her sick husband with that romantic love which it had been her sin and misfortune to bestow elsewhere, she could not have watched quietly in that darkened chamber. She would have fled away from the patient's presence to fling herself on the ground somewhere, wholly abandoned to her anguish. But she had never loved George Gilbert: only that womanly tenderness, which was the chief attribute of her nature, that sympathetic affection for every thing that was suffering or sorrowful, held her to the invalid's bedside. She was so sorry for him, and she was so horribly afraid that he would die. The thought that she might step across the darksome chasm of his grave into those fair regions inhabited by Roland Lansdell, could not hold a place in her heart. Death, the terrible and the unfamiliar, stood a black and gaunt figure between her and all beyond the sick-room. Edith Dombey and Ernest Maltravers were alike forgotten during those long days and nights in which the surgeon's rambling delirious talk only broke the silence. Isabel Gilbert's ever-active imagination was busy with more terrible images than any to be found in her books. The pictures of a funeral cortège in the dusty lane, a yawning grave in the familiar churchyard, forced themselves upon her as she sat watching the black shadow of the perforated lantern that held the rush-light, looming gigantic on the whitewashed wall.

And, thinking thus of that dark hour which might lie before her, she thought much less of Roland Lansdell than in the days before her husband's illness. She was not a wicked woman; she was only very foolish. The thought that there was a handsome young country gentleman with a fine estate and fifteen thousand a-year waiting to be her second husband, if death loosened her present bondage, could not have a place amongst those tender poetical dreams engendered out of her books. A woman of the world, hardened by worldly experience, might have sat in that dusky chamber watching the sick man, and brooding, half remorsefully, half impatiently, upon the thought of what might happen if his malady should have a fatal ending. But this poor sentimental girl, nourished upon the airiest fancies of poets and romancers, had no such loathsome thoughts. Roland Lansdell's wealth and position had never tempted her; it had only dazzled her; it had only seemed a bright and splendid atmosphere radiating from and belonging to the Deity himself. If, in some dreamy rapture, she had ever fancied herself far away from all the common world, united to the man she loved, she had only pictured herself as a perpetual worshipper in white muslin, kneeling at the feet of her idol, with wild-flowers in her hair. The thought that he had fifteen thousand a-year, and a superb estate, never disturbed by its gross influence her brighter dreams; it was not in her to be mercenary, or even ambitious. That yearning for splendour and glitter which had made her envious of Edith Dombey's fate was only a part of her vague longing for the beautiful; she wanted to be amongst beautiful things, made beautiful herself by their influence; but whether their splendour took the form of a boudoir in May Fair all a-glow with wonderful pictures and Parian statues,* rare old china and tapestry hangings, or the floral luxuriance of a forest on the banks of the Amazon, was of very little consequence to this sentimental young dreamer. If she could not be Mrs Dombey, sublime in scornful indignation and ruby silk velvet, she would have been contented to be simple Dorothea,* washing her tired feet in the brook, with her hair about her shoulders. She only wanted the vague poetry of life, the mystic beauty of romance infused somehow into her existence; and she was as yet too young to understand that latent element of poetry which underlies the commonest life.

In the mean time a very terrible trouble had come to her—the trouble occasioned by her father's presence in the neighbourhood of

Graybridge. Never, until some days after his apprehension at Liverpool, had Mr Sleaford's wife and children known the nature of the
profession by which the master of the house earned a fluctuating
income,—enough for reckless extravagance sometimes, at others,
barely enough to keep the wolf from the door. This is *not* a sensation novel. I write here what I know to be the truth. Jack the
Scribe's children were as innocently ignorant of their father's calling
as if that gentleman had been indeed what he represented himself—
a barrister. He went every day to his professional duties, and returned at night to his domestic hearth; he was a very tolerable
father; a faithful, and not unkind husband; a genial companion
amongst the sort of men with whom he associated. He had only
that awkward little habit of forging other people's names; by which
talent, exercised in conjunction with a gang whose cunningly-
organised plan of operations won for them considerable celebrity, he
had managed to bring up a numerous family in comparative comfort
and respectability. If any one had been good enough to die and leave
Mr Sleaford a thousand a-year, Jack the Scribe would have willingly
laid down his pen and retired into respectability; but in the mean
time he found it necessary to provide for himself and a hungry
family; and having no choice between a clerk's place with a pound a
week and the vaguely-glorious chances of a modern freebooter,* he
had joined the gang in question, to whom he was originally made
known by some very pretty little amateur performances in the
accommodation-bill line.*

Never, until after his apprehension, had the truth been revealed
to any one member of that Camberwell household. Long ago, when
Jack the Scribe was a dashing young articled clerk, with bold black
eyes and a handsome face,—long ago, when Isabel was only a baby,
the knowledge of a bill-discounting transaction which the clerk designated an awkward scrape, but which his employers declared to be
a felony, had come suddenly upon Mr Sleaford's first wife, and had
broken her heart. But when the amateur artist developed into the
accomplished professional, Isabel's father learned the art of concealing the art. His sudden departure from Camberwell, the huddling of
the family into an Islington lodging, and his subsequent flight to
Liverpool, were explained to his household as an attempt to escape
an arrest for debt; and as angry creditors and sheriffs' officers had
been but common intruders upon the peace of the household, there

seemed nothing very unnatural in such a flight. It was only when Mr Sleaford was securely lodged within the fatal walls of Newgate,* when the preliminary investigations of the great forgeries were published in every newspaper, that he communicated the real state of the case to his horror-stricken wife and children.

There is little need to dwell upon the details of that most bitter time. People get over these sort of things somehow; and grief and shame are very rarely fatal, even to the most sensitive natures. 'Alas, sweet friend,' says Shelley's Helen, 'you must believe this heart is stone; it did not break!'* There seems to be a good deal of the stony element in all our hearts, so seldom are the arrows of affliction fatal. To Isabel the horror of being a forger's daughter was something very terrible; but even in its terror there was just the faintest flavour of romance: and if she could have smuggled her father out of Newgate in a woman's cap and gown, like Lady Nithisdale,* she might have forgiven him the crimes that had helped to make her a heroine. The boys, after the first shock of the revelation, took a very lenient view of their father's case, and were inclined to attribute his shortcomings to the tyranny and prejudice of society.

'If a rich cove has a jolly lot of money in the bank, and poor coves are starving, the rich cove must expect to have it forged away from him,' Horace Sleaford remarked moodily, when debating the question of his father's guilt. Nor did the hobbledehoy's sympathy end here; for he borrowed a dirty and dilapidated copy of Mr Ainsworth's delightful romance from a circulating-library, and minutely studied that gentleman's description of Newgate in the days of Jack Sheppard,* with a view to Mr Sleaford's evasion of his gaolers.

It was not so very bad to bear after all; for of course Jack the Scribe was not so imprudent as to make any admission of his guilt. He represented himself as the victim of circumstances, the innocent associate of wicked men, entrapped into the folly of signing other people's names by a conspiracy on the part of his companions. Hardened as he was by the experiences of a long and doubtful career, he felt some natural shame; and he did all in his power to keep his wife and children dissociated from himself and his crimes. Bitterly though the cynic may bewail the time-serving and mercenary nature of his race, a man can generally find some one to help him in the supreme crises of his fate. Mr Sleaford found friends, obscure and vulgar people, by whose assistance he was enabled to get his family out of the way before his trial came on at the Old Bailey. The boys, ever athirst for information of the Jack-Sheppard order, perused the daily record of that Old Bailey ordeal by stealth in the attic where they slept; but Isabel saw nothing of the newspapers, which set forth the story of her father's guilt, and only knew at the last, when all was decided, what Mr Sleaford's fate was to be. Thus it was that she never saw Mr Lansdell's name amongst those of the witnesses against her father; and even if she had seen that name, it is doubtful whether it would have lived in her memory until the day when she met the master of Mordred Priory.

No language can describe the horror that she felt on her father's sudden appearance in Midlandshire. Utterly ignorant of the practices of prison-life, and the privileges of a ticket-of-leave,* she had regarded Mr Sleaford's dismal habitation as a kind of tomb in which he was to be buried alive for the full term of his imprisonment. Vaguely and afar off she saw the shadow of danger to Roland, in the ultimate release of his enemy; but the shadow seemed so very far away, that after the first shock of Mr Lansdell's story, it had almost faded from her mind, blotted out by nearer joys and sorrows. It was only when her father stood before her, fierce and exacting, hardened and brutalised by prison-life, a wretch for ever at war with the laws he had outraged,—it was only then that the full measure of Roland Lansdell's danger was revealed to her.

'If ever I come out of prison alive, I will kill you!'

Never had she forgotten the words of that threat. But she might hope that it was only an empty threat, the harmless thunder of a moment's passion; not a deliberate promise, to be fulfilled whenever the chance of its fulfilment arose. She did hope this; and in her first stolen interview with her father, she led him to talk of his trial, and contrived to ascertain his present sentiments regarding the man who had so materially helped to convict him. The dusky shadows of the summer evening hid the pallor of her earnest face, as she walked by Mr Sleaford's side in the sheltered hollow; and that gentleman was too much absorbed by the sense of his own wrongs to be very observant of his daughter's agitation.

Isabel Gilbert heard enough during that interview to convince her that Roland Lansdell's danger was very real and near. Mr Sleaford's vengeful passions had fed and battened upon the solitude of the past years. Every privation and hardship endured in his prison-life had been a fresh item in his long indictment against Mr Lansdell, the 'languid swell,' whom he had never wronged to the extent of a halfpenny, but who, for the mere amusement of the chase, had hunted him down. This was what he could not forgive. He *could not* recognise the right of an amateur detective, who bore witness against a criminal for the general benefit of society.

After this first meeting in Nessborough Hollow, the Doctor's Wife had but one thought, one purpose and desire; and that was, to keep her father in ignorance of his enemy's near neighbourhood, and to get him away before mischief arose between the two men. But this was not such an easy matter. Mr Sleaford refused to leave his quarters at the Leicester Arms until he obtained that which he had come to Midlandshire to seek—money enough for a new start in life. He had made his way to Jersey immediately after getting his release, and had there seen his wife and the boys. From them he heard of Isabel's marriage. She had married well, they said: a doctor at a place called Graybridge-on-the-Wayverne—and important man, no doubt; and she had not been unkind to them upon the whole, writing nice long letters to her stepmother now and then, and sending post-office orders for occasional sovereigns.

Heaven only knows with what difficulty the poor girl had contrived to save those occasional sovereigns. Mr Sleaford demanded money of his daughter. He had made all manner of inquiries about George Gilbert's position, and had received very satisfactory answers to those inquiries. The young doctor was a 'warm' man, the gossips in the little parlour at the Leicester Arms told Jack the Scribe; a prudent young man, who had inherited a nice little nest-egg—perpetually being hatched at a moderate rate of interest in the Wareham bank—from his father, and had saved money himself, no doubt. And then the gossips entered into calculations as to the value of Mr Gilbert's practice, and the simple economy of his domestic arrangements; all favourable to the idea that the young surgeon had a few thousands snugly invested in the county bank.

Under these circumstances, Mr Sleaford considered himself entirely justified in standing out for what he called his rights, namely, a sum of money—say fifty or a hundred pounds—from his daughter; and Isabel, with the thought of Roland's danger perpetually in her mind, felt that the money must be obtained at any price. Had her husband been well enough to talk of business-matters, she might have made her appeal to him; but as it was, there was an easier and more speedy method of getting the money. Roland, Roland himself, who was rich, and to whom fifty pounds,—large as the sum seemed to this girl, who had never had an unbroken ten-pound note in her life,—must be a very small matter; he was the only person who could give her immediate help. It was to him therefore she appealed. Ah, with what bitter shame and anguish! And it was to deliver up the money thus obtained that she met her father in Nessborough Hollow on the night of that dismal dinner at Lowlands. The idea of telling Roland of his danger never for a moment entered her mind. Was he not a hero, and would he not inevitably have courted that or any other peril?

She thought of his position with all a weak woman's illogical terror; and the only course that presented itself to her mind was that which she pursued. She wanted to get her father away before any chance allusion upon a stranger's lips told him that the man he so bitterly hated was within his reach.

CHAPTER X

' 'TWERE BEST AT ONCE TO SINK TO PEACE'*

After that farewell meeting with Mr Sleaford in Nessborough Hollow, a sense of peace came upon Isabel Gilbert. She had questioned her father about his plans, and he had told her that he should leave Midlandshire by the seven o'clock train from Wareham on the following morning. He should be heartily rejoiced to get to London, he said, and to leave a place where he felt like a fox in a hole. The sentimental element was by no means powerfully developed in the nature of Jack the Scribe, to whom the crowded pavements of Fleet Street and the Strand were infinitely more agreeable than the wild roses and branching fern of Midlandshire.

His daughter slept tranquilly that night for the first time after Mr Sleaford's appearance before the surgeon's door. She slept in peace, worn out by the fatigue and anxiety of the last fortnight; and no evil dream disturbed her slumbers. The odic forces must be worth very little after all, for there was no consciousness in the sleeper's mind of that quiet figure lying among the broken fern; no shadow, however dim, of the scene that had been enacted in the tranquil summer moonlight, while she was hurrying homeward through the dewy lanes, triumphant in the thought that her difficult task was accomplished. Only once in a century does the vision of Maria Martin* appear to an anxious dreamer; only so often as to shake the formal boundary-wall of common sense which we have so rigidly erected between the visible and invisible, and to show us that there *are* more things in heaven and earth than our dull philosophy is prepared to recognise.

Isabel woke upon the morning after that interview in the Hollow, with a feeling of relief still in her mind. Her father was gone, and all was well. He was not likely to return; for she had told him, with most solemn protestations, that she had obtained the money with extreme difficulty, and would never be able to obtain more. She had told him this, and he had promised never again to assail her with any demands. It was a very easy thing for Jack the Scribe to make that or any other promise; but even if he broke his word, Isabel thought, there was every chance that Roland Lansdell would leave Midlandshire very speedily, and become once more an alien and a wanderer.

The Doctor's Wife was at peace, therefore; the dreadful terror of the past fortnight was lifted away from her mind, and she was prepared to do her duty; to be true to Mr Colborne's solemn teaching, and to watch dutifully, undistracted by any secret fear and anguish, by George Gilbert's sick-bed.

Very dismal faces greeted her beside that bed. Mr Jeffson never left his post now at the pillow of his young master. The weeds grew unheeded in the garden; and Brown Molly missed her customary grooming. The gardener had thrown half a load of straw in the lane, below the doctor's window, so that no rumbling of the wagon-wheels carrying home the new-mown hay should disturb George Gilbert's feverish sleep, if the brief fitful dozes into which he fell now and then could be called by so sweet a name.

Mr Pawlkatt sat looking at his patient longer than usual that morning. George Gilbert lay in a kind of stupor, and did not recognise his medical attendant, and sometime rival. He had long since ceased to be anxious about his poor patients in the lanes behind the church, or about any thing else upon this earth, as it seemed; and now that her great terror had been lifted from her mind, Isabel saw a new and formless horror gliding swiftly towards her, like a great iceberg sailing fast upon an arctic sea. She followed Mr Pawlkatt out of the room, and down the little staircase, and clung to his arm as he was about to leave her.

'Oh, do you think he will die?' she said. 'I did not know until this morning that he was so very ill. Do you think he will die?'

The surgeon looked inquisitively into the earnest face lifted to his—looked with some expression of surprise upon his countenance.

'I am very anxious, Mrs Gilbert,' he answered gravely. 'I will not conceal from you that I am growing very anxious. The pulse is feeble and intermittent; and these low fevers—there, there, don't cry. I'll drive over to Wareham, as soon as I've seen the most important of my cases; and I'll ask Dr Herstlett to come and look at your husband. Pray try to be calm.'

'I am so frightened,' murmured Isabel, between her low half-stifled sobs. 'I never saw any one ill—like that—before.'

Mr Pawlkatt watched her gravely as he drew on his gloves.

'I am not sorry to see this anxiety on your part, Mrs Gilbert,' he remarked sententiously. 'As the friend and brother-professional of your husband, and as a man who is—ahem!—old enough to be your father, I will go so far as to say that I am gratified to find that you— I may say, your heart is in the right place. There have been some very awkward reports about you, Mrs Gilbert, during the last few days. I—I—of course should not presume to allude to those reports, if I did not believe them to be erroneous,' the surgeon added, rather hastily, not feeling exactly secure as to the extent and bearing of the law of libel.

But Isabel only looked at him with bewilderment and distress in her face.

'Reports about me!' she repeated. 'What reports?'

'There has been a person—a stranger—staying at a little inn down in Nessborough Hollow; and you,—in fact, I really have no right to interfere in this matter, but my very great respect for your husband,—and, in short——'

'Oh, that person is gone now,' Isabel answered frankly. 'It was very unkind of people to say any thing against him, or against me. He was a relation,—a very near relation,—and I could not do otherwise than see him now and then while he was in the neighbourhood. I went late in the evening, because I did not wish to leave my husband at any other time. I did not think that the Graybridge people watched me so closely, or were so ready to think that what I do must be wrong.'

Mr Pawlkatt patted her hand soothingly.

'A relation, my dear Mrs Gilbert?' he exclaimed. 'That, of course, quite alters the case. I always said that you were no doubt perfectly justified in doing as you did; though it would have been better to invite the person here. Country people will talk, you know. As a medical man, with rather a large field of experience, I see all these little provincial weaknesses. They will talk; but keep up your courage, Mrs Gilbert. We shall do our best for our poor friend. We shall do our very best.'

He gave Isabel's tremulous hand a little reassuring squeeze, and departed complacently.

The Doctor's Wife stood absently watching him as he walked away, and then turned and went slowly into the parlour—the empty, miserable-looking parlour, which had not been used now for more than a week. The dust lay thick upon the shabby old furniture, and the atmosphere was hot and oppressive.

Here Isabel sat down beside the chiffonier, where her poor little collection of books was huddled untidily in a dusty corner. She sat down to think—trying to realise the nature of that terror which seemed so close to her, trying to understand the full significance of what Mr Pawlkatt had said of her husband.

The surgeon had given no hope that George Gilbert would recover; he had only made little conventional speeches about calmness and fortitude.

She tried to think, but could not. She had only spoken the truth just now, when she cried out that she was frightened. This kind of terror was so utterly new to her that she could not understand the calm business-like aspect of the people who watched and waited on her husband. Could he be dying? That strong active man, whose rude health and hearty appetite had once jarred so harshly upon all her schoolgirl notions of consumptive and blood-vessel-breaking heroes! Could he be dying?—dying as heroic a death as any she had ever read of in her novels: the death of a man who speculates his life for the benefit of his fellow-creatures, and loses by the venture. The memory of every wrong that she had ever done him—small wrongs of neglect, or contemptuous opinions regarding his merits—wrongs

that had been quite impalpable to the honest unromantic doctor,—
crowded upon her now, and made a dull remorseful anguish in her
breast. The dark shadow brooding over George Gilbert—the dread
gigantic shadow, growing darker day by day—made him a new creature in the mind of this weak girl. No thought of her own position
had any place in her mind. She could not think; she could only wait,
oppressed by a dread whose nature she dared not realise. She sat for
a long time in the same forlornly listless attitude, almost as helpless
as the man who lay in the darkened chamber above her. Then,
rousing herself with an effort, she crept upstairs to the room where
the grave faces of the watchers greeted her, with very little sympathy in their gaze.

Had not Mr and Mrs Jeffson heard the reports current in
Graybridge; and was it likely they could have any pity for a woman
who crept stealthily at nightfall from her invalid husband's house to
meet a stranger?

Isabel would have whispered some anxious question about the
patient; but Matilda Jeffson frowned sternly at her, commanding
silence with an imperious forefinger; and she was fain to creep into
a dark corner, where it had been her habit to sit since the Jeffsons
had, in a manner, taken possession of her husband's sick-bed. She
could not dispute their right to do so. What was she but a frivolous,
helpless creature, fluttering and trembling like a leaf when she es-
sayed to do any little service for the invalid?

The day seemed painfully long. The ticking of an old clock on
the stairs, and the heavy troubled breathing of the sick man, were
the only sounds that broke the painful silence of the house. Once or
twice Isabel took an open Testament from a little table near her, and
tried to take some comfort from its pages. But she could not feel the
beauty of the words as she had in the little church at Hurstonleigh,
when her mind had been exalted by all manner of vague spiritualistic
yearnings; now it seemed deadened by the sense of dread and horror. She did not love her husband; and those tidings of heavenly
love which have so subtle an affinity with earthly affection could not
touch her very nearly in her present frame of mind. She did not love
her husband well enough to pray that something little short of a
miracle might be wrought for his sake. She was only sorry for him;
tenderly compassionate of his suffering; very fearful that he might
die. She did pray for him; but there was no exaltation in her prayers,

and she had a dull presentiment that her supplications would not be answered.

It was late in the afternoon when the physician from Wareham came with Mr Pawlkatt; and when he did arrive, he seemed to do very little, Isabel thought. He was a gray-whiskered important-looking man, with creaking boots; he seated himself by the bedside, and felt the patient's pulse, and listened to his breathing, and lifted his heavy eyelids, and peered into his dim blood-shot eyes. He asked a good many questions, and then went downstairs with Mr Pawlkatt, and the two medical men were closeted together some ten or twelve minutes in the little parlour.

Isabel did not follow Mr Pawlkatt down-stairs this time. She was awed by the presence of the strange physician, and there was nothing in the manner of the two men that inspired hope or comfort. She sat quite still in her dusky corner; but Mrs Jeffson stole out of the room soon after the medical men had quitted it, and went slowly down-stairs. George was asleep; in a very sound and heavy sleep this time; and his breathing was more regular than it had been—more regular, but still a laboured stertorous kind of respiration that was very painful to hear.

In less than ten minutes Mrs Jeffson came back, looking very pale, and with traces of tears upon her face. The good woman had been listening to the medical consultation in the little parlour below.

Perhaps Isabel dimly comprehended this; for she got up from her chair, and went a little way towards her husband's housekeeper.

'Oh, tell me the truth,' she whispered imploringly; 'do they think that he will die?'

'Yes,' Matilda Jeffson answered, in a hard cruel voice, strangely at variance with her stifled sobs, 'yes, Mrs Gilbert; and you'll be free to take your pleasure, and to meet Mr Lansdell as often as you like; and go gadding about after dark with strange men. You might have waited a bit, Mrs Gilbert; you wouldn't have had to wait very long—for they say my poor dear master—and I had him in my arms the day he was born, so I've need to love him dearly, even if others haven't!—I heard the doctor from Wareham tell Mr Pawlkatt that he'll never live to see to-morrow morning's light. So you might have waited, Mrs Gilbert; but you're a wicked woman and a wicked wife!'

But just at this moment the sick man started suddenly from his sleep, and lifted himself into a sitting position. Mr Jeffson's arm was about him directly, supporting the wasted figure that had very lately been so strong.

George Gilbert had heard Matilda's last words, for he repeated them in a thick strange voice, but with sufficient distinctness. It was a surprise to those who nursed him to hear him speak reasonably, for it was some time since he had been conscious of passing events.

'Wicked! no, no!' he said. 'Always a good wife; always a very good wife! Come, Izzie; come here. I'm afraid it has been a dull life, my dear,' he said very gently, as she came to him, clinging to him, and looking at him with a white scared face,—'dull—very dull; but it wouldn't have been always so. I thought—by and by to—new practice—Helmswell—market-town—seven thousand inhabitants—and you—drive—pony-carriage, like Laura Pawlkatt—but—the Lord's will be done, my dear!—I hope I've done my duty—the poor people—better rooms—ventilation—please God, by and by. I've seen a great deal of suffering—and—my duty—'

He slid heavily back upon William Jeffson's supporting arm; and a rain of tears—passionate remorseful tears never to be felt by him— fell on his pallid face. His death was very sudden, though his illness had been, considering the nature of his disease, a long and tedious one. He died supremely peaceful in the consciousness of having done his duty. He died, with Isabel's hand clasped in his own; and never, throughout his simple life, had one pang of doubt or jealousy tortured his breast.

CHAPTER XI
BETWEEN TWO WORLDS

A calm came down upon the house at Graybridge, and for the first time Isabel Gilbert felt the presence of death about and around her, shutting out all the living world by its freezing influence. The great iceberg had come down upon the poor frail barque. It almost seemed to Isabel as if she and all in that quiet habitation had been encompassed by a frozen wall, through which the living could not penetrate.

She suffered very much; the morbid sensibility of her nature made her especially liable to such suffering. A dull remorseful pain gnawed at her heart. Ah, how wicked she had been! how false, how cruel, how ungrateful! But if she had known that he was to die—if she had only known—it might all have been different. The foreknowledge of his doom would have insured her truth and tenderness; she could not have wronged, even by so much as a thought, a husband whose days were numbered. And amid all her remorse she was for ever labouring with the one grand difficulty—the difficulty of realising what had happened. She had needed the doctor's solemn assurance that her husband was really dead before she could bring herself to believe that the white swoon, the chill heaviness of the passive hand, did indeed mean death. And even when she had been told that all was over, the words seemed to have very little influence upon her mind. It could not be! All the last fortnight of anxiety and trouble was blotted out, and she could only think of George Gilbert as she had always known him until that time, in the full vigour of health and strength.

She was very sorrowful; but no passionate grief stirred her frozen breast. It was the shock, the sense of horror that oppressed her, rather than any consciousness of a great loss. She would have called her husband back to life; but chiefly because it was so horrible to her to know that he was there—near her—what he was. Once the thought came to her—the weak selfish thought—that it would have been much easier for her to bear this calamity if her husband had gone away, far away from her, and only a letter had come to tell her that he was dead. She fancied herself receiving the letter, and wondering at its black-edged border. The shock would have been very dreadful; but not so horrible as the knowledge that George Gilbert was in that house, and yet there was no George Gilbert. Again and again her mind went over the same beaten track; again and again the full realisation of what had happened slipped away from her, and she found herself framing little speeches—penitent, remorseful speeches—expressive of her contrition for all past shortcomings. And then there suddenly flashed back upon her the too vivid picture of that death-bed scene, and she heard the dull thick voice murmuring feebly words of love and praise.

In all this time Roland Lansdell's image was shut out of her mind. In the dense and terrible shadow that filled all the chambers of her brain, that bright and splendid figure could have no place. She thought of Mr Colborne at Hurstonleigh now and then, and felt

a vague yearning for his presence. He might have been able to
comfort her perhaps, somehow; he might have made it easier for her
to bear the knowledge of that dreadful presence in the room up-
stairs. She tried once or twice to read some of the chapters that had
seemed so beautiful on the lips of the popular curate: but even out
of that holy volume dark and ghastly images arose to terrify her, and
she saw Lazarus emerging from the tomb livid in his grave-clothes:
and death and horror seemed to be every where and in every thing.

After the first burst of passionate grief, bitterly intermingled with
indignation against the woman whom she believed to have been a
wicked and neglectful wife, Matilda Jeffson was not ungentle to the
terror-stricken girl so newly made a widow. She took a cup of scalding tea into the darkened parlour where Isabel sat, shivering every
now and then as if with cold, and persuaded the poor frightened
creature to take a little of that comforting beverage. She wiped away
her own tears with her apron while she talked to Isabel of patience
and resignation, submission to the will of Providence, and all those
comforting theories which are very sweet to the faithful mourner,
even when the night-time of affliction is darkest.

But Isabel was not yet a religious woman; [the faith that is stronger
than death was not hers in this hour of terror; she was only trying to
be good—only trying, after her own simple, half-childish fashion, to
resemble those holy and happy creatures whose pure lives she had
heard Mr Colborne describe, dwelling with tender, rapturous earnestness upon the perfection of their existence here, the splendour
of their reward hereafter. She was only trying to be good; and the
new current of her life had been disturbed by George Gilbert's
death, as by a sudden tempest.]* She was a child again, weak and
frivolous, frightened by the awful visitant who had so newly entered
that house. All through the evening of her husband's death she sat
in the little parlour, sometimes trying to read a little, sometimes idly
staring at the tall wick of the tallow-candle, which was only snuffed
once in a way—when Mrs Jeffson came into the room 'to keep the
scared creature company for a bit,' she said to her husband, who sat
by the kitchen-fire with his elbows on his knees and his face hidden
in his hands, brooding over those bygone days when he had been
wont to fetch the dead man from that commercial academy in the
Wareham Road.

There was a good deal of going in and out, a perpetual tramp of hushed footsteps moving to and fro, as it seemed to Isabel; and Mrs Jeffson, even in the midst of her grief, appeared full of some kind of business that kept her astir all the evening. The Doctor's Wife had imagined that all voice and motion must come to an end—that life itself must make a pause—in a house where death was. Others might feel a far keener grief for the man that was gone; but no one felt so deep an awe of death as she did. Mrs Jeffson brought her some supper on a little tray late in the evening; but she pushed it away from her and burst into tears. There seemed a kind of sacrilege in this carrying in and out of food and drink while he lay upstairs; he, whose hat still hung in the passage without, whose papers and ink-bottles and medical books were all primly arranged on one of the little vulgar cupboards by the fireplace. Ah, how often she had hated those medical books for being what they were, instead of editions of *Zanoni* and *Ernest Maltravers*! and it seemed wicked even to have thought unkindly of them, now that he to whom they belonged was dead.

It was quite in vain that Mrs Jeffson urged her to go upstairs to the room opposite that in which the surgeon lay; it was quite as vainly that the good woman entreated her to go and look at him, now that he was lying so peacefully in the newly arranged chamber, to lay her hand on his marble forehead, so that no shadow of him should trouble her in her sleep. The girl only shook her head forlornly.

'I'm afraid,' she said, piteously—'I'm afraid of that room. I never thought that he would die. I know that I wasn't good. It was wicked to think of other people always, and not of him; but I never thought that he would die. I knew that he was good to me; and I tried to obey him; but I think I should have been different if I had known that he would die.'

She pulled out the little table-drawer where the worsted socks were rolled-up in fluffy balls, with needles sticking out of them here and there. Even these were a kind of evidence of her neglect. She had cobbled them a little during the later period of her married life,—during the time of her endeavour to be good,—but she had not finished this work or any other. Ah, what a poor creature she was, after all!—a creature of feeble resolutions, formed only to be broken; a weak vacillating creature, full of misty yearnings and aspirings—resolving nobly in one moment, to yield sinfully in the next.

She begged to be allowed to spend the night downstairs on the rickety little sofa; and Mrs Jeffson, seeing that she was really oppressed by some childish terror of that upper-story, brought her some blankets and pillows, and a feeble little light that was to burn until daybreak.

So in that familiar room, whose every scrap of shabby furniture had been a part of the monotony of her life, Isabel Gilbert spent the first night of her widowhood, lying on the little sofa, nervously conscious of every sound in the house; feverishly wakeful until long after the morning sun was shining through the yellow-white blind, when she fell into an uneasy doze, in which she dreamt that her husband was alive and well. She did not arouse herself out of this, and yet she was never thoroughly asleep throughout the time, until after ten o'clock; and then she found Mrs Jeffson sitting near the little table, on which the inevitable cup of tea was smoking beside a plate of the clumsy kind of bread-and-butter inseparably identified with George Gilbert in Isabel's mind.

'There's somebody wants to see you, if you're well enough to be spoken to, my dear,' Matilda said, very gently; for she had been considerably moved by Mrs Gilbert's penitent little confession of her shortcomings as a wife; and was inclined to think that perhaps, after all, Graybridge had judged this helpless school-girl creature rather harshly. 'Take the tea, my dear; I made it strong on purpose for you; and try and cheer up a bit, poor lassie; you're young to wear widow's weeds; but he was fit to go. If all of us had worked as hard for the good of other folks, we could afford to die as peaceful as he did.'

Isabel pushed the heavy tangled hair away from her pallid face, and pursed-up her pale lips to kiss the Yorkshirewoman.

'You're very kind to me,' she said; 'you used to think that I was wicked, I know; and then you seemed very unkind. But I always wished to be good. I should like to have been good, and to die young, like George's mother.'

It is to be observed that, with Isabel's ideal of goodness there was always the association of early death. She had a vague idea that very religious and self-denying people got through their quota of piety with tolerable speed, and received their appointed reward. As yet her notions of self-sacrifice were very limited; and she could scarcely have conceived a long career of perfection. She thought of nuns as creatures who bade farewell to the world, and had all their back-hair cut off, and retired into a convent, and died soon afterwards, while they were still young and interesting. She could not have imagined an elderly nun, with all a long monotonous life of self-abnegation behind her, getting up at four o'clock every morning, and being as bright and vivacious and cheerful as any happy wife or mother outside the convent-walls. Yet there are such people.

Mrs Gilbert took a little of the hot tea, and then sat quite still, with her head lying on Matilda Jeffson's shoulder, and her hand clasped in Matilda's rough fingers. That living clasp seemed to impart a kind of comfort, so terribly had death entered into Isabel's narrow world.

'Do you think you shall be well enough to see him presently, poor lassie?' Mrs Jeffson said, after a long silence. 'I shouldn't ask you; only he seems anxious-like, as if there was something particular on his mind; and I know he's been very kind to you.'

Isabel stared at her in bewilderment.

'I don't know who you're talking of,' she said.

'It's Mr Raymond from Conventford. It's early for him to be so far as Graybridge; but he looks as pale and worn-like as if he'd been up and about all night. He was all struck of a heap-like when I told him about our poor master.'

Here Mrs Jeffson had recourse to the cotton-apron which had been so frequently applied to her eyes during the last week. Isabel huddled a shabby little shawl about her shoulders; she had made no change in her dress when she had lain down the night before; and she was very pale and wan, and tumbled and woebegone, in the bright summer light.

'Mr Raymond! Mr Raymond!' She repeated his name to herself once or twice, and made a faint effort to understand why he should have come to her. He had always been very kind to her, and associated with his image there was a sense of sound wisdom and vigorous cheerfulness of spirit. His presence would bring some comfort to her, she thought. Next to Mr Colborne, he was the person whom she would most have desired to see.

'I'll go to him, Mrs Jeffson,' she said, rising slowly from the sofa. 'He was always very good to me. But, oh, how the sight of him will bring back the time at Conventford, when George used to come and see me on Sunday afternoons, and we used to walk together in the cold bare meadows!'

That time did come back to her as she spoke: a gray colourless pause in her life, in which she had been—not happy perhaps, but contented. And since that time, what tropical splendour, what a gorgeous oasis of light and colour, had spread itself suddenly about her path! a forest of miraculous flowers and enchanted foliage that had shut out all the everyday world in which other people dragged out their tiresome existences—a wonderful Asiatic wilderness, in which there were hidden dangers lurking, terrible as the cobras that drop down upon the traveller from some flowering palm-tree, or the brindled tigers that prowl in the shadowy jungle. She looked back across that glimpse of an earthly paradise to the old dull days at Conventford; and a hot blast from the tropical oasis seemed to rush in upon her, beyond which the past spread far away like a cool gray sea. Perhaps that quiet neutral-tinted life was the best, after all. She saw herself again as she had been; 'engaged' to the man who lay dead upstairs; and weaving a poor little web of romance for herself even out of that prosaic situation.

Mr Raymond was waiting in the best parlour,—that sacred chamber, which had been so rarely used during the parish surgeon's brief wedded life,—that primly-arranged little sitting-room, which always had a faint odour of old-fashioned *pot-pourri*; the room which Isabel had once yearned to beautify into a bower of chintz and muslin. The blind was down, and the shutters half-closed; and in the dim light Charles Raymond looked very pale.

'My dear Mrs Gilbert,' he said, taking her hand and leading her to a seat; 'my poor child—so little more than a child,—so little wiser or stronger than a child,—it seems cruel to come to you at such a time; but life is very hard sometimes—'

'It was very kind of you to come,' Isabel exclaimed, interrupting him; 'I wanted to see you, or some one like you; for every thing seems so dreadful to me. I never thought that he would die.'

She began to cry, in a weary helpless way, not like a person moved by some bitter grief; rather like a child that finds itself in a strange place, and is frightened.

'My poor child, my poor child!'

Charles Raymond still held Isabel's passive hand, and she felt tears dropping on it; the tears of a man, of all others the last to give way to any sentimental weakness. But even then she did not divine that he must have some grief of his own—some sorrow that touched him more nearly than George Gilbert's death could possibly touch him. Her state of feeling just now was a peculiarly selfish state, perhaps; for she could neither understand nor imagine any thing outside that darkened house, where death was supreme. The shock had been too terrible and too recent. It was as if an earthquake had taken place, and all the atmosphere round her was thick with clouds of blinding dust produced by the concussion. She felt Mr Raymond's tears dropping slowly on her hand; and if she thought about them at all, she thought them only the evidence of his sympathy with her childish fears and sorrows.

'I loved him like my own son,' murmured Charles Raymond, in a low tender voice. 'If he had not been what he was,—if he had been the veriest cub that ever disgraced a good old stock,—I think even then I should have loved him as dearly and as truly, for *her* sake. Her only son! I've seen him look at me as she looked when I kissed her in the church on her wedding-day. So long as he lived, I should have never felt that she was really lost to me.'

Isabel heard nothing of these broken sentences. Mr Raymond uttered them in low musing tones, that were not intended to reach any mortal ears. For some little time he sat silently by the girl's side, with her hand still lying in his; then he rose and walked up and down the room with a soft slow step, and with his head drooping.

'You have been very much shocked by your husband's death?' he said at last.

Isabel began to cry again at this question,—weak hysterical tears, that meant very little, perhaps.

'Oh, very, very much,' she answered; 'I know I was not so good as I ought to have been; and I can never ask him to forgive me now.'

'You were very fond of him, I suppose?'

A faint blush flickered and faded upon Isabel's pallid face; and then she answered, hesitating a little,

'He was very good to me, and I—I tried always to be grateful—almost always,' she added, with a remorseful recollection of rebellious moments in which she had hated her husband because he ate spring-onions, and wore Graybridge-made boots.

Just the slightest indication of a smile glimmered upon Mr Raymond's countenance as he watched Isabel's embarrassment. We are such weak and unstable creatures at the very best, that it is just possible this man, who loved Roland Lansdell very dearly, was not entirely grieved by the discovery of Isabel's indifference for her dead husband. He went back to the chair near hers, and seated himself once more by her side. He began to speak to her in a very low earnest voice; but he kept his eyes bent upon the ground; and in that dusky light she was quite unable to see the expression of his face.

'Isabel,' he began, very gravely, 'I said just now that life seems very hard to us sometimes,—not to be explained by any doctrine of averages, by any of the codes of philosophy which man frames for his own comfort; only to be understood very dimly by one sublime theory, which some of us are not strong enough to grasp and hold by. Ah, what poor tempest-tossed vessels we are without that compass! I have had a great and bitter grief to bear within the last four-and-twenty-hours, Isabel; a sorrow that has come upon me more suddenly than even the shock of your husband's death can have fallen on you.'

'I am very sorry for you,' Isabel answered, dreamily; 'the world must be full of trouble, I think. It doesn't seem as if any one was ever really happy.'

She was thinking of her own life, so long to look back upon, though she was little more than twenty years of age; she was thinking of the petty sordid miseries of her girlhood,—the sheriff's officers and tax-gatherers and infuriated trades-people,—the great shock of her father's disgrace; the dull monotony of her married life; and Roland Lansdell's sudden departure; and his stubborn anger against her when she refused to run away with him; and then her husband's death. It seemed all one dreary record of grief and trouble.

'I am growing old, Isabel,' resumed Mr Raymond; 'but I have never lost my sympathy with youth and all its brightness. I think, perhaps, that sympathy has grown wider and stronger with increase of years. There is one young man who has been always very dear to me—more dear to me than I can ever make you comprehend, unless I were to tell you the subtle link that has bound him to me. I suppose there are some fathers who have as deep a love for their sons as I have for the man of whom I speak; but I have always fancied fatherly love a very lukewarm feeling compared with my affection for Roland Lansdell.'

Roland Lansdell! It was the first time she had heard his name spoken since that Sunday on which her husband's illness had begun. The name shot through her heart with a thrill that was nearly akin to pain. A little glimpse of lurid sunshine burst suddenly in upon the darkness of her life. She clasped her hands before her face almost as if it had been actual light that she wanted to shut out.

'Oh, don't speak of him!' she said, piteously. 'I was so wicked; I thought of him so much; but I did not know that my husband would die. Please, don't speak of him; it pains me so to hear his name.'

She broke down into a torrent of hysterical weeping as she uttered this last entreaty. She remembered Roland's angry face in the church; his studied courtesy during that midnight interview at the Priory, the calm reserve of manner which she had mistaken for indifference. He was nothing to her; he was not even her friend; and she had sinned so deeply against the dead man for his sake

'I should be the last to mention Roland Lansdell's name in your hearing,' Mr Raymond answered presently, when she had grown a little quieter, 'if the events of the last day or two had not broken down all barriers. The time is very near at hand, Isabel, when no name ever spoken upon this earth will be an emptier sound than the name of Roland Lansdell.'

She lifted her tear-stained face suddenly and looked at him. All the clouds floated away, and a dreadful light broke in upon her; she looked at him, trembling from head to foot, with her hands clasped convulsively about his arm.

'You came here to tell me something!' she gasped; 'something has happened—to him! Ah, if it has, life is *all* sorrow!'

'He is dying, Isabel.'

'Dying!'

Her lips shaped the words, and her fixed eyes stared at Charles Raymond's face with an awful look.

'He is dying. It would be foolish to deceive you with any false hope, when in four-and-twenty hours' time all will be finished. He went out—riding—the other night, and fell from his horse, as it is supposed. He was found by some hay-makers early the next morning, lying helpless, some miles from the Priory, and was carried home. The medical men give no hope of his recovery; but he has been sensible at intervals ever since. I have been a great deal with

him—constantly with him; and his cousin Gwendoline is there. He
wants to see you Isabel; of course he knows nothing of your husband's death; I did not know of it myself till I came here this
morning. He wants to see you, my poor child. Do you think you can
come?'

She rose and bent her head slowly as if in assent, but the fixed
look of horror never left her face. She moved towards the door, and
seemed as if she wanted to go at once—dressed as she was, with the
old faded shawl wrapped about her.

'You'd better get your housekeeper to make you comfortable and
tidy, while I go and engage a fly,' said Mr Raymond; and then
looking her full in the face, he added, 'Can you promise me to be
very calm and quiet when you see him? You had better not come
unless you can promise me as much as that. His hours are numbered, as it is; but any violent emotion would be immediately fatal.
A man's last hours are very precious to him, remember; the hours of
a man who knows his end is near make a sacred mystical period in
which the world drops far away from him, and he is in a kind of
middle region between this life and the next. I want you to recollect
this, Isabel. The man you are going to see is not the man you have
known in the past. There would be very little hope for us after
death, if we found no hallowing influence in its approach.'

'I will recollect,' Isabel answered. She had shed no tears since she
had been told of Roland's danger. Perhaps this new and most terrible shock had nerved her with an unnatural strength. And amid all
the anguish comprehended in the thought of his death, it scarcely
seemed strange to her that Roland Lansdell should be dying. It
seemed rather as if the end of the world had suddenly come about;
and it mattered very little who should be the first to perish. Her
own turn would come very soon, no doubt.

Mr Raymond met Mrs Jeffson in the passage and said a few
words to her before he went out of the house. The good woman was
shocked at the tidings of Mr Lansdell's accident. She had thought
very badly of the elegant young master of Mordred Priory; but
death and sorrow take the bitterness out of a true-hearted woman's
feelings, and Matilda was womanly enough to forgive Roland for the
wish that summoned the Doctor's Wife to his deathbed. She went
upstairs, and came down with Isabel's bonnet and cloak and simple
toilet paraphernalia; and presently Mrs Gilbert had a consciousness

of cold water splashed upon her face, and a brush passed over her tangled hair. She felt only half-conscious of these things, as she might have felt had they been the events of a dream. So presently, when Mr Raymond came back, accompanied by the muffled rolling of wheels in the straw-bestrewn lane, and she was half-lifted into the old-fashioned, mouldy-smelling Graybridge fly,—so all along the familiar high-road, past the old inn with the sloping roof, where the pigeons were cooing to each other, as if there had been no such thing as death or sorrow in the world,—so under the grand gothic gates of monastic Mordred, it was all like a dream—a terrible oppressive dream—hideous by reason of some vague sense of horror rather than by the actual vision presented to the eyes of the sleeper. In a troubled dream it is always thus,—it is always a hidden, intangible something that oppresses the dreamer.

The leaves were fluttering in the warm mid-summer wind, and the bees were humming about the great flower-beds. Far away the noise of the waterfall blended with all other summer sounds in a sweet confusion. And he was dying! Oh, what wonderful patches of shadow and sunlight on the wide lawns! what marvellous glimpses down long glades, where the young fern heaved to and fro in the fitful breezes like the emerald wavelets of a summer-sea! And he was dying! It is such an old, old feeling, this unwillingness to comprehend that there *can be* death any where upon an earth that is so beautiful. Eve may have felt very much as Isabel felt to-day, when she saw a tropical sky, serenely splendid, above the corpse of murdered Abel.* Hero may have found the purple distances of the classic mountains, the yellow glory of the sunlit sands, almost more difficult to bear than the loss of her drowned lover.* But it is only when a Napoleon dies that there is tempest and stormcloud, young trees uprooted by the whirlwind, and general desolation in unison with the dread terror of a great man's death.

There was the same solemn hush at Mordred Priory that there had been in the surgeon's house at Graybridge; only there seemed a deeper solemnity here amid all the darkened splendour of the gracious rooms, stretching far away, one beyond another, like the chambers of a palace. Isabel saw the long vista, not as she had seen it once, when *he* came into the hall to bid her welcome, but with the haunting dreamlike oppression strong upon her. She saw little glimmering patches of gilding and colour here and there in the cool gloom of the shaded rooms, and long bars of light shining through the Venetian shutters upon the polished oaken floors. One of the medical men—there were three or four of them in the house—came out of the library and spoke in a whisper to Mr Raymond. The result of the whispering seemed tolerably favourable, for the doctor went back to his companions in the library, and Charles Raymond led Isabel up the broad staircase; the beautiful staircase which seemed to belong to a church or a cathedral rather than to any common habitation.

They met a nurse in the corridor; a prim, pleasant-looking woman, who answered Mr Raymond's questions in a cheerful business-like manner, as if a Roland Lansdell or so more or less in the world were a matter of very small consequence. And then a mist came before Isabel's eyes, and she lost consciousness of the ground on which she trod; and presently there was a faint odour of hartshorn and aromatic medicines, and she felt a soft hand sponging her forehead with eau-de-Cologne, and a woman's muslin garments fluttering near her. And then she raised her eyelids with a painful sense of their weight, and a voice very close to her, said,

'It was very kind of you to come. I am afraid the heat of the room makes you faint. If you could contrive to let in a little more air, Raymond. It was very good of you to come.'

Oh, he was *not* dying! Her heart seemed to leap out of a dreadful frozen region into an atmosphere of warmth and light. He was not dying! Death was not like this. He spoke to her to-day as he had always spoken. It was the same voice, the same low music which she had heard so often mingled with the brawling of the mill-stream; the voice that had sounded perpetually in her dreams by day and night. [She forgot that it was a wickedness to have loved him. All her remorse, all her penitence, was gone like a thing that had never been. She was Gretchen, she was Alice,* she was any thing that is ignorant and loving and foolish; and he was not dying!]*

She slipped from her chair and fell upon her knees by the bedside. There was nothing violent or melodramatic in the movement; it seemed almost involuntary, half unconscious.

'Oh, I am so glad to hear you speak!' she said; 'it makes me so happy—to see you like this. They told me that you were very, very ill, they told me that—'

'They told you the truth,' Roland answered gravely. 'Oh, dear

Mrs Gilbert, you must try and forget what I have been, or you will never be able to understand what I am. And I was so tired of life, and thought I had so little interest in the universe; and yet I feel so utterly changed a creature now that all earthly hope has really slipped away from me. I sent for you, Isabel, because in this last interview I want to acknowledge all the wrong I have done you; I want to ask your forgiveness for that wrong.'

'Forgiveness—from me! Oh, no, no!'

She could not abandon her old attitude of worship. He was a prince always—noble or wicked—a prince by divine right of his splendour and beauty! If he stooped from his high estate to smile upon her, was he not entitled to her deepest gratitude, her purest devotion? If it pleased him to spurn and trample her beneath his feet, what was she, when counted against the magnificence of her idol, that she should complain? There is always some devoted creature prostrate in the road when the car comes by; and which of them would dream of upbraiding Juggernaut* for the anguish inflicted by the crushing wheels?

The same kind hands which had bathed Mrs Gilbert's forehead half lifted her from her kneeling attitude now; and looking up, Isabel saw Lady Gwendoline bending over her, very pale, very grave, but with a sweet compassionate smile upon her face. Lord Ruysdale and his daughter had come to the Priory immediately after hearing of Roland's dangerous state; and during the four-and-twenty hours that had elapsed, Lady Gwendoline had been a great deal with her cousin. The hidden love which had turned to jealous anger against Roland's folly regained all its purer qualities now, and there was no sacrifice of self or self-love that Gwendoline Pomphrey would have hesitated to make, if in so doing she could have restored life and vigour to the dying man. She had heard the worst the doctors had to tell. She knew that her cousin was dying. She was no woman to delude herself with vain hopes, to put away the cup for a while because it was bitter, knowing that its last drop must be drained sooner or later. She bowed her head before the inevitable, and accepted her sorrow. Never in her brightest day, when her portrait had been in every West-end print-shop, and her name a synonym for all that is elegant and beautiful,—never had she seemed so perfect a woman as now, when she sat, pale and quiet and resigned, by the deathbed of the man she loved.

During that long night of watching, Mr Lansdell's mind had seemed at intervals peculiarly clear,—the fatal injuries inflicted upon his brain had not blotted out his intellect. That had been obscured in occasional periods of wandering and stupor, but every now and then the supremacy of spirit over matter reasserted itself, and the young man talked even more calmly than usual. All the fitfulness of passion, the wavering of purpose—now hot, now cold, now generous, now cruel,—all natural weakness seemed to have been swept away, and an unutterable calm had fallen upon his heart and mind.

['I never thought I could come to this, Gwendoline,' he said. 'O God, have pity upon me! What presumptuous stuff I have talked about the limits of possibility, the transformations of matter! and how utterly powerless I was to comprehend such a change as that which has come to me during the past few hours! I have sneered at good men's records of deathbed repentances, and all that simple pious prosiness which Christian men and women talk when they are dying; and yet—and yet, Gwendoline, the change has come, and I think I see a little way farther than of old. Something,—oh, so vague and shadowy, that no words of mine can tell of it,—something opens all at once before my eyes. You have been out riding on a stormy day, haven't you? and have seen the dull low sky closing in all the earth, dense and impenetrable, until suddenly there has been just a little cleft in the darkness, and you have seen through to the higher heavens beyond,—oh, so far above that low brooding sky, which seemed just before the uttermost boundary of the universe. I have been under the low sky a long time, my dear; but I think there is a cleft in the darkness now, and I can see just a glimpse of the splendour. I do not feel as if I were dying. I do not believe this change which is so near me is the kind of death I once believed in. It is not the end, Gwendoline. The light that has come to me is strong enough to show me as much as that. It is not the end.']*

Once, on waking from a brief doze, he found his cousin watching, but the nurse asleep, and began to talk of Isabel Gilbert. 'I want you to know all about her,' he said; 'you have only heard vulgar scandal and gossip. I should like you to know the truth. It is very foolish, that little history—wicked perhaps; but those provincial gossips may have garbled and disfigured the story. I will tell you the truth, Gwendoline; for I want you to be a friend to Isabel Gilbert when I am dead and gone.'

And then he told the history of all those meetings under Lord Thurston's oak; dwelling tenderly on Isabel's ignorant simplicity, blaming himself for all that was guilty and dishonourable in that sentimental flirtation. He told Gwendoline how, from being half amused, half gratified, by Mrs Gilbert's unconcealed admiration of him, so naïvely revealed in every look and tone, he had, little by little, grown to find the sole happiness of his life in those romantic meetings; and then he spoke of his struggles with himself, real earnest struggles—his flight—his return—his presumptuous belief that Isabel would freely consent to any step he might propose—his anger and disappointment after the final interview, which proved to him how little he had known the depths of that girlish sentimental heart.

'She was only a child playing with fire, Gwendoline,' he said; 'and had not the smallest desire to walk through the furnace. That was my mistake. She was a child, and I mistook her for a woman— a woman who saw the gulf before her, and was prepared to take the desperate leap. She was only a child, pleased with my pretty speeches and town-made clothes and perfumed handkerchiefs,—a schoolgirl; and I set my life upon the chance of being happy with her. Will you try and think of her as she really is Gwendoline,—not as these Graybridge people see her,—and be kind to her when I am dead and gone? I should like to think she was sure of one wise and good woman for a friend. I have been very cruel to her, very unjust, very selfish. I was never in the same mind about her for an hour together,—sometimes thinking tenderly of her, sometimes upbraiding and hating her as a trickstress and a coquette. But I can understand her and believe in her much better now. The sky is higher, Gwendoline.'

If Roland had told his cousin this story a week before, when his life seemed all before him, she might have received his confidence in a very different spirit from that in which she now accepted it: but he was dying, and she had loved him, and had been loved by him. It was by her own act that she had lost that love. She of all others had least right to resent his attachment to another woman. She remembered that day, nearly ten years ago, on which she had quarrelled with him, stung by his reproaches, insolent in the pride of her young beauty and the knowledge that she might marry a man so high above Roland Lansdell in rank and position. She saw herself as she had been, in all the early splendour of her Saxon beauty, and wondered if she really was the same creature as that proud worldly girl who thought the supremest triumph in life was to become the wife of a marquis.

'I will be her friend, Roland,' she said presently. 'I know she is very childish; and I will be patient with her and befriend her, poor lonely girl.'

Lady Gwendoline was thinking, as she said this, of that interview in the surgeon's parlour at Graybridge—that interview in which Isabel had not scrupled to confess her folly and wickedness.

'I ought to have been more patient,' Gwendoline thought; 'but I think I was angry with her because she had dared to love Roland. I was jealous of his love for her, and I could not be kind or tolerant.'

Thus it was that Isabel found Lady Gwendoline so tender and compassionate to her. She only raised her eyes to the lady's face with a grateful look. She forgot all about the interview at Graybridge; what *could* she remember in that room, except that *he* was ill? in danger, people had told her; but she could not believe that. The experience of her husband's deathbed had impressed her with an idea that dangerous illness must be accompanied by terrible prostration, delirium, raging fever, dull stupor. She saw Roland in one of his best intervals, reasonable, cheerful, self-possessed, and she could not believe that he was going to die. She looked at him, and saw that his face was bloodless, and that his head was bound by linen bandages, which concealed his forehead. A fall from his horse! She remembered how she had seen him once ride by upon the dusty road, unconscious of her presence, grand and self-absorbed as Count Lara; but amongst all her musings she had never imagined any danger coming to him in that shape. She had fancied him always as a dauntless rider, taming the wildest steed with one light pressure of his hand upon the curb. She looked at him sorrowfully, and the vision of his accident arose before her; she saw the horse tearing across a moonlit waste, and then a fall, and then a figure dragged along the ground. She had read of such things: it was only some old half-forgotten scene out of one of her books that rose in her mind.

No doubt as to the nature of Mr Lansdell's accident, no glimmering suspicion of the truth, ever entered her brain. She believed most fully that she had herself prevented all chance of an encounter between her father and his enemy. Had she not seen the last of Mr Sleaford in Nessborough Hollow, whence he was to depart for

Wareham station at break of day? and what should take Roland Lansdell to that lonely glade in which the little rustic inn was hidden,—a resting-place for haymakers and gipsy-hawkers?

She never guessed the truth. The medical men who attended Roland Lansdell knew that the injuries from which he was dying had never been caused by any fall from a horse; and they said as much to Charles Raymond, who was unutterably distressed by the intelligence. But neither he nor the doctors could obtain any admission from the patient, though Mr Raymond most earnestly implored him to reveal the truth.

'Cure me, if you can,' he said; 'nothing that I can tell you will give you any help in doing that. If it is my fancy to keep the cause of my death a secret, it is the whim of a dying man, and it ought to be respected. No living creature upon this earth except one man will ever know how I came by these injuries. But I do hope that you gentlemen will be discreet enough to spare my friends any useless pain. The gossips are at work already, I daresay, speculating as to what became of the horse that threw me. For pity's sake, do your best to stop their talk. My life has been sluggish enough; do not let there be any *esclandre* about my death.'

Against such arguments as these Charles Raymond could urge nothing. But his grief for the loss of the young man he loved was rendered doubly bitter by the mystery which surrounded Roland's fate. The doctors told him that the wounds on Mr Lansdell's head could only have been caused by merciless blows inflicted with some blunt instrument. Mr Raymond in vain distracted himself with the endeavour to imagine how or why the young man had been attacked. He had not been robbed; for his watch and purse, his rings, and the little trinkets hanging at his chain, all of them costly in their nature, had been found upon him when he was brought home to the Priory. That Roland Lansdell could have counted one enemy amongst all mankind, never entered into his kinsman's calculations. He had no recollection of that little story told so lightly by the young man in the flower-garden; he was entirely without a clue to the catastrophe; and he perceived very plainly that Roland's resolution was not to be shaken. There was a quiet determination in Mr Lansdell's refusal, which left no hope that he might be induced to change his mind. He spoke with all apparent frankness of the result of his visit to Nessborough Hollow. He had found Isabel there, he said, with a

man who was related to her,—a poor relation, who had come to
Graybridge to extort money from her. He had seen and spoken to
the man, and was fully convinced that his account of himself was
true.

'So you see the Graybridge gossips had lighted on the usual
mare's-nest,' Roland said in conclusion; 'the man was a relation,—
an uncle or cousin, I believe,—I heard it from his own lips. If I had
been a gentleman, I should have been superior to the foul suspicions
that maddened me that night. What common creatures we are,
Raymond, some of us! Our mothers believe in us, and worship us,
and watch over us, and seem to fancy they have dipped us in a kind
of moral Styx,* and that there is something of the immortal infused
into our vulgar clay; but rouse our common passions, and we sink to
the level of the navigator who beats his wife to death with a poker in
defence of his outraged honour. They put a kind of varnish over us
at Eton and Oxford; but the colouring underneath is very much the
same, after all. Your King Arthur, or Sir Philip Sidney, or Bayard,*
crops up once in a century or so, and the world bows down before
a gentleman; but, oh, what a rare creature he is!'

'I want you to forgive me,' Roland said to Isabel, after she had been
sitting some minutes in the low chair in which Lady Gwendoline
had placed her. There was no one in the room but Charles Raymond
and Gwendoline Pomphrey; and Mr Raymond had withdrawn himself to a distant window that had been pushed a little way open, near
which he sat in a very mournful attitude, with his face averted from
the sick-bed. 'I want you to forgive me for having been very unjust
and cruel to you, Mrs Gilbert—Isabel. Ah, I may call you Isabel
now, and no one will cry out upon me! Dying men have all manner
of pleasant privileges. I was very cruel, very unjust, very selfish and
wicked, my poor girl; and your childish ignorance was wiser than my
worldly experience. A man has no right to desire perfect happiness:
I can understand that now. He has no right to defy the laws made by
wiser men for his protection, because there is a fatal twist in the
fabric of his life, and those very laws happen to thwart him in his
solitary insignificance. How truly Thomas Carlyle has told us that
Manhood only begins when we have surrendered to Necessity!* We
must submit, Isabel. I struggled; but I never submitted. I tried to
crush and master the pain; but I never resigned myself to endure it;

and endurance is so much grander than conquest. And then, when I had yielded to the tempter, when I had taken my stand, prepared to defy heaven and earth, I was angry with you, poor child, because you were not alike rash and desperate. Forgive me, my dear; I loved you very much, and it is only now, now when I am dying, that I know how fatal and guilty my love was. But it was never a profligate's brief passion, Isabel. It was wicked to love you; but my love was pure. If you had been free to be my wife, I should have been a true and faithful husband to my childish love. Ah, even now, when life seems so far away; even now, Isabel, the old picture rises before me, and I fancy what might have been if I had found you free.'

The low penetrating voice reached Charles Raymond, and he bent his head and sobbed aloud. Dimly, as the memory of a dream, came back upon him the recollection of that time in which he had sat amongst the shadows of the great beech-trees at Hurstonleigh, with the young man's poems open in his hand, and had been beguiled into thinking of what might happen if Roland returned to England to see Isabel in her girlish beauty. And Roland had returned, and had seen her; but too late; and now she was free once more,—free to be loved and chosen,—and again it was too late. Perhaps Mr Raymond seems only a foolish sentimentalist, weeping because of the blight upon a young man's love-story; but then he had loved the young man's mother,—and in vain!

'Gwendoline has promised to be your friend, Isabel,' Roland said by and by; 'it makes me very happy to know that. Oh, my darling, if I could tell you the thoughts that came to me as I lay there, with the odour of leaves and flowers about me, and the stars shining above the tall branches over my head. *What* is impossible in a universe where there are such stars? It seemed as if I had never seen them until then. [It used to be so difficult to me to believe. I think all the *ignes fatui* of the world must have glimmered and danced before my eyes, so that I could not see those unspeakable lights above. They all went out at once, the foul marshy exhalations, like the lamps in a theatre when the curtain goes down. I am changed, Isabel; but it is no earthly conversion achieved by books and sermons. When God pleases, He says, Let there be light; and the fool is wise. That raising of the dead in Jerusalem was only typical of the miracles which were to come afterwards. Have you ever read the letters of some condemned wretch waiting the hour of his

execution? What an exaltation pervades them! The unhappy creature can scarcely spell, perhaps; but he pours out long ungrammatical
rhapsodies about heaven and glory; and you shrug your shoulders,
and cry, Cant! hypocrisy! And yet it *may* be real, after all. No
ordinary man, sound in health, presumptuous in the expectation of
a long life before him, can understand the feelings of a man who is
face to face with death. Death, which loses the worst of its terrors
when we begin to feel that it is not the end! Only when we are very
close to the gate can we see the far country beyond. I remember
when I was a little boy I used to think the world was flat, like a great
prairie; so that the too presumptous traveller, coming to the edge of
it, tumbled over headlong into chaos. I smile even now when I think
of that foolish fancy; but perhaps some of my fancies since that time
have been very little wiser than that.']*

He rambled on thus, with Isabel's hand held loosely in his. He
seemed to be very happy—entirely at peace. Gwendoline had proposed to read to him; and the parish rector had been with him,
urging the duty of some religious exercises, eager to exhort and to
explain; but the young man had smiled at him with some shade of
contempt in his expression.

'There is very little you could read from that book which I do not
already know by heart,' he said, pointing to the Bible lying open
under the clergyman's hand. 'It is not your unbeliever who least
studies his gospel. Imagine a man possessed of a great crystal that
looks like a diamond. His neighbours tell him that the gem is price-
less—matchless—without crack or flaw. But some evil thing within
the man suggests that it may be valueless after all—only a big beautiful lump of glass. You may fancy that he would examine it very
closely; he would scrutinise every facet, and contemplate it in every
light, and perhaps know a good deal more about it than the believing possessor, who, feeling confident in the worth of his jewel, puts
it safely away in a strong box against the hour when it may be
wanted. I know all about the Gospel, Mr Matson; and I think, as my
hours are numbered, it may be better for me to lie and ponder upon
those familiar words. The light breaks upon me very slowly; but it
all comes from a far distant sky; and no earthly hand can lift so
much as the uttermost edge of the curtain that shuts out the fuller
splendour. I am very near him now; I am very near "the shadow,
cloaked from head to foot, who keeps the keys of all the creeds!" '*

The conscientious rector thought Mr Lansdell a very unpromising penitent; but it was something to hear that the young man did not rail or scoff at religion on his dying-bed; and even that might have been expected of a person who had attended divine service only once in six weeks, and had scandalised a pious and well-bred congregation by undisguised yawns, and absent-minded contemplation of his filbert-nails during the respectable prosiness of a long sermon.

The rector did not understand this imperfect conversion, expressed in phrases that sounded the reverse of orthodox; but the state of matters in that death-chamber was much better than he had expected. He had heard it hinted that Mr Lansdell was a Freethinker*—a Deist*; even an Atheist,* some people had said; and he had half anticipated to find the young man blaspheming aloud in the throes of his dying agony. He had not been prepared for this quiet deathbed; this man, who was dying with a smile upon his face, murmuring alternate fragments of St John's gospel and Tennyson's *In Memoriam.** Addison* himself, holding up his own bearing as a model for all Christian mankind, could scarcely have conducted himself more respectably than this cynical young lounger, whose life, vaguely reported at county dinner-tables, had scandalised all Midlandshire.

'I was with my mother when she died,' Roland said by and by, 'and yet could not accept the simple faith that made her so happy. But I daresay Saul had seen many wonderful things before that journey to Damascus.* Had he not witnessed the martyrdom of Stephen,* and had yet been unmoved? The hour comes, and the miracle comes with it. Oh, what an empty wasted life mine has been for the last ten years! because I could not understand—I could not see beyond. I might have done so much perhaps, if I could only have seen my way beyond the contradictions and perplexities of this lower life. But I could not—I could not; and so I fell back into a sluggish idleness, "without a conscience or an aim." I "basked and battened in the woods." '*

The rector lingered in the house even after he left Roland's chamber. He would be summoned by and by perhaps, and the dying man would require some more orthodox consolation than was to be derived from Mr Tennyson's verses.

But Roland seemed very happy—happier than he had been since his early manhood, when he had made his one brief struggle to do something good for the working-man. There was a brightness upon his face, in spite of its deathlike pallor—a spiritual brightness, unaffected by any loss of blood, or languor of that slow pulse which the London physicians felt so often. For some two or three hours after the struggle in Nessborough Hollow he had lain stunned and unconscious; then he had slowly awakened to see the stars fading above the branches over his head, and to hear the early morning breeze creeping with a ghostly rustling noise amidst the fern. He awoke to feel that something of an unwonted nature had happened to him, but not for some time to any distinct remembrance of his encounter with Mr Sleaford.

He tried to move, but found himself utterly powerless,—a partial paralysis seemed to have changed his limbs to lead; he could only lie as he had fallen; dimly conscious of the fading stars above, the faint summer wind rippling a distant streamlet, and all the vague murmur of newly-awakening nature. He knew as well as if a whole conclave of physicians had announced their decision upon his case,— he knew that for him life was over; and that if there was any vitality in his mind, any sense of a future in his breast, that sense, so vague and imperfect as yet, could only relate to something beyond this earth.

['I know that I am dying, and yet there is no death in my mind,' he thought. '*Is* there something afterwards— something beyond the last pulsation of the heart? Oh, phrenologists, who teach us that the noblest sentiments of our minds are only so much gray matter, perishing eternally with the benumbing of our spinal marrows,— physiologists, preachers of the doctrine which makes the universe an ascending-scale of mechanical progression, and man, at his best and brightest, nothing more than the latest development of the tadpole and the civilised half-brother of the gorilla,—I wonder whether you are all wrong, after all. Are only the little children wise? Are the ignorant foolish creatures that I have seen mumbling simple supplications in the dusky aisles of Belgian cathedrals,—are they nearer the light than all the princes of modern science, who take the soul out of a man's breast, and tell him of what stuff it is made?']*

Very rambling fancies filled Mr Lansdell's mind as he lay amongst the bruised fern, with the wild-rose brambles and blossoms above him. He knew that his life was done; he knew that for him all interest in this earth and its creatures had ceased for ever; and a perfect calm came down upon him. He was like a man who had possessed a great fortune, and had been perpetually tormented by doubts and perplexities about it, and who, waking one morning to discover himself a beggar, found a strange relief in the knowledge that he was penniless. The struggle was all over. No longer could the tempter whisper in his ear, urging him to follow this or that wandering exhalation of the world's foul marsh-lands. No more for him irresolution or perplexity. The problem of life was solved; a new and unexpected way was opened for him out of the blank weariness which men call existence. At first the thought of his approaching release brought with it no feeling but a sense of relief. It was only afterwards, when the new aspect of things became familiar to him, that he began to think with remorseful pain of all the empty life that lay behind him. He seemed to be thinking of this even when Isabel was with him; for after lying for some time quite silent,—in a doze, as they thought who watched him,—he raised his heavy eyelids, and said to her,

'If ever you should find yourself with the means of doing great good, of being very useful to your fellow-creatures, I should like you to remember my wasted life, Isabel. You will try to be patient, won't you, my dear? You will not think, because you are baulked in your first pet scheme for the regeneration of mankind, that you are free to wash your hands of the business, and stand aloof shrugging your shoulders at other people's endeavours. Ten years ago I fancied myself a philanthropist; but I was like a child who plants an acorn over-night, and expects to see the tender leaflets of a sapling-oak sprouting through the brown earth next morning. I wanted to do great things all at once. My courage failed before the battle had well begun. But I want you to be different from me, my dear. You were wiser than I when you left me that day; when you left me to my foolish anger, my sinful despair. Our love *was* too pure to have survived the stain of treachery and guilt. It would have perished like some beautiful flame that expires in a tainted atmosphere. Impure love may flourish in a poisoned habitation; but the true god sickens and dies if you shut him from the free air of heaven. I know now that we should not have been happy, Isabel; and I acknowledge the mysterious wisdom that has saved us. My darling, do not look at me with those despairing eyes; death will unite us rather than separate us, Isabel. I should have been farther away from you if I had lived; for I was tired of my life. I was like a spoilt child, who has possessed all the toys ever devised by mortal toymaker, and has played with them all, and grown weary of them, and broken them. Only his nurses know what an abomination that child is. I might have become a very bad man if I had lived, Isabel. As it is, I begin to understand what Tennyson means. [I used to read him only in a critic's cynical spirit, or rather in the narrow-minded spirit of that literary Janus,* who is himself an author, and pretends to possess the disinterestedness necessary to criticise the writings of other people, while he only disguises his malice and jealousy under the mantle of affectedly-impartial criticism. I used to steal Tennyson's metres and pretty tricks of style, and twist them into my own pitiful mulings; and now, only now, I begin to understand how much more than a poet he is.]* He has written the gospel of his age, Isabel. He has told me what I am: "an infant crying in the night; an infant crying for the light; and with no language but a cry." '*

These were the last words that Roland Lansdell ever spoke to the Doctor's Wife. He fell back into the same half-slumber from which he had awakened to talk to her; and some one—she scarcely knew who it was—led her out of the sick chamber, and a little way along the corridor into another room, where the Venetian shutters were half open, and there was sunshine and splendour.

Then, as if in a dream, she found herself lying on a bed; a bed that seemed softer than the billows of the sea, and around which there were curtains of pale green silk and shadowy muslin, and a faint odour like incense hovering about every thing. As in a dream, Isabel saw Lady Gwendoline and the nurse bending over her; and then one of them told her to go to sleep; she must want rest; she had been sorely tried lately.

'You are among friends,' the soft patrician voice murmured. 'I know that I wronged you very much, poor child; but I have promised *him* that I will be your friend.'

The soft curtains fell with a rustling noise between Isabel and the light, and she knew that she was alone; but still the dream-like feeling held her senses as in a spell. Does not simple, practical Sir Walter Scott, writing of the time of his wife's burial, tell us that it was all like a dream to him; he could not comprehend or lay hold of the dread reality? And is it any wonder, therefore, if to this romantic girl the calamity that had so suddenly befallen her seemed like a dream? He was dying! every one said that it was so; he himself spoke of his death calmly as a settled thing; and no one gainsayed him. And yet she could not believe in the cruel truth. Was he not there, talking to her and advising her? his intellect unclouded as when he had taught her how to criticise her favourite poets in the bright summer-days that were gone. No, a thousand times no; she would *not* believe that he was to die. Like all people who have enjoyed a very close acquaintance with poverty, she had an exaggerated idea of the power of wealth. Those great physicians, summoned from Savile Row,* and holding solemn conclave in the library,—they would surely save him; they would fan that feeble flame back into new life. What was medical science worth, if it was powerless to save this one sick man? And then the prayers which had seemed cold and lifeless on her lips when she had supplicated for George Gilbert's restoration took a new colour, and were as if inspired.

She pushed aside the curtains and got up from the bed where they had told her to sleep. She went to the door and opened it a little way; but there was no sound to be heard in the long corridor where the portraits of dead-and-gone-Lansdells—all seeming to her more or less like him—looked sadly down from the wainscot. A flood of hot sunshine poured into the room, but she had no definite idea of the hour. She had lost all count of time since the sudden shock of her husband's death; and she did not even know the day of the week. She only knew that the world seemed to have come to an end, and that it was very hard to be left alone in a deserted universe.

For a long time she knelt by the bedside praying that Roland Lansdell might live—only that he might live. She would be contented and happy, she thought, to know that all the world lay between her and him, if she could only know that he lived. There was no vestige of any selfish desire in her mind. Childishly, ignorantly, as a child might supplicate for the life of its mother, did this girl pray for the recovery of Roland Lansdell. No thought of her new freedom, no foreshadowing of what might happen if he could be restored to health, disturbed the simple fervour of her prayers. She only wanted him to live.

The sun sloped westward, and still shone upon that kneeling figure. Perhaps Isabel had a vague notion that the length of her prayers might prevail. They were very rambling, unorthodox petitions. It is not every mourner who can cry, 'Thy will be done.'

Pitiful and weak and foolish are some of the lamentations that rise to the Eternal Throne.

At last, when Isabel had been some hours alone and undisturbed in that sunlit chamber, an eager yearning to see Roland Lansdell once more came upon her,—to see him, or at least to hear tidings of him; to hear that a happy change had come about; that he was sleeping peacefully, wrapt in a placid slumber that gave promise of recovery. Ah, what unspeakable delight it would be to hear something like this! And sick men had been spared before to-day.

Her heart thrilled with a sudden rapture of hope. She went to the door and opened it, and then stood upon the threshold listening. All was silent as it had been before. No sound of footsteps, no murmur of voices, penetrated the massive old walls. There was no passing servant in the corridor whom she could question as to Mr Lansdell's state. She waited with faint hope that Lady Gwendoline or the sick-nurse might come out of Roland's room; but she waited in vain. The western sunlight shining redly through a lantern in the roof of the corridor illumined the sombre faces of the dead Lansdells with a factitious glow of life and colour; pensive faces, darkly earnest faces— all with some look of the man who was lying in the chamber yonder. The stillness of that long corridor seemed to freeze Isabel's childish hopes. The flapping of a linen blind outside the lantern sounded like the fluttering of a sail at sea; but inside the house there was not so much as a breath or a whisper.

The stillness and the suspense grew unendurable. The Doctor's Wife moved away from the door, and crept nearer and nearer the dark oaken door at the end of the corridor—the ponderous barrier that shut her from Roland Lansdell. She dared not knock at that door, lest the sound should disturb *him*. Some one must surely come out into the corridor before long,—Mr Raymond, or Lady Gwendoline, or the nurse,—some one who could give her hope and comfort.

She went towards the door, and suddenly saw that the door of the next room was ajar. From this room came the low murmur of voices; and Isabel remembered all at once that she had seen an apartment opening out of that in which Roland Lansdell lay—a large pleasant-looking chamber, with a high oaken mantel-piece, above which she had seen the glimmer of guns and pistols, and a picture of a horse.

She went into this room. It was empty, and the murmur of voices came from the adjoining chamber. The door between the two rooms was open, and she heard something more than voices. There was the sound of low convulsive sobbing; very subdued, but very terrible to hear. She could not see the sick man, for there was a little group about his bed, a group of bending figures, that made a screen between her and him. She saw Lady Gwendoline on her knees at the bottom of the bed, with her face buried in the silken coverlet, and her arms thrown up above her head; but in the next moment Charles Raymond saw her, and came to her. He closed the door softly behind him and shut out that group of bending figures. She would have spoken; but he lifted his hand with a solemn gesture.

'Come away, my dear,' he said softly. 'Come with me, Isabel.'

'Oh, let me see him! let me speak to him! Only once more—only once!'

'Never again, Isabel,—never upon this earth any more! You must think of him as something infinitely better and brighter than you ever knew him here. I never saw such a smile upon a human face as I saw just now on his.'

She had no need of any plainer words to tell her he was dead. She felt the ground reel suddenly beneath her feet, and saw the gradual rising of a misty darkness that shut out the world, and closed about her like the silent waters through which a drowning man goes down to death.

CHAPTER THE LAST

'IF ANY CALM, A CALM DESPAIR'*

Lady Gwendoline kept her promise. What promises are so sacred as those that are made to the dying, and which become solemn engagements binding us to the dead—the dead whom we have wronged, most likely; for who is there amongst us who does not do some wrong to the creature he most tenderly loves? Gwendoline Pomphrey repented her jealous anger against her cousin; she bitterly lamented those occasions upon which she had felt a miserable joy in the probing of his wounds. She looked back, now that the blindness of passion had passed away with the passing of the dead, and saw herself as she had really been—unchristian, intolerant, possessed by a jealous anger, which she had hidden under the useful womanly mask of outraged propriety. It was not Roland's sin that had stung her proud spirit to the quick: it was her love for the sinner that had been outraged by his devotion to another woman.

She never knew that she had sent the man she loved to his death. Inflexible to the last, Roland Lansdell had kept the secret of that fatal meeting in Nessborough Hollow. The man who had caused his death was Isabel's father. If Roland had been vindictively disposed towards his enemy, he would, for her sake, have freely let him go: but no very vengeful impulse had stirred the failing pulses of his heart. He was scarcely angry with Jack the Scribe; but rather recognised in what had occurred the working of a strange fatality, or the execution of a divine judgment.

'I was ready to defy heaven and earth for the sake of this girl,' he thought. 'I fancied it was an easy thing for a man to make his own scheme of life, and be happy after his own fashion. It was well that I should be made to understand my position in the universe. Mr Sleaford was only a brutal kind of Nemesis waiting for me at the bottom of the hill. If I had tried to clamber upwards,—if I had buckled on my armour, and gone away from this castle of indolence, to fight in the ranks of my fellow-men,—I need never have met the avenger. Let him go, then. He has only done his appointed work; and I, who made so pitiful a use of my life, have small ground for complaint against the man who has shortened it by a year or two.'

Thus it was that Mr Sleaford went his own way. In spite of that murderous threat uttered by him in the Old Bailey dock, in spite of the savage violence of his attack upon Roland Lansdell, he had not perhaps meant to kill his enemy. In his own way of expressing it, he had not meant to go too far. There is a wide gulf between the signing of other people's names, or the putting an additional *y* after the word *eight*, and an unauthorised O after the numeral on the face of a cheque—there is an awful distance between such illegal accomplishments and an act of deliberate homicide. Mr Sleaford had only intended to 'punish' the 'languid swell' who had borne witness against him; to spoil his beauty for the time being; and, in short, to give him just cause for remembering that little amateur-detective business by which he had beguiled the elegant idleness of his life. Isabel's father had scarcely intended to do more than this. But when you beat a man about the head with a loaded bludgeon, it is not so very easy to draw the line of demarcation between an assault and a murder; and Mr Sleaford did go a little too far: as he learned a few days afterwards, when he read in the *Times* supplement an intimation of the sudden death of Roland Lansdell, Esq., of Mordred Priory, Midlandshire.

The strong man, reading this announcement in the parlour of a low public-house in one of the most obscure purlieus of Lambeth, felt an icy sensation of fear that he had never experienced before admidst all the little difficulties attendant upon the forging of negotiable autographs. *This* was something more than he had bargained for. This Midlandshire business was murder, or something so nearly resembling that last and worst of crimes, that a stupid jury might fail to recognise the distinction. Jack the Scribe, armed with Roland Lansdell's fifty pounds, had already organised a plan of operations which was likely to result in a very comfortable little income, without involving any thing so disagreeable to the feelings of a gentleman as the illegal use of other people's names. It was to the science of money-lending that Mr Sleaford had turned his attention; and during the enforced retirement of the last few years he had woven for himself a very neat little system, by which a great deal of interest, in the shape of inquiry-fees and preliminary postage-stamps, could be extorted out of simple-minded borrowers without any expenditure in the way of principal on the part of the lender. With a view to the worthy carrying out of this little scheme, Mr Sleaford had made an appointment with one of his old associates, who appeared to him a likely person to act as clerk or underling, and to double that character with the more dignified *rôle* of solicitor to the MUTUAL AND COÖPERATIVE FRIEND-IN-NEED AND FRIEND-INDEED SOCIETY; but after reading that dismal paragraph respecting Mr Lansdell in the supplement of the *Times*, Jack the Scribe's ideas underwent a considerable change. It might be that this big pleasant metropolis, in which there is always such a nice little crop of dupes and simpletons ready to fall prone beneath the sickle of the judicious husbandman, would become, in vulgar parlance, a little too hot to hold Mr Sleaford. The contemplation of this unpleasant possibility led that gentleman's thoughts away to fairer and more distant scenes. He had a capital of fifty pounds in his pocket. With such a sum for his fulcrum, Jack the Scribe felt himself capable of astonishing—not to say uprooting—the universe; and if an indiscreet use of his bludgeon had rendered it unadvisable for him to remain in his native land, there were plenty of opportunities in the United States of America for a man of his genius. In America—on the 'other side,' as he had heard his Transatlantic friends designate their country—he might find an appropriate platform for the MUTUAL AND COÖPERATIVE FRIEND-IN-NEED AND FRIEND-INDEED SOCIETY. The genus dupe is cosmopolitan, and the Transatlantic Arcadian would be just as ready with his postage-stamps as the confiding denizen of Bermondsey or Camden Town. Already in his mind's eye Mr Sleaford beheld a flaming advertisement of his grand scheme slanting across the back page of a daily newspaper. Already he imagined himself thriving on the simplicity of the New-Yorkers; and departing, enriched and rejoicing, from that delightful city just as the Arcadians were beginning to be a little impatient about the conclusion of operations, and a little backward in the production of postage-stamps.

Having once decided upon the advisability of an early departure from England, Mr Sleaford lost no time in putting his plans into operation. He strolled out in the dusk of the evening, and made his way to some dingy lanes and water-side alleys in the neighbourhood of London Bridge. Here he obtained all information about speedily departing steam-vessels bound for New York; and early the following morning, burdened only with a carpet-bag and the smallest of portmanteaus, Jack the Scribe left Euston Square on his way to Liverpool, whence he departed, this time unhindered and unobserved, in the steam-vessel *Washington* bound for New York. And here he drops out of my story, as the avenging goddess might disappear from a classic stage when her work was done. For him too a Nemesis waits, lurking darkly in some hidden turning of the sinuous way along which a scoundrel walks.

'If any calm, a calm despair.' Such a calm fell at last upon Isabel Gilbert; but it was slow to come. For a long time it seemed to her as if a dreadful darkness obscured all the world; a darkness in which she groped blindly for a grave, where she might lie down and die. Was not *he* dead? What was there left in all the universe now that he was gone?

Happily for the sufferer there is attendant upon all great mental anguish a kind of numbness, a stupefaction of the senses, which in some manner deadens the sharpness of the torture. For a long time

Isabel could not think of what had happened within the last few troubled weeks. She could only sit helpless and tearless in the little parlour at Graybridge while the funeral preparations went quietly on about her, and while Mrs Jeffson and the young woman, who went out to work at eighteenpence a-day, came in every now and then to arouse her from her dull stupor for the trying-on of mourning garments which smelt of dye and size, and left black marks upon her neck and arms. She heard the horrible snipping of crape and bombazine going on all day, like the monotonous accompaniment of a nightmare; and sometimes when the door had been left ajar, she heard people talking in the opposite room. She heard them talking in stealthy murmurs of the two funerals which were to take place on successive days—one at Graybridge, one at Mordred. She heard them speculate respecting Mr Lansdell's disposal of his wealth; she heard the name, the dear romantic name, that was to be nothing henceforward but an empty sound, bandied from lip to lip; and all this pain was only some portion of the hideous dream which bound her night and day.

People were very kind to her. Even Graybridge took pity upon her youth and desolation; though every pang of her foolish heart was the subject of tea-table speculation. But the accomplished slanderer is not always a malevolently disposed person. He is only like the wit, who loves his jest better than his friend; but who will yet do his friend good service in the day of need. The Misses Pawlkatt, and many other young ladies of standing in Graybridge, wrote Isabel pretty little notes of condolence, interlarded with quotations from Scripture, and offered to go and 'sit with her.' To 'sit with her;' to beguile with their frivolous stereotype chatter the anguish of this poor stupefied creature, for whom all the universe seemed obscured by one impenetrable cloud.

It was on the second day after the surgeon's funeral, the day following that infinitely more stately ceremonial at Mordred church, that Mr Raymond came to see Isabel. He had been with her several times during the last few days; but he had found all attempts at consolation utterly in vain, and he, who had so carefully studied human nature, knew that it was wisest and kindest to let her alone. But on this occasion he came on a business errand; and he was accompanied by a grave-looking person, whom he introduced to Isabel as the late Mr Lansdell's solicitor.

'I have come to bring you strange news, Mrs Gilbert,' he said. 'News that cannot fail to be very startling to you.'

She looked up at Charles Raymond with a sad smile, whose meaning he was not slow to interpret. It said so plainly, 'Do you think any thing that can happen henceforward upon this earth could ever seem strange to me?'

'When you were with—him—on the last day of his life, Isabel,' Mr Raymond continued, 'he talked to you very seriously. He changed—changed wonderfully with the near approach of death. It seemed as if the last ten years had been blotted away, and he was a young man again, just entering life, full of noble yearnings and aspirations. I pray God those ten idle years may never be counted against him. He spoke to you very earnestly, my dear; and he urged you, if ever great opportunities were given you, which they might be, to use them faithfully for his sake. I heard him say this, and was at a loss to understand his full meaning. I comprehend it perfectly now.'

He paused; but Isabel did not even look up at him. The tears were slowly pouring down her colourless cheeks. She was thinking of that last day at Mordred; and Roland's tenderly-earnest voice seemed still sounding in her ears.

'Isabel, a great charge has been intrusted to you. Mr Lansdell has left you the bulk of his fortune.'

It is certain that Mr Raymond expected some cry of surprise, some token of astonishment, to follow this announcement; but Isabel's tears only flowed a little faster, and her head sank forward on the sofa-cushion by her side.

'Had you any idea that Roland intended to leave his money in this manner?'

'Oh, no, no! I don't want the money; I can do nothing with it. Oh, give it to some hospital, please; and let the hospital be called by his name. It was cruel of him to think that I should care for money when he was dead.'

'I have reason to believe that this will was made under very peculiar circumstances,' Mr Raymond said presently; 'when Roland was labouring under a delusion about you—a delusion which you yourself afterwards dispelled. Mr Lansdell's solicitor fully under-stands this; Lord Ruysdale and his daughter also understand it; and no possible discredit can attach to you from the inheritance of this fortune. Had Roland lived, he might very possibly have made some alteration and modifications of this will. As it stands, it is as good a will as any ever proved at Doctors' Commons.* You are a very rich woman, Isabel. Lady Gwendoline, her father, and myself are all legatees to a considerable amount; but Mordred Priory and the bulk of the Lansdell property are left to you.'

And then Mr Raymond went on to explain the nature of the will, which left every thing to himself and Mr Meredith (the London solicitor) as trustees, for the separate use and maintenance of Isabel Gilbert, and a great deal more, which had no significance for the dull indifferent ears of the mourner. There had been a time when Mrs Gilbert would have thought it a grand thing to be rich, and would have immediately imagined a life spent in ruby-velvet and diamonds; but that time was past. The blessings we sigh for are very apt to come to us too late; like that pension the tidings of which came to the poet as he lay upon his deathbed.

Mordred Priory became the property of Isabel Gilbert; and for a time all that Shakesperian region of Midlandshire had enough to employ them in the discussion of Mr Lansdell's will. But even the voice of slander was hushed when Mrs Gilbert left England in the company of Lord Ruysdale and his daughter for a lengthened sojourn on the Continent. I quote here from the *Wareham Gazette*, which found Isabel's proceedings worthy of record since her inheritance of Mr Lansdell's property.

Lady Gwendoline had promised to be the friend of Isabel; and she kept her word. There was no bitterness in her heart now; and perhaps she liked George Gilbert's widow all the better on account of that foolish wasted love that made a kind of link between them.

Lord Ruysdale's daughter was not the sort of woman to feel any base envy of Mrs Gilbert's fortune. The Earl had been very slow to understand the motives of his kinsman's will; but as he and his daughter received a legacy of ten thousand pounds apiece, to say nothing of sundry old Cromwellian tankards, and Queen-Anne tea-pots fashioned by Paul Lemeri,* old-fashioned brooches and brace-lets in rose-diamonds, a famous pearl-necklace that had belonged to Lady Anna Lansdell, a Murillo and a Rembrandt, and nineteen dozen of Madeira that connoisseurs considered unique, Lord Ruysdale could scarcely esteem himself ill-treated by his late nephew.

So Mrs Gilbert was permitted to possess her new wealth in peace, protected from all scandal by the Ruysdale influence. She was permitted to be at peace; and she went away with Lady Gwendoline and the Earl to those fair foreign lands for which she had pined in the weedy garden at Camberwell. Even during the first bitterness of her sorrow she was not utterly selfish. She sent money to Mrs Sleaford and the boys—money which seemed enormous wealth to them; and she instructed her solicitor to send them quarterly instalments of an income which would enable her half-brothers to receive a liberal education.

'I have had a great sorrow,' she wrote to her stepmother, 'and I am going away with people who are very kind to me; not to forget— I would not for the world find forgetfulness, if such a thing was to be found; only that I may learn to bear my sorrow and to be good. When I come back, I shall be glad to see you and my brothers.'

She wrote this, and a good deal more that was kind and dutiful, to poor Mrs Sleaford, who had changed that tainted name to Single-ton, in the peaceful retirement of Jersey; and then she went away, and was taken to many beautiful cities, over all of which there seemed to hang a kind of mist that shut out the sunshine. It was only when Roland Lansdell had been dead more than two years, that she began to understand that no grief, however bitter, can entirely obscure the beauty of the universe. She began to feel that there is something left in life even when a first romantic love is nothing but a memory; a peace which is so nearly akin to happiness, that we scarcely regret the flight of the brighter spirit; a calm which lies beyond the regions of despair, and which is unruffled by those vague fears, those shadowy forebodings, that are apt to trouble the joyful heart.

And now it seems to me that I have little more to do with Isabel Gilbert. She passes away from me into a higher region than that in which my story has lain,—useful, serene, almost happy, but very constant to the memory of sorrow,—she is altogether different from the foolish wife who neglected all a wife's duties while she sat by the mill-stream at Thurston's Crag reading the 'Revolt of Islam.' There is a great gulf between a girl of nineteen and a woman of five-and-twenty; and Isabel's foolish youth is separated from her wiser wom-anhood by a barrier that is formed by two graves. Is it strange, then, that the chastening influence of sorrow has transformed a sentimental girl into a good and noble woman—a woman in whom sentiment takes the higher form of universal sympathy and tenderness? She has faithfully employed the trust confided to her. The money bequeathed to her by the ardent lover, who fancied that he had won the woman of his choice, and that his sole duty was to protect her from worldly loss or trouble,—the fortune bequeathed under such strange circumstances has become a sacred trust, to be accounted for to the dead. Only the mourner knows the exquisite happiness involved in any act performed for the sake of the lost. Our Protestant creed, which will not permit us to pray for our dead, cannot forbid the consecration of our good works to those departed and beloved creatures.

Charles Raymond transferred to Isabel something of that affection which he had felt for Roland Lansdell; and he and the orphans, grown into estimable young persons of sixteen and seventeen, spent a great deal of their time at Mordred Priory. The agricultural labourer, who had known the Doctor's Wife only as a pale-faced girlish creature, sitting under the shelter of a hedgerow, with a green parasol above her head, and a book in her lap, had good reason to bless the Doctor's Widow; for model cottages arose in many a pleasant corner of the estate that had once been Roland Lansdell's— pretty Elizabethan cottages, with peaked gables and dormer windows, and wonderful ovens, that would cook a maximum of provision by the aid of a minimum of fuel. Allotment gardens spread themselves here and there on pleasant slopes; and coming suddenly upon some woody hollow, you generally found yourself face to face with the Tudor windows of a schoolhouse, a substantial modern building, set in an old-world garden, where there were great gnarled pear-trees, and a cluster of beehives in a bowery corner, sheltered by bushes of elder and hazel. [Even the dreaded innovation of steam-ploughs and threshing-machines brought no discontent to the farmers round Mordred.]*

Sigismund Smith appeared sometimes at Mordred Priory, always accompanied by a bloated and dilapidated leathern writing-case, unnaturally distended by stuff which he calls 'copy,' and other stuff which he speaks of as 'proofs.'

Telegrams from infuriated proprietors of penny journals pursue him in his calm retreat, and a lively gentleman in a white hat has been known to arrive per express-train, vaguely declaring his intention of 'standing over' Mr Smith during the production of an urgently-required chapter of *The Bride of the Bosphorus; or, the Fourteen Corpses of the Caspian Sea.*

He is very happy and very inky; and the rustic wanderers who meet a pale-faced and mild-looking gentleman loitering in the green lanes about Mordred, with his hat upon the back of his head, and his insipid blue eyes fixed on vacancy, would be slow to perceive in him the deliberate contriver of one of the most atrocious and cold-blooded schemes of vengeance that ever outraged the common dictates of human nature and adorned the richly-illustrated pages of a penny periodical. Amongst the wild-roses and new-mown hay of Midlandshire, Mr Smith finds it sweet to lie at ease, weaving the dark webs of crime which he subsequently works out upon paper in the dingy loneliness of his Temple chambers. He is still a bachelor, and complains that he is not the kind of man to fall in love, as he is compelled to avail himself of the noses and eyes, ruby lips, and golden or raven tresses—there are no other hues in Mr Smith's vocabulary—of every eligible young lady he meets, for the decking out of his numerous heroines. 'Miss Binks?' he will perhaps remark, when a lady's name is mentioned to him; 'oh, yes; *she's* Bella the Ballet-Girl (one of Bickers's touch-and-go romances; the first five numbers, and a magnificent engraving of one of Landseer's* best pictures, for a penny); I finished her off last week: she poisoned herself with insect-powder in a garret near Drury Lane, after setting fire to the house and grounds of her destroyer; she ran through a hundred and thirteen numbers, and Bickers has some idea of getting me to write a sequel. You see there *might* be an antidote to the insect-powder, or the oilman's shop-boy might have given Bella patent-mustard in mistake.'

But it has been observed of late that Mr Smith pays very special attention to the elder of the two orphans, whom he declares to be too good for penny numbers, and a charming subject for three volumes of the quiet and domestic school; and he has consulted Mr Raymond respecting the investment of his deposit-account, which is supposed to be something considerable; for a gentleman who lives chiefly upon bread-and-marmalade and weak tea may amass a very comfortable little independence from the cultivation of sensational literature in penny numbers.

EXPLANATORY NOTES

6 *St Bartholomew's*: St Bartholomew's Hospital, London, where medical students were trained.

7 *There are prisoners and prisoners . . . the fire of their own souls*: this passage is cut from the stereotyped edition (hereafter *SE*).

8 *a clarence-and-pair*: a closed four-wheel carriage with seats for four. Its name is a compliment to the Duke of Clarence (later William IV).

9 *Mr Gilbert's feet*: in *SE*, paragraph ends here.

11 *sensation author*: see the discussion of sensation fiction in the Introduction, pp. ix–xii.

13 *They had their own idea . . . private life*: this passage is cut from *SE*.

22 *blocks for the accommodation of many an imaginary Anne Boleyn and Marie Antoinette*: the second wife of Henry VIII of England and the wife of Louis XVI of France were both beheaded.

27 *She had been taught a smattering of every thing*: the ensuing critique of Isabel's inadequate education is repeated in numerous novels by women in the mid-nineteenth century. See, for example, George Eliot's comments on the education of Dorothea Brooke and Rosamund Vincy in *Middlemarch*.

28 *Bulwer*: Edward Bulwer-Lytton (1803–73), aristocrat, member of parliament, novelist and man of letters, with whom Braddon conducted an interesting correspondence (see Robert Lee Wolff, 'Devoted Disciple: The Letters of Mary Elizabeth Braddon to Sir Edward Bulwer-Lytton, 1862–1873', *Harvard Library Bulletin*, 22:1 (Jan. 1974), 1–35, and 22:2 (Apr. 1974), 129–61). Bulwer had several bestsellers early in his career, including *Pelham* (1828), an exploration of dandyism, and *Paul Clifford* (1830), the story of a gentleman highwayman and an example of the 'Newgate novel' (after the Newgate prison in London), a sub-genre of fiction depicting criminal low life. Isabel is an avid reader of Bulwer's novels, and his characters loom large in her private mythology.

Dickens: Charles Dickens (1812–70) dominated the fiction market in the mid-nineteenth century, with his own writings and through his editing of magazines such as *Household Words* (1850–9) and its successor *All the Year Round*. Several of his characters figure large in Isabel's fantasy life.

Thackeray: William Makepeace Thackeray (1811–63), another successful novelist whose characters people Isabel's private world.

John Brodie: John Browdie, a bluff Yorkshireman, the son of a corn-factor, in Charles Dickens's *Nicholas Nickleby* (1839).

Zanoni: (1842), a novel by Edward Bulwer-Lytton. Set in Italy, a Greek island, and revolutionary Paris, this novel tells the story of Zanoni, who is rumoured to possess the elixir of life and to have used it to prolong his own youthfulness. It is a tale of passion and the supernatural in which two men (Zanoni and a young Englishman, Clarence Glyndon) compete for the love of Viola Pisani (an opera singer) and for possession of Zanoni's secret. The novel ends with Zanoni sacrificing his immortality to save Viola.

28 *Lord Steyne*: a sharp-tongued and menacing aristocrat, and one of the several men whom Becky Sharp tries to manipulate in her attempt to make her way in Society in Thackeray's *Vanity Fair* (1848).

Hookee Walker: an early Victorian expression (origin unknown), used to indicate incredulity at a tall story or untrustworthy statement.

29 *Florence Dombey*: the heroine of Charles Dickens's *Dombey and Son* (1848). Deprived of her mother and brother Paul through their premature deaths, and coldly rejected by a father who is only interested in a male heir to carry on the family firm, Florence spends a lonely childhood and adolescence, alleviated only by her friendships with lower-class characters. Polly Toodle, the railwayman's wife who nurses her younger brother; Walter Gay, her father's employee, whom after much tribulation she eventually marries; Solomon Gills, Walter's uncle and a maker of nautical instruments, and his friend Captain Cuttle.

little Paul: Florence Dombey's brother, a sickly, strange, and preternaturally wise child, who seems to be constantly awaiting the early death which duly claims him in a highly wrought death scene.

Dombey: Mr Paul Dombey (the Dombey of Dickens's *Dombey and Son*) is only interested in a male heir, and denies his motherless daughter Florence the love she craves.

Augustine Caxton: the father of the narrator of Bulwer-Lytton's novel *The Caxtons: A Family Picture* (1849). Caxton the elder is constantly preoccupied with his great work in progress, a history of human error.

Rawdon Crawley: the slightly disreputable soldier son of Sir Pitt Crawley (who employs her as a governess), whom Becky Sharp ensnares into marriage in Thackeray's *Vanity Fair*. The circumstances of his marriage and his experience of fatherhood make Crawley a sadder and a wiser man before he dies a premature death of fever on Coventry Island, of which he has become governor.

Captain Cuttle: a retired sailor, 'very salt-looking man indeed' (ch.4), who befriends Florence Dombey in Dickens's *Dombey and Son*.

noble-hearted Walter: a sound-hearted young man, employed as a clerk by Dombey and Son. His love for Florence Dombey leads to his being sent off to the West Indies. He is presumed lost in a storm, but returns to claim Florence in marriage.

delirious Byron at Missolonghi: George Gordon, Lord Byron (1788–1824), author of many of Isabella's favourite poems. Byron left England in

1816, outraged by the hypocrisies of English Society. He led a colourful and peripatetic life, and died of a fever at Missolonghi in April 1824 after joining the Greek rebels in 1823.

The Girl with the Golden Eyes: *La Fille aux yeux d'or* (1834–5) by Honoré de Balzac, the third part of his *Histoire des treize* and one of the *Scènes de la vie Parisienne*. *La Fille* is a mystery story whose plot turns on the sensational disclosure that the two lovers of Paquita Valdes are in fact half-siblings, the daughter and son of the profligate Lord Dudley. It also offers an analysis of the materialism of contemporary Paris.

Ernest Maltravers: (1837), a novel by Edward Bulwer-Lytton. Together with its sequel, *Alice, or the Mysteries* (1838), *Maltravers* is a *Bildungsroman*, whose eponymous hero, a rich young student of Kantian philosophy, shelters with a criminal, Luke Darvil, when he becomes lost on the moors. He helps Darvil's beautiful daughter, Alice, escape, lodges her in an isolated cottage, and begins to educate her. After she has been se-duced by Maltravers, the pregnant Alice is seized by her father and taken to Ireland. In the following eighteen years Maltravers pursues his philosophical quest, and has numerous adventures and romances in a variety of European locations, before returning to England, where he becomes a member of parliament and is reunited with Alice (now Lady Vargrave).

Eugene Aram: (1832), a novel by Edward Bulwer-Lytton, based on a true story. Eugene is a guilt-ridden scholar who, prior to the novel's action, during a period of extreme poverty, had been an accomplice to a mur-der. His past catches up with him and he is denounced on his wedding day. He is sentenced to death and his bride dies of shock. The novel was condemned as immoral by several contemporary reviewers.

Bride of Lammermoor: (1819), a novel by Sir Walter Scott, third in the series *Tales of My Landlord*. A tale of star-crossed lovers in which Lord Ravenswood and Lucy Ashton fall in love despite a deep-seated enmity between their families. During Ravenswood's absence abroad Lucy's mother bullies and tricks her into marriage with Lord Bucklaw. Shortly after the marriage Lucy stabs her husband and dies insane. Ravenswood is swallowed up by quicksands as he rides to fight a duel with Lucy's brother and husband.

31 *like Edith Dombey in Mr Hablot Browne's grand picture*: Dickens's *Dombey and Son*, like many of his novels, was illustrated by Hablot K. Browne ('Phiz').

the Lancet: an important journal for the medical profession.

32 *the Great Exhibition*: since the story begins in 1852, this must refer to the Great Exhibition of 1851. 'The Great Exhibition of the Industry of All Nations' was held on a fourteen-acre site on the northern edge of Hyde Park in London.

36 *Prince Louis Napoleon . . . days of his exile*: Emperor Napoleon III (1808–73), was known as Louis Napoleon until he became emperor in 1852. In

the early 1830s, and after his failed invasion of France in 1836, he lived in London.

42 *hegira*: hijra or hejira, the flight of Mohammed from Mecca to Medina in AD 622 which inaugurated the Muslim era.

43 *An inexpressible melancholy . . . unalloyed regret*: this passage is cut from *SE*. It refers to the death of Thackeray in 1863.

44 *the Law-List*: an annual publication containing statistics connected with the legal profession.

45 *Heart of Midlothian*: (1818) a novel by Sir Walter Scott, second in the *Tales of My Landlord* series. The title refers to the popular name for the old Edinburgh Tollbooth or prison, and the plot links the story of the Porteous riot of 1736 to that of Jeannie and Effie Deans. The latter is sentenced to death for infanticide, and her sister walks to London to seek a pardon for her from Queen Caroline. Effie's story has a tragic nemesis when the child whom she had been falsely accused of murdering (but who had been stolen by a gypsy) kills his own father, the aristocrat who had married Effie following her reprieve.

Wandering Jew: a legendary Jew condemned to wander the world until Christ's second coming as a punishment for having insulted Christ as he bore his cross to Calvary. This legend appears in many literary works in the nineteenth century, including Eugène Sue's *Le Juif errant* (1844–5), and *Salathiel* (1839), a romance by George Croly.

46 *Jeannie Deans*: see note to p. 45, *Heart of Midlothian*, above. Jeannie is generally reckoned to be one of Scott's most vividly realized characters.

Papal Bull: an official letter or written instruction from the Pope.

Lollards: followers of John Wyclif (1320?–84), a religious reformer who attacked both the organization and the teachings of the papacy. Wyclif made an English translation of the Bible.

Caesar Borgia: Cesare Borgia (1476–1507), favourite son of Pope Alexander VI. An early advocate of Italian unity, and notoriously violent.

Ignatius Loyola: (1491–1556), dedicated himself Knight of the Blessed Virgin and undertook a pilgrimage to the Holy Land. On his return to Paris he founded the Jesuit order with its vows of chastity, poverty, and obedience. The Jesuits were staunch defenders and enforcers of Catholic orthodoxy against would-be reformers. Loyola is the author of *Spiritual Exercises*, a manual of devotion and rules for prayer and meditation.

47 *Box and Cox*: (1847) a farce by John Maddison Morton (1811–91).

Guilbert de Pixérécourt: Rene Charles Guilbert de Pixérécourt (1773–1844), prolific writer of stage melodramas in the 1830s. Translations of his work became an important part of the repertoire of the English melodramatic theatre in the nineteenth century.

48 *Racine or Corneille*: Jean Racine (1639–99) and Pierre Corneille (1606–99), major French dramatists and poets.

the Vicar of Wakefield: (1766) a novel by Oliver Goldsmith, which tells of the trials and tribulations (including bankruptcy, seduction, and abduction) of the family of the unworldly Reverend Dr Primrose. All ends happily.

50 *Sometimes he was honourable enough . . . welcome to people the place with fiends*: Robert Lee Wolff notes that Braddon here attributes one of her own habits to Smith. See Robert Lee Wolff, *Sensational Victorian: The Life and Fiction of Mary Elizabeth Braddon* (New York, 1979), 131.

53 *'love some bright peculiar star, and think to wed it'*: Shakespeare, *All's Well That Ends Well*, i. i. These words are spoken by Helena, who is expressing her unrequited love for the high-born Bertram: '. . . there is no living, none, | If Bertram be away. 'Twere all one | That I should love a bright particular star | And think to wed it, he is so above me.'

57 *Tilda Price's glorious sweetheart*: another reference to John Browdie in Dickens's *Nicholas Nickleby*. Tilda Price is the miller's daughter whom John marries. (See also note to p. 28.)

58 *I do not know . . . dazzled, and confounded*: this passage is cut from *SE*.

63 *the innocent Leporello*: Leporello is the servant of Don Giovanni in Mozart's opera.

66 *Mr George Combe*: (1788–1858), phrenologist, lecturer, and writer on phrenology (the study of the mental faculties, based on the theory that each separate mental faculty has its own organ and location in a particular region of the brain. Hence the shape of the cranium was thought to be a guide to the development of these organs and faculties).

Greenacre: James Greenacre (1785–1837), a manufacturer of 'amalgamated candy' for medical purposes who was hanged for wife-murder (he was married five times).

71 *Pinnock's pleasant abridgments of modern and ancient history*: William Henry Pinnock (1783–1843) was an educational writer and publisher who enjoyed great success with his abridgements of Goldsmith's *Histories of England, Greece and Rome*, and the *County Histories* series.

72 *Normans*: inhabitants of Normandy who 'Normanized' Britain first by dynastic marriages and then, in 1066, by conquest.

Plantagenet monarchs: English kings from Henry II (1133–89) to Richard II (1367–1400).

Mary Queen of Scots: (1542–87), daughter of James V of Scotland and Mary of Guise. Succeeded her father in 1542, and married Francis II of France in 1558, the year in which she laid claim to the English throne. She returned to Scotland in 1561, following Francis's death (1560), and was involved in much sexual and political intrigue. She married Henry Stewart, Earl of Darnley (1565), and was implicated in his death, after which she married her lover, the earl of Boswell (1567). She was executed in 1589.

72 *fair Princess Mary, Queen of France and wife of Thomas Brandon*: Mary of France (1496–1538), daughter of Henry VII and Elizabeth of York. Married first Louis XII and then, following his death, Charles (not Thomas) Brandon, Duke of Suffolk.

Heptarchy . . . Corday: the Heptarchy was the collective name for the seven English kingdoms that existed from the sixth to the ninth century. Charlotte Corday (1768–93) was an admirer of the writings of Jean-Jacques Rousseau, and a passionate advocate of liberty and republican ideals. Angered by the excesses of the French Revolution, she determined to end them by eliminating Marat, whom she stabbed in his bath on 13 July 1793.

young princes of the House of York . . . smothering business: Edward V (1470–83) and Richard, Duke of York (1472–83), sons of Edward IV. Murdered in the Tower of London on the orders of Richard III.

Henry Esmond: the hero of Thackeray's complexly plotted historical novel, *The History of Henry Esmond Esq., A Colonel in the Service of Her Majesty Queen Anne, Written by Himself* (1852). Henry's father's concealment of the true circumstances of his son's birth robs Henry of his aristocratic birthright, but he proves himself one of nature's aristocrats through his brave deeds and his chivalrous love for Rachel Esmond (the wife of the man who has inherited Henry's estates).

Steerforth: James Steerforth, the dashing, self-indulgent schoolfriend of Dickens's David Copperfield, who seduces Little Em'ly (the niece of David's old nurse, Peggotty) to whom David had introduced him.

Bill Sykes: criminal associate of Fagin in Dickens's *Oliver Twist* (1838), who murders Nancy, the prostitute who had befriended Oliver. This reference provides yet another example of the way in which Isabel romanticizes the plots of fiction and converts villains into heroes, rewriting Dickens's low-life villain into the Count Guillaume de Syques.

73 *ΑΝΑΓΚΗ*: the Greek word for fatality.

Beatrix: the daughter of Rachel Esmond, and sometime competitor with her mother for the affections of the hero of Thackeray's *Henry Esmond*. (See also note to p. 72.)

74 *Miss O'Neill*: Eliza O'Neill (1791–1872), an Irish actress whose roles included Juliet in *Romeo and Juliet* at Covent Garden in 1814 and Lady Teazle in Sheridan's *School for Scandal*. She gave up the stage following her marriage to William (later Sir William) Becher.

75 *Mrs Siddons*: Sarah Siddons (1755–1831), perhaps the most renowned tragic actress of the nineteenth century.

L.E.L.: Letitia Elizabeth Landon (1802–38), an extremely successful poet in her day. Landon wrote poems in which creative women (often orphans), rejected in love and by the world, dramatize their feelings.

78 *a Florence Nightingale, or a Madame de Laffarge*: Florence Nightingale (1820–1910) rebelled against the restrictions of the domestic existence of

the upper-middle-class woman and became famous for her nursing work in the Crimean War and as a reformer of the nursing profession. Madame Lafarge was given a life sentence with hard labour for the murder of her husband in 1840. (She was subsequently pardoned by Napoleon. She wrote two books protesting her innocence in 1841 and 1853.)

lure some recreant Carker . . . denounce and scorn him: in a dramatic scene in chapter 54 of Dickens's *Dombey and Son*, Edith Dombey spurns Carker, her husband's manager, who has ensnared her into going away with him. Like Isabel, Edith remains chaste despite appearances to the contrary, and against all the expectations of her would-be lover.

81 *Childe Harold*: *Childe Harold's Pilgrimage* (1812, 1816, and 1818), a poem by Byron which describes the reflections of a pilgrim who (rather like Lansdell) is sated with a life of revelry and seeks to distract himself from his world-weariness by travelling in distant lands.

Lara: Lara is Conrad, the hero of Byron's poem 'Lara'. He is a pirate chief who returns in disguise to his lands in Spain. Lara/Conrad is thought to embody Byron's own conception of himself. 'Lara' is a sequel to 'The Corsair'.

82 *Pierian waters*: Pieria, near Mount Olympus, is the home of the Muses.

83 *'Yes, poor little girl . . . they see*: cut from *SE*.

I daresay Beatrice . . . did make Benedick wretched: a reference to the sparring partners in Shakespeare's *Much Ado About Nothing*.

84 *Shakespeare's play and Monk Lewis's ballad!*: the references are to the heroine of Shakespeare's late romance *Cymbeline* and 'The Fair Imogine', a poem by Matthew Gregory Lewis (1775–1818), best known for his Gothic Novel *The Monk* (1796).

86 *the very ultima Thule of bliss*: cut from *SE*. Earlier versions have 'the very acme of bliss'. *Ultima Thule* means the highest or lowest limit, the uttermost point or degree attained or attainable. *Ultima* is the Latin word for final, last. Thule is the ancient Greek and Latin name (first found in Polybius' account of the voyage of Pytheas), for a land six days' sailing north of Britain, supposedly the most northerly region in the world.

88 *Did she love him? . . . very tolerable, after all*: cut from *SE*. The passage contains the novel's second reference to Hablot Browne's illustrations for Dickens's *Dombey and Son* (see note to p. 31). Isabel's curious imagining that her life would have been improved if only she had had a father to strike her and cast her off as Mr Dombey had Florence is yet another example of her overactive reading.

90 *Blondin*: Charles Blondin (Jean-François Gravelet, 1824–97), acrobat, high-wire walker, trapeze artist, and juggler, star of the London music-hall in the 1860s.

91 *Yankee levee*: a levee is an official morning reception at which dignitaries

receive visitors. From the eighteenth century Yankee was used to refer to New Englanders.

91 *Joseph and his Brethren*: refers to the biblical story of Joseph, whose father, Jacob, made him a coat of many colours. Joseph was hated by his brothers for being the best-loved son (see Gen. 37 ff.)

98 *Jane Eyre*: the spirited orphan heroine of Charlotte Brontë's novel of the same name (1847), who flees Thornfield Hall, the home of her erstwhile employer, Edward Rochester, when he confesses, on the day of their planned wedding, that he already has a wife. Jane faces starvation rather than compromise her love and her principles by living as Rochester's mistress.

Masaniello: (Tommas Aniello) a fisherman who led the revolt of the people of Naples against their Spanish rulers. After initial success the revolt was subdued and Aniello was assassinated. The story of the revolt appears in Daniel Auber's opera *La Muette de Portici* (1828).

102 *Shelley*: Percy Bysshe Shelley (1792–1822), a radical and a Romantic poet. Author of several of Isabel's favourite poems.

Cooper: James Fenimore Cooper (1789–1851), an American seaman who became a leading novelist. Best known for his 'Leatherstocking Tales', a series of novels (including *The Last of the Mohicans*, 1826) depicting the life of the early American Frontier.

Lever: the Irish novelist Charles Lever (1806–72), sometime physician and editor of the *Dublin University Magazine*. His prolific fictional output included military novels and tales of Irish life.

Edgar Ravenswood and Lucy: see note on *The Bride of Lammermoor*, p. 30.

103 *Zuleika*: the heroine of Byron's 'The Bride of Abydos' (1813). Zuleika, the daughter of Pasha Giaffir, is married against her will to Karasman, a rich ruler whom she has never met. She confides in her brother Selim, who reveals that he is, in fact, her cousin, whose own father has been murdered by Zuleika's father (Selim's father's brother). Selim asks Zuleika to share his life as a pirate, but he is struck down by her father. Zuleika dies of grief.

Amy Robsart: the heroine of Sir Walter Scott's *Kenilworth* (1821), another tale of a woman tricked into a secret marriage and the complications ensuing from this which result in the death of the much-misunderstood and suffering heroine.

Medora: a character in Byron's 'The Corsair' (1814), who dies of grief upon hearing of the supposed death of her beloved, the pirate chief Conrad.

wandering Jamie: it is possible that Braddon is misremembering Robert Burns's song 'Wandering Willie' (to the tune of 'The Bashful Lover'). This song tells how Willie 'wandering through the wood' comes upon the sleeping form of the 'blooming Nelly' 'Who for her favour he had sued'. Willie 'gaz'd, he wish'd | He fear'd, he blush'd | And trembl'd where he stood.' After gazing and trembling for three stanzas, Willie plucks up courage to kiss Nelly, and pursues her when she rushes off in fright: 'He vow'd, he pray'd | He found the maid | Forgiving all, and good.'

107 *all the houris in Mahomet's Paradise*: a houri is a nymph of the Muslim Paradise.

Mr Tennyson's King Arthur: Alfred Lord Tennyson (1809–92) wrote numerous poems on the mythical King Arthur and his court. The first four books of his Arthurian poem, *The Idylls of the King*, were published in 1859.

Mudie's: a lending or 'circulating' library, founded by Charles Edward Mudie in 1842. Borrowers paid an annual subscription to obtain books in person or by post.

108 *They had very little to say to each other . . . rides his own hobby-horse*: these three paragraphs on the awfulness of a marriage in which the husband and wife have nothing to say to each other are cut from *SE*.

110 *Mr Buckstone's bright Irish heroine*: a reference to one of the characters of John Baldwin Buckstone (1802–79), English actor, dramatist, and theatre manager who helped establish the fashion for domestic melodrama in the 1830s.

113 *'She only said, "My life is weary!"'*: a mis-quotation from Tennyson's poem 'Mariana' (1830), the lament of a woman (based on Mariana from Shakespeare's *Measure for Measure*) who forlornly awaits the arrival of a lover who does not appear. Tennyson's poem actually reads: 'She only said, "my life is dreary | He cometh not," she said; | She said, "I am aweary, aweary, | I would that I were dead."'

119 *a kind of indoor Cleopatra's galley*: cut from *SE*. A reference to Cleopatra's gilded barge as described by Enobarbus in Shakespeare's *Anthony and Cleopatra*, II. ii: 'The barge she sat in, like a burnished throne, | Burn'd on the water. The poop was beaten gold . . . | . . . She did lie in her pavilion, cloth-of-gold, of tissue, | O'erpicturing that Venus'.

the Row: Rotten Row, in Hyde Park, where fashionable Society rode.

125 *I have been at Hampton Court . . . as if people lived in them*: cut from *SE*.

Vandyke: Sir Anthony Van Dyck (1599–1641), Flemish artist, court painter to Charles I, best known for his portraits.

Gobelin tapestries: tapestries made in the Gobelins factory in Paris (or in the style of those made there).

Tintoretto: the Venetian painter Jacopo Robusti Tintoretto (1518–94).

126 *Lady Clara Vere de Vere*: the subject of Tennyson's poem 'Lady Clara Vere de Vere' (1842). The poem, addressed by a man to a heart-breaking aristocratic lady, portends developments in Braddon's plot and its scheme of values. The final stanza reads: 'Clara, Clara Vere de Vere, | If time be heavy on your hands, | Are there no beggars at your gate, | Nor any

poor about your lands? | Oh! teach the orphan-girl to sew, | Pray Heaven for a human heart, and let the foolish yeoman go.'

126 *Joanna of Naples*: a painting by Tintoretto.

Hood's haunted house: 'The Haunted House' is a poem by Thomas Hood (1799–1845).

127 *steam-farming*: farming with steam-driven implements.

128 *When Lord Dundreary declares . . . universal attribute of the mind*: this sentence is cut from *SE*. Lord Dundreary is a character in *Our American Cousin* (1858), a play by the successful dramatist Tom Taylor. Dundreary is an idle, brainless fellow with long drooping whiskers (a style of moustache later known as a Dundreary, or Dundreary whiskers).

129 *Alfred-de-Musset-ism*: Alfred de Musset (1810–57) was a French poet, dramatist, and writer of fiction, and lover of George Sand and (briefly) Louise Colet. His early verse was inclined to Byronic posturing. The poems written after the break-up with Sand dramatize the poet's sufferings.

130 *a mixture of Tennyson and Alfred de Musset*: volume versions add 'and Edgar Allan Poe' after Tennyson.

Balfe's music: Michael William Balfe (1808 –70) was a violinist, composer, and conductor of Italian opera.

131 *Murillo*: Bartolome Esteban Murillo (1617–82), Spanish painter of devotional subjects and genre scenes of street children.

133 *Look at Swift . . . in fiction*: refers first to three eighteenth-century satirists who published letters addressed to women: Jonathan Swift, who addressed the letters which make up his *Journal to Stella* to Esther Johnson; Laurence Sterne, who wrote a series of romantic letters to Eliza Draper (a married woman with whom he fell in love in 1766 when she was on a two-month leave from India); Sir Richard Steele, who published his letters to his second wife (Margaret Scurlock, 'Dear Prue') who for much of their marriage lived in Wales while her husband lived mainly in London. Byron's wife, Anna Isabella Milbanke, outraged by his conduct (including an incestuous affair with his half-sister Augusta), obtained a legal separation from him. Byron responded with poems such as 'Lines on Hearing that Lady Byron was Ill', which includes lines such as 'Thou hast sown in my sorrow and must reap | The bitter harvest in a woe as red'. The sentence on Steele is cut from *SE*.

as Astarte watched with Manfred: Manfred, the eponymous hero of Byron's poem, lives a life of remorse in the Alps, an outcast from society, wracked with guilt for 'some half-maddening sin' – an incestuous affair with his sister Astarte. The latter appears to him in a vision and foretells his imminent death.

Mrs Gamp: a comic character, given to drink and malapropisms, in Dickens's *Martin Chuzzlewit*.

134 *Ascot cups*: prize horse races held at Ascot in Berkshire and attended by fashionable society.

136 *like a modern Laocoon family without the serpents*: Book 2 of Virgil's *Aeneid* tells the story of the last days of Troy. Laocoon, a priest of Apollo, warns the Trojans against allowing into the city the wooden horse left by the Greeks (ostensibly as a gift to the goddess Minerva). Laocoon and his two sons were killed by two serpents which came from the sea.

138 *Chastelar*: Chastelard, a French nobleman who fell in love with Mary Queen of Scots and followed her to Scotland. He was executed after being found in her room.

Pamela: the heroine of Samuel Richardson's novel, *Pamela* (1740), who is pursued by her employer, Lord Booby. Having successfully evaded his attempts to seduce her, she becomes his wife.

Guido: Guido Reni (1574–1642), an artist who specialized in melodramatic and sentimental religious painting.

140 *'Oh, my cousin, shallow hearted'*: from Tennyson, *Locksley Hall*, lxxii.

vis inertiae: literally, the power of inactivity. Here a resistance to change.

141 *pour se distraire*: 'in order to amuse or distract himself'.

Mirabeau: Honoré Gabriel Riquetti, Comte de Mirabeau (1749–91), politician and orator in revolutionary France, an advocate of limited monarchy.

Life of Robespierre: published in 1848.

143 *the labour of Sisyphus*: Sisyphus, the legendary king of Corinth, who chained death in an attempt to avoid dying, was punished in the Underworld by being made to roll a heavy stone up a hill. The stone always rolled down just as he approached the top.

the toil of the daughters of Danäus: the fifty daughters of Danaus, king of Argos, were promised in marriage to the fifty sons of Aegyptus (their uncle). All except Hypermnestra fufilled their promise to their father to kill their husbands on their wedding night. Their punishment was to be sent to Hades where they were to fill a sieve with water.

Stuart Mill: probably John Stuart Mill (1806–73), philosopher, political reformer, and proto-feminist. The reference may be to James Stuart Mill (father of the above), a utilitarian and political economist.

Maculloch: (McCulloch in volume versions) it is unclear whether Braddon is referring to John Maculloch (1773–1835), sometime president of the Geological Society, or John Ramsay McCulloch (1798–1864), statistician, political economist, and author of an 'Essay on the Circumstances which determine the Rate of Wages and the Condition of the Labouring Classes' (1826).

144 *St Stephen's*: the location of the House of Commons in Westminster, London.

accepted the Chiltern Hundreds: an application for the Chiltern Hundreds is a device by which a sitting member of parliament resigns his seat.

151 *Watteau*: Jean-Antoine Watteau (1684–1721), one of the most important eighteenth-century French painters, particularly well known for his *fêtes-champêtres*, scenes of elegant leisure in a park setting.

151 *Raffaelle*: Raffaello Sanzio (1483–1520), Italian painter of portraits and devotional scenes, especially madonnas.

152 *Nemesis*: downfall caused by retributive justice.

153 *It was all weary . . . failure*: cut from SE.

   Alas for Roland . . . field: cut from SE.

154 *Sir Reginald Glanville*: a character in Bulwer-Lytton's *Pelham* (1828), who is falsely accused of a murder of which he is subsequently cleared by Henry Pelham's detective work.

155 *Edith Dombey in the grand Carker scene*: see note to p. 78 above.

   '*I'm very sorry that you are not well!*': *Othello*, III. iii.

   pleaded for Cassio: a reference to Desdemona's pleading with Othello (III. iii) on behalf of Cassio, the man with whom Iago falsely accuses her of betraying her husband.

156 *Ruth Pinch . . . John Westlock*: 'cheerful, tidy, bustling, quiet little Ruth', the domestic heroine of Dickens's *Martin Chuzzlewit*, with whom John Westlock (her brother Tom's erstwhile colleague) falls in love as she keeps house for Tom in picturesque poverty.

157 *Madame de Staël*: Anne-Louise Germaine (1766–1817), novelist, literary theorist, and political pamphleteerist. She moved in high political circles and had numerous love affairs.

   St Helena: the island to which Napoleon was exiled.

158 *Revolt of Islam*: (1818) a poem by Percy Bysshe Shelley. Originally titled *Laon and Cythna*, it was written after the fall of Napoleon had brought widespread misery to the poor. According to Shelley the poem illustrates 'the growth and progress of an individual mind aspiring after excellence and devoted to the love of mankind', and its 'impatience with all oppressions under the sun'. Cythna, committed to the liberation of her sex, allies herself with Laon to incite the people of Islam to rise up against their oppressors. After initial success the rebellion is put down and Laon and Cythna are burned at the stake.

159 *Giaour*: the hero of Byron's poem *The Giaour* (1813) which tells the story of Leila, a female slave who is cast into the sea as a punishment for unfaithfulness to her Turkish lord, Hassan. Her lover, the Giaour, avenges her by killing Hassan, and then retires to a monastery in grief and remorse.

160 *Shelley's own skylark*: a reference to Shelley's poem 'To a Skylark'.

167 *Leonidas*: king of Sparta, the hero of the defence of the pass at Thermopylae against the army of Xerxes (480 BC).

170 *Cuyp-like*: Aelbert Cuyp (1620–91), a Dutch landscape painter whose study of light influenced English artists.

172 *Rembrandt hues*: Rembrandt van Ryn (1606–69), Dutch painter and etcher generally considered to be a master of light and shade. He used vivid lighting effects and a glossy finish in many of his works.

fusee-boxes: boxes for large-headed matches.

buhl: wood inlaid with elaborate patterns of tortoiseshell, ivory, brass, etc.

marqueterie: decoration made with thin pieces of wood, ivory, metal, etc., fitted ,together to form a design on furniture.

filigree-work: ornamental work consisting of delicate tracery.

Chelsea . . . Palissy ware: all kinds of decorative china, porcelain or earthenware.

Vandevelde: it is unclear from the context to which of the Van de Veldes Braddon refers here, William the Elder (1611–93), William the Younger (1633–1707), or Adriaen (1636–72). All three were painters of ships and marine scenes. William the Younger was the best known and had a great influence on English marine painting. Adriaen painted landscapes and atmospheric beach scenes.

Fyt: Jan Fyt (1661–1), Flemish painter and etcher of hunting scenes, best known for his detailed and textured still lives of creatures killed in the hunt.

Greuze: Jean-Baptist Greuze (1725-1805), French painter of sentimental and moral genre scenes. Produced several titillating and suggestive paintings of apparently innocent young girls.

Spagnolettis: Jose or Juseppe de Ribera (1590–1652), nicknamed Spagnoletto (little Spaniard), painted a series of philosophers depicted as beggars or vagabonds. He employed a tenebrist style, using dark tonalities.

174 *Lance-like*: in the style of George Lance (1802–64), a painter of still life.

'such stuff as dreams are made of': from Prospero's speech in Shakespeare's *The Tempest*, IV. i. 'We are such stuff as dreams are made on, and our little life | Is rounded with a sleep.'

175 *the dew berries which Titania's attendants gave to Bottom*: in Shakespeare's *A Midsummer Night's Dream* Titania, queen of the fairies, becomes enamoured of Bottom (a 'rude mechanical' wearing an ass's head) after her eyes have been treated with a magic potion. She orders her attendants to 'Feed him with apricocks and dewberries | With purple grapes, green figs and mulberries'.

rout-cakes: rich cakes usually made for use at a reception or festivity (rout).

fricandeau: fried or stewed meat (usually veal) served with a sauce.

176 *Sterne's donkey*: presumably a reference to the dead ass whose passing is sentimentally lamented by one of the characters encountered by the narrator of Lawrence Sterne's *Sentimental Journey through France and Italy* (1768).

176 *Flodden*: site of a battle in 1513, in which James IV of Scotland was killed and his armies (despite their superior numbers) were defeated by the English.

Fontenoy: (1745) a battle in the war of the Austrian Succession, in which an army led by the Duke of Cumberland defeated a superior French force led by Marshall Saxe.

the Peninsular: the war fought against Napoleon in the Spanish–Portuguese Peninsula, 1808–14.

the 'Phaynix': Phoenix Park in Dublin.

180 *a diamond edition of the works of Thomas Moore*: a special edition of the works of the poet Thomas Moore (1779–1852), author of *Lalla Rookh* (1817).

184 *Zuleika, kneeling for ever at Selim's feet*: see note to p. 103.

Castor and Pollux: the twin sons of either Zeus and Leda, or Leda and her husband Tyndareus. They are represented in literature as both courageous mortals and as gods who protect sailors. Pollux was a noted boxer.

flâneur: an urbane stroller of the city streets.

185 *Carlyle's French Revolution*: *A History of the French Revolution* (1837) by Thomas Carlyle. A colourful and partial account of the dramatic events in France, beginning with the death of Louis XV and taking in the fall of the Bastille, the constituent and legislative assemblies, Louis XVI's flight to Varennes, and the trial and execution of the king and queen, through to Napoleon Buonaparte's subduing of the revolt of the Vendemiaire in 1795.

Lamartine's Girondists: the French poet Alphonse (Marie Louis) de Lamartine (1790–1869) became a member of the provisional government in the Revolution of 1848.

the chiefs of the Mountain and the martyrs of the Gironde: the Chiefs of the Mountain were the Montagnards, a group of Jacobin extremists known as the Mountain or the Left because they sat on the upper benches of the assembly to the left of the president. Many of them were executed in the Reign of Terror in 1793. The Girondists were a group of deputies from the Gironde serving in the legislative assembly of 1791–2 and the convention of 1792–5 who were sympathetic to provincial rather than Parisian government and aroused the hostility of Robespierre.

186 *the feast of St Partridge the martyr*: the game bird shooting season traditionally begins on 1 September.

188 *Horace Walpole's Inspired Idiocy*: Walpole (1717–97) made Strawberry Hill into a Gothic castle and established a printing press there. He is the author of the Gothic tale *The Castle of Otranto* (1764) and of *The Mysterious Mother* (1768), a tale of incest. His literary reputation rests mainly on his letters.

192 *Desdemona might have pleaded for him all day long*: another reference to Desdemona's pleading with Othello (III. iii) on behalf of Cassio.

196 *Bell's Life*: a well-known sporting journal which developed from Pierce Egan's *Life in London and Sporting Guide* (1824). *Bell's Life* was incorporated into *Sporting Life* in 1859.

the favourite for the Oaks: the horse best-fancied to win the Oaks, a race run at Epsom race course.

201 *Heaven knows . . . repented*: cut from *SE*.

202 *stuffy entresol chambers*: an entresol is a low storey placed between the ground floor and the first floor of a building (a mezzanine).

203 *John of Gaunt*: (1340–99), first Duke of Lancaster. Son of Edward III. England's greatest landowner and controller of a large army. Very influential in a turbulent time in English politics. His son seized the throne from Richard II and reigned as Henry IV.

Tudors: the Lancastrian ruling dynasty, founded by Henry VII. Its badge was the red rose.

210 *Marcus Curtius*: according to legend, after soothsayers had foretold that a chasm which had appeared in the Roman Forum could only be filled by Rome's greatest treasure, he leapt into it fully armed, claiming that arms and valour were the greatest treasures of Rome.

211 *Louise la Vallière*: the mistress of Louis XIV who bore him four children. When Louis took another mistress in 1667 she took refuge in a convent in order to avoid scandal. She subsequently embraced the spiritual life, retiring with the Carmelites to live a life of austerity and penitence.

212 *Marryat's phantom captain turned landsman*: a reference to *The Phantom Ship* (1839) a novel by Captain Frederick Marryat (1792–1848).

cabinet-picture: a picture 'of such beauty, value, or size, as to be fitted for a private chamber, or kept in a cabinet' (*OED*).

213 *Louis the Well-beloved*: Louis XV (1710–74), king of France 1715–74.

Ingénue at the Français: a player of female juvenile lead roles at the Comédie Français theatre.

217 *'Oceans should divide us'*: these words are spoken by Julia, the heroine of *The Hunchback* (1832), the most popular of the plays of James Sheridan Knowles (1784–1862). Julia was first played by Fanny Kemble and the role was extremely popular with nineteenth-century actresses. The words used by Braddon occur in an impassioned speech in IV. ii: 'In the same house with me, and I another's? | Put miles, put leagues between us. The same land should not contain us. | Oceans should divide us— | With barriers of constant tempests—such | As mariners durst not tempt! O Clifford! Rash was the act so light that gave me up, | That stung a woman's pride, and drove her mad— | Till in her frenzy she destroyed her peace!'

220 *T. R. D. L.*: the Theatre Royal, Drury Lane, in London.

222 *the miller's daughter on the banks of Allan Water*: it is possible that Braddon

is referring to Robert Burns's 'By Allan Stream I Chanc'd to Rove' (to the tune of 'Allan Water'), in which a lover sings of his bonnie Annie who pledges her eternal love for him: 'Her head upon my throbbing breast, | She, sinking, said: "I'm thine for ever! | While monie a kiss the seal imprest— | The sacred vow we ne'er should sever.' (There is nothing in Burns's poem to suggest that Annie is a miller's daughter.) Alternatively, this might be a reference to Edward Ball's play, *The Miller of Derwent Water* (1853).

223 *Hamlet's solemn question*: refers to Hamlet's famous soliloquy ('To be or not to be') in *Hamlet*, III. i.

224 *cerulean lights*: sky-blue or azure lights.

226 *I think . . . newspapers*: cut from *SE*.

Aristides: an Athenian general and statesman who was ostracized as a result of conflict with other leaders. The process of ostracism was decided by popular vote. Plutarch notes that when asked by Aristides (who was incognito) whether he had ever been harmed by the man on whose fate he was voting (i.e. Aristides) one such voter replied in the negative, adding that it vexed him to hear Aristides referred to as 'the just'.

Diogenes: a Greek philosopher of the fourth century BC. The chief proponent of the Cynic school of philosophy which held that happiness could derive only from virtue, and from renouncing conventional needs. He practised this philosophy by living in a tub.

Junius Brutus: Marcus Junius Brutus, a Roman Republican leader who helped to plan Julius Caesar's assassination in 44 BC.

227 *Ah, what a sweet . . . snubbed*: cut from *SE*.

228 *d'oyleys*: small ornamental mats used at dessert.

230 *the Corsair*: Conrad the pirate chief, hero of Byron's poem 'The Corsair' (1814).

'Once more the gate behind me falls': this is the first line of Tennyson's poem, 'The Talking Oak' (1842).

'dark and cold and dreary': another reference to Tennyson's poem 'Mariana'. See note to p. 113.

231 *the rules of Lindley Murray*: Lindley Murray was an American-born grammarian and author of a number of standard textbooks widely used in English schools in the nineteenth century: *the English Grammar* (1795), *Reader* (1799), and *Spelling Book* (1804).

232 *the national school*: a school run by a national school society such as the Church of England National Society. There was no fully state-run national system of education until Forster's Elementary Education Act of 1870.

'left a Corsair's name . . . crimes': the concluding lines of Byron's 'The Corsair'.

235 *young Caxton's . . . Life of Robert Hall*: a reference to Edward Bulwer-

Lytton's novel *The Caxtons: A Family Picture* (1849). Robert Hall (1764–1831) was a Baptist minister who created a sensation with his *Modern Infidelity considered with respect to its Influence on Society*.

236 *It is impossible . . . delightful books*: cut from *SE*.

240 *'My love's a noble madness'*: John Dryden, *All for Love* (1678), II. i.

241 *There is always 'mine ancient' . . . the delinquent*: a further reference to Shakespeare's *Othello*. Othello addresses the treacherous Iago with this term.

242 *C'est selon!*: it all depends.

243 *The British Gazetteer*: an alphabetically organized geographical guide to Britain.

244 *galère*: business.

He was not at all angry . . . lodgment?: cut from *SE*.

245 *Rousseau*: Jean-Jacques Rousseau (1712–78), French writer and philosopher who held that man was by nature virtuous, free, and happy, but was corrupted by the inequalities of a property-owning society.

Messrs Moxon: Edward Moxon (1801–58) set up as a publisher in 1817. Moxon published Southey, Wordsworth, Tennyson, and Browning.

247 *Friar Lawrence*: in Shakespeare's *Romeo and Juliet* Friar Lawrence counsels Romeo Montague against becoming involved with Juliet Capulet because of the feud between their families.

248 *Beatrice . . . Dante*: Beatrice was the name which Dante Alighieri (1265–1321) gave to the woman whom he celebrates in *Vita Nuova* and *Divina Commedia*.

Leonora . . . Tasso: Byron uses the story of the poet Torquato Tasso's love for Leonora d'Este in 'The Lament of Tasso'.

as vague as the showman's notion of the rival warriors at Waterloo: the narrator of Thackeray's *Vanity Fair* – part of which is set at the time of Waterloo – describes himself as a showman. Alternatively this may be a reference to the staging of some spectacular theatrical or dioramic re-enactment of a scene from the battle.

Is there not . . . delicious: cut from *SE*.

She could not . . . umbrageous branches: cut from *SE*.

249 *Hildegonde*: possibly a reference to Huldegund, the beloved of Walter of Spain, hero of the epics *Waltharius* and *Waldere*, and referred to in the *Nibelungenlied*.

250 *Raleigh*: Sir Walter Ralegh (*c*.1554–1618), poet, courtier, and explorer, and sometime favourite of Elizabeth I.

252 *Waller . . . Sacharissa*: Edmund Waller (1606–87) wrote a number of poems in praise of 'Sacharissa' (Lady Dorothy Sydney), whom he unsuccessfully wooed after the death of his first wife.

253 *Lumley Ferrers*: an unscrupulous character in Edward Bulwer-Lytton's

Ernest Maltravers (1837) and *Alice, or the Mysteries* (1838). After plotting against Ernest, he is finally murdered by his own henchman, Cesarini.

257 *Koh-i-noor*: a very large Indian diamond said to be 2,000 years old which became part of the English crown jewels in 1849 following the annexation of the Punjab.

258 *Queen Mab*: a reference to 'Queen Mab' (1813), a poem by Percy Bysshe Shelley in which the fairy queen shows Ianthe the past history of the world and discourses on its miserable state (attacking 'kings, priests, and statesmen') before revealing a better future in which (according to Shelley) 'all things are recreated, and the flame of consentaneous love inspires all life'.

Millais-like figure: a reference to the painting style of John Everett Millais (1829–1860), a member of the Pre-Raphaelite Brotherhood who painted romantic and literary subjects and genre scenes.

259 *pianissimo*: very softly.

261 *Helena . . . Bertram*: the central characters of Shakespeare's *All's Well That Ends Well*. Bertram is forced to marry Helena after she chooses him as her reward for curing the King of a dangerous illness. Immediately after the marriage Bertram deserts her to enlist to fight with the Duke of Florence, claiming that she may not call him husband until she obtains the ring from his finger and is with child by him. By a clever trick Helena achieves both of these feats, and a penitent Bertram accepts her as his wife.

Viola . . . Zanoni: a reference to Bulwer's novel. See note to p. 28.

262 *Beatrice Portinari . . . Viola . . . Leila . . . Gulnare Zelica*: Beatrice Portinari is Dante's Beatrice. Viola is (presumably) Viola Pisani, the heroine of Bulwer-Lytton's *Zanoni* (see note to p. 28); Leila is the murdered heroine whom Byron's Giaour avenges (see note to p. 159); in *SE* Medora, who dies of grief at the reported death of her lover, Conrad (in Byron's poem *The Corsair*), is substituted for Gulnare (also in love with Conrad), who slays his enemy, the Seyd (see note to p. 103); Zelica is the heroine of 'The Veiled Prophet of Khorassan', one of the oriental tales in Thomas Moore's 'Lalla Rookh' (1817). Half-crazed by the apparent death of her lover, Azim, Zelica is tricked into marrying Mokanna with promises that the marriage will gain her entry to Paradise. Azim returns to punish Mokanna, but mistakenly kills Zelica, who dies in his arms.

265 '*For love himself took part against himself*': from Alfred Tennyson's 'Love and Duty' (1842). Tennyson wrote this poem in 1840 when he broke off his engagement to Emily Sellwood because of financial difficulties and her family's opposition to the match. The line used here occurs in the following context 'For love himself took part against himself | To warn us off, and Duty loved of Love— | O this world's curse,—beloved but hated—came | Like Death betwixt thy dear embrace and mine, | And crying 'who is this?' behold thy bride, | She pushed me from thee.'

267 *Father Newman*: John Henry Newman (1801–90), Anglican priest and leading figure in the Anglo-Catholic Oxford Movement, who converted to Roman Catholicism and was received into the Church of Rome in 1845. His *Apologia pro Vita Sua* was published in the same year as *The Doctor's Wife*.

268 *the monk in Hugo's Notre Dame*: in Victor Hugo's *Notre-Dame de Paris* (1831), Claude Frollo, an archdeacon of the cathedral, employs Quasimodo (a hunchback he has befriended) to kidnap Esmeralda (a gypsy dancer with whom he is enamoured). Frollo subsequently stabs Esmeralda's rescuer, with whom she has fallen in love, and incriminates her. Frollo, in turn, is killed by Quasimodo as he (Frollo) watches Esmeralda's body hanging from the gallows.

Undine: in the fairy romance 'Undine' (1811) by Friedrich Baron de la Motte Fouque, Undine is a sylph who is brought up by a fisherman and his wife after their own daughter is lost and thought drowned. Undine marries Huldbrand (a knight), who subsequently becomes attached to Bertha, a haughty young woman who is in fact the fisherman's lost daughter. Huldbrand marries Bertha after Undine has been taken back into the sea by her angered fairy relatives, but he is subsequently killed by a kiss from Undine,who rises from the well.

271 *Tasso*: Torquato Tasso (1544–95), Italian poet, author of the epic *Gerusalemme Liberata*.

277 *Mr Longfellow's typical rivulet*: a reference to Henry Wadsworth Longfellow (1807–82). Longfellow's poetry, especially 'The Song of Hiawatha', is full of rivers which separate a land of innocence and plenty from a darker, drearier world.

heartless Faust . . . trusting Gretchen: against the promptings of his better self, and at the behest of the devil, Faust seduces Gretchen, who subsequently dies in the first part of Johann Wolfgang Goethe's *Faust*

Robert the Devil: the father of William the Conquerer and the subject of many legends connected with his violence and cruelty, including the mistreatment of his wife.

278 *Steerforth . . . simple Em'ly . . . noble Pegotty's broken heart*: see note to p. 72.

Surrey Theatre: in the mid-nineteenth century the Surrey Theatre (situated south of the Thames in Blackfriars Road, London) was famous for sensational melodrama and spectacular stage effects.

280 *grave Judge Brandon*: Richard Brandon, the executioner of Charles I and other Royalists.

scarlet letter: the letter A (for Adultery) which Hester Prynne is made to wear as a mark of her sin of bearing a child out of wedlock and refusing to name the father in Nathaniel Hawthorne's novel *The Scarlet Letter* (1850).

281 *The day had been . . . before her*: cut from *SE*.

281 *dioramic picture*: the diorama, invented by Daguerre and first exhibited in Paris in 1822, came to London in 1823. By looking down a long tunnel (of thirty or forty feet) at a large flat picture painted on opaque and translucent material, a seated audience was given an illusion of depth through the use of special lighting at front and back. It was particularly effective for producing landscape and crowd scenes in the theatre.

Henry von Kleist: Heinrich von Kleist (1777–1811), a German writer who led a restless and troubled life wandering Europe, beset (after his reading of Kant) by a sense of the futility of his goal of acquiring intellectual knowledge. On 21 November 1811 he committed suicide after shooting Henriette Vogel in response to her request to shorten her sufferings (she had an incurable disease).

282 *Benjamin Webster . . . Sarah Woolgar*: Webster (1797–1882), a member of a large theatrical family, was an actor, manager, and playwright. He took over the lease of the Haymarket in 1837 and the Adelphi in 1844, opening the New Adelphi in 1859. Sarah Jane Woolgar (Mrs Alfred Mello, 1824–1909) was an actress who made her debut at Webster's Adelphi in October 1843. She appeared in a number of adaptations of Dickens's novels and in the melodramatic repertoire.

the words of the poet: Braddon paraphrases Tennyson's *In Memoriam: A.H.H.* (1850): ' 'Tis better to have loved and lost | Than never to have loved at all' (Canto xxvii).

284 *Irving*: Sir Henry Irving (1838–1905), a noted actor and theatre manager.

285 *Mary Magdalene*: after Jesus cast out seven devils from her she accompanied him and the twelve disciples when they went 'preaching and shewing the glad tidings of the kingdom of God' (Luke 8).

Whitefield . . . the miners at Kingswood: George Whitfield (1714–70) was leader of the Calvinistic Methodists and a popular missionary preacher, who at various times preached among the working classes in Bristol and the West Country.

Danton: Jacques Danton (1759–94), French statesman of the revolutionary period. Member of the first Committee of Public Safety which was replaced by Robespierre's Grand Committee in 1793.

286 *Cromwell*: Oliver Cromwell (1599–1658) the Lord Protector, leader of the Parliamentarians against the Royalists.

John Law: (1671–1729) escaped from prison after being sentenced to death for killing 'Beau' Wilson in a duel. He fled to France, where he established the first French bank (1716). In 1719 his scheme to convert the French national debt failed, bringing widespread ruin.

Luther: Martin Luther (1483–1546), leader of the Reformation in Germany.

Wesley: John Wesley (1703–91), leader of Methodism and noted preacher.

Mr Austin Colborne . . . wiser: cut from *SE*.

should feel this influence, as she had felt others?: *SE* reads 'should be touched and melted by Mr Colborne's eloquence?'

287 *cab and tiger*: a one-horse carriage introduced into London in the nineteenth century and a liveried servant who rides with his master or mistress.

288 *'And now I live, and now my life is done!'*: from 'Elegy' composed by the English Roman Catholic conspirator, Chidiock Tichborne (*c*.1558–86) in the Tower of London as he awaited execution.

289 *Diana and Endymion*: Endymion was the shepherd with whom the goddess Diana became enamoured as she saw him sleeping on Mount Latmos. She caused him to sleep for ever so that she might always enjoy his beauty.

291 *Scarron . . . Rochefoucauld . . . Swift . . . Voltaire . . . Wilkes . . . Mirabeau*: all writers who at some point railed against women. Paul Scarron (1610–60), French burlesque poet, novelist, and dramatist, who also railed against the artificiality of contemporary literature; François, Duc de La Rochefoucauld (1613–80), French moralist and author of *Reflexions ou sentences et maximes morales* (1665)—a series of gnomic sentences analysing human motives, the chief of which he found to be egoism; Jonathan Swift (1667–1745), satirist and critic of human vanity and folly, Voltaire, pseudonym of François-Marie Arouet (1694–1778), philosopher, satirist, moralist, historian, dramatist, poet, and pamphleteer, author of *Candide* (1759), a satire on the optimism of Rousseau; John Wilkes (1727–97), politician, member of the Hell Fire club at Medmenham Abbey, who published the obscene *An Essay on Woman* (1764); Mirabeau, see note to p. 141.

292 *All manner of vague fashionable fancies . . . wife*: cut from *SE*.

odic force: C. F. von Reichenbach developed the theory of the 'odyle force' or 'od' to explain the flow of spiritual influence from the minds of telepathists, mediums, mesmerists, and clairvoyants (mesmerism and spiritualism were particularly in vogue in the 1850s and 1860s).

animal-magnetism: another theory associated with spiritualism and mesmerism.

295 *Christie and Manson*: a well-known London auctioning house.

Tokay: a sweet heavy wine from Tokay in Hungary.

296 *Pitt*: this reference could be to any one of several famous Pitts, but is most likely to William Pitt (1759–1806), who became chancellor in his twenty-second year and prime minister in his twenty-fifth.

298 *Peel*: Sir Robert Peel (1788–1850), reforming politician, member of parliament, founder of the Peace Preservation Police and of the modern Conservative party. Died of injuries sustained when thrown from his horse.

Palmerston: Henry John Temple, third Viscount Palmerston (1784–1865), had several periods of office as prime minister, and was still serving in that capacity when *The Doctor's Wife* was published.

298 *Wolfe*: James Wolfe (1727–59) rapidly rose to the rank of major-general but died young of battle wounds after leading his men in a successful attack on Quebec.

Wellington: Arthur Wellesley, first Duke of Wellington (1769–1852), led the troops who routed Napoleon at Waterloo. He was also a politician and statesman.

Emile Augier: (1820–89), a French dramatist who criticized both the bourgeois philistinism and the aristocratic arrogance of the Second Empire.

299 *Sterne's Sentimental Journey*: Laurence Sterne's *Sentimental Journey through France and Italy* (1768), in which the narrator meets with sentimental adventures and takes delight in everything he encounters, in contrast to the splenetic Smelfungus (based on the novelist Tobais Smollett) and Mundungus (based on Dr S. Sharp) whose travels left him 'without one generous connection or pleasurable anecdote'.

Dickens's Uncommercial Traveller: *The Uncommercial Traveller* (1860), a collection of tales and sketches of places and manners, in which Dickens depicted institutions in need of reform.

William Beckford's delicious blasé letters ... Vathek: William Beckford (1759–1854), who developed Fonthill Abbey as an elaborate Gothic fantasy, was the author of *Vathek* (1786), a fantastic oriental tale, and also of *Dreams, Waking Thoughts, and Incidents* (1783, revised 1834) and *Recollections of an Excursion to the Monasteries of Alcobaca and Batalha* (1835), a series of letters from various parts of Europe which demonstrate the author's powers of description and his ironic observation of life.

303 *It is all very well ... wrong*: cut from *SE*.

Launcelot: in Arthurian legend, medieval romance and Tennyson's poems, the most romantic of the Knights of the Round Table. He was the lover of Queen Guinevere, thus betraying King Arthur (her husband). His relations with Guinevere are strained by his involvement with Elaine, the Fair Maid of Astolot.

305 *Mr Nash to Goldsmith ... '... take no manner of notice of the lady'*: Richard (Beau) Nash (1674–1762) established the assembly rooms at Bath, served as master of ceremonies and drew up a code of dress and etiquette. The reference here is to Oliver Goldsmith's *The Life of Richard Nash* (1762): ' "The only way to make love now," I have heard Mr Nash say, was to take no manner of notice of the lady, which method was found the surest way to secure her affections.'

306 *the famous Spanish fleet in the Critic*: Richard Brinsley Sheridan's *The Critic, or a Tragedy Rehearsed* (produced in 1779) centres on a rehearsal of *The Spanish Armada*, an absurd, sentimental, and bombastic historical drama written by the critic Puff.

307 *Dora Spenlow*: the childlike wife of the eponymous hero of Dickens's *David Copperfield*.

respectable Samuel Rogers: Samuel Rogers (1763–1855) was a successful poet with a wide acquaintance in the literary world. *Recollections of the Table Talk of Samuel Rogers* was published in 1856.

delightful Lionel in Rosalind and Helen: Lionel is the persecuted husband of Helen in Shelley's poem 'Rosalind and Helen: a Modern Eclogue' (1819) Rosalind's history involves an incestuous love and a tyrannical father. Helen's family life is destroyed by the political persecution of her husband. The two women end up living together.

309 *Tillotson's sermons*: John Tillotson (1630–94), sometime archbishop of Canterbury, and the author of lucidly written and widely read sermons.

312 *Dr Robert James Graves*: (1796–1853), president of the Irish College of Physicians and author of *Clinical Lectures on the Practice of Medicine* (1848), which gained him a reputation in Europe.

316 *Squeers*: the schoolmaster in charge of the Yorkshire school—Dotheboys Hall—in which Nicholas suffers in Dickens's *Nicholas Nickleby* (1838–9).

321 *She thought . . . uplifted hand*: this sentence, which refers to famous affecting death scenes in Dickens's *Dombey and Son* and *David Copperfield*, is cut from *SE*.

Madame de Chantal . . . St Francis de Sales: Jeanne Françoise Fremyot (Barrone de Chantal, 1572–1641) met François de Sales (1567–1622) after she was widowed, and placed herself in his spiritual care. Under his direction she founded the female Order of the Visitation in Annecy. It is possible that these figures were in Braddon's mind at this time because of the relatively recent founding of the Salesian Society (in 1859). The Society of St Francis de Sales was dedicated to the Christian education of youth.

322 *Lucretia . . . Tarquin*: the beauty of Lucretia, wife of Tarquinius Collatinus, so captivated Sextus (the son of Tarquin, king of Rome) that he raped her. As a result, Lucretia killed herself and the Tarquin family was expelled from Rome.

You see, Mr Lansdell . . . cowardice: cut from *SE*.

Mireille's phantom city: Mireille is the eponymous heroine of a Provençal poem (written in Occitan) by Frédéric Mistral (1830–1914). This is yet another story of thwarted lovers. Mireille dies in the arms of Vincent (from whom her parents had separated her) after she has had a vision in which the Saintes Maries have told her that earthly suffering is a necessary precursor to heavenly happiness. Michel Carré adapted the poem as an opera which was performed at the Théatre Lyrique in 1864.

323 *a Madonna by Giorgione*: Giorgio Barbarelli, or Giorgio del Castelfranco (*c*.1475–1510), a Venetian painter and pupil of Giovanni Bellini.

Lauzun . . . Brummel: Armand Louis de Gontant-Biron, Duc De Lauzun (1747–93), was a soldier, rake, and adventurer who was brought up in the household of Madame de Pompadour. George (Beau) Brummel (1778–

1840) was a friend of the Prince Regent (George IV) and leader of London fashion.

323 *Did not D'Alembert . . . peaceful pleasures of geometry*: serial version does not include this sentence. Jean Le Rond D'Alembert (1717–83) was a philosophe and distinguished mathematician.

325 *borrowed from the pages of a poet . . . at his worst*: *SE* has: 'borrowed from the misty pages of Shelley'.

326 *Good heavens . . . refused to me!*: cut from *SE*.

garde-chiourme: a warder of galley slaves.

333 *'I'll not believe but Desdemona's honest.'*: *Othello*, III. iii.

335 *the Thunderer*: the nickname given to *The Times* newspaper in the nineteenth century on account of the style of one of its writers, Edward Stirling (1773–1847).

George Sand: pen-name of Lucile-Aurore Dupin, Baronne Dudevant (1804–76), novelist and woman of letters, well known for her unconventionality, the lover of the poet Alfred de Musset and the composer Chopin.

Springheeled Jacks . . . John Mittons . . . Tom and Jerry: men-about-town. Tom and Jerry were central characters in Pierce Egan's *Life in London* whose names became synonymous with riotous living.

Crimean war: (1853–6), in which the French and British resisted Russian attempts to expand into Turkey and the Danubian Provinces. The war was the subject of much press comment. Although the allies were successful, the British conduct of the war was widely held to reveal great incompetence in the military.

Indian rebellion: the Indian mutiny of 1857, which began when Bengali soldiers shot their British officers and marched on Delhi to restore the Mughal emperor. The rebellion spread to Agra, Cawnpore, and Lucknow and smouldered on until spring 1859.

337 *ben trovato:* well-found.

canard: a hoax, false report, or extravagant story calculated to mislead.

339 *Helen*: Helen of Troy, whose beauty supposedly caused the Trojan wars.

343 *Major Pendennis*: the uncle and guardian of the hero of W. M. Thackeray's *The History of Pendennis* (1848–50), who saves his nephew from an unsuitable youthful marriage to an actress and generally offers wise counsel.

346 *Fagin*: the leader of the gang of young pickpockets who ensnare Oliver in Dickens's novel *Oliver Twist* (1837–8).

Manfred: melancholy hero of a verse play by Lord Byron (1817).

347 *Harold Skimpole*: a character in Dickens's *Bleak House* who refers to himself as a child, relies upon the goodness of others for his sustenance, and refuses to accept any responsibility for his own actions.

ignis-fatuus light: 'foolish fire'. A phosphorescent light which flickers over marshy ground, and which seems to move elsewhere when it is approached. This property led to the belief that the light was the work of a sprite intent upon leading travellers astray. Metaphorically the *ignis fatuus* is a delusive aim or hope.

349 *Spartans . . . Persians . . . Thermopylae*: a reference to Herodotus' *History of the Persian Wars*. The Spartans, together with the Thespians and Thebans, were slaughtered as they attempted to defend the Pass of Thermopylae against the much larger forces of the Persians.

357 *Parian statues*: the island of Paros was renowned for its white marble. Parian denotes a fine white porcelain used for making statuettes.

simple Dorothea: a virgin martyr of the fourth century whose saint's day is 6 February.

358 *freebooter*: an adventurer who goes about in search of booty or plunder.

the accommodation-bill line: a fraud involving accommodation bills, which were a way of raising money on credit.

359 *Newgate*: the most famous prison in England in the nineteenth century. Located in the city of London, it replaced Tyburn as the place of public executions in 1783.

'*"you must believe this heart is stone; it did not break!"*': the words 'you must believe | This heart is stone, it did not break' are actually spoken by Rosalind in Shelley's 'Rosalind and Helen: a Modern Eclogue' (1819).

Lady Nithisdale: Winifred Maxwell, Countess of Nithsdale petitioned George I in 1716 for the life of her husband (William Maxwell),who had been sentenced to death for his part in the first Jacobite rebellion (1715). When this failed she helped her husband escape from the Tower of London and subsequently joined him in Rome. She later wrote a narrative of his escape.

Jack Sheppard: Harrison Ainsworth was the author of numerous historical novels and tales of criminal life, including the history of the eighteenth-century cracksman Jack Sheppard.

360 *ticket-of-leave*: prisoners could be released on a sort of parole system known as a ticket-of-leave. Tom Taylor wrote a celebrated melodrama entitled *The Ticket-of-Leave Man* (1863).

362 ' *'Twere best at once to sink to peace'*: from canto xxxiv of Alfred Tennyson's *In Memoriam: A.H.H.* (1850), a poem in memory of his friend Arthur Henry Hallam who died suddenly aged 22. This is one of several references to this poem.

363 *Maria Martin*: this is probably a reference to Maria Marten, whose body was found hanging in the Red Barn on the farm belonging to the Corder family at Polstead near Ipswich. Maria had borne children to two of the Corder sons. William Corder (the younger of the brothers) was hanged for her murder. A melodrama, *The Red Barn*, based on Maria's story (and representing her as an innocent maiden seduced by a man of

property) was first performed in 1828 and enjoyed considerable popularity.

370   *the faith that is stronger . . . sudden tempest*: cut from *SE*.

379   *Eve . . . Abel*: the story of the slaying of Eve's son Abel by his brother Cain is told in Genesis 4.

Hero . . . drowned lover; Leander, the lover of Hero (a priestess of Aphrodite), used to swim across the Hellespont at night in order to visit her, but he was drowned during a storm. The distraught Hero threw herself into the sea. Christopher Marlowe and Thomas Hood both wrote poems on this subject.

380   *She forgot . . . not dying*: cut from *SE*.

Gretchen . . . Alice: Gretchen, see note to p. 277. Alice is the seduced and betrayed heroine of Bulwer-Lytton's *Ernest Maltravers* and *Alice, or the Mysteries* (see note to p. 30).

381   *Juggernaut*: one of the names of Krishna. An idol of Krishna was dragged in a great cart in an annual Indian festival in which many devotees would throw themselves beneath the cart's wheels to be crushed.

382   *'I never thought . . . the end'*: cut from *SE*.

386   *Styx*: the river in Hades over which the shades of the departed were ferried by Charon.

King Arthur . . . Sir Philip Sidney . . . Bayard: all models of chivalry. King Arthur is the legendary king of Britain, who founded the Round Table to further his particular model of heroism and chivalry. Sir Philip Sidney (1554–86) was a courtier, soldier, and poet. Pierre de Terrail, Seigneur de Bayard (c.1473–1524), was the 'chevalier sans peur et sans reproche' (the knight without fear and without reproach), who won fame in the Italian campaigns of Charles VIII and Louis XII.

Carlyle . . . Necessity: a reference to Thomas Carlyle's *Sartor Resartus* (1833–4). Carlyle's protagonist, Teufelsdrockh, 'directly thereupon began to be a man' after passing through the 'Everlasting No', a process which involved annihilating self, embracing the actual, duty, and work.

388   *It used to be so difficult . . . wiser than that*: cut from *SE*.

'the shadow . . . all the creeds!': from Alfred Tennyson's *In Memoriam*, canto xxii.

389   *Freethinker*: one who finds that religious belief contradicts reason, and refuses to accept conventional authority in the matter on religion.

Deist: one who rationally accepts the existence of a Supreme Being, but does not accept the supernatural aspects of religion.

Atheist: one who denies the existence of God.

In Memoriam: *In Memoriam: A.H.H.* (1850) by Alfred Tennyson.

Addison: Joseph Addison (1672–1719), poet, dramatist, essayist, and Whig statesman.

Saul . . . journey to Damascus: Saul of Tarsus, also known as Paul, was converted to Christianity by a vision experienced as he was travelling to Damascus to continue his persecution of the early followers of Jesus.

martyrdom of Stephen: Stephen, a deacon of the early Christian Church was stoned to death after being arraigned by the Council of Jerusalem for bearing false witness.

'basked and battened in the woods': canto xxxv of Tennysons's *In Memoriam: A.H.H.*

390 *'I know that I am dying . . . it is made?'*: cut from *SE*.

392 *I used to read him . . . poet he is*: cut from *SE*.

Janus: in Roman mythology Janus is the god of gates and doorways, usually depicted with two faces (facing in opposite directions).

'an infant crying in the night': canto iv of Tennysons's *In Memoriam: A.H.H.*

393 *Savile Row*: a fashionable London address for well-connected doctors (like Harley Street).

395 *'If any calm, a calm despair'*: *In Memoriam*, canto xi.

401 *proved at Doctors' Commons*: Doctors' Commons is the building in the city of London used by the College of Doctors of Civil Law.

Queen-Anne teapots fashioned by Paul Lemeri: Paul De Lamerie (1688–1751) is described by Christopher Lever in *Goldsmiths and Silversmiths of England* (London, 1975) as probably the finest worker in silver and gold that England has ever known. Born in Bois-le-Duc, De Lamerie accompanied his Huguenot parents to England when they fled from religious persecution in France. He was particularly well known for his pieces of silverwork with large flat undecorated surfaces in the so-called 'Queen Anne' taste.

403 *Even the dreaded innovation . . . farmers about Mordred*: this sentence is cut from *SE*.

404 *Landseer*: Sir Edwin Henry Landseer (1802–73), English painter of animal portraits noted for their detail.

The Oxford World's Classics Website

www.worldsclassics.co.uk

- Information about new titles
- Explore the full range of Oxford World's Classics
- Links to other literary sites and the main OUP webpage
- Imaginative competitions, with bookish prizes
- Peruse *Compass*, the Oxford World's Classics magazine
- Articles by editors
- Extracts from Introductions
- A forum for discussion and feedback on the series
- Special information for teachers and lecturers

www.worldsclassics.co.uk

American Literature

British and Irish Literature

Children's Literature

Classics and Ancient Literature

Colonial Literature

Eastern Literature

European Literature

History

Medieval Literature

Oxford English Drama

Poetry

Philosophy

Politics

Religion

The Oxford Shakespeare

A complete list of Oxford Paperbacks, including Oxford World's Classics, OPUS, Past Masters, Oxford Authors, Oxford Shakespeare, Oxford Drama, and Oxford Paperback Reference, is available in the UK from the Academic Division Publicity Department, Oxford University Press, Great Clarendon Street, Oxford OX2 6DP.

In the USA, complete lists are available from the Paperbacks Marketing Manager, Oxford University Press, 198 Madison Avenue, New York, NY 10016.

Oxford Paperbacks are available from all good bookshops. In case of difficulty, customers in the UK can order direct from Oxford University Press Bookshop, Freepost, 116 High Street, Oxford OX1 4BR, enclosing full payment. Please add 10 per cent of published price for postage and packing.